THE

# PHILANGELUS

THE FIRST TALE

BRIAN PRATER

Mr. Macabre Publications



Cover design and illustration by Jeff Brown Graphics

Book interior typesetting by Brian Prater

Interior illustration by Galilee Bürger

Author photo by Chris Pitts

First edition, 2024

Hardback ISBN: 979-8-9892737-0-6

Paperback ISBN: 979-8-9892737-1-3

Electronic edition ISBN: 979-8-9892737-2-0

# CONTENTS

For my beloved bride,
who kept patience while I wrote and rewrote,
for my beloved mother,
who brought me succor when I most needed it,
and for my dear father,
who always supported and believed in me

# PART I: NIGHT

# CHAPTER I
## CHUCK'S CHOICE

October 13, 2016
Mt. Pleasant, South Carolina

*"How do you know? Don't do this, Chuck!"*

Chuck's front door slammed back against the wall as he burst into the room. He liked the loud bang it made. It hurt his ears, and he wanted to feel something other than the pain inside, even if it was physical pain. He'd arrived home from school later than usual, having decided to take all the books in his locker home with him so his mother wouldn't have to pick them up herself on Monday. He would never have to see Wando High again. That thought gave him comfort. He hadn't paid attention to where he was going when he stomped into the house, until he found himself before the door to his mother's bedroom. He stood stock-still a moment. It was quiet on the other side. His mother wasn't home.

*"Out looking for a job maybe?"*

Chuck sneered, surprised such an optimistic thought would cross his mind. More likely she was out banging her latest meal ticket. Another deadbeat drunk with a mean backhand. Chuck preferred him high. He was pacified when high.

His mother's absence suited him fine. It was perfect. He would just leave her a note. He grabbed some paper and a pen out of his backpack and went to sit at the kitchen table. It was covered with so much crap he couldn't even see its surface. He headed for his bedroom instead, but stopped. Turning back to the table, he shoved the debris out of his way, hearing several moldy bowls and glasses shatter as they hit the floor.

This no consequences thing was all new to him. It felt good. He cleared off a chair and sat down. It took him longer than he'd expected to begin, spending a full five minutes staring down at the blank sheet without writing a word. He'd thought this note would be easy to write. Maybe even exhilarating. There was nothing to hold him back anymore. There would be no more anxiety or injuries. He would be free. He and his mother would both be free. And now he could finally let her in on his plan through this message. He knew he wouldn't be getting the chance to tell her later. But, he couldn't think how to start such a letter. There was so much to say, yet no simple way to say it.

*"Come on! There are plenty of better ways to handle this. Why not ask for help?"*

There was his doubt of the plan again. But he was ignoring that now. He'd been over it a hundred times in his head, and this was the best way to improve both his and his mother's situations.

*"The only way."*

That was better. He just needed to keep focused. Keep from faltering now that he was getting so close to the freedom he craved. It ended up taking over an hour to finish the note once he started writing. When he looked up at the clock, it was already 4:30.

Shit! He had to get a move on! The drunk would be home soon. He couldn't be caught unprepared. He folded up the paper and wrote "Mom" on the top, leaving it on the table for her to find later. Rushing back to her room, he ripped open her closet door. It was in here. The last thing he needed to complete his plan. He'd left it on the top shelf.

Pulling piles of musty clothes out of his way, he spotted the shoe box and slid it carefully off the shelf. Unwrapping the newspaper inside, he held the Glock 17 up to the light. It was one of the few things his real father had left behind when he'd skipped town eleven years ago.

*"Fitting it should now be the tool for the job at hand, considering it came from the first drunk junkie to knock Mom up, eh?"*

Chuck smirked at the thought. He'd secretly taken the gun out of its box numerous times before to learn how it worked. He'd even smuggled it out of the house and practiced shooting in the woods once, just to be certain it would fire. After ensuring there was a bullet in the chamber and the safety was off, Chuck headed to his bedroom. He thought better of it halfway there and turned back into the master. His mother and the drunk wouldn't go to his room.

He sat on the foot of their bed, faced the door, and breathed deeply, trying to slow his heart rate. Now that the moment of truth had arrived, he felt hesitant.

*"It's not too late! Put the gun back, Chuck. They wouldn't have to know how close you came. You can still turn this whole thing around."*

He thought about that for a moment.

*And what? Let things go on like they always have? No. The world doesn't change. At least my world doesn't. Sometimes, you've just gotta take matters into your own hands.*

He tightened his grip on the Glock, feeling an adrenaline rush from the expectation. He began to sweat. His determination rose. It would happen at any moment!

*"What about God?"*

He stopped his steady breathing, caught off-guard by the question.

*"What if there's a God and life beyond this life? Divine justice and all that? What if there is a consequence to this action you can't escape? What if there's even a Divine Savior Who can help you?"*

He'd never considered factors like that when hatching his plan. He wasn't raised with any religion. He'd only ever been inside of a church with Jack and Kevin when they were kids. Even then, he hadn't understood half of what he saw there. But now existential questions entered his thoughts, almost as if they were being pressed into his mind whether he liked it or not. As he sat pondering them, something else started ringing through his thoughts. He tried concentrating on it and realized it was one word.

*"Delusion . . . Delusion . . . Delusion, Chuck. A wonderful little bedtime story to keep kids happy when they go to sleep at night. Kids who had better parents and better childhoods than you. A Divine Hero to inspire their imaginations. A Fictional Character in a cosmic joke, like Mr. Wilkerson's always saying at school. You have a chance to experience real freedom here, Chuck. Not the imagined freedom of religion. It only takes one act. One little tug on the trigger. Then all your troubles are over. Your misery will be over."*

Tears were rolling down Chuck's cheeks. But he'd felt his determination return with those words of encouragement. The last beating he'd received from the drunk flashed through his mind. That was the final push.

Before he had the chance to second-guess the plan again, he jammed the gun into his mouth and pulled the trigger.

Jack Dacre jerked awake with a scream caught in his throat.

He could have almost sworn he'd heard an actual gun blast in the moment between sleep and consciousness. But it was just a dream, he reassured himself as he got his bearings. The first thing his eyes fell on when they snapped open was his laptop. He must have left it running the night before, because the screen was up.

The background was doing its usual rotation of pictures every seven seconds, switching between images of some of his favorite movies and musicians. Shots of Bob Marley, Eminem, Lady Gaga, Kesha and other pop stars were interspersed with shots from *The Terminator, Predator, The Lord of the Rings, The Dark Knight,* and *The Avengers.* Had his head been clearer, he might have wondered why the screen was up now when it had been closed before he'd gone to sleep. He sat up, more familiar surroundings coming into focus, then fell back on the pillow, taking a deep breath. What the fuck had induced a nightmare like that?

He hadn't hung out with Chuck Nelson in years. Their only interactions since middle school had been brief and in passing. Sure, they still sat near each other in the occasional class. Jack couldn't help but notice Chuck's annoying habit of tapping on the back of his chair leg with his foot whenever seated directly behind him. But that was about the extent of their relationship now. Jack had let it die on purpose years ago. So from what conscious material had his brain concocted such a fucked up dream this morning?

He shook his head thinking about it, deciding he didn't care for the answer as much as he did ridding himself of the nightmare's memory. It was putting him in a funky mood he couldn't classify. Was it sadness, dread, disappointment, or something else? Maybe a mix. A weird in-between of general negativity. He sat up again, feeling his head throb as the hammer of the early morning cracked down on it.

*Dad's right,* he thought. *Nothing good happens after midnight. Not until at least . . . eleven in the morning.*

He chuckled bitterly as he swung his legs onto the floor and hung his head low, rubbing the sleep from his eyes. He was about to lay his head back on the pillow and cuddle into the inviting arms of unconsciousness once again, when sixty pounds of Labrador Retriever came bursting into the room, pummeling him over as it leaped onto the bed. He let the family pet chase him back onto his pillow in her attempts to lick his cares away.

"You know, that's rude. We really need to teach you the concept of personal space."

He covered his face with his sheet as the assault of affection continued.

*"Sto-op it!"*

He laughed as the dog pawed his face through the cover. Finally, he wrapped his arm around her neck and pulled her down next to him.

"Go to sleep," he ordered. "Nobody's supposed to be up at this ungodly hour."

The canine rolled onto her back, sniffing into his ear with her cold nose until he got the message and rubbed her belly. After that, she was calm, settling her upside down head on the pillow next to his. Before either of them could cross back into dreamland, an even less welcome alarm bell entered the room, assaulting the serenity of man and man's best friend together.

"Time to get up, Jack," his mother hollered as she swung his door open and flipped on the overhead light.

In truth, she probably hadn't raised her voice an octave above its normal volume. But, with Jack about to slip back into regaining his few precious minutes of lost rest, he couldn't help but angrily raise the covers over his head once more to blot out its unwelcome ringing.

"Come on, son. It's eight o'clock."

That was a lie and Jack knew it. His mother would often tell him it was a later time than it was when she was trying to get him up on a school day. He'd caught on to the trick years ago. Of course, back when it used to work, there had been a couple of instances where he'd jumped up and begun dressing in a panic, which his mother and sister had found rather amusing.

"I'll meet you downstairs for breakfast in five minutes," Lorelai continued. "If I have to come up here again, I better not find you still in bed!"

Jack made sure he heard her heeled shoes click down the stairs before uncovering his face again. He looked at Ruby, still lying on her back, though with her upside down brown eyes open and staring into his.

"Well . . . shit," he muttered.

He rolled off the bed, stumbling his way out the door and halfway down the hall to the bathroom. His sister, Chloe, emerged from her own room, already having showered, blow dried, put on makeup, and dressed.

"Really, Jack?" she asked, seeing him bumbling around half-naked.

"You're just jealous of my raw magnetism," he said in a groggy voice before closing the door.

"Yeah. You should really teach me your ways," she shot through it as she passed.

Jack relieved himself, rubbed more sleep from his eyes, and glanced at his appearance in the mirror, seeing the reason for Chloe's gibe. Apparently, his bed had become an electric chair overnight. He turned on the sink and splashed water over the jungle atop his head. It took almost a minute of fighting before it stopped standing back up. Once it did, he wiped his face off with a washcloth and headed back to his room.

There was a linen button-up on the floor Chloe had given him for his birthday that looked and smelled clean enough. He pulled it on, rolling the sleeves, before digging through the laundry basket Lorelai had dropped in his room three days ago, which he'd never bothered to put away. He found a pair of jeans and sauntered down to breakfast—the only good thing about mornings as far as he was concerned.

Lorelai had put out a plate of bacon and eggs on the kitchen island for each of them. He took a seat and glanced at the clock on the far wall. 7:45. So, his mother had been lying to get him up earlier. He felt a surge of self-satisfaction for recognizing her trick.

"Well, the dead lives!" she said from the counter.

"The dead and *buried* would have heard you, Mom. Thanks for breakfast."

"You're welcome."

She sat down and they both folded their hands, saying grace together. Jack let

Lorelai lead as he'd not yet fully rediscovered the power of speech since waking up.

"What classes do you have this semester again?" Lorelai asked him as they started eating.

Taking a long gulp of milk, Jack found his normal voice.

"English, biology . . . oh and I'm finally taking psychology. That's the one you and Dad said I might like, right?"

Lorelai smiled. "You're already so good at figuring out what people are thinking. Figured a formal sharpening of your tools would actually make you scary. Like it then?"

He nodded. "It's definitely the most interesting class I've ever had. For once, I sometimes look forward to reading from a textbook . . . Sometimes."

Lorelai rolled her eyes. "Why do you hate school so much, son?"

"Like I've said a thousand times, it's *boring!*"

"But you like solving puzzles and figuring out the ends of mysteries before they're over. How come you don't—"

"Exactly!" Jack interrupted. "I like learning about interesting stuff. Fun stuff. School rarely has the ambition to try and be either."

Lorelai chuckled. "But you're liking psychology so far?"

"So far. From what the teacher said, it sounds like the chapter on abnormal psych will be the—"

Jack's words were interrupted as something crashed into him from behind, knocking the breath from his lungs. His heart skipped a beat. He grasped the island, nearly falling sideways off his stool into Lorelai's lap. He jerked his head around once he'd regained his balance. His plate of bacon and eggs was empty.

"*RUBY!*" he roared, taking off after the fleeing dog.

Lorelai burst out laughing.

*"Get back here! I'm gonna kill you, you hear me! Get back here! Sit!"*

Jack's yelling did no good as the dog made loops around the house, going from the living room, to the dining room, to the kitchen, then back to the living room, all while chewing and swallowing her loot.

"She's never . . . done *that* . . . before," Lorelai sputtered through fits of giggles.

Jack couldn't help cracking a smile himself, though still giving chase to the mischievous mutt.

Jack was still fretting over having to eat cereal instead of the rest of his original breakfast as he drove to school.

Wando High was in a scenic locale of wilderness. The largest high school in the state, it had over three thousand seven hundred students enrolled, with the campus itself covering one hundred ten acres of modern, well-kept facilities. When Jack arrived, the parking lot was already crowded with the honking cars of students trying to find a spot. Not bothering to waste his time joining in, he parked his Jeep Cherokee on the side of the road next to campus and walked across the lawn, heading for Room 101. His English teacher always flashed a welcoming smile to students when they entered. Jack noticed it didn't seem as warm today, as though she were forcing it. He was too tired to dwell on it, taking a seat next to Kevin.

"What up?" he greeted. "You look like I feel."

Kevin smiled through the exhausted look on his face. "And just think, we only have . . ." he checked his phone for dramatic effect, "about seven more months of this until summer break!"

"Doomsayer. Don't fuckin' remind me."

"You started it."

Before slouching down in his chair, Jack scanned the room to see if Chuck Nelson had arrived yet. He wasn't seated in his corner desk behind Jack's. It looked like he wasn't hanging out anywhere else in the room either.

"This is a weird morning," Jack said. "You know how I woke up today? Had a nightmare about Chuck killing himself. Fuckin' disturbing."

"Chuck *Nelson?*" Kevin asked. "Shit! We ain't even hung out with him since middle school. What happened in the dream?"

"He came home, wrote his mom a note, pulled a gun from a closet, and blew the back of his head out. Think I almost screamed out loud when I woke up. I've never had a dream so vivid before. It was like I could hear his thoughts in it."

"Shit, that is fucked up! Where'd that come from?"

"No clue."

Jack's weird feeling of negativity started to come back. He wanted a new topic of conversation.

"Hey, on a lighter note, guess what arrived in the mail over the weekend?"

"New game?"

"Well, next to that, it doesn't sound very exciting. No, The Citadel approved me."

Kevin's eyes widened. "You mean . . ."

Jack nodded. *"Full* scholarship! Everything paid for."

"No shit!" Kevin shook his head. "Man, I haven't even spent time thinking about where I want to go and you've already got a free ride offered. You gonna accept?"

"Of course!"

"So you're definitely set on the whole military tactician idea then?"

"Something like that. Seemed the most exciting job I could think of at this point."

Kevin shook his head again, laughing. "How are you thinking that far ahead? I haven't even thought about what I want for lunch."

"They told us to start applying to places by last year." Jack shrugged. "I just wanted to get it out of the way."

"Bullshit! You're always thinking ten steps ahead. That's why I never beat you at *Call of Duty*. Hey . . . wait a minute."

"What?"

"You didn't get interested in the military because of that, did you?"

"Video games? No. That'd be stupid. It was movies."

Kevin laughed. "Wait, you serious?" he asked, seeing Jack's straight face.

Jack broke, laughing himself. "Actually, kinda."

"Okay. Explain."

Jack leaned back in his chair. "Remember when we were kids, what you, me, and Chuck all wanted to do when we grew up?"

"Man, I don't remember! We were too busy pretending to fight evil and slay monsters."

"That's exactly what I'm talking about. We wanted to be heroes, beat up bad guys, save the world, that kind of thing."

"Yeah, that's what any kids who grow up watching superhero movies want. What does that have to do with choosing a career at seventeen?"

"When they told us to start thinking about what we'd want to do with our lives last year, all I could think of that actually interested me was the stuff I'd have said when I was a kid." Jack laughed. "You remember how much I wanted to be Van Helsing when it came out?"

Kevin chuckled. "I do remember that. That was your favorite for years. You were so hopeful his job at the Vatican was real."

He laughed harder as he remembered how Jack had begged his parents to get him a black leather trench coat for Christmas that year.

"Yeah well, unfortunately there are no vampires or werewolves to be slain on a holy crusade in real life. Still, it got me thinking how I'd love to do an adventurous job instead of one where I'm sitting behind a desk eight hours a day. And the only scenarios I could think of were being a cop, a firefighter, or something in the military. Since I didn't want to be just a guy who takes orders, I figured a military commander of some kind. You know, the guy who plans out the attack. Anyway, that's how The Citadel's scholarship happened."

"Yeah, but be honest. *Call of Duty* had something to do with it, right?"

Jack couldn't help a smile breaking over his face as he nodded his head from side-to-side. "Well, maybe that and . . ." Jack veered off, losing his train of thought as his and Kevin's eyes drifted toward the door.

Jenny Wright, Becky Hall, and April Evans had entered the room giggling. Both boys swept their gazes over them before abruptly turning back toward one another, as though a sensor would go off within the girls that would GPS track their lines of sight back to their sources if they hovered them over the clique too long. Instead, Jack's and Kevin's eyes met each other, conveying a silent message between them.

*Shiiit! What I wouldn't do to get me some of that! Then again, a million dollars delivered to my front door would be nice too. And just about as likely.*

"Is Jenny still dating Brad?" Jack whispered.

"Last I heard. Course, I could flip a coin over whether or not those two were together and it could be either answer, depending on the time of day."

Jack's shoulders shook up and down as he tried to stifle a laugh.

"So what were the movies that interested you in the military?"

"*Captain America* was one."

"Which one?"

Jack looked at Kevin with a wry expression, as Naomi Ackermann entered the classroom and took one of the last empty seats on his other side.

"Come on," Jack said. "Don't you know me well enough? I hated the first one. The last two all the way."

"Speaking of movies to hate, did you finally see *X-Men: Apocalypse*?"

Jack nodded, as Naomi glanced over, neither boy noticing her.

"Well?" Kevin asked.

"I liked it."

"What?" Kevin and Naomi said in unison, making both boys look her way.

After their silence went on a moment too long, Naomi said, "Sorry to interrupt. I'm a fan."

Jack and Kevin kept staring.

"So . . ." Naomi said, "you liked the movie?"

"Yeah," Jack said at last. "Not my favorite, but it was up there for me."

Naomi wrinkled her nose. "Ugh, I thought it fell so far below the bar the last two had set."

"That's what I've been saying," Kevin said.

"I still like *Days of Future Past* more," Jack said. "That was probably the best *X-Men* movie ever. But I'd been waiting for them to do Apocalypse as the villain for years. And I don't know why people were so down on his performance. I thought he was menacing. I loved it when he and Professor X had a mental battle inside their heads!"

Naomi nodded. "That part was cool. I'll give you that. But Apocalypse's motivation was so unclear."

"Why do people keep saying that?" Jack demanded. "He thinks he's God and he wants to rule the world. Pretty basic villain stuff."

"Yeah. Basic and uninteresting," Kevin said.

"Alright, alright!" Jack waved his arms in submission. "I'm clearly outnumbered. At least we can all agree it wasn't as bad as some other franchise movies that came out this summer."

Kevin and Naomi laughed, nodding their heads.

"Good one for horror movies though," Jack said.

"Yeah?" Kevin asked. "You and Chloe see 'em all again?"

"Most of them. *The Conjuring 2* was one of the best we've seen in a long time."

"Oh, no thank you," Naomi shook her head and shivered.

Jack grinned. "Not a horror fan, huh?"

"Wouldn't know. I've never seen any. Too scary!"

Jack laughed. "You just need the right company."

Naomi smiled, brushing a lock of hair behind her ear. "Yeah? Well, I never really had anyone around who'd want to watch them."

"You should tag along with my sister and me. We've been watching them our whole lives."

"That's because they're weird," Kevin said. "Don't let him suck you in too."

"Shut up!" Jack said. "You watch plenty yourself."

"Not like you two freaks."

Jack shoved him. "Fuck you! You know you're—"

"Good morning, Wando High School," the principal's voice rang out over the loudspeaker, interrupting Jack. "I'm afraid I have to start the day off with some very sad news. As some of you may already be aware . . . we lost one of our students here over the weekend."

Jack looked up at the speaker in the corner, along with everyone across the room who'd still been talking.

"I'd like us all to take a moment of silence for Chuck Nelson."

Jack went numb. A cold sheet of silence settled itself over the entire campus, stifling several people's breath.

*What . . . the fuck?* Jack thought.

He must have misheard.

"I heard it was a suicide," Jenny whispered to April a few chairs away.

"Yeah, that's what they were saying at the front office this morning," Becky answered her. "His mom was coming in to pick up the stuff from his locker."

Jack looked at Kevin, whose face had turned paler than it already was. Kevin returned his gaze.

"What . . . the fuck?" he echoed Jack's own thought in a whisper.

Naomi turned to glance at Chuck's empty seat behind Jack's. Jack heard his neck creak as his head swayed from side-to-side while his mind spun. The principal had been mistaken. Chuck was just late. He was late all the time! Sometimes he didn't show up at all. As for the rumor Jenny was spreading, what did she know? She'd probably never deigned to look at Chuck before.

"Thank you," the principal spoke from the loudspeaker again. "For anyone who may wish to stop by the office and speak to one of the school counselors, there will be one available at any time today until five-o'clock."

The teacher stood up after the principal's message ended, a somber expression on her face. Jack realized the reason her smile had seemed feigned when he'd entered.

"I know he was in this period," the English teacher addressed the class. "So, if anyone feels the need to do that now, feel free."

Nobody moved. Jack couldn't tell if his body felt weightless or so heavy he was paralyzed. He didn't waste energy considering the question. He was too busy trying to process a thousand different thoughts at once, all trying to shove their way to the forefront of his brain. It was as if they all got stuck against each other in the doorway and none of them made it under the foyer light of his reason. Instead, his mind felt numb. He was unable to consider any single thought.

The one that finally surfaced first was a realization about his body after all. The news of Chuck's death had brought a physical effect with it. His stomach felt tight and a little queasy. For some reason, this sick feeling jogged other thoughts into action. The ones he'd been both curious and dreading to consider.

"Did you *know?*" he heard Kevin ask.

He turned to see his friend staring at him.

"Was that some sick, twisted way of telling me?" Kevin went on. "Did you know Chuck was . . . gone?" Kevin furrowed his eyebrows. "No, you couldn't have—"

"Of course not!" Jack interrupted. "Did I look like I knew 'til just now? No, but . . . we don't even know what happened yet. Let's go outside." He stood up. "I think Kevin and I will take you up on that, Miss Sanger," he said, as Kevin rose and headed for the exit with him.

The teacher waved the two boys on as they left, acutely aware of everyone staring at them as they did.

"Alright, class. Unless there's anyone else, turn to page two-seventeen," the two boys barely registered her saying as they passed. "We're going over a contemporary of Shakespeare's today. Christopher Marlowe."

Jack shut the door behind them, walking a few paces down the hall. Neither had any intention of going to the school offices and they made sure they were out of earshot before talking. Jack was first.

"This can't be right!"

"Dr. Stopes didn't even say anything about what happened!" Kevin ranted. "Maybe we should go to the offices and ask him."

"I doubt he'd give us details."

"Yeah, but he could at least confirm if it was a suicide or not!"

"I can't—that can't be true! Chuck wouldn't—"

"How would *we* know that?" Kevin demanded. "We distanced ourselves from him years ago! What if there was something we could have done if we were still—"

*"Stop! Don't do that!"*

Jack found himself pacing, tapping the fingers on his right hand against his thumb one by one. First the index, then the middle, then the ring, then the pinky, and back to the ring, middle, and index, repeating the process over and over.

"This is not on us!" he declared. "And we don't even know what happened yet. What if it was a car accident or something?"

*"Jack!"*

Jack stopped and looked Kevin in the eyes.

"What?"

"He can't be just . . . gone!"

# CHAPTER II
## DOUBT

Jack continued to feel numb the rest of the day.

He'd eaten lunch with Kevin in silence. Kevin had looked much the same as Jack thought he must look. Heading to last period, neither even bothered to look up curiously when they passed Brad Mason cornering Jenny in the hallway.

Brad's face was inches from hers, which was beginning to stream tears. The tears might have been of fear or sadness. Maybe both. If either passerby had cared to venture a guess, each would have assumed the couple had broken up again, or were on the verge of it, and Brad was none too pleased about it.

Jack and Kevin might have dared approach to see if Jenny needed rescuing. Brad was a football player, but the pair could probably take him together. That had been the Jack and Kevin before this particular afternoon. Since English class, nothing had done much more than half register in their minds. They passed the feuding couple without pausing and entered the science classroom. The only acknowledgment of the situation outside its door from Jack was a single thought passing through his head.

He wondered why Jenny had never tried for anyone else if she was so indecisive about Brad. She could have gotten any guy in the school she wanted. As soon as Jenny was out of his sight, she was out of his mind, which turned back to Chuck Nelson and ways in which he might have kept their friendship from fading out years ago. He'd done his best all day to try not to go down those avenues of thought, but he couldn't help it. All he could do now was come up with about a hundred different ways he might have seen signs of what was coming and prevented it.

Searching for a distraction, he tried occupying himself with what Mr. Wilkerson was doing in the back. The rotund biology teacher was standing behind the lab counters setting up some kind of experiment, or cleaning one up from his previous period. He did teach chemistry too, and there weren't as many lab exercises involved in biology class as far as Jack knew. It was just as well. Jack preferred a lecture to a lab assignment today. He could focus more on his thoughts.

"How're you doing?" someone asked behind him.

Jack jumped, turning to see Naomi was seated near him.

"Oh," he breathed, feeling his pulse slow back down. "Sorry, what'd you say?"

"I asked how you were. You and Kevin were friends with Chuck Nelson right? You never came back to English this morning, and I didn't see you the rest of the day. You okay?"

Jack didn't know how to respond to that. Luckily, he was saved by the bell. It got Mr. Wilkerson trudging back up to the front of the room, calling the class to attention. A couple of tardy students rushed in at the bell's tune, including Jenny, who grabbed a seat between Becky and April near the front. From the looks of things, she'd done her best in the bathroom to hide any evidence she'd been crying. Since her two acolytes were busy flirting with a couple of the football players, neither noticed her red cheeks or puffy eyes.

"Talk later, I guess," Jack said to Naomi, though he had no intention of restarting the conversation she'd tried to initiate.

"Alright, e'erybody shut up now," Mr. Wilkerson boomed his usual greeting. "We've got a lot to cover today, and I don't have time for . . ." The teacher looked around the room. "Wait a minute. Darris isn't here! Guess you could all go on chatting a few more minutes. We might even be able to finish early."

Jack chuckled along with several other students. It was the first time he'd smiled since that morning. He was grateful to the science instructor for that.

"Alright, seriously though," Mr. Wilkerson called everybody back to silence. "You'll all remember from our first day that biology is a term meaning 'the study of life.' Well—"

His words were interrupted by the door bumping as though someone had used their whole body to push it open instead of just turning the handle.

The teacher inhaled a deep breath. "Oh, well. Speak of the Devil and he shall appear, I suppose."

Jack and half the room laughed as Darris Denham stumbled into the classroom.

"Thanks for deciding to join us, Darris!"

"Sorry, Mr. Wilkerson, I forgot which one was your room," Darris answered, climbing over book bags, purses, and people's ankles to reach the center of the desks.

"You forgot?" the instructor asked. "Funny, I seem to remember you knew where it was when you took this class last year, and the time before that, and before that."

"Oh, it's just that I thought they would have made you principal by now, sir," Darris retorted. "But I guess you turned it down when you realized you wouldn't get the privilege of seeing me every day, huh?"

The other students stifled laughter.

"Oh, I'm sure if I were the principal I'd still get to see you just about every day, Darris."

Nobody stifled their laughter at that.

"Alright, sir! Alright! Score one for you and counting," Darris shot back, smiling.

"Speaking of scores, if you want to be playing football this semester, you better not be slacking off. I'll be giving Coach Wilkes updates on how you're doing."

"Oh, come on!"

"I'll tell you what," Mr. Wilkerson said, "bribe me, and I'll think about going back on that."

"Alright. Wait, let me write that down before I forget." Darris opened his backpack and searched for something. "Shiiit . . . anybody got an extra pen?"

The room chuckled again.

"Alright, that's enough," the teacher called for everyone's attention. "Let's talk some science. Darris, try to keep up."

Darris jerked his head back. "Bitch—" he started to say.

But Mr. Wilkerson bulldozed over him, having already wasted enough time bantering. If he did hear the beginnings of Darris' final remark, he chose to ignore it.

"Today we're going to be talking about what many scientists think of as the beginning of the modern study of biology. The evolutionary theory. Now, does anyone here know what evolution is?"

After a few moments of silence, Becky spoke up. "Isn't it the study of how species change over time and when new species appear?"

"Yes, exactly that," Mr. Wilkerson said, picking up a marker and beginning to write on the whiteboard.

Jack took advantage of the teacher's back being turned and checked his phone, continuing to search for what he'd been looking for on the internet since that morning. Some mention of Chuck's death in the local news. Specifically how he'd died.

"Evolution is defined as 'change in the gene pool of a population from generation to generation by such processes as mutation, natural selection, and genetic drift,'" Mr. Wilkerson finished writing out the definition while the class copied it down.

Although Jack was only half-listening, continuing to scroll through his phone, he was recording every bullet point the teacher put up on the board in his notebook.

"Now, we'll be covering all three processes in this class," the teacher continued. "But I want to focus today on probably the most disputed of the three: natural selection."

He wrote out another definition on the board. Finally, a headline caught Jack's eye.

*Mt. Pleasant Teen Suicide—Some are Already Saying It Will Influence Mayor Derry's Meeting with the Governor to Discuss State Gun Regulation*

Jack felt his lunch writhe in his stomach, but clicked on the link anyway.

"Natural selection is defined as 'a natural process that results in the survival and reproductive success of individuals or groups best adjusted to their environment, which leads to the perpetuation of genetic qualities best suited to that particular environment.'" Mr. Wilkerson paused after writing. "What that's basically talking about is how species—including humans—adapt to their environment over time." He turned around to face the class. "Can anyone give me some examples of how different populations of humans have adapted to their environments over time?"

No one answered. Jack wasn't about to. He'd read enough of the article to confirm it was about Chuck. He'd also read enough to confirm his . . . was it a fear reality would somehow match his dream or a relief? Either way, Chuck had killed himself and he'd used a gun to do it. But it had happened on Friday. So Jack's dream would have occurred later, meaning it wasn't a premonition. Still . . . what was it then? Had he actually dreamed something that had happened in real life without any prior knowledge? How? Why?

His head swirled again as it had that morning. Somehow Mr. Wilkerson's lecture cut through it. Jack found himself hanging on his every word out of a desperate yearning for some normality to return to his day.

"How about skin color?" the teacher suggested.

Darris volunteered an answer. "People in Africa are black, 'cause it's so hot there."

"Yes. Good. One reason people have darker skin in hotter countries is to protect them from the sun, as opposed to people in colder, less sunny environments. From the beginning of the human race until now, the process of natural selection has determined what we would look like today. Why do we have two arms and two hands? Why do we have four fingers and a thumb on each hand?"

*Because that's just the way God made us,* Jack thought absently, trying much harder than he usually needed to pay attention.

Anything to keep his mind off the article on his phone. Acknowledging it would make what happened that morning all too real, and his morning had been too weird to be real. And too tragic.

Mr. Wilkerson looked him in the eyes. "Because natural selection determined it," he stated, as though he'd heard Jack's thought and corrected him.

Jack stared back into his eyes. The teacher looked away, but he had Jack's full attention now.

"This brings us to why I said natural selection has been disputed since it was originally hypothesized. Not everyone was ready to believe it at first, even in the scientific community. But, to understand why, you need to know the story of evolution. It was first theorized in the nineteenth century, by a guy named Charles Darwin." Mr. Wilkerson wrote the name up on the board. "Darwin published his theory in a book called *On the Origin of Species*. But he got into some trouble for it with the Christians of his day."

Jack had been paying such close attention to what the teacher was saying that this last statement almost seemed to sting him. His head began to throb.

"A lot of people—especially the religious—at first rejected the idea that humans were just another mammal and that our origin is not unrelated to the other animals. Now, up until Darwin's time, what did people believe about how humans originated?"

He paused, waiting on the students' replies. A few of them mumbled different things, all basically giving the same answer. The teacher heard each one of them, tuned to understand murmuring after years of practice as a high school instructor.

"That's right. They believed a," he made quotation marks in the air with his fingers, "'Higher Being' had created mankind. In other words, they believed in creation rather than evolution. However, the scientific discoveries begun by Charles Darwin have since proven that we were not created by any Higher Being."

Jack sat unmoving in his chair. The feeling of numbness coursed through his entire body with a vengeance this time. Mr. Wilkerson's last words were taking time to sink in, as though his brain were having trouble processing them. He'd heard them, but it was like he didn't know where to file them in his head. Instead, they sat there repeating over and over in his short-term memory, almost ringing in his ears.

*Not created by any Higher Being. Not created. No Higher Being. No. Not. Nothing! No Higher Being. Nothing! There's nothing out there!*

The teacher had made the statement so matter-of-factly. Maybe there was some mistake, or Jack had misheard. The instructor plunged onward with his lesson, his declaration apparently no more significant to him than explaining to the students two plus two equals four. Jack kept waiting for him to elaborate on his point regarding the existence of God, but he'd moved on to explaining the difference between something called macro and microevolution. Once Jack's feeling of numbness subsided, it was replaced with a new feeling. Fear.

*If there's no God, then there must be no afterlife,* he thought. *And if there's no afterlife, where is Chuck now? Just . . . gone?*

Abruptly, violently, the feeling of fear was replaced by something else. Something that felt like it flowed through Jack's very veins. Anger. Who did Mr. Wilkerson think he was declaring there was no God? Of course there was! There had to be!

*"Are you sure?"* asked a little voice in the back of his head. *"What proof have you of that? Have you ever seen anything concrete that proved to you beyond the shadow of a doubt there's a God? Or do you believe it just because it's what Mommy and Daddy always told you?"*

The mental mallet bashed against Jack's mind without warning. As fast as it had come, the feeling of anger within him was replaced with fear again. How was he so certain God existed? The horror of that idea coupled with Chuck's death threatened to overwhelm him. It reared up in his mind like the head of some disgusting monster emerging from beneath the waves of his unconscious to consume his every conscious thought.

Doubt proceeded to pervade every crevice of his mind as he sat wrestling against it, losing himself in the tidal wave of its onslaught. When the bell rang to signal the end of the school day, the students flooded toward the doors together. Jack floated through the sea of his classmates, still attempting to grasp an intellectual life-preserver that could secure his peace of mind. It was no use.

Skeptical questions kept drowning out all other thoughts.

Jack awoke feeling groggy, sitting up slowly but not rising from the bed, instead sitting on its side waiting for the blood to stop rushing to his head and give him back his vision.

He hoped the nap had helped. He hadn't planned on falling asleep when he'd thrown himself down upon entering his room, but he wondered if sleep had calmed him enough to be able to think more clearly. His drive home had been silent, with no music. He'd wanted the distraction Katy Perry or Eminem might bring, but there was no distraction to be had from this. He needed answers. He couldn't ignore the kinds of questions making a feast of his brain. Biology class had only been their appetizer. During the drive, they'd proceeded to the entrée.

*"What if it's all a fantasy?"* the cognitive beating had pummeled him. *"What if God's just another Santa Claus or Tooth Fairy, and now it's time to grow up, face the truth? There's no evidence for a happy-go-lucky party in the clouds after death, Jack. There's only the weight of the earth from six feet under. But you won't feel it. You won't feel anything more than Chuck does now."*

*NO!* Jack had thought back, his anger defibrillated to life again from conclusions like these. *God isn't something made up like the Easter Bunny. People don't go to church every weekend for children's myths! They go for God! He's a different matter.*

*"But what proof have they of His existence? Have any of them ever witnessed a miracle? Have you? Has anyone in your family ever seen God or any indication He's really there? Or are you simply trusting the word of a two-thousand-year-old Book written by the poor, superstitious men of an ancient Middle East? After all, how do you personally know the Bible to be a trustworthy source?*

*You know from your study of ancient pagan mythologies at Divine Savior that they had similar creation and redemption stories. The Bible's not even original! How then could it have been revealed by a Deity and not be the mere work of men copying other men who invented stories before them?"*

The doubts stayed with Jack all the way home.

*"And haven't you heard before that some parts of the Bible are metaphorical?"* he'd remembered as he'd parked in the driveway. *"How do you know which parts the authors intended to be taken literally? When deciding if you believe in something or not, what's important are the facts, Jack. Not metaphors."*

*There may be metaphors in the Bible,* Jack had reasoned to himself as he'd stomped across the front porch to the door, *but I seriously doubt the literal existence of an afterlife is among them. As far as Chuck's fate is concerned—*

*"Chuck's fucked, Jack,"* a thought interrupted before he could stop it. *"Chuck's fucked."*

Jack had opened the door and entered, finding himself in his mother's embrace before he knew what hit him.

"I heard about what happened," she said. "You didn't have to finish the school day. You should have come home this morning."

"Yeah," he said, "woulda spared me . . ."

He'd left his thought unfinished. He hadn't felt ready to discuss what had happened in biology class yet. Questioning the family's religion over Chuck's death was enough for his own mind to wrestle with for one afternoon. He didn't need to know how his parents or sister would react. He needed to figure out what he made of it himself first. Lorelai had drawn back to look him in the eyes, but he'd found himself avoiding hers, as though she'd read his thoughts if he met them.

"You need anything?" she asked. "We can have your favorite for dinner tonight. Your Dad and Chloe will be home soon. They're—"

"I think I want to lie down," he interrupted. "I'm kind of exhausted."

With that, he'd brushed past her and headed up the stairs.

As his head cleared from the nap, he caught a whiff of the Mexican food his mother had promised wafting up the stairs. Ground beef and refried beans mingled together to make his mouth water. He wondered how long he'd been out. He glanced over at the clock on his nightstand. It was unplugged for some reason.

Frustrated, he searched for his phone. Both his pockets were empty. Looking for it on the bed, he was surprised at how dark it had grown since he'd fallen asleep. The only light in the room was a sliver of moonlight peeking in through his window. This wasn't enough for him to see his bed covers. He felt around to see if the phone had fallen out while he'd slept, only to remember stowing it in his backpack after reading the article on Chuck. The backpack was by the front door where he'd tossed it after arriving home.

He got up and felt his way toward the hall bathroom, squinting his eyes. The only thing he could make out in the moonlight was his doorknob reflecting it back at him. He had to move across the room slowly, careful not to stub a toe on his desk chair as he slid his feet across the floor. Its hardwood creaked beneath him, reminding him he'd never successfully sneak out of the house at night should he ever try.

He stopped when he smelled something burning. His mother never overcooked food. He reached out to turn the door handle, but the room went dark for half a second. A shadow passed behind him, blocking the light from the window. He felt his private parts suck themselves in at the same time. Gooseflesh stood up on his neck and rippled down his spine.

*Fuck!* he almost gasped aloud, holding his breath.

He jerked his head around so fast, he cricked his neck. Warmth and pain massaged it together, but he didn't let himself cry out. He was straining his ears to hear who was in the dark with him. For the next several moments, all he could hear was his own heart pounding in his ears. Nothing he could see in the room appeared out of the ordinary from the dim light provided by the sky's fingernail.

"Chloe?" he finally called.

No one answered.

He wasn't surprised. Why would his sister be sitting in his room while he slept? Besides, he'd never heard the floor creak when the shadow had passed. Whatever had made it wasn't a person.

The shadow passed before the window again, from outside of it. It was a bird flying back-and-forth. He let his breath out at last, laughing at how jumpy he'd become. His afternoon had done a number on him. He wasn't someone prone to scare easily. It was the main reason Chloe enlisted him to see horror movies with her. He was someone whose arm she could grab without reacting when the jump scares happened.

He grabbed the doorknob and trudged down the stairs, deciding to use the bathroom in the main floor hallway when he saw how dark the upstairs hall had grown. He just felt more comfortable being closer to everyone else at the moment. Shit, he was jumpy! Afraid of the dark, like a fucking four-year-old. He'd have made fun of anyone else being this way at his age. Still, it was only when he'd reached the bottom step of the staircase that he remembered to take full breaths again.

He paused once more as he passed the kitchen. It was empty. And neither the stove nor the oven were on.

"The fuck?" he murmured, walking through its entryway, beginning to tap the fingers on his right hand back-and-forth across his thumb.

No one was there. But he could have sworn he'd smelled Mexican food before. Even something burning. He didn't hear anyone in the living room beyond the kitchen.

"Mom? . . . Dad?"

No answer.

"Chloe?"

Nothing.

"Ruby?"

Nothing. Not even the sound of the dog's toenails pounding the wood floors in response to his beckoning.

"'Megan . . . Uncle Frank?'" he quoted Kevin McCallister from *Home Alone*, probably because quoting a comedy made him feel more at ease. "'Uncle Frank, *is this a joke? . . .* Where *are* you guys?'" he finished the line in a high pitched voice, perfectly imitating Macaulay Culkin's character and chuckling to himself.

He was reading too much into things. He walked out the kitchen's screen door into the backyard, figuring his family must be outside. It slammed shut louder than usual, almost as if someone had pulled it closed behind him. He jolted, glancing back at it with angry eyebrows. He hadn't even felt a gust of wind.

"Cheap piece of shit," he muttered before turning back to the yard.

Maybe the others had decided to do a fire pit tonight. Actually, that sounded like a good idea. He wouldn't mind sitting by the flames in a lawn chair this particular evening. Maybe they could even eat out there. The pit roared from across the yard, stoked to a blaze. He felt a jolt of excitement at the idea of roasting marshmallows over it. But there were no signs of life around it.

By all appearances, his only company was the clicking of the crickets. Where had everyone gone? With the fire looking as good as it did, the family should be out enjoying it. And why hadn't anyone bothered to wake him up for it?

Suddenly, inexplicably, he had a strong feeling he was being watched. The feeling grew with each passing moment. He stepped across the back patio, peering across the grass. His mother's gazebo in the middle of the lawn was dark. The only life on it was the reflection of the flames dancing up and down its pillars. These illuminated half a face staring back at him, peeking around the front pillar.

Jack choked on his breath.

After a moment, his heart slowed back down. The face was that of the life-sized mannequin of Frankenstein's Monster. He and Lorelai had tied the decoration to the gazebo themselves two weeks prior. The mannequin was designed to look like it was spying on anyone who approached. The fire had made it look different. More sinister. Besides that, it had cast its shadow across the gazebo's floor.

Given that the gazebo was also decorated with cobwebs and a mechanical bat hanging from the ceiling, he couldn't fault himself too much for being startled. He wasn't used to the different look of the backyard yet. Not at night.

On Halloween, the bat would be turned on and its eyes would light up red as it flapped its wings and flew around in circles on its string. It too had an enlarged shadow because of the flames. At least it was still at the moment, hanging lifeless.

Jack scanned the rest of the yard for anything out of the ordinary other than the rest of the holiday decorations. There was a scarecrow toward the left corner swaying in the wind, tilting slowly from side-to-side, almost as if it was considering him. Jack knew its face wore a smile. He'd helped his father set it up. The caress of the fire's curling fingers bounced off its face in a way that made it appear to sneer at him now. Shadows swam over its face in such a constant state of change, it appeared to reorient its expression every few seconds. None of the looks it was sending his way were friendly.

Feeling a chill, Jack turned away, focusing instead on the area of the yard with trees. More rubber bats and spiders hung from their branches, along with sheets fashioned into ghosts. There was even a battery powered swing which, when turned on, would move as though it were swinging by itself. For some reason, it was moving now.

Jack furrowed his brow, annoyed someone had left it running. They were trying to save its battery for Halloween itself. Still, he wasn't about to go over and turn it off until he'd made certain he was alone.

Along the ground beneath the tree branches, ghoulish plastic hands and heads had been staked in, making it appear as though zombies were rising from their graves. There were fake gravestones to go with them two rows of which were lined with cobwebs that formed a trail from the back yard around the side of the house to the front. It would lead trick-or-treaters to the gazebo.

The Dacres would have a bobbing for apples contest there for the neighborhood on Halloween Night. Jack had helped Lorelai build and paint some of the headstones years ago. There were puns such as, "I. B. Rising," "I. B. Back," and "C. U. Soon" written on most of them. Off to the side of the trail opposite Jack's, three square bundles of hay were stacked to form shelves. The Dacres had placed several fake pumpkins on these, to be joined by real ones should the family get to carving any this year. The pumpkins were providing the only light in the yard other than the fire pit and moon at the moment.

The little lamps within them had been set to a timer that would turn them on at dusk. Some pumpkins had square teeth. Some, sharp. Some wore surprised or sad faces. Others didn't have faces at all, but featured shapes like owls or willow trees. If Jack had his way, he was even going to buy a fog machine and place it behind the hay bushels on Halloween, just to give the party even more atmosphere. That was when he saw it.

There was something standing behind the hay bushels.

He stopped tapping his fingers, every joint in his body locking in place at once. At first he thought it might be his imagination. He blinked a couple of times, trying to clear his vision. The more he stared, the more a vague silhouette came into view.

It stood just out of reach of the pit and pumpkins' light. Some*one* was standing beyond the light, Jack corrected himself. Someone very tall and lean, with shoulders hiked up almost above their head. Very round shoulders. Almost too round and broad to be normal. Contrasting with the rest of the silhouette's blackness, he could see thin, bone white hair hanging behind the shoulders, billowing in the wind. The hair was so thin it looked fake. The figure might have been another Halloween decoration. But Jack knew his family's decorations. Nothing had been placed behind the hay bushels, and the Dacres didn't have any mannequins shaped like what he saw.

He noticed the crickets had stopped clicking. There was no sound in the air but the subtle flicker of the flames off to his right. Not a peep issued from the dark shape's direction. He thought of saying, "hello," to see who was there, but knew that was stupid. This was no one he knew, and whoever it was was standing in his backyard. Trespassing.

Who the fuck was standing in his backyard staring at him right now? And where the fuck was his family? He was about to run back in the house when something else broke the paralyzed silence for him. A scream from somewhere off in the distance. A long, pained scream.

He thought it sounded masculine. Could it have been his father's? Another scream, this time from somewhere way off behind him. It sounded like someone being tortured. A sound of severe pain mixed with utter terror.

The first scream had made him draw breath, but he still hadn't made a sound himself, nor removed his eyes from the figure standing in front of him. He wasn't going to give whoever it was the chance to move in on him without his seeing. The second scream behind him startled him enough to turn a little. He was afraid there might be more intruders who'd get the drop on him from that direction while the one in front of him caused a distraction. He still didn't take his eyes fully off the person in front of him. That was good, because they moved at the sound of the second scream too.

The shadowy silhouette drew back from the hay bushels farther into the darkness where Jack started losing sight of his outline. He could tell the trespasser was moving toward the side of the house. His movement was strange, like he was hobbled over, maybe limping.

Was it someone who'd escaped whoever was tormenting people out in the dark and was looking for help? Or was it one of the tormentors? Had they been injured by whoever they'd taken? Were they now pursuing them? Either way, with the figure moving away, Jack was about to run back inside to dial the police. The intruder changed direction, swaying oddly back-and-forth, moving toward him.

Another scream of agony tore through the silent night, this time much closer, thrusting Jack into action. He dove for the screen door, ripped it open, and slammed the inside door behind him, turning its deadbolt. He then bolted himself into the living room, headed for his backpack to retrieve his phone.

Halfway past the couch, someone grabbed his shoulders. He yelled in surprise. All the lights came on at once, almost blinding him.

*"Jack!"* someone screamed in his face.

He yelped like a child again.

*"Jack!"*

The face of his father appeared before him as his eyes adjusted.

"Dad," he registered. *"Dad!"* he yelled. *"There's someone outside!"*

"What?"

*"Someone . . ."*

He left his thought unfinished, noticing for the first time that his mother and Chloe were standing in the room too, looking at him as though they'd seen a ghost.

"Someone . . . was screaming!" Jack finished.

"Yes," his mother nodded, an expression of concern on her face. *"You* were screaming, Jack."

# CHAPTER III
## NIGHT TERRORS

Jack sat alone reading from his psychology textbook at a small side table during lunch the next day.

The cafeteria was noisy. Darris and a bunch of other football players were seated at a long center table next to his, entertaining several cheerleaders. Brad and Jenny were among them, and Jack guessed they were together for the moment. Darris must have been telling some amusing stories, because the whole table would occasionally burst out laughing at him. None of this was distracting Jack. He was too immersed in what he was researching.

It seemed his mother had been correct in her guess as to what had happened to him the night before. After doing research online, she'd told him what she thought when he came down for breakfast that morning. Did it not apply to him, he might have found the subject material fascinating. It had made his hair stand on end when his family had told him what had happened from their perspective. How he'd come down the stairs into the living room while they were all watching TV and stood in front of them with a blank expression on his face. Then, after several moments of staring at them like a psycho, unresponsive to anything they said, how he'd begun screaming at the top of his lungs. His father was only able to rouse him after shaking his shoulders and yelling in his face.

According to his textbook's description, night terrors—also called sleep terrors—were nightmares so intense people awoke screaming and sometimes flailing about from them. The sleeper could be harder to awaken than usual. These episodes could be paired with sleepwalking, and they could be induced by stress. Jack had endured a fair share of that the day before.

There was one glaring symptom that didn't line up with his experience. The book said night terrors, as opposed to nightmares, usually involved amnesia after the episode. Or, at the very least, the dreamer would only remember a single visual scene or image. Jack remembered everything about his dream, so much so he wouldn't have minded forgetting it.

At least there was some good news. Night terrors only required medical intervention if they persisted, started disrupting rest to a debilitating degree, or there was a threat of injury to the dreamer. They usually stopped on their own, without involving a doctor or a therapist. That was good, because Jack didn't feel like dwelling on it. He was certain it was Chuck's death that had brought it on. Still, this conclusion left one question unanswered.

What was he to make of the dream about Chuck's suicide? He'd had no idea Chuck had died when he'd had that nightmare, nor had he been stressing over what Mr. Wilkerson had said yet. So, was that dream a night terror or a normal nightmare? Nothing about it had felt normal. It had felt as vivid as the dream about the intruder. Then again, he hadn't sleepwalked or awoken screaming from that one. But was that because things were getting worse . . . and would continue to?

He closed the textbook, wishing he could get his mind off morbid subjects for a few minutes of his day. He'd hoped sleep and maybe even his scare the previous night would have jogged the eschatological doubts from his brain. He'd hoped in vain. They'd returned to the forefront of his mind as soon as he'd awoken that morning, as though they'd been levitating just above his unconsciousness, waiting to latch back onto his every waking thought and drain the life from him again. He jumped when Kevin set his tray down across from him.

"Hey," Kevin greeted without much enthusiasm.

"Hey," Jack muttered back.

Both sat without speaking further a few minutes, eating slowly.

"You hear about Chuck's funeral?" Kevin finally asked.

"Yeah. My mom said it was this Thursday, somewhere downtown. Saint Philip's, I think."

"Yeah," Kevin said.

"Fat fuckin' asshole gave me detention again today," they overheard Brad say at the next table. "That sonofabitch needs to get laid."

"Shoulda heard him in class yesterday," Darris said. "Went off on God and everything."

Jack stopped chewing. So did Kevin. They turned their heads to hear better, eyeing one another as they did.

"What do you mean?" Brad asked.

"Yeah, he was talking about how science proved there was no God a long time ago."

Brad stared, then shook his head. "I don't know about all that."

"Who the fuck does? And what's it matter anyway? Ain't like God's here speaking up for Himself. Figure if He really cared, He'd take care of Mr. Wilkerson without needing us. Maybe then I'd finally get a free pass on his class!"

The table laughed again before dispersing to take their trays to the trash cans.

Jack and Kevin remained at theirs, looking down at their half-eaten food. Kevin looked back up when Becky passed their table on her way out, after which he was the first to start eating again. Jack kept his gaze downward.

*Where is God in all this?* he wondered.

If He was real, why couldn't he find Him? Why wasn't He helping him and Kevin out with everything they were dealing with? It wasn't like he needed Him to appear and declare His presence in some miraculous way, just nudge their thoughts in the right direction. Of course, a miracle would be pretty awesome. He pictured a robed, white-bearded Figure opening the sky, kicking in Mr. Wilkerson's door, and taking over teaching the class that afternoon. He managed a half-smile at the daydream.

"Mom and I got into it over that yesterday," Kevin said, tilting his head toward the table where the others had been seated.

"Huh?" Jack asked, coming back to reality. "Over what?"

"Religion. I told her I'd go to Chuck's funeral, but I was done with going to church after that."

Jack was stunned. He and Kevin had gone through ten years of Catholic school together and had been parishioners of St. John the Baptist's Cathedral for as long as he could remember. For Kevin to walk away from his faith just like that . . . He tried not to let his shock show on his face or be heard in his voice.

"Really?" he asked, hoping he sounded nonchalant. "What brought that on?"

"Would a *Good* God have allowed what happened to Chuck?" Kevin asked, then shook his head. "I'd think if God existed and was really All-Good, Chuck would be here right now."

Jack was silent. He didn't know what to say.

Kevin shrugged his shoulders. "Plus, I think I was already pretty much there even before this week. What happened to Chuck and then what Mr. Wilkerson said in class yesterday just put the final nails in it for me. I realized I had no more reason to believe in God. I've never seen any evidence for what they taught us at Divine Savior, but there's plenty of evidence religion's something people made up to keep other people well-behaved."

Jack was having a hard time keeping his face neutral while processing this. He still didn't know what to say. So he continued to say nothing.

Kevin went on, "Anyway, Mom didn't take it too well. Course, once I gave her some arguments she had no answer for, it shut her up. My guess is she'll probably reload her guns with Father Murphy this weekend and come argue with me again. But I've heard his sermons enough to know he won't have shit to say either."

"So what were your arguments?" Jack asked after a moment.

Kevin took a bite of mashed potatoes before answering. "I told her that if God really was Perfect on His own, like the Church taught us, then He wouldn't have needed to create us, or create anything for that matter. So, the fact that we and the universe are here at least makes it seem like God isn't Perfect by Himself." He swallowed his food. "I also reminded her how we'd always been taught God's Infinite and can do anything. But to say something's all-powerful is a contradiction."

"What do you mean?" Jack asked.

Kevin swallowed the potatoes. "If something were all-powerful, then could it create something more powerful than itself?" he asked before swallowing. "If it could, then it clearly wasn't the most powerful thing in the first place, because now there's something more powerful than it. And if it can't, then it clearly has limits and is not all-powerful, because I was able to name something it couldn't do."

Jack was speechless. Kevin just shrugged again, as though this hadn't been difficult for him to work out.

"That got her off my back for now at least. You're welcome to use the arguments yourself with your parents if you need. It did wonders for me."

"So you're happy letting go of religion then?"

"Fuck yeah! If Catholicism's false, so are all the rules it tells us to obey. I for one can't wait to get a girlfriend now that I don't have to worry about fucking her being a *sin.*" He wrinkled his nose at the last word, as if it excreted a stench coming out of his mouth. "Anyway, it's way better to me than thinking so many things we like to do are things we'll be punished for in a future life."

Jack pondered Kevin's conclusions. He agreed day-to-day life might be easier without the rules of morality. After all, it was their Catholicism that got him and his family up at the ass-crack of dawn on Sundays to go to Mass. The thought of a religionless world was attractive. But its attractiveness soon imploded for him as he played it out in his mind.

"What about death?" he asked.

"What about it?"

"The thought of there being nothing after death doesn't scare you?"

"Sure it does. But there's nothing I can do about that. Best thing I can do is enjoy life to the fullest while I'm still around, since I'll only live once."

Jack reflected another moment. "That's not good enough for me. I'd always want more. Even if I lived a thousand years, it wouldn't be enough when I finally came to the last day of life and it all had to come to an end."

"I know what you mean, man. But, like I said, ain't nothing we can do about it."

"We could look for evidence of God's existence. What about the dream I had about Chuck's death before I ever knew he was dead?"

"I've thought about that," Kevin said, pausing before taking another bite of food. "I'd say it was a coincidence. Wild, crazy, and statistically unlikely, but still a coincidence. You wouldn't have thought anything more of it than a random, fucked up dream if Chuck were still here."

"But he's *not* still here," Jack pointed out. "We found out he shot himself the same day I dreamed he'd shot himself. You really think that was just a coincidence?"

"You really think it couldn't have been?"

"Sure it could have been, but—"

"See," Kevin interrupted. "You admit it could have been a coincidence. So what's the problem thinking it was?"

"Because it could have also been something else. Maybe it's even more likely it was something else, given the wild, statistical chances I'd happen to dream a suicide on the same day we learn it actually happened."

"Okay," Kevin said. "For the sake of argument, let's play this out then. What are the other possibilities of what the dream could have been?"

"Maybe a warning from God?" Jack suggested.

"But you had the dream after Chuck had died," Kevin reminded him. "What would be the point in His telling you about it then, if it wasn't to prevent the suicide? Unless it was just to torture you with the news, in which case, God would be pretty cruel and not anyone I'd want to worship. And, regardless, that's not evidence for His existence."

"Okay, so maybe it was sent to torture me," Jack said. "Maybe it wasn't from God, but . . . from something else. Something evil."

Kevin chuckled. "What, like the Devil?"

"Yeah . . . maybe like the Devil."

"But you have about as much evidence the nightmare came from the Devil as I do in thinking it was a coincidence. And since we know coincidences happen, and I've never seen any more evidence for the Devil's existence than I have for God's, *I* conclude your dream must have been a coincidence."

Jack sat in silence.

"It didn't feel that way to me," he said. *"But I know what you're gonna say,"* he added before Kevin could interject. "Feelings aren't logic and they can mislead us."

"Exactly," Kevin pointed. "Crazy people feel what they believe is true too. Doesn't make it so."

"Yeah, I guess you're right. The dream about Chuck wouldn't be enough to prove the spiritual anyway. Speaking of which though, you should hear the dream I had last night."

A bell rang, breaking into their conversation.

"Oh crap!" Kevin grabbed his tray. "C'mon, we're late!"

"I'll catch up with you in a second. Gonna finish this real quick." Jack indicated his half-eaten chicken sandwich.

"Tell me later about what happened last night?" Kevin asked.

"Yeah."

Kevin walked away, dumping his tray in the trash can and heading to his next period. Jack remained where he was, with no intention of finishing his lunch. He'd lost his appetite. Since the day before, he'd felt like he was starting to lose everything. First Chuck died. Then he'd begun to lose his faith. Now he'd learned Kevin might have already lost his. What was happening to his world?

He closed his eyes, massaging his forehead. When he opened them again, he stared at the doors Kevin had just gone through. He wanted to do something to help him, but he didn't know what he could do. He supposed he could pray. Pray Kevin found his faith again. Pray they both found their faith again.

"Our Father . . . Who art in Heaven . . ." he began.

*"Are you so certain of that, Jack?"* asked the little skeptical voice in his head.

"Hallowed be Thy Name;"

*"How can Something which doesn't exist have a Name?"*

"Thy kingdom come,"

*"Hahahaha!"*

"Thy will be done, on Earth as it is in Heaven."

*"Heeheeheeheehee!"*

"Give us this day our daily bread,"

*"Well, if He is real, what was the 'daily bread' He gave you yesterday when He threw you to the wolves?"*

"and forgive us our trespasses, as we forgive those who trespass against us;"

*"You mean like Mr. Wilkerson? Do you forgive him? How about Chuck?"*

"and lead us not into temptation, but deliver us from evil."

*"But can He deliver you from doubt, Jack? There's the real question. And, if so, where is He now? I don't see him."*

Jack got up and left the cafeteria, feeling like he'd just pushed a boulder up a mountainside.

Wind blew through St. Philip's Graveyard at a harsher pace than normal, sending leaves crunching under the Dacres' feet.

Jack was forced to fold his arms. He should have worn a thicker suit. But why would he have expected a chill in the air this early in the year? From the looks of things, no one else had. He could see tourists crossing back-and-forth through the cemetery's iron fence sporting shorts and T-shirts. They looked cold too. He supposed real fall was upon them, given this first hint of winter's bite. He tried distracting himself from his discomfort by focusing more on his surroundings.

St. Philip's was one of the oldest graveyards in the city, with headstones and mausoleums dating back centuries. He knew Colonel William Rhett, who'd been known as "Scourge of the Pirates" and who'd brought the infamous Blackbeard to justice, was buried here somewhere. In addition, John C. Calhoun's grave was here. So were the graves of Charles Pinckney and Edward Rutledge, signers of the Constitution and Declaration of Independence. To Jack's surprise, Chuck had been provided a mausoleum. Apparently, he had some uncle or grandparent who'd been a wealthy member of the Episcopal Church and had bought the plot for the family.

*Of course the generosity came after his death,* Jack thought. *Where was all the help for Chuck when he was still alive?*

Jack rubbed his neck, trying to suppress his anger. He knew it was only because he was blaming himself for what he hadn't done while Chuck was still living. But, glancing across the mourners at Chuck's mother, his guilt and anger were only fed. She looked like a woman who'd been run over by a train, twice, as though the first time hadn't been enough.

Jack couldn't say the same for the man standing next to her. It wasn't Chuck's father. He assumed it was Mrs. Nelson's latest boyfriend. He was gazing in no particular direction with a blank expression on his face. It didn't look like shock or grief. That was made all the clearer by contrasting it with Mrs. Nelson's next to him. It looked more like he was in a daze. Jack wondered if he was drunk or maybe high. As far as he was aware, he'd never seen anyone drunk or high up close. If he had to guess, he was seeing it now.

He wondered what kind of home life Chuck had lived in the years since he and Kevin parted ways with him. He stopped thinking about that good and quick. It brought back the guilt.

He tried focusing on who else was attending the funeral. He recognized a few of Chuck's aunts and uncles. Kevin and his parents were standing next to Mrs. Nelson and her spaced out boyfriend. Next to them stood Naomi Ackermann. Why was she there?

She glanced up and smiled at him, as though knowing through some intuition he was looking her way. Taking half a second to react appropriately from being caught staring, he smiled back, then jerked his head to the left, stepping away from the gathering. Taking his cue, she followed.

The funeral officiant was busy preaching a sermon in front of the mausoleum before the pallbearers placed the coffin inside. No one noticed the two teenagers slipping away. Jack waited until they were a safe distance from the mourners, under the shade of a nearby oak tree, before he said anything.

"What brought you here? I didn't think you knew Chuck very well."

"We sat in the same classes together for years," she said. "I wanted to pay my respects."

"That's . . . very kind of you."

For some reason, this made him start to choke up. He hadn't yet cried over Chuck's death. He wasn't going to let it be now, in front of a girl from school he barely knew. Stifling the urge to let his inner turmoil bust through the surface, dragging his dignity along with it, he looked away from Naomi. He fixed his gaze on the winding cords of the oak tree, stretching up and over them with their moss hanging down like laundered sheets, providing them privacy.

"I'm sure he would have appreciated it," he managed after a few moments of silent fisticuffs between his will and his emotions. "Actually, he probably wouldn't have believed it." He smiled at her. "A girl from school coming to his funeral I mean. Don't think he ever had much luck with the ladies."

She smiled, looking down, and Jack wondered if he'd seen her blush.

"I doubt he'd have even expected Kevin and me to be here," he said, turning away again.

This statement had brought the tears welling back up to the brim of his eyelids once more, ready to pour over should they lose any of their rigidity. He felt her hand press the back of his shoulder, surprised she'd been comfortable enough to make such a gesture. The unexpectedness of it was probably all that had kept him from losing it then and there.

"You guys have a falling out or something?" she asked in a tender voice he appreciated.

"Not so much. It was more a gradual drifting apart. But it was a deliberate one on my and Kevin's part. About sixth grade, Chuck started acting out more. Getting suspended from school all the time. Having brushes with the cops. Things like that. He'd always had a temper, but at that point he was displaying some real anger issues. Kevin and I could tell our parents were getting uncomfortable with it. We were too. So we stopped doing as much with him. Even stopped inviting him to sleepovers and birthday parties. It seemed to go alright. He never confronted us about any of it. We figured we'd made it seem like a natural parting of ways due to differing interests."

Jack took a breath, realizing he'd been monologuing for almost a full minute. He'd never had the chance to say any of this out loud to anyone before. Hearing himself tell the story to a newcomer . . . he felt all the more like a jackass for abandoning his friend when he'd clearly been in need. Why hadn't he seen it sooner?

Naomi squeezed his shoulder, as though sensing his anguish. "So, you three were close friends before sixth grade then, huh?"

"Three best friends," he said. "Kevin and I went to Divine Savior School up until high school. Chuck was always public, but we met him at a park one Saturday when we were kids. He was playing *Lord of the Rings* too. Once we discovered that common interest, we were thick as thieves."

Jack smiled at the memories.

"When we'd act out the movie at the park or in one of our backyards, Chuck was always Gimli. Actually, looking back, I'm guessing he gravitated to him because he was the angrier character and it gave him an excuse to chop things with a toy ax. I'd usually be Aragorn, 'cause I liked the sword more as a weapon." He chuckled now. "Plus I always wanted to marry a mythical princess like him. Kevin would be Gandalf, 'cause he liked finding sticks to make into his staff."

"'*Yoooou shall nooot paaass!*'" Naomi quoted.

Jack laughed. "Exactly. Kevin used to do that all the time whenever he'd find a new stick outside."

"Sounds like a fun childhood."

"It was. At least for me and Kevin. Not so much for Chuck. His dad left him and his mom. Actually that was the same year we met him I think, or somewhere around there. I think that's where stuff started spiraling for him. Course, I think I'm only just realizing that now, looking back."

"Well, judging from the look of the guy with Mrs. Nelson now . . . I thought that was his dad, but I guess it's his stepdad. Anyway, he doesn't exactly look like the best father to have."

"I don't think they're married. But yeah. I noticed the look of him too. Not someone I'd care to meet, much less live with. I wish I'd understood what was going on with Chuck sooner. If Kevin and I knew more about a troublesome home life that involved abuse or something, we wouldn't have . . ." Jack couldn't finish.

Naomi stepped around his shoulder, facing him now. "This isn't your fault, Jack. It's nobody's fault. Chuck must have been very troubled, but I doubt what happened had anything to do with you or Kevin."

It was taking more and more mental energy for Jack to keep his cool while he looked Naomi in the eyes. He shifted his weight in an attempt to steady himself.

"I have no way of knowing that. Maybe things would have been different if we hadn't shunned him. Chuck could have leaned on us. He needed us and we weren't *there*—" his voice cracked and faded on the last word.

The buildup inside him finally boiled over. He didn't gasp or sob. Tears just rolled silently down his cheeks. He turned away from Naomi again. She kept her hand on his shoulder, as though giving him permission, but was gracious enough not to step over and look him in the face this time.

He breathed haggardly, which might have just been his grief, but was probably also the result of his week of fitful sleep. There hadn't been a decent night's rest since Monday. Naomi allowed him the time he needed to calm down. It wasn't brief. The tears kept coming as he thought over his years of friendship with Chuck, knowing that chapter of his life had been brought to an unexpected and definitive end this time. As he tried to distract himself with anything other than memories, he noticed a peculiar figure standing a short distance from the rest of the mourners.

A short man with bone white hair who looked to be in his early sixties, wearing clergyman's attire, but not like any Jack was used to seeing. He had the usual white collar over black, but he wore a robe instead of dress clothes, and the buttons going down the robe were a light rose color. So was the Victorian-looking sash around his waist that hung down the side of his legs, with tassels at its bottom. The minister's attire made him look like someone who'd just stepped through a time portal from the nineteenth century. Jack liked it. The man looked like he was praying. To Jack's surprise, he made the sign of the cross before turning to depart the graveyard.

He was a Catholic priest, but not one Jack recognized. What was a Catholic priest doing at an Episcopal funeral? He didn't know. Regardless, it had been enough of a distraction that his weeping had stopped. The look of the priest had made him feel comforted, as though things were going to be okay. He brushed the tears from his face before turning back to Naomi.

"Sorry."

"Don't be sorry! You lost your childhood best friend!"

This statement almost made the tears begin again, but Jack controlled himself. "Should we rejoin the others?"

"If you want, but . . ." She broke off.

"What?"

"Nothing. I don't know," she said. "You're right. Let's get back. I haven't said hi to Kevin yet."

"Me neither."

They made their way toward the mourners again. It looked like the pallbearers were about to place Chuck's body in the mausoleum. Jack didn't want to miss it, but he found he also wanted to keep talking to Naomi. She made him feel comfortable being himself.

"Hey, are you doing anything for Halloween?" he asked without fully thinking it through before the words leapt from his lips.

She looked a little surprised by the question. "Nothing I'd planned yet. It's still a couple weeks away isn't it? Why do you ask?"

"My family usually has a party with friends and any trick-or-treaters who come by. There's a bobbing for apples contest in the backyard and stuff."

"Oh, that sounds fun!"

"Yeah? Well, if you're interested. Kevin should be there too. It'd be fun to chat under more cheerful circumstances."

She smiled. "Sounds good!"

# CHAPTER IV
## THE PUMPKIN CALLER

*What could have been going through Chuck's mind when he'd decided to end his own life?*

The question bothered Jack for the next forty-eight hours after the funeral, even as he helped his mother set the table for Saturday's dinner. Nothing seemed to get it out of his head. He knew he could never kill himself. But he imagined Chuck would have said the same thing, once upon a time. So what had brought him to the point where he'd found dying was better than living?

That had set Jack wondering whether Chuck had believed in an afterlife or not. He remembered Chuck coming with him and his family to church when they were kids, but he realized he didn't know if Chuck's own family was religious. It wasn't a subject that had come up between three young boys during sleepovers. For all Jack knew, Chuck and his mother had been atheists. He supposed that, for atheists, suicide wouldn't be as insane a notion. If an atheist found his life had grown intolerable, he could always opt out of it for oblivion instead. To Jack's mind, this was still a repulsive notion compared with the idea of eternal life. But Jack hadn't lived Chuck's life. Would he hold a different opinion if he had?

He shuddered.

"Alright, everybody! Dinner!" his mother called into the living room, snapping him out of his thoughts. She smiled at him. "Thanks for helping set up, son."

"No problem," he muttered, seating himself in his usual spot at the table.

He was quiet while they all listened to Chloe prattle on for twenty minutes about two of her co-workers who'd broken up the night before. There had been all the drama at work that day. He tuned most of it out. He found the story trivial compared to the problems he was facing. Maybe he'd have had more sympathy for the couple a week earlier. Now their story was just irritating. Death jumping out from around a corner to punch him in the face had changed his perspective on a few things.

When Chloe paused to take a breath and a few bites of food, Lorelai turned to him. "You've been awfully quiet, son. What's on your mind?"

The question caught him off guard. For some reason, it felt invasive, as though his mother had demanded insight into his most private thoughts. He didn't know why his internal reaction was so extreme. He was probably just tired.

"Plenty," he said. "But I don't want to interrupt a good story once it's been started." He smiled at Chloe, who smiled back.

"No, I've been going on too long already. You look like you want to talk."

"Not really," he said.

"You sure?" she pressed. "You haven't said much at all lately."

"Well, it hasn't exactly been my week."

"You know . . ." His mother hesitated, which was unusual. "If you wanted to talk to someone about what's happened, your dad and I would support you."

"You mean a therapist?" Jack asked.

"It would be quite understandable after what's happened."

Jack considered for a moment while everyone looked at him. His father had glanced up when his mother had mentioned therapy and nodded his agreement.

"Thanks for the offer," Jack said. "But I don't think a shrink's what I need. I can't do anything to change the fact that Chuck's . . . gone. Besides, his death's not the only thing that's been on my mind this week."

"What is it then?" his father spoke for the first time.

Jack was quiet another moment. He supposed he couldn't hide his doubts forever, and they weren't going away on their own. It was time to open up.

"Well, it was actually something my biology teacher said."

"Mr. Wilkerson?" his father asked.

"Yes . . . He claimed that . . . God doesn't exist. He said science proved as much a long time ago."

"Oh." Dale Dacre smiled, an unimpressed expression on his face. "That all?"

"Well, you can't let that upset you, son," Lorelai said, taking a bite of her chicken marsala. "You're in a public school now. You're going to have to expect to run into people with different beliefs than you."

*I know. I know,* " Jack said, a little too harshly. "It's not like I thought everyone at Wando was Catholic, but it still made me mad."

"You can't get mad just because someone's an atheist, Jack," his father said.

"I wasn't mad because he's an atheist. I was offended because he preached his atheism in the classroom as though it was a cold hard fact."

"So what?" Chloe said. "You just ignore it and move on."

Jack turned to her, his frustration growing. "Just like that, huh?"

"Well, what do you want me to say?" she asked. "What difference does letting it upset you make? It doesn't change anything."

"Wow!" Jack laughed, shaking his head. "Am I glad the Prophets and Evangelists of the Bible didn't have your attitude. Christianity would've never extended beyond the Middle East, much less reached this country. They went to death in defense of their faith, and you're telling me I shouldn't even be bothered to stand up for it in a classroom!"

Jack's whole family laughed at him.

"That has nothing to do with this, Jack," Lorelai said. "Who was talking about Prophets and Evangelists? We're just talking about you."

"You're telling me you wouldn't have been the least bit angry if it had been you who had to sit there and listen to a lecture based in atheism?"

"No," Dale answered him before Lorelai could. "And you'd better be putting whatever the teacher wants on his tests. I don't want your grade in his class slipping and your scholarship with The Citadel put in jeopardy just because you don't like what the man personally believes."

"Even if the answers he wants on his tests are a *lie?*" Jack demanded.

"You don't have to believe his opinions yourself," Dale said, "but you do have to maintain your A in his class."

"Just keep thinking about how you'll be done with it in December," Lorelai encouraged. "Then you won't ever have to deal with this teacher again."

*"That's not the point!"* Jack argued. "I'm not worried about my grade. I could pass any of Wando's classes even if I slept through them. You know that. It's the principle of the thing. Why should I have to bow down and accept whatever a teacher throws at me, even if it's bullshit?"

*"Because,"* Lorelai raised her own voice, *"like your father said, he's the one who's in charge of your grade . . . And that's the last I want to hear about it,"* she added, seeing he was about to argue back.

Jack grabbed his plate and rose from his chair. "I'm finished. Thanks for dinner."

He put the plate in the kitchen and stormed up to his room.

Jack replayed the conversation over and over again in his head for the next fifteen minutes.

Trying to open up hadn't brought him any comfort the way he'd hoped. Little did his family know the anger he'd been directing toward Mr. Wilkerson was what he felt toward himself for doubting his faith. He supposed that, if his teacher's statement hadn't initiated such an internal struggle within his own mind, he would have just felt sorry for a person who didn't believe in God. Yet here he was, struggling to keep his head above water while attempting to swim through a sea of anxiety over the matter.

*"It's all an old metaphysical fairy tale full of miraculous legends, paradoxes, and nonsense!"* the little voice in his head protested.

He closed his eyes, massaging the sides of his forehead to help himself concentrate through it.

*"You only think Catholicism's the correct religion, because it's the one you were raised with. If you'd been born into an atheistic family, you'd be on a quest to prove that side right instead!"*

*I'm not trying to think with a biased mentality!* Jack thought back. *I'm trying to think objectively! To look at both Catholicism and atheism objectively!*

*"Then why are you still praying?"*

Jack opened his eyes as the question popped into his head, taken aback. It was true. He'd been praying more. After what had happened to Chuck, he'd found himself praying during any pocket of free time in his day, usually for answers to the questions he couldn't figure out.

*"Why do you pray if you're honestly assessing both sides objectively? Seems to me you should wait until you've confirmed there's a God before you try communicating with Him. Otherwise, you're wasting your time, not to mention your breath."*

Jack thought about that a moment. It seemed to make sense.

*"But so does this. If there's a God, and He really is all people say He is, then praying's the only way you're going to find Him. You can't reach up to Him. He can only reach down to you. How else are you to communicate that you're seeking Him, except by telling Him? You're like an astronaut stranded in space, unsure if NASA can still hear you or not. You keep talking anyway on the off-chance they can."*

Jack nodded. That made sense too. And since the thought had for once stifled his unremitting doubts, he closed his eyes and laid back on his bed, trying to rest.

*"Yes, dream,"* the voice came back. *"That's all you can do. For that's all sweet religion is. Just various versions of mankind's dream of a better and everlasting existence, contrasted with the dark reality of his brief moment in the sun. After all, what is one human lifespan compared with the vastness of time, Jack? But the blink of an eye."*

Jack tucked his head between his hands, curling into a fetal position. "Shut up!" he argued with himself. "Just . . . for once . . . shut the hell up!"

There was a small knock at the door. He was grateful for the interruption. Nonetheless, his voice still came out tersely when he answered.

"Who is it?"

Chloe cracked it open. "Still mad, huh?" She smiled timidly.

He sat up. "No, I just like stomping up the stairs every once in a while for exercise!"

"Okay! Okay! No need for the sarcasm. I just thought I'd suggest dropping the class if you dislike the teacher so much."

"Can't. Biology's a required science, and Mr. Wilkerson's the only one at Wando who teaches it. Besides, we're way past add-drop deadlines, and I only have one more semester after this. I have to take it now. Otherwise I won't be able to take physics in the spring and graduate on time."

"Too bad. Well, good luck dealing with him I guess. Anyway, I came to tell you someone's at the door for you."

Jack furrowed his eyebrows. "Who? Kevin?"

"No. Nobody I know. But I think they're from school." She eyed him with a half-smile, raising an eyebrow. "A girl. Said she talked to you at the funeral."

"Naomi? How'd she know where I live?"

Chloe shrugged. Jack passed her and went downstairs, skipping steps along the way. He opened the front door and started to greet her, but it wasn't Naomi standing on the threshold waiting for him.

A tall silhouette stood on the porch just beyond the reach of the foyer light. A silhouette he recognized all too well, though he'd only seen it once before. It should have been illuminated when he opened the door, but no light extended out to the porch. It was as if it were repelling light, refusing to reveal the figure who stood on it. It made it impossible for Jack to see anything of the visitor other than very round shoulders and thin bone white hair. The only light visible on the porch issued from a pumpkin in the stranger's right hand. The face carved into it had thinly slit eyes, giving it a sly expression. Its mouth was carved into a grin, one side of which curved higher up its cheek than the other. The flame within it burned fiercely, flickering in such a way that its face seemed to move.

Jack was paralyzed for half a second as he took in the sight. But he soon sprung into action, slamming the door shut and frantically bolting its lock. He turned around to scream for help, but the entire house had gone dark behind him. He was alone. There was a scratching from the door's other side. It sent tingles echoing up and down his spine. They were enough to make him look back at the door without thinking.

Through its decorative window, he could see the specter of his nightmare still standing on the front porch, peering in from the other side. He held the pumpkin below his chin and lifted its top off. The flame within poured up over his features, illuminating them for the first time. Jack's breath froze in his throat, unsure whether to suck in or exhale, almost making him cough. It was as if all his worst nightmares from childhood had become incarnate and presented themselves to him in a single moment.

A grinning, dead face leered back at him. It had black skin stretched so thin the cheeks protruded outward, leaving the eye sockets sunken. Despite this, the skin was still wrinkled, even on the fiend's bald head. It had no eyebrows or lashes. No nose or ears. Only holes where they should have been, making its face appear more like a skull. The eyes were milky white, with no pupils or irises, standing out against the dark skin along with the hair hanging off the back of its head. The only other color besides these were its yellowing, chipped teeth.

Jack got a good look at these as the creature's grin widened, stretching its skin even farther over its facial muscles in a disgusting way. He tried to run, but his legs wouldn't work, nor would his neck muscles, which forced him to continue looking into those lifeless eyes. His voice was working though, enough for him to scream at the top of his lungs.

*"NO! NOOOO! HELP MEEE! HELP MEEEEEE!"*

Suddenly, everything went blurry as an earthquake obscured his vision. He awoke to his mother's terrified face inches from his. She'd been shaking him.

*"Jack! Wake up!"*

He blinked hard a few times. *"I'm up! I'm up!"* He breathed out a long sigh. "I'm awake," he reassured, more to himself than anyone else.

"Another night terror," his mother said.

Jack couldn't tell if it had been a question or a statement. He didn't care. He was too busy trying to slow his breathing and heart rate down, wiping cold sweat from his forehead.

"Are they supposed to terrify him or us?" Chloe asked, standing behind Lorelai with Dale. "'Cause it's doing a good job freaking me out."

*"Fuck you, Chloe!"* Jack shouted. *"You try having one!"*

"Hey, I wasn't—"

"Alright! Alright!" Lorelai interrupted the siblings, quashing the argument before it could go further. "Are you alright, son? You made it all the way down the stairs again. That worries me. You didn't fall this time, but . . . it could always happen if you're sleepwalking. Maybe we should put some kind of a lock on—"

Jack cut her off by shoving his way past her to take a seat on the bottom steps, still gasping for air. He could see the grinning, leering face of the monster so vividly in his memory that he avoided looking up at the front door's window.

"I don't even remember falling asleep!" he said. "How long has it been since I left dinner?"

"Half an hour, forty-five minutes maybe?" his father said.

Jack plunged his face into his hands, raking his fingers through his hair. "What the fuck's happening to me?" he whispered.

Lorelai stooped down in front of him. "Our offer from earlier still stands, son. If a therapist could help . . . maybe a professional could stop these . . . episodes."

Jack didn't look at her. "I'll think about it," he said after a few seconds. "But I still feel like what I need is . . . something else. I don't know who has the answers for what I'm dealing with. I do want to talk to someone, but about more than just grief."

"Great!" Lorelai smiled, standing up. "Now, I think we could all use some sleep."

Jack's face darted up. "I don't want to go back to sleep right now!" he almost yelped, sounding far more panicked than he'd intended.

There was no denying it. Not only was he having trouble sleeping. Now he was afraid of sleeping. Afraid of who—what—he might meet when faced with the insides of his eyelids.

"I'll stay up with you," Chloe volunteered. "We can watch a comedy or something."

"Yeah, that sounds good," Jack agreed, getting up and heading for the couch in the living room.

His parents didn't argue.

"You sure you don't need anything else?" Lorelai asked.

"I just want to get my mind off the whole thing right now," Jack said, as Chloe joined him on the couch.

"Okay, well, don't stay up too late. Remember, we have Mass in the morning."

She and Dale turned and headed upstairs, but Jack had glanced in their direction. What she'd said had helped him figure out who he did want to talk to.

Dale weaved around traffic, steering through the inner city of downtown Charleston.

It was a typical drive through the historic South Carolinian metropolis. Slow, with constant stops. Tourists walked in droves through the palmetto tree-lined streets, filing in and out of antique shops, fancy clothing stores, quaint brunch spots, archaic hotels, distinguished theatres, scenic graveyards, picturesque museums, and grand, nineteenth-century houses that had been converted into luxurious restaurants. Even if a driver were a local and knew all the hidden side streets, it made little difference. The pedestrians crossed the roads as though the vehicles weren't there, forcing drivers to jam on the brakes. As if they weren't enough to delay the traffic, there were also the stop lights about every quarter mile. And the narrow lanes—which hadn't been expanded since being built to accommodate carriages over a hundred years earlier—changed randomly into turn-only lanes and parallel parking spots. Yet, Dale was patient with this poorly planned mess of roads. He knew its rhythm.

Jack wasn't so patient this morning, fidgeting in his seat. His father took the right off King Street onto Broad, and the Cathedral of St. John the Baptist at last came into view. Its black iron gate parted to allow entry into the parking lot. The church was a gothic edifice of brown stone, constructed in 1890. It was long and narrow, with numerous parapets and buttresses along its sides, always giving it the resemblance of an ancient sea vessel to Jack. The steeple atop it was crowned with a giant gold cross, which he knew could be seen from the harbor, having caught sight of it before in the family's speed boat.

After parking, the family clambered their way through the small vestibule at the back of the church and into its nave. It was lined with great pillars on each side, giving the impression they'd just stepped into ancient Roman times. The walls featured soaring stained glass windows, sending a river of colors cascading off the white marble floor. The sanctuary at the front was flanked by two side chapels, one of which housed the baptismal font. The stone piece rose from the floor in the shape of a pedestal crowned with a gold dome-shaped lid.

The Dacres dipped their hands in the smaller holy water fonts behind the pews, crossed themselves, and made their way to their usual spot on the nave's left side. Jack entered the pew last, seating himself apart from the rest of the family. He knelt down to pray for the few minutes before the ceremony began. Chloe noticed the change in his demeanor from his usual behavior on Sunday mornings. The previous week, she'd had to wake him during the homily when he'd started drooling on himself. Father Murphy's droning had worked its magic again.

After a few minutes, the bell clanged from the tower and everyone rose from their seats. Three boys and two girls dressed in black robes with lacy white shirts over them processed down the aisle. The priest followed. Father Murphy was a middle-aged man wearing thick glasses and green vestments. Upon reaching his chair in the sanctuary, he led the congregation through the opening prayers, after which they all sat down to hear the Scripture readings of the day.

"A reading from the Book of Wisdom," the lector's voice resounded through the church. "Who can know God's counsel, or who can conceive what the LORD intends? For the deliberations of mortals are timid, and unsure are our plans. For the corruptible body burdens the soul, and the earthen shelter weighs down the mind, that has many concerns. And scarce do we guess the things on Earth, and what is within our grasp we find with difficulty; but when things are in Heaven, who can search them out? Or who ever knew your counsel, except you had given wisdom and sent your holy spirit from on high? And thus were the paths of those on earth made straight."

Jack sat tense and unmoving, feeling the words had been directed at him, as though God were reaching out to him after all. His deliberations over the last week had been timid, and his mind did feel weighed down by the many questions he was unable to answer. But, the reading sounded like it was saying no one could hope to know God's plans or counsels without the guidance of His Holy Spirit, which only He could give.

*But I already knew that,* he prayed. *That's why I'm here . . . to ask for Your help.*

Father Murphy soon stood up and walked over to the ambo to read the Gospel passage for the day.

"A reading from the Gospel according to Saint Luke," he stated in his characteristic monotone. "Great crowds were traveling with Jesus, and he turned and addressed them, 'If anyone comes to me without hating his father and mother, wife and children, brothers and sisters, and even his own life, he cannot be my disciple. Whoever does not carry his own cross and come after me cannot be my disciple.'"

Jack was stunned at Christ's words. He didn't remember ever hearing this part of the Bible before. What did Jesus mean by "hating" one's parents and siblings? Wasn't hate supposed to be what He always preached against? Jack sat down after the reading, feeling more confused than ever, hoping Father Murphy would elaborate on what the passage meant.

He knew Jesus often spoke metaphorically, teaching truths in the context of parables, but the truths within the metaphors were usually obvious to him. This time, he found himself unable to solve the puzzle. While Father Murphy preached, Jack stayed more focused than he ever had. But the clergyman never addressed Christ's strange declarations. Instead, he kept reiterating how much Jesus loved everyone, with no references to any of the day's readings. Jack found himself growing more and more impatient and frustrated.

He knew Jesus loved everyone. He'd retained that lesson since he was about three years old. Today, he needed some kind of assurance that what Catholics believed made sense!

After fifteen minutes of rambling, the priest stepped down from the ambo. Jack went through the rest of the Mass feeling a sense of defeat. He couldn't picture Father Murphy lasting long against the arguments of someone like Mr. Wilkerson, or even Kevin. It seemed his friend was right to feel justified in his position. His mother was never going to get what she needed from the priest to win against his atheistic arguments. Neither was he.

When one of the altar servers rang a bell from the front, signaling the consecration was about to take place, Jack glanced up, watching the cleric pick up a round white wafer from the altar. This was supposed to be the moment in which the priest transformed the bread and wine into the literal Body and Blood of Jesus Christ.

As Father Murphy raised the Host for all to see, Jack wondered for the first time in his life if he were really looking at Jesus or just a brittle little cracker.

# CHAPTER V
# THE MYSTERY PRIEST

*"You're just grasping at straws! You could read anything and find a way to interpret it as related to your own situation, Jack! Those ambiguous Old Testament readings were designed that way. People find in them whatever they want all the time. Why do you think there are so many different religions founded around the Bible?*

*If you wanted, you could start seeing supernatural signs all over the place, in everyday life. It's called a self-fulfilling prophecy, dumb-ass! But if you do that, people will think you're crazy. And they wouldn't be wrong would they? Because that would be crazy."*

Ever since the Mass on Sunday, the skeptical voice in Jack's head never seemed to leave him alone. It was like it had been bolstered. He could feel himself spiraling down into an ever deepening despair. He went through day-to-day tasks wondering if there were any real meaning or ultimate purpose behind them.

Sitting at his desk in English class, he gazed out the window at a mockingbird making its nest in a tree branch. It was a sunny morning. Lush leaves decorated the bushes. Dazzling clouds painted the sky. The sight was gorgeous and should have brought him peace. All he could do was question whether such a picture had been crafted by a Being of higher intelligence, or was simply the result of a random assortment of atoms across the universe. Despite the sight's beauty, he kept thinking about the Psalm read at Chuck's funeral.

"Though I should walk in the midst of the shadow of death, I will fear no evils, for Thou art with me. Dark be the valley about my path."

Variations of the verses had been repeating in his mind for days.

*I walk in the midst of the shadow of death . . . I will fear no evils . . . Dark be the valley . . . Dark is my path . . . I fear evils . . . But Thou art with me . . . Thou art with me.*

*"He wouldn't be with you though, Jack,"* came the skeptical voice he'd grown to loathe so much. *"You shunned Chuck, helping drive him to despair and suicide. Would Jesus have done that? Would Jesus be pleased with that? No. You're marked*

*now. Your soul reeks of sin. Probably mortal sin. You've even doubted God's existence. What would He have to do with you now?"*

Jack shuddered. He had failed Chuck in a grave way. He and Kevin both. And now, they were abandoning their faith. Maybe that was it. Maybe that was the reason he couldn't seem to find God when he needed His help so much. Maybe he'd been unable to discern His presence because he was in the state of spiritual death.

Was that why he was losing his faith in the first place? Was God punishing him? Another shiver tickled its way down his spine. He knew there was only one way to have serious sins erased from the soul. Confession to a priest. But he hadn't been to Confession in years.

*There's no way I'm doing that!* he thought.

Then second-guessed himself.

*Why not? Maybe I could finally get some straight answers if I confess all these doubts. Priests are the ones who're supposed to know about this stuff anyway. Maybe I was too quick to judge Father Murphy's competency on Sunday. He could have something to offer.*

*"And what exactly are you going to do? Show up at the church office and say you want to confess your sins?"* The voice laughed.

Jack was terrified by the prospect. But the alternative of being condemned kept running through his mind. If there was a chance Hell was real, he'd rather be safe than sorry.

*Yeah,* he thought back. *Why not?*

Chuck's signature tapping on the back of his chair interrupted his deliberations, irritating him. He was trying to concentrate! The tapping was really getting annoying—

Jack jolted, making Naomi jump beside him.

He tore his head around to look behind them. Chuck wasn't seated in the corner desk behind him. Chuck was dead. No one was sitting behind him. There was no one anywhere behind them in the room. And no one present could have gotten the right angle to kick the back of Jack's chair without him seeing it. But he knew he hadn't imagined the tapping.

Chuck's tapping.

Jack stared at the empty desk. *Was he losing his fucking mind?* Maybe he should take his parents up on their offer for therapy.

"What?" Naomi asked beside him.

"I just thought . . . did you feel anything behind us just now?"

She looked at Chuck's old desk. "No . . . What is it, Jack? You're freaking me out!"

"Just . . . could have sworn I felt someone kick the back of my chair just now, the way Chuck used to."

Naomi stared at the desk, then back at Jack. "Maybe it was just memory association. Muscle memory or whatever. You know? How sometimes you feel your phone vibrating in your pocket when it's not even there, but you're just used to feeling texts come in all the time?"

"Yeah . . . maybe," Jack said.

He didn't feel the least bit convinced by her rationalizing. There was nothing for it. He needed to talk to someone who could provide answers.

If not a counselor, then Father Murphy would have to do.

Jack pulled into St. John's parking lot, feeling like a performer on stage just before the curtain lifted.

He turned off the engine, but remained in his Jeep. This was crazy. What was he doing here? He'd been going back-and-forth on his decision to seek Confession the whole drive over. It wasn't too late. He could turn around and go home right now—no harm, no foul.

He hadn't made himself look like a fool in front of anyone yet. No one would ever have to know he'd been here. The keys were still in the ignition. Jack shuffled them between his fingers, teetering on the decision to pull them out or turn the car back on before being noticed. What would this really accomplish?

*"If you leave now, you'll always wonder what might have happened had you stayed and asked the priest your questions."*

Jack knew that was true, but he was still apprehensive. Couldn't he just go to Confession another day? Were there any officially scheduled times at the parish, when Father Murphy would already be waiting in the confessional and never had to see his face or know his name?

*"You know that's just an excuse. You'll keep putting it off, and end up never going."*

Whether it was hammering doubts at him or telling him what to do in order to satisfy those doubts, the little voice of reason in Jack's head was really beginning to annoy him.

*Yes, I would,* he thought. *Just under less awkward circumstances!*

*"Stop procrastinating. Look at what the last week's been like. YOU NEED AN-SWERS NOW, JACK!"*

Jack rubbed his forehead, almost feeling those last words hit him. The mental assault demanded satisfaction.

*"Don't you remember how you felt after confessing last time?"*

He looked up. He did remember. It had been before his Confirmation in seventh grade. He'd felt refreshed. Lighter even. As though a weight had been lifted from his shoulders.

He yanked the key from the ignition.

Jack marched into the office on the opposite side of the parking lot from the cathedral and approached the receptionist's desk.

An elderly lady with short gray hair and thick glasses was seated in front of him.

"Can I help you?"

Her voice was sweet. It put him more at ease.

"Yes. I'm a parishioner here and was wondering if Father Murphy might be around?"

"Oh, I'm sorry. He's out of town until tomorrow evening."

"I see . . ."

Jack could hear the defeat in his voice for himself. So it was no wonder the receptionist's expression changed to one of concern.

"You can leave a message for him if you like," she offered.

"No thanks. I was actually going to ask if he'd hear my confession. I guess I'll try catching him another time."

"Oh, well if Confession was all you needed, I'm sure Monsignor Bamonte would be willing to hear it."

"Who?"

"Monsignor Bamonte. He arrived at the parish a few weeks ago. He's staying at the rectory with Father Murphy. I can phone him and see if he's in his office if you like."

"Sure," Jack said. "Thank you."

She picked up her phone and dialed an extension. After a few moments in which Jack caught himself holding his breath, she spoke into the receiver.

"Monsignor, there's a gentleman here who'd like to go to Confession. Do you have time?"

Jack waited.

"Yes . . . Okay . . . Alright, that works fine." She hung up and looked at Jack with a smile. "He'll be right out. You can wait in that chair in the corner if you like."

She pointed behind him.

"Thanks a lot!" Jack said, taking a seat.

"My pleasure!"

Two minutes later, the clergyman emerged from a hallway on Jack's left. Jack tilted his head back in surprise. It was the mystery priest he'd seen in the graveyard at Chuck's funeral. He was still dressed in the archaic attire.

"You're a younger man than I expected," the monsignor welcomed in a soft voice.

Jack rose from his chair, holding out a hand in greeting. "Jack Dacre."

The priest shook it. "Monsignor Adrian Bamonte."

"Good to meet you. I didn't realize we had another priest around."

"Well I've only been in town a few weeks. I haven't had a chance to meet many of the parishioners yet. But come! Your timing was perfect. I was just headed out for a walk to take in some of Charleston's sights. Why don't you join me and we'll do Confession along the way."

"Sure." Jack followed him outside. "You know, I have seen you once before, a few days ago, at St. Philip's Cemetery. You were at Chuck Nelson's funeral. Did you know him?"

"No. I read about what happened to him in the news and decided to stop by his funeral when I realized how close it was. Thought he wouldn't mind the extra prayers. Did you know him then?"

Jack was coughing, trying to stifle the emotions Monsignor Bamonte's act of kindness had stirred in him. "We were childhood best friends."

The monsignor bowed his head. "I'm sorry for what you must be going through. I'll keep you and your loved ones in my prayers."

"Thank you . . ." Jack gulped, forcing his feelings away. "So, are you here to replace Father Murphy or something?" He realized he hoped the answer was yes.

"No. Don't worry. Your rector is here to stay. I'm just here as a favor to Bishop Richard. He and I are old friends and he asked me to come down and help out, since the Diocese of Charleston was short-staffed. I'm actually a priest of the Archdiocese of Washington." They exited through the churchyard's iron gates onto the sidewalk of Broad Street. "So, why don't we begin?" the monsignor asked.

Jack nodded.

"In the name of the Father, and of the Son, and of the Holy Spirit," the priest initiated the Sacrament.

Crossing himself along with him, Jack took a deep breath. "Bless me, Father, for I have sinned. It's been . . . four years since my last Confession."

The clergyman nodded, his kindly expression remaining.

Feeling encouraged, Jack went on, "I'm lost in doubt. I've been seriously questioning whether or not God exists, and it's been driving me crazy."

He'd finally admitted it to someone out loud. Pausing, he looked Monsignor Bamonte in the eyes to see his reaction. The priest just nodded again, his expression neutral.

"The thought of there being nothing after death terrifies me! I haven't been able to put my mind at ease about it."

"Was your friend Chuck's death the catalyst for these thoughts?"

"Yes, but there was another part to it. I just started my senior year of high school, and my new biology teacher made a statement in class that science has proven God doesn't exist. At first I was angry and wanted to argue with him. But, I hesitated. I realized I wasn't so sure myself. I was raised Catholic. I've grown up praying and going to Mass every Sunday. But that's just it! My faith was inherited, not obtained. I believed in God, because people told me He was real."

"And now you need to experience Him for yourself, given what's just happened to your friend. You need some tangible, personal reassurance of it all, because you've realized other people's reassurance isn't good enough anymore," the monsignor finished for him.

"Yes, exactly!" Jack said.

The priest nodded. "What you're going through is quite normal, especially given the circumstances. Many people around your age and even a little older have reconversion periods when they question their beliefs. It's not something to be ashamed of. It's actually an opportunity for your faith to grow. Your mind wants to reach the next stage of its maturity. And, like any other growth process, it can be painful while you're going through it."

"Tell me about it," Jack said. "It feels like a crisis."

"Well crises usually bring out either the best or the worst in people. It's up to you to decide how this experience ends up changing you. But it doesn't sound to me like you're guilty of any sin. I believe you're what I like to call an inquirer, not a doubter."

"What's the difference?"

The priest smiled. "Glad you asked. Inquirers and doubters may both ask the same questions. But the inquirer wants the truth, no matter what it is. Even if it's a truth he won't like. The doubter wants to be confirmed in what he prefers to believe. The inquirer is what the Church would like all of her curious children to be. It's never a sinful thing to sincerely ask why something is as it is. It can only lead to a greater understanding and appreciation of Truth. Take a look at Psalm Fifty-Two, for example. It begins, The fool said in his heart: There is no God." The cleric paused a moment. "I take that passage as saying a fool is someone who doubts the existence of his Creator according to his will, not his reasoning."

Jack's heartbeat sped up with excitement at having found someone who thought analytically. He was glad he'd come to the church office on this particular afternoon after all. He wondered what he'd have gotten from Father Murphy.

"The failure to keep an open mind to any and all possible explanations," Jack said, "instead of being biased from the start."

"Exactly," the cleric said. "So which would you say you are?"

"Definitely the inquirer. I admit, I want it to be true that Catholicism's based on fact. But I'm not interested in deluding myself. I want the truth, even if it's that God's not real." He paused. "Although . . . I'm not sure how I'll handle it if that's the case."

"Well then, let's see what we can do for you. Why don't we start where your trouble began? You said Chuck's death got you asking questions, but you also said your biology teacher's statement pitting science against religion spurred on your internal conflict. Yes?"

"Yes, sir."

"So, other than the death of your friend making you ask the questions people naturally wonder when they lose a loved one, would you say the struggle in your mind is also an inability to reconcile faith with reason?"

"I guess so."

"Alright. Let me ask you this then, just so I can best understand. How would you personally define faith?"

Jack didn't answer immediately. He felt like he was taking a pop quiz all of a sudden. He thought back to his schooling at Divine Savior.

"I've heard it called 'the evidence of things unseen.'"

"Is that your definition or just one you've heard? Do *you* think of it that way?"

Jack wrinkled his nose. "No. I don't think I like that definition. I guess the best I can come up with myself is 'belief in the unseen.' But, still, that's just a statement of what it is. It doesn't help me have it."

"I know, but one thing at a time. I still want to clarify your definition. Would you say faith is blind?"

Jack shifted his bottom jaw to one side. "What do you mean?"

"Are you familiar with the notion of taking a leap of faith?"

"Sure. I've heard the phrase before."

"And would you say taking a leap of faith is how we come to accept our Catholic beliefs?"

Jack wasn't sure what the monsignor was looking for, and for some reason he felt like he'd be disappointing him if he gave the wrong answer. He wasn't used to feeling incompetent. But Divine Savior had never gone into more detail about the definition of faith than they already had.

"I . . . suppose so," he answered.

The priest smiled. "Guess again."

Jack mentally kicked himself, but the cleric didn't seem to mind his answer.

"Faith isn't wishful thinking or a blind hope that our religion is true," he explained. "There is no leap of faith in Catholicism. Sadly that's how many Catholics today think we come to believe though. It's just another version of Pascal's Wager.

Don't suppose you've ever heard of that?"

"No," Jack said, as they turned down the sidewalk of Market Street, heading toward East Bay.

"It basically says that, even if you don't know God exists, it's safer to bet on it. If you're wrong, and there's no God to greet you after death, you won't know the difference at that point and you'll have lived a good life. On the other hand, if you're right, you'll have won Heaven. And, of course, if you bet there's no God and you're wrong, you lose happiness with Him for eternity and end up in Hell. Therefore, it's ultimately safer to wager God exists."

Monsignor Bamonte paused, allowing Jack to ponder everything he'd said.

"Do you see the flaw in that argument?"

"It definitely doesn't satisfy me. That's for sure. I don't want to go through my life hoping my faith's justified. I need to know what I believe is true in order to be at peace."

The monsignor nodded his head. "Precisely why Pascal's Wager is a flawed outlook. It treats faith as if it's a gambling chip. But divine faith's a gift given by God to man, not by man to God. No one can reason his way to it. The kind of faith we're talking about is something wholly separate from reason. But, in Pascal's Wager, the person pretends to have divine faith, as though they could feign it before God and trick their way into Heaven.

If you really think about it, what Pascal's actually encouraging is—as you said—hope. And hope's different from faith. It's confusions like this that cause atheists to sometimes pessimistically define our Faith as 'belief despite the evidence.' But Catholic faith would be better defined as 'trust based on good reasons.'"

Jack thought for a moment, deeply. He'd never heard insights such as this monsignor was dolling out like candy at a parade.

"You keep calling it divine faith," he said, "as if there are different types."

"There are. There are two. Human and divine. Unlike divine faith, human faith can be obtained through reason. Examples of it would be the trust you have in people like your doctor, your teachers, or your parents. You'd believe your doctor if he told you a certain prescription medicine would be helpful to you in order to recover from a sickness wouldn't you?"

"Of course."

"Why?"

"Because he's been to medical school, studied diseases, probably dealt with other people who've been cured of the same illness with the same medicine."

"Right. You'd believe him because you trust he's qualified and has your best interests at heart. You trust your teachers and parents when they tell you things, because you have no reason to doubt them. Most of what you learn from your textbooks in school is even based on faith. Have you ever personally seen things like the pyramids of Egypt, the Great Wall of China, or Vatican City?"

"Not personally, no. But I've seen pictures."

"So you believe those things exist based on the testimony and evidence provided to you by others. Not by your personal firsthand experience."

"Sure."

"That's an example of human faith. You trust, or have faith, that those things exist and that the people in your life are telling you the truth, because you have no reason to doubt their trustworthiness and because there's strong evidence supporting their claims. Whether we realize it or not, we base a lot of our day-to-day decisions on faith."

They arrived at the Pineapple Fountain in Charleston's Waterfront Park, pausing a moment to take in the sight. The tri-level fruit was pouring water into a pool surrounding it at the bottom, while sprinklers next to it spouted more water up in several directions. Kids were running back-and-forth past the streams, daring each other to get wet, to many a mother's chagrin. Jack chuckled, watching one toddler who couldn't have been more than two dart toward a sprinkler, only to be snatched up by his mother at the last second.

A gust of wind washed over Jack's face, slapping the flaps and tassels of Monsignor Bamonte's clothes into waves. It carried the smell of salt with it from the harbor just beyond. The water looked calm today. There were no white caps dusting its surface. The clouds in the sky matched its serenity. They were drifting lazily, accessorized with golden hues at their contours.

Jack found himself smiling. But the smile soon faded. The sights started him wondering again whether there was really a Divine Artist behind it all. The priest made his way down the line of palmetto trees along the sidewalk. Jack followed.

"Okay," he said, catching up. "That's all clear enough. So what's divine faith then? I'm guessing it's the type we're professing at Mass when we recite the *Creed*?"

"Yes. And the simple difference between the two types is that the first is based on the testimony and reliability of other people. The second's based on the testimony and reliability of God Himself. People can be mistaken. God can't.

That's why divine faith's actually the more reliable of the two. But it requires more than just our reason to possess it. Reason alone only acknowledges as true the things evident to it, such as what's experienced through the five senses or simple concepts, like two plus two equaling four. To have divine faith requires not only sound reasoning but also the assent of the will. That's because the articles of the Catholic religion are not self-evident like those simpler truths. Only the man who's willing to believe in Divine Revelation will be able to."

"Well I'm definitely willing. It's my reason that's having trouble accepting it."

"I know. You wouldn't have sought out a priest otherwise. I just wanted to make sure you understood what divine faith is, since it's what you seek. Let's get back to your story. You're having trouble adhering to both science and religion, seeing them as opposed to each other in this case?"

"That's right."

"So I assume what you seek to satisfy your doubts is something supernatural. Would witnessing a miracle be enough for you?"

Jack thought a moment about his answer before giving it.

"I don't mean to sound like Doubting Thomas, or to repeat his mistake. But . . . yes. I suppose you could put it that way. Well, no actually. It's not like I'm demanding a miracle from God. I just want Him to give me whatever it is I need to believe in Him, and nothing more."

"That prayer's very wise of you," the priest commended, "because a miracle might not satisfy you, even if God were to give you one."

Jack raised his eyebrows. "What makes you say that?"

"Look at the Apostles. They witnessed Christ perform plenty of miracles. Yet they continued to doubt Him. Peter himself denied ever knowing Him when the going got tough, and that was after he'd already seen Him raise the dead."

Monsignor Bamonte paused, eyeing Jack's face.

"I don't bring that up to discourage you, Jack, but to encourage you that you're in good company. You're not the first follower of God to experience what you're going through."

Jack pondered everything the cleric had said so far. But another doubt he'd been having came back to him. He was about to bring it up, when Monsignor Bamonte beat him to it.

"But I'm guessing one of the things you're having doubts about is whether or not the events recorded in the Bible are true, since you're questioning the very existence of God."

"Yes actually. The New Testament was written by Christ's followers. So of course they'd paint the most glorified picture of Him and speak of miracles! Their writings would be biased. Maybe even propaganda. 'Cause it was their goal to get everyone to follow Him."

"Very shrewd, Jack." The monsignor smiled. "Very shrewd."

Encouraged that the priest didn't seem annoyed, Jack was emboldened to go on. "Also, I've heard in sermons before that the Bible's sometimes metaphorical. How do I know which parts are supposed to be taken literally and which are only symbolic?"

The clergyman's smile widened. "I do like the way you think."

They reached the end of the road, arriving at the Charleston Battery Park. More palmetto and oak trees filled it, surrounding a large gazebo in its center like soldiers guarding their king. Cannons and cannonballs dating back to the War of 1812 were scattered among them across the grounds.

The park offered one of the best views in the city. Resting on the southernmost tip of the Charleston peninsula where the Ashley River met the Cooper, it was half surrounded by water. From here, a person could stand atop the seawall and gaze out at Castle Pinckney, Fort Sumter, and the Sullivan's Island Lighthouse on the far side of the harbor.

"Here, let's take a rest over there," Monsignor Bamonte suggested, nodding across the street at a bench under a large oak in the park. Sitting in silence a few moments, taking in the scenery and watching several families picnicking and playing with their dogs, the priest said, "Let me ask you this, Jack. If the Apostles were propagandists, why would they paint themselves out as such cowards when they wrote the story of Christ's life years after His death? You'd think they'd want to look more like heroes to their readers."

Jack was silent.

So the monsignor continued. "When soldiers reported to the Pharisees on Easter morning that Jesus had risen from His grave, they bribed them to say His Apostles had come and stolen the body in the night. But why would the Apostles have been willing to later die for Jesus if they'd only stolen His body as a ruse? If Christ wasn't really Who He said He was and didn't actually rise from His own death, why die for Him after He'd been executed? Remember, the Apostles were the men who fled from His side before His Crucifixion. Why suffer prison, torture, and death for a Messiah Who'd promised to rise from the dead and then hadn't done it?"

Jack could see the logic in the argument. And, for the first time in weeks, his skeptical mind was quiet, with no counterargument to offer.

"Also," the monsignor went on, "why would so many later disciples of Christ be willing to go to their deaths if they weren't convinced beyond the shadow of a doubt that the Resurrection had occurred? The martyrs of the early Church who were devoured by lions in the Roman Colosseum hadn't personally known Christ during His lifetime. They'd only heard His Apostles preach about Him. Why would they believe such a tale as a Resurrected Man unless the Apostles themselves performed miracles to authenticate their claims? Would you be willing to be fed to lions if you weren't certain of Heaven?"

"Not at all," Jack said.

"And yet, the martyrs were more than willing. They were joyful over it." The priest paused again to let Jack think before going on. "It's true that some parts of the Bible are meant to be taken in a metaphorical sense, but not the Four Gospels. The only metaphors to be found in those Books are Christ's parables, not His miracles. Do you really think the Apostles and Christian converts would have refused to deny Jesus' Divinity, even to the point of death, unless they'd witnessed literal miracles?

These people didn't go to execution over a mere idea or new philosophy. There'd be no point in dying for an idealist once he was gone. They died because they believed they'd rise in a literal sense from their own deaths."

"That . . . is a very compelling argument," Jack said.

Listening to Monsignor Bamonte calmly break things down step-by-step put his mind more at ease than it had been in a very long time. He felt a weight was being lifted off his shoulders. He was also beginning to get the sense he'd encountered someone with an intellect unlike anyone he'd ever known. The priest smiled, rising from the bench, heading back down the park's path toward the street, with Jack following.

"Food for thought," the cleric said. "Enough to last you a while I hope. But we've gone and lost ourselves in a theological discussion and forgotten this is a confession. What sins did you need to cleanse your soul of today, my son?"

Jack took a deep breath. This was the part he'd been putting off and the reason he'd brought up his doubt first. The doubt was easier to talk about. He didn't know if he'd make it through this.

"I . . ." he tried to begin, but took another breath, unsure how to say what he felt. "It was . . . It's partly my fault what happened to Chuck Nelson."

He exhaled. His emotions churned inside him like they had at the funeral. They'd boil their way to the surface again if he wasn't careful. He looked at the priest, who only nodded, an unreadable expression on his face.

"Could you tell me more about that?"

As though the cleric had opened a floodgate that was already primed to burst asunder, Jack launched into the whole story of his and Chuck's friendship. He went through the years of their childhood, then described how he and Kevin broke their friendship off with him in middle school. By the time he finished, he looked up to find he and the monsignor were on Church Street, standing next to the iron fence of St. Philip's Graveyard. Chuck's mausoleum was less than thirty feet away.

Jack's eyes widened at the sight. He hadn't noticed the direction they'd been heading as he'd recounted his tale, too lost in his own narrative. He wondered if the clergyman had led them this way on purpose.

"I'm sorry for what's happened to you, Jack," Monsignor Bamonte said after stopping, looking over at the mausoleum to which Jack's own eyes were nailed. "Suicide is a poison that spreads through many lives beyond the one who dies by it. But, in this case, it wasn't you who first mixed that poison. Maybe there was some lack of charity in how you distanced yourself from your friend, and maybe not. Like you said, he seemed to be getting dangerous, and you and Kevin were scared. Either way, it's not your fault Chuck decided to kill himself.

It sounds to me like his unhappiness was already present when you were still friends. In any case, no matter what part we might play in our friends' bad choices, their choices are always their own, for which they alone are responsible. You're not at fault for this, Jack."

A sob escaped Jack's throat.

"I just miss him," he whispered, continuing to stare at Chuck's quiet resting place. "I miss him, and I could have had so much more time with him in the past five years if I hadn't abandoned him."

"You feel guilty because you wonder if things might have been different. Those are normal thoughts to have when we lose a loved one. But it doesn't make you guilty of how you lost them."

Jack nodded without turning to the priest, letting the tears fall from his eyes.

"Was there anything else you wanted to confess?"

Jack wiped the tears from his cheeks. "I lashed out at my sister the other night. I felt badly about that later."

"Alright. For your penance, I'd like you to go into the cathedral once we get back and go before the tabernacle. While you're there, I want you to make an appeal to the Mother of God that she help take away your guilt and your doubt, alright? Let's get Mary fighting the battle with you so you're sure not to lose it. Think you can do that?" he asked, taking Jack's hand in what the teenager thought was meant to be a handshake before he felt him press a holy card into it.

"Yes, sir," Jack said, pocketing the card to look at it later.

"Now, if you'll make an act of contrition, I'll give you absolution."

"Sorry. I don't remember that prayer."

"It's alright. Any prayer of repentance will do. Why don't you try this one?"

The cleric quoted him a short formula, which Jack repeated.

"Lord, I do believe. Help my unbelief."

Monsignor Bamonte raised his right hand over Jack's head and recited a formula in a different language. Jack thought it might be Spanish, but it didn't sound quite right.

"Amen," Jack responded at the end of the prayer.

"Your sins are forgiven, my son. Go now in peace."

It was a pleasant transition from the noisy street outside to the stillness inside when Jack closed the front door of the cathedral behind him.

There was no one else in the church, and he realized it felt much more like a sacred place to him that way. In the piercing silence, his doubts of the previous days seemed to be swept away, as though they'd been unable to cross the threshold with him. Walking up to the foot of the sanctuary, his footsteps echoed back to him off the walls, skipping along uninterrupted on the hushed air.

He glanced up at the stained glass windows while passing them, taking in their brilliance as though he'd never seen them properly before. Those near the ceiling featured portraits of saints from different eras. Saint Francis of Assisi, Saint Benedict of Nursia, Saint Teresa of Ávila, Saint Mary Magdalene, and several others looked down on him as he made his way toward the front. The lower windows portrayed scenes from the Scriptures. Their animated colors were a most welcome sight after his dark days. It was as if he were being welcomed home by celestial family members after a long and unexpected journey.

He knelt down in the front pew and looked to the tabernacle. It was a small structure that resembled a miniature house, located above the high altar in the back of the sanctuary. It had a decorative gold door about a foot and a half tall, behind which were housed the Hosts that had been consecrated during Mass. There was a large red candle next to it that was always kept burning, even when no one was present in the church. Jack remembered learning about it at Divine Savior. It was called the sanctuary lamp and served as a signal that Jesus was physically within the tabernacle at the time, under the appearance of the unleavened bread.

As Jack stared at the little golden house, he experienced a mixture of emotions. He was ashamed for having doubted Christ, but still curious as to whether or not He truly lingered behind that door. He sat contemplating it a few minutes, before noticing there was a new statue of the Blessed Virgin Mary in front of the right side chapel, behind the baptismal font. Father Murphy must have just had it put in, because it hadn't been in the church the previous weekend. It was about four or five feet tall, matching the statue of Saint Joan of Arc in front of the side chapel on the opposite wall.

The Blessed Mother was gazing heavenward while standing on clouds and a crescent moon above three baby angels. Her face displayed so much bliss Jack wondered whether or not such serenity was even possible. But what intrigued him most about the statue was that Mary's hair was uncovered. Every other depiction Jack had ever seen of her always featured either a hood or veil on her head. This one showed thick, flowing brown locks reaching down past her back. Seeing a kneeler in front of it, he rose from the front pew to get a closer look.

Kneeling down, he couldn't keep his gaze off her face. After a moment, he cast his head down in a low bow, ashamed to look into the eyes of the Mother of Him Whose very existence he'd questioned. Five minutes might have passed in which he didn't move. It seemed like moments to him.

Finally, he breathed an almost silent prayer. "Hail . . . hail, full of grace!" he whispered, feeling unworthy to address her by name. "If you and your Son are there, help me to know it! Lead me out of the darkness, to the truth! Guide me out of the dark path . . . to the light of truth!"

When he opened his eyes, he saw there were a few pamphlets tucked into the kneeler's cubbyhole. Among them was a large index card featuring two pictures side-by-side. Jesus holding His Sacred Heart next to Mary holding her Immaculate one. The two figures each extended a hand in blessing, holding their Hearts in the others. The Virgin's had a crown of white roses surrounding it. Christ's was crowned with thorns.

Picking the card up, Jack was mesmerized by their stirring expressions. Their eyes caught his attention most. Both had blue irises that appeared animated. All his memories of Chuck, along with the guilt he felt over his doubts, seemed to resurface at once, like waves from the deep of his unconscious at last crashing onto the shore of the present moment.

He felt a single tear roll down his cheek and watched it fall onto the holy card, landing directly over the Blessed Mother's Heart. He found the courage to gaze up at the statue again. When he did, he could have sworn he saw a smile of pity appear on its face.

His analytical mind immediately explained it away as a trick of the light from the windows. He rose from the kneeler and headed back down the center aisle of pews toward the double doors. On his way, he remembered the holy card the monsignor had given him and pulled it out of his pocket. It pictured the Blessed Sacrament on the front, housed in a monstrance atop the altar. Within the Ivory Orb, he could see the faint outline of Jesus' face.

He flipped it over and froze in his tracks. His breathing stopped. The hair at the top of his scalp prickled, as though someone were tickling him from above. He felt like he had when he'd heard the first reading at Mass on Sunday.

The inscription on the back of the holy card read: *"I am the Light of the World. He that followeth Me walketh not in darkness but shall have the light of life."*

# CHAPTER VI

## THE DARK MIST OF ALL HALLOWS' EVE

Jack had been dozing on his English textbook for a solid hour when he rolled over on his bed.

He'd fallen asleep reading an excerpt from a play by Christopher Marlowe. *The Tragical History of Doctor Faustus*, assigned for a test on Friday. He was awakened when the textbook page he'd been lying atop was pulled over on top of his head as he turned, glued to his cheek with saliva.

"Ugh!" he grumbled, slapping the page away and sitting up.

The sun had set while he slept. The faint glow of the late October twilight had given way to the harsh red tint of his alarm clock which filled the room. Lorelai had gifted him the comically oversized and enthusiastically loud device some years ago. She'd hoped it would aid her daily struggle to pry her son from his bed. Every morning he was confronted by the enormous numbers. They loomed, crimson and condemnatory, announcing just how late he was in the most unforgiving way possible. At the moment, they read 9:43 pm.

Feeling the numb beginnings of a headache, Jack collapsed back onto his pillow with a groan. Pressing on with his studies was out of the question. Still, it was an early night in the Dacre household. His parents and Chloe would be downstairs watching TV for another hour at least. Jack found he had no desire to join them. He considered going downstairs for a snack, but his lethargy got the better of that decision too. He rose to brush his teeth before turning in for the night.

While he stood at the hall bathroom's sink, Ruby sat on his foot and gazed up at him in adoration. She was never subtle when asking for attention. Perhaps she sensed her favorite human wasn't quite himself. Jack managed a quick pet on her head before traipsing back to his room.

Her tags clinked cheerfully in his wake. As he settled down under his covers and rolled onto his right side, she leapt into the bed with him, assuming her usual spot nestled behind him. No overwhelming cosmic dilemmas tonight. Only the softness of her fur and his pillow, all accompanied by the canine's gentle breathing.

For someone whose brain never turned off, Jack was comfortably blank as his eyes closed and he drifted toward unconsciousness. But there was one spark left in his cerebral engine after all, because his half-conscious mind registered that he'd neglected to close the bedroom door on his way back from the bathroom. He squinted his eyes open, considering whether or not he had the energy to bother with it tonight. The cool sheets were so relaxing. Gazing out the doorway, wondering whether or not the sounds of the living room television would intrude on his sleep, his eyes snapped open all the way.

Ruby was standing in the doorway, the fur on her back electrified, her tail sticking straight back. She glared in his direction. Jack's heart sped up to violent speed. Ruby was right behind him in the bed!

How was she also standing in the doorway? And why was she looking so fierce? His joints locked up. There was still something breathing on the back of his neck.

He felt his mattress sink at its center behind him, indicating something heavier than his yellow Lab. The breathing changed, growing deeper. Its pace slowed, as though in anticipation. Ruby issued a shrill bark from where she stood, and Jack saw she was staring past him, at whatever had followed him into bed. Her ears were back. She was baring all her teeth.

*What the fuck had crawled in bed with him?*

He wanted to turn over. His limbs were unresponsive to the intention. Maybe he didn't dare. Or was he unable to move?

Hot, wet breath bathed the back of his exposed neck now.

Was the breath wet, or was the dampness his own sweat? His mind was screaming at him to move. He was still unable. The only movements he could feel were internal, as his bladder and bowels nearly let go. His chest started to shake.

His eyes squeezed shut when a guttural growl vibrated his entire backside. Whatever made it sounded bear-sized. He shot a desperate glance toward the doorway, putting all his hopes in man's best friend. But Ruby had dipped low, her tail disappearing between her legs as she backed down the hallway. The vicious snarling grew louder. She let out a last pitiful yelp and fled down the stairs, abandoning him.

Jack hoped with all the rational thoughts he had left that his parents or Chloe had heard Ruby's cries, or would at least notice her come dashing down the staircase, and come up to investigate.

*No. No one will come!* he shrieked in his mind. *Because this isn't real. Wake up! You know it's another night terror. Wake up!*

The growling moved closer, up behind his ear now. He found himself wishing it was a night terror. It felt too real.

*Stop thinking like that!* he told himself. *You know they can feel real at the time. It isn't. It's not real! It's not real! It's not real! Wake up!*

The scream he couldn't scream thrashed around inside him like a rat in a trap.

It was worse than having it scratch its way up through his vocal cords. A roar broke from the horror hovering behind him, rustling his hair. All the life returned to his limbs at once. He nearly flew across the room to the doorway, half-falling his way down the stairs.

Before he'd made it to the bedroom's threshold, he'd heard heavy claws gash the mattress where he'd been lying a moment before.

Of course, there had been no gashes in Jack's mattress when his family had come up to investigate after calming him down.

There was no evidence a monster had been in his bed at all, because night terrors left no physical evidence other than sweaty sheets and the terrified dreamer. Jack had been more frightened of this episode than any before. This time, it wasn't just that he didn't remember falling asleep. He couldn't remember waking up either. He supposed he had when he'd jumped from the bed. After all, he'd felt like he couldn't move before that, probably because he'd still been asleep and his body had needed to catch up with his mind. Still, there hadn't been a distinct moment this time where he knew sleep had ended and consciousness had returned. That worried him.

How was he supposed to distinguish reality from dreams if the dreams felt just as real? He spent most of the next day considering the question. When he wasn't concerned over the night terrors, he was concerned over existential questions. His doubts had returned, despite his conversation with Monsignor Bamonte.

The priest's advice had helped for a time, but new contradictions to the existence of an afterlife had arisen to rage their way through his mind. Every time he thought he'd solved one of them, another objection would pop up in its place, which would send him back to speculating, all preventing him from enjoying any substantial period of peace. Each question just seemed to beget more questions. The ones he'd mostly been focused on this time revolved around the existence of the soul.

If it was as much a part of human beings as their bodies, why couldn't it be demonstrated scientifically? How would he prove its existence to someone like Mr. Wilkerson if they were engaged in a debate? He found himself imagining this scenario all through biology class, while the instructor reviewed DNA strands and how genetic traits are passed through parents to offspring.

He pictured himself somehow having a perfectly rational and demonstrable answer to anything the teacher could object. And, of course, he'd be demonstrating all these rational arguments in front of the whole class so they too could see the irrationality of Mr. Wilkerson's position. But this was a pipe dream.

Maybe Monsignor Bamonte could do it. Maybe. But he didn't feel the least bit confident in himself at besting the instructor in his own field.

The only thing that managed to bring some brightness into Jack's day had been looking forward to the party that night. It was October 31st. His favorite holiday had arrived.

He'd given Naomi the address at school. Excitement coursed through him as he pulled his costume out of the closet, wondering what she'd think. Neither of them would tell the other at school what they were going as until the other said first, and neither had caved. So it remained a mystery.

Jack was going as a grotesque looking gargoyle. He'd always loved the scary costumes, especially masks that clung tight to the skin, where you couldn't tell from where the person's eyes were looking out at you. The particular mask he'd found at the costume store this year was of two faces melded together at the sides, trying to pull apart from each other in opposite directions. One wore an expression of pain. The other, fury.

There were four eyes on the mask altogether. A pair for each face. His own eyes would be looking out the two closest to the center of the mask, each from a different face, just to throw people off. Both faces had fangs and a pair of curved horns protruding out their foreheads, giving the mask four horns in all that curved around the back of Jack's head in various directions.

The bottom of the mask would go all the way down over Jack's chest, covering it with an exposed bloody ribcage. Chunks of flesh appeared to hang off it. Attached in a clasp under this would be the tips of the skeletal batwings that would hang over his shoulders and down to his ankles like a cape. He'd have a black robe on under all these accessories. He'd even bought a pair of clawed gray-skinned gloves to match the mask and wings.

He smiled as he spread the costume pieces out on his bed. Naomi would never have guessed this. It was the best costume he'd seen at the store that year. He'd forgotten how scary it looked. He'd be giving the neighborhood trick-or-treaters quite the fright when they came around the corner of the house to bob for apples this time. He'd already pegged the hay bushels as a good spot to set up.

He'd stand beside them, hold up a plastic scythe he'd bought that stood taller than his head, bow his face downward, and pretend to be a decorated mannequin. Then he'd wait for passersby to draw near, before jumping or reaching toward them, giving them a jolt. The pranks were one of his favorite parts of Halloween.

It had started in the seventh grade when his father had built a vampire coffin big enough for him to fit inside. That year, he'd dressed up as Count Dracula and waited to lift the lid and pop up at the trick-or-treaters when they walked past.

Ever since, he'd always come up with a new trick to pull on the neighborhood.

The previous year, he'd dressed as Frankenstein's Monster, the costume covering every inch of his skin, and pulled up a lawn chair beside the family's mannequin of the same monster. He'd sat by the front door where his parents were handing out candy, pretending to be another stuffed decoration. He'd even hung some hay out his sleeves to complete the effect. Then he'd jumped up once people were sure he was artificial.

This year's prank had been inspired by his first night terror. It was his way of taking some control back to his life and of associating something besides the figment in his dream with the pumpkin-decorated hay bushels. Snapping the wings over his chest, he pulled on the mask and grabbed the scythe, ready for action. Grinning from ear to ear underneath the double-faced monstrosity, he heard Chloe ascending the stairs. He tiptoed out his doorway and across the hall, waiting for her to round the corner when she reached the second level.

When she did, he lunged forward with a growl, bringing his fake weapon to bear over her head. She screamed. Then smacked him hard on his shoulder.

*"You little fuckface!"* she yelled, while he laughed hysterically from behind the mask.

"Here," he leaned forward, pointing a finger over his cheek, "give us a kiss."

She shoved him out of the way, not without a smile escaping her, and went to her room. "I'll get you back!" she called after him.

"Sure!" he laughed, descending the stairs.

He took up his post at the hay bushels after reminding his mother to come get him when either Kevin or Naomi got there, and started having his Halloween fun.

Trick-or-treaters trickled in at a steady rate over the next hour.

Dale periodically refilled the apple buckets in the gazebo and kept watch over the party. Lorelai was busy inside making brownies, cookies, and cupcakes decorated with orange and black icing. Chloe soon joined her, coming down dressed as a steampunk version of Little Red Riding Hood. A speaker at a back window blasted horror movie themes and holiday related songs out into the backyard. At the moment, it was playing *This is Halloween* by Danny Elfman.

Jack had gotten his fog machine. It was set up next to him, and the effect was working great. Swirls of mist billowed up around him as he stood stone still, waiting for groups of unsuspecting victims. Oftentimes, after being pranked, groups of trick-or-treaters would wait around for the next one to come along, joining in the laughter for themselves.

Lorelai came out to tell Jack that Naomi had arrived.

"Okay," he whispered, "send her out, but don't tell her where I am. Tell her I'm at the gazebo and she can help me run the bobbing for apples contest."

"Got it."

When Naomi came out onto the back patio, Jack saw she was dressed as Maleficent. She had the cap with horns, the staff at her side, everything. She looked as though she'd walked straight off the movie set. As Jack had expected, she took the path of fake headstones to get to the gazebo, the trail continuing to do what it was designed to do. March people right past him. When she came close, he leaned forward and swung the scythe downward in front of her. She yelped, drawing back.

"Fancy seeing you here, Mistress of All Evil," he greeted. "Didn't you know there's only room for one staff-wielding wraith at this party?"

*"Jack?"* she exclaimed, beginning to laugh. "Whoa! You got me good! I could have sworn you were another decoration."

"That's the idea, m'lady." He spun his free hand at the wrist and took a slight bow. "When it comes to trick-or-treat, I prefer trick."

She laughed again, and he took off his mask.

"Want to try *the—*" he started to ask, when something heavy thumped down on his shoulder from behind hard enough to hurt.

He gasped, spinning around. There weren't any decorations behind him that could have fallen over, and it would have been impossible for a party guest to sneak up on him. He was already in the ideal spot to see everyone arrive, whether they entered the backyard through the house or around the side from the front.

*"Whoa shit!"* he screamed.

A dark figure stood behind him, fog curling up around it. His heart skipped, fearing the fiend of his nightmares had returned to its original haunt. Had he somehow fallen asleep while standing up waiting on trick-or-treaters to pass? Could he never be secure in knowing if he was awake or not?

There was something different about the shape of the silhouette this time. It was wearing a fedora, and its shoulders weren't as broad. Looking down, he saw it had grabbed his shoulder with a hand of bladed fingers. It leaned forward into the orange glow of the pumpkins atop the hay bushels. Jack drew back from the grotesque face of Freddy Krueger.

"Welcome to my nightmare, *bitch!*" the horror movie villain declared in Kevin's voice.

"Fuck me!" Jack breathed in relief, then heard Chloe and his mother come out of the darkness to join in Naomi and Kevin's laughter.

Lorelai was snapping pictures of Jack's reaction, while Chloe had to bend over she was laughing so hard.

"How'd you get behind me?" Jack demanded.

"Circled far enough out and came through your neighbor's yard." Kevin grinned, stretching the prosthetics glued on his face.

Jack leaned his scythe on his shoulder, tossed his mask on one of the hay bushels, and clapped his gloved hands together. "Gotta say. That was good. Congratulations. Ya got me."

Kevin high-fived Chloe with the clawed Freddy glove.

"Not the only master of Halloween now, are you?" he said to Jack.

"Jack, put your mask back on," Lorelai said. "I want a picture with all three of you in costume while the fog machine's still running. Hey, you and Naomi match well with all the horns."

They all took group and individual photos. Afterward, several of the braver trick-or-treaters approached to request pictures with Jack and Kevin. It made the boys feel like celebrities, probably a little too much. Kevin's prosthetics and Naomi's makeup prevented either of them bobbing for apples, so Jack joined them for candy apples inside.

"Want to go on a walk?" Naomi asked Jack when Kevin went to the bathroom at one point. "I've never seen this neighborhood, and it looked like there were some pretty cool decorations around the block."

"Sure," Jack said.

"It's good to see you in such a better mood than usual," Naomi said as they wandered through the twisting streets tapping their staffs on the ground before them like walking sticks. "I don't think I see you smile half this much at school."

"School's never been that interesting to me. This though. This is my night!"

"Thanks for inviting me."

"Thanks for being a listening ear for me at Chuck's funeral. That wasn't exactly me at my best."

"I wouldn't expect you to be at your best at a friend's funeral. How've you been since?"

Jack thought about his answer, deciding how much he wanted to tell her. "Tired a lot. Haven't been sleeping well."

"Understandable."

They were silent as they walked past the next two houses and turned a corner back onto Jack's street, until Naomi shook her head.

"It's weird thinking how many classes I sat near Chuck and how he's just . . .

gone," she said. "I just hope, wherever he is now, he's in a better place."

"Me too . . ." Jack hesitated, trying to figure out how to word his next thought, or if he should voice it at all.

"What?" Naomi asked.

Jack shook his head. "I don't know. I don't want to sound insensitive."

"About me or Chuck?"

"Chuck."

"What about him?"

Jack focused on the gnarled roots breaking up through the sidewalk in front of them, avoiding her eyes. "I worry for the fate of his soul . . . I mean . . . with his last act being suicide and all . . . but who knows what kind of mental state he might have been in, right? He might not even have been aware of what he was doing at the time."

Naomi shuddered as they stepped over the roots. "I never thought of that."

Jack furrowed his eyebrows, then shook his head again. "I guess there's no way to know one way or the other."

They were both silent.

"It's sad that his being mentally ill is a *best case* scenario at this point," Jack said. "But, if it were me, I'd rather face God knowing I'd taken the life He gave me in a delusional state than with a full knowledge of what I was doing."

"I really never thought of it that way," Naomi said. "That is sad."

"Yeah . . . Just the nature of having free will, I guess. Our choices have consequences. I can't imagine what Mrs. Nelson must be going through."

They approached Jack's house, and he found himself distracted by a squirrel climbing down the oak tree in his front yard. It was looking at him with caution, unsure if it should proceed.

"Survival instinct," he mumbled to himself upon observing the rodent's hesitation. "Instinct . . . Free will . . ." He waded further into the thought. *"A proof!"* he declared.

"Huh?" Naomi turned to him.

"Sorry, just thinking out loud."

"'Bout what?" she asked, biting into her candy apple.

"What Mr. Wilkerson said the day I found out Chuck died. Remember when he claimed the study of biology disproves the existence of the spiritual."

"Yeah." She furrowed her eyebrows. "I was annoyed by that."

"I was too. But . . ." Jack stopped walking, his mind making connections. "Humans are different from every other animal on the planet because of our free wills . . . and the fact we have free will might just prove we have souls!"

"That's . . . interesting. How do you figure that?"

Jack's mind was racing now. "Yeah, think about it! Animals make every choice based on instinct. But humans are the one species that doesn't. And if we're truly free in our choices, then we're clearly not just physical beings. We must have souls! If the thought processes of the brain were purely electrical and chemical reactions, then a person's choices would be completely determined by their biological functions and there'd be no such thing as a free choice."

"That's amazing! Where'd you learn that?"

He looked at her. "Didn't. Thought of it just now. Been doing a lot of thinking on these subjects since Mr. Wilkerson's comment."

"You should bring it up to him in class. Challenge him."

Jack was jolted out of his musings by her statement. "No, I can't do that . . . I don't feel confident I have all the answers."

"You seem ready to me. I could never come up with that. You really think he'd have an answer to what you just said?"

"Don't know. But I don't want to find out the hard way. I wouldn't want to enter a fight I didn't feel confident I could win. There's still a lot for me to learn before I'd feel ready to challenge an atheist to a debate."

After helping his mother and Chloe load dishes from the party, Jack trudged up the stairs at ten, feeling as though his stomach were the heaviest part of his body.

He'd probably had one or two more cupcakes than he should have—fuck it, three more cupcakes than he should have. He threw his mask on his bed and unclipped the wing cape, opening the closet. He shifted several hangers of clothing aside to fit the wings on their own hanger when something hit him on the head from above.

*"Ow!"* he yelled, taking a quick step back as it landed on the floor in front of him.

It was a small box, the lid of which had snapped open upon landing. He rubbed his head in annoyance, looking up. It must have fallen off one of the shelves above his clothes racks, jostled when he'd shifted them. He didn't know how it would have been jostled. It had never fallen before.

He didn't recognize it. It must have been up there a while. He leaned down to pick it up and return it to a shelf, but stopped halfway, recognizing an item inside it. Something he hadn't seen in years.

He pulled the holy card out in stunned disbelief, one he thought had been long lost. He'd received it as a gift from an old rector of St. John's when he was three years old. His first holy card. The one that had started him collecting them up through third grade.

It portrayed a winged angel with long blonde hair, wearing white garments and a flowing blue cape. The warrior was brandishing a sword with a gold hilt, looming over a cowering red monster with black bat wings and horns on its forehead. Even though he'd been so young, Jack could still remember being captivated by the picture upon first viewing it and asking his mother about the two figures displayed on it. It was his earliest memory.

Lorelai had explained it was Saint Michael the Archangel throwing the Devil out of Heaven. Jack had remained fascinated by the angelic warrior from that day forward, even chosen him as his patron saint at Confirmation ten years later. Staring at the depiction of Satan beneath Michael's heel, Jack realized consciously for the first time that the existence of demons was part of what he was questioning by doubting his Catholic beliefs.

He backed up to sit on the bed. Then stood again when he sat on something. His gargoyle mask had been crumpled. He stuck his free hand inside it to beat it out so it would retain its shape for future use, but hesitated once more. Taking a seat, he looked back-and-forth from the mask to the card in his other hand. He had to admit the faces attempting to pull apart from each other on the mask—faces that had hidden his own for a good portion of the evening—were demonic in appearance. He didn't know how well he'd conquered his fear by pranking people in the same spot he'd first dreamed up his own monster.

The mask he'd used to do it and the holy card he now compared it to just reminded him of the creature, which he thought of for the first time as a demon. He figured Kevin's prank dressed as *the* dream demon of cinema was probably helping to steer him that way. Still, he was surprised he hadn't thought of the fiend he so feared to meet when closing his eyes as a demon before. It was a pretty damn good way to describe it.

If Catholicism were true, and his recent doubts were a spiritual struggle, wouldn't it be demons who'd want to make him lose the fight? Could demons be involved in his problems? Even causing them? He stared a few more seconds at the dual faces of his mask. Their expressions were that of pure agony and rage. Hell illustrated before his eyes.

He chucked the mask into the trash can under his desk. Next year, maybe he'd just attend the Halloween party as a superhero or something. Looking back to the card, he continued gazing at its depiction of the Devil. Could demons really be the villains behind the evil in the world? Could they be to blame for its lack of belief? And his own?

In a flash, his skeptical mind latched onto the thought, going to work at poking holes in the conjectures of his musings.

*"It's just another damn theory added to other theories! Once again, there's no*

*proof! Do you really expect me to believe in demons? All you've done is add more fantastical creatures to the fairy tale of religion, the same way people added elves to the Santa Claus story! I need something more serious and tangible than hypothetical daydreams to convince me God exists!"*

*I am serious!* Jack argued back mentally. *If I'm right, if the Devil's behind anything that goes on in the world, don't you think being skeptical about it is exactly how he'd want people to react?*

*"Don't you think believing in things without proof is exactly why no one takes religious people seriously?"* the voice countered.

*I didn't say I believed it. Just that it would make sense . . . if only it could be proven . . .*

Comical images of horned, animated monsters with red skin running around chasing village people with pitchforks entered Jack's mind. Did the Church really expect him to believe in such Saturday morning cartoons?

*"Well, no. Real demons wouldn't be like that. They'd be more like what you've seen in all those horror movies you and Chloe watch. Like . . . well, like you were just thinking, what you've been seeing in your night terrors."*

Jack ruminated another moment, his gaze still transfixed by the holy card.

*Yeah,* he thought. *If demons were real, they wouldn't be mischievous little fantasy characters. They'd be murderous, psychopathic creatures whose paths I'd never want to cross.*

*"Maybe you already have. What if they are responsible for your doubts, Jack?"*

A wave of trepidation glided down his spine, then up his stomach, becoming slight nausea. Without consciously thinking about it, he flipped the card over in his hand, finding some relief in what he saw written on the back. He turned around from his sitting position on the bed and knelt on the floor, facing the crucifix hanging on the wall above his headboard.

"Saint Michael the Archangel," he prayed, reading from the card, "defend us in battle! Be our protection against the wickedness and snares of the Devil! May God rebuke him, we humbly pray! And do thou, O Prince of the Heavenly Hosts, by the power of God, thrust down to Hell Satan and all the evil spirits, who roam through the world seeking the ruin of souls. . . . *Amen."*

Jack let out a breath with the final word, thinking he would feel better. He didn't. A splitting headache struck him out of the blue, to the point he could feel his forehead begin to perspire. The sweat was cold. He dropped the card facedown on the bed, stood up, and turned off the light. He needed to lie down *now.*

Maybe his poor diet of the evening was catching up to him. Both his head and his stomach were killing him. He felt he'd vomit if the headache grew any worse. It did. He couldn't even make it to the bed. He dropped to the floor at its foot, curling up into a fetal position, praying for sleep to come take the pain away. Despairing thoughts burned their way through his mind. In their wake, they incinerated all the comfort Monsignor Bamonte had imparted that had helped him regain somewhat of a grip on belief.

No matter how hard he tried, he couldn't remember anything the priest had said now. The headache was jumbling his memories. The more he tried to focus on them, the worse the mental strain made the headache. It was like trying to see through a thick fog.

His mind resounded with negative commentaries. Monologues on death, oblivion, and a Godless world. Any reasons for faith seemed like a small tent he and the priest had pitched together that was now being blown over by the stark reality of nothingness beyond its feeble walls. Jack felt the worst he had since first learning of Chuck's suicide.

He told himself he just needed to sleep it off. That was all. The headache and stomachache would go away if he could only rest.

It took another few minutes, but he drifted off—his physical ailments departing him the moment he crossed the threshold of unconsciousness.

When Jack awoke, it was with a violent gasp.

He couldn't tell how long he'd been out or why he'd jolted in his sleep, but he felt refreshed now. He thought it must be morning. There was a faint light peeking into the—

Jack raised his head, blinking, then sat bolt upright. He wasn't in his room. He had no idea where he was. It was a bedroom of some sort. He'd been lying on the floor at the foot of a bed fit for a king.

It was a canopy style with four wooden corner posts shaped like wings. They supported a roof from which hung transparent gold curtains to enclose the mattress. Its gold comforter and pillows featured bizarre symbols all over them, none of which he recognized.

To the bed's right, mounted on stands, were two medieval-looking breastplates with matching pairs of boots on the floor beneath them. One set silver. The other bronze. They were glowing.

Jack blinked a few times, wondering if he was seeing clearly. But they were glowing. They were what was making the room look like early morning. It looked to be dark outside.

Jack stood up, a panic rising in his stomach. He'd been kidnapped! He noticed his clothes had been replaced with wool rags of a musky scent. He was wearing a tattered, long sleeve gray shirt and brown pants.

He racked his brains, trying to recall the last thing he could before waking in this strange room. He remembered the Halloween party, walking with Naomi, coming up to his room, feeling ill, and . . . falling asleep on the floor. That was it. That was all he could remember.

Had he been taken from his home in his sleep? Maybe. Maybe his kidnappers had drugged him so he wouldn't wake up. On that note, maybe he'd even woken up the next day, gone somewhere else, and then been kidnapped. And maybe he didn't remember any of that now, because he'd been drugged when taken, so that the last thing he now remembered was falling asleep on Halloween night.

How long had he been missing? What day was it now? Where the fuck was he?

A pair of curtains on the far side of the bed billowed in the wind with what looked like a terrace beyond them. Creeping toward them, Jack peered through, checking if anyone was outside. The place was deserted.

Cautiously, he slipped through, hoping there might be a way out of . . . wherever this was, and a place he could phone home.

Once he exited onto the balcony, an entirely new concern presented itself.

He was still asleep. That was all. Or at least sleepwalking again and only half awake. No way this was real.

No fucking way.

The beginnings of another night terror. But, as he reached up and pinched his cheek hard, he winced with real pain.

*Definitely feel awake,* he thought.

But that was impossible. What he saw on the horizon had no other rational explanation. His breathing sped up with his heart rate. He had to struggle to remain calm. He squeezed his eyes shut. Nothing was different when he reopened them. He tried blinking hard a few times. Nothing changed. He'd awoken in a strange new world.

A world where it was daylight in several locations across the horizon, but night in others . . . at the same time. There were multiple points where the change from one to the other seemed so abrupt he couldn't discern how the sun was illuminating some places but cut off from others. When he scanned for the sun itself, or even the moon or stars, he couldn't find them. White clouds and blue sky were clear over the places experiencing daytime, but there was no solar source for it. Tracing the daylight to its origin, he saw the brightest spots were places on the ground instead of in space.

He blinked slowly again. Then again. Still nothing changed.

His mind couldn't take it anymore. He went back in the room, looking for another way out, trying to forget about the horizon, deciding he had to be on drugs. It was the drugs making him see things. The horizon would clear up back to its normal appearance once they were flushed from his system. But to get them flushed, he had to escape.

He tiptoed to the only door in the room. It looked heavy, with a strong iron knob. He turned the bolt, holding his breath in hope it wouldn't be locked from the outside. It turned with no resistance.

He breathed and pulled slowly, praying it wouldn't creak. He peered out into a grand stone hallway. It was pristine like the bedroom. Medieval looking. Were his kidnappers fucking royalty? Where had they taken him, Europe? If not for the circumstances, he'd have admired the surroundings. As it was, he didn't have time to consider them. He stepped out and stalked down the hall.

As he proceeded, the passage seemed to narrow. He couldn't be sure whether it did or not. It might have been an adrenaline rush, a paranoid imagination, or the drugs again. Maybe all three in combination.

Around its first corner, the hall changed from stone to rotting wood. There were gaps along its walls, floor, and ceiling. It was much darker than the stone section. His breathing felt way too loud as he stood, unsure how he'd navigate the wooden hall without making noise, or worse, falling through the floor.

He had no other choice. He pressed onward, trying to stay on the most stable looking planks. He passed a ramshackle door on his right that hung ajar from a single hinge, glancing into the room beyond. It didn't appear to be a way out. Just a shabby holding cell, he guessed. He continued down the hall, passing another door in much the same condition, until he rounded another corner and found a rickety stairway. It led down into darker shadows.

He felt a chill like he was growing ill, a cold sweat breaking over his forehead. He tried the stairs. The top step uttered a loud creak under his weight, tattling on his position. He stopped, holding his breath again. No one came running.

He tested the strength of the side rail, squeezing and shaking it as much as he dared. It might be the only thing left to hold him up if the stairs gave out from under him. When he felt ready, he started down to the second step. Then he heard something.

Someone else in the house. He stopped. Weeping echoed up the staircase from somewhere below. It sounded like a young girl, maybe a toddler. It was a heartrending sound. Jack wondered if he was the only kidnapping victim in the place.

He hurried the rest of the way down the stairs as fast as he could, keeping his footfalls as light as possible beneath him. His anxiety rose with every creak. When he reached their bottom, he thought he'd reached the bottom level of the building. There was a door across from him with a window on it. He could see the outside beyond. His heart hammered with exhilaration when its knob turned without resistance. He was about to make a mad run for it, when another sob reached his ears. He hesitated.

He couldn't leave the girl.

His compassion and self-preservation instincts battled it out for several seconds, keeping his leg muscles locked in place. He could bring the police back with him later. But what if it was too late for her by then? Or what if he couldn't find the place again, being that he was all fucked up on drugs at the moment? They might make him lose his sense of direction.

He took a deep breath, letting the door handle go, backtracking into the haunted-looking house.

The girl's cries seemed to be coming from its opposite end. He passed an enormous grandfather clock in what appeared to be a dining room. He couldn't have imagined a creepier one. It looked like something Dr. Jekyll's alter ego would buy at an antique shop. All the rooms he passed through were in no better condition than the rotten hallway and staircase. He traced the toddler's sobs through a living room. But, just as he thought he was about to find her, her cries receded somewhere behind him.

He figured she was moving around, looking for a way out like him. He jumped when the grandfather clock chimed behind him. It echoed in his ears, making it harder to focus on the little girl's location. Listening intently in-between its tolls, he picked her voice up again. She was at the stairs. When he got to them, she sounded like she'd gone up them. He hesitated before climbing them again. He could be cutting off his own getaway. His instincts screamed at him to run for the door.

He went up the stairs, taking them on all fours to try and distribute his weight. Halfway up, he jolted when the girl's weeping started reverberating off the walls, sounding like it was echoing from every direction. And she wasn't just crying anymore. She was saying something to herself, repeating it over and over like a prayer.

He couldn't make out what it was over the echoes. She was close. Maybe just around the corner at the top of the staircase. Since her cries had grown so loud, he took advantage of them and bolted up the rest of the stairs, hoping they'd muffle his footsteps.

When he turned back down the wooden hallway, there was no one there. Her voice had moved to its opposite end. He sucked in air through his nose, growing frustrated. But he wouldn't call out for her to stop moving. Not in this place that looked more like a carnival's Halloween extravaganza than a house designed to be a family home.

It sounded like whatever she kept repeating rhymed. Her words were so jumbled together, he couldn't be sure. He could only pick out a few of them here and there. He started examining the best route to climb his way back through the rickety hall when he stopped dead. One of her words jumped out at him plainer than any.

His own name.

Spooked out of his search, he stopped trying to locate the girl and put all his focus into discerning what she was saying.

*"From the deep bolgias of the abyss*
*Cometh a dreaded black mist"*

Jack edged his way to the hallway's wall. Her voice was getting easier to hear.

*"A subtle nightmare*
*Thy soul to tear"*

He pressed himself against the wall. His sweat increased, accompanied with a fresh wave of nausea.

*"Endeavor not to flee*
*He shall always find thee"*

Jack's breathing stopped. His joints felt frozen in place again.

*"Now doth a dark specter arise*
*To serve the Lord of Flies"*

The echoing lessened. Her words grew clearer. She was getting closer to him now. Jack wished she'd move away.

*"His schemes are unknown, but sinister*
*To please his unholy master"*

She was right around the next corner.

Jack forced his legs to work and circled to face her. What he saw made him feel as though his heart had stopped, or was racing so fast he could no longer feel a pause between its beats. He'd found what had been crying, and it wasn't a little girl.

The only similarity it had to a toddler was its size. It was crouching against the wall with its back to him ten feet away. From behind, he would best describe it as a giant bat. Its arms were winged and it was covered in tiny black fur with large pointed ears protruding from the sides of its head. The creature was undoubtedly what he'd been tracking. He heard it whimpering in the child's voice.

Abruptly, it jerked its head up and sniffed the air. Jack's eyes widened. It turned its head slowly to face him, rising up on its haunches.

No bat, nor any animal of Earth, ever had a face like it. It had large fangs for teeth that hung over its lips. But its eyes! Its eyes were the eeriest part. They were those of a human, except the pupils were drawn in tight, the irises a sickening lime in color.

When the imp beheld Jack, a wicked smile spread over its face, and, as it recited the final lines of its ballad, a deeper, alien voice issued alongside its imitation of an innocent's, making Jack's blood run cold.

> ***"Never before have you encountered such a foe***
> ***The demon who shall lay waste to all you know . . . Jack."***

Jack was rooted where he stood, afraid if he moved he'd provoke the monster to a chase.

When the imp finished speaking, it crouched back to all fours and scuttled up the wall. Jack stepped backward as the little beast hooked its long, webbed fingers and clawed, gnarled toes into the ceiling, crawling upside down toward him. His heart pounding, he was about to launch himself down the stairs without a care of falling, when the pygmy climbed instead up into one of the holes in the ceiling.

He heard it moving around inside the walls behind him next. He dashed in the opposite direction, which took him back toward the pristine section of the house. The stone hall was clear when he tore around its corner. He almost knocked the bedroom's door off its hinges as he hurtled into it at the hallway's end. He slammed it shut behind him, turning to lean against it while catching his breath. But he never caught his breath.

He held it, seeing the room was almost entirely shrouded in black mist now. He stared, wondering if he should turn around or stay put. He'd never seen fog that was black before. The stuff could be poisonous. Then he remembered the imp's poem mentioning a "dreaded black mist." He pressed himself harder against the door, trying to get as far from it as he could. A swirl of it moved toward him, stopping inches from his face.

He felt pinned. The mist lingered several seconds, taking a shape. Jack thought the shape looked familiar. His eyes widened when he recognized it. A face he'd only seen once before, but that had left enough of an impression he'd never forget it. The face of his incarnate nightmares.

Suddenly, the monster lunged out at him.

Its mouth of chipped teeth was open, ready to take a bite out of his cheek. Jack tried to scream. No sound came out. Fear had stolen the volume from his breath.

*"Get out,"* a calm voice commanded from somewhere to Jack's right. The monster and the mist vanished.

# CHAPTER VII
## INCORPOREAL SIGHT

The voice sounded familiar, but Jack couldn't place it with his heart racing as it was.

It felt like it would burst at any moment. He turned to see who'd spoken, and his terror increased.

The creature that stood before him resembled a man, but it was no man. It stood at Jack's height, clothed in a white gi for a shirt, the absence of sleeves revealing toned arms. The two folds of its shirt closed over its chest in a V-neck that tucked down into a silver belt, forming a long flap that hung in front of its legs to its ankles. There was a parallel flap hanging behind them. It wore silver boots and wrist bracers over its pants and forearms, much like the armor hanging beside the bed. But the creature's ancient attire didn't startle Jack as much as its appearance.

It had straight, dark hair hanging over its ears and the back of its neck, ruffled but still perfectly ordered somehow. It had a clean-shaven square face with a strong jawline and cleft chin. Its eyes were an exotic aqua, making them both intriguing and frightening at the same time. But its clothes and skin! They were luminescent, as though its form was composed of different shades of light. And hanging from its shoulder blades were a giant pair of feathered white wings.

Even this wasn't what unsettled Jack the most. It was the experience of the being's presence. It was overpowering. It gagged him from screaming. It was as though Jack's skin had come alive and was shifting over his body everywhere. His every instinct induced him to flee, but he couldn't, no matter how much he tried. He thought the feeling must be how an ant felt the first time a human's shoe crashed down over its world, changing how it saw things from its tiny vantage point.

The winged being approached, and power returned to Jack's legs at once. He moved away, tripping over a corner of the bed, since he couldn't remove his eyes from the sight before him. He fell hard, but there was no pain. He clawed his way backward across the floor on palms and heels.

The creature stopped its advance at Jack's hesitation and smiled. "Don't be afraid, Jack."

As quick as the fear had washed through his body, the creature's statement inundated it with bliss that counteracted it and went to work slowing his heart. He caught a whiff of a sweet scent wafting off the creature, which—like its voice—carried an air of familiarity with it, though Jack was still unable to place it. He felt he could sit and bask in this feeling forever.

The shining man laughed, a sound which only sent Jack into further ecstasy. He wanted to ask the creature who—or what—it was, but found it impossible to form words in the midst of his euphoria. Without uttering a word itself, the luminescent newcomer seemed to give him permission to speak, as though it had some power over his mind.

It came out in a half-whisper when Jack finally stammered his questions. "Who . . . who are you? What is this place? Where'd that . . . *thing* go?"

When he spoke, Jack was startled to hear his voice echoing. The strange thing was the echo had resounded before he'd spoken, and both voices seemed to come from within him instead of one reflecting back to him off the walls.

"Fear not," the creature said. "It won't be returning tonight. We're in your bedroom. And by the way, it's still All Hallows' Eve. You were only asleep a few hours before those wretches woke you. As for who I am, I believe you already know the answer to that, Jack. Don't you recognize my voice?"

Jack did and he knew why. It was much more distinct, but it was the same voice. The voice he'd known through the years that would sometimes admonish him to carry out or avoid certain actions. The voice that had comforted him in his darkest moments, especially in recent weeks. The voice he now realized he'd often mistaken for his own thoughts.

But the possibility—even the suggestion of the possibility—was too much for his mind to bear. It would just be too good to be true. Yet here was the proof standing in front of him.

"You're . . ." he started to answer, but the premature echo of his own voice occurred again, making him hesitate to go on speaking.

His companion waited, looking expectant.

Deciding to ignore the echo for the time being, Jack finished. "My guardian angel," he breathed, barely able to let it sink into his mind until he'd said it aloud.

"I am," the angel nodded. "But you may call me Dathiel."

Jack still couldn't believe it. "This is a dream, right? Like, the opposite of a night terror?"

"Does this feel like a dream, Jack?"

Jack reached up and pinched his cheek as he had earlier. Just like before, he felt the pain. But now he noticed it felt less sharp than it should have.

"Maybe. I feel strange. Like my sense of touch is dulled or something. And I can hear some kind of internal echo every time I speak."

"Your sense of touch is different at the moment, but only because you're experiencing two receptions of input through it at once. Every sense, except vision, will seem different through incorporeal sight, because they're only partially supplanted by it. As for your voice, you're hearing your thoughts before you speak them."

*"What?"*

Jack decided this was another dream after all. That's why it felt so surreal. He didn't want it to be. But it had to be.

"No it's not," Dathiel said, as though he'd heard the thought. "I know it's a lot to take in, and your ever-so-analytical mind can't stand that. But I assure you, it's real. So is everything you've been undergoing of late. You'll have to accept that on your own, Jack. I can help you understand your gift, even cope with it. But I can't make you accept the reality of it. That's for you, and you alone."

"Gift?"

"Incorporeal sight," Dathiel repeated. "That's what Our Father calls it. A charism He doesn't give to many of His followers the way He's gifted it to you."

"What is it?" Jack asked, wondering why he was even humoring this conversation.

It was just a dream. Still, it was the best dream he'd ever had, and he didn't want it to end. The angel's presence felt so wonderful. So tangible. He couldn't remember ever feeling anything like it before, awake or asleep. It felt . . . real. He knew what lucidity felt like, and he felt lucid at the moment. He started doubting whether or not he was dreaming. But what other explanation was there? This was all too crazy!

"Why is it so crazy?" Dathiel asked.

Jack's head drew back in surprise, gazing up at the angel from the floor.

"Is this not what you were hoping was real? God, the soul, life beyond death, unseen helpers like me?"

"Did you just . . . are you reading my mind?"

The angel tilted his head. "Yes and no. I don't possess cardiognosis. So the thoughts of your heart's deep recesses and the affections of your will are off limits to me. But I can make conjectures as to what you're probably thinking." A half-smile came over Dathiel's face. "And we angels are rarely wrong in those conjectures, especially about people we've known their whole lives."

"So you can't read my mind, but . . . you can read me . . . like . . . how a psychologist would?"

"I suppose the comparison suffices. Though our powers of perception would put even the greatest of psychologists to shame. To you, it would still seem like we were reading your mind."

"So what am I thinking right now?"

"You were just thinking about the scene in the first episode of the *Sherlock* television series, where Watson initially observes Sherlock Holmes' detective skills in action. You happened to last view that episode on August eleventh—your birthday. You watched it with Chloe. You were remembering the nacho dip she made for you, which you enjoyed so much you just made a mental note to convince her to make it again soon. That brought Ruby to mind, because she was pining at the bowl of dip the whole time it sat in-between your laps on the couch. Now you're trying to remember if anyone fed Ruby tonight. Don't worry. Your father did."

Jack's jaw had dropped. "You can read my mind!"

Dathiel gave another half-smile. "I know it seems that way, but I promise that was all deduction. We angels have far more to go on than humans when it comes to drawing conclusions about what people are thinking."

"Like what?"

Dathiel tilted his head to the other side now. "Are these really the questions you want to ask me first, Jack?"

"No," Jack admitted. "I've got about a million more important ones. But I'm curious. How did you do that?"

The angel shrugged. "Very well. What you say and how you say it reveals much of what you're thinking, such as your tone, the inflections of your words, and the speed at which you speak them. But a human psychologist would use those same indicators to infer his conclusions. In addition, I can instantly observe every one of your bodily functions. And not just the obvious ones on the outside, but on the inside too. They give much of what you may be thinking away, since all your body's operations are conducted by the same organ—your brain. And your thoughts also pass through that. It also helps that I happen to be your guardian. I know your disposition—with all its little giveaways—even better than your parents."

Jack started laughing, feeling more of his former terror from the monster encounter fade as he did. "Okay! Okay!" he said, shaking his head. "Point made."

"Not entirely," Dathiel observed.

Jack looked him in his aqua eyes.

"You enjoyed that demonstration, but it was just a little self-indulgence for you wasn't it? You're still doubting. You still think this is a dream. You think I can tell what you're thinking because I'm part of your subconscious myself."

"Would explain everything," Jack said.

The angel swept a wing out in front of him and brushed it across Jack's face. Its force sent Jack falling farther backward onto his elbows.

"*Hey!*" he yelled.

"That feel like a dream?"

"Look, I'd like to believe you, but how am I supposed to be sure? How can I prove it to myself?"

"Why don't you switch back to corporeal sight? You know of any dreams you can shift in and out of at will?"

"What?"

Dathiel stuck both wings out in front of him, hooked them under Jack's armpits, and stood the youth up before him. The whole motion was so smooth, Jack didn't register what was happening until it was over.

"I told you, the Father gave you a different version of incorporeal sight than he has most others. One of those differences is your control over it. Switch from it if you will, back to corporeal sight."

"What do, corporeal and incorporeal, even mean?" Jack asked, a little nervous at being so close to the luminous specter.

"Physical and spiritual. You're seeing the spiritual side of creation right now. Take a look at the material side again, if that's what you need to be convinced you're awake."

"How?" Jack asked, not wanting to upset him further.

"Will it."

Jack complied, wishing everything around him were normal. His surroundings went black. He started to panic, worried he'd gone blind. But his eyes soon adjusted to the darkness. He saw he was back in his bedroom, standing at the foot of his bed where he'd fallen asleep. His sense of touch returned to normal. He felt the coolness of the hardwood floor beneath his feet. The only lights in the room came from the moon outside and the digital clock on his nightstand. It read 2:00 in the morning. He reached out and put his hand on the wall to confirm he was conscious, then slapped his face. Stinging pain followed, even more so than the times he'd pinched himself. He flipped the switch by the door and squinted as familiar surroundings lit up around him.

"I'm awake," he said aloud, hearing no echo this time.

He sat down on his bed, breathing heavily a few minutes. He tried to get his mind around all he'd just experienced. He was conscious now, but had he just dreamed encountering demons and an angel in a medieval mansion? Dathiel had told him to will to see normally again. Had that been his mind's way of waking itself from the dream, or had he just had an authentic miraculous experience? He thought about what the angel had begun explaining.

If he really had a gifted ability to see the spiritual part of creation, could he turn it back on by willing it too? Now that he knew he was awake, he wished he could see the angel's beauty again. Feel his presence, if only for a moment. It would confirm the visitation had occurred.

He jolted when the room around him changed. He was sitting on the decorative bed in the much larger bedroom he'd seen before. Dathiel was standing beside him.

Jumping up in alarm at the instantaneous switch of scenery, he nearly swore, but held back at the sight of the guardian.

"See?" Dathiel grinned.

Jack stood still, staring at the angel without saying anything. Dathiel remained silent too, returning his gaze.

When Jack spoke again, he noticed the echo in his voice had returned. "You're . . . *real! This is all real!*"

The guardian nodded. "As real as you."

Jack dashed forward in a moment of elation, desiring to touch—perhaps even hug—his lifelong protector from Heaven. But he stopped himself, remembering something that had stood out to him once during a Bible lesson at Divine Savior. In the story of the burning bush, God wouldn't permit Moses to approach His presence without first removing his shoes in reverence. There were no shoes on Jack's feet, but he wondered if it wasn't permissible to approach or touch a sacred creature like the one who stood before him without permission first. Dathiel must have read this thought, because he raised a hand and grabbed Jack's arm, pulling him into an embrace.

As he did, he raised his wings, spreading them around him. Jack was amazed by their size. They could have enveloped him.

"It's refreshing to see this much happiness course through you again, Jack. It's been such a long time since you let your mind rest."

Jack sighed in relief beneath the shelter of the wings. The angel's clothing felt strange. He backed out of the hug, looking them over. They were made of a material he couldn't identify. He'd best describe it as a combination of chain mail and tiny fish scales. It looked coarse but was soft to the touch. Dathiel saw what he was examining.

"My clothes are hardly what will mystify you most about the world as you see it now. Take a look at yourself."

He gestured to something behind Jack, who turned to see an ornate, gold mirror in the same location of the room where a much plainer, smaller mirror hung on the wall of his bedroom. He approached and viewed his reflection. He recognized the person looking back at him, but he looked older than seventeen now. Mid-twenties perhaps. Maybe even thirty. His complexion was the same but clearer, with no traces of acne. He even saw a hint of luminescence exuding from his skin, like his guardian's, though not nearly as bright.

The raggedy garments he wore made him look like a peasant from the Middle Ages. He noticed his shoulders looked broader beneath them. He pulled off the shirt and was stunned to see his upper body was heavily muscled now. There was a symbol imprinted on the center of his chest. He would have called it a tattoo, but it was glowing, composed of white light rather than ink. After hesitating a few moments, he touched it. Although it shined, it gave off no heat. It felt the same as the rest of his skin. It looked like a capital M written in a decorative fashion. He had no idea what it might mean. He'd never seen it before.

Dathiel walked up behind him, glancing over his shoulder. "What you're seeing is not your body, but your soul."

"You mean I don't really look like this?"

"Oh, you do. Just not to corporeal sight. Check for yourself. Remember, you have the ability to switch between two manners of vision now."

Jack turned back to the mirror and willed to see with "corporeal sight" as Dathiel called it. He flinched as everything around him changed again. He was staring into his plain, small mirror on the wall, still wearing the Halloween costume he'd fallen asleep in earlier that night. He pulled its velcro attachments open and slipped off the black robe and T-shirt underneath, examining his much more familiar upper body. Slim and healthy enough, but not muscled the way he'd seen it a moment ago, and with no symbol on the chest.

Understanding the concept now, he willed to switch back to incorporeal sight. The room changed, along with his physique. He was gazing again at a bodybuilder in the mirror. He grinned, switching back to his regular sight, then again to his gifted one, and back-and-forth several more times, like a child playing with a light switch. He couldn't believe the differences between his two appearances.

"Alright, Jack!" Dathiel laughed. "I think you have the hang of it."

"So . . . everything I'm seeing right now is spiritual?"

"Yes. But everything you see that's naturally incorporeal appears in a way you could have imagined it to look, so that your mind's able to grasp it. In other words, what is spiritual appears to have a material form, since it's impossible for humans to imagine anything spiritual as it actually exists. When they try, they always end up applying some tangible form to it, like an animal or figure of light."

"Okay. I think I follow." Jack paused. "What is it with that internal echo every time I talk? I don't hear an echo when you speak."

"I told you, it's your thoughts before you speak them out loud. I have no echo because I don't really have a body. This winged form you see is just your gift's way of showing you a bodiless mind. If the echo bothers you, just mentally direct what you want to tell me. I can hear your thoughts when you will me to."

"Okay," Jack thought, and didn't hear any accompanying echo this time. "Why does my soul appear so different from my body?"

"It looks older because you've already received the Sacrament of Confirmation, which brought it to maturity. And it appears so strong because you've nourished it of late, with the Sacrament of Confession. That brought it back to the magnificence with which it shined at your Baptism. You've also kept it healthy since then, through daily prayer and practice of the virtues." Dathiel's expression changed to that of a proud parent. "With that, by the way, I am most pleased."

Jack smiled and wondered if he was blushing when his cheeks heated up. "Thanks," he said, feeling emotion well up inside him.

The expression Dathiel was wearing made him want to cry. Not tears of sadness, but joy at having put such a look on so magnificent a creature's face. To distract himself, he moved on to his next question.

"So . . . what's this?" He indicated the symbol on his chest.

"The sacramental seals of Baptism and Confirmation," Dathiel said. "You'll bear them for eternity. That's why you only had to receive those two Sacraments once."

Jack looked down at his chest. "Seals? As in more than one? I only see one symbol."

"Maybe at first glance. They overlap each other. The Seal of Baptism appears as a cross. Christ's symbol. The Seal of Confirmation is a combination of the capital letters A M A standing for, Ave Maria, Alleluia. Mary's symbol. Once fully initiated into the Church, the soul carries seals marking it as a child of both the Father and Mother of Christendom."

Gazing at them in the mirror, Jack could now distinguish the cross, the capital M, and the two capital A's—the horizontal line in both A's being the same horizontal line of the cross. He liked how the mark could appear as four distinct characters, but at the same time be viewed as a single symbol. Studying it, he noticed something else shining in his peripheral vision and glanced over at his desk.

The holy card of Jesus and Mary he'd found in the church the day of his confession was glowing. So was the one of Saint Michael he'd dropped on the foot of his bed. He picked up the one featuring Christ and His Mother. They looked different through incorporeal sight. Mary was much more beautiful, and Christ more handsome. Their skin was darker. Their noses were different. And their eyes were gold instead of blue.

"Before we venture outside," the guardian interrupted his gazing, "I think it would be wise to put on your armor."

"My armor?" Jack asked, putting the card back on his desk.

Dathiel motioned to the breastplates that hung beside the bed.

*"Those are mine?"*

"Take a look through corporeal sight. What do you think they are?"

Jack switched back to his normal manner of vision and found he was looking at his nightstand. The only things on it were his bedside lamp, his digital clock, and a Dean Koontz novel, *Darkness Comes,* which he'd been meaning to start a few weeks ago, but hadn't gotten to in the aftermath of Chuck's death.

"I don't know," he said, switching back to incorporeal sight.

"Look harder. Try inside the nightstand."

Jack flipped his sights and bent down to open the nightstand's single drawer.

Rummaging through it, he didn't find many things he'd think of as armor in a spiritual sense. There were old photographs, pens and pencils, rubber bands, a blank journal he'd received as a birthday present a few years ago, and—

"My Confirmation medals!" he exclaimed out loud, switching again to his gifted sight and turning to Dathiel. "The breastplates and boots are my cross and Saint Michael medal."

"That's right. Blessed medals will often manifest as armor through your charism."

Jack marveled.

"Put them on."

"Both of them at once? How?"

"You're still thinking in corporeal terms, Jack. You'll see! Just slip on the chain."

Jack switched his vision and grabbed the chain the cross and medal hung from out of the drawer. Before placing it over his head, he switched back to incorporeal sight, curious to see what it would look like as he donned the armor. He saw that he was holding the bronze breastplate. The silver one had disappeared.

"Hey, where'd the other one—"

Before he'd finished his question, the silver breastplate materialized in his hands as the bronze disappeared, changing into light and receding into the silver.

"O-o-oh no way!" Jack laughed.

The guardian looked amused at his wonder. Jack slid the chain over his neck and watched as he slipped the breastplate over his head. The moment it was secured, he jumped in surprise as the boots materialized on his feet, beginning as white light and solidifying into armor.

Dathiel patted his back. "What do you think?"

Jack looked at his reflection in the mirror, feeling awestruck. Both muscled and armored, he appeared ready to engage in ancient warfare.

"I think . . . I think I'm going to have fun with this!" He grinned. "So I'm guessing I'm wearing both sets of armor right now, even though I can only see the silver one?"

"Now you're catching on! If you wish the other to come to the forefront of your defenses, just will it to rise to the surface."

Jack stared into the mirror, waiting to see the bronze armor. It immediately materialized, the silver breastplate and boots dissolving into light behind it.

*"I'm going to have so much fun with this!"* he exclaimed.

The armor wasn't even cold against his skin. It felt a perfect temperature. It also felt pliable.

"What's this made of? It's light. Even flexible. But I don't feel anything when I bang on my chest."

"Still thinking in terms of physics, Jack?"

Jack looked up and laughed. "Right. So which is which?" He looked down. "I mean—"

"The silver armor is the cross. The bronze, the armor of Prince Michael."

Jack examined the intricate details on the two breastplates, switching back-and-forth between them. The angel walked over to where his bedroom window would have been located, spreading the curtains and exiting onto the large balcony beyond. Jack soon turned and followed, amazed this time at how royal the terrace appeared now that he was calmer and could take the time to appreciate it.

"So this is all just my bedroom?"

"Yep." The angel leaned on the stone railing with both hands, looking out over the trees at the horizon.

"Why does it look so much bigger than it does physically?"

"Localities will often appear more populated through your gift with all the spirits it enables you to see. We don't exactly take up space. But, since you behold us as having bodily forms now, environments have to materialize as larger to accommodate everyone."

"I see. So what's the deal with the sky? Why are night and day divided like that? I couldn't find the sun earlier."

The angel smiled, and Jack felt the overwhelming sense of bliss start to overtake him again, almost making him forget his question.

"No, your gift won't show you the stars as the sources of light in the universe. The sun is the corporeal light of the world. The Son of God is the Spiritual Light. Did He not remind you of that after your penance in the cathedral?"

Jack was shocked at hearing that occasion brought up. He'd been alone in the church that day, and he hadn't told anyone about his experience there. He had to remind himself it was his ever-present bodyguard from God who addressed him now. He realized he'd never truly been alone in his life.

"What you now see illuminating select places across the Earth is Christ Himself, from within the tabernacles of Catholic churches."

Jack traced the sources of daylight down to the ground again. "No kidding." He noticed several of the bright points were surrounded by a dense cluster of buildings. "What's that city?" He pointed.

"Where we're headed tonight."

Jack turned to the guardian. "It's two in the morning! I can't take off now."

Dathiel laughed, and Jack barely held himself together at hearing the sound. Tears wanted to burst forth from his eyes.

"I didn't mean I needed you to physically travel there, Jack. Tell me, why do you think I appear with wings to you?"

Jack thought a moment.

"Well . . . even in paintings and statues, angels are usually portrayed with them.

So I guess it's because it's how I'd have imagined you, right? Didn't you say it was my imagination and memory that this 'charism' draws from?"

"Indeed. But the reason artists portray us with wings in the first place happens to be the same reason I appear with them to you."

Jack was puzzled. "Why? Have artists all seen their guardian angels too?"

Dathiel chuckled. "No. Not many of them anyway. They paint and sculpt us with wings, because wings denote our swiftness. As pure minds, we travel at the speed of thought."

"The speed of thought." Jack pondered.

"Yes. Think about how fast your thoughts move from one thing to another. You may imagine being here in your bedroom in one instant, then in New York City in the next, and perhaps standing on the moon after that. If I willed it, I could actually travel to each of those places as fast as I considered them."

"Teleportation," Jack said.

"The name will do," Dathiel said. "Though it's more often referred to as 'agility' by the theologians. I tell you this, because you'll travel in the same way with your new gift. Where you perceive yourself doesn't have to match where you are physically. Your location through incorporeal sight will correlate to where your attention's focused."

Jack was intrigued. "Are you saying what I think you're saying?"

Dathiel smiled his half-smile, and Jack thought he looked a little mischievous.

"I suppose it'll be easier to understand it by doing it." The angel stepped up on the railing. "Follow me," he instructed, before diving headfirst off the balcony.

He kept his wings tucked in close until just before hitting the ground, at which point he swerved upward and extended them, landing almost without a sound. Jack was captivated by the spectacle. His guardian's wingspan must have been fifteen feet wide.

Dathiel turned and looked back up to the balcony. "Come on, Jack."

There was no staircase leading to the ground from the terrace and it was at least three stories high. Jack turned to head back inside his room and descend through the house, but hesitated as he wondered if the pigmy demon might still be around. Before he could deliberate much on his options, the angel called to him again.

"Where are you going?"

Jack glanced back over the railing. "Meet you out front."

"Just jump," the guardian invited, as though it should have been an obvious option.

"I don't have wings, Dathiel!"

"You don't need them for a drop of that distance."

"Are you kidding? This must be fifty feet up!"

"Exactly. Your soul's strong enough to make that leap."

The angel disappeared and instantly reappeared right in front of Jack, crouching on the railing with his hand held out, nearly causing the teenager to fall backward in surprise.

"Now come on," he said, as though there was nothing extraordinary about what he'd just done.

The look in the guardian's eyes inspired a trust within Jack that was hard for him to fathom. Without thinking, he grabbed his hand, then realized what he'd done as he felt himself being pulled toward the railing.

"Wait a minute, Dathiel! I—"

He screamed as he was hurled off the balcony and fell tumbling in circles toward the ground.

As he neared the end of his fall, something kicked in, and he spun himself around to land feet first in the dirt below. He'd formed a small crater as his weight slammed into the earth. Yet, somehow, he didn't feel jolted by the drop.

Dathiel landed beside him a moment later. "That's one way to teach a child to walk."

Jack looked at him in disbelief.

With another mischievous smile, the angel threw his hands up in a shrug. "What?"

Jack raised a finger. *"Not . . . funny!"* he panted.

The guardian appeared to be holding back laughter. "I don't know, Jack. You looked pretty funny from where I was standing!"

*"Not . . . funny!"* Jack repeated, placing his hands on his knees and trying to catch his breath, but unable to hold back a smile himself.

"You're fine, Jack! You're still standing at your window."

"What?"

Jack willed to see normally again and found himself alone in his bedroom at the windowsill, looking out through the curtains into a moonlit night. His heart skipped when his door slammed open behind him. The monsters had returned!

So he thought for a split second. But when he turned around, it was to find his father stumbling in, a haggard expression on his face. Dale Dacre blinked furiously as the light hit his eyes, looking back-and-forth across the room.

"You alright, son? Your mother and I heard you screaming again."

"Oh." Jack couldn't help letting a laugh of relief escape him. "No. Well, yes, I did scream. But it's fine. It wasn't a night terror."

He tried to think of something to say without lying, but also without admitting the real reason for his outburst.

"You know those dreams you have when you're almost asleep and suddenly have a sensation of falling? You could say I just experienced a little bit of that. Just catching my breath."

Dale looked relieved. "Oh. Yeah, I know what you mean. I hate those things! You need anything?"

"No, I'm fine. Sorry I woke you."

"It's alright. Goodnight."

"Love you!"

His father closed the door. Jack switched to his supernatural sight, perceiving himself back outside again. He was standing in broad daylight next to Dathiel on a much larger front lawn than the Dacres actually owned.

The guardian wasn't making any effort to hold back his laughter now. "That was close!"

*"Are you crazy?"* Jack yelled, being sure to only do it mentally this time.

"A lover of fun, but never crazy, Jack. You really think I'd physically throw you out a window?" He laughed harder, clapping his hands and ruffling his wings. "With guardian angels like that, who'd need demons?"

Jack looked down at his hands. "So, I guess I'm having an out-of-body experience, huh?"

"Actually, no. Your soul's still attached to your body."

"Then how am I seeing myself as outside my bedroom?"

"Because, again, your soul is spiritual. It might be bound to your body, but it isn't otherwise bound by time, mass, volume, or any laws of physics. Its attention can travel, like I said."

Jack laughed. "I don't know if I understand this gift, but I'm most definitely going to have fun with it!" He glared at his guardian. "And I'm also definitely going to get you back!"

"I look forward to it, old boy!"

Jack stepped from the crater he'd formed, testing his legs. They felt alright, but his sense of touch was off.

"What was it you were saying about how this charism affects my other four senses?"

"A bizarre experience isn't it, feeling all those sensations at once?"

"Yeah. I can feel the ground under my feet, but I can still feel my bedroom floor under them too."

"Yep, your gift doesn't just show you spiritual creation. It allows you to interact with it. You'll experience things through it, but also remain somewhat aware of what's going on around you in the physical world. Sight's the only sense it completely overtakes."

Jack stopped walking around the lawn and—without switching to corporeal sight—physically stepped backward, feeling his way along the bedroom floor, until the back of his legs hit the bed and he sat down. He'd vaguely heard the hardwood floor creaking under his feet. But, through the whole movement, he'd seen no motion with his eyes. They were focused on the oak tree in his front yard. He reached out and put a hand on its bark, sensing its rough touch through his fingers. At the same time, he physically reached down and felt the covers on his bed, half-perceiving their soft touch through the same fingers.

"This is . . . so weird," he said.

"I wager you'll find yourself saying that another time or two before the night's over," the guardian said, stepping up beside him.

He slipped a hand under Jack's arm and tugged him toward the far edge of the lawn.

"Come. We must be on our way. It's already late. And since you're only just getting adjusted to your gift, we'll be traveling the distance to the castle the long way. Point-to-point, instead of teleportation."

"The castle?" Jack asked, hurrying along beside him.

"You'll see," Dathiel said.

But the guardian paused, throwing a hand across Jack's chest to stop him in his tracks. They'd reached the far side of the yard, and the angel was glowering at something across the street. Jack was startled at how his expression changed from what it had been a moment before. He followed his gaze, seeing the daylight end a few paces in front of them.

Beyond the veil of darkness, Jack saw a small cloud of impenetrable black mist. It looked like the mist the demon had lunged at him from earlier. It made the night around it appear as though it were mere twilight. Jack gasped, his heart rate speeding up as panic bit through his chest.

The mist receded backward as Dathiel continued glaring at it, disappearing around the corner of the decrepit house it had been lingering beside. The house looked as haunted as the hall and stairs where Jack had met the pigmy. Jack was about to ask the guardian about the mist when the ground shook. A bolt of lightning struck a block away, half-blinding and discombobulating him.

It sent him falling backward hard enough to slam his head into the ground, at the same time falling physically back on his bed and blacking out.

"You're alright, Jack," Dathiel roused him.

Jack opened his eyes, finding himself held up in the angel's arms.

*"What . . . was that?"* he asked, barely hearing the sound of his own voice.

"Nothing that concerns tonight's journey. Come." The guardian spread his wings and shot thirty feet upward, hovering in the air above Jack's head.

"And how exactly am I supposed to follow you that way?" Jack asked, craning his neck.

"Try to keep up of course." Dathiel grinned. "I'll fly slow."

With that, he turned and took off down the street, flying at least sixty miles per hour.

*"Hey, you said slow!"* Jack yelled, running after him.

The Heavensent spirit was already past the roof of the last house on the road, disappearing over the tree line. Jack started sprinting and was alarmed as the houses on each side of him became a blur. He found himself at the opposite end of Hidden Lane in less than four seconds, sliding to a stop, stunned by his speed.

"Seems you can keep up after all, eh?"

Jack turned to see Dathiel perched on a large tree branch nearby. "How did I . . . ?"

"The breadth between weakness and might is far greater when it comes to the spiritual realm. The more virtuous a soul, the more its strength, speed, agility, and stamina increase—not to mention the more pleasing its appearance is to behold." He stood up on the branch. "You can leap higher now too. Come on up."

Jack looked at him. The limb he stood upon must have been fifteen feet high. To humor him, Jack obeyed his direction, crouching down and jumping as hard as he could. He sailed upward, landing on the branch next to his guardian. His eyes were wide when he looked down at how far the ground was below them now.

"Trust me yet?" Dathiel asked.

Jack noticed how thin the branch was under his feet. Yet he wasn't nervous. He felt calm, as though he'd done this many times.

"Try your strength," the angel proposed, tossing him something. It was a rock almost as large as Jack's fist. "Crush it."

Jack held up the stone and squeezed, watching in astonishment as it crumbled in his hand. He glanced up, seeing his guardian was wearing a half-smile once more. He returned a grin of his own.

*"Tag! You're it!"* Dathiel thumped him on the chest as he propelled upward off the tree.

The strike pushed Jack off-balance and he fell backward. His hands shot out and caught a branch on his way down. He swung himself around in a complete flip, landing back where he'd stood before. The entire movement felt natural, as though it were instinct rather than a conscious action.

"Oh, that's how it is, huh?" he whispered upon recovering from the surprise.

He bounded his way up the rest of the tree with a fluidity that would have evoked envy from an Olympic gymnast. He leapt upward from the highest bough, grasping at the flaps of Dathiel's clothing. The guardian hovered teasingly just out of reach. When Jack jumped again, the angel shot downward among the branches, easily dodging his charge as they sailed past each other.

Never losing sight of his target, Jack hopped from tree to tree, shimmying up and down branches as though he'd been born to move that way. Dathiel glided and dove his way through boughs and over rooftops with Jack hot on his heels for several blocks, until the youth began closing the distance between them. Jack leapt off a roof at top speed, arms open wide to catch his companion from behind. Just as he was about to grab him, the angel flapped one of his wings back and brushed him aside as though he were a piece of tissue paper. Jack tumbled sideways through the air with no control over his direction for a few moments, until he flipped himself around, ready to land on his feet and continue the pursuit. Dathiel caught both his ankles before he ever hit the ground and pulled his legs out from under him, dragging him high into the air, laughing hysterically all the way.

"Hahahoho! Thought you could catch *me*, Jack?"

Jack struggled in vain against his guardian's grip. "No fair! You have two extra limbs!"

"Indeed I do. And not afraid to use them."

He swung Jack around in circles a few times, then tossed him skyward.

*"WHOOOA!"* Jack bellowed when he plummeted downward, seeing he was hundreds of feet above the trees now.

The guardian caught him by the wrists just in time, heaving him out of his dive and flying him horizontally a few feet above the ground.

"Come now, Jack. Let's see who's really the fastest this time!"

He let him drop. Jack wasted no time, sprinting at sixty miles per hour almost as soon as his feet made contact with the Earth. Dathiel was ten feet ahead of him, flapping his wings rapidly, flying in a straight line. Jack put his head and shoulders forward, running as fast as he could, soon realizing they'd already traveled half of Mt. Pleasant.

The angel spun his body around face up and glanced back at him. *"Feeling tired yet?"*

*"Not in the least!"* Jack shouted.

It was true. Since it was his mind racing, the only thing that felt strained was his concentration. It was taking a great deal of focus to keep pace with the guardian. Dathiel soon veered off to the right and landed on the wall of an abandoned looking stone building. Only half of it remained intact, as though it had been the subject of a bombing. Jack jumped up and landed beside him, while he surveyed the horizon.

They were within one of the areas covered by darkness. Every building appeared as though it had been left over from the Middle Ages, and each was rundown. Jack could see beyond them to a city in the distance that was illuminated by the daylight emanating from the churches. Its buildings looked archaic in design too, but better kept, like they were new.

"The world certainly looks different now," he said. "The houses—even my clothing—appear medieval."

"You're seeing the world in a way God sees it now, divided up between His kingdom and the kingdom of darkness. Environments will always reflect the spiritual state of those who inhabit or own them. People's choices will determine what the world looks like to you."

"That's . . . different," Jack said.

"Is it really?" Dathiel asked, looking at him. "Did not Christ reveal two millennia ago that the Kingdom of God was not to be found in some far off place, but within men's hearts?"

They reached the outskirts of the pristine city Jack had seen in the distance a few minutes later, and the youth barely recognized Charleston.

Dathiel hadn't been kidding when he said the world would appear bigger through his gift. The buildings were much more imposing. Many of the roads were nothing more than dirt paths or cobblestone, and there were stagecoaches parked everywhere. Jack couldn't spot any cars.

"What's with all the carriages? I know Charleston has horse-drawn tours, but there aren't this many in town."

The angel chuckled. "Those are cars."

"Wha-at!" Jack laughed. "Why does everything seen through this ability have such an ancient look to it?"

"To remind you that, although technology is constantly changing, human nature has not."

They rounded a corner onto a street where night was reigning and Jack halted at the sight before them, his stomach tightening. A horde of walking corpses were milling around, most limping on half-decayed legs.

*Zombies!* he thought. *A freaking zombie apocalypse!*

He grabbed his guardian's shoulder, wanting the angel to fly them up and away. Dathiel stayed put.

"Close," he said in response to Jack's thought. "Dead souls. People who've fallen from grace."

The crowd of the dead were wandering everywhere. Jack didn't see a way through them on the ground. Not without touching them. So many repulsive smells wafted over from them to infest his nose that he didn't want to get any closer. It was as though someone had opened an old gym bag in his face. The street reeked of old sweat and skunk.

"Don't be afraid," Dathiel said. "They'll do you no harm. They can't see you."

"No kidding," Jack said. "They don't seem to have the eyes for it."

He'd been looking closely, and all the zombies had hollow eye sockets. That was their commonality, but there was more that differentiated them. Some had boiling sores and rashes all over their skin. Some were obese. Others frail, looking like they'd blow over at the slightest wind. Still others were both obese and frail, being fat in their limbs and skinny at their bellies. These hobbled around like they were on strings being controlled by a puppet master.

Those who drew Jack's attention most were running around like rabid animals, twitching and attacking others, even hitting and biting themselves. He backed up a few paces when one of them neared him, gnawing its fingers off before tearing out its hair. The smell of skunk excreting from it forced him to cover his nose.

Something about it caught his eye. He gasped, immediately regretting the action as it brought the soul's foul stench in contact with his tongue. There was a bone white cross traced on its chest.

"Hey! How is someone whose soul is dead marked with the cross?" he choked out.

"I told you the Baptismal Seal was eternal," Dathiel said.

Jack looked at him with raised eyebrows, then looked back at the horde, noticing others bearing the sacred mark. Some even bore the additional Seal of Confirmation, marking them as Catholics. None of their marks shined the way Jack's did, but they still weren't easy to miss on the souls' darkened skin.

"Come," the guardian said, heading into the crowd as though he meant to go through it. "Our destination lies this way."

Jack didn't follow. The angel turned back.

"They won't bother you, Jack. They're unaware of our presence. Just stay close behind me."

Reluctantly, Jack obeyed, holding his breath, before realizing it wasn't necessary. Since his charism was only half bringing scents through his nostrils, he was able to breathe shallowly and avoid taking in as many odors from what he was witnessing through it. His guardian pushed their way through the wandering dead, who indeed didn't seem to perceive them. Jack tried his best to stay right behind him and refrain from touching any of the repulsive spirits.

Despite his best efforts, one of them bumped into him. He almost gagged, as it brushed its way past. Its skin felt like rotted leather. It never even bothered to glance up as it jostled him.

Staring after it, he thought it might be a woman. He'd been having trouble discerning between male and female among the corpses with their various levels of decay, but this one's hair—what was left of it anyway—was longer. Its ragged garments more feminine. He realized why she'd declined to raise her head. She was a hunchback. Her neck protruded out before her chest, disabling her from looking up.

"So," Dathiel said from in front of him, having looked back to see what was keeping him, "even through incorporeal sight, Jenny Wright still distracts you, eh, Jack?"

Jack turned to him. "You're kidding, right?"

"I'm afraid not."

"But this . . ." He had to stop himself from saying "thing." "This soul barely resembles Jenny!"

"That's why Christ said the condemnation of the fallen would be His failure to recognize them. That's how much vice deforms the soul." He glanced over Jack's shoulder. "Three guesses who the souls accompanying her are."

Jack saw the two other zombies walking with Jenny, and he didn't need more than one guess as to their identities. Even outside of school, she was still surrounded by her lackeys. Becky and April.

Curious, he followed them a few paces. Like all the rest, none of them possessed eyes. All three girls had rashes and sores. Jenny had large bald spots on her head where the hair had fallen out because of them. Becky and April's faces were performing a strange phenomenon. They kept changing their shape. They'd go from fat, to thin, to round, to angular, then back to fat, and the cycle would repeat in no discernable order. After watching several of these cycles, Jack realized they were morphing into other people's faces, including each other's and Jenny's.

"Why do Becky and April's faces keep changing like that?"

"Envy," Dathiel said. "The faces of the jealous are always striving to change into the faces of those whom they envy. That vice is—among other things—a crime against identity."

Jack coughed, covering his nose and mouth behind his arm. "They smell like vomit!"

"Yes. Each vice has its own scent and symptom. You'll come to recognize them all if you pay attention. Now come on. It's getting late."

He flew up and perched on a nearby street lamp, which Jack's sight manifested as a pole with a flaming lantern hanging from it. Jack jumped over several of the dead in a single bound and caught the pole under where the angel crouched atop it, holding himself on it above the throng. He felt like a monkey, or Spider-Man. Figured he'd probably look like them too, if the crowd below could see him.

"You know," he said, glancing down at Jenny as she hobbled along, "at first I only felt . . . disgust at this sight. But now that I've seen them up close, I feel pity for these souls."

"Jenny is a sad case," Dathiel said. "She thinks no one can ever love her, not unconditionally. So she destroys herself in various ways. She's living out Hell here on Earth. I've seen more and more Catholics succumbing to the pitfalls she does."

Jack looked up at him. "Jenny's Catholic?"

The angel nodded. "Born, raised, and educated the same as you were."

Jack looked down at her before she and her posse turned a corner. He'd had no idea Jenny Wright of all people suffered from such despair. She was probably the most popular girl at Wando High.

"How can so many of these people be Catholic and live in this state?"

"That's for you to discern. But I'll tell you this. If they were to die physical death in their current condition, their sacramental seals would mark them as traitors in Hell, and their sufferings there would be all the more intensified for it."

Jack glanced back up at the guardian. His face, illuminated under the flickering lantern, had gone pale. Dathiel returned his look of shock with a solemn expression.

"To whom more is given, more is demanded, Jack."

The words stomped up the porch of Jack's ears like military personnel come to bang on his eardrum and demand his compliance with a draft.

"What's to be demanded of me then . . . after receiving something like incorporeal sight?"

Dathiel stared down at him before answering. It was only for a moment, but it felt much longer to Jack. The spirit's gaze seemed to pierce deeper into his heart than he'd said angels were able to see.

"As someone initiated into the fullness of Truth, and endowed with such a charism? . . . *Much!*" the angel declared. "Much, Jack. Your struggle with doubt was not the only reason you were bequeathed such an extraordinary gift. You're called to a great and grave destiny."

# CHAPTER VIII
## THE CASTLE AND THE MAID

Dathiel turned and took flight down an alley, leaving Jack brooding on his last words.

When he leapt off the street lamp to follow, he turned onto Clifford Street among another throng of souls. Some of these were alive. Unlike the dead, they looked human. Some were pale, as though they were falling ill. Others looked normal. None glowed the way Jack did. A grand white castle stood before them, lined with pillars on its front and topped with turrets and towers. Its highest point must have been a hundred feet up.

"Whoa! Is that where we're headed?" Jack asked Dathiel.

"That little nook? No. That's the Lutheran castle named for Saint John. But, as you can see, it's not one of the sources of daylight in the world. The Blessed Sacrament's not housed within."

They approached its front gates, and Jack was surprised by its state of disrepair. There were missing sections of wall where large chunks of its stone had been strewn across the courtyard. He was about to ask why, when Dathiel flew up to the corner of its roof. He followed, scaling its walls by jumping from balconies and windowsills, finding grips in ways that were superhuman. He caught up to the guardian in a matter of seconds.

The angel pointed to the east over the rooftops. *"That's* where we're headed."

Jack turned around and grew wide-eyed. A few blocks away stood a brown castle that dwarfed the one they balanced upon. The prominent bastion shined from within, emitting daylight around itself as well as to several far-off areas. There were multiple turrets and parapets along its sides on which he could see glowing figures patrolling. Numerous angels also circled in the air over and around its perimeter.

Dathiel took flight once more, speeding toward it. Jack got a running start, leaping over an alley to the next building and continuing to travel in like manner from roof to roof. He screamed in exhilaration with every jump, until he landed on the street next to his guardian, directly in front of the enormous fortress. He had to let his eyes adjust a few moments to the midday light they now stood within.

"I present to you—as we blessed behold it—the Cathedral of Saint John the Baptist," Dathiel declared.

Jack was already staring up in sheer awe. Even the gold cross crowning the steeple was larger and higher than before. There was a winged figure standing beside it, gleaming brighter than his guardian, or any other angel he could see. Lowering his gaze, he beheld a wide moat of brilliant flowing water surrounding the castle. He couldn't find the source of its light. It was clear, but also glowing, not appearing illuminated by any separate source. He had trouble taking his eyes off it. He felt his mouth water with thirst the longer he stared.

Dathiel approached the moat's edge. Jack saw no way to cross at its front without swimming. There were several small bridges along the castle's sides leading to doorways, but the drawbridge to its main entrance was up. Raising a hand, Dathiel signaled two angelic sentinels standing with spears on each side of it. One of them grabbed the handle of a large wheel next to him and began turning. The bridge lowered slowly, landing over the water with almost no sound, which surprised Jack, given its gigantic size.

As they made their way across, the illustrious angel atop the steeple flew down and alighted between the sentinels at the opposite end. He shined so brightly, it had looked as though a spotlight were passing over the face of the castle when he'd descended. The newcomer approached and met them at the bridge's center.

Jack felt more overwhelmed by his presence than he did Dathiel's. His guardian bowed his head, and Jack did the same. The angel was most regal. He was clothed in a gold breastplate over maroon robes and was of a short, stocky build, with brown skin and black hair that hung down past his shoulders.

"This is an unexpected surprise, Prince Avdiel!" Dathiel greeted. "I hadn't counted on such a formal welcoming party."

"Nonsense," the resplendent angel said. He looked at Jack with a smile. "So, this is the recipient of the charism."

Dathiel turned to Jack. "Jack Dacre—Prince Avdiel, Guardian of the Diocese of Charleston."

Jack felt all the more self-conscious hearing these credentials and bowed his head again, trying to think of the best formal greeting he could muster. "Pleased to meet you," was all he came up with.

"No need to be nervous, Jack," Avdiel reassured. "We've been around each other many times before. My duties often bring me to the cathedral. It's an honor to finally meet you, officially."

"An honor for me too," Jack said.

Avdiel smiled. "Enjoy your visit."

"You're leaving already?" Jack asked, more disappointment in his voice than he'd anticipated.

"I'm afraid so. I do apologize for the brief introduction, but I'm here to meet with the bishop's guardian tonight. I'm sure we'll be seeing more of each other in the coming days."

Jack smiled, and the prince spread his wings, flying up to a large window on a small bastion across the street, disappearing inside. Jack assumed the smaller castle must have been the bishop's residence. It was located in the same place as it was through corporeal sight, across the street from the church.

"Why would he be honored to meet me?" Jack asked, as they continued across the drawbridge. "It's not like I've done anything special."

"That so?" Dathiel chuckled. "Well, he's been watching you over the years. We all have. And we've long awaited the day you'd be meeting us."

"He looked Indigenous."

Dathiel nodded. "He's been guarding this land a long time."

Dathiel thanked the guard who'd lowered the bridge as they passed and ascended the front steps, opening the doors to the castle. Pouring from the top of the doorway, covering the entrance, was a cascade of the same shining water Jack had seen in the moat. At the floor, it flowed down through a crack so not a drop splashed outward beyond the threshold. Jack saw no way to enter without being soaked.

Dathiel stepped through without hesitation, and Jack shrugged, holding his breath and following. He was amazed at how perfect the water's temperature felt. It was neither too cold nor too hot, but perfectly refreshing. Even more amazing was that he came out on the other side of it dry. He felt rejuvenated, like it'd been his first bath in weeks. He smelled better, even felt stronger than he had a moment ago, like his muscles had all just gotten a pump.

He only had a moment to notice all this, because once he saw what was beyond the bright cascade, his attention was pulled in a hundred different directions.

The cathedral's interior was far more complex than its physical appearance.

It had several levels, with staircases and balconies. The pillars were larger. There were more pews. The windows shined brighter, and there seemed to be activity in every nook and cranny. Angels and luminescent wingless figures—who Jack assumed were human saints—bustled to-and-fro, occupied with various tasks. His eyes darted everywhere, trying to take it all in.

There was something different about the windows other than their increased size and splendor. The figures depicted in them were the same, but their faces were changed. The faces of Jesus and Mary looked identical to his holy card back home, as though the card and windows had been designed by the same artist. The gold trimmings along the walls and pillars—which had been plaster moldings sculpted to resemble grapevines, three leaf clovers, oak leaves, and lilies before—were now living vines with real fruit and flowers growing from them. They complemented the place with an array of new colors and smells. The baptismal font at the front was now a large tri-level fountain spouting glowing water up in four directions.

Jack realized the luminescent liquid must be holy water. It flowed over the edge of each level of the fountain until it reached the bottom. At that point, he assumed it traveled through the floor and supplied the moat outside. Despite all this, his eyes were first and foremost drawn to the source of the castle's light. The tabernacle.

It looked the same, but was now large enough that a grown man would fit inside it. Jack stared in hesitant anticipation, waiting to see if *He* would step out to greet them. Dathiel walked ahead and knelt on the bottom step leading up to the altar before it. Jack followed and knelt beside him.

"I brought you here tonight so that your first venture upon receiving your gift could be to offer a prayer to His Majesty," Dathiel said. "First, you should thank Him for bestowing it. Secondly, you'll want to request wisdom to use it wisely. And you'll want to beseech aid for the coming battles."

Jack didn't say anything, directing all his attention to the One before them. Taking the guardian's advice, he thanked Him for the reception of an ability he would otherwise never have dared request. His prayer wasn't so much formed into words as it was a simple willingness for the Savior to look into his heart and see his appreciation for all the marvels he'd witnessed so far.

Next, he reluctantly turned his thoughts to the "coming battles" Dathiel had mentioned. He assumed he'd been referring to the demons who'd invaded his home earlier in the night. He shuddered at the memory, hoping he wouldn't have to face them again if he prayed hard enough for protection.

Contemplating the shining tabernacle, he burned with curiosity as to whether or not the Deity would emerge from the small house to directly answer his prayers. After all, if incorporeal sight enabled him to see what was normally unseen by human eyes, wouldn't it now reveal to him the Son of God instead of a piece of bread? Wouldn't he now be able to see the Eucharist for What—Who—It really was?

The questions were at least a distraction from thinking about the monsters who'd haunted him. Soon the light emanating from the tabernacle's veiled door made his eyes water, and he was forced to glance away. He surveyed the rest of the sanctuary. He and Dathiel knelt near the statue of Saint Joan of Arc. Like the windows, it had changed. The silver armor she'd been wearing before was now a suit of white armor. Her hair was darker and styled in a pixie cut. The face's features were different. Prettier, but also younger. She could have been his age. Jack did a double take when the head of the statue turned toward him.

"Did your mother never teach you it's impolite to stare?" the statue—which had become a living person—asked in a French accent.

Jack jumped up from his kneeling position, as the former sculpture hopped down off her pedestal. Stranger still, now that she'd moved away from it, he saw the statue remained on the stand behind her, as if the real person had walked out of her own representation. She laughed at him.

"What, big brave Jack Dacre afraid of a maid?" She tilted her head. "You should be."

She shined brighter than the angels and was exceptionally more beautiful. Yet Jack didn't feel as paralyzed by her presence as he did each time he'd passed close to one of them. Her scent was different too. It was like the smell of cream, but with a spicy edge.

After a few seconds, he found his voice again. "You just . . . caught me off guard."

"It's not me you need to be on guard against."

Dathiel had remained knelt in prayer with his eyes closed through the whole ordeal, either undisturbed or unaware of everything that had just occurred around him. Since he only continued to pray, Jack took it as a cue he was free to speak without bothering him.

"Saint Joan, I presume?"

"What gave it away?" She raised an eyebrow.

Jack smiled.

"You can call me, La Pucelle or Maid, if you like. Most saints do. And you, the recipient of the latest charism in the Militant. A pleasure to make your acquaintance."

She extended her hand with the palm facing the floor. Jack wasn't sure if he should shake it or take it in his hand and kiss it. He knew that's what they did in the olden days. But Joan of Arc had lived in medieval times. He thought the whole kissing a lady's hand thing had been more of a Victorian practice. Playing it safe, he took her hand and helped her down the steps from the sanctuary.

"I thought you could use all the celestial friends you can find now," the saint said. "Your new gift will bring you more than just wonders from Heaven."

She passed him, walking toward one of the staircases leading up to a balcony along the side of the castle.

Jack followed. "Are you referring to the battles Dathiel said were coming my way? What exactly should I be expecting?"

She turned halfway up the stairs. "What do you think Hell's reaction will be to the man who can now plainly see so many secrets of the cosmos?"

Jack didn't answer. He didn't want to answer.

"Let me give you an ancient piece of advice," she said. "One that sums up the last few years of my own lifetime on Earth." She turned, heading up the stairs again as she remarked, "If you want peace, prepare for war."

Jack felt a sick sensation in the pit of his stomach looking up at her from the bottom step. Without saying anything, he ascended the stairs after her. It wasn't until they'd both ascended their fourth set of stairs to a balcony that circled the castle near its ceiling that either said any more.

"War," Jack breathed, "with Hell . . . But . . . how am I supposed to battle demons? They're not tangible. I can't shoot, stab, or punch them."

"Spiritual warfare's psychological. You'll fight them with your mind."

*"How?"*

She didn't answer. Jack was about to protest, when he was distracted by a cohort passing them. A group of angels accompanied a saint who looked as glorious as Joan, though his appearance was quite different. He was an old man dressed in a black, hooded robe with deep, chestnut eyes and a bald head. The only hair on him were his bushy eyebrows and a gray mustache and beard that hung all the way down to his chest.

Jack didn't catch what he was saying to the angels, but he was surprised by the commanding voice such a short man possessed. The winged spirits seemed to be reverentially taking orders from him. Joan led him on until they stopped near a set of double doors with another cascade of holy water pouring before them. She swiped out her free hand, and the doors swung open behind the water, as she pulled Jack outside.

He found himself standing on a terrace high above street level. The view of the world from here was even more mesmerizing than it had been from his bedroom window. Charleston had grown enormous. Judging from the way Joan chuckled, he imagined his awestruck face must have resembled a child's on Christmas morning. He felt more like he was looking out over a fantastical kingdom than the little city of Charleston he'd grown up knowing. The multiplication of day and night within distances a few miles apart added to its outlandish appearance.

As far as he could tell, the Cathedral of Saint John the Baptist was now the tallest structure in town. From where he stood, every other building was visible, including all the other castles. A few shined daylight from within, and he figured they were other Catholic churches. The rest must have been Protestant. They all had one thing in common he could see. They'd all endured damage. He leaned over the railing and observed the cathedral was no exception. Angels were busily repairing openings in the walls with new stones.

"Why do all the churches look like they've had a wrecking ball taken to them? I noticed the same thing earlier when Dathiel and I passed a Lutheran castle."

Joan nodded. "Because only some of that castle's members are virtuous. The strength of any stronghold for souls depends upon all its inhabitants to uphold it. The more degenerate a castle's members, the more incorporeal enemies are enabled to enter and wreak havoc, snatching what they can."

"By 'incorporeal enemies' you mean demons?" Jack asked.

Joan didn't say anything, just pointed into the sky. His eyes followed her course. Flying high above them were countless angels. He could tell by their glow. But, in the outer darkness, where night reigned, he saw flocks of what he'd mistaken earlier for large black birds. Some of them even dared enter the realms of daylight, dive-bombing the ground like birds of prey hunting field mice.

He glanced back at Joan. "So those are—"

"Yes."

He looked up again, his breathing quickened. "And I'm guessing, unlike the dead souls of the living, they can see me?" He jerked his head back in her direction, desperation creeping into his tone. "And you're saying they can even enter the *churches?* Because if churches aren't safe from them, what is? Are there any safe havens in the world? What are we supposed to do if—"

"Peace, Jack! Your fear will be your first misstep in a downfall if you don't conquer it." She gazed into his eyes with a boldness he feared he'd never possess. "You have Dathiel. And me. That suffices. Besides, this castle is much safer than other fortresses. God Himself resides here, in the Flesh. When the Lord of Creation is physically Present, demons are a great deal more hesitant to draw near."

"Indeed," a voice spoke from behind them.

They turned to see Dathiel perched atop the archway over the doors they'd exited. He was crouched down with his chin on his hands, his wings overhanging each side of its small roof.

"How did you—" Jack started to ask, but stopped at the angel's smile. "Right. The speed of thought."

"Yes," the guardian said. "The speed you'll be returning home with tonight. It's very late now, and I can't have you sleeping the entire day away. After all, it's a feast day. Given that, Monsignor Bamonte will be too busy to meet with you. So I'd like you to come here to the cathedral the following day at exactly three o'clock. He'll be coming by for meditation at that time.

Wait for him. Tell him everything you've experienced tonight and everything we've told you. Leave nothing out. But, tell no one else of your charism until you've first told the priest. He'll know how best to guide you from there. Be sure to then obey any instructions he gives you to the letter."

"Do I really have to go now?" Jack complained. "This feels like the safest place."

"It is," Joan said. "But you can't hide forever under a steeple. You now behold visibly how much of this world remains in the darkness of the Devil's contempt.

You must go and do whatever you can for the lost souls you encounter out there. Do that, and we'll do what we can to protect yours."

Jack was looking her in the eyes. There was no fear in them. Only strength. He didn't feel any of it himself.

"I'll try," he said. He looked up at Dathiel. "So . . . teleportation then? Or agility—whatever you call it."

The guardian hopped down in front of him. "It's quite simple. Just concentrate your thoughts on where you wish to go. Then will to go there."

"Dorothy and her ruby slippers then. Got it." Jack gazed out over the horizon, admiring the view from the terrace one last time. He closed his eyes, trying to soak into his soul all the light he could from the tabernacle in the castle below.

Then he focused his thoughts on home.

When Jack opened his eyes, he was standing back in his now larger-than-life front yard.

Looking up and down his street, he was dismayed to see his lawn was the only one on Hidden Lane being illuminated by the Blessed Sacrament. All other houses were decaying, evidently inhabited by deceased souls. He turned to the more cheerful sight of his own residence and was astonished by the size of the medieval mansion. He hadn't had time to admire it from the outside before he and Dathiel had—

His thoughts froze.

He was looking at the dilapidated section of the house, remembering what it indicated. He sprinted up the yard and yanked open the front door. He raced up the rickety staircase, remembering the doorways he'd passed in the wooden section of hallway. Knowing the physical layout of his house, it struck him what those rooms must be.

He came to the first door hanging from a single hinge and nudged it open. He smelled the kinds of scents he'd been expecting, and dreading. Old sweat, vomit, sewage, another overpowering odor he couldn't identify. Whatever it was, it was the worst stench he'd ever inhaled. He took a deep gulp of cleaner air and stepped into the bedroom.

Its size and the familiar placement of the furniture told him it was Chloe's room. She lay on a broken cot, motionless. He left almost as soon as he'd entered, unable to bear the sight for more than a moment. He wanted to scream and break down where he stood. Instead, he did what he least wanted to do in that moment.

Proceeded down the hall to the next door. His heart breaking with each step, he squeezed his eyes shut as he turned its handle.

The overpowering scents that rose up to greet his nostrils when the door swung inward told him all he needed to know. He opened his eyes and beheld the souls of his parents lying on a stone slab. They were in the same state as Chloe.

Deformed and dead.

# CHAPTER IX
## SPIRITUAL COMBAT

Jack's eyes remained closed as he strained to slip back into unconsciousness and relive the previous night's dream.

It had been such a wonderful dream, though it had begun and ended as a nightmare. He knew he was awake now. He could feel the mattress beneath him. Turning over, he thought the reason for the nightmarish parts might have been because he was closer to consciousness at the beginning and end. Closer to surfacing back up to the stark misery of real life.

Submitting to the inevitable, he opened his eyes, allowing the last remnants of the dream to slip away from his mind despite his best efforts to cling to them. As his bedroom came into full focus, so did his memory. He sprung up to a sitting position, remembering he'd fallen asleep on the floor the first time.

His heart skipped at the prospect that his adventure with an angel had been real. He willed to see through incorporeal sight, jolting when he found himself in the room decked out for royalty. He was still arrayed in armor. Having encountered demons in his own home, he'd never removed his medals from around his neck. After what Saint Joan had told him, he didn't think he ever would.

"Peace, Jack. You worry too much," his guardian said from the balcony.

*"Dathiel!"* Jack rushed to the terrace. *"It was all real!"*

The angel laughed. "I should hope so. Otherwise, I'm in trouble."

Jack surveyed the horizon, beholding once more the strange divisions of night and day. "It looks different out there than last night," he said.

"Because people's souls have changed. Since last night, some have come back into grace. Others fallen from it. You'll find the appearance of your surroundings as fickle as the waves of an ocean now."

Dathiel's mention of souls reminded Jack how his night ended. He turned to look down at the other bedroom windows of the household. His heart sank.

"So . . . my family . . ."

His guardian looked at him with a somber expression. "I didn't want my first revelation after meeting you to be bad news, Jack. You were so relieved to learn your faith was true, and you'd just been attacked by demons. But, yes. I'm afraid you're the only member of your family who belongs to God's kingdom. It's been that way for a long time."

Jack didn't look at him. His gaze was fixed on the decayed section of his home. "How long?" he asked.

Dathiel said nothing. Jack jerked his head in the angel's direction.

"How long have they been . . ." He couldn't bring himself to say the word dead. "Like that?" he finished.

The guardian's gaze was the only thing holding Jack together.

"Your parents have lived in death since before you were born. Chloe, since you were thirteen."

Jack felt his body grow cold as goosebumps stood together across it like an army formed to riot an injustice. "What were their sins?" he asked, not recognizing his own voice with its flat tone.

"That is not for me to reveal. But, if you must know, your gift can help reveal them."

"The symptoms," Jack remembered. "And the smells."

"Yes. Incorporeal sight shows you the types of sins burdening souls. You just have to pay attention to match the symptom with the category."

"There was one smell I didn't recognize. All of my family has it. Gotta be the worst odor I've ever inhaled."

"Rotting flesh," Dathiel said. "A scent of the worst kind of sin."

Jack stared out at the horizon, refusing to turn toward his door. If he went downstairs, he'd have to face the full reality of his loved ones' condition.

"It's almost time for school anyway, Jack," the angel urged him on, reading his thoughts and emotions. "You'll need to leave soon. And you should eat something before you go."

Jack took a deep breath and rose physically from his bed. He threw on a pair of jeans and a linen T-shirt before descending to the main level of the house. Everyone was in the kitchen.

"Jack wakes up on his own? And *early?*" his father observed. "Huh, maybe I should buy a lottery ticket today."

"Just in time. You want eggs?" his mother called.

"Can make you coffee too, if it'll keep this trend going," Chloe said. "It'll be more peaceful for all of us without having to hear Mom shout up the stairs every morning."

Jack remained standing at the foot of the stairs. There were echoes every time one of them spoke. He realized his gift enabled him to hear the thoughts at the forefront of other people's minds too. He didn't consider the implications of this. He was too distracted by what he saw. He wasn't sure if it was more repulsive or saddening to him.

What should have been the kitchen was unrecognizable. The colors were muted. Half the wall and roof were missing, exposing the room to the outside. And, what should have been his father, mother, and sister were nothing but corpses milling around without eyes. Their skin was gray, great bald patches and bulging sores on their heads and bodies. Their teeth were rotten. Their frames obese. Chloe exhibited the symptom of envy. He recognized some of the faces hers were periodically morphing into as a few of her friends. He almost leapt back in disgust when one of the zombies turned and spoke to him again.

"You want scrambled eggs or an omelet, son?" he heard it echo in his mother's voice.

He switched to corporeal sight. The wretch before him transformed into Lorelai. He sank down on one of the stairs behind him, fighting back tears, realizing now what he'd seen saddened more than disgusted him.

"Jack? You alright?" Lorelai asked.

Everyone turned to look at him.

"Sorry," he managed without having his voice crack. "I . . . I'm not very hungry . . . I think I'll get going early."

He stood and headed for the door.

"Whoa! Why off so suddenly this morning?" Lorelai pursued him outside.

"Hey! You need to at least drink something!" he heard his father shout from the kitchen island.

"Jack? Won't you be needing this?" Lorelai held up his backpack, which he'd left by the front door.

"Thanks." He doubled back to grab it and hurried to his Jeep.

"And you should at least take a water bottle with you." She went back into the house to retrieve one.

Jack viewed his Jeep through incorporeal sight. It was a roofless carriage that looked to be made of brass and gold. Dathiel was perched on its right front corner.

"You do have time to eat something you know," he said.

"I can't. I'm not ready to face them yet."

"Face who, son?"

Jack turned to see Lorelai had returned carrying a bottle and realized he'd spoken out loud to Dathiel. "Nothing. Gotta go."

She tossed him the water. "Have a good day at school then."

He hopped in the Jeep and took off as fast as he could without skidding. His mother was no fool. He could tell she knew something was up from her expression in his rear view mirror. He couldn't have that discussion with her right now. How was he even supposed to broach the subject?

*Hey, Mom! Last night, God granted me the ability to see your souls, and I noticed none of you have been to Confession in a while. So tell me, what are the mortal sins I see eating away at you?*

He shook his head, laughing bitterly at the prospect. Maybe Monsignor Bamonte could give him advice on how to handle it. That was, of course, if he could even convince the priest about what had happened. Attempting to get his mind off the inevitable conversations to come, he switched to incorporeal sight as he drove out of his neighborhood. It was strange to see carriages moving at the speed of cars, and with no animals pulling them. The more pristine ones were all helmed by souls in grace. The old, rickety ones were driven by the dead. It was such a weird sight to him seeing zombies that could drive. There was nothing like that in movies. Dathiel was still perched on the corner of his own carriage, with the guardians of other living drivers riding the same way on the coaches of their charges. Every angel had an expression of vigilance on his face, checking back-and-forth, scanning for potential threats.

Dathiel turned to Jack. "Don't worry. Monsignor Bamonte will help you manage your new situation."

"Why are there no angels accompanying the dead souls?" Jack asked, not wanting to discuss his family. "I thought everyone in the world had a guardian, no matter their religion or spiritual state."

"They do. And the guardians of the deceased you see are always around. It's just that their charges have shunned them. So their angels have left them to their sins out of respect for their free will. They never cease looking on from a distance for an invitation to bring them back to grace though."

Jack turned onto the Arthur Ravenel Bridge. It was always a busy freeway, but now it was teaming with a parade of fantastical creatures on antiquated vehicles. Even the bridge itself appeared out-of-date.

Dathiel turned around again. "You might want to use corporeal sight while driving, Jack."

Almost immediately following the warning, Jack felt the carriage bump and heard a honk from behind him. Switching his vision, he saw he was drifting into the median while driving twenty miles under the speed limit. He adjusted, realizing the difference in scope of the world's two manifestations had thrown him off.

He drove the rest of the way to school without using his supernatural vision again.

When Jack switched back to using his charism after arriving at school, he cried out, taking several steps backward both spiritually and physically.

To corporeal eyes, Wando High was a rather ordinary brick edifice. To Jack's eyes, it had been replaced by several dark fortresses. Black spires jutted out from their roofs in odd directions, each looking as though it were hewn from volcanic rock. The grass and plants were gone, replaced by exposed dirt. Peppered across the grounds were holes that looked as though they led down into tunnels. Surrounding the perimeter of the campus was a tall stone wall composed of the same material as the bastions, with sharp spikes lining its top, making escape on foot look impossible. Jack felt as though he was suddenly trapped in some medieval concentration camp.

Jumping at a titanic crash behind him, he turned to see a black gate rising and slamming back down every time another coach entered the decrepit courtyard in which he stood. Most carried the souls of the dead. The few living souls on campus besides Jack looked unhealthy, but since there were still a handful, the night was balanced out to appear as twilight. What little light did reach them was further blocked by billows of black smoke. It emerged from the mouths of the tunnels, from the windows of the fortifications, even from cracks in their walls, making the school look like a factory of some kind. The stench of the fumes assaulted Jack's senses, but not as much as the sheer noise of the place. And it wasn't the students causing the ruckus. It was what most filled Jack with terror.

Everywhere across the grounds and rooftops, even clinging to the sides of the citadels, were inhuman spirits that were unmistakably demons.

They appeared under various shapes and sizes. There were black ones, gray ones, brown ones, green ones—every shade evoking a sense of corruption to Jack's mind. Some had horns. Some had fur. Some were slimy. Others more reptilian, crawling around on arms alone, their bodies those of serpents below the chest. Some were humanoid. Others appeared nothing close to human. Some had the webbed wings of bats and circled above, swooping down and gashing souls with their talons. Others were earthbound and stalked back-and-forth in groups, latching onto students like packs of hungry wolves, all the while screaming crude abuses and threats.

Jack spotted a familiar looking soul pass by his carriage. Jenny Wright. She was still walking with a hunch. Now he saw why. Dogging her was a gray demon who hobbled along on two legs much the same as she did. He was bald and had what resembled a long goatee hanging from his chin. On second glance, Jack saw it was a pair of horns that curved inward, the tips of which glowed orange like hot pokers.

He bobbed his head up and down and side-to-side, searing cuts into his own chest, drawing black blood, laughing as he did it. Jack watched as the monster dealt blow after vicious blow to Jenny's head, beating her down into her constant stance of submission. With each punch, he heard the hateful spirit speaking to her.

"You know, Brad wouldn't look at other girls if you were more satisfying to him, cunt. Haven't you ever thought that maybe you've gotten a little boring? He's not the reason the excitement's gone from the relationship. You are, bitch! He's gonna take a better deal as soon as it comes along if you don't do something about it soon."

A scraping sound to Jack's left distracted him. He gasped as a slimy, legless creature dragging its own entrails behind it clawed and scooted its way toward him. It had a hungry look in its eyes.

He snapped out of incorporeal sight, jumped back in his Jeep, peeled backwards in the opposite direction from which he'd seen the demon coming, and tore off down the street.

*"Where were you?"*

"Calm down. I was right there beside you. You were too distracted to notice."

"Well what am I supposed to do? I can't go back there! *I can't!*"

"Yes, you can, because I'll be with you, like I always am. You've been through the place before. You can survive it. But, now maybe you understand why you've come to hate the place so much, even before incorporeal sight."

Jack leaned back in the swivel chair in front of his bedroom desk, both of which his gift revealed to appear much more elegant.

"So . . . Wando's a demonic stronghold or something?"

Dathiel nodded. "A lot of schools are these days. Satan has his claws dug into every facet of society into which he can hook them, and education's one of his high priorities."

Jack stared at the floor, thinking about his scholarship to The Citadel. In less than a year, he'd never have to go back to Wando if he didn't desire. But that seemed too far away. Couldn't he be done now? Never have to face the place again starting today? That got him thinking about his plans to join the military, hoping to be some kind of tactician, and a realization struck him.

"It is a brilliant strategy," he said, looking up into Dathiel's exotic eyes. "On the Devil's part I mean. Get us thinking the way he wants us to while we're still young and more impressionable. Then he shouldn't have to worry as much about having problems from us in the future."

"And society stays the way he wants it," the angel finished for him. "That's why he considers you a threat."

Jack sat forward in his chair. "Me! What did I do to get his attention?"

"It's more what you could potentially do to his kingdom. As for what you've already done, you've been resisting his regime. Have you not felt attacked of late? Especially since Mr. Wilkerson's statement? Who do you think is responsible for the doubts you've been wrestling with? Who do you think you've really been wrestling with?"

Jack leaned back again, to the point his chair almost tilted over on its axis. The Devil, responsible for his crisis of faith? He'd considered that before. As he pondered it again, a hypothetical entered his mind.

If he were the Devil, what would his perspective be? What would his strategy be? He played out the scenario.

If he were the Devil, who'd pledged his everlasting hatred for God and declared war against Him, how would he best draw people away from their Creator? Simple. Convince them no such Creator existed. Atheism seemed like pure genius when thought of as a demonic tactic. Satan wouldn't have to put any effort into making people neglect God if they never knew He was there.

As Jack mulled it over, he hit another brilliant stroke. It would also be beneficial to the Devil to convince the world he himself didn't exist. It would be his field day! Once belief in both God and demons was gone, the idea of right and wrong would soon follow them into obscurity. How much easier would it be to tempt mankind to every kind of sin if they no longer believed in sin? Kevin was a prime example of the result.

Jack turned his thoughts to world history, applying his theoretical scenario. How long had atheism been around? He was pretty sure it was a relatively new phenomenon that had only come about as a widespread belief within the last few hundred years. Before that, people had always held to some kind of religious belief, whether monotheistic, polytheistic, or pantheistic. People who only believed in what could be experienced through the five senses . . . That was new to the equation.

It dawned on him that if atheism was Satan's brainchild, it might be his greatest triumph to date.

"And he wouldn't have needed to rush in bringing it about either," Dathiel interjected, clearly having been following the line of Jack's thoughts. "Since he's immortal, he could take his time, planning and implementing it over the course of centuries, until it became widespread. Now it has. This secular society is firmly within his grip."

Jack stared at the angel, in awe at both the genius and the horror of it.

"So . . . I was right last night then," he said. "The Devil caused atheism."

The guardian nodded. "He's worked very hard over the past several hundred years to accomplish it, and will in turn work hard to keep the belief strong. That's why the demon who was in your room last night tried to make you feel like a religious fanatic for even thinking of your scenario."

Jack sat up straight. "What?"

Dathiel held his gaze. "As *I* told you last night, real demons aren't like what you'd see portrayed in a kid's TV show. They're more like what you've seen in all those horror movies you and Chloe watch."

"Like what I've been seeing in my night terrors," Jack repeated in a whisper, remembering the words popping into his head. Several quiet seconds passed before he spoke again. "Your voice is one I've heard in one form or another many times before last night, isn't it?"

The guardian nodded.

"But you aren't the only one I've heard. Not the only one who's been suggesting things to me lately, are you? There are others. The not-so-friendly voices in the back of my head."

The angel nodded again. "And with your charism, you can see them now."

Jack's eyes widened. "Are you telling me there's been—"

He went silent, hearing faint steps on the stairs outside his door. They grew louder. Closer. He turned toward the door in fear of what might be about to come through it. When it swung open, he breathed a sigh of relief for the first time yet at seeing his mother's rotting soul. He flipped back to corporeal sight.

"So I went by your school and officially signed you out," Lorelai told him. "How're you feeling?"

Jack was still catching his breath and took a moment before answering. He could see the concern on her face.

"A little better, I guess. Thanks for doing that. I just didn't think I'd make it through school today."

"You need anything?"

"No thanks."

"You sure? I can make you a sandwich or something."

"I'm fine," he insisted, wishing she'd leave so he could return to his other conversation.

"Okay, well, call if you need me."

"Thanks. I will."

After she'd gone downstairs, Jack switched back to his charism. The angel was gone. Disappointed, he relinquished it and closed his eyes in an attempt to clear his mind and lower his stress level. When he opened them again, they landed on the gargoyle mask he'd thrown in the trash can under his desk. He felt exposed. Vulnerable. What could he do if *Satan* was the one hounding his beliefs? Like he'd said to Saint Joan, demons were invisible. Immaterial.

How could a person fight against something like that?

Flipping through his psychology textbook that evening, Jack figured getting ahead on some reading might take his thoughts off his fears a while.

The subject remained his favorite of the semester, and the class had finally reached what sounded like the most interesting chapter to him. *Abnormal Psychology.* He'd seen enough movies portray mental disorders that he was excited to find out which ones, if any, were accurate. He skimmed through OCD and bipolar disorder, already familiar with those, but read more slowly when he came upon two less familiar to him: dissociative identity disorder and schizophrenia. He perused the textbook's definition of schizophrenia.

*A brain disease the symptoms of which include agitation, emotional blunting, social withdrawal, unusual behavior, hallucinations, and delusions. The symptoms usually begin during young adulthood. The disease's causes are unknown, but they appear to be both environmental and genetic. Contrary to past public perception, schizophrenia is not caused by poor or abusive parenting. Its treatment involves intense interpersonal therapy and neuroleptic medication.*

Feeling a cold sweat break out on his forehead, Jack read on.

*People with schizophrenia hear voices and see things which are not there. They often believe other people to be reading their minds or planning to hurt them. This leads many persons with schizophrenia to live in paranoia and great terror. They may become extremely agitated when they discuss what they are actually thinking. They may engage in one simple activity for hours on end or may sit perfectly still and become non-responsive to external stimuli.*

Jack dropped the book, jumping at the sound it made hitting his desk. He didn't even remember picking it up while reading. When it landed, a note card was blown off the desk and fluttered to the floor. He picked it up, flipping it over, seeing it was the picture of Jesus and Mary he'd taken from the cathedral. He felt somehow distanced from it now, as though it was part of a dream to which he'd been clinging but from which he was at last awakening, whether he wanted to or not. He wiped the perspiration off his forehead and remembered the last time he'd felt the inexplicable sick feeling he was now. He switched to incorporeal sight.

The curtain to the terrace was shrouded by a cloud of black mist. It blocked the light from outside, leaving his soul the only source of illumination in the room.

The fog receded, at last unveiling the complete form of the monster hidden at its center.

It was mosquito-like in appearance, standing hunched, its head protruding in front of its chest. Yet it stood seven feet tall. It wore tattered gray rags for clothing. They didn't do much to cover up its spindly limbs or emaciated ribcage. Its bone white hair hung from the back of its head all the way to its waist. It had a tail with a narrow, razor sharp arrowhead at its end. Its legs were in three segments, with paws for feet. Its hands resembled a human's, other than the long length of the fingers and the black talons on their tips. Looking behind its back, Jack saw why its shoulders always looked so round to him when he'd seen its silhouette in his night terrors. He hadn't been seeing shoulders. He'd been seeing wings. They were feathered like the angels' Jack had come to know, but as jet black as the monster's skin.

It held a black spear in its right hand like a staff. The weapon split to form two shards at its top end. The spikes encased a glowing red ball at their base. The ball was the source of the black mist. Jack saw it sucking the fog back in, as the evil spirit revealed itself.

Jack stood erect, hoping he was giving off an impression of bravery by not running. The truth was, he didn't feel courageous at all. The experience of this creature's presence inundated him with far more fear than any he'd seen that morning.

*Satan himself,* Jack thought.

"I was wondering when I'd be seeing you again," he said, his voice almost shaking.

The monster smiled the same eerie grin that had haunted his dreams for weeks. He found he wanted the thing to just speak already! Its silence was too terrifying. When it finally did, Jack caught glimpses of a forked tongue behind its teeth.

"You would have seen me sooner," it said in a raspy Russian accent. "But you weren't ready to face the truth until now."

Its voice was calm. Unnerving. Jack thought it was how a talking corpse would sound.

"What truth would that be?" he asked, his every muscle tense, unsure what he would do should the enemy make a move against him.

"My identity."

"You're a demon. Maybe the Devil himself. What more do I need to know?"

The creature laughed, a coarse sound that made Jack's shoulders tighten.

"Is that what your guardian angel told you? Or, should I say, what you've been telling yourself?"

"What do you—"

Jack's words were cut short as the fiend sprung at him. It thrust its spear out to bring it down on his head. The scepter struck him across the face. He felt the pain of a physical blow inasmuch as his second sight affected his sense of touch.

The monster began beating him repeatedly with it. Jack experienced a sense of worthlessness. He felt there was nothing he could do to help himself or ever be happy again. Where was Dathiel when he needed him? The thought of his guardian brought more vicious attack. He started having trouble picturing the angel's face in his mind.

As he tried to process what was happening, he thought the experience of the thrashing felt familiar. It was the same experience he'd been having over the last few weeks whenever battling doubts or guilt. He realized he'd been Hell's punching bag before, many times. With this realization came an emotion that conflicted with his fear and feelings of inadequacy. Fury.

"I will *not* be a victim anymore!" he thought, as the monster raised its spear to belt him over the head again.

Abruptly, he caught the weapon, stopping it mid-swing. It was as though the movement had been instinctual instead of a conscious action.

"Interesting," the fiend said, sounding unimpressed.

*"I'm through . . . doubting . . . for you . . . ANYMORE!"* Jack shouted mentally, watching in amazement as he thrust the spirit back while springing to his feet.

"Most interesting," it mused. "You are quite the fighter, Jack. It's the only reason I'm still here."

Jack ignored the creature's words. He was too busy wondering how he'd just held back the Devil. In his astonishment, he remembered what Saint Joan of Arc had said. Spiritual warfare was psychological. He could fight demons with his mind. Combating demons . . . *was a battle of wit and ideas! An argument!*

A warm boost of confidence coursed through him. The spirit before him cackled, bringing its weapon swinging forward. Jack concentrated his thoughts into resisting despair . . . and blocked the spear before it hit his face, catching it between his arms as he crossed them in the shape of an X.

*"Get out!"* he demanded, hoping the words would have the same effect as when Dathiel had spoken them.

"I'm afraid that's impossible, Jack. Not if you wish to hold onto sanity."

"Who are you?"

"Oh I think you know. You've always known deep down, but the knowledge is finally coming to the surface now that you've discovered the name of your condition. You were just reading about it. Do the symptoms not all line up?"

"That's bullshit," Jack resisted, but his arms gave a little and the spear pressed closer to his face.

"Is it now?" The creature smiled, displaying its broken teeth. "You've been suppressing your emotional draw to women. You've been withdrawing socially from your family more and more. Your behavior has become erratic and agitated, as you see from their reactions when you are around them. You're a young adult. And . . . let's not forget the big one . . . you've started seeing and hearing things no one else can. I hit every symptom yet?"

"You don't honestly think . . ." Jack struggled to finish the thought as the spear pressed even closer to his forehead. He closed his eyes, feeling sweat break out on it again. "I'm going . . . to fall for that . . . do you?"

His soul pushed the spear back several inches in the opposite direction. He'd thought the comeback, but without much confidence. He couldn't hold the spear at bay much longer. It began gaining ground toward its target again.

Jack felt a deep dread rising from the pit of his stomach. He knew his opponent was only voicing a concern he'd kept buried in the far recesses of his subconscious since meeting Dathiel. And the fiend could see his true reaction, no matter how well he tried to conceal it. His arms weakened under the spear's pressure until it touched his face. But it hadn't pierced him yet.

"You're not so sure are you?" The monster said, pushing.

"I *will not*—" Jack started.

The monster drew the head of the spear back to throw him off-balance and attempted to trip his legs out from under him with its tail. Jack jumped as it swung beneath him.

"But you're determined not to accept the truth," the fiend spun his spear up to swipe at his head again. "That's why you've been hiding behind this black mist every time I surface."

"*I!*" Jack raised an arm to block the spear, but was faked out as his opponent changed the direction of its swing and struck him instead in the ribs with the bottom of it.

"You dread me, Jack," the creature's words pierced his mind with the blow of its weapon, "but not for the reason you imagine. You think your fear is based on me being this primordial monster, condemned to the pits of an inferno from which parents teach their children to pray for protection at night, when . . . in reality . . . you fear me because *I'm you*, Jack! Your voice of reason personified."

Jack was stunned for a moment by the blow of the creature's words, failing to understand what it was playing at.

"What are you talking about?" he demanded, refusing to let the pain overwhelm him.

The mental resistance on his part manifested by his hitting the spear away and swinging his leg around to kick the monster in the face. He was amazed by his agility. But he missed his intended target. Instead, the fiend dodged by backflipping around with surprising agility of its own for a creature its shape. It then proceeded to bounce off the walls and even Jack himself as its arguments manifested in more attacks.

"Did you really think you had a supernatural gift from God?" The monster clucked its forked tongue. "Sorry. Just a brain disease. And I'm the only part of your brain that's aware of it. I've been trying to reach you all day, Jack. Especially since it hit full force last night." The monster uppercut him on the chin. "Are you ready to listen yet, or are you going to repress me with your imagination again?"

"What the hell are you *talking about?*" Jack fought back, but with clumsily placed punches, all of which missed.

He wasn't offering counterarguments. He was just attempting to stonewall. Maybe that was his problem. But he couldn't find a loophole in what his enemy was saying!

"What did you think the angels and saints represented?" it demanded. "You've always had a creative imagination, Jack. By the way," it stopped hitting him for a moment and looked itself up and down, "a spear? Black mist? Taloned fingernails? A Russian accent? You certainly know how to portray a villain! If I were really the Devil, don't you think I'd appear a little less . . . cliché? You could have at least tried to be original."

*"Lies!"* Jack fought back, but his punches and kicks continued to miss, while the diabolic spirit landed blow after blow upon him.

"No, Jack. Defense mechanisms. Fantastical beings leading you down the rabbit hole of insanity. But you mustn't follow them. Please! I know that, in this case, the truth is uglier than the lie. I agree, it would be wonderful if everything you've come to believe was true. If each little thing in life had meaning. If it was all part of one, grand adventure with a final destination beyond death. But none of what you're seeing is real! And I simply can't let you live the rest of your life in this fantasy you've created for yourself. Otherwise you'll end up in an asylum, truly imprisoned.

It's not too late! Schizophrenia's not incurable. Not in your case. I know this, because I'm still here. I'm the one section of your brain that's resisting it. But I won't last forever, Jack!"

The two foes dueled across the bedroom and out onto the terrace, Jack on the defensive the whole way.

"You're seeing my arguments as attacks? As hellish temptations against you? Then stop me, Jack! After all, we're one inasmuch as you're one with Dathiel and the others. Cease visualizing my position as an assault and end portraying me in this monstrous form."

Suddenly, the creature backed off, calmly placing the spear by its side. As Jack watched, it transformed before him into a tall, jolly Franciscan friar. Its gray rags morphed into a gray habit and its spear changed into a simple wooden walking stick with two gnarled branches at the top in place of the prongs.

"Bullshit! *You* did that!" Jack accused, his words manifesting as a wide swung punch.

"No," his enemy countered the blow, drawing past it with superhuman speed and striking his unguarded face with the stick, forcing him all the way to the ground with it.

As he lay on his back, he was hit by the demonic friar over and over, hearing each blow as a statement, much as he'd seen Jenny receive that morning.

*"You* control me, just as you control everything else you're seeing. You've been making your projections tell you what you want to hear. Your imagination wishes to believe in Catholicism and so is manifested as celestial spirits who confirm it's all true. Meanwhile, you keep visualizing your skeptical side that's grounded in reality as demons, so that anything we tell you to the contrary you can dismiss as the deceits of Hell. It's a clever tactic, Jack. But let's cut the bullshit already, huh?"

*"No,"* Jack protested, but in a weaker voice and to no avail.

He was pinned down. His breaths came in shallow gasps as he writhed on the floor. His thoughts were sporadic. He couldn't focus for any length of time before suffering another onslaught. He kept trying to remember Monsignor Bamonte's arguments for belief, but couldn't recall any of them at the moment. He felt like a sailor who'd fallen overboard in a storm and was now being tossed about and drowned among treacherous waves. When the evil spirit at last paused between two accusations and he had a chance to think, he grasped one more time for any flaw he could discern in its position before the barrage was renewed.

*"NO!"* he screamed with more force this time, spiraling up feet first and kicking his attacker in the face just as it was about to swing the stick down on him again.

He flipped over and landed on the railing, swinging his fists at the friar's head, hoping to catch it by surprise. His mind just wasn't fast enough to keep pace with a fallen angel's. The spirit countered every one of his strikes with its stick.

"What about everything I've learned through the saints I see?" Jack threw out a kick. "Even the word, incorporeal, was something I'd never heard before Dathiel said it last night!"

"Yes, you had," the fiend blocked his rebuttal with a kick of its own as it leapt into the air.

It followed through and hit him in the ribs again, displaying a level of prowess far beyond Jack's skill as it landed on the railing beside him.

It swung its stick at him. "You received ten years of Catholic education before Wando. You may not consciously remember everything you heard taught in the classrooms of Divine Savior, but it's all there in your memory. And, as you've learned in psychology class, even if a person isn't paying particular attention to something at the time, what their ears hear is still recorded in their brain. It's just buried in the subconscious. Just because you can't recall all your religious studies at will doesn't mean your schizophrenia couldn't bring them up. The human brain is a very complex organ. You know that."

Jack blocked the fiend's arguments with his arms as best he could, but he saw bruises forming on them as his mind continued to weaken. The diabolic monk flipped up and brought its heel down toward his head. Jack dodged, but his shoulder still caught the brunt of the kick. Refusing to allow the pain of it to slow him down, he punched the evil spirit again, putting all his bitterness behind his fist. The monk spun up into a roundhouse kick and knocked him off the railing. He went whirling in a circle back onto the terrace.

"What about demonic possession?" Jack used his momentum to swing around and trip the friar's feet out from under it. "How do you explain that phenomenon if you and your kind aren't real?"

"Simple," his opponent countered, doing a backflip before Jack's leg ever touched it and landing of its own accord on the terrace in front of him. "You were just reading about its scientific name. Dissociative identity disorder. It's a psychological problem, not a spiritual one. To fix it, you'd need a therapist, not a witchdoctor armed with medieval superstitious incantations."

*"You're wrong!"* Jack fought back, but with ever-waning strength.

Perceiving it, the monk took advantage of his weakness and landed a vicious crack on the side of his head with the stick. Jack went down, hard, at the same time physically making his way over to his bed from his desk and curling into a ball. The Franciscan mutated back into the black monstrosity. Dark mist issued from the red globe on its spear. It enshrouded Jack, as the evil spirit stabbed at him with its tail. Everything it had said seemed to line up perfectly. Jack couldn't find any holes in its story. As the fiend kicked and battered him with the scepter, his breastplate cracked in several places.

"Look at what's become of you, Jack. You'd even go so far as to manifest me as another part of the fantasy. That's why you seek to suppress me in this fog. You know that, if I'm left unrestrained, I can eventually cave the fiction in on itself every time. I already have! You already know the truth. Those angels and saints you've been hallucinating, they're the part of your mind clinging to a lie.

You have to learn to cope with what I represent. Reason. Reality. The exposing of religion's absurdity. If you really wanted me to go away, you'd have made me disappear a long time ago. But you said it yourself, you want the truth, no matter what it is. Well, here it is, Jack. There is no God. No angels or saints. No fairy tale place you get to go after death. There's only this world. The material. The *provable!*

It's harsh. It's ugly. It's disagreeable to your sentimentality. But it's the fucking truth, Jack. And I'm begging you . . . accept it now before all your sanity's gone and live the remainder of your life in freedom from delusion. That's the logical choice to make if you only get to live once, isn't it?"

The monster leaned down over him.

"I trust you'll see that soon. You're too intelligent a person to indulge a fantasy forever. I just hope it's soon enough. Just think, on the bright side, once you let it go, you won't have to see this creature you've imagined up anymore. Until then . . ." the fiend slid its tail around Jack's throat and pointed one bony finger at his forehead, "I'll be right here."

Jack felt himself being dragged across his terrace to the balcony. The spirit spread its wings, taking flight and towing him along behind it through the air. As they ascended, it continued to monologue.

"Poor boy. You're sick. Sick in the mind."

It flapped its wings loudly. They slapped Jack's face while he struggled to breathe, feeling like a man who'd hanged himself and was now being carried off to his eternal lot by the Grim Reaper.

"And I am the cure. But you need to stop interfering with me and let me do my work of healing your brain. Follow my voice to find your way out of hallucination, Jack. It's the voice of reason."

The monster ceased its ascent and hovered in midair, looking back down at the dangling teenager. It released its grip.

Jack tumbled toward the ground hundreds of feet below, screaming, falling asleep on his bed before he ever saw himself land.

# CHAPTER X
## BIOLOGICAL EVOLUTION

Jack stayed out sick from school again the next day.

Wando High was the last place he could bear to see after the night's experience. He'd even been angry when his mother had awoken him to check if he felt better, sleep feeling like his only refuge from the trials of life. After his parents left for work, it refused to return to him.

He got up to distract his thoughts in some other way. He drove aimlessly through Mt. Pleasant for a while, trying to come up with something to do. Eventually, he wound up in Charleston, parked beside the cathedral.

Turning the engine off, he sat a few minutes, unsure what he'd intended in coming to the church. He stepped out to go in and visit the tabernacle. Saint John's was empty inside. He took a seat in a pew and brooded in silence, closing his eyes and burying his face in his hands. His fear that he'd deluded himself came crashing down on him. For twenty-four hours, one glorious day, he'd been convinced Heaven was real.

Now the rug had been pulled out from under him again. Of course, if everything the monster had said was a lie, and it was in fact Satan who'd crawled up from Hell to derail his faith, Jack couldn't help but admire his strategy. Imagining things from the Devil's perspective again, the fallen angel's suggestions would be the cleverest way he could think to renew his doubt at this point. Mulling it over, he initiated incorporeal sight for the first time since the fight. The castle was just as beautiful and bright as he'd beheld it through his so-called charism before. Dathiel was standing at his side.

"Why is it you're here now, but were nowhere to be found last night?" Jack asked, trying his best not to sound accusatory in case he really was addressing a prince of the Heavenly Court.

"I may be your guardian, but this is not my battle, Jack. It's yours. I've prevented thousands upon thousands of would-be attackers from reaching you in your brief seventeen years on Earth so far. But Our Father has to allow some to break through. Otherwise, how would you grow in holiness?"

"How do I know you're real? What if I'm just crazy and having a conversation with myself right now?"

"Do you really believe that?"

Jack ran his fingers through his hair, yanking a handful of it as he did. *I don't know what to believe anymore!* It's not like I've ever been supernaturally gifted or schizophrenic before. I have no previous experiences to compare this to."

He heard a door open and close behind him.

"Well, maybe this'll help," the angel soothed. "I told you you'd be meeting the monsignor here today."

Jack turned to glance behind him through corporeal sight. It was Monsignor Bamonte who'd entered, dressed in his usual black cassock and rose-colored fascia. Jack checked his phone and saw it was exactly 3:00. His heart skipped at the realization that a projection of his unconscious couldn't have prophesied the clergyman would be coming over to the church at that very moment on that very day. But, a moment later, one word rang through his mind, slapping his hopes back down. He could already hear the fiend from his night terrors throwing it in his face, should he ever fight him on it. Coincidence.

The monsignor lived and worked next door. It wasn't unlikely he might often visit the church. Walking up the center aisle, the priest spotted Jack and sat in the pew behind him.

"Nice to see you again, Mr. Dacre!"

Jack smiled, but without much energy, unable to fully hide his mental weariness. "You too, Monsignor."

"You look beat. How is everything?"

Jack lowered his eyes to the floor. "Beat," he repeated, then chuckled. "That's a good way to put it. Beat . . . in more ways than one."

"Something happen since we last spoke?"

Jack massaged his forehead. "So much. Honestly, I wouldn't even know where to start."

"Usually easiest to start at the beginning."

Jack took a deep breath, feeling his stomach sink at the thought of what he was about to tell the priest. He didn't know how he'd react, and he rather liked their rapport as it was. He didn't want to see the look on his face when he found out he was batshit crazy.

His voice got caught in his throat a few times as he began to narrate his past forty-eight hours. He took his time, trying not to forget any details. The cleric's face grew more serious as he went on. He must have talked for twenty minutes. Monsignor Bamonte listened attentively, interrupting only if something needed clarification. Jack found it hard to read the priest while he spoke.

"Now, I'm not sure if it's ever been demons at all," he finished. "I'm not sure if any of it is what I thought it was. What if it's all in my head? What if I'm insane? The one I fought last night claimed I'm schizophrenic, and that it and everything else I've been seeing are hallucinations. It said it's the part of my brain that's fighting the disease, like some mental white blood cell."

"So now you're not only dealing with doubts about the existence of God . . . you're questioning your sanity too," the priest summed up for him.

"Yeah," Jack breathed, feeling tired after all his talking.

The monsignor nodded his head, appearing deep in thought. He studied Jack, his expression impervious to emotion as it had been while Jack recounted his tale. At last, he voiced an opinion.

"The way I see it, there are only four possibilities to consider about what you've told me. They're the same four logical considerations the Church herself uses to investigate when anyone claims to have experienced a miracle. The first would be that the person is lying." The priest smiled. "I don't think I have to worry too much about that one. You seem sincere to me, Jack. So, if we were to rule that one out, it leaves the other three. The second possibility is that the person hallucinated, which is exactly what you're already thinking could have happened."

"So what are the other two alternatives?"

"One is that it is an authentic miracle from God. Only prayer and patience would be able to discern that."

"And the fourth?"

The monsignor pursed his lips, appearing to carefully choose his next words. "There's always the chance the entire thing is a deception of the Devil. Scripture does tell us Satan and his minions may appear as angels of light in order to mislead us. I don't say that to put you on edge, only to keep you open-minded and considering every possibility. If you have received a supernatural ability, God would take no offense at you first taking time to ensure it didn't come from His enemy. In fact, a life of studying the history of the Church and the lives of the saints would tell you He expects nothing less."

Jack pondered the monsignor's words, feeling a mixture of trepidation, curiosity, and determination all at the same time.

"Well . . . I don't like the idea the Devil's gotten in my head at all. But, even if this whole thing did turn out to be his trick, at least that would be proof he was real and that God must therefore be real too. I think the hardest thing to figure out is still whether or not I'm experiencing something otherworldly or if I'm just crazy."

He saw a slight reaction in the cleric's face at his words this time. He couldn't be sure, but it looked like surprise.

"I agree," the priest said. "And I promise I'll do what I can to help you with that. Of course, my knowledge of mental illness only goes so far. I do have some experience, but I'm not a psychologist."

"Right, I wouldn't expect you to be. So . . . if we were to keep things in your area of expertise, let's say, for the sake of argument, incorporeal sight was something put in me by either God or Satan. What would be the best method of discovering which one it was?

The evil spirit I fought seemed desperate to get me to doubt it, almost to the point I'd be inclined to think it's not from Hell. I'd figure the demons would want me to embrace it if it was of their design. Still . . . it'd also be a really clever form of reverse psychology for Satan to throw doubt on his own trick in order to get me to rely on it as though it were sacred."

Monsignor Bamonte smiled. "Very insightful. My advice for discerning between the celestial and the diabolic would be to follow the counsel Christ Himself gave in the Gospel about those matters."

Jack perked up, not realizing the Bible contained an answer for his specific situation.

"You will come to know the origin of something by its fruits," the priest said, "meaning the effects it produces over time. In the meantime, I'd advise not publicizing what you've told me, but keeping it between you, myself, and your family."

"Okay," Jack agreed, though with no real intention of saying anything to his family until he knew for sure if his "charism" was real or not.

If it was, he had no idea how he'd tackle telling them about how it revealed their souls. If it wasn't, then there'd be no need to start such an awkward conversation.

"Of course," the monsignor said, "we've only talked about how you'd discern whether this, incorporeal sight, is from God or the Devil. As you pointed out, the first thing to discern is whether this whole thing's not a product of your mind."

"Right," Jack said, his voice sounding desperate in his own ears. He felt the wide divide between his mind and peace had returned. "But I have no idea how to find that out."

"Don't worry. The mystics have some advice for you on that."

Jack looked the cleric in the eyes. "Mystics?"

"The saints who received supernatural gifts in life, like the one you're describing. Saints like John of the Cross and Teresa of Ávila would advise a person in your situation to ignore any kind of otherworldly phenomena until you'd discerned where it was coming from. If what you have is from the demonic and you ignore it, they'll eventually stop presenting it to you. The demons don't like when their antics are ignored. They'd soon give up and try attacking you in some other way.

If what you have is from God, then it'll remain with you whether you acknowledge it or not, because God doesn't change His mind. And if what you have is a mental illness, you won't be able to ignore it. So . . . whatever incorporeal sight is, ignoring it for a while should show us something about its nature.

With that in mind, I propose we proceed as though you didn't possess it at all. I'll meet with you at regular intervals to see how things are going and, in the meantime, teach you some objective reasons to believe that I'd teach anyone who came to me with your doubts. That should help with your questions about God's existence."

Jack sat back in his pew, surprised at the relief he felt wash over him at the priest's suggestion. His only regret was the thought of not seeing Dathiel or Joan of Arc for a while. Real or not, he couldn't deny the comfort their presence had brought him.

"That sounds good to me, Monsignor."

The priest nodded. "I'm glad you're open to the idea. How about trying to go a straight two weeks without consciously tapping into this ability, then come see me and tell me how it went. Think you can do that?"

"Shouldn't be a problem if I'm really the one in control of it."

"Also, if you're willing, I'd like you to start keeping a daily journal. Begin with Halloween night and record everything you've told me and anything that occurs from now on. Bring the journal with you to our meetings and I'll review it."

"Alright . . . There is one other thing I was thinking might help."

"Yes?"

"Would . . . would an evaluation from a psychologist be a good idea? That way I could be officially tested for schizophrenia? My mother's already offered me to see a professional because of my friend's suicide."

"That sounds great! I'd say you should definitely take her up on that. And if you're comfortable telling them about what you've told me, then yes. Hopefully they'll be able to help with discerning whether your experiences are purely mental."

Jack smiled as another wave of relief washed through him, unfurling his stomach from its tightened position. He felt he was regaining some of the ground he'd lost the previous night. Maybe mental order could be restored after all.

"In the meantime," the priest said, "I can offer you your first lesson in what I guess we'll call 'reasons to believe' if you have a few minutes."

Jack turned more toward the cleric in his pew. "I'm all ears!"

"Alright."

The clergyman paused, closing his eyes and massaging his forehead a moment. Jack thought it almost looked like he was listening for directions. He supposed he was saying a silent prayer.

He began. "In speaking with you last time, I believe I picked up on something. Am I correct in thinking you have a fear—or maybe let's use the word, hesitancy—when it comes to the empirical sciences?"

"What do you mean, like . . . I see science as something threatening to Catholic teaching?"

"Yes. Would you say that's your position?"

"You could say that . . . yeah."

The priest nodded. "I suspected as much. And it's not surprising, given it was in a science class your crisis of faith began. But science isn't faith's enemy, despite the fact that, sadly, both atheists and Christians sometimes think so. Tell me, if Divine Revelation's true and some particular hypothesis of an empirical science correct, how would the two ever possibly contradict each other?"

"They . . . couldn't."

"Precisely. So the only time science could contradict Catholicism is if it's incorrect about something. And, believe me, no one fears fallacious science more than scientists themselves. It's their job to seek the truth and be accurate. When understood properly, science and religion are both avenues to understanding God, ourselves, and the world around us. They're not fundamentally opposed, as many think. In your case, biological evolution is the stumbling block. I suppose you believe it contradicts creation and the Book of Genesis?"

"Yes, sir."

"It doesn't. It's possible to accept both as true. And there are plenty of Catholics who do."

*"Really?"*

The monsignor nodded. "Even Darwin himself was a Christian. Pope Benedict XVI once stated that there are many scientific proofs in favor of evolution, which appears to be a reality we can see and which enriches our knowledge of life and being. Other popes over the last century spoke highly of evolution's study too. Pope Pius XII and Saint John Paul the Great both noted there's no opposition between faith's understanding of creation and the evidence of the empirical sciences."

The cleric paused a moment, allowing Jack to process before continuing.

"Also, *The Catechism of the Catholic Church* states that investigations into the origin of life on Earth should hardly cause us anxiety, but—on the contrary—invite us to even greater admiration for the greatness of the Creator, prompting us to give Him thanks for all His works and for the understanding and wisdom He gives to scholars and researchers."

*"How?"* Jack demanded. "I mean, that's all great news if it's true. But . . . how do belief in creation and the theory of evolution not conflict with each other? Mr. Wilkerson seems to think so. And I don't see how they'd line up myself."

"I'm afraid you're both mistaken then. Likely your teacher has never read Genesis closely, or—if he has—he lacked the Catholic Church's interpretative guidance. Let's take a look at it while we're on the subject."

Without pulling out a Bible or even a phone to browse a version online, the monsignor again proceeded to quote citations verbatim, without a reference before him.

"Genesis chapter three, verse nineteen states: 'the Lord God *having formed out of the ground* all the beasts of the earth and all the fowls of the air.' Further up in verse seven it says: 'the Lord God formed man *of the slime of the earth* and breathed into his face the breath of life, and man became a living soul.'"

The priest smiled, looking Jack in the eye.

"And who's to say how much *time* God took in forming man before breathing an immortal soul into our first father, Adam? Time is of no consequence to Him. Perhaps the forming of man from slime is Sacred Scripture's way of describing the biological evolution of complex organisms from lesser ones. Perhaps evolution is just our way of describing God's method in bringing about life. Perhaps the random changes in biology that scientists call 'natural selection' are actually the fine-tuning of an Intelligent Designer. There are many scientists who think so.

Francis Collins for one—who was director of the Human Genome Project—referred to the genetic code as 'the language of God.' And without the genetic code, evolution would be impossible. Then, Anthony Flew—who was formerly an atheist—wrote that the coded chemistry in DNA couldn't be explained without belief in an Intelligent Cause, since meaningful information doesn't just randomly emerge from collections of molecules."

Jack sat silent and stunned. It must have shown on his face, because Monsignor Bamonte started laughing.

"Surprising what one can find in the only Book we call 'the Living Word,' eh?" the priest said. "That is, when one bothers to search. Don't feel too badly though. Most people don't bother."

Jack looked around his biology classroom while he waited for class to begin, wondering which idea of the place upset him more, whether it was just a plain, physical space of four walls and a ceiling where the myth of God was discredited, or part of a dark castle of Hell where invisible enemies lurked unseen waiting to corrupt the minds of youth.

There was nothing he could do to conclude which at the moment. Either way, he despised the place. At least Monsignor Bamonte's two week challenge made it easier for him to go back to school, knowing he wouldn't have to come face-to-face with monsters.

"There you are, Jack!" Naomi smiled, taking her seat near his. "Haven't seen you since the party."

"Sorry. I was out sick the last couple of days."

"Oh, sorry to hear. You feeling better?"

"Good enough I guess. I miss anything exciting with . . .?" He jerked his head in Mr. Wilkerson's direction, who was standing at the whiteboard writing out definitions.

Naomi chuckled. "No, nothing I've noticed. It's been pretty uneventful."

"Alright, e'erybody shut up now," Mr. Wilkerson called the class to attention. "It's time to review for your midterm. It's going to cover everything up through last week. I've written its main sections on the board, so copy them down. For the first part—biological evolution—who can tell me how the theory of evolution originated?"

Darris volunteered an answer. "Charles Darvin—"

"Darwin," Mr. Wilkerson corrected. "Go on."

"He figured out humans came from smaller organisms and didn't just appear out of nothing, like Christians had thought."

"Very good. Yes, Charles Darwin's theory led scientists to realize that the firings of natural selection eventually brought humans into existence."

Angered at hearing the subject of a discrepancy brought up again, and feeling better prepared to argue with what he'd learned from the monsignor, Jack raised his hand.

"Yes, Jack?" the teacher called on him.

"Just wondering how evolution *automatically* discredits the creation spoken of in the Bible's Book of Genesis."

"Glad you brought that up," the instructor said without even pausing to think. "As you'll all recall, evolution wasn't widely accepted at first. Teaching it in classrooms was even outlawed here in the United States. But it's been scientifically proven since then, while religion has remained unconfirmed." The teacher smiled before adding one last comment. "Personally, I find it funny books like the Bible tell us miracles used to occur all the time, with God appearing and speaking to people pretty often. Yet, ever since the invention of things like video cameras, that never seems to happen anymore."

Approving laughter erupted from a few of the students across the classroom.

"Anyway," Mr. Wilkerson continued, "to answer your question more specifically, Jack. One major leap forward for Darwin's theory was the Scopes Monkey Trial of 1925. John Scopes was a teacher who'd violated the law against teaching evolution in the classroom and was put on trial for it. His defense attorney, Clarence Darrow, argued with his opponent, William Bryan, on the stand. Bryan had claimed everything in the Bible was true. But, when Darrow questioned him about how the age of certain rocks—which geologists had determined to be millions of years old—didn't line up with the Christian belief that the Bible revealed Earth to be roughly six thousand years old, Bryan had no answer. Darrow then went on to point out numerous places where the Bible even contradicts itself, let alone science. Needless to say, evolution was soon instilled in school textbooks while the prejudices of religion were removed."

The teacher went on with the review, either failing to notice or choosing to ignore that Jack's question had been more of a challenge. Jack didn't speak up again. He had no facts to quote against what the teacher had said. Instead of exposing Mr. Wilkerson's position as faulty to the other students, it seemed all he'd accomplished by his objection was help reinforce it.

"Good try," Naomi whispered to him.

"Not good enough," Jack whispered back.

That night, Jack had another night terror.

It began with him walking in the middle of a desert, before he stumbled down a sand dune, putting him before a dark cave at the base of a mountain. He wasn't sure at first why he was supposed to fear the place, but he knew he was. As he approached the cave's mouth, unable to control where his legs took him, several of the creatures he'd seen upon viewing Wando High through incorporeal sight were spewed forth. Cackling, they surrounded him, as though playing some diabolic form of Ring Around the Rosie.

Two of the monsters stood out to Jack from the others. These he hadn't seen before. He was sure of it, because he would have remembered them. They were the weirdest and most frightening of the bunch.

The first looked more human. Almost too human, which might have been what disturbed Jack so much. Even the stare of its gray eyes seemed too relatable. It was clothed only in a loincloth of what looked to Jack like the Spanish moss that hung from trees around the Carolinian Lowcountry. Its skin had been burned to a brown shade. Its head retained a few locks of shoulder-length blonde hair that clung to it in patches. The only inhuman things about it were its pointed ears and the batwings on its back, which had been sliced in half down the middle and were now dripping black blood as it danced and twirled around. It flashed a grin at him, and Jack saw most of its teeth had been knocked out.

The second new monster was much more grotesque in appearance. It was a brown minotaur with the face of a clown that was dressed like a stage magician. Crimson horns curved up from its forehead in front of a black top hat. The bestial right half of its body stood out from its more human left half, literally. A muscled arm with a long-fingered, clawed hand and a leg with a hoof for a foot were tearing out of its magician's tuxedo near its middle. The tuxedo clothed its left side with no problem, the beast's left hand being of normal size and wearing a white glove, while its left foot wore a dress shoe. Jack couldn't see much of its midsection where minotaur morphed into magician. The demon was cloaked in a black cape with what looked like a red interior.

Despite all this grotesquerie, what was most haunting about the monster to Jack was its face. It was the minotaur's, but its fur was painted over with a white base, red rims around its black eyes, a green nose, and a blue smile stretching over its cheeks. Mean looking fangs were gnashing at Jack from the middle of the painted smile.

At some unknown signal, the first creature grabbed a whip hanging curled up at the hip of its loincloth and lashed it out at Jack, catching him by the neck and pulling him forward to faceplant in the sand. The other demons lunged inward, closing their circle the moment he hit the ground. They held him down, the minotaur yanking his head up by his hair so he was forced to face the cave. As he watched and waited, almost knowing what would happen before it did, the evil spirit he'd fought the night after Halloween emerged.

Its tattered gray rags billowed in a cold gust of wind. The black feathers of its wings bobbed up and down in unison like a thousand black hands bidding the other monsters settle down their roars and cackles. The fiend smiled its ghastly grin, reaching a hand out to Jack, as if offering help. It seemed more like an enticement to enter with it into the darkness behind it.

When Jack tried breaking free of its minions' hold on him, the spear-toting leader shook its head in disappointment.

"You'd choose madness over truth, Jack?" It clucked its forked tongue. "So much for the honesty of Christians."

It spread its wings and flew up to the peak of the mountain. Jack's captors lifted him to look up at it. Perching on the rock, the monster kept its wings spread and raised its scepter, which shot bolts of red lightning down at Jack. When they struck him, his whole form went rigid. He would have screamed if he could, but his vocal cords felt like they were contracting along with all the other muscles in his body. Despair overtook him.

It was only then he realized he was screaming, as he sat up in bed, cold sweat all over him. His sheets were what had been binding his limbs. Not the hands of demons or the strike of a nightmarish red lightning. He struggled to unwrap himself, twitching when the light switched on above him.

*"Fuck, Jack! It's just me!"* Chloe said from the doorway.

He was breathing too hard to respond. His parents walked up behind his sister in the hallway.

*"Another one?"* his mother asked, a worried expression on her face. "Thank God

you're seeing the doctor tomorrow."

# CHAPTER XI
## MADNESS OR MALEVOLENCE

Dr. Rasput seemed a welcoming enough man.

His Queen Street office was painted a warm tan color and there were paintings of sea shores and fishing docs spread over the walls. He'd greeted Jack and Lorelai in the lobby before showing Jack to their session. He turned on a white noise machine and placed it just outside the door before closing it and sitting opposite Jack, who'd taken a place on his couch.

The couch was leather. Cold. Jack never found leather furniture relaxing. Not when fall was becoming winter. The pillows on the couch were nice. One of them had a furry texture to it. He found himself rubbing it on his lap while waiting for the session to begin. He didn't know how therapy was supposed to start.

He felt the flutters of butterfly wings tickling the inside of his stomach. He knew he had no reason to be nervous. He should have been excited. He might be about to get some straight answers on what was going on with him. Still, the jitters came. He distracted himself from succumbing to them by looking over Dr. Rasput's bookshelves. There were volumes on psychotropic drugs, marriage counseling, adolescent therapy, treatment research, and more.

He scanned for books on schizophrenia, not finding any. He hoped he'd chosen the right doctor. He'd insisted on a Catholic therapist, and Dr. Rasput was apparently the only one in the area who was Catholic, qualified to counsel, and could prescribe medication if necessary.

"So," the doctor began, pulling Jack's eyes back in his direction, "I understand you've lost someone close to you recently."

Jack smiled, hoping it appeared polite. "Y-yes," he stuttered.

His nerves really were getting to him. It was frustrating. He was not someone to let fear control him. Why should therapy make him nervous enough to stutter if seeing monsters never had?

"One of my best friends during childhood, Chuck Nelson," he said without stuttering a single syllable this time. "My mom tell you anything else when she called in?"

"Just that you've been suffering what you both believe are night terrors ever since. That you seem tired a lot. Not much else. I noticed you said Chuck was a best friend during childhood . . . Was he not your best friend anymore?"

Jack shook his head. "Not for years. But it wasn't really Chuck I came to talk to you about. That's just what my mom thinks."

"Oh?"

Jack surveyed the doctor a moment, trying to read him. This was the part making him nervous. The revelation that would either unite or separate him from the psychiatrist. The doctor wasn't as impassive as Monsignor Bamonte. Even through the sunlight reflecting off his glasses, Jack could see kind eyes. They made him look open, a listening ear. Still, that didn't mean he was trustworthy. For that, Jack would need to do some probing.

"Before we get into that, I had a few questions. I hope you don't mind. I just wanted to get to know you a little first before spilling all my deepest secrets."

"Absolutely," Dr. Rasput said. "That's part of the first session with any patient. And, in case your mother didn't pass this on already, I want you to know anything you tell me in here stays between us. The only reason I'd be forced to break confidentiality is if you told me something that indicated you were a danger to yourself or others."

Jack nodded. "Good to hear. I read online that you were a Catholic. That was a big part of why I chose to see you. Some of what I've been dealing with crosses into the realm of religion. I've been speaking with a priest about it already. But . . . we think it might also cross into the medical field. So, I wanted to know where you were coming from when it came to your religious outlook, just so we're all on the same page and looking at my problem from all possible angles. You are Catholic, right?"

After a moment of processing all Jack had just laid on him, the doctor nodded his head. "I am."

"Okay, if I may ask . . . what's your outlook on supernatural occurrences?"

The doctor tilted his head and pursed his lips. "What do you mean by my outlook?"

"Do you believe in them?"

"That's an interesting question. I wonder . . . what makes you ask?"

"It relates to why I'm here. I wanted to gauge your exact religious outlook to know where you're coming from. I'm guessing, as a Catholic, you believe in the supernatural, right?"

Dr. Rasput slowly shook his head. "No. As a Catholic, I can't say I do."

Jack's heart sank, but he kept his face neutral to hide his disappointment and confusion. "You don't believe in miracles?"

"Oh yes! I believe in miracles. I thought you meant things like conjuring stuff from thin air or ghostly apparitions."

Jack was silent a moment, even more confused now. "You don't believe in otherworldly things, but . . . you believe in miracles?"

"That's one way to put it, yes," the doctor said, shifting in his armchair and crossing his legs. "Maybe I'm misunderstanding your question."

"I mean things like . . . I guess, what you'd find in the Bible. The parting of the Red Sea, the feeding of the five thousand, the Resurrection of Christ, things like that. Do you believe in those things?"

"Absolutely."

"Oh . . . okay. That's why I was confused. I mean . . . wouldn't you call those supernatural events?"

The doctor nodded and shifted in his chair again, uncrossing his legs and leaning forward. "I see. I see what you mean now I think. Let me clarify. No, I wouldn't call those supernatural myself. I actually took a Biblical exegesis class in college that addressed the difference I think you're getting at. The miracle I see in the feeding of the five thousand is the miracle of sharing the food that the people were hiding in their sacks. That's similar to the miracle of Christ living on in our hearts that we call, the Resurrection."

The doctor paused a moment, gazing up toward the right corner of the room, appearing to think back.

"The parting of the Red Sea's a little more difficult to make sense of. But my professor had a pet theory on that one. It may have referred to a great wind that forced the tide back farther than usual."

Jack felt more perplexed than ever. "So . . . if I'm understanding you right . . . according to your schooling, the miracles spoken of in Catholicism aren't about supernatural occurrences then? Meaning Jesus didn't physically rise from the grave and didn't literally multiply five loaves of bread and two fish into enough pieces to feed a crowd of five thousand?"

The doctor nodded. "Correct. The supernatural interpretation of those passages would be a medieval understanding that modern scholarship has since reinterpreted to align with today's scientific understanding."

Jack leaned back into the couch's chilly cushion, the leather feeling sticky on the back of his neck. It pulled at the skin there any time he shifted. He realized he'd started to sweat.

"What about things like angels and demons?" he asked. "What do you make of it when Scripture mentions them?"

"You mean, what do I think they are?"

Jack nodded.

The doctor tilted his head and puckered his lips again. "I'd say they're a manifestation of the human figures' consciences. Like how movies and cartoons sometimes show the little devils and angels on people's shoulders directing them what to do. They were the Scripture authors' way of illustrating what was going on internally for the human characters in their stories."

Jack couldn't believe his ears. "So you see them more as literary devices? Not actual beings?"

"Yes."

"What about things like death, and Heaven, and Hell?" Jack demanded, sitting forward, trying—but probably failing—not to show his rising indignation at what he was hearing. "Do you believe life goes on after death?"

The doctor shifted back in his chair, crossing his legs again, his expression looking . . . well, looking rather like Mr. Wilkerson's when he spoke about Christianity. It was an expression of skepticism Jack had come to know all too well, and to loathe. That pull at the corners of the mouth that almost wanted to become a condescending smile but which was held back the moment before it formed into one.

"Maybe it would help if we focused on why you've come to see me, Jack. You mentioned your problem related to these questions somehow. I can't help you if you don't tell me what's bothering you."

*Real subtle evasion,* Jack thought, as his right hand fingers began tapping across his thumb.

Index to thumb, middle finger to thumb, ring finger to thumb, pinky to thumb, ring finger again, and so on. The tapping sped up the more Jack thought about what he should say next. He didn't trust this doctor. He had crazy ideas he'd never encountered before. Why did he feel more like he was talking to his biology teacher than someone akin to Monsignor Bamonte? That was the whole point in requesting a psychiatrist who shared his beliefs! But what could he do about it now?

Dr. Rasput was his only option, and he hadn't come to therapy to hold back what was on his mind. That would be a waste of both their time, not to mention his parents' money. He wanted a professional's opinion, one way or another. Yet he felt despair welling up inside him. The opinion was going to be biased. If the doctor didn't really believe in miracles, how could he have an open mind to the possibility one had occurred? He noticed Dr. Rasput looking at his right hand. He stopped tapping his fingers.

"Something's happened to me," he said. "Something I'm unsure about the nature of. I'm not sure if it's supernatural or psychological."

"Oh?" the doctor asked, leaning forward, appearing interested.

This surprised Jack. He'd expected him to look closed off. But his expression looked open again. The skepticism was gone. Now his eyes only displayed compassion, as though he was eager to allay anything ailing Jack. Maybe there was hope after all. Maybe Dr. Rasput would change his mind once he'd heard Jack's story.

But, as he went through his tale, Jack picked up subtle expressions that showed him what the psychiatrist really thought. Because of this, he summarized his story in far less detail than he had for the monsignor, wanting to get the session over with as soon as he could. His stomach was feeling achy. The butterflies had metamorphosed into wasps that were stinging him from within, urging him to get things over with here so he could just go home and figure things out for himself.

He held out details such as the demons—especially fighting with one—and what Dathiel had told him about his "destiny." He didn't tell him his supposed ability enabled him to discern the state of people's souls and that he could hear some of their thoughts through it. He only told the doctor how he'd started seeing angels and saints, what Dathiel had explained to him about how this gift worked, and how the world and people looked different to him when he used it.

"That's interesting," Dr. Rasput said when he was done.

He rose from his armchair, pulling the swivel chair from behind his big mahogany desk that was perched to give him a view over Queen Street. He wheeled it over to a cabinet of drawers on the far side of the room. Opening one from a key in his pocket, he sat down and started rummaging through it.

"So what do you think?" Jack asked. "It sound like schizophrenia to you?"

"It could be," the doctor said without turning around. "Or it could be some other form of psychosis. Have you taken any drugs lately?"

"No, sir."

"Anything medicinal? Whether for depression, sleep, injury, or anything like that? It doesn't have to be an illegal drug."

"No, nothing like that. I don't take drugs."

"And you're not currently on any prescriptions?"

"No."

The doctor nodded his head, still without looking over his shoulder, swiveling back around as soon as he'd found what he was looking for.

"Good. This won't be mixed with anything else and have unforeseen side effects then. I'm going to write you a prescription for a trial of thorazine. It's an antipsychotic medication used to treat disorders that include schizophrenia and manic depression. So if either of those really are your core issue, this can start to fight it. It can also help with nausea and anxiety. So it may lessen those symptoms for you too."

"So you think my problem is psychological then?"

The doctor looked him in the eyes from behind the corner of his desk where he was writing and nodded. "Whatever it is, yes. I think it has to do with either your brain or your mood, or both. What exactly it is and what caused it we'll need more time to determine. It was probably triggered by your recent tragedy. But we'd have to have a lot more meetings and do a lot more talking to get to the bottom of that. In the meantime though, this should help you deal with the immediate symptoms. If it works for you, I'll write you a prescription for a refill at our next session."

Jack took the paper slip the doctor handed him and thanked him, hoping time was about up. He could tell he'd gotten as much as he was going to get out of the session.

"Are there any possible side effects I should be aware of?" he asked. "I mean, if I don't actually have any kind of mental illness, would taking this hurt me in that case?"

The doctor rattled off his answer as though he'd memorized it from a script.

"Side effects can include a number of different things. They'll be listed in full on one of the sheets I'm sending home with you and your mother. The most severe ones include insomnia, anxiety, weight gain, blurred vision, dizziness, and motor restlessness that can include mood agitation along with it." The doctor hesitated a moment. "On the rarest of occasions, a patient can suffer psychotic symptoms or catatonic states. But again, that's very rare. Hopefully you won't experience any of those. If you do, call me immediately."

Jack nodded, his eyes going bleary as they wandered the bookshelves again. The side effects sounded like those he'd hear on an infomercial for sore throat medicine or something simple like that, where not only were the side effects worse than a sore throat, they included a sore throat.

*You know,* he'd think when he saw such a commercial, *I think I'd just ride out my sore throat.*

He almost laughed at this thought, but held it back. He didn't want to have to explain a random outburst to the doctor. Right now, all he wanted to do was wrap up and leave. He didn't like the idea of taking such a powerful medication afterward, but he had to know whether he'd experienced a psychological sickness or a real supernatural phenomenon.

Still, unless this thorazine did wonders for him, he didn't think he'd be returning to see the psychiatrist again.

Jack started taking the thorazine the next morning, and took the next two days off school.

During this time, Lorelai found herself on the phone more times than she bothered to keep count, whether it was with the psychiatrist's front desk secretary, the psychiatrist himself, or the family doctor. After the first day, she was on the verge of taking Jack to the emergency room. Jack insisted this was unnecessary, at least during the moments he was lucid enough to insist it.

This lack of lucidity didn't lend credibility to his judgment. When he wasn't present to his family, he was ranging from jittery states to catatonia. Lorelai didn't know which frightened her worse, Jack displaying uncontrollable motor tics or becoming unresponsive to those around him, like he was in a trance. The worst incident came near the end of the second day.

Jack was sitting on the living room couch watching TV in one of his stupors, not really taking much in from what was happening on the screen in front of him. He thought he heard a TV from upstairs coming through the ceiling. He looked up, puzzled. Chloe wasn't home at the moment, and his parents were in the kitchen. So, who'd turned on a TV up there? The more he listened, the less sure he became it was a television at all.

"Hello?" someone was calling. "Can anyone hear me?"

Jack narrowed his eyebrows while he looked up, which pinched together much slower than they would have under normal circumstances. Little motions and reactions had been taking more effort for him to perform.

"*I'm stuck!*" the voice called.

Jack thought he recognized it, but couldn't place it.

"*I can't see in here!*"

Jack's grip on the living room couch's armrest tightened. He recognized the voice now. He hadn't heard it in a while. That's why it hadn't registered at first.

"Wait," it said. "I can see light now."

There were shifting sounds in the ceiling, like there was someone moving around inside it. Jack raised his eyebrows.

"I think I can see you," the voice called. "Here! In the vent!"

Jack looked to the air conditioning vent on the ceiling and thought he saw it vibrating, like someone was trying to knock the cover off from behind. A shiny black point emerged between one of its cracks. He recoiled, thinking a cockroach was crawling out of it. But it wasn't a bug. It was wiggling like a finger, beckoning him.

Four more black fingers emerged through other cracks on the cover. It was ripped inward. A head popped out from the hole left in the ceiling. Chuck Nelson shot Jack an upside down grin.

"Jack old boy! Good to see you! How long's it been, man?"

Jack didn't say anything. His mouth and throat had gone dry. He couldn't have spoken if he'd wanted. Chuck frowned, which looked like a smile from Jack's view.

"Why the somber face? Oh . . . is it because I'm not supposed to be here anymore? You're right. Sorry. I forgot. I'll just make myself scarce."

With that, Chuck somehow forced an arm out of the ceiling next to his head.

There was a gun in his hand. He pointed it at Jack, whose heart raced, thinking he was about to shoot him.

"Here's to you, Jack, and to old friendships."

Chuck turned the gun into his own mouth and pulled the trigger, blasting blood and brain matter across the ceiling behind him. Jack moaned but never made it to a full scream. Chuck's head and arm hung from the vent, swinging back-and-forth a few times before coming to a dead rest.

The gun was still clutched in his hand, aimed at the floor. After a few seconds, he sprung to life again, smiling that upside down smile. Jack didn't register when the next changes took place, or whether they'd been gradual or instant, but Chuck's skin turned gray and decayed. He looked like he'd already been in the grave a while.

"How you like that, Jack? *Still here and dead!*" He broke into hysterics.

Jack was fighting to breathe. Chuck tilted his head sideways.

"What?" he asked, as blood ran from his mouth up his upside down face and dripped from his forehead to the living room floor, while brain matter dripped from the back. "Don't like my new look?"

The ceiling slumped around him, and Chuck fell to the floor in front of Jack on his back. Jack jumped, drawing his legs up under him, not wanting to touch the talking corpse. Chuck's lifeless eyes stared up at him a moment, and Jack thought the fall might have finished the job the bullet couldn't. But his dead friend soon sat up and turned around on his knees to face him.

"I'm only like this because you and Kevin abandoned me when I needed you, Jack." Chuck's voice started to rise. "Blew out my head. Now I'm dead. *You fled, and now I'm dead! Blew out my head. Now I'm dead! YOU FLED, AND NOW I'M DEAD!*"

Suddenly, demons burst their way through the walls and ceiling, even emerged from the TV behind Chuck. Others crawled around from the hallway. They looked like the ones Jack had seen at Wando and in his night terrors. At the same time, he thought they looked different somehow. Fuzzy. And the ones coming out the TV were made of the same colors that made up the screen.

Maybe it was just blurred vision on Jack's part. Either way, in a matter of seconds, the room was demolished and overrun by the monsters. They destroyed the light fixtures as they tore their way through the ceiling. The room went dark.

They were clawing their way toward Chuck and Jack. Chuck spread his arms, as though he'd expected them. They bit and clawed at him until they'd ripped off all his clothes. One demon that had a face crossed between a pig and a toddler stuck its head under Chuck's legs and latched onto his penis, its upside down eyes leering up at Jack from there.

"This is my lot now, Jack," Chuck said. "Thanks a bunch!"

As soon as he'd finished speaking, the demons shredded him, tearing off limbs in various directions. They devoured his remains in a matter of moments like a pride of hungry lions. They turned toward Jack, clawing their way forward. Squealing and gasping for air like a pig faced with its slaughter, Jack jumped up to the back of the couch.

*"NO! NO! NO! NOOO!"* he screamed, turning to open the window, slamming it with his elbow when he realized he didn't have time to open it.

It cracked but didn't break. When his parents rushed in from the kitchen, they found what he'd been trying to do. The trouble was, the window behind the couch had no latch. It didn't open. It had never possessed that feature, and Jack knew that. This sent Lorelai into another fit of near hysteria.

The only thing that kept her calm on the outside was she had to seem strong in order for her and Dale to calm Jack down. When he'd turned back around, the salivating monsters that had been ready to eat him alive were gone. The room was intact. Even the vent on the ceiling was back in place. Only his parents were there.

He didn't want to hang around to see if the monsters would come back, so he finally agreed to let them take him to the hospital. Any reason to get out of the house at that point sounded good to him. As his parents helped him to the car, Jack noticed something. He saw it even through his shock at what he'd just seen in the living room minutes ago. There was a certain look in his father's eyes.

Dale Dacre meant to sue Dr. Rasput for everything he could get. It wouldn't be the first lawsuit his father had ever initiated and it probably wouldn't be the last. Jack couldn't blame him. In fact, he thought he might agree with this course of action. But his head was swimming.

He knew he wasn't in the right state of mind to weigh in on decisions like that at that moment.

Jack was agitated during his first hour at the hospital.

He couldn't seem to sit still. He'd answered a few of the nurse's and doctor's questions in a curt manner, impatient they didn't already know what to do. Once Dale and Lorelai were able to take over, Jack fell asleep in the hospital bed, not realizing how tired he'd become.

The doctor wanted to keep him overnight for observation. When he awoke later, he wasn't sure of the time. It was still dark. His father had stayed with him, sleeping in an easy chair with a freestanding lamp behind it in the corner of the hospital room next to Jack's bed.

They'd actually restrained him to its side rails! He was still able to reach over to the table next to him to retrieve things. It had been when he'd grabbed the glass of water off it he'd noticed the straps on his arms. He was bound to the bed, unable to even get up and go to the bathroom without the permission of someone else.

*Didn't they know he'd been the victim here?*

He guessed his attempts to flee the living room out a window that never opened had given his family quite the scare. They only wanted to keep him safe, even if it had to be from himself, he reasoned. Still, the less rational side of his brain—the part that was maybe busy flushing the thorazine from his system—kept feeling resentment over the restraints.

His mood got better the more he woke up. The ice water pouring down the sluice of his throat rinsed more of the negative thoughts away. He started to feel safe within the restraints, as though nothing could get to him while he was being held by them anymore than he could get to anything else in the room. Looking around at his quiet surroundings, his breathing slowed.

The room was shrouded in shadows. There was a TV hanging near the ceiling. Its blank black screen made him feel better. He could still picture the multicolored shapes crawling out of his own back home. There was a green potted plant on the windowsill, its giant leaves reaching out in all directions like the triangular tentacles of a botanical octopus. The sliding glass door of the room was covered by a curtain. There was a sink just inside it for the nurses. For some reason, Jack's attention was most drawn to the far corner of the room opposite the one his father was sleeping in.

He soon realized why. It was so dark, his sight couldn't pierce all the way to the corner. It gave him the distinct feeling someone or something was watching him out of it, hiding within its shadows, just outside the gaze of the streetlamps peering in through the window. Like something was waiting to reach out and pull him into the corner's unending dark should he ever get up to use the bathroom next to it.

*But no one else is here,* he told himself. *It's just me and Dad.*

This did nothing to shake the feeling they weren't alone. He craned his neck to try and see the back of the corner, hearing every joint within it creak like the rattle of loose screws. He stared long and hard. Was it a vague silhouette he saw forming from the shadows? A familiar silhouette? Tall, dark, with only two colors contrasting its blackness? That of long white hair and a smile of broken yellow teeth? Or was it just his imagination? Even another side effect of the thorazine?

His breathing sped up alongside his pulse. He tried to tell himself it wasn't there. There was *nothing* there! Nothing in that corner! Nothing within that all-consuming darkness!

He was just seeing what he expected he'd see after what he thought he'd seen in his living room earlier. That was all. If he concentrated, the nightmare would vanish.

But it wouldn't vanish. The longer he stared, blinking several times to clear his eyes, the more he was sure the fiend of his night terrors stood in the room watching him. As dark as the corner was, the monster's skin was darker. As if to confirm for Jack it was there, the creature raised its arm and waved at him. Jack yanked at his restrains, pulling in the opposite direction, trying to jump from the bed and run for the sliding glass door. The sound woke his father, who reached up and turned on the lamp standing behind his chair.

"Jack? . . . Good, you're awake. How're you feeling."

Jack didn't answer. The moment the light turned on and put the opposite corner of the room in full view, the silhouette he was convinced he'd been seeing disappeared. Its vanishing act was so sudden, he wondered if the shadows in the room had been playing a trick on his eyes. He noticed the window behind the potted plant was open. The streetlamps outside might have cast its shadow in a funny way across the corner. A slight gust of wind might have moved the plant so its shadow looked like it was waving at him.

"Could you . . . turn the light back off a second?" Jack asked his father.

Dale did. "Sorry. Should have warned you it was coming on. But you startled me when you moved."

Jack wasn't listening. He was staring into the corner. The plant was casting a shadow. It could have been what he'd seen. But it didn't look to be exactly the same shape from before. Then again, he'd shifted his position on the bed when he'd yanked against his restraints. The angle he was looking at it from now might be different. He laid his head back on his pillow, unsatisfied.

"Okay, you can turn the light on now. Thanks."

His father turned on the lamp and got up to alert the nurse Jack had roused. Jack lay brooding, staring at nothing in particular, refusing to look at the far corner of the room anymore. Was it madness or malevolence stalking his mind? Whichever it was, he felt it was coming for him.

Soon.

# CHAPTER XII
## THE PRINCE AND THE POWER

Jack had to stop and marvel upon entering Monsignor Bamonte's office, feeling as if he'd walked into a small museum.

Vivid oil paintings hung on every wall. Statues lined the tables and shelves. Everywhere he turned there was either a Madonna and Child, an angel, a saint, or a Biblical scene looking back at him. The wall to his right was made up of books, many of them having the antique look Jack suspected he'd only see in the old libraries of Europe, kept behind glass and under lock and key, to be gazed at but never handled. He could think of only one word to describe the place, especially after his experiences over the past weeks: sanctuary.

He felt more relaxed the moment he crossed the threshold than he ever had in Dr. Rasput's office. Safer. He thought he could lose himself in the contents of this place and forget about life's problems for a whole afternoon.

"Why don't you take a seat," the clergyman offered.

Jack had been so wrapped up in the décor he'd failed to notice the priest's desk, or the couch and armchairs placed out for guests. He took a seat on the couch. The cleric settled into one of the chairs, beginning the meeting with a brief prayer, before glancing up to address Jack.

"So how did things go for the past two weeks?"

"Normal except for one rough patch," Jack said. "I met with a mental health professional like we discussed and he prescribed some meds for me, but there were some serious side effects. I wound up in the hospital."

"Really? I'm sorry to hear. You're doing better now?"

"Yes, sir. The side effects went away once the drugs were out of my system."

"What kind of side effects?"

Jack leaned his head back, nodding it from side-to-side, but stopped when his head throbbed with the jerkiness of the movement. He was too sleep deprived even for that gesture.

"Oh, so many," he said. "I don't even know if I caught them all. I wasn't all there for a couple of days. Moodiness, maybe some blurred vision, jitteriness . . . but I seem to have had some of the rarest too. Catatonia . . . even visual hallucinations."

"Hallucinations," the priest repeated. "Did it seem like the same thing you'd experienced before?"

Jack hesitated before answering. "I've thought a lot about that. It's an important question. *The* question really."

Jack stared down, not meeting the priest's eyes a few seconds. Monsignor Bamonte thought he looked whipped. The bags under his eyes were dark. Jack looked up and met his gaze again.

"I can't be sure. But . . . I want to say, no. The hallucinations I had on the meds were so trippy. They just seemed . . . too trippy. Whole bodies sliding out of vents. Stuff coming out of televisions. Don't get me wrong, the stuff I saw before was weird. But it still seemed like it had an order to it, you know? It could all be explained and made sense in its own way. There were rules. The stuff I saw while on thorazine . . . That was just . . . weird. And I knew it at the time, but even more after it was out of my system. Anyway, I did manage to do what you asked."

"You haven't engaged in incorporeal sight at all in two weeks?"

Jack shook his head.

"Was that difficult for you?"

Jack pushed out his bottom lip and shook his head. "No. Other than what happened with the meds, things have been normal. The only other things hard about the last two weeks have been my usual doubts. And my night terrors are still bad."

"Night terrors?"

"Yes—oh, I guess I've never mentioned those to you before. They started the day I found out my friend died. I started having these . . . sleepwalking episodes and nightmares so bad I sometimes wake up screaming. I've had so many now, I've lost count. Most of them feature the monster I told you about last time. The one I fought. The one I thought might be the Devil himself. He's usually the one torturing me in them. And it doesn't help that I can't always tell if I'm awake or not."

"Hmm," the priest mused. "Can you tell me more about them?"

"Sure. Sometimes when I'm having one, I'll get up and do stuff or have conversations with people, all while being partially asleep. In one of them, I thought I was talking to my sister from the top of the stairs before she turned into a demon and tried to drag me down them. When I snapped awake screaming, I found myself standing at the top of the stairs in real life, about to fall down. They're different than what I was telling you about last time though. Incorporeal sight was something I'd never experienced before Halloween. Of course . . ." Jack smiled, and the monsignor noted again how exhausted he looked, "I'm probably the person least likely to know what's going on with me. If I'm really crazy, I can't trust myself, right?"

The priest had cocked his head while Jack had spoken. "So you'd never had these night terrors in your life before? Never been prone to vivid dreams at previous times of stress?"

Jack shook his head, slowly, so it wouldn't throb this time. "No. But I read stress can induce them. And I have experienced more stress than ever before. I read it is strange they'd start now when they've never happened before though. They're supposed to be more common for young kids, not someone my age." Jack shrugged. "Then again, not every seventeen-year-old loses a friend to suicide and starts questioning their whole worldview on the same day. If anything could trigger night terrors in me, I guess that was enough."

The priest nodded. "I guess so. Are they why you look so tired?"

Jack gave a brief smile that once again enunciated his fatigue without the need for words. "You noticed. Guess it's gotten too hard to hide. Yes, they're making my stress over everything else worse. I've been losing more and more sleep because of them, which isn't helping my moods or ability to concentrate. I hate feeling like I'm going to see demons every time I close my eyes! It's made me afraid just to go to bed."

Monsignor Bamonte nodded, wearing an expression Jack hadn't seen before. At least, not to the degree he saw it now. He thought it looked like compassion, but his exhaustion was making his ability to read faces sluggish.

"Yes," the priest said, "that sounds exhausting. I'm sorry to hear that."

"Thanks."

Jack took a deep breath, realizing how much he'd been talking. Despite noticing this and thinking he should probably shut up already and let the monsignor speak, his motormouth kept revving back up and firing off more words. Maybe it was because the priest was the only tangible person he felt comfortable enough to be open with. Not even Dr. Rasput had achieved that level of rapport.

"I have felt exhausted a lot lately . . . and tense. I'm sure the dreams will go away once I work out my doubts though . . . and my guilt I guess."

The mysterious expression came over Monsignor Bamonte's face again. Jack was sure it was compassion this time. In the next moment, his face turned back to neutral.

"If you don't mind talking a little more about them, may I ask—have they always been demonic in nature?"

"You mean, have they always been about demons?"

"Yes."

Jack considered this a moment. "I guess so. When they started, I just thought of them as monsters. But, I see them as demons now. You could say they were demons from the beginning. Actually, when they first started, I was almost convinced I was awake when I'd get attacked, until I did some research and discovered night terrors can seem real at the time."

"I see. And this all started around the same time as your crisis of faith?"

"Same day actually."

"I'm sorry you've had to deal with so much hardship at once. If you like, I can give you a blessing for healing. Maybe it'll help you sleep."

Jack nodded emphatically. His head didn't even ache with the movement.

"Anything that might help!"

The priest grabbed a purple stole off the back of his chair and wrapped it over his shoulders. He raised his right hand toward Jack, who bowed his head in response. He glanced back up when the cleric recited the blessing in a foreign tongue. It sounded like the same one he'd used in Confession.

"What language was that?" Jack asked when he was done.

"Latin," Monsignor Bamonte said, replacing the stole on the back of his chair. "So, other than these night terrors and drug-induced delirium, you said you've had no other unusual experiences since we last met?"

Jack shook his head.

"Haven't felt the need to use incorporeal sight in a two-week hiatus, or felt pulled into it even?"

"Well, I have missed some of what I saw through it. The saints and angels I mean. But I didn't want to go against your advice. So no. It's been no problem."

"Do you think you still have the ability to tap into it?"

"I don't know. I wouldn't know unless I tried."

"Why don't you?"

Jack was surprised by the request. He saw something new in the cleric's eyes. Was it vigilance?

"Now?" he asked.

"Yes. I think this is as good a time as any. Plus I can be here to check reality for you and let you know what I observe from the outside."

After a moment of hesitation, during which Jack's brain roared like a blender, mixing the emotions of trepidation, curiosity, and excitement together to the point he couldn't separate them anymore, he willed to see through his "charism" for the first time in two weeks. His vision changed instantly. The office before him expanded, growing far more brilliant, so much so he had to shield his eyes until they adjusted to the luminous beings present with them. Dathiel stood on his left, but he barely seemed to shine compared with the other spirits in the room.

Monsignor Bamonte appeared much younger. It took Jack a few moments to recognize him with jet-black hair and an absence of wrinkles. His armchair had become more of a throne. He wore a silver breastplate and wrist bracers with a white, long-sleeved cloak hanging down to his ankles. Stranger still, Jack noticed both his thumbs and index fingers glowed as though made of white light, similar to the sacramental seals he'd seen on his chest. At the priest's left stood an angel clad in gold armor with an angular face, blue eyes, and wavy blonde hair that hung down to his chin. His presence felt stronger than Dathiel's, though not as overwhelming as Prince Avdiel's. But it was the creature to the right of the monsignor that was most affecting Jack.

Though it was lying down, he could tell it must have been the size of a small horse when standing. It was canine in appearance and resembled a mixture of wolf and German Shepherd. It's fur and the two large feathered wings on its sides were white, while it's yellow eyes stirred something deep in Jack's heart. A feeling of both awe at the creature's fierceness and admiration at its beauty. Its presence was the strongest he'd felt, even more so than Avdiel's.

"Ye-yes!" Jack stuttered, snapping himself back to seeing only an elderly Monsignor Bamonte before him. He panted as though he'd just taken a sprint. "I've definitely still got it."

"Are you alright?" Monsignor Bamonte leaned forward. "Wait, were you using it?"

"Yes," Jack answered, continuing to gulp air. "And we weren't alone."

"What did you see?"

"Dathiel was here. So was another angel I assumed must be your guardian. But there was a third creature with them. Something unlike anything I've seen before. Its presence was . . . too much to bear!"

"Did it feel threatening?"

"No, I wouldn't say that. Just . . . overwhelming. All the angels have felt that way when I'm near them, but not to this degree."

The cleric leaned back in his chair, his expression still unreadable to Jack. "I didn't observe any physiological change in you until you gasped. You just appeared to be looking at me the same as before."

"What does that mean?"

"I don't know . . . I'm still not sure what to make of this, incorporeal sight, yet. But . . . if you're alright with one more assessment today. We've seen what ignoring it does. Perhaps we should try testing it."

Jack looked with uncertainty at the priest. "I thought we just did. How do you mean?"

"You say you saw my guardian angel in the room with us. Why don't you try asking him how long it's been since my last confession and what I confessed when I went?"

After another long moment, during which Jack prepared this time by steadying his breathing as though he were about to run a marathon, he nodded.

"Okay . . . I'll try. But if the other creature's still here, I can't promise I'll be able to speak."

"It's alright. Do what you can. If it's too much, don't overwork yourself."

Jack took one more deep breath and peeked at the world he saw behind the world. All was the same as before. The office was now a chamber. The winged hound still sat calmly beside the priest. Jack turned toward his guardian, hesitant to converse with either of the spirits flanking the clergyman. They were too glorious. Dathiel encouraged him with a glance and nod. Without saying anything aloud that Monsignor Bamonte would hear, Jack greeted the blonde angel on his left in the most respectful way he could and asked if he was the priest's guardian.

"We're both his guardians," the winged hound answered. "And you needn't fear to address me, Jack. Any angel will be happy to meet you."

Jack was surprised to hear the hound's voice was soft, not at all what he would have expected from a creature its size, if he would have expected it to speak in the first place.

"Then you're an angel too?" he asked, taking a few seconds to muster the courage.

"Indeed. I'm a Power. A member of an Angelic Order high above the rank of most guardians, who specialize in dealing with the fallen angels."

Jack wanted to ask just how many different kinds of angels there were, but he remembered Monsignor Bamonte was waiting.

"Well, my princes, may I ask when your charge last went to Confession and what he confessed?"

It was the blonde angel who answered this time. "Tell the monsignor he has four guardians. Myself, Meriel the Archangel. Lupe here of the Order of Powers. And Nuri and Jehoash of the Seraphic Order, who are standing guard outside. Our charge last heard confessions this past Wednesday and last attended the Sacrament as a penitent himself ten days ago, on a Friday afternoon at three o'clock. It was the bishop who heard his confession. Regarding what he confessed..." The Archangel shrugged. "We forget."

Understanding little of what the angels had meant about "Orders" Jack bowed his head to them and blinked, seeing no more than an elderly priest in an armchair again. He repeated what he'd heard verbatim, scrutinizing the cleric's reaction. Monsignor Bamonte's face never changed, other than a slight raising of his eyebrows, as Jack named and described the four spirits.

"Is that right?" he asked when the clergyman said nothing.

As the priest answered, Jack couldn't tell from his tone whether he was convinced or not. He seemed as calm and collected as ever.

"I'm reserving judgment as to what exactly I think for now. But, I do think it's safe for you to begin using this ability again and keeping everything you experience through it recorded in your journal. The fruits it produces are what will give us its source at this point."

"You want me to use it?"

Jack hadn't expected that advice. He thought about the experience of the angel called Lupe, then about his encounters with the fallen spirits, particularly the beating he'd received two weeks ago.

"I don't know if I'm ready for that, Monsignor!"

"Which is precisely the reason I'm giving you permission. But remember this, Jack. Prayer is your number one coping strategy now. Turn to it constantly. If anything or anyone you encounter tries to dissuade you from it, treat it as an agent of the Devil. And be sure to keep me updated about anything serious that happens, good or bad. I'm going to give you my personal number so you can reach me more easily."

Stepping out into the cathedral parking lot from the church offices, still stunned at Monsignor Bamonte's counsel, Jack figured the church was as safe a place as possible to begin testing his strange ability.

He hoped he'd be far enough away from Lupe in there. He went in and sat at the edge of a front pew, close to the tabernacle. He switched his vision and stood in wonder at what appeared before him.

He was outside the castle in what he thought was the parking lot, judging from its position. It had transformed into castle grounds. What had been a blacktop lined with cars had become an attractive meadow, sprinkled with giant trees and carriages. The office buildings behind him had turned into a row of small stone garrisons. Off to his left, what had been a bench with a statue of the Blessed Virgin in front of it was now a garden with an archway of multicolored roses leading into it, many of shades he'd never seen in the physical world. Beyond, in the garden itself, he saw trees and bushes covered in flowers of various types. Some were much larger than normal. Some were glowing. And, similar to the angels and saints themselves, some looked like they were made of light. Jack wanted to venture in and explore, but Dathiel pulled him in the opposite direction.

"I know the courtyard can be an enticing place to wander, Jack. But you'll have more time for that after your meeting. Hello, by the way." The angel grinned.

"Good to see you again," Jack smiled. "What is that place?" He indicated the area beyond the archway.

"Our Lady's rose garden. I'll take you to see it sometime. But first we—" The guardian paused mid-sentence, glancing upward like he'd heard something. "Oh!

Seems there's another who wishes to meet you first. Come!"

Dathiel grabbed his hand, pulling him forward a step. In the next instant, they were standing in Jack's front yard.

"Why'd you bring us here?" Jack asked.

"Someone summoned us. Look." Dathiel pointed at the house.

Jack thought it was glowing like a Christmas ornament for half a second. Then he realized something was shining from behind it, so brightly the rays of light it was casting danced outward for hundreds of feet. They twirled about the house, as though a projector was featuring a drive-in movie on the back of his home.

"Go on," Dathiel encouraged. "He'll be guiding us from here to our original destination."

Without asking any more questions, Jack ran forward, bounding his way up to the roof by bouncing off windowsills. He almost tripped a couple of times in his excitement. He thought it might be the Occupant of the tabernacle Himself, come out to meet him at last.

When he peered down over the roof's edge, he saw the light was shining from within his mother's gazebo. Although clean and pristine to physical sight, with its white pillars and polished wood benches, Lorelai's prized backyard ornament appeared ill-kept and haunted now. Indeed, the whole of the backyard reflected the apparent spiritual state of the rest of his family. Its usually lush bushes and trees were dead and barren. There was no longer grass growing anywhere. It seemed his own soul only affected the front yard.

Jack found he wasn't bothered much by this sad state of affairs. At the moment, he was too distracted by the beautiful voice singing from within the gazebo. He recognized its song as an old Advent hymn he'd always loved. It was one of his favorites to hear around Christmas time.

*"O come, O come, Emmanuel!*
*And ransom captive Israel*
*that mourns in lonely exile here*
*until the Son of God appear.*

*Rejoice, rejoice, O Israel!*
*To thee shall come Emmanuel!*

*O come, Thou Dayspring, come and cheer*
*our spirits by Thine advent here;*
*disperse the gloomy clouds of night,*
*and death's dark shadows put to flight.*

# THE PHILANGELUS


*Rejoice, rejoice, O Israel!*
*To thee shall come Emmanuel!*


*O come, Thou Rod of Jesse, free*
*Thine own from Satan's tyranny;*
*From depths of Hell Thy people save,*
*and give them victory o'er the grave.*


*Rejoice, rejoice, O Israel!*
*To thee shall come Emmanuel!"*


Jack realized he'd been leaning over the edge of the roof unmoving, having lost all track of time. The singing was the most wonderful thing he'd ever heard in his life. He wiped a couple of tears from his eyes and jumped down to ground level in a single bound, landing in front of the gazebo.

*"Jack!"* the singer from within it exclaimed, grabbing him up in a bear hug as though he was an old friend.

Jack hadn't had time to get a clear look at the visitor. All he knew was it was the brightest and tallest figure he'd met. From the way his joints were clenching up while everything else in his body went a little haywire too, he guessed it was another angel. Pulling his head back to get a better look, he saw it was a giant. Its head was nearly scraping the gazebo's ceiling.

Though Jack was sure he'd never met this one, there was something familiar in the experience of his presence. All the fear in his heart was transformed into a mirth that seemed like memory. A memory of . . . well, Christmas time as a small child. The giant's scent even carried these memories to him, as he inhaled the smell of chocolate kisses, pine needles, and chocolate chip cookies.

He didn't feel as overwhelmed as he had in Lupe's presence. Yet he was certain this spirit was superior to the winged hound somehow. He couldn't explain why. Shocked though he was at being scooped up by the stranger, he couldn't help laughing at his greeting. When he did, he felt inundated by the sensation of joy the spirit's presence provided, like his laughter had opened the gate into his heart. He knew he would very much like this angel, whoever he was.

"Uh . . . hi!" he said when he regained his voice.

The angel laughed, letting him drop so he was able to get a full view of him. Jack's eyes widened. He might not have been the most exotic angel he'd met, but he was the most beautiful. He was eight feet tall. The curly hair hanging over his ears looked as though it were composed of gold, complimenting his olive skin. He wore a white breastplate over a short-sleeved blue robe that revealed arms built like a weightlifting champion's. And, though his face appeared youthful, his bright emerald eyes exhibited the wisdom of ages.

"Ah, it's good to be back in Charleston again!" the giant expressed, spreading his arms and throwing his head back.

As he did, more light spread from him to dispel the darkness seeping from the dead houses surrounding the wasteland of a backyard. Dathiel chuckled, landing next to Jack, looking as though he was affected by the newcomer's presence as much as him. His jaw looked flexed. Tears were forming in his eyes, and he couldn't seem to help his laughter.

"It hasn't been that long, my prince!" the guardian said.

"Oh, I think Jack here would disagree," the giant said, pulling the boy to his side. "You've been under vicious attack of late, no?"

"Sure," Jack said distractedly, still enjoying the delights supplied by the giant's presence.

"I thought so. I'd been begging Our Lord and Lady to hurry up and grant you your charism since the day the demons first moved against you. Or at least to let me visit you more often and scare them off."

"We've met before?"

"Plenty of times! But I've been awaiting a face-to-face ever since your Baptism."

"You were at my Baptism?"

"I'm present at every Baptism. I'm patron of the Sacrament."

"Forgive me, Jack," Dathiel intervened. "May I introduce, Prince Gabriel the Archangel."

Jack looked up into the giant's emerald eyes, awestruck. "Gabriel . . . as in . . .?"

Gabriel smiled. "Yeah, that Gabriel."

Jack assumed a less informal stance. The Archangel laughed at his self-conscious gesture.

"Oh don't feel intimidated by me, Jack. I'm the one honored by the roles God bestowed on me."

"I hate to cut the reunion short," Dathiel said, "but shouldn't we be moving along? Jack will have to be getting home soon."

"Yes," Gabriel said. "Let's get to the Third Gate. He'll meet us there."

"Third Gate?" Jack asked. "Where's that?"

"Up." Gabriel pointed skyward.

Jack's eyes followed his finger and saw what must have been millions of demons circling high above them. The sky always seemed littered with them, like an upside down kitchen floor someone had spilled garbage all over that was now infested with ants.

"Really?" he asked.

"Don't worry," Gabriel soothed. "That's why I'm here to escort you. Watch this!"

The Archangel stepped out from under the gazebo and spread his wings, forming a strong gust of air that forced Jack and Dathiel to take a few steps backward. His wingspan must have been twenty feet. He spiraled upward in ever widening circles. The dark spirits in the sky scattered in all directions, giving him a wide berth, as he ascended all the way to the clouds.

"Up we go, Jack." Dathiel spread his own wings and held out a hand.

"Hold on," Jack said, still hesitant. "Where exactly are we going?"

"You'll see, but we're pressed for time. Your mother will get worried if you're gone too long. Take my hand."

Jack didn't, only continued to stand there, deliberating.

"You'll want to come with us, Jack. If fear of Hell's forces disturbs you, this is one acquaintance you'll be glad to have."

Jack finally obeyed. Dathiel launched into the air, Jack dangling by his side. He grabbed the angel's other hand with his free one as he physically reached out to balance himself against the pew's handrail in front of him, his equilibrium thrown off by what he was seeing through incorporeal sight. The gazebo, backyard, and Dacre home all shrank below them.

He yelled in exhilaration as they rose higher than the guardian had ever flown him before. The entire Tri-County area was visible. Soon he was able to look up and down the coastline. Glancing up to where they were headed, he was shocked to see castles and outposts built upon the clouds.

"What the—*WHOA!*" he yelled.

Dathiel had released his grasp as they passed over the tip of a low nimbus. Jack flailed his arms and legs, his stomach doing summersaults. But his fall was broken only a second after the angel let go, and he rolled to a stop on something soft. He lifted his head. He'd come to rest near the edge of the cloud, the floating mountain's substance feeling similar to fine sand under him. He stood up shakily. The cloud was solid. It held him. Dathiel landed on a crevice above him.

Jack didn't look at him. He was looking down. It was strange to see light shining up from below the cloud instead of from a sun above it. Having the chance to observe the surrounding citadels more closely now, he saw there were numerous angels peopling them, all more resplendent than the guardians of persons he'd met on Earth below.

"A world built over the world!" Jack marveled.

He turned to see Gabriel was perched in a fissure of cloud above Dathiel.

The Archangel smiled. "Follow me."

He took flight, heading higher up the mountain, with Dathiel in tow. Jack ran and jumped from crevice to crevice and roof to roof, as his two guides led him up through the aerial metropolis. Scaling the side of a lookout tower, he glanced over at a section of the sky enveloped in night. The gray clouds there supported dark structures similar to the ones he'd seen at school. He was disappointed to see demons patrolling them. The good angels weren't the only ones who ruled the skies.

He refocused his attention on Gabriel and Dathiel, trying not to lose sight of them among the myriads of other angels flying to-and-fro between the celestial fortresses. It wasn't difficult to keep track of the Archangel. He shined the brightest of anything in the clouds.

As he paced them, rising ever higher across the white peaks, valleys, and plains, they eventually glided off the edge of the nimbus and headed straight into the side of the next one. Jack hesitated on the edge from where they'd leapt, unsure what they were thinking. It looked as though they were both about to faceplant. Just before they collided with the mountain, a tunnel swirled open before them, out of which poured yellow light. The angels sailed inside, disappearing into its radiance.

Jack took a few steps back to get a running start, charging as fast as he could toward the chasm between himself and the tunnel. The gap must have been forty feet wide. He bellowed with all his might as he hurtled through the air, almost missing his mark, losing his footing when he landed at the tunnel's entrance. He screamed when he started to slip backward and fall out.

Two strong hands grabbed both his arms just in time, pulling him the rest of the way inside. With a grin each, Dathiel and Gabriel turned, running along the luminescent pathway. Jack followed right behind, trying to calm his breathing.

The tunnel twisted until it curved up to an almost vertical angle. Jack had to use both his hands and feet to keep up. The direction changed to horizontal again, and he saw an opening before them. The three exited into the bottom of a ravine, and Jack craned his neck upward in astonishment.

Nestled between two walls of cloud was a gate of solid gold. It was three hundred feet tall and a hundred and fifty feet wide. Shining white pillars lined its front, and it was adorned with precious stones of every color, even many foreign to Earth, like the flowers Jack had seen in the cathedral's rose garden.

Strange creatures patrolled its top. Some were large winged hounds like Lupe. Others looked more humanoid, while still appearing canine, whether from elongated faces and snouts, having the eyes of wolves, having tails, or just appearing hairier than people. Despite their unusual forms, Jack couldn't deny each had a wild beauty to it. He guessed they were angels too. Powers. That was what Lupe had called himself.

"So, are these the famous Pearly Gates?" Jack asked his two escorts.

"I suppose you could call them that if you like," Gabriel said. "This is the gateway between the worlds of the Third and Second Hierarchies of angels."

"Yeah I don't know what any of that means," Jack said.

Both angels laughed.

"You'll have to learn a little about how the Choirs of Heaven are structured," Gabriel said.

"I'd like to," Jack said, looking at him, but Gabriel didn't elaborate. "I take it this is the Third Gate you mentioned then?" Jack asked, turning back to it after a moment.

"Yep," Dathiel said.

"So, who are we here to meet?"

"Your—" But Dathiel was cut off.

A commotion had arisen among the wolf-like angels. They sounded excited by something on the other side and started scurrying about their business faster.

*"Open the gates!"* a gruff one barked.

As the entrance parted in the middle, the three visitors were bathed in a gold light that outshined even Gabriel. Squinting through the blinding brilliance, Jack could just make out the silhouette of another eight foot tall winged figure stepping out onto their side. When the doors closed, the new arrival's gold light continued forcing him to squint. As his eyes adjusted, he saw this angel had olive skin and gold hair too, albeit perfectly straight and hanging down to the bottom of his shoulder blades. His face was angular, with high cheekbones that exuded maturity. Though it was mainly from his sapphire eyes Jack sensed this was a most wise and perceptive being.

His arms were large and muscular. He wore a crimson robe and cape that hung down to his ankles along with his wings, and the crown upon his head—as well as his breastplate, boots, and the cross-shaped hilt of the broadsword sheathed across his back—were all gold. The crown was bedecked with small rubies. These matched a large one embedded on the chest of his breastplate.

The experience of the angel's presence hit Jack full force. He felt pervaded with courage and a profound sense of security. Fear now seemed a half-forgotten dream he remembered only in order to laugh at its absurdity. He'd already suspected this one's identity. Now he felt certain. As if to further confirm him, his own bronze breastplate surfaced from beneath his silver one as soon as the newcomer stepped out from behind the gates. Dathiel was right.

Jack couldn't think of a better saint to help him conquer dread of the demonic.

# CHAPTER XIII
## THE NINE ORDERS

Dathiel turned to Jack. "Jack, this is—"

"Saint Michael . . . the Prince of Angels," Jack interrupted in a near whisper.

Michael smiled. "Sharp eye, Jack."

His voice was deep but gentle. Jack found it soothing.

Dathiel smiled. "I thought you might recognize your patron! May I present our leader, the Terror of Demons."

Jack genuflected and bowed his head, taking a deep breath, realizing he'd been holding it before. The prince gave off a strong scent of rosemary. Michael bent down and extended a hand. Jack looked up to see he was smiling. And, unless he was misreading it, the Archangel's expression showed admiration for him. He took his hand, and the prince pulled him to his feet.

"After your battles of late, I thought it was time I made my presence known to you, brother."

Jack's face grew warm at such an icon referring to him so familiarly. He wondered if he was blushing. If so, Michael was discreet enough to ignore it.

"Battles of late . . . yes." Jack almost had trouble remembering his encounters with demons now. "I didn't expect the Prince of Heaven himself to take a personal interest, much less take time out to visit."

Michael wrapped a wing around him and Jack felt bathed in the rosemary fragrance. He guided him along the cloud away from Dathiel and Gabriel, who withdrew, as though this was meant to be a private meeting for Jack.

"Well, I am your patron saint, Jack. Besides that, I take a personal interest in any baptized soul harassed by infernal forces. And time is of no consequence to me. I exist outside it. So, I have as much time as you can spare to speak with you. I imagine you have many concerns now that you possess incorporeal sight."

"That's . . . one way to put it."

Jack was trying his best to stay focused when all he wanted to do was bask in the glory of the Archangel's presence. It filled him with a serenity that brought with it a zeal for adventure. Had someone told Jack of this experience beforehand, he would have thought the two sentiments too different to be mixed. Feeling them now, he couldn't imagine having one without the other.

"Then I suppose we'll begin with the immediate issue," Michael said. "The demon who's been attacking you."

Jack shuddered, his memory pulling him somewhat back to reality despite his resistant will.

"I know," Michael soothed, reading his emotions. "You're afraid. But it's alright. Without fear, there'd be no such thing as courage."

"I don't know if I have the courage for this," Jack said. "The demons at Wando were terrifying enough, but the one who's been attacking me at home . . . He always feels so much worse!"

"He is."

"His presence is overwhelming! Like it's the Devil himself!"

"It's not Satan. Just another of his minions. But the spirits you've seen at school only fell from the lowest Order of angels. The one you fought was Head of the Powers before the Fall."

Jack nodded his head without understanding what Michael meant. The angels he'd met kept throwing terms like, Order, and, Powers, around like he was supposed to understand what they referred to. He had no idea what they were all talking about.

Michael must have seen this, because he smiled and winked. "But you have no idea what I'm talking about, right?"

Jack smiled and raised his hands in a dumbfounded gesture. There was no faking comprehension to an angel. In that moment, Jack was grateful none of his schoolteachers had ever been angels. There'd never have been any getting away with pretending to pay attention in class while daydreaming about something else.

"Allow me to give you a crash course in the Hierarchies of angelic beings."

"Please," Jack said, fascinated again by the prospect of learning more about his supernatural

*—provided you're not crazy—*

acquaintances.

"There are nine of what we call Orders or Choirs of angels in Heaven," Michael said. "Listed from highest to lowest, they are the Seraphim, the Cherubim, the Thrones, the Dominations, the Virtues, the Powers, the Principalities, the Archangels, and the Angels. These Nine Orders are grouped into Three Hierarchies. The first three I named form the Supreme Hierarchy. The next three form the Middle. The last three, the Lower." Michael indicated the golden gate behind them. "This is the gate that separates the world of the Middle Hierarchy from that of the Lower. You can see there are Powers patrolling it, as they're the lowest Order within the Middle Hierarchy."

He guided Jack to the edge of the cloud. They were standing on the highest one in the sky. Jack could see across the floating cities to the end of the horizon in every direction.

"The bright angels you see populating these castles atop the clouds are Principalities, as they're the highest Order in the Lower Hierarchy and we're standing at the height of that realm. It's their duty to guard corporeal places on earth, such as houses, neighborhoods, cities, dioceses, even whole continents and bodies of water."

"So, I guess Avdiel is a Principality then," Jack said. "Since he's guardian of the Diocese of Charleston."

"Precisely. My brother spirits are grouped into their respective Orders based on their specific knowledge or activities. But no two angels are actually equal. We're different from humans in that regard."

"How do you mean?"

Michael paced the edge of the cloud with his hands held behind his back. Jack followed beside him.

"Humans all share the same nature. Human nature. So each of you may be your own individual, but you're all of the same species. When it comes to us though, each has his own nature, making each of us a unique species. That's why we all have different effects on you when you encounter us. For the first time in your life, not only are you meeting creatures of higher natures than a human, but each is as different from the next as a dog is from a tree."

Jack let another smile escape him as he put a hand up to the side of his head and signaled an explosion, showing Michael he'd just blown his mind. The prince laughed, a gesture that almost sent Jack's mind into overdrive.

"Oh that may happen a time or two more now that you can see this side of creation."

"So what about the other Orders then?" Jack asked. "Did you say the lowest was just called 'Angels?' Because I thought you were all collectively called angels. What happened, run out of fancy names when you got to number nine?"

Michael bellowed another sonorous laugh. "Actually, it was named thus just to confuse you."

"It's working."

Michael chuckled. "Allow me to answer your question with a question."

"Why simplify things now?"

"What do you think the word 'angel' means?"

Jack shook his head. "Couldn't tell ya."

"It's a Greek word for, messenger. So, all the Orders can collectively be called angels, because we're all messengers in some capacity. The more technical name for angelic spirits—which the theologians of the Middle Ages applied to us—is intelligences. Use that name if it will help you keep the names of the Orders straight in your mind. As for the Ninth Order itself, they're simply called Angels because they're often people's direct messengers from God. It's from them most humans' guardians are selected. Dathiel hails from that Choir."

"But not every human," Jack observed. "None of Monsignor Bamonte's guardians identified themselves as being from the Order of Angels."

"Right again, because important persons are assigned intelligences from a higher Order. Usually the Archangels. Hence, the monsignor was given the Archangel Meriel at conception. His other three came later."

Jack thought he heard distant footsteps coming from somewhere above them. He looked up, confused. They were already standing on the highest mountain in the sky. Even if there had been another cloud above them, the footsteps sounded as though they were on a hard surface, not the soft substance of the airborne cities' grounds. Focusing in on them, he discerned the sound wasn't coming through incorporeal sight. Someone was walking around in the choir loft above the pews in the church.

"Excuse me, my prince."

Jack gave a slight bow of the head to Michael and switched to corporeal sight. He checked the time on his phone. It was almost 4:30. If he remembered correctly from the announcements after Mass the previous weekend, the choir would be starting its practice soon. He didn't have much longer to talk in silence.

"So, you said the demon who's been haunting me was Head of the Powers?" he asked when he'd switched back to incorporeal sight, wishing to get all the vital information he could while he could still hear.

"He still is," Michael said. "Commander of the fallen ones at least. All the angels who fell to damnation retain their natures and ranks. So they still possess the abilities natural to an intelligence. Abilities humans would call preternatural or magic, because they're above your own nature. What demons lack are supernatural powers. Those only come through divine grace."

"So, you're saying Hell's forces are also organized according to the Nine Orders?"

Michael nodded. "Because the demons are still angels. The only difference between them and us is not what we are, but what we do. Whether we're good or evil."

Jack laughed, and Michael glanced at him inquiringly.

"I was just thinking, you banished the Devil from Heaven because he rejected God and thought he could do things better. Yet he didn't even change the ordering of his subjects after the fact. He's a hundred percent unoriginal! A ripoff!"

Michael joined in his laughter. "And forever too stubborn to admit it! Believe me, I tried convincing him."

Jack heard someone else enter the church behind him to his left. He needed to hurry.

"So," he said, "my attacker on Halloween . . ."

"His name is Mephistopheles. He's the primary demon who's been tormenting you with doubts."

"Mephistopheles . . . That name rings a bell."

"It should. It's used in an English play by Christopher Marlowe. *The Tragical History of the Life and Death of Doctor Faustus.* You read it in English class this semester."

"Right! The story about the man selling his soul to the Devil. Mephistopheles was the demon he summoned to draw up the contract!"

Michael nodded. "The play was inspired by an old German legend that has its origins in reality. The character of Faustus is based on an actual person, who indeed willingly surrendered himself to darkness, was enslaved, and eventually taken by Mephistopheles. If you wish to know more about him, I suggest you ask Monsignor Bamonte. He'll be familiar with the name. In the meantime, I warn you to be vigilant. He's a very cunning and dangerous opponent.

The main characteristic of the blessed Powers is courage. Mephistopheles and his fallen Powers retain that trait. Only they use their boldness to go out against God's stronger followers now, instead of protecting them. But they aren't blunt instruments who use brute force to accomplish their ends. They're clever and will use your own strengths and weaknesses against you in order to poison your mind. Remember, spiritual warfare is primarily psychological. The Powers are especially adept at it, being originally created to be the law enforcers of Heaven." Michael turned to look up at those patrolling the top of the golden gate. "Or, as the other Orders affectionately call them, the Hounds of Heaven and God's Guard Dogs."

Jack glanced up with him. "Guess that's why they appear canine to me, huh?"

"It is. In fact, the damned Powers are largely responsible for the origin of werewolf legends."

Jack jerked his head toward Michael. *"You're kidding!"*

The prince shook his head, his expression sober. "The idea of a man transforming into a wolf existed in several cultures. It was present in the Roman Empire and Greece, and goes back as far as ancient Mesopotamia, extending over numerous times since then. Why do you think accounts of lycanthropy are so persistent over that many places and eras? Because, as with many legends, they have some basis in fact. When people claimed to have witnessed their loved ones or neighbors change into ferocious wolf creatures, what they'd really witnessed were demonic apparitions and illusions. The Powers wanted to sow mistrust and superstition among humans.

Such extraordinary manifestations are sometimes permitted by the Father for some greater good He has planned. But it's rare. These days, demons in the West work harder at convincing people they don't exist instead of trying to incite fear. It makes capturing souls easy for them."

"Yeah, I noticed," Jack mumbled.

"Of course, you can see them now. So, for you, they've reverted back to terror tactics."

"Well, it's working."

"And that's unsurprising with how powerful Mephistopheles is. But you were at the point of hysterics before he made his appearance on Halloween."

"Yes. Because of the imp." Jack shivered as he remembered its leering, grinning face.

"He fell from the Angels, Jack. A demon of that Order shouldn't be able to intimidate you. You've grown strong enough in virtue to be far more threatening to him. That's why he fled from the sight of you."

"What? When did he—"

"He wasn't chasing you when he crawled toward you on the ceiling that night. He was trying to hide. His job of delivering Mephistopheles' message was forced on him. The grin he flashed at you was a bluff. He was scared."

Jack felt a chill slither its way down and around his spine as the bat creature's poem echoed through his memory.

*Never before have you encountered such a foe . . . The demon who shall lay waste to all you know . . . Jack!*

Michael considered him, reading what he was remembering and observing its emotional effect. "Come with me," he said. "Let's extend our little walk down to the Earth's surface."

He placed a hand on Jack's shoulder. In the next moment, they were both standing on the peak of the Arthur Ravenel Bridge overlooking the Cooper River. Jack could see most of Charleston from here. It must have been the highest point around for miles. But he wasn't paying attention to the view. He drew closer to Michael's side, attempting to hide under his wing. Flying around them, obscuring most of the view, were thousands upon thousands of evil spirits. The monstrosities screamed blasphemies and obscenities of every kind, pouncing on the souls in the carriages and rickety boats beneath them.

"You allow their displays of aggression to overwhelm you," Michael said next to Jack in the same calm tone as before, as though the flocks of abominations surrounding them were no more than flocks of birds flying by. "Have any of them touched you, or even flown near you?"

"*No . . .*" Jack yelled, having a hard time hearing his own voice over the chaos. "*They don't seem to have noticed me yet.*"

"Oh they've noticed us. They're pretending to ignore us in the hopes we'll ignore them and move on without doing them any harm. They're surveilling us very closely while trying not to attract our attention."

Jack covered his ears, watching the demons attack minds below them like swarms of angry bees, biting chunks off souls, even tearing off their limbs. *If this is them being subtle, I'd hate to see them try to attract attention!"*

"As with the pygmy and those you've seen at Wando, these spirits are amongst the lowest Order of demonic ranks. They're mostly bark and little bite for someone as strong as you. They prefer to scavenge dead souls, avoiding the virtuous the way gnats avoid a fire. Observe . . ."

Michael spread his wings as though he were about to take flight. All the dark spirits Jack could see dove into the river and surrounding marshlands with the speed of shooting stars. Some fled as far as Charleston, taking refuge in the buildings on the outskirts of the city. In an instant, the world grew silent. By all appearances, the Archangel had cleared the entire countryside by his gesture.

"Whoa," Jack said, hearing an internal echo as he did.

Michael smiled at his awe, folding his wings down again. "When you have the power of One Who's Infinite behind your actions, Jack, who can stand against you?"

Jack didn't see a single demon in the sky or on the streets as Michael flew him on his back to St. John's Castle.

He did spot a few cowering indoors through windows, as though a hurricane were passing through town. He'd have laughed if he wasn't so awestruck. He couldn't believe where he was. Riding on Saint Michael the Archangel's back, like a mystical knight riding a griffin. He almost shed tears, feeling like he was living out a childhood dream. He thought one or two might have escaped his eyes. If so, they'd been dried by the wind whipping past his face before they landed.

Michael dropped him off on the castle's roof. Bidding him farewell, he assured him he'd be close by if ever he needed to call upon him. Jack watched the Archangel soar back up toward the clouds like a giant golden eagle, captivated by the spectacle. Afterward, he wandered the castle's roof, pacing its perimeter, pondering all his patron had told him. He enjoyed the sight of the angels gliding around in circles above the fortress. Eventually, Dathiel flew down from among them.

"Think you're ready to face the dark fortress of Wando High now?"

"Not much choice, even if I'm not," Jack said. "But . . . I guess. I wish I felt better prepared to face this . . . Mephistopheles. Michael said Monsignor Bamonte would know more about him."

"That's not surprising. Michael's the one who guided you to the priest in the first place. It was him who convinced you to get out your Jeep and go to Confession the day you met him."

"Really? I guess the Prince of Heaven's been taking a personal interest in me longer than I thought, huh?"

"Since the day of your Baptism. Even before that really. And it was him who struck down Mephistopheles on Halloween night."

"What are you talking—" Jack paused and thought a moment. "The lightning that struck! That was Michael?"

"Yep. Mephistopheles recognized you could see us now and was leaving to inform his master. Michael prevented it and bound him so he's now unable to reveal that bit of information to any of his more powerful comrades. If Satan were informed of either your charism or the fact that his nemesis is your patron saint, he might send an even more powerful agent against you. Or worse, come after you himself."

"Hold on. Does the Devil really not know Saint Michael's my Confirmation Saint?"

Dathiel shook his head. "He and his minions are well-informed about what goes on up here. But they don't know everything that happens on Earth. And the identity of Jack Dacre's patron is one of many particulars we've concealed from them until the proper time. Your acquaintanceship with Monsignor Bamonte's been hidden too, from all except Mephistopheles and his underlings here in town."

"And incorporeal sight?" Jack asked.

"Any demon you encounter will recognize you can see them, which is why we're keeping you from meeting any who'd be too much for you and any powerful enough to meet directly with Satan about it."

Jack chuckled, if for no other reason than to lessen his anxiety at the thought of encountering demons again. "Well, Michael definitely made his point clear on Halloween!"

Dathiel chortled. "He wasn't about to let Mephistopheles of all demons interfere with his plans. I think he may have taken Satan's sending him after you as a personal affront. Other than Lucifer, he was one of the angels our prince personally threw down from Heaven."

"Really? There a story there?"

Dathiel shot him a smile. "Isn't there always?"

Jack smiled back.

"The former Head of Heaven's Powers had let his ambition get the better of him," Dathiel elaborated. "That's why he sided with Lucifer's mad plot of rebellion against the Creator. When Michael led those of us loyal to the Father against the apostates, Mephistopheles tried to block our way to their leader." Dathiel's smile widened, and he shook his head. "He's regretted the day he stood in Michael's way ever since."

Jack's smile widened too. "I can imagine. After meeting him, I'm glad he's on our side."

"Which brings me to the last bit of advice I'll leave you with before your return to Wando." The guardian flapped his wings twice as he leapt off the corner of the castle's rooftop, perching on a turret several feet across from them. He looked back at Jack, while other angels dove and circled above and below him. "During the war in Heaven, the battle cry of the angels faithful to the Father was 'Who is like God?' It was our response to Lucifer's arrogant assertion that he would be 'like the Most High,' which you can find recorded in the Sacred Scriptures."

Dathiel paused, turning to look up at the floating cities on the clouds divided in their allegiances by the light shining up from the Catholic castles. He appeared lost in his memories of the angelic war. Jack wasn't sure if his expression was one of reminiscence or horror. Maybe both. At last, he snapped out of it and looked back at Jack.

"In Hebrew 'Who is like God' translates 'Mikha'el.' In English, 'Michael.'"

"No way!" Jack exclaimed. "I never knew that."

Dathiel nodded. "Your patron's very name was our call to arms and our motto. He was the first to declare it in opposition to Lucifer. So, when under siege by fallen angels, say it with conviction. Even Satan himself still trembles at its utterance."

Jack hadn't said a word all morning.

His drive was silent. He hadn't bothered to turn on the radio. Nearing his destination, he decelerated the Jeep and switched to incorporeal sight to confirm Dathiel was with him.

The black wall of Wando loomed before them, intruding on Jack's view like the wall of a prison for souls, which—he supposed—it was. His carriage rolled up. The heavy gate yawned open, releasing cries of the repugnant spirits from the bowels of the fortress within.

Jack took a deep breath and drove through, hearing the gate slam shut behind him, clipping the back of his vehicle as it did. He heard and felt it grind against the back bumper. Sparks flew.

"Terror tactics," he whispered to himself. "Antics."

Continuing to employ his new sight as he parked and exited the coach, he kept an eye out for any actual attacks. The demons hadn't seemed to notice his entrance. They seemed focused on the weaker souls arriving. The charade didn't fool him. After what he'd witnessed atop the Ravenel Bridge, he knew they'd be watching any souls in grace, and none on campus shined like he did.

The other living souls looked pretty much the same as they appeared corporeally, with the addition of cuts and bruises. As Jack and Dathiel approached the main entrance to the school, not a single fallen angel came near them. The front doors of this central stronghold manifested to Jack's sight as grotesque sculptures of gargoyles, serpents, and scorpions. It was hard to discern the seam between the doors through them. A knocker hung from each. One from the nostrils of a gargoyle head. The other from the mouth of a snake.

Jack was about to pull the one on the right, when both doors swung open for him. Ear-splitting sounds of torture and cackling spewed forth from the darkness inside, hitting his chest like a gust of wind. He stood rooted to the spot.

"Yes, you have and will see horrible things, Jack," Dathiel said next to him. "Horrible things. But, remember, it's God Who's enabled you to witness the unseen. That includes the demonic. You've received this charism while still a student of Wando, because He intended it that way. You're witnessing the devastation demons wreak on these poor souls every day, because it's what He wants you to see."

Jack turned to him. "God *wants* me to see all this mutilation? *Why?*"

To his surprise, the guardian smiled. "You're asking the right questions, Jack. Now go on or you'll be late for class."

Jack took one final gulp of cleaner air before crossing the school's threshold. He felt like Jonathan Harker about to enter Dracula's castle. The difference was, Jack would be doing it aware the place was dangerous. The deep breath hadn't helped, but he was out of time.

He stepped into the halls of horrors.

# PART II: MORNING

# CHAPTER XIV
## HALLS OF HORRORS

"Damn, she's hot! Ah man, if only I could—"

"You just need another hit. You can always get clean later when—"

*"Hahahaha!* There's another notch on your belt! Everyone said she was an uptight bitch too! My ass! Can't wait to tell 'em all about thi—"

"Damn, I need a drink."

*"Bastard's not getting away with giving me a D! Screws up my whole record! Wait 'til my parents tear into the school board and—"*

"It's alright. She doesn't need to know—"

*"Son of a bitch is gonna get it in the ass for this! No one back stabs me and gets away with—"*

"Tonight you'll nail her. Just keep wearing her down. She's gotta give it up sometime. I wonder if weed would help relax her enough to—"

"Look at them flocking around her like she's worth the time! How does a bitch like that get a guy like—"

*"FUUUUUUCK! What the fuck am I supposed to do if—"*

"Fuckin' cum-dumpsters. Only reason they should ever be opening their mouths is to suck my—"

"No one ever has to know. And no one will. Just keep your mouth sh—"

Jack covered his ears, dropping incorporeal sight, unable to take anymore of the screaming. As he and Dathiel had made their way to the English wing, the stone corridors had been lit just enough by torches along the walls for him to witness the grotesqueries taking place around them. Deceased souls were huddled together in corners, occasionally darting out to find a new spot for cover. Demons crawled along the walls and ceiling in pursuit, taunting their prey before lunging down to mutilate them. The students' shouts of misery haunted Jack.

Passing by, he'd caught bits of what the evil spirits were saying to them when they struck. One thing he'd gleaned, the demons weren't just supplying proposals to people's thoughts. They often spoke as if they were the person talking to themselves. He guessed it made victims more suggestible if they thought they were coming up with the ideas. The scary thing was, it was working. Once the students succumbed to the demons' temptations, Jack saw them become culpable for them. The infernal monsters would then tear chunks out of their souls. He shuddered as he wondered how many times in life his own imaginings had been the whim of an evil spirit at his ear.

It wasn't until he'd been seated at his desk in English several minutes that he mustered the courage to use his ability again. Demons entered the room alongside their victims while they gathered for class. He vaguely heard the sound of his desk legs scraping across the floor as he physically pushed himself backward, hoping the monsters wouldn't come any closer. He would have fled outright again if not for Dathiel's presence.

The serpentine demons he'd seen two weeks ago were among the newcomers. Some coiled themselves around the souls afflicted with rashes and sores, petting their heads as if they were property. The rest slunk and slithered around the legs of other students, scratching them sensuously, flicking their forked tongues out as though whetting their appetites. Jack saw sores appear anywhere a snake's tongue or talon struck and realized they were presenting temptations to the souls with each touch. When Kevin arrived and took his seat next to him, Jack saw he was a walking corpse too. Covered, like so many others, in rashes, boils, and sores.

*No!* Jack thought. *Does everyone I know have to be dead to God?*

He listened more closely to the serpentine demons, trying to figure out the nature of their temptations and identify the sins rashes, boils, and sores signified. A belligerent voice boomed across the classroom, cutting off all other sound. Jack turned to see a burly demon enter alongside an especially restless soul. The victim was twitching and biting his knuckles, reminding Jack of the zombies he'd seen running around the street like rabid animals on Halloween night. The scent of skunk burned its way up his nose, making him cough. Given how the demon fueling the symptoms was acting, he guessed he'd identified the signs of wrath. Flipping momentarily over to his regular sight, Jack saw the soul he'd been looking at was Brad Mason.

"That figures," Jack mumbled to himself, flipping back.

The bell rang, and the rest of his classmates trickled in, dispersing to their seats. Two of the newcomers stood out to him from the rest of the crowd. A girl and her guardian angel. Besides her attire, which resembled that of a traveler from the Middle Ages, Naomi looked the same. The angel next to her was a winged youth with curly, flaming red hair clothed in a green robe. He looked no older than eleven or twelve.

"Good to see you, Jack," the little guardian said, holding a hand out. "Paviel's the name. Glad Naomi has an acquaintanceship with you."

"Yes . . ." Jack said, shaking his hand after a moment. "So am I. Nice to meet you."

Paviel beamed. Jack noticed several of the demons in the room scowling at them, especially the big one with Brad. Apparently, they were none too pleased with Jack's ability to see them and to interact with their enemies. He imagined what pissed them off most was the genuine moment of enjoyment he'd experienced when Paviel had walked up to him. The guardian gave off the scents of apple cider and cinnamon, reminding Jack of some of his favorite things about Fall.

The fallen spirits didn't approach to do something about Jack's mood shift. Dathiel and Paviel were glaring at them, as though daring them to try. They all soon went back to what they'd been doing. Jack overheard a familiar voice from somewhere among them. He'd only heard it once before, but he hadn't forgotten it. The gray hunchbacked demon he'd seen badgering Jenny in the parking lot was hacking away at her dignity once again. She must have been on the far side of the room, because he couldn't see her. Once the other demons realized it was getting to Jack, they parted to let him witness the harassment, sneering in his direction.

*"Slut! Break up with him and it's just back to square one. You really think every other guy's not exactly the same? Men are men! Be grateful you have one at all. Better than being a fat, unwanted bitch like so many others. Just fuck him and shut the fuck up once in a while, and maybe he'll stick around."*

The hunchback's comrades cackled, joining in the abuse.

Jack's blood boiled, but he didn't know how to help, if he even could.

As infuriating as all Jack witnessed throughout the day was, none of it compared to his last period.

The science wing was now the lowest part of the school to his eyes. Descending with Dathiel, he thought they must be deep underground by the time they neared Mr. Wilkerson's classroom. Like most places, the biology room appeared different. It was a dungeon.

It was dark, illumined only by a few fires burning in the lab from holes in the floor where the wood had been broken up. He saw pentagrams and other strange symbols scratched into the tabletops. There were cobweb covered jars of different shapes and sizes filled with dark brown and green liquids. One was filled with a red one that looked eerily like blood. Most of the jars had fingers, livers, hearts, pieces of brain, or other body parts floating in them, making Jack feel he'd just discovered Dr. Frankenstein's laboratory. Something he'd have thought fun under very different circumstances. The rest of the jars were filled with what he could best describe as liquid gold. These had shards of base metal sitting on the table next to them.

Jack was as hesitant to enter the room as he'd been to enter the school at the beginning of the day. He started to draw back, figuring he'd cut his last class and head home. Dathiel grabbed him by the arm and led him inside.

"You can't avoid the place forever, Jack. You'd have to face what it is and what they do here sooner or later."

Jack let his guardian guide him to his chair. It had chains on it, resembling the kind of chair they'd bind a criminal or crazy person to in medieval times. He didn't like it. Not one bit! He wanted to leave and never return to this room again. A demon sitting next to a fire in the back snickered upon sensing his fear. It was spider-like in appearance. It had extra limbs poking out of its abdominal area, a bald fuzzy head, and pincers for a mouth.

"I don't think the lad likes it down here, prissy sissy," it said to Dathiel, its pincers clicking together when it spoke. "You should have kept him concealed from our sight. No matter. I'll enjoy hearing his screams."

Dathiel ignored the comment. Jack sat in his chair facing away from the foul-looking thing, resolving that—whatever should happen—his reaction would not be a scream. He heard the tardy bell go off as though from a distance, and a soul he hadn't seen yet, but had been anticipating seeing all day, entered the room. Its appearance confused him. It wasn't at all what he'd expected. Mr. Wilkerson didn't look much different.

The only differences incorporeal sight was showing Jack were empty eye sockets and paler skin. Skin the color of death, like a heavyset Count Dracula, if Dracula wore raggedy khakis and a button-up shirt left loose around the collar. But Jack saw none of the symptoms of vice he'd started to recognize on other souls. There were no boils or sores, no morphing face, not anything deforming him other than the absence of eyes. The teacher didn't even smell that bad. He couldn't tell if Mr. Wilkerson's soul was dead or just blind and ill.

*But he has to be dead!* Jack thought.

He'd been sure the atheist would exhibit all the symptoms of vice. He'd been waiting to see an abomination walk through the door. Ready to hold his breath at its vile stench. Ready to avert his eyes from its monstrous appearance.

The black-and-white looking version of Mr. Wilkerson took a seat at his desk, greeting the class just as good-humored as ever, no demons accompanying him. Jack fretted, wondering again if incorporeal sight was authentic. It was betraying its own rules as they'd been explained to him.

A black mist entered the room and he forgot what he was thinking about, clutching his desk, whitening his knuckles. An arrowhead tail slithered out from the fog up Mr. Wilkerson's leg and around his shoulder. It pierced the side of his forehead.

"Alright, e'erybody shut up now," Jack heard both the teacher and Mephistopheles say in near unison, as the teacher rose from his desk. "I have your midterms back," the voices continued together. "And a lot of you didn't do too well on the first section." Jack noticed Mephistopheles was speaking a half-second before Mr. Wilkerson. "So we're going to go over it as soon as they're passed out. With it already being Thanksgiving break tomorrow, some of you need to step it up if you don't want to repeat this class."

As the teacher walked up and down the front row of desks handing out tests, Jack watched in horror as the tail of the Power enshrouded in mist was pulled with him like some infernal HDMI cable plugged into his head. A shiver ran up Jack's back. His neck tightened. He started physically shaking. He didn't like being this close to the monster who'd so viciously beaten him.

The only thing that kept him from running out the room shrieking his head off was the presence of Dathiel and Paviel. They were once again the only blessed intelligences present. All other students were accompanied by fallen ones.

"Now," the dual voices went on, "who can tell me the exact definitions of evolution and natural selection? Anyone? Because a number of you got those wrong."

Becky raised her hand and recited the textbook answers verbatim, to the congratulations of both the teacher and the evil spirit behind him. Jack felt fury intermix with his fear, certain now of what he'd suspected Mephistopheles was doing. He glanced down at his midterm. He'd aced it for answering its questions exactly how he knew Mr. Wilkerson wanted. Now he knew the teacher wasn't the only one who'd wanted it.

He shoved the test to the far end of his desk, disgusted with himself. He'd compromised what he really thought for the sake of a stupid fucking number on a stupid fucking piece of paper! But, since he didn't dare raise a hand to publicly challenge the biology instructor's lesson this time, his anger had nowhere to go. He was forced to stew in silence. He noticed something while he did. Something that was enough to distract him from his anger. The other demons in the room shuffled away the moment it reared up within him, like they were afraid.

He smiled to himself at the thought, but it wasn't enough. He couldn't speak up. He had no new facts to quote. He hadn't forgotten how the teacher had been ready for his objection last time. With what he could see now, he wondered if it had been Mr. Wilkerson he'd been pitted against.

As if in answer to this thought, all the demons in the room turned their heads at the same time to stare at him, smiles on their faces. The tail unplugged itself from Mr. Wilkerson's head, and the opaque mist drew backward. Jack looked on the grinning, skull-like face of his tormentor for the first time since it had thrashed him about his own bedroom.

"Yes," Mephistopheles said, "you should have watched your step before challenging a professor, Jack. If you knew as much about the universe and its workings as he does, you'd be an atheist yourself instead of sitting there projecting something like me onto him."

The demon drove his tail back into the teacher's skull and resumed his lecture, even managing to weave a few sacrilegious jokes into it, to the amusement of most other students and spirits in the room. More black mist discharged from the red ball on the Power's spear, enveloping everyone in the room except Jack, Naomi, and their guardians. Either Jack had lost his mind, or most of his classmates were trapped in the snares of Hell.

He wasn't sure which thought disturbed him more. He also couldn't help but notice how melodramatic it sounded to him either way. Had he really become part of some dark fairy tale, or was this not how a teenager would imagine a teacher and a class he'd come to resent? He could have laughed out loud at how ridiculous the whole thing would look from the outside. He could have laughed out loud, if he didn't feel both his faith and his friends' eternal salvation were hinged on his figuring it all out. He relinquished incorporeal sight, unsure if he felt like laughing, weeping, or throwing his desk against the wall.

*Maybe it's all just the last remnants of puberty,* he thought, and then did laugh under his breath.

Naomi looked at him with a curious expression.

He shook his head, signing for her to forget it.

When the final bell rang, Jack almost dashed out the door.

He couldn't have been more ready for a week away from Wando. He rushed to his locker to grab the rest of his books, eager to get to his Jeep and leave the campus in the dust.

"Hey, Jack," someone said behind him.

He turned to see Naomi. "Hey," he said, continuing to stuff textbooks in his backpack. "What's up?"

She smiled, awkwardly, if Jack wasn't mistaken. He'd never seen her smile like that before.

"Going anywhere for Thanksgiving?" she asked.

"Nah. Most of my extended family lives around here. We usually just gather at one of our houses." He zipped his bag shut and threw it on his back.

"Well . . . if you're not busy that night—after Thanksgiving dinner I mean—and you're free, my family's having some friends over later, if you're not busy that is."

Jack stopped fiddling with his locker combination, noticing Naomi's stance was different than usual too. She looked as if she didn't know what to do with her hands. Had she just done what he thought?

"Sure," he said. "Sounds like fun."

*"Great!* People should be showing up around seven or so. See you there!" She started walking away, her pace quicker than normal.

He smiled. "So where's, there, exactly?" he called after her.

"Oh, right!" She turned back. "Here." She handed him a torn off piece of paper. "That's the address. And my number's on there too, in case you get lost."

He looked up at her. "That's what GPS is for."

She smiled. "Right."

Jack thought he saw her cheeks turning red.

"Well, I'll see you there hopefully," she said, turning and walking away even faster than before.

Watching her go, the concerns that had weighed him down in class didn't seem so unbearable all of a sudden. He headed through the hall in the opposite direction feeling lighter, even with the added weight of his backpack. He rounded a corner and spotted Jenny emerging from one of the girls' bathrooms. She'd been crying again. Jack saw the red around her eyes.

A pang of pity stabbed his heart. He switched to incorporeal sight to see if her distress was because of the usual culprit. The hunchbacked demon appeared next to her, as his surroundings transformed into Gothic corridors. The creature was shouting insults. Jack transitioned back to regular sight, not wishing to listen to them this time.

Instead, he prayed a *Hail Mary* for Jenny's happiness. To his surprise, she stopped walking, as though a deep thought had come over her. Her face showed the strain of someone who was trying to remember something that had just slipped their mind. After a moment, she continued down the hallway, glancing over when they passed and greeting him with a smile and hello.

Curious at her abrupt change in demeanor, he utilized incorporeal sight one more time. The demon wasn't with her now. And there was a gaping hole in the wall that hadn't been there a moment ago. Its edges were smoldering, as though it had been burned open. Jack would have guessed the hunchback itself had charged through to the other side, except the hole wasn't large enough for the wretch to fit through it. He examined it more closely, getting the feeling he'd just missed something dramatic in the few moments he wasn't using his second sight.

Suddenly, the hunchback lunged out of a dark corner on the hall's other side, shoving Jack over. *"Bastard! Don't you ever fucking try that again!"*

Panicking, Jack crawled backward on his elbows.

*"Fucking Catholics with your hypocritical inclinations toward compassion and defilement. She's mine, bitch! Find your own whore!"*

The demon kicked Jack in the face, and he felt a pang of worthlessness, as if there was nothing he could do for Jenny, much less any other students. He couldn't even help himself. He tried crawling away from his assailant when it paused between batterings to glance up and down the hall, checking if Dathiel was coming to his rescue. His guardian wasn't around. There was no one else in the shadowy corridor, human or otherwise. The hunchback came at Jack again, kicking him hard in the stomach. Jack's mind was inundated with feelings of inadequacy. When he saw the demon bringing its fist down to belt him over the head, he cried out in prayer.

*"God help me!"*

He caught the monster's wrist. He blinked. His attacker looked as stunned as him.

*"Get your hands off me!"* it shouted, yanking its arm free and swinging it around to punch him.

*"Father!"* Jack prayed in desperation, and countered the assault with a block and shove this time, forcing the hunchback backward onto the floor.

Cursing, the monster rose and stared him down. "I don't recall giving you permission to fight back, boy."

*Fight back* . . . The words repeated in Jack's mind, as he realized his counter-attacks were his prayers for help.

There was another way to resist spiritual assault. One he hadn't known in his last brawl. Maybe spiritual warfare wasn't just about mental concentration and argumentation. Prayer could be used to fight. Prayer was his coping strategy. Hadn't that been what Monsignor Bamonte had told him? Turn to it constantly, he'd said. If anyone tried to dissuade him from it, he should treat it as . . . an agent of the Devil.

He looked the gray monstrosity in the eyes. It reared back its arm for another punch. Jack supplicated heavenly aid once more, and caught it by the wrist again.

*"Boy! I told you to get your damn hands off me!"*

Zeal built up in Jack's chest. His grip tightened, his former self-loathing drowned out by the new feeling. The hunchback roared like a caged lion.

*"Let go! LET GO OF ME!"*

It clawed at his arm with its free hand, howling in pain. When that proved ineffective, it punched away at his face. Jack only continued tightening his grip, barely feeling the hunchback's strikes now. His skin and armor seemed to harden against them. He bent the demon's arm backward, forcing the loathsome spirit to its knees. Every insult he'd ever heard it shout at Jenny came flooding into his memory, fueling his rising indignation.

"Will you never learn when it's time to *SHUT THE HELL UP?*" he shouted over the creature's threats.

He raised his own fist and dealt a brutal blow to its face. The demon reeled, looking dazed. After a moment, it recovered and snarled its outrage. Jack responded by clutching its wrist tighter, until he felt his fingers crush through it. The hunchback's hand fell twitching to the floor. Jack looked down in disbelief at what he'd done, watching the hand disintegrate into smoldering sparks and ashes, disappearing.

The monstrosity screamed, falling backward in pain. All that was left at the end of its forearm was a stump dripping black blood. It crackled off sparks, some of it disintegrating too.

*"What have you done? You son of a bitch! I'll kill you! I'LL KILL YOU! I'm gonna rip you limb from fucking limb!"*

"Father, defend me!" Jack prayed.

As he did, he saw himself kick the demon in the chest, sending it sailing through the hallway's stone wall into the cafeteria on the other side. Shocked and scared though he was by what was happening, his curiosity and anger both overruled his apprehension, and he stepped through the opening in the wall to pursue his enemy. The hunchback lay sprawled on the floor between the cafeteria's long tables. Incorporeal sight revealed them to be made of driftwood, like something Jack would expect to see on a pirate ship.

The hunchback was surrounded by a group of other evil spirits. They glanced up when Jack entered, and he started second-guessing his decision to give chase. Among them were the serpentine demons, muscular demons of wrath, and a group of slimy, slug and toad-like spirits he'd seen surrounding the students during lunch. Though these differed in shape and size, their common features were that none had eyes or ears and they all had gaping maws filled with rows upon rows of sharp teeth. He'd concluded at lunch that their forte was temptations of gluttony, judging from how they'd encouraged the students to either overeat or starve themselves. While the demonic horde looked him over, assessing the situation, the hunchback roused from its stupor.

*"That shitbag's trying to steal my prey! Kill him!"*

Three of the wrathful spirits charged Jack from the front. It was a diversion. One of the serpents was attempting to slither around behind him for a surprise attack. Somehow he was aware of the strategy, though he'd never been in a physical fight before. Without so much as a glance behind him, he brought his heel backward into the viper's face, launching it upward to chest height and elbowing it over a table—all while never taking his eyes off the opponents before him.

The three muscled demons hesitated upon seeing what he'd done, but only for a second. When they lunged, Jack watched in astonishment as he countered every one of their attacks like some sort of ninja. One of them swung its leg out in an attempt to trip his feet from under him. He jumped, spinning into the air and bringing his own foot around to collide with the side of the spirit's head. The brute fell into its two comrades and they all went down together.

With the situation escalating out of control, the rest of the surrounding demons closed in to subdue the troublemaker together. Having observed the effect of his simple prayers for help, and being up against so many enemies at once, Jack decided to try a formula prayer. He recited another *Hail Mary*, since it had bothered the hunchback so much. As he said it, a ball of fire formed in his palm, growing to the size of a large apple. It was made of pure flame, but it felt hard as rock.

When he finished praying it, the ball launched from his hand and pierced the chest of one of the burly demons. It left a gaping, crackling hole through which Jack could see to the other side. The spirit wailed and fell writhing to the ground, disintegrating in a matter of moments. Jack now knew what had made the smoldering hole in the corridor's wall before. The demons remaining ceased their approach, backing away from him. He smiled and recited the *Hail Mary* two more times, gripping a fireball in each hand. He threw them at a couple of nearby serpents before they had a chance to launch themselves, and chaos erupted across the cafeteria.

His opponents scattered in all directions. Many fled, while a few pushed against them, trying to get closer to Jack and put him down before things grew worse. Others yelled they were going for reinforcements. Those who remained accused them of being weak and cowardly. As these bolder monsters rushed him, Jack prayed the *Our Father*, curious to see how it would manifest itself. Instead of a ball of fire, a ball of lightning formed in his palm. He shot it at one of the slug-like demons. It not only disintegrated, streaks flew off its hide as it burned, hitting several other spirits standing in close proximity. Jack couldn't help laughing.

"Now that's what I call an electric eel!"

He snapped back to attention a millisecond later, needing to focus in order to make his prayers powerful enough. The remaining adversaries were closing in. He prayed the Lord's Prayer with even more fervor. The lightning ball grew larger. He held it up with both hands. It shot out multiple bolts in several directions, frying approaching demons who yelped and retreated like whipped dogs. He leapt ten feet into the air and threw the ball at the largest spirit he could spot, afterward landing atop one of the tables to get a better view of how many threats were left.

Just when he'd assessed there were eight demons remaining, a dozen more entered the cafeteria from all entrances. Apparently, those who'd fled before weren't bluffing about going for backup. As the new arrivals charged, Jack tried praying the *Apostle's Creed*.

Everything in front of him went blurry. At first he blinked, thinking something was happening to his eyesight. But, as he looked around, he saw he was surrounded by what looked like a circular heat wave emanating from his soul and expanding outward. It made a deep roar like thunder, forming cracks in the floor and walls when it came into contact with them. It washed over the demons, and they began to scream and claw at the air, stumbling around like drunkards.

Jack realized they couldn't see anymore. And, judging from how they all kept shouting at one another without ever answering, he guessed they'd been deafened too. By all appearances, any spirit the shockwave had touched was completely discombobulated and in a state of hysterics. If there hadn't been so much adrenaline pumping through his veins, Jack would have found the scene hilarious.

Watching a spirit of wrath who'd been closest to the table he stood upon, he observed the effect of the shockwave wearing off. Its eyes focused on him and it snarled. Figuring the discombobulation must be a temporary effect and that he was missing his window of opportunity, he launched into action. He leapt off the table and slammed both boots into the angry spirit's chest. The demon was knocked backward off its feet, and he used its momentum to springboard into a second opponent, grabbing its neck and swinging himself around its body. This forced it to twirl and slam face-first into the ground, while he ended up standing atop its back.

He vaulted into the next group of monsters and—using his agility—propelled and ricocheted himself from demon to demon, bouncing across the entire cafeteria like a pinball. He knocked them all to the ground one by one in a matter of seconds without ever touching the floor himself. When he landed, the only enemy left standing was Jenny's tormentor.

It had retreated to a corner when Jack started employing Catholic formulas. Jack tilted his head as he looked it in the eyes, savoring the expression of dread on its face when it realized there was no one left to protect it. Still cradling its arm, the hunchback dashed toward the exit.

Jack's soul was faster. He rammed into it as hard as he could with his shoulder, sending it tumbling into the air and crashing through the opposite corner of the room. He jumped up to the hole it had left and prepared to follow it outside. The monster had rolled almost all the way to the football stadium.

Jack bounded down from the wrecked wall and sprinted after it across the desolate wasteland his sight revealed Wando's lawn to resemble. The creature stood to get its bearings and saw him coming. It decided to stand its ground this time, storming out to meet him head on, cursing all the way.

When they collided, the demon didn't even slow Jack down. Its feet left the ground, and he crashed them both through the bleachers onto the football field. They separated as they rolled to a stop. Jack was the first back on his feet. He pounced on the monster before it could rise, stomping his foot down on its back and grabbing the two horns hanging from its chin. His skin had grown so tough during the battle he didn't even feel any burn from the glowing tusks, though steam rose from his palms as his fingers closed around them. The spirit howled in pain while he twisted and tugged at its head with all his might.

*"This . . . is . . . what . . . happens,"* Jack yelled through gritted teeth, *"to . . . those . . . who . . . defile . . . THE INNOCENT!"*

With a final heave, he wrenched the hunchback's head off. The body began disintegrating beneath him. He tossed the likewise crackling head aside. It smoldered into nothing before ever hitting the ground.

He took a deep breath, relaxing his muscles. Even physically, he'd grown tense during the battle. Turning back toward the bleachers, he saw he wasn't out of the woodwork yet. Hundreds of demons were spilling over them like a black tide sweeping the field. He started to run, but they overtook him in a matter of seconds, several of them latching onto his arms and legs, while two of them grabbed his head, forcing it down into the dirt. He felt a shortness of breath as one of their hands closed over his mouth, attempting to crush his face. His eyes widened when he saw it was the spider-like demon he'd seen in biology class.

*"And this,"* the suffocating spider shouted, *"is what happens to those who dare defy the rulers of this kingdom!"*

The insectoid ground his cranium deeper into the earth. He felt his former zeal waning under the onslaught. He prayed the *Hail, Holy Queen* in a desperate attempt to regain it, and a multitude of laser beams shot out from every part of his soul, slicing through his attackers like a hot knife through butter. The spider's limbs went flying. Black blood and screams of agony spewed from its mouth. The beams coming from Jack were of every color, including those he'd only seen through his new eyesight. The demons drew back, some of them not fast enough, as they were slashed in half.

Jack rose from the ground to face those left. The beams swiveled around him while he did, protecting him on all sides, making him feel like a rotating disco ball. They petered out after he finished the prayer. But their damage was done.

The situation was now a deadlock. The remaining demons circled at a distance, determining how best to proceed. Jack prayed another *Our Father* and *Hail Mary*, keeping the lightning and fireballs simmering at his sides in each hand, waiting for any of the monsters to venture another assault. None dared.

*"What are you all waiting for?"* a winged beast demanded, landing among its comrades. *"It is but one soul!"*

The newcomer flew at Jack, and he prepared to hurl the lightning at it. But Dathiel descended, landing atop the approaching hell beast, crushing it to pieces under his heels. The guardian stood between Jack and the other wayward spirits.

*"The fight is over, princes,"* he bellowed. *"Return to your stronghold."*

The demons stayed where they were, appearing unsure what to do. Each looked to others for direction. Exchanging expressions of scorn for the angel, they seemed to collectively make up their minds and stalked forward.

"Well," Dathiel said, bringing his fists up as four blades extended from each of his wrist bracers over his knuckles, "if that's the way it has to be. I was hoping we'd go this way."

The monstrosities closed in, but the celestial intelligence cut into them first. Jack was floored by how smoothly he dispensed with enemies. He even used his wings to slap and bat them aside. At a point, he crossed his arms over his chest and hovered into the air, spinning into the diabolic creatures like an out-of-control helicopter. Heads and limbs were slashed off and sent tumbling in all directions. The angel made his charge's fighting style appear clunky and inefficient by comparison. In less than a minute, he'd slain every demon on the field, with any who'd still been on the sidelines fleeing back into the depths of the school.

Dathiel lowered his arms to his sides and the blades retracted. "Well, that was adventurous!" He turned to Jack. "Time to go."

Jack didn't move, staring at him with a raised eyebrow.

Dathiel smiled. "What?"

Jack gave a half-smile back, shaking his head. "Nothin', Wolverine."

Dathiel laughed. "Hey, don't blame me for how your gift portrays me in battle. It's filtered through your imagination, not mine."

"Any other tricks hidden up your sleeves?"

"Plenty. But you've got your whole life to discover them. Right now, we really should leave before they alert the chieftain."

*"Chieftain?"* Jack asked, physically hurrying out the school building and running across the grass to his Jeep.

"The demon who oversees Wando High. Unlike those you just fought, he's a fallen Archangel. You can expect he'll want retribution for this. Speaking of which," Dathiel beamed at him as he climbed onto the corner of his carriage, "you were fantastic! I'm proud of you!"

"I had no idea I could do any of that!" Jack said, throwing his backpack into the backseat.

"Wouldn't have guessed ordinary life could be so extraordinary, huh? You're developing a better skill for spiritual warfare. I've never seen you engage in it with such zeal before."

"Yeah, the experience did feel familiar . . ." Jack paused as he flipped back to regular sight to find the ignition and turn the key, "but it's been harder in the past."

"Well, today's opponents were small fish," Dathiel said, his wings trailing in the wind as the carriage tore down the street. "They were mostly assaulting you with temptations of the flesh. But you've had your passions under control a while now. You're more used to dealing with the intellectual attacks of Mephistopheles."

"Thank God *he* wasn't around just now," Jack praised, buckling his seat belt as he sped away from the campus.

"Not this time. But you need to prepare for greater battles. This was only a light skirmish compared with what's to come."

# CHAPTER XV
# THE ARMORY

Lorelai hadn't even crossed her front door's threshold after arriving home from work that evening before her son was hitting her with questions about where he could purchase religious medals.

"There's that new convent of Dominican nuns on Sullivan's Island," she said. "They have a gift shop I think."

"I'm going there," Jack said, heading out the door. "Where is it exactly?"

"I'm sure it's closed by now, son. They'll be open tomorrow."

"Alright, then I'm heading out there first thing in the morning."

"How 'bout I take you?"

Jack's mind was somewhere else as he sat in the passenger seat beside Lorelai.

He hadn't said a word since they got in the car. She noticed he kept glancing over at the right front corner of the hood and moving his lips slightly. He must have been praying again. He'd been doing a lot more of that lately. He'd been acting strange too.

"So," she interrupted, "why the sudden urgency for medals?"

He looked over at her and his eyes seemed to focus. He didn't answer at first.

"I'll need them," he said after a few seconds. "All the protection I can get."

"Protection from what, son?"

He pursed his lips, as though careful in choosing his next words. "Well, what else do sacramentals protect us from? The Devil."

She laughed. "And has the Devil been bullying you?"

His face turned serious. She could tell she was about to lose him again.

"You don't know the half of it," he almost whispered.

"Alright," she said, not knowing what else to say.

They were silent for a time. She tried to think of the best way to get him to open up.

"So," she tried, "what exactly has been going on with you?" She saw him look over at her in her peripheral vision, like he was considering her.

"I guess I'd say I'm prioritizing my life better," he said. "That's why the sudden interest in the Faith. I've come to realize how important it is."

"Yeah? What set that off?"

"Chuck's death. And my teacher denying it at school."

"Well, that's nice." She paused again. "So, why does your faith have to make you so quiet and serious all the time? You barely speak around us anymore."

He was silent. She wondered if she'd made him close up again. Had she pushed too far too fast? She never could tell with teenagers what was going to set them off.

"You have any big secrets in your past you've never told me about?"

The question caught her off-guard. "No . . . what do you mean?"

"Dark secrets?" Jack pressed. "Things you wouldn't want your kids to know?"

Lorelai laughed. "Well, if I didn't want you to know, why would I tell you?"

"Seriously," Jack said without cracking a smile in return.

Lorelai felt at a loss. "Like what? Have I ever killed anyone or robbed a bank? That kind of thing?"

"Well . . . have you?"

She laughed harder. "No. You don't have to worry about the police coming for your mother, Jack. No deep dark secrets here. What makes you ask something like that anyway?"

He smiled, chuckling himself now. The laughter seemed feigned to her.

"Nothing," he said.

There was silence again, until he asked another strange question.

"When's the last time you or Dad went to Confession."

His inquiries were so random, she didn't know what to think of them. "I don't know. Not for years. Why?"

"I found out recently every Catholic's supposed to go at least once a year, but I don't think we've ever done that."

"Oh that's just a guideline, son. We're fine."

*"No."*

He surprised her with the forcefulness of his response.

"It's not a suggestion. It's a requirement. And a person shouldn't be going to Communion if they're aware of even one mortal sin on their soul. But all of us go every week."

"Well, if you're so worried about it, why don't you go to Confession then?"

"I did. Went last month for the first time in years. Can't tell you how much it's helped. But . . . I wasn't really talking about me . . . Can you really tell me with confidence that—after not going to Confession for years—there's not a single reason you might need to go now?"

The questions were beginning to irk her. Her temper rose with her voice.

"Where is all this coming from, son? You go to Confession once and suddenly become a doom-and-gloom preacher of fire and brimstone?"

"Deflection, Mom. You didn't answer the question."

Her grip tightened on the wheel. She heard its leather squeak like a dying mouse under her fingers.

"That's enough, Jack. Sorry I asked!"

He sighed and his tone softened. "I'm not trying to attack you, Mom—"

"Well you're doing a bang-up job of that, aren't you?" she interrupted.

"I'm only asking out of concern for you. I've learned a lot I didn't know about the Church's teachings in the last month, and realized I hadn't been living according to all of them either."

"Well I've been a Catholic a lot longer than you, son. You don't need to worry about me."

Jack's voice changed to its militant tone again. "How can you tell me not to worry about you? Would you not worry about me if I was in some kind of trouble?"

She laughed with a bitter edge. "I'm not in trouble, son. I haven't gone to Confession, because I don't have anything to confess."

Jack was the one who laughed with the bitter edge now. It fueled her anger.

"I seriously doubt that, Mom. Not with how many temptations surround people all the time. Everybody's got something they can bring to the confessional. Especially if they haven't been in years."

"That's enough!"

"Mom, I'm on your side here—"

*"Enough!"* she cut in. "I don't want to hear another word about this! You understand me?"

"You know, the more defensive you get, the more it just makes me think you have something to hi—"

*"JACK! I SAID ENOUGH!"*

The rest of the drive to the convent passed in tense silence. Lorelai could have kicked herself. It hadn't been her best attempt at connecting with her son.

Jack could have kicked himself as he exited the car. It hadn't been his best attempt at connecting with his mother. He'd been too forward in his queries and come across like a fanatical, holier-than-thou bigot. He couldn't blame his mother for perceiving it that way, because it was exactly how he'd felt. He was never going to get anything out of her so long as he appeared to be either prying or preaching, which, he supposed, was what he'd been doing. But he was at a loss in trying to think of a better way to discover a person's secret sins. Those wouldn't come up in casual conversation, especially between mother and son. He knew he had the knowledge that could help save her soul. What he lacked were the tactics to pass it on.

Perhaps Monsignor Bamonte could give him pointers. Of course, there was also the fact he was Lorelai's teenage son. That wouldn't incline her to take any advice from him seriously. On top of it all, Jack knew Lorelai Dacre was a strong-willed—fuck it—*stubborn* woman.

He should know. He'd inherited the personality trait himself. When they argued, they were equivalent to a couple of wolves locked in a cage together, vying for the alpha position. It tended to make one or both of them the source of most family feuds. But Lorelai's obstinacy was breaking a whole new level of frustration in him this time. It was hindering him from possibly rescuing her from damnation. It was a high stakes round, and he had to win. Still, he had to admit to himself he'd let his own impatience get in the way.

He tried taking his mind off his family a while by examining the convent before them through his new eyesight. It was aesthetically pleasing enough to natural vision. A stone building resembling a castle. His other sight revealed it to be all the more majestic and populated by blessed spirits. Following his mother around to a side door leading into the gift shop, he was surprised by its size. He'd expected a small alcove with a few trinkets. The sisters' store contained numerous stands filled with holy cards, medals, religious statues, and walls of books. Surveying the place through his ability, he realized what it was in spiritual terms.

He saw nuns in the back repairing blessed objects. They were armored, like him. And the objects they were handling appeared as armor, even a few weapons, as the sisters hammered and welded them back together. The unblessed products on sale looked the same as they did to corporeal sight, but Jack could see what they'd become once blessed from what he saw the sisters repairing.

"An armory!" he said mentally.

"The best kind," said a voice behind him in a French accent. "And a forge."

"Princess Joan!" he almost said audibly, turning around.

She wasn't alone. Accompanying her was the short elderly saint he'd seen ordering angels around in the cathedral on Halloween.

"I didn't think it would take long before you came seeking more sacramentals," Joan said. "Now you know their importance firsthand."

"No kidding," he said, eyeing the other saint. He had rather stern features. "Wouldn't happen to have any recommendations as to what I should get do you?"

It was the elderly saint who answered, his voice as gruff as Jack remembered. "Well we didn't come down to hand out flowers, did we?" he said in an accent Jack didn't recognize.

Jack bowed his head in the saint's direction, sensing he was not one to cross.

"Jack Dacre—Saint Benedict of Nursia," Joan introduced.

"Pleasure to meet you," Jack greeted.

Benedict smiled. "You didn't come for pleasure, Jack."

"True," Jack said. "So what's the best armor around here for protecting against demons?"

"You'll want some of the essentials," Joan said. "Ask the sisters for the Brown Scapular of Our Lady of Mount Carmel, a Miraculous Medal, the Jubilee Medal of Saint Benedict here, and the Medal of the Holy Face."

"And those'll protect me against vendetta from Wando's chieftain and Mephistopheles?"

"Only if you enable them to, boy," Benedict said. "Sacramentals aren't magic talismans. In addition to a priest's blessing, their effectiveness relies on the strength of the wearer's faith. That's why Self-Loathing's first blows penetrated your breastplates more than his later ones. You'd willed to resist him by then."

"Self-Loathing?"

"The hunchback you decapitated."

"So that was his name . . . Makes sense based on what I felt when he attacked me, and the kind of stuff I always heard him saying to Jenny."

"Can I help you find anything?" Jack heard a soft voice echo behind him.

He turned and beheld a dazzling sight. Before him stood a figure wearing a white hooded cape and a suit of armor covering every inch of skin. The suit looked like it was made of diamond. It had rubies for eyes. He swapped his visions and saw it was a young nun, probably not even in her mid-twenties yet. She wore glasses and white garments, with a black veil almost completely covering her light brown hair.

"Sorry," he said when he realized she was waiting for his answer. "Yes actually. I was looking for . . ."

He'd already forgotten most of the items Joan had mentioned. Transitioning sights again so she could repeat them, he rattled them off to the sister.

"Yes, we have those in stock," the nun said. "They'll be over here."

She led him to the back of the gift shop, passing Lorelai on the way, who was speaking with one of the older sisters. The young nun rummaged through a container filled with silver medals.

"Here's the Medal of the Holy Face." The young sister handed Jack a small silver piece no larger than a nickel. "Here's the Brown Scapular."

She bent down, grabbing a plastic bag from the bottom of the container stand. Inside were two rectangular pieces of wool cloth about two inches long attached to each other by two wool strings. One of them featured a picture of the Blessed Virgin Mary handing the Scapular to a monk while supporting the Christ Child on her knee.

On the second was written: "Whosoever dies clothed in this Scapular shall not suffer eternal fire." In smaller print at the bottom, it read: "The Scapular Promise from Our Lady of Mt. Carmel."

*"What?"* Jack exclaimed. "Is this true?"

"What, the promise? Oh yes," the sister said. "Our Lady appeared to Saint Simon Stock in the year . . . 1251, I believe, and presented him with the Brown Scapular, promising that anyone who died wearing it would never be damned. That's what's depicted there." She pointed at the illustration. "The Order of Carmelites have worn it as their habit ever since. This is a miniaturized version of it that anyone may wear and receive the same benefit, as long as they have a priest enroll them."

*"Why doesn't everyone in the world wear one of these?"* Jack exclaimed.

The sister laughed. "You're asking the wrong person. I myself do. The Dominican Scapular anyway."

She gripped a white cloth hanging over her shoulders. It went halfway past her knees in front and behind. It looked like an apron.

"So that's a full-size scapular?"

"Yep. I'm pretty sure every order has their own."

"So is that how this one's worn?" Jack indicated the small scapular in the bag. "With one of the pieces over the chest and the other over the back?"

"Yep." The sister rummaged through another stand of medals. "Hmm, it looks like we're out of Miraculous and St. Benedict Medals here. We do have the St. Benedict in sterling silver, but it'll be more expensive."

"That's fine," Jack said. "I'm guessing it'll be more durable that way, and I don't intend to stop wearing it anytime soon."

She smiled at him. "What brought you seeking these specific medals today?"

He thought about how to answer for a moment. "I've felt . . . under spiritual attack lately. And, a friend of mine recommended these sacramentals could help."

She glanced into his eyes, and something in hers made him think she wasn't unfamiliar with his plight. "Well, if you're dealing with the demonic, the Jubilee Medal is definitely one to go with. It even originated as a shield against evil."

Scanning the sterling silver section of medals, she unlocked the plastic door of the stand, pulled a box off one of its shelves, and handed it to him. The medal inside was the same size and shape of the Holy Face Medal but contained many intricate details. On its front, it pictured Saint Benedict himself holding a cross in one hand and a book in the other. To his left a raven was taking flight. On his right stood a cracked chalice with a serpent inside it. Across the rest of the medal, stuffed in just about any space they would fit, were letters and words written in a foreign language.

"There should be an explanation of it in here," the sister said, opening the box after handing Jack the medal. She pulled out a folded paper that had been underneath it. "Here we go. The book Saint Benedict is holding is the Rule for Monasteries, since he's considered the Father of Western Monasticism. The raven is flying away with a loaf of poisoned bread an envious enemy had sent to him. The serpent and chalice represent a poisoned drink his own monks tried to murder him with. It shattered when he said a blessing and made the sign of the cross over it before drinking, after which he abandoned the traitorous brothers . . ." She looked farther down the paper. "As for all the symbols, around the edge of the medal's front are the Latin words: *Eivs in obitv nostro praesentia mvniamvr.'*"

Jack followed along on the medal itself as she read.

"That translates: 'May we be strengthened by his presence in the hour of our death.' It says here Saint Benedict is believed to be a very powerful patron for the dying." She scrolled down more of the description. "On the back of the medal, printed on the cross in the center, are letters that stand for the Latin prayer: 'May the Holy Cross be my light! May the Dragon never by my guide!'" She scanned down to the bottom of the pamphlet. "Ah, here's the part I was looking for. Around the edge of this side are printed letters representing the Latin for: 'Begone Satan! Never tempt me with your vanities! What you offer me is evil. Drink the poison yourself!'" She folded the paper and slipped it back in the bottom of the container. "That should tell you a little of why this medal's so potent against the diabolic."

"You're telling me!" Jack examined the minute details for himself. "I'll take it."

"Alright." She put the medal back in its box.

"So what about the Holy Face Medal? Any significant history behind it too?"

"The face pictured on it is the imprint of Jesus' face from the Shroud of Turin," she said, stepping around behind the cash register, which had a glass top displaying decorative cross necklaces underneath it.

"What's that?"

"The cloth His Body was wrapped in during the three days in the tomb before the Resurrection."

"Wait, the Church has that?"

"Yes. It's in Rome."

"So this would be an image of Christ's actual face then!"

Jack looked more closely at the medal. It resembled the way he saw Jesus pictured in images through incorporeal sight.

"It is," the nun nodded. "Saint Thérèse of Lisieux is said to have had a great devotion to it. She's a big part of why the medal became so popular."

The sister reached under the counter beneath the lit necklaces on display to an area Jack couldn't see and pulled out a basket, holding it out for him to look. There was a small pile of silver and blue oval medals inside. The Blessed Virgin was pictured on them with her hands spread while she stood atop a globe, crushing a serpent's head under her foot.

"I usually save these for visiting priests and seminarians, since I only have a limited number. But, something tells me you'd do well to have one yourself."

Jack looked up from the basket. "What are they?"

"Miraculous Medals that were blessed by Pope Leo XIII in 1884. He's the pope who wrote the Prayer to St. Michael you probably grew up praying. Actually, he wrote that the same year these were blessed."

She dropped one of the medals into his hand as his eyes widened. He held it in his palm as though it were a delicate ornament.

"Are you serious?" he asked.

"Yes. One of my ancestors was a priest who worked in the Vatican at the time. He had a bag full of these blessed by the pope while there. They've been passed down for generations in my family since. I took some with me when I became a nun to give out to clergy. Since they're blessed, I can't sell them. I only give them as gifts."

"That's too generous, sister! I can't take this!"

"Don't sweat it! As you can see, I have plenty left. And I already wear my own."

"Well . . . I can't thank you enough. I'll be glad to be armored in this! I'll wear it the rest of my life if I can help it."

She smiled, as he examined the sacramental.

"Latin printed around the edge of this one too it looks like."

"Yes. That'd be because they came from Rome originally. But every Miraculous Medal has the same prayer circling its edge: 'O Mary conceived without sin, pray for us who have recourse to thee.'"

Jack looked up. "I've heard that one before."

"I'm sure you have. Other than the crucifix itself, this is probably the most popular medal in the Church. Its proper name is actually the Medal of the Immaculate Conception. But, when it first came around in 1830, it quickly became known as the Miraculous Medal because of how many graces manifested for those who wore it."

"I guess I can go ahead and put it on, if it's already blessed." Jack said, pulling his chain out from under his shirt.

"I can attach it for you. I have the tools back here." The sister grabbed two pairs of needle nose pliers from under the counter. "Do you want me to go ahead and put the others on too?"

"Sure. Thanks." He slipped the necklace off and handed it to her. "By the way, I don't think I asked your name."

"Oh, sorry—Sister Jane," she said, fastening the medals onto his chain.

"Jack Dacre. Thanks again for your help."

She handed the chain back to him, and he placed it over his head, switching to incorporeal sight to see how the Miraculous Medal would manifest. Much like Saint Michael's and his cross, it appeared as a breastplate and boots. These were bright blue. The breastplate emitted thin multicolored rays of light similar to those he'd seen issue from his soul when he'd prayed the *Hail, Holy Queen* during his fight. He ran his fingers through them, finding they brought no harm to him, though he suspected the demons wouldn't be so lucky.

"Found what you needed, son?" Lorelai asked, walking up behind him.

He switched back to corporeal sight.

"Absolutely!"

# CHAPTER XVI
## DEMONIC NAMES AND DEMONIC GANGS

"Michael told me you'd be familiar with the name," Jack said.

It was evening. He'd met the monsignor at his office to deliver his journal and have his medals blessed. In catching him up on what had been happening and mentioning the name, Mephistopheles, as the identity of his oppressor, the priest had raised an eyebrow.

"Yes," Monsignor Bamonte said. "Anyone who's familiar with *Faustus* would recognize it."

"The English play based on the German legend," Jack nodded. "Michael told me about that. But he said you'd know more."

The cleric stared, considering him again, as he folded his hands over his lap.

"Well I can tell you the meaning of the name. There are a few scholars speculate. Some say it comes from the Hebrew words for 'destroyer,' 'liar,' and 'falsehood plasterer.' Others say it comes from a Greek phrase for 'he who shuns the light.' And a third theory combines Greek and Latin to translate 'noxious bile,' or, 'poison.'" He shrugged. "But, whichever meaning you go with, they're all obviously appropriate descriptions for a demon. From what you've described about him, they all fit."

Jack was again amazed at the clergyman's knowledge of facts off the cuff. "You know, you quote things word-for-word like that a lot. You have a photographic memory or something?"

The edges of the priest's lips quivered. "No. Just . . . a good one."

"Well you're right. It does fit. For one, this demon shuns the light. He's usually hiding in his black mist when I encounter him. Do you know if *Faustus* is the only historical documentation of him?"

Monsignor Bamonte leaned back in his swivel chair behind his desk. "Hard to say. His is one of the more obscure demonic names I'm familiar with. But it does come down to us from Tradition as one of the greater opponents for Christians to be on guard against."

"One of? You know other names?"

"Sure. Satan's not the only devil mentioned in Scripture. There's Legion, Moloch, Asmodeus, the Astaroth. That's just a few off the top of my head, but there are plenty of others in the Bible alone. They're usually mentioned as gods or goddesses of the pagan nations."

"Wait, I was always taught pagan idols were just statues, or images, or other lifeless objects people worshiped."

"Yes," the priest nodded, "they were. But oftentimes the statues were inhabited by evil spirits who'd speak or perform wonders through them. That's why the pagans attributed power to them in the first place."

"Huh . . . I always wondered as a kid how people could be so stupid as to think a statue affected things like the weather. I remember being really shocked when they wouldn't convert to Judaism after seeing the prophets perform miracles."

Monsignor Bamonte chuckled. "Well, now you know why they clung to their idols so desperately, and why the True God had to perform those miracles to convince them otherwise. Imagine how slow you'd be to change your mind if you'd already seen a statue do things like change the weather or conjure fire. Remember, when Moses changed his staff into a snake as proof of his message to Pharaoh, the pagan priests were able to perform what looked like the same feat. They conjured a couple of snakes by the power of devils."

The priest's chair squeaked as he leaned farther back.

"Getting back to your own story and some of the demons you say you've encountered, if they're the real thing, I wouldn't be surprised if the temptations you think are their forte are actually their names too. Less powerful fallen spirits are often named for their function. So, for example, the slug-like demons would probably go by the name, Gluttony."

"All of them?"

"Yes. You said you've seen them working in groups most of the time?"

Jack nodded.

The priest did too. "That'd also line up with what we know about real demons. They tend to have a gang mentality. The members will all identify themselves by the name of their leader. So, if a spirit other than the one you've already met were to call itself Mephistopheles, that would just mean he's of Mephistopheles' party and under his command. This is especially common when you're dealing with demons who specialize in a function. So, there are multiple evil spirits named Pride, Wrath, Gluttony, and the like. You say you defeated one called Self-Loathing, but I guarantee you there are others out there who still bear the name."

"You sound like you've had a lot of experience with this stuff . . ."

The monsignor gave a quick half-smile. "Well, as a Dominican Tertiary, I've studied my fair share of angelology. Besides that, yes. I've had some personal experience with the preternatural and supernatural in life."

"Really?" Jack sat forward in his armchair. "There any interesting stories there?"

"Maybe one or two. But I'd rather stay focused on yours for the moment."

"So you think what's happening to me is something supernatural then? A gift from God?"

The monsignor's face went stoic again. "I'm still reserving a judgment on that until we've discerned it further. But I don't want you to worry yourself too much over it. Just continue using the ability and recording what you see in your journal once I get it back to you. I'll have an opinion for you soon enough. There is something I want to bring up regarding its use. You say you've spoken to the demons you see when you've encountered them?"

Jack was the one who gave a half-smile this time, recalling with satisfaction what he'd said to Jenny's tormentor. "We've exchanged . . . a few words, yeah."

"I'd caution you against that. If they're the real thing, dialoguing with fallen angels can be a very dangerous venture. It could even open the door to becoming possessed."

*"Whoa!* I had no idea—"

"It's alright. I know you didn't. That's why I'm giving you the friendly warning now. But, I'm surprised Dathiel wouldn't have already told you this, if he's really your guardian angel . . ."

*"Yeah! So am I!"*

"Why don't you ask him why he didn't."

Seeing the clergyman meant right then, Jack switched to incorporeal sight, letting his eyes adjust from the dim office to the bright chamber it revealed. Lupe and Meriel were there. His own guardian was absent, but there was someone else standing at his side.

"Prince Michael!" Jack bowed his head. "I didn't expect to see you here."

"Dathiel's on an errand for me. I'm standing in. And I'm always close by during these meetings. I'm the one who chose Monsignor Bamonte as your spiritual director."

"Spiritual director?"

"Spiritual guide, if you prefer. The person who helps to guide you toward growth in your relationship with God. They're quite necessary as one advances through the life of the spirit. And I do have an answer for him. Tell him I've obtained from Our Immaculate Lady the dispensation to converse with evil spirits when necessary, but only when employing your charism.

As someone who bears the burden of seeing the demonic through your senses, it will be necessary for you to have more direct interaction with them than most. Hence, Our Lady has pledged it will never open you to possession and that no demon will be permitted to deceive you beyond what your mind can handle. To be valid, this dispensation does require your director's approval. Let his voice be the voice of Christ for you in the world."

"Well . . . thanks for the favor, my prince . . . Sorry to ask, but," Jack smiled sheepishly, "do you think you could repeat all that so I can pass it along?"

After giving the message verbatim to the monsignor, he switched back to corporeal sight and waited to see what he'd say. The priest had his elbows propped up on his desk and was leaning his chin on his folded hands, appearing deep in thought.

"I'll have to get back to you on that one," he said. "I need to take a few days to consider and pray about it." He squinted his eyes at Jack, as though a new thought had struck him. "I have an idea though. You say Michael is here with us now?"

"Yes, sir," Jack said.

"Well then, ask him to send me some outward sign that makes it clear it's truly his and Mary's will, and I'll grant the dispensation before you return to school."

"Will do," Jack said. "I hope you get what you need. Speaking of school, that reminds me of another question I've been meaning to ask you. How does the Catholic Church reconcile the six days of creation with how old scientists say the Earth is? Mr. Wilkerson said the Bible reveals Earth to be about six thousand years old, but that scientists have determined it's much older. He referred to a trial where a . . . William Bryan, I think his name was, couldn't account for the disagreement. It seems like an area where science and religion do conflict this time."

The cleric smiled, shaking his head. "No. Not if you know the context. William Bryan was a fundamentalist, and fundamentalists believe that's what the Bible reveals because they interpret everything in the Scriptures literally. But, if you do that, you're bound to run into errors. The Catholic Church interprets many passages symbolically, including the account of the six days. She takes it to mean six periods—each of an indeterminate amount of time—in which God did His creative work. Since God's outside of time and exists in an 'Eternal Now' you might say, all of time as we know it is present to Him at once.

That's why Saint Peter states in his Second Letter that one day with the Lord is as a thousand years and a thousand years as one day. The reason so many people think they see discrepancies between Genesis and modern discovery is because they're treating the Bible like a science textbook. But there's a quote from Pope Benedict XVI that sets such an approach straight. The Bible isn't meant to be a manual of natural science.

Genesis is more concerned with why life came to be than how. All we need to take from its revealed truth is that God created the cosmos out of nothing, then formed man out of its created material, after which He breathed an intellectual soul into him, thus making the human animal like Himself. Beyond that, Scripture needn't answer exactly how God formed humanity, nor how many moments, or years, or centuries He may have chosen to do it over. Those answers are for man to discover himself, through science. Nature is as much a book written by God as the Bible. In fact, you and Charles Darwin share a similarity in that vein."

Jack sat back in his chair and raised his eyebrows, waiting for the priest to elaborate. He didn't like being compared with the father of the evolutionary theory. It had brought him too much grief.

Monsignor Bamonte smiled at his reaction. "By hypothesizing evolution, he was simply seeking truth like you are, Jack."

Jack looked down, his instinct leading him to immediate distaste for the notion. But, was he just projecting his opinion of Mr. Wilkerson, with all his sarcastic comments, on everyone associated with science now?

"And, regarding the Scopes Monkey Trial," the priest said, "it's not true that Bryan gave no answer to Clarence Darrow, like your biology teacher told you."

Jack jerked his head back up, leaning forward in his seat, shocked and intrigued Mr. Wilkerson had finally been mistaken about something. A mistake that could be empirically proven to boot.

Monsignor Bamonte went on, "When confronted with Darrow's evidence, Bryan was just forced to admit the days of creation may not necessarily have been six, solar, twenty-four hour days." The priest spread his hands in a shrug. "But Catholics have known that as far back as the second century."

Jack was beginning to think there wasn't a single challenge to the Church's beliefs that would intimidate the cleric. "You have an answer for everything don't you, Monsignor?"

The priest smiled at him. "The important thing to remember is that there always is an answer, Jack. Even if you don't know it at first, you can find it. Now," he stood from his chair, "you told me you had some medals for me to bless, yes?"

Jack pulled his chain out from under his shirt and removed it from his neck, placing it on the desk.

"Ah, I see you've retrieved a St. Benedict Medal." The priest nodded. "That'll suit you well in your present endeavors."

"Also," Jack placed the bag with the scapular in it on the desk, "Sister Jane said you had to 'invest' me in this?"

"The Brown Scapular. Yes, there's an investiture so you're able to share in the promise attached to it. Of course, understand it doesn't mean you're dispensed from keeping all the Commandments and practices of the Faith. It just means Our Lady will somehow guarantee that you do." He laughed. "Not that I'm worried you'll be too much of a problem when it comes to that."

Jack smiled. "No, I don't think so."

"Give me a moment," the priest said, reaching down into a drawer under his desk and pulling out a decorative bucket with a gold aspergillum in it. "I'll need to whip up some holy water for all these blessings."

He stepped outside to fill the bucket from a sink, after telling Jack to search his shelves for a book titled, *Rituale Romanum*. Jack found it after a couple of minutes. It was an ancient-looking leather-bound volume. When the monsignor returned, he flipped through it and held his right hand over the water he'd brought back.

"Water made by God, I purge you of evil, in the Name of God the Father Almighty, in the Name of Jesus Christ, His Son, Our Lord, and in the power of the Holy Spirit. Become now water blessed to banish all power of the enemy and to conquer and dispel that enemy himself with his fallen angels, by the power of the same Lord Jesus Christ, Who shall come to judge the living and the dead and the world by fire."

"Amen," Jack responded when the monsignor paused.

He watched through incorporeal sight as the blessing continued. Rays of white light emitted from the monsignor's glowing thumb and index finger, entering the water, which transformed into the luminescent liquid flowing throughout the castle next door. It started moving within the bucket, like it had a life of its own.

"Grant that everything in the homes or other buildings of the faithful that is sprinkled with this water may be freed of all uncleanness and be freed from harm," the cleric continued. "Let no harmful spirit abide there, nor breath of corruption approach, and may all the snares of our hidden enemy vanish. If there be anything which threatens either the health or the peace of those living there, may the sprinkling of this water put it to flight. Grant that the well-being sought by calling on Your Holy Name may be defended from all attacks, through Christ our Lord."

Monsignor Bamonte flipped to another section of the book and turned his attention to Jack's Medal of Saint Benedict.

"Our help is in the Name of the Lord." He pointed to Jack's response on the page.

"Who made Heaven and Earth," Jack intoned.

"I cast out the demon from you, creature medal, by God the Father Almighty, Who made the heavens and the earth and the seas and all that they contain. May all power of the adversary, all assaults and pretensions of Satan, be repulsed and driven afar from this medal, so that it may be for all who use it a help in mind and body; in the Name of the Father Almighty," the priest began making the sign of the cross several times over the medal, "of Jesus Christ, His Son, Our Lord, of the Holy Spirit, the Advocate, and in the love of Our Lord Jesus Christ, Who is coming to judge both the living and the dead and the world by fire."

"Amen," Jack prayed.

The clergyman prayed silently a moment, but Jack heard him saying an *Our Father* through incorporeal sight. As he watched, the lightning ball that formed in his spiritual director's hand struck the medal, until it had diffused itself into it. There were a few more responses between the two of them, and the monsignor finished with a final prayer. While he did, Saint Benedict himself appeared out of nowhere, and the medal changed into a pair of silver wrist bracers. Each was lined and decorated with the Latin phrases written on the front and back of the medal.

"Wear these," the saint told Jack, "and, in battle, hold them before you in defense, concentrating on the prayers inscribed therein. Anything your enemies should cast at you will be deflected back upon them."

Benedict disappeared as suddenly as he'd arrived. Monsignor Bamonte performed a simple blessing over the Holy Face Medal, there being no formal one in the *Rituale*. When he waved the sign of the cross over it and sprinkled the holy water, it transformed into a round handheld mirror with a gold handle. Saint Joan appeared this time, explaining to Jack that the mirror could shrink to the size of a quarter for carrying or expand to the size of a full body. Whenever anyone would gaze into it, they would see themselves as God saw them. Thus, demons would flee before it, their reflection reminding them of their eternal loss.

Jack held it up, and the mirror grew large enough for him to see his entire face. He could distinguish every tiny flaw on it much more vividly than in the mirror in his bedroom. Joan recommended it as a good way to monitor when it was time for a devotional Confession. When Jack put his chain back around his neck, the wrist bracers formed on his forearms. He slid the mirror beneath one of them as it assumed a size apt to fit there. Investiture in the Scapular was the only thing left. He pulled the wool vestment from its package, as Dathiel showed up just in time to stand with Michael at his side.

Monsignor Bamonte instructed him to kneel and flipped through the *Rituale* again. "Lord, show us your mercy."

"And grant us your salvation," Jack read.

"Lord, heed my prayer."

"And let my cry come unto Thee."

"The Lord be with you."

"And with your spirit."

"Let us pray: Lord Jesus Christ, Savior of the human race, sanctify by Your right hand this habit, which is to be worn by Your servant in love and devotion to You and Your Blessed Mother, Our Lady of Mount Carmel. By her intercession may he be defended from the evil foe and persevere in Your grace until death. We ask this of You Who live and reign forever and ever."

"Amen."

The cleric sprinkled the scapular with holy water and placed it over Jack's head. As he did, Jack witnessed it materialize into a pair of brown pants—replacing his tattered pair—and a hooded, ankle-length robe. He realized what the white cape and robe must be that he saw Sister Jane and Monsignor Bamonte wear through his gift. The nun had said the Dominican Scapular was white. Jack's own brown cloak covered everything but his wrist bracers, which remained on the outside of its sleeves.

"Take this blessed habit," the priest entreated him, "and call on the Most Holy Virgin, that by her merits you may keep it spotless, be protected by her from all adversity, and attain everlasting life."

*"Amen,"* Jack prayed more vigorously than ever.

"By the power granted me, I receive you as a partaker of all the spiritual favors which, by the merciful help of Jesus Christ, are enjoyed by the religious of the Order of Carmelites; in the Name of the Father, and of the Son, and of the Holy Spirit."

"Amen."

"May Almighty God, Creator of Heaven and Earth, bless you, He who graciously chose you for the confraternity of Our Lady of Mount Carmel. We pray to her that in the hour of your death she will crush the head of the ancient serpent, so that you may finally possess the palm and crown of the everlasting inheritance; through Christ Our Lord."

"Amen."

"Well . . ." Monsignor Bamonte took a deep breath, removing the stole he'd worn for the blessings, "I think we've run out of prayers. I think you could walk through machine gun fire wearing all that . . . But I wouldn't try."

Jack burst out laughing, standing from his kneeling position.

"Of course . . ." the priest squinted his eyes in thought when their laughter died down. "These sacramentals are mostly defensive aren't they? What you still lack is a tool to go on the offensive against the forces of darkness for a change."

"But I thought you said that was dangerous."

"Directly challenging or communicating with demons can be dangerous. That's not what I'm talking about. There's an ancient sacramental you've yet to wield. The Church's greatest treasure and Heaven's most powerful weapon, second only to the Mass and Eucharistic Adoration. Satan himself fears nothing more than when it's taken up against him. It was even called 'the scourge of the Devil' by Pope Adrian VI."

Jack felt anticipation welling up in his chest. "What is it already, Monsignor? Don't keep me in suspense!"

The priest reached under his cassock and pulled a small object from his pocket, showing him.

Jack stayed vigilant as the days rolled toward Thanksgiving, expecting retaliation for his actions at school any time, but feeling better prepared for it with his new garment and armor.

The scapular was a most peculiar addition. He could swear it changed texture on occasion, sometimes feeling like it was made of silk or cotton, other times feeling like wool or leather. Stranger still, sometimes the hood would disappear altogether, as though melting into the rest of the robe. The cloak also seemed to move on its own, even when there was no wind to blow it and he was standing still. At first, Jack thought he was imagining it, until one day he reached back to pull the hood up and it wrapped itself over his head before his hands ever touched it. Curious, he'd practiced willing it to move and realized it acted like an extra limb. Through mental command, he could make it flap or do things like wrap around to cover his face without his having to lift it up.

*"Eat your heart out, Dracula!"* he'd exclaimed the first time he'd managed this. *"I don't even have to lift my arm to pull off your move!"*

The first night he'd gone to bed wearing it, the cloak had cocooned him and hardened into a stone substance to shield him while he rested. He'd never felt so secure sleeping since childhood. He'd felt as though he were wrapped in the arms of Mary herself. All this made him curious to see what the scapular would do for him in battle. Michael told him it was both lightning and fireproof and would be even stronger against a demon's blows than most of his breastplates. No evil spirits had shown up for him to find out firsthand. Still, he remained on edge, figuring they'd strike the moment he dropped his guard.

In this constant state of tension, he'd almost forgotten about his invitation from Naomi. He remembered it on Thanksgiving Day itself, thirty minutes before he was supposed to arrive. He'd rushed out to his car, punching the address into his GPS, grateful to see she lived in Mt. Pleasant too.

The driveway was lined with the cars of other guests when he arrived. He parked on the street, scanning the area through his second vision. To his surprise, the household appeared whole, with no rotten parts to it at all. When he knocked on the door, it was Naomi who answered.

"You made it!"

"Somebody said there was free food here," he said.

She laughed. "Typical guy. Offer food, and they come running. Yeah it's in the dining room."

Soon she was leading him around the different gathering areas of the home, introducing him to other guests. He checked every room he entered. No demons were present. Other than the souls of a few of the visitors, there was nothing dead in the house at all. The place was vibrant with life. He started to relax, enjoying the first down-to-earth conversations he'd had in a long time. Eventually, he and Naomi made their way to the back porch. The two of them sat talking on a wooden bench, for how long, he had no idea. He wasn't keeping track of time anymore.

"I haven't been able to unwind this much in a while," Jack said. "Thanks for the invite."

She nodded. "It's nice to see Jack Dacre emerge from his shell every once in a while."

"Hey! I'll have you know my shell's quite warm and cozy, thank you very much."

"Wouldn't know, would I? It's always closed."

"Well it's open for business now. Happy?"

"Depends. Does that mean I'm invited in?"

Jack became aware of how close she was sitting to him. At the same time, he realized they were the only ones left outside.

"What makes you so interested in an invite?" he asked.

*What the fuck was that?* he thought. *That's the best you could come up with?*

"What makes you so hesitant to give one?" she asked.

Her voice had dropped almost to a whisper. She'd turned to face him, leaning her head forward. His heart rate was trying to compete with the speed of a hummingbird's wings. He felt sure she would see his shirt fluttering up and down because of it. It was his move, but he didn't know what to do. It wasn't butterfly wings tickling the inside of his gut. It felt more like the tentacles of an octopus were wrapping around his intestines and squeezing his breath short.

"Didn't know anyone was knocking at my door," he said.

*Where . . . the fuck . . . am I getting these lines?* he wanted to scream at himself.

She smiled. "Knock, knock."

*Well, at least she's as cheesy as me. How is this working?*

He could see she was waiting for him to lean in. He guessed that was his next step. But something made him hesitate. A feeling. One that told him to hold back. It wasn't that he thought kissing her would be wrong, but for some reason he felt it wasn't his place. Frustrated at being frozen by indecision in this critical moment, he flipped his eyesight over to the incorporeal to catch whatever demon might be attempting to confuse him.

He didn't see any. The backyard was bright with daylight. Maybe it really was his own stupidity making him hesitant.

He jolted when he saw something large take flight out the corner of his eye. By the time he'd jerked his head around, it had sailed over the roof of the house. He tried sniffing the air to see if its scent had been sweet or rancid. All he could smell was Naomi's fragrant soul. Neither of their guardians were in sight. So he couldn't ask one of them. Maybe it had been one of them who'd just flown off. He gritted his teeth, as stuck as before. If it had been an angel who'd stopped him, then he'd know his hesitation was well-founded. On the other hand, it could have been a fallen spirit trying to ruin his and Naomi's moment.

"Jack? What is it?" he heard Naomi's voice echo.

He dropped incorporeal sight, realizing his tension was showing all over his face. No doubt the opposite expression she'd been hoping to see on it at that moment.

"Sorry," he said.

He leaned back on the bench, away from her face.

"Hey, what's wrong?" She nudged his arm. "The shell's closing up again."

"Life it seems is catching up with me."

"What? Why?" She half-laughed, but he could hear the disappointment through it. "What's changed in the last thirty seconds?"

He felt his phone vibrate in his pocket and didn't even have to read the text from his mother when he saw the time on its clock.

"I'm sorry," he said again, standing up. "Looks like I'm being summoned."

He left, spending the entire drive home brooding over how the situation might have gone if he'd been able to get his head out of his ass.

Jack surveilled the horizon, standing on the railing of his terrace, vigilant for the impending attack.

He'd watched for the last half hour as day and night shifted from place to place. More often, the darkness overtook the light. It was still more than he could see looking out the window with his normal eyesight. The blackout stretched across the entire Tri-County Area.

The Dacres had all been watching TV earlier in the evening when there'd been a titanic thunder crash and the power had gone out. Chloe had lit candles while they waited for it to return. It never had. Hours had gone by and it was still out. Everyone else had gone to bed. Jack remained awake.

The blackout seemed like a foreboding omen. It was his last night before returning to school. He stood guard, attentive to any disturbances. From his vantage point, he could see plenty of demons across the sky, but Hidden Lane was quiet. His robe billowed in the wind, having assumed a light texture. Not what he'd expect from it if enemies were closing in. He kept its hood up anyway should anything manage to creep up and strike him from behind.

After ten more minutes of inactivity, he decided it was time to get some sleep. He was about to switch visions when the demons in the sky changed their flight patterns. They started flocking out in all directions. He watched to see what had stirred them up. Soon a bright figure appeared on the horizon, flying toward him. He made out its shining gold hair and thought it was Michael, but saw he was mistaken once the approaching Archangel was within a hundred meters. Feeling a carefree attitude wash over him as the intelligence landed on the railing beside him, he welcomed him with a greeting he'd have found corny on any other occasion. He couldn't help it. The angel's presence put him in a goofy mood.

"What brings such a distinguished guest to my humble abode, my prince?"

"Ha ha ha!" Gabriel gave a mock laugh, folding his wings behind him. "I see someone knows the efficacy of flattery."

"We are in the South." Jack jumped down from his perch. "I'd offer you sweet tea and boiled peanuts or something. But, you know, your lack of a body and all."

"My, someone is in a good mood. I'd probably pass anyway. Besides, I've come to offer you something. News that should put you more at ease regarding the morrow. Your dispensation's been validated. You'll be receiving a call from Monsignor Bamonte within the hour."

Jack turned. "I take it Michael gave him his sign?"

The Archangel guffawed. "Loud and clear! It'll have the electric companies scratching their heads a while longer."

"Wait, are you saying—did Michael cause the blackout?"

"Well, not directly. But you could say he was the secondary cause. Don't worry. You'll have your power back by morning. In any event, you should be hearing from your spiritual director soon."

Jack laughed, shaking his head. "The prince certainly knows how to send a message doesn't he? Is subtlety even in his playbook?"

"You've met him. What do you think?"

They both laughed.

"Kidding aside, he's the best tactician I know amongst the intelligences," Gabriel said. "Why do you think we all rallied behind him when Lucifer rebelled? He's subtle enough that none of the demons in your life know he's here. Not even Mephistopheles."

"That so?"

Gabriel shook his head. "Not a whisper of him. There's no other angel I'd rather follow into battle. Speaking of battle," he plopped down cross-legged on the railing, hanging his wings over the edge, "I hear you were quite successful with the Angelic Salutation the other day."

"The what?" Jack asked, grabbing the railing and swinging his legs over to sit next to the Archangel.

"The Angelic Salutation. My greeting to Our Lady recorded in the Scriptures."

Jack thought a moment. "Oh, the *Hail Mary?* Yeah, it was successful all right! I never imagined I'd see prayers themselves manifest through my gift. And I definitely wouldn't have expected fireballs!" He almost laughed again, amazed at how fast his mood had shifted with the arrival of his visitor.

"That's only the form it takes in battle," Gabriel said. "It's how the damned perceive it. We blessed perceive it another way."

"As what?"

"Why don't you see for yourself? There are no enemies around right now."

Jack closed his eyes, focusing on each word as he recited the ancient formula. Gabriel bowed his head, joining him.

"Hail Mary, full of grace, the Lord is with thee. Blessed art thou amongst women, and Blessed is the Fruit of thy womb, Jesus. Holy Mary, Mother of God, pray for us sinners now and at the hour of our death. Amen."

Jack was watching his right hand in astonishment. It wasn't a fireball that formed in it, but the most beautiful and fragrant red rose he'd ever seen. It shined, composed of nothing but light. Yet it felt solid in his palm.

"This is one of the roses I saw in the garden beside the castle!"

"Yes," Gabriel said, taking it in his own hand. "Our Lady keeps many of the faithfuls' prayers there."

"I still need to visit. I've never gone inside."

"No time like the present," the prince said, wrapping one of his wings around him, blocking his view of the horizon.

When he removed it a moment later, they were both standing in the cathedral's courtyard at the garden's arched entrance. The Archangel led the way inside, placing Jack's prayer in a bush full of other red roses. The colors given off by the flowers growing on the trees and bushes danced around the cobblestones of the pathways like living rainbows. The beams looked like the ones shining from his blue breastplate.

"I take it the rainbows are the *Hail, Holy Queen* prayer?" Jack asked, reaching out to touch one.

"That's right."

When Jack's fingers came in contact with it, he was surprised to feel warmth this time. Another surge of cheerfulness coursed through him. The two visitors made their way to the heart of the garden, where they came upon a gazebo standing in its center. It was much bigger and prettier than the one at Jack's house. Its pillars were lined with roses and lilies. They took a seat on its steps.

"Do any of these flowers ever wilt?" Jack asked.

"Never in all eternity. Our Lord and Lady treasure each one forever. Although, there is one way a flower could die."

Jack glanced over.

"If the person who prayed it were to be condemned to Hell at death. Every prayer a person has ever said stands as a testament in their favor at their judgment.

If they were to ultimately fall to punishment instead of ascending to reward, their prayers would no longer live on anymore than their souls would."

Jack gazed up into the trees, feeling a sense of foreboding at the Archangel's words. He thought again about what Dathiel had said regarding his, great and grave destiny. The whole idea of death, eternity, and salvation versus damnation scared the hell out of him. But, the idea of atheism terrified him more. A chance at everlasting happiness was better than no chance at all. Lost in thought, Jack took a moment to notice there were glowing fruits hanging in the trees alongside the flowers.

"Are the fruits how the Lord's Prayer manifests to heavenly spirits?" he asked.

"No. That one appears as the lilies you see around the garden. The fruits are another prayer. One you'll learn soon."

"But why fruit? Spirits don't eat."

"True, true! But that prayer manifests that way to represent how it nourishes souls and heals Our Lord and Lady's Hearts."

"What are they like? Jesus and Mary I mean."

The Archangel smiled, leaning his elbow on the step behind him and tilting his head back, as though Jack had asked him about his favorite hobby. The experience of his presence started to get overwhelming again. Jack had to struggle to stay focused on what he was saying.

"Christ is quite the Optimist. Charismatic . . . Long-suffering. And, little known to many of the earthbound, has quite a sense of humor. Mary is . . . lovely, the very embodiment of sweetness. I'd never observed a human like her in the history of the human race until she was conceived, and there's been none like her since. You know, I was her guardian angel in life."

"No, I didn't know that."

"Yes, that's why it was me who announced her destiny to her. And she was younger than you when I did. Only fourteen years old and asked to bear the Savior of the World. Ponder that should you ever question whether you're too young to handle the destiny God's asking of you."

Jack heard his phone ring from a distance, but didn't want to leave the conversation.

"That would be the call you've been waiting for," Gabriel said. "Better take it."

Reluctantly, Jack relinquished incorporeal sight, taking a few seconds to find the phone, his bedroom being so much darker than the garden he'd just been seeing.

"Hello, Monsignor."

"Mr. Dacre."

"I hear you have news for me."

There was a pause. "Really? Who told you that?"

"Saint Gabriel the Archangel. He's just been to visit me. He says you've received the sign from Michael you were waiting for."

There was another pause, longer this time. "Maybe you have friends in high places after all, Jack. Yes, I'm satisfied enough to grant you the dispensation. But, I want you to contact me immediately should anything become too much for you. Battling the demonic is no joke. Even if it were, Satan doesn't have a sense of humor."

"Thank you. I will. And I know. The last thing the demons have made me do is laugh." Jack hung up the phone and glanced out his window in the direction of Wando. "Won't be long now."

# CHAPTER XVII
## DELUSION AND RACISM

The fortress of Wando High was silent.

Jack had never heard it that way through incorporeal sight before. He and Dathiel stood listening outside its wall. The only sound was the rising and shutting of the gate as carriages trickled in for the students' first day back to school.

"I'd expected guards posted along the perimeter," Jack said. "Maybe I was flattering myself."

"No, not in this case. More likely they're just hiding."

"Well at least it's quiet now. That's a welcome change."

"No more peaceful though. As long as Delusion and his minions remain in control here, the minds of the students are still coming to their doom."

"Delusion?"

"It's one of the names the chieftain calls himself. He goes by, Labyrinth, too."

"Delusion . . . Labyrinth . . . And I thought Gluttony and Self-Loathing were weird name choices."

"Self-identity's one of the many things lost in the chaos of the Abyss. It's surprising the damned call themselves by names at all."

"Well I don't care what his name is," Jack declared, making his way toward the gate. "I think it's time we had words."

"You're bolder than usual," the angel said, pacing alongside him.

"I've been thinking about what that demon said to me the other day. How they're the 'rulers of this kingdom.' Maybe it's time a new kingdom was established here."

"So what's the plan, boss?"

Jack smiled, putting on a thick Southern accent. "Simple. I'm just gonna walk in and tell 'em 'bout Jesus."

"Blunt, but valiant. I like it."

They stepped under the gate. The grounds appeared abandoned. There wasn't a single evil spirit in sight, and Jack heard no activity from within the black citadels. All was quiet. Behind them, the gate rattled open again. A carriage entered the grounds bearing a single occupant. Jack had rarely seen Jenny arrive at school without Brad. As she exited the carriage and made her way across the wasteland, he observed her soul walked upright now, though still a corpse.

"Jenny looks better," he said.

"She's finally made a real break from her boyfriend. They won't be getting back together again. Your prayers helped her take that final step, which was also a step back towards sanctity for her. The relationship with Brad had been holding her from that."

"Then I can help bring dead souls back to life," Jack turned to the angel. "With prayer."

The guardian nodded. "Just keep in mind, it may be a long, hard road for some."

Jack glanced up at the dark spires before him with renewed determination. "Then I'll start with cutting the head off the snake that's poisoning these particular souls. Which one is Delusion?"

Dathiel looked over at the largest fortress. "I don't think I'll need to point him out."

Hundreds of diabolical monsters emerged at once from within the battlements. Many of them wore armor and toted medieval swords, spears, or battle axes. Jack had never seen a show like this from them before. He felt some of his former courage wane. They were giving no pretenses this time for his being the object of their focus. He stood his ground, hoping he still appeared brave.

The hordes stirred, opening their ranks, as their chieftain came forth from among them. Jack recognized the demon. He'd seen him in one of his night terrors. The one who was a mixture of clown, magician, and minotaur.

"So," Delusion said in a voice that sounded half-human and half-animal, "it really is Jack Dacre who has my soldiers so agitated."

"Delusion, I take it," Jack said. "Or do you prefer, Labyrinth? I'm confused."

Although it was subtle, Jack saw the demon go rigid at his mention of its names, making the cape wrapped over its chest billow. Apparently, it hadn't expected him to know them. The monster glanced at Dathiel with clear hatred in its dead eyes.

"It's *Mr.* Delusion to a student, you impudent little shit! Think of me as the real principal around here."

"Not for long," Jack said.

Delusion bellowed a derisive laugh. "You have one clash here where you come out lucky and you think you own the place, do you?" The demon raised his bestial hand. "You've freed no one by your efforts, boy. All of them will one day be damned alongside my little band here. Just ask Chuck how much fun we've been having at the barbecue. I'm sure he'll have plenty of stories to tell, including how he threw himself into my arms at the end."

Jack's fist tightened.

Delusion smiled, the blue paint of his clown makeup stretching farther up his cheeks. "That's right, Jack," he said, grabbing the top hat off his head and doing a bow and curtsy, flapping his cape out with his free hand. "I'm the one who tempted that particular example of God's defective creativity to suicide."

Jack felt ready to tear the deformed clown to pieces. The monster saw his anger.

"Go ahead, boy. Take a swing! You think I'll go down as easily as those you fought before? They were familiars. This time, you face a lord of demons!"

Several of his so-called familiars came forward to defend him, brandishing their spears. The minotaur raised and lowered his arms, signaling them to stand down.

"Stay your weapons, boys. Daddy's going to show you how to properly handle a Catholic."

Jack's cloak flared up around him, and he saw Delusion take an almost imperceptible step backward, betraying his boast for arrogance. He was clearly uncomfortable around a scapular.

"I'll take that challenge," Dathiel said. "If it's a fight you want from my charge, I'm sure he'll oblige. But your minions will be staying out of it so long as you wish me to remain on the sideline."

Delusion jerked his head in the angel's direction. "And I have your word you'll not step in if he only faces me?"

"Indeed. And the word of a blessed angel can be trusted, no?"

"Let's get on with this," Jack declared. "I have a class to attend."

He prayed the *Apostle's Creed*, sending out a shockwave that shook the ground and obliterated any dead trees in the area. Delusion and his demons fled backward, avoiding the touch of the prayer. Dathiel flew up and seated himself on the branch of a tree that had been far enough away to remain standing.

"Better," Jack said. "That gives us some breathing room."

The chieftain came forward again. "If you're worried about tardiness, Jack, why don't you go ahead to class?" He chuckled. "After all, classrooms are such a special place for you and me."

Jack glared at him, waiting for the demon to expound on whatever private joke he was enjoying, but preparing to strike as soon as he started monologuing, already having heard enough of his bullshit.

Delusion tilted his head, the blue grin on his face widening again as he bared his fangs in another smile. "Have you ever seen anything concrete that proved to you beyond the shadow of a doubt there's a God? Or do you believe it just because it's what Mommy and Daddy always told you?"

Jack froze in strategizing his next move, recognizing the minotaur's words.

"What if it's all a fantasy?" Delusion continued taunting. "What if God's just another Santa Claus or Tooth Fairy, and now it's time to grow up, face the truth?"

Jack knew where he'd heard the statements before. They were what had gone through his head the day his crisis of faith had begun after Mr. Wilkerson declared there was no God.

Delusion saw his recognition. "Right again, Jack. I was there to assist in instigating all your pain." He spoke his next words in the biology teacher's voice. "They believed in creation rather than evolution. However, the scientific discoveries begun by Charles Darwin have since proven that we were not created by any Higher Being." The demon resumed his normal voice with a cackle. "I like to make my rounds to the classrooms on occasion. Ensure everyone's receiving their proper indoctrination."

Hearing a perfect replica of the statement that had haunted him more than any other words in his life blended a mixture of fear and fury within Jack like he'd never known before. They rose together through his chest as he exhaled. He wouldn't have been surprised if he'd breathed fire.

"I'm going to . . . *thoroughly* enjoy it when I rip your—"

Jack's words were cut off when Delusion rammed his horns into his chest, bunting him backward across the wasteland. As he slid on his back through rough mud, his robe changed to a leather texture to soften the scraping. He'd carelessly allowed the minotaur to do what he'd been planning to do, get him talking and use it as a diversion. That wouldn't happen again!

He reached up and dug his hand into the mud, utilizing his momentum to backflip onto his feet. He had little time to spare. Delusion was already running at him again. The demon flung out his gloved hand and pulled a black-bladed machete crackling out of thin air. The weapon looked as though it were composed of volcanic rock, like the fortresses. He swung it down at Jack's head.

Jack concentrated on remaining in a calm state of silent prayer as he raised his arms, blocking each of the monster's strikes with his new wrist bracers. Though Delusion was stronger, faster, and more agile than any demon he'd fought the last time, he managed to avoid every swing he took at him. The machete deflected off his Sacramental of Saint Benedict as though bracer and blade were two magnets repelling each other.

Jack returned his enemy's aggression, taking swings at him with his fists whenever there was an opening. The demonic prince reacted as quickly as he did, dodging and blocking his jabs. Although not permitted to join in themselves, the chieftain's surrounding vanguard kept the fight closed in by their ranks, shouting jeers and blasphemies in an attempt to distract their master's opponent.

As the battle continued, it started raining. Jack felt drops of water hit him both through incorporeal and corporeal sight, prompting him to make his way inside the school building. Capitalizing on this moment of distraction, Delusion caught him off-guard, kicking him in the chest with his hoofed foot. Jack landed in the mud amidst the laughter of the surrounding monsters. Undeterred, he feigned getting up, but instead threw out his hand, reciting the Lord's Prayer. A streak of lightning shot from his palm into Delusion's chest. It sent the demon falling backward, giving him time to regain his own footing. As a pleasant bonus, when he stood, all the mud slid off him, as though it were unable to cling to his cloak.

Delusion rose to his own feet, his singed fur and tuxedo still smoking. *You think you're the only one with power, boy?* he roared, raising his humanoid hand with the white glove on it.

Jack barely raised his own arm in time as streaks of red lightning shot from the demon's fingertips. Jack's wrist bracer drew each of the bolts to itself like a conductor, after which it fired them back at Delusion. The minotaur howled in pain, ceasing his attack, smoking even more than before.

"What are you imagining will come of this, Jack?" the chieftain demanded upon recovery, glaring at him with his dark, red-rimmed eyes. "You think once you've defeated me and my minions all the souls at this school will suddenly become good little Bible-thumpers?"

"That'd be a trip, wouldn't it?" Jack said, keeping his bracers at the ready should the demon be trying to distract him again.

He recited the Angelic Salutation and launched a fireball at him. The chieftain shot a ball of fire from his own hand, surprising Jack. It collided with his in midair. Delusion's was obliterated, but his own came out smaller on the other side and had been knocked off-course just enough to miss its target. It flew instead into scattering bystanders. The minotaur hurled another ball directly at Jack. His scapular wrapped around him from behind and slapped it away.

Jack crouched forward, spreading his arms, daring his enemy to make another move. "Come on."

"You first," Delusion said.

With that, he spread his cape, unveiling what was hidden underneath it. The monster's chest—which Jack had expected would be divided down the middle between minotaur and magician like the rest of his body—wasn't there. Instead, there was what looked to Jack like a black hole with white mist swirling in lines toward its center. The center looked—no, *felt*—to Jack like it was beckoning him. There was a pull to it. The longer he gazed into the open cape, the deeper the black hole seemed to sink into forever.

Despair threatened to overwhelm him. Nothingness. He felt sure he was staring into nothingness. This was what there was beyond the moment of death. This was what had passed through Chuck's mind after the bullet, and it was now all he knew. This would be what everyone knew after their brief dance with life.

Jack wanted to look away, to shed the feeling the gaze of the abyss filled him with. When he did manage to glance partly above it, it was to meet Delusion's dead eyes. He'd drawn close to him without realizing. So close! Close enough to touch him! He wasn't sure if he'd walked toward the demon or been dragged by the pull of his center. All he could feel was the nothingness of despair reaching out to him from it. It was some kind of demonic hypnotism. He needed to resist. He tried praying the *Apostles' Creed.*

"I believe in . . ." He couldn't get the rest of the words out.

*One God! I Believe in One God!* he wanted to shout.

But, did he? The void into which he stared seemed to prove otherwise. It felt to him like what atheists had figured out and accepted a long time ago. Something believers were still deluding themselves over, dancing around on the precipice of it all their lives, pretending they'd never fall in. But everyone would fall in eventually, because its doorway was death.

*No!* Jack wanted to protest, but was unable. *I believe . . . I . . . believe . . . in . . . in . . .*

He still couldn't manage it. He couldn't lie to himself, much less to God. How could he claim belief in a Deity Whose existence he hadn't finished working out for himself yet? That would be premature and dishonest. Even if He was out there, surely God wouldn't favor the prayer of a man who said he believed with his lips, but doubted in his heart. And he couldn't hide his heart from God.

Jack dragged his gaze to the upper rim of the black hole again, seeing he was even closer to Delusion. Soon he'd be close enough that he'd be swallowed into the unending depths of his chest. He tried remembering a different prayer, one he could pray with more honesty.

*Any* other prayer! None came to mind. He was a fucking cradle Catholic and no prayer formulas would come to mind!

*"Help!"* he cried in a mouse of a voice.

The abyss drew him closer. Delusion brought the two sides of his cape up around him, ready to envelop him in darkness. It reminded Jack of when Monsignor Bamonte would raise a hand over his head to bless him, or when he'd given him absolution the day they'd met. That sparked a memory. He'd forgotten a prayer formula that day too. *The Act of Contrition.* The priest had told him any prayer of penitence would do, and he'd provided one. A simple one. A short one. It flashed into Jack's mind like lightning.

*Lord, I do believe. Help my unbelief.*

"Lord I do . . ." Jack started to pray.

His feet stopped sliding over the mud. The prayer had paused his advance toward the demon. Delusion's face contorted in frustration. But Jack couldn't finish. He couldn't say that prayer with honesty either. He wasn't sure he believed. That was the whole reason he couldn't get through the first line of the *Creed.*

He started sliding toward Delusion again. The demon's face relaxed, his smile returning. Any prayer would do, the priest had said. Any prayer would do. And the one he'd provided—the only one Jack could think of at the moment—wasn't a strict formula, was it? Could he amend it to fit his present need?

*"Lord . . ."* he began again.

He was able to close his eyes, cutting his gaze off from Delusion's chest at last. The feelings of despair started vanishing the moment he couldn't see it. His thoughts cleared a little. He remembered the demon's jab about Chuck. This thing, this beast, had prompted the murder of one of his best friends! Anger shoved the rest of his despair aside.

"Lord, I want to believe," he whispered, then shouted, *"Destroy my unbelief!"*

As he spoke the words, they manifested in his uppercutting Delusion's chin just before the demon could close his cape around him. The monster fell backward into a group of his minions, looking stunned.

*"Bet you never got that reaction from Chuck, did ya, ya fucking ass-wipe?"*

Delusion recovered faster than Jack expected and shot him with red lightning. Jack failed to block it this time, flying backward onto his back. The strike stung like a bitch. With it, despair fought to overcome his anger again.

He refused to let it. He was going to rip this demon apart like he'd done to Self-Loathing, maybe down the middle. Who ever thought of combining a minotaur with a stage magician anyway? Jack rose with a primal roar, unable to form words, ready to aim all his loathing at the wretch in the top hat. He saw what he thought might be fear in the demon's eyes as it retreated backward, disappearing into the hellish crowd behind him.

"Your guardian said my familiars couldn't join the fight," Jack heard his voice moving among his host. "He didn't say anything about my using them for cover."

Jack ignored his words, focused instead on pinpointing their location. But every time the minotaur spoke, he sounded as though he was somewhere new. Suddenly, he dashed out from the demonic circle with superhuman speed and struck Jack, vanishing again as fast as he'd appeared. Jack recovered and prepared to pursue him into the mob, when his enemy ran out from behind him, striking the back of his head this time. Jack dove after him, but Delusion was swifter than he looked with such a misshapen body, and his soldiers kept getting in the way. They never struck Jack for fear of Dathiel, but they did make his job of targeting their leader harder. Jack stalked among them, keeping an eye out for the slightest flash of a white face, brown fur, or a magician's cape.

It was difficult. The other monsters kept shifting among themselves to disorient him. Remembering his Holy Face Medal, he had an idea that would at least keep him guarded from behind. He pulled the quarter-sized mirror out from beneath his wrist bracer, and it grew to full size. He slung it over his shoulder facing outward, forcing anything standing behind him to stare into it.

The demons closest to him howled, drawing away from their wretched reflections. He smiled at their reaction. Before long, he spotted the chieftain out the corner of his eye, hiding under the wings of two of his soldiers. He pretended not to see him, waiting until the monster charged. When he did, opening his cape to try and lure Jack in again, the youth slung the mirror around like a shield, forcing the demon to look into the black hole for himself.

Delusion half-roared, half-screamed his agony, closing his cape and cowering down into a whimper. Jack whipped the mirror back out to his side and willed his Miraculous Medal to surface from beneath his other armor. Its light beams cut into the chieftain, and he screamed in more pain and fury.

"What's the matter?" Jack taunted. "Not as fun when it's you staring up your asshole?"

Delusion didn't say anything, only turned and ran toward one of the holes in the ground that were always billowing black smoke. Jack sprinted into pursuit, bowling demons aside with his wrist bracers and mirror if they tried to get in his way, keeping their chieftain's flowing cape in view. Delusion entered the hole, and Jack followed, seeing he'd been right to think they were entrances to underground tunnels. From the looks of it, they formed an interconnected series, probably leading into the dungeons under the school.

The satanic lord turned a corner and Jack briefly lost sight of him. When he rounded it himself, the monster had disappeared. Jack slowed his pace, knowing his quarry had to be close. He was no doubt hiding among his minions again. He passed by a group who seemed more interested in the soul they were huddled around and feeding upon, when Delusion lunged out to scratch his face with his clawed hand. Though he left no mark with his talons, the blow stunned Jack enough that the chieftain had time to retreat again.

"Welcome to my labyrinth, boy," the dark prince's words echoed through the tunnels. "Tell me, if this is a game of cat and mouse, which of us is the cat and which the mouse?"

"Always been more of a dog person myself," Jack said, tracking his enemy's voice to a large cave into which several of the tunnels opened.

As he searched it, the minotaur lunged from another group of his soldiers who'd been huddled in a corner. This time, Jack turned and caught his fist before it connected with his face.

"Does this answer your question?" he asked, shrinking the mirror strapped on his arm and landing a punch of his own between the fallen Archangel's eyes.

Delusion growled and backhanded him across the cheek with his free hand hard enough that Jack's grip slipped off him, enabling the demon to dart back among his followers. Jack wasn't about to lose him again. As the other spirits crowded in, attempting to block their master from sight, he used them to gain a better vantage, leaping up and stepping across their heads and shoulders while they yelled in protest.

Once he was close enough to their chieftain, he jumped from a demon of wrath's head and hurled himself into the fleeing wretch, knocking him to the ground and getting a grip on his cape. The prince was quick to respond, spreading the cape and wrapping it around Jack. He flung the cocoon toward the wall, hurling Jack out of it to slam his head and collapse to the ground. The throw didn't hurt Jack as much as it would have if it were physical, but he was disoriented from it long enough for Delusion to vanish. Growing tired of this hit-and-run guerrilla style of warfare, he prayed for guidance.

"Glory be to the Father, and to the Son, and to the Holy Spirit. As it was in the beginning, is now, and ever shall be, world without end. Amen."

Jack realized he'd never recited this prayer before while using incorporeal sight, because he was as surprised as the surrounding evil spirits when a ball of white light formed in his hand and exploded like a flash grenade. He felt he should have been blinded, but his eyesight was fine. The demons on the other hand hadn't fared so well. They were howling and scratching at their eyes, which were smoking. The prayer had even singed the skin of those closest to its explosion. Smiling, Jack prayed the formula again, this time launching the ball of light from his palm into a group of spirits farther down the tunnel. As it blew, they were all blinded.

"Alright, Delusion," he whispered. "Let's see how you fare in the dark."

He moved through the tunnels, throwing light out ahead of him every few minutes once he realized the prayer's effect was temporary. The fallen angels roared their fury every time, but they didn't dare lash out for fear of the consequences. Jack scrutinized each blinded group as he crept past, trying to be stealthy in his hunt. Although unseen, his position didn't always go unnoticed. Some of the monsters would sniff the air when he drew close and call out his location. He sped up his search, never staying in the same place for long.

He threw another ball of light around a corner. The angry screams of unsuspecting spirits sounded. He whipped around the corner to find the new passage was teaming with demons not only on the ground but on the walls and ceiling too. Delusion sprung down from a cluster of them and vaulted toward a wooden door at the opposite end of the tunnel, shielding his eyes as he ran.

*"Gotcha!"* Jack breathed, giving chase.

The demonic prince crashed through the door, entering a spiral stone staircase that must have led back up into the black castles above. Jack ran up it after him, shooting fire and lightning balls along the way. He kept missing because of the circular shape of the tower they were ascending. Frustrated, he threw himself against a wall and propelled off it into the opposite one, ricocheting back-and-forth between them up the stairwell, overtaking Wando's chieftain in a matter of seconds.

When he collided into him from behind, it knocked them both through a window. He lost his grip on his quarry as they fell through the air. They landed on the roof of an adjacent spire, the chieftain grasping a protruding spike before rolling over its edge. Jack barely caught its ledge. He was left hanging by one hand over the ground several stories below.

Laughing, Delusion released his grip on the spike and slid the rest of the way down to the ledge like a bully on a playground coming to gloat over the kid who'd fallen off the slide. *"Dumbass teenager! Shoulda thought that through a little more, eh?"*

He cackled, raising his hoofed foot to stomp Jack's fingers. Before he got the chance, Jack kicked against the wall of the tower to swing himself upside down and bring his heel colliding into the demon's face. The blow knocked Delusion off-balance, and he fell back on the roof, finding Jack standing over him a moment later.

"Shoulda taken your own advice," Jack said.

The minotaur roared, pulling his machete out of midair again and swinging for Jack's head as he lunged upward. Jack dodged, but Delusion was only slicing in order to buy himself time to climb to a higher position. As Jack pursued him up the slanted roof, the monster turned and shot red lightning down. Jack rolled out of the way, avoiding it in the nick of time. When Delusion tried again, he raised his wrist bracer, sending the bolts flying back into the monster's face.

*"You motherfucking bread-worshipper! I'm going to rip you and all your damn little classmates to pieces!"*

Gaining a good foothold, Jack launched himself up to Delusion's height with one leg, bringing his other foot into the demon's chin from below. The chieftain was stunned and lost his grip on both his weapon and the rooftop. He tumbled down to the edge. Jack backflipped alongside him, catching him by one of his horns and dangling him over the side. After a moment, the demon came to.

Jack was the first to speak. "Now that we're in a better position to talk . . ."

*"Release me!"*

Jack raised his free hand and formed a fireball in it. "When you fall by my hand, demon, it won't be to the ground."

"What do you want?"

"To take my time and watch you burn slowly. I'm guessing you extended the same courtesy to my friend."

Jack almost choked up on this last sentence, but he held it together. This wretch was not going to see him vulnerable.

"I thought you Christians believed in mercy." Delusion smiled. "Isn't vengeance supposed to be our way?"

"Those your chosen last words?" Jack asked, raising his hand higher to slam the fireball down on the minotaur's head.

The demon saw he was serious. Jack saw the change on his face.

*"I can grant you the school, Jack!* Let me go, and I'll forswear it to the students' guardian angels. Send me back to Hell, and Satan will just send another, and then another, to take my place, no matter how many of us you bounce. It's his school, boy. But right now, it's under my authority. If I give that authority over willingly, the angels may just keep it longterm. What do you say? Cut me down for your own gratification, or play the long game for the sake of the souls here who still have a chance to be redeemed?"

Jack stared at him. Quiet. Thinking. Then the fire in his hand grew larger. He laughed. To his amusement, the laugh looked like it rather terrified the fallen Archangel.

"You think this is an interrogation room where criminals get to make deals? You think I'd deal with the Devil? You think there's any way this ends without your head impaled on a spike at Hell's gates, warning all your little brothers and sisters down there not to fuck with my friends? You think I'd believe a fucking word you said? Mark my face, Delusion, and mark its bullshit meter. It's about to be the last thing you ever see in this world."

Jack's burning fist flew at the minotaur's face.

*"I'M NOT YOUR GREATEST THREAT IN THIS TOWN, JACK!"* Delusion cried, still trying to stave off the inevitable.

Jack's hand stopped midway. He'd been curious what the chieftain would say if he ignored his first offer.

"I was there, but I didn't *lead* the attack against you that day in class!" Delusion went on. "You should be more worried about your own soul than those you see here. You've got a far greater beast than me on its scent. Did you think someone like you would go unnoticed by the Lord of Hell?"

"I guess not," Jack said. "That must be why he's sent the prince of his Powers after me, huh?"

He saw the hope drain from the chieftain's face at the realization he already knew Mephistopheles' identity.

"Don't worry," Jack said. "I'll send him down to join you at the barbecue soon."

Anger flashed across the minotaur's features now. His clown smile curved downward with his lips. But it soon turned upward again.

"But you've lost every battle with *him* so far, haven't you, boy?"

Jack glared at him, and the demon saw he was a millisecond from driving his ablaze fist down into his face.

*"Only because you didn't know his weakness!"* Delusion sputtered.

"Yeah? And what might that be?"

"You're never going to beat him in combat without knowing his fear."

*"Spit it out, demon! I don't have all day!"*

A roar echoed from the sky, sounding across the entire campus. Jack jerked his head upward. Delusion put his hand out and summoned his machete back into it, slicing off the horn Jack was gripping, cackling as he fell toward the ground. Sheathing his weapon back out of sight, he caught hold of the tower wall.

*"Now you've done it, Jack!"* he called back up as he crawled along the wall like some grotesque cockroach. *"Your antics here have attracted the attention of our local Principality!"*

Jack flung the fireball at him, but he scurried around the tower just in time. The ball only blew stones out of its wall where the demon had been a moment before. Jack looked for a way to pursue him. He was *not* about to lose Chuck's tempter.

He gasped when a hand clutched his shoulder from behind.

Thinking it was the demonic Principality Delusion had warned him about, Jack breathed a sigh of relief when he turned to see it was Dathiel who'd prevented his pursuit.

"Follow me," the guardian instructed, flying off the roof's ledge.

*"How?"* he called after him.

His scapular began billowing, as though it wanted him to grab it. He complied, and the cloak spread out on each side of him like a cape. Understanding as if by intuition what to do next, he leapt from the ledge and used the robe like a parachute, gliding along behind Dathiel as the angel descended to the ground. If he hadn't been so pumped with anger from his fight, he would have enjoyed the ride. He was too focused to stop and appreciate the fact his cloak enabled him to glide. They landed behind one of the fortresses, and the cloak shrunk in size to fit his form again.

"Stay close," Dathiel said, wrapping a wing around him. "I can conceal us from their sight."

The angel went transparent as they turned the corner. Jack could barely see him.

"Are you invisible to them?" he whispered.

"We both are, so long as you remain under the wing. Stay quiet though. They can still hear us."

A demon passed close by, but didn't seem to notice them as he approached an alcove in a tower wall. "The boy is busy in class now, master," he spoke into the dark crevice.

It was true. Physically, Jack was seated in his English classroom. But—little known to the demons apparently—he was still using incorporeal sight.

The familiar scampered away, and Delusion emerged from his hiding place. In the meantime, the demonic Principality he'd warned Jack about landed with a thud in the middle of the wasteland, making no effort to be subtle in his visit. Dathiel's cloaking trick was working, because the demon had landed not twelve feet away from where he and Jack stood.

Jack recognized this monster too. He'd seen it in the same night terror where he'd first seen Delusion. It was the one with the whip on its hip that had pulled him to the ground in it. Looking next to his moss loin cloth, Jack saw he was carrying the whip with him today too. Delusion strode out to meet his superior, walking past Jack and his guardian without so much as a glance in their direction. His soldiers hastened away to a safe distance, leaving the two commanders free to meet without interruption. The chieftain approached with caution, but also with an underlying hatred, irritated at yet another demon on the grounds more powerful than himself. He'd had more than his fill of that with Mephistopheles commandeering his underlings whenever it struck his fancy.

"Welcome, Baal Racism," Delusion greeted as he knelt and bowed his head.

He observed the Principality's curled whip with trepidation. He'd seen him use it on souls before, each crack inciting racist thoughts within them. But he'd also seen him lash his own kind with it. He was in no mood to be humiliated in front of his familiars for a second time today.

Racism waved away the chieftain's greeting. "You may dispense with the pretenses, *Baal.*" He emphasized the title, making it sound more like an insult than an honor to the Archangel. "They'll neither increase my patience nor decrease your chances of being demoted yet again. I've heard tell the Catholic boy is still stirring up trouble, even more so than before. I've warned you to keep him subdued!"

Delusion was infuriated by the accusation, but struggled to conceal his temper for fear of the whip. "I was under the impression Baal Mephistopheles was in charge of Jack Dacre's case . . ."

Racism's next movement was so swift, Delusion didn't have time to brace himself. The Principality grabbed his whip and flung it out toward the minotaur's face. It lashed him across the cheek, adding a black gash above his painted blue grin.

"Taking a tone with me, clown?" He whipped him again.

*"No, my baal!"* Delusion cried, throwing up his hands. "I merely assumed the Prince of Powers wouldn't want us interfering with his work!"

Racism looked across the grounds at Delusion's soldiers, then down at the minotaur's missing horn. "Your wounds and recent decrease in subordinates tell more than your lying tongue. I seem to remember more familiars than this upon my last inspection. The boy's handiwork, I presume?"

Delusion nodded. He'd never get a lie past Racism.

"So, it seems you've been assuming you may interfere with Mephistopheles' prey after all." Before Delusion could answer, Racism backhanded him to the ground with his free hand. *"If I have to come back to this motherfucking backwater outpost of yours about this again, you'll spend the rest of your damnation roasting in the pits, with no enterprises on Earth whatsoever! You hear?"*

The chieftain writhed as he was kicked and lashed with the whip. He struggled to crawl away, but Racism put his foot down on his throat. The Principality switched from yelling to a calm tone so abruptly, Jack thought it was how a psychopath must come across.

"Look at you, the fantastic deluder. Tell me, how does a demon who once specialized in thwarting priests and corrupting seminarians come to be exiled to overseeing a mere public high school anyway?" Delusion squirmed under his heel, unable to form coherent words. "What's that?" The Principality bent down. "Speak clearly now. You're babbling like a nigger." He increased the pressure on the minotaur, almost crushing his throat, before slapping his own forehead, as though a memory had struck him. "Oh, yes! I remember! You managed to lose an entire order of priests back to the Enemy, didn't you? An order whose hearts had been safely confined to our kingdom for years. Disturbing to think what the Dark Master's reaction would be if you were to let yet another of his coveted prizes slip through your fingers, eh? Especially if it's only a barely catechized teenager."

Racism feigned a shudder. "A disturbing thought indeed!" He smiled. "But, if I must, I'm sure I could bear witnessing what the Master would do to you, Delusion. For old times' sake." He lifted his foot, allowing Delusion to claw his way out from under him. "Fortunately, he's too clever a tactician to leave a cracker like you in charge. From now on, unless instructed otherwise, you and your minions will leave the Catholic to the care of our . . . *guest.*" Racism almost spat the last word, betraying his own distaste for the presence of a demon more influential than himself in his territory. "Stay on the rest of the students and ensure they're kept from the influence of his prayers," he commanded. "Any questions?"

"Well, now that I have *your* permission," a voice said in a Russian accent from behind Racism.

The Principality turned to find himself face-to-face with Mephistopheles. Jack gasped aloud. Luckily, it was muffled by Racism's own reaction. Jack hadn't seen the Power's approach. He thought he must have materialized where he stood, because there was no way he could have missed it.

Two streaks of red lightning shot from each spike on Mephistopheles' spear, hitting the other two demons. Racism fell beside Delusion, both of them writhing on the ground now. Mephistopheles let it go on a few more seconds, then withdrew the lighting.

"Very good, pups. Now you're ready for class. Time you both listen to the real teacher."

"Speaking of class, yours is about to start," Dathiel whispered to Jack. "No need to be around for what comes next. You won't miss anything important here. Demons just love to pick on each other."

"I want to see this," Jack protested. "I'd rather it be me, but as long as someone's beating Delusion." He turned to the angel. "As far as I'm concerned, he murdered Chuck! I'll kill him! I'll kill them all!"

"God's justice will rain down on Delusion and his conspirators in good time," the guardian said. "For now, keep up with your studies."

Reluctantly, Jack obeyed.

# CHAPTER XVIII
## THE PHILANGELUS

There was no escape, no way to stall facing his fear any longer.

Jack knew the dreaded confrontation had arrived. There'd be no running away this time. Naomi took her seat at the desk next to his. She neither acknowledged nor looked at him as she did. After a few seconds, in which a curtain of silence hung between them, he knew he'd have to be the first to push it aside.

"Great party the other day!" he said.

"Yeah," she said in a monotone, still without looking at him.

The curtain wouldn't open. He thought he'd be smothered by it if he kept trying to get through it.

"Everyone else have fun?"

"Sure."

She opened her textbook, seeming more interested in its contents than ever before. Jack said nothing else for several minutes while Miss Sanger explained the family feuds between Romeo and Juliet's families, asking the students if they could think of any other literary examples of star-crossed lovers. His chest felt tight and his stomach felt light. He couldn't get enough air through this fucking curtain!

He guessed he'd fucked up worse than he'd imagined. He tried to interest himself in his own textbook. It wasn't exactly filled with his genre of entertainment. Even if it had been, he doubted there was much that would distract him from the palpable tension erupting out of the person next to him.

*What more's going to be thrown at me this morning?* he thought. *The hordes of Hell aren't enough? I have to deal with a first not-a-fight with my first not-even-my-girlfriend too? And how is it this feels worse?*

He took two slow deep breaths, trying to calm down, knowing it was the fight he'd just been in that had him rattled. Too bad no one else had seen it. If they had, maybe they'd cut him a break for fumbling on other things, like failing to take the cue to kiss them at the right moment! Not able to stand it any longer, he spoke again. He'd cut through the fucking curtain if he had to.

"Hey, sorry I had to leave the party so suddenly the other night. It was my mom on the phone hounding me to come home."

"Oh. Well it's cool," Naomi said in the same dispassionate voice from before.

Her jaw twitched.

*Yeah, you look completely cool with it,* Jack thought, pretending not to notice.

"I was hoping we could hang out again soon though," he said. "You busy after school?"

She looked him in the eyes at last. He thought he saw a glint of excitement pass over hers, but it was so quick he wasn't sure. They went back to a deadpan in the next moment.

"I've got something tonight."

"Oh." He tried not to betray his disappointment. "Well, maybe some other time then."

He went back to browsing his English book, but could see she was still looking at him in his peripheral vision.

"Maybe Friday night?" she offered.

His head whipped back to meet her gaze. *"Really?"* he sputtered, mortified at how high pitched his voice had come out.

*Smooth, Jack. Real fuckin' smooth.*

"I mean, sure. I'm free then."

"What'd you have in mind?"

The first thing Jack did when he arrived home that afternoon was switch to incorporeal sight to share his excitement with Dathiel.

The guardian knew about everything happening in his life. He could share in the celebration of all his victories, both against demons and his recouping the status quo with Naomi. Jack hadn't used his ability since that morning. He'd wanted to wait until he was far away from Wando so he wouldn't have to hear the demons catcalling him about his Friday plans. When he opened his eyes to the intangible world into which he had a private entrance, he saw his usually bright front yard was overcast.

Racism, Delusion, and several of their minions sprung out from surrounding houses and bushes, striking him down before he had a chance to react. He hit the ground hard at a buck from the minotaur's remaining horn. The blow hurt more than any he'd received from him that morning, as though the demonic prince had grown stronger since then. That, or he himself had somehow grown weaker. Worst of all, Mephistopheles was with them.

The Power approached and stood over him, leaning on his spear like a walking stick. "What are you doing, Jack? We've got real problems here, and you're busy trying to play house with a girl. She's a distraction we can't afford."

"There is no *we*, you piece of shit!"

Jack tried to rise and punch the fiend, but Delusion and Racism kicked him in the stomach together. In that moment, he wished he could strangle Mr. Wilkerson for starting all this. A repugnant taste passed through his mouth. He coughed, spitting blood onto the grass. His eyes widened. He'd never seen his soul bleed before. What did that mean? Souls weren't bodies. How could they bleed? Laughing, Wando's chieftain stepped down on his shoulder blade with his hoof, forcing his face into what he'd just spit out.

*"Come on, Jack!"* Mephistopheles pleaded. "How long are we going to play this game of denial before you accept the truth? I need you to be strong if you're to be cured. Right now, you look about as strong as a beached guppy."

*"The only cure I need is from you, demon!"* Jack struggled to yell through a mouthful of grass and dirt. *"Once I have enough faith, I'll fuckin' crush you with it! It'll be you facedown in the dirt when I'm done with you!"*

"Faith, huh?" Mephistopheles mused. "You mean the 'trust based on good reasons' the priest told you about? Because all I've seen you engage in lately is pure imagination. Only there would you come up with such a *'delusion'* of grandeur as a great destiny you're being called to by the Invisible Man in the sky. And you've certainly created compelling villains for your little fiction, haven't you?" The monster waved an arm, indicating himself and the spirits holding him down. "Complete with names and backstories. You're set up as quite the superhero in this adventure story too. Just need a mask and an alter ego name and you're done. You've even romanticized a friend's suicide into a murder that needs avenging. What, you come up short on two dead parents in an alley?" Mephistopheles cackled. "Sound like a child's daydream to you yet? Oh, and don't forget to add a damsel to be won over by the end. But apparently you're already working on that angle too, huh?" The monster shook his head, still laughing. "I'm sorry, Jack, but how do you ever expect to hold down a relationship while still suffering such out of hand psychosis? Didn't you ever see *A Beautiful Mind?*"

Jack's anger boiled. He pushed harder against Racism and his familiars, managing to make it to his knees and stare the Power in the face while they held him.

"You want trust based on good reasons?" he demanded. "Something clearly outside my imagination? What about the sign Monsignor Bamonte said he'd received allowing me to speak with *your* kind?"

"Did he ever tell you what it was?" Mephistopheles slapped him across the face with a wing and kicked him back down into the dirt with his comeback. "Unless it was some kind of divine vision, how is that proof of the supernatural? And if he were to tell you it *was* a vision, then I'd question his sanity too."

Jack felt himself weakening under the monsters' weight atop him, once again unable to find holes in his tormentor's arguments. He seemed right. Although he'd been using his supposed gift from Heaven for over a week now, he still couldn't be sure whether or not what it showed him was real. Suddenly, the pressure on his back lifted and he was able to raise his head. The demons were retreating back into the shadows of the surrounding houses. They issued warnings from the darkness as they left.

"You can suppress me, Delusion, and his horde all you want, Jack," he heard Mephistopheles taunting. "But we'll remain with you until you cast off this *self*-delusion."

"Or go completely mad," Delusion whispered.

The last of the evil spirits vanished into the shade and the clouds dispersed. The Dacres' front yard shined again. Jack was infuriated he didn't yet have the weapon Monsignor Bamonte had recommended to him. He couldn't wait to bring it against his enemy's detestable spear! But, when he'd mentioned to his mother he was headed out to Song of the Angels Convent again to buy one, she'd stopped him with the phrase, "Christmas is coming." She'd always used that saying whenever forced to drop a hint to one of her kids not to buy something in the weeks leading up to the holiday. So he'd have to wait a few more weeks. As far as he was concerned, they couldn't pass soon enough.

He spat the blood and dirt out of his mouth and climbed to his feet, managing to crack a bitter smile at the irony of his situation. When he was a child, he'd always anticipated Christmas so he could open his presents. But, back then, the gifts had been more of want than necessity, and they certainly never served a life-preserving purpose. Now, he anticipated the approaching Christmas in order to open one gift. A gift he required to defend his very soul. He touched his bottom lip, saw there was still blood on it, and spat again.

"Are you alright?" Dathiel asked from behind him.

Jack turned around as the angel landed, figuring he was why the demons had retreated. "Thanks."

"Wasn't me who chased them off this time."

"Who then?"

"You have many patrons looking out for you, Jack. You'll meet them all in time. But I'm afraid today's defender couldn't stay."

"What's this?" He showed Dathiel his crimson fingertips. "Souls don't bleed!"

"I know. The injuries you see inflicted on spirits are your gift's way of illustrating their imperfections and suffering. You bled because your enemies succeeded in tempting you to commit venial sin."

"*What sin*—" Jack stopped before finishing the thought, knowing the answer from Dathiel's glare. "Right. The wrath directed at Mr. Wilkerson."

"That was one of them," the guardian nodded. "Remember, Jack, the living can always repent so long as they're drawing breath in this world. There's hope even for a soul such as Wyatt Wilkerson. Your anger over your situation is not unfounded, but it would be better directed at those who're truly responsible, who happened to be the ones attacking you in the first place."

"Oh, trust me, I'm angry at them too," Jack said, leaning against the oak tree and putting his hands on his knees. He took several deep breaths. "But . . . shouldn't I be practicing charity toward everyone? Even the demons?"

Dathiel checked over his wounds, feeling his back where Delusion had stomped him.

"They're beyond redemption," he said after a moment. "They've already been judged. They'll never repent and therefore are deserving of your disdain. But you should never insult them the way you did Mephistopheles just now. They're still angels by nature. You should detest their motives, but never their being."

Jack raised an eyebrow. "So, you're telling me I should hate them, but . . . at the same time . . . not hate them?"

Dathiel chuckled. "To hate someone is to wish Hell upon them for eternity. So if we were speaking of human evildoers who still walk the Earth, I'd tell you to hate what they do but love them as persons made in God's image. Since we're talking about those who're already damned, your hatred is an agreement to the justice of God's judgment and therefore just. So, no, I'm not telling you to desist from hating the demons. Just don't malign their dignity as intelligences.

You can be angry with them. Even call their decision to stand against the Almighty stupid, since there's nothing more idiotic. But don't stoop to mudslinging their personhood, else you'll distance yourself from the Creator by mocking His creation."

Jack shook his head. "Okay, now I'm just more confused."

The angel laughed again. "Just hate what they do but not what they are, and don't let them rile you up beyond your own self-control."

"Got it. That's all you had to say!" Jack started laughing too, but stopped when pain shot through his stomach where Delusion and Racism had kicked him. "Anything you can tell me about this, Racism, demon? Every time I think I've got enough to be concerned about, something else pops up!"

"He oversees all the demons in the Charleston Diocese. That's the territory assigned him by Satan. When the Church first dawned on Earth, the Devil reshaped his own kingdom to mimic her structure and try to combat her efforts. Every diocese now has both an angelic guardian and a demonic one trying to undermine him. They both strive to make the people within it reflections of themselves, like parents with children. Knowing the history of South Carolina, you can see how much Racism has succeeded in his goal."

"That's . . . a bit of an understatement!" Jack said.

He remembered learning in school how South Carolina had been one of the most outspoken states on retaining slavery in the nineteenth century and the first state to secede from the Union. His mother had even pointed out Fort Sumter during their drive back from Song of the Angels, telling him the first shots of the Civil War had been fired there. If what Dathiel was saying was true, the fallen Principality was the instigator behind all of it.

"So, tell me this," Jack said, "'cause I've been curious about why demons exist at all. If intelligences are so *intelligent*, how was it any of you came to reject Heaven when it was offered? Even I can see the obvious choice to go with there, especially given the alternative."

"Then you're wiser than some of the brightest of us were," Dathiel said, pressing Jack's side to determine the extent of his bruising. "But then, knowledge and wisdom are different, eh? The latter being how you choose to use the former. Still, your question merits consideration." The angel tilted his head to the side, examining where Mephistopheles had struck him across the cheek. "It shocked even Michael when some of our peers fell. What transpired at the dawn of our creation was the very pinnacle of insanity. We came to call it 'the dilemma of creation.'"

"What is tha—*Ow!*" Jack winced when Dathiel touched what was clearly a bruise.

"Pray the Lord's Prayer with sincerity," Dathiel instructed.

Jack complied. As he went through the formula, he watched Dathiel drawing a large white lily from his palm. When he finished, the angel squeezed its petals, dripping white liquid from its center onto his wounds and into his mouth. He felt relief from his injuries the moment the liquid touched them.

"What'd you just do?" he asked.

"After God Himself, it was more you. The Lord's Prayer can erase all venial sins when prayed with enough devotion."

Jack realized he had yet another reason to anticipate his Christmas gift.

"I'll take the rest of the lily's dew to soothe the souls in Purgatory," the angel said, beginning to fade into the daylight surrounding them.

"Wait!"

Dathiel came back into full view. "Yes?"

"Tell me more about this 'dilemma of creation' first. You make it sound like God made a mistake. What exactly happened at your dawn? How did Satan and his minions fall?"

Though they were aqua and luminescent, somehow Dathiel's eyes darkened. "That's a macabre story, and a long one." He paused. "And, at the same time, a short one, I suppose." He stared at Jack another moment, as though considering before saying more. "I can tell you enough to help you understand the answer to your original question."

He elaborated.

When he was done, Jack raised a hand and made an exploding gesture next to his head, showing his mind had again been blown.

The next few weeks felt like they dragged on purpose.

Jack wasn't sure if it was because of his anticipation of Christmas or the constant harassment from demonic enemies. Probably both. At least he and Naomi were on good terms. Neither of them had brought up the disaster of their almost-first-kiss on Thanksgiving, but they were speaking. That was enough for Jack.

When Christmas Eve finally rolled around, he felt he'd been running a marathon through a dense jungle filled with thorns and hidden pitfalls. Dathiel had needed to patch up fresh wounds on him several more times. Thankfully, it was a tradition in the Dacre family that the kids could open one present after Mass the night before Christmas. Jack knew which one to pick.

He'd even convinced his parents to let him open it before leaving for church, since he'd need to have it blessed by a priest. His mother told him the one he wanted was the small box with light blue wrapping paper. The rest of his family watched as he untied the bow and tore it open, removing the lid from a white case inside. He pulled out a rosary.

It had red beads, a silver chain, and a Miraculous Medal as its centerpiece. The beads sparkled beneath the light of the Christmas tree next to the couch as he held it up, resembling rubies. Lorelai approached, putting her chin on his shoulder from behind.

"I spoke to one of the sisters when we went to Song of the Angels about a good gift idea," she said. "She recommended this when I told her I didn't think you had a rosary. Apparently, it's a symbolic one. There's supposed to be an explanation inside the box."

"I love it already!" Jack exclaimed.

She squeezed his shoulders. "Oh, and here. This goes with it."

She handed him a black drawstring bag that felt like it was made of velvet. It resembled the money pouches he'd seen in pirate movies.

"For keeping it in a safe place."

Jack knew where that safe place would be for him. In his pocket, on his person, where he'd have access to this "weapon" at all times.

Riding to the cathedral for Christmas Eve Mass, Jack read the explanation that had come with his present.

He was relieved to see it included instructions on how to pray the Rosary. It'd been so long since he'd last done it, he'd forgotten how. He didn't even remember the names of the different Mysteries from Mary and Jesus' lives he knew were supposed to be called out at the beginning of each set of ten beads. All he remembered was the Twenty Mysteries were split into four categories of Five Mysteries each. The Joyful, Luminous, Sorrowful, and Glorious.

He skimmed over their descriptions. There was too much to memorize all at once. For the time being, he read the description of the rosary itself. The crucifix at its bottom was called the papal crucifix and was a miniature replica of the one crowning the pope's staff. The beads were seven millimeter Bohemian crystals, multifaceted and iridescent. Jack had already witnessed this trick when holding them up in front of the Christmas tree's lights. They reflected different colors of the rainbow when they twirled. All the rosary's symbolism lay in these colors.

The red beads were meant to be reminiscent of both the Blood of Christ's Passion from the Sorrowful Mysteries and the Tongues of Fire from the Glorious. The beads' iridescence was meant to bring to mind the light of the Luminous Mysteries. The colors of the rainbow were a reminder of the sign of God's promise to Noah after the Great Flood, that He would never again drown the world over mankind's fallen nature, which—as of the Joyful Mysteries—His Son had come to Earth to restore. The pamphlet also noted it was fitting the rainbow be reflected on a rosary, since Mary herself was the new sign from God, holding back His wrath from striking mankind down for sin.

Jack finished reading right as the car pulled into the church parking lot, smiling when he thought of one more symbolic connection between his present and the rainbow on his own. Noah's sign was given to represent God's promise against further mass destruction. When Monsignor Bamonte had recommended he start praying the Rosary, he'd affectionately called it "the weapon of mass construction."

Climbing out the car, Jack surveyed the courtyard through his alternate vision. Numerous spirits approached the castle for the Vigil Mass, in addition to the living people in attendance. He continued viewing things through incorporeal sight all the way inside, anticipating the change of surroundings that astounded him so much when he'd first watched the Mass through it. Once Father Murphy, the altar servers, and their guardian angels all processed up the aisle—and as soon as the priest began the Liturgy with the sign of the cross—the walls of the castle melted away and Jack could no longer see an end to the crowd surrounding the altar. The ceiling had disappeared too. Vibrant clouds hovered in its place just above the multitudes, carrying saints and diverse angelic creatures from their various Orders.

Jack gazed up at them, unable to keep his eyes on them very long because of their brilliance. The floating mountains stretched upward as far as his eyes could see. He could barely make out the ones holding the Powers. Yet he could tell there were others beyond even those, no doubt supporting the higher Choirs. Father Murphy had also changed. He was no longer visible. His form emitted blinding white light as intense as that coming from the tabernacle.

Dathiel had explained everything happening the first time Jack witnessed all these phenomena. The Mass, he'd said, was the Sacrifice of Calvary itself made present on the altar. So to attend it was to stand as close to the foot of the Cross as the Blessed Mother, John the Apostle, and Mary Magdalene. Since it was outside of time and space—Christ's Act having transcended all of history—Jack could now see everyone in the world who was attending the Liturgy, as though all Catholic churches had become one. He could perceive everyone in Heaven because the Sacrifice was eternally present to them too.

Dathiel told him to try not to think of each Mass as an individual ceremony, but as the same one every time, in which he participated alongside anyone who ever had or would. He remembered going to the bathroom at one point the previous week and doing a double take over what happened when he crossed the cathedral's threshold while the Mass was being celebrated. From the outside, the castle was its usual size. When he'd stepped back inside, it appeared to again extend endlessly.

As for the change in the celebrant's appearance, Dathiel told him whenever they performed any of the Seven Sacraments, Catholic priests acted *"in persona Christi."* Literally, "in the person of Christ." Thus, Jack's charism was revealing it to be Jesus Himself Who stood at the altar. Knowing this, Jack had later been confused when it came time for the consecration of the bread and wine and he hadn't seen any change in them. Rather than shine as It always did from within the tabernacle, the round Wafer had continued to look the same after Father Murphy had spoken the words over it. When Jack brought up to his guardian how his gift seemed to contradict the Catholic teaching of transubstantiation in this instance, Dathiel laughed.

"Your gift reveals unseen realities to your eyes, Jack," he'd said. "But did you really expect it would have power over the One Who gave it to you? He manifests and hides when He wills. Incorporeal sight can't force Him to reveal himself. Whenever you see Christ through your gift, it's because He permits it. But, more to the point, you're forgetting something about transubstantiation. Or, perhaps you never thought of it before. What exactly does it imply?"

Jack had given him a puzzled look. "It's when the bread and wine transform into the Body and Blood of Christ. Every Catholic knows that."

"So what does it mean when you look upon the Host after the words of consecration have been spoken over It?"

Jack had stared at him, unsure what he wanted. "That you're looking at Jesus. That's what I'm saying. Why don't I see—"

"Hold on." Dathiel had raised a finger. "You're right, but what's another way you could put it?"

Jack was at a loss. So the angel answered for him.

"The bread no longer exists after the consecration. It's been replaced by Christ. And yet, the Eucharist continues to resemble bread doesn't It?"

"Yes."

"Well then, why are you astonished at seeing What looks like bread through your supernatural vision? It's already a miracle you see What looks like bread through corporeal sight."

Jack had thought at length on his guardian's words ever since, especially when attending Mass. But then, as if to keep him on his toes, the wafer had disappeared at the moment of consecration the previous week, and Father Murphy had looked to be holding nothing in his hands.

Dathiel had stirred beside him in the pew. "See! The bread's gone. Now, only Christ remains."

"But I don't see anything now."

"Now you see Him, now you don't. And until your faith is strong, you won't," the angel had teased. "Is seeing nothing when you know Someone's there really more miraculous than seeing bread you know isn't?"

Jack had shaken his head, realizing the spiritual realities he could see would always have new surprises to throw at him.

"The Mass and Eucharist are the deepest Mysteries in Heaven, on Earth, or under it, Jack," Dathiel had said. "Even a seraphic intellect can't pierce them any more than the Lord wills. Don't feel you're being inadequate. Just humble yourself, contemplate them with as much focus as you can muster, and God'll supply what you lack."

Jack had taken him at his word and was now paying close attention to all that occurred before him on the altar. When the consecration arrived, he was caught off guard yet again. The Host began shining in the priest's fingers.

"Ah, looks like He's giving you a glimpse beyond the veil today," Dathiel whispered beside him. "A little Christmas gift, I suppose."

Upon receiving Communion, the Host continued to shine from within Jack for fifteen minutes. His armor hardened along with his skin and muscles. His blue breastplate gave off more colored rays of light than before. He felt stronger than ever.

It was always the most rejuvenating experience of his week.

When Mass ended, Jack slipped away from his family.

They were headed to drop off presents at his aunt and uncle's house. At first, his parents had protested his staying behind, but he wanted the chance to test his rosary out after having it blessed. What better place to do it than from the church?

They'd be picking him back up after their visit, which gave him roughly one hour. That should be enough. He'd seen Monsignor Bamonte helping hand out Communion with Father Murphy during Mass. He couldn't have gotten far. The church was already emptying. But he was having trouble finding the priest. He switched to incorporeal sight, figuring it'd be easier to track his soul with how it shined. Dathiel grabbed his arm, pulling him toward the wall instead.

"Don't worry," the angel said. "We'll catch the monsignor soon enough. Right now, there's someone else who'd like to see you."

"Who?" Jack asked, physically seating himself in a pew near the front.

"Just follow me."

The guardian ushered him into an alcove off to the right and down a flight of spiral stairs that led to a wooden door. Stepping through a cascade of holy water in front of it, Jack found himself on one of the bridges beside the castle. They crossed over the moat and Dathiel led him toward the rose garden.

As they approached its arched entryway, Jack was frozen by the appearance of two more angels who stood on each side of it. They affected him so much Dathiel had to help him walk up to them. They were different than any intelligences he'd yet encountered. Even Michael's presence hadn't paralyzed him like this. He couldn't seem to speak in their presence, and if he wasn't mistaken, Dathiel was struggling with the same things.

The two spirits were human in form, but each had a face far too breathtaking to be of Earth. The one to the right looked Chinese. He wore an aqua robe and had long hair, with a clean-shaven face. The other was short and stocky, with green eyes and a long red beard and mustache that hung past his shoulders along with his hair. Jack thought he looked like a dwarf from a Tolkien story, except both angels had six wings on their backs and every strand of their hair was composed of fire, down to their eyebrows and lashes.

"Hello, Jack," the bearded one greeted. "I am Jehoash, one of Monsignor Bamonte's other guardian angels. Pleased to make your acquaintance."

"Good . . . t-t-to . . . m-meet you t-t-t-too," Jack stuttered while Dathiel supported him.

It felt like Dathiel was providing the strength to speak, or maybe it was Jehoash himself. Jack couldn't have moved his jaw otherwise. The Asian angel stepped forward, taking his free arm. Even through his robe, Jack could feel his touch was like fire and ice at the same time.

"And I am Nuri," the angel said. "The last of the monsignor's guardians."

"You're . . . b-both . . . f-from the highest Order of angels then . . . r-right?" Jack asked. "S-S-Sss." He stopped and cleared his throat, trying his best to speak. "Seraphim?" he finally managed.

"Correct," Jehoash said, as the four of them walked through the small tunnel of multicolored roses that led inside the garden.

"So . . . s-s-six wings, huh?" Jack tried to make conversation to take his mind off how intimidated he felt. He thought he might burst out of his skin at any moment. "There a . . . r-r-reason for th-that?"

"As a matter of fact, there is," Nuri said. "It's for the purpose of humility. Our Choir's main duty is to perpetually adore the holiness of the Most High. We use the bottom two to cover our feet out of reverence, the middle two for flight, and the top two to cover our faces. Gazing on the Almighty's face is overwhelming even for us."

Jack couldn't imagine anything overwhelming these spirits, but he didn't argue, and he didn't have time to ponder it. When they entered the garden, a monster emerged beside them from around the corner of the archway. It startled Jack to its presence when it grunted as loud as a bear. Turning, he screamed.

*"Whoa! What the fu— . . . what is that?"* he yelled, lunging away, almost knocking Nuri over.

Jack had never seen a creature like it. Not even in science fiction or fantasy movies. The beast had four faces. The front of its head was a man's, while a lion's face looked out at him from its right. An eagle's protruded from the back of its head. And, as it rotated until the human face gazed directly at him, he saw an ox's face emerging from the left side. Each face was separated by a mane of hair in-between them that connected at the bottom and covered the creature's chest. It walked on all fours, with the front half of its body being that of the lion and the rear being the ox's. It flapped four eagle wings on its back.

"Peace, Jack!" Nuri reassured. "He means you no harm. He's a Cherub. Another of the angels from the Supreme Hierarchy."

"From the Order of Cherubim," Jack repeated Michael's lesson, mostly to himself, trying to distract his mind from melting. He felt if he didn't keep talking, his sanity might slip away from him altogether. "The Order below yours. The second highest."

"Precisely," the beast answered for itself in a deep voice from its lion face. "Forgive my startling you, Jack. We're only here to escort you along with our seraphic brethren."

The lion had been speaking and looking at him while its body paced beside them, the direction of its steps guided by the eyes of the human face in front. It was so strange.

"We?" Jack asked, wondering if the beast was in fact four angels fused into one.

Then he heard another guttural grunt from behind him. He turned to look past Nuri at a second Cherub. This one stood upright on two legs and all its faces were positioned to look in the same direction, with the eagle being atop the other three. Its feet were that of the eagle and its arms were winged like one, but it had a second pair on its back, still giving it four wings in all like the first Cherub.

"Yes," the first Cherub answered from the eagle face behind its head as it took the lead of Jack, Dathiel, and the two Seraphim. "There are quite a few of us in the garden tonight."

Jack noticed the eagle spoke with the same voice as the lion and realized that, despite its numerous visages, the Cherub must be a single person. Recovering from his initial shock, he took a moment to look over the unusual newcomers. He found himself appreciating the seamlessness of their blends. Though he should have thought them deformed, there was something brilliant and natural in how their various parts went together. His group neared the heart of the garden and he spotted several more of them, all heading in the same direction, as though they'd been waiting to join the little caravan. Some of them had skin resembling burning coals. Others had eyes all over their bodies, even lining their wings.

A blinding light emanated from somewhere nearby, distracting Jack. It was coming from the gazebo. They turned a corner that put it in view and he had to cover his face. The brilliance lessened when they emerged into the garden's center, accommodating Jack's eyes the way Christ in the tabernacle always did the closer he came to it. Angels of various Orders were scattered about the place. Besides the Seraphim and Cherubim, there were youths with two wings who looked eleven or twelve. Others resembled toddlers of three or four. He guessed they were Principalities. He saw Avdiel shepherding them. Jack's didn't linger on them long, not once he glanced at the light's source in the gazebo. Gabriel stood under its roof next to a being more beautiful than any angel or saint.

A woman clothed in a white robe and gold belt with a blue cape trimmed in gold. She had an olive skin tone, a high forehead and cheekbones, a pointed chin, a long straight, perfectly formed nose, and dark lashes and eyebrows encircling chestnut golden eyes that sent serenity coursing through Jack's mind. Her dark hair was abundant and smooth, with tints of red in it from what he could see. He couldn't tell how long it hung down her back. It was partially covered by a white veil atop her head. Her age was hard to determine. There was something youthful about her, but he sensed something maternal too. She could have been anywhere from eighteen to thirty. As with all celestial persons he'd met, she was composed of various shades of light, but she appeared more solid than the others, even Joan and Benedict.

If his education hadn't told him otherwise, Jack could have imagined mistaking the maiden for God. The experience of her presence seemed to suggest it. He felt prevented from going any closer. Yet, it was a different experience than with the angels. Instead of the instinctual fear that froze up his joints and mind upon encountering them, the lady's presence filled him with a sense of warmth that loosened his thoughts and muscles, almost making him collapse where he stood. It reminded him of being a young child when his mother would bathe him. He'd always loved the feeling of the hot water as it poured across his limbs when she filled the tub. It was his favorite part of the bath. The lady's presence was like a magnification of that. He felt washed over by the warm sentiments of peace and love. But he felt something else with them. Unworthiness. He felt guilty even looking at her and diverted his eyes downward.

He knew who this was. He'd seen her in enough paintings and stained glass windows throughout the blessed kingdom, but she was far more breathtaking in person. He was not ready to meet her, but Dathiel grasped his arm, attempting to guide him forward as Jehoash and Nuri led the way.

"No," he protested in a whisper, pulling his arm from his guardian's grip.

He fell to his knees, seeing the bottom step of the gazebo in front of them. He hadn't even noticed the angels had led him that close already. He'd been too mesmerized by the sight of the woman to feel his feet treading toward her. Keeping his head bowed low, he closed his eyes. A tremble thundered through him, stirring up his emotions.

*Fitting,* he thought. *Didn't the very corpses under the Earth get stirred out of their graves on Good Friday in sorrow to the Mother of the Crucified? Why should my own body react any differently?*

He couldn't face her! Not now! Not yet! Not before he'd found his faith and made up for his doubt. He'd keep his eyes low until she'd passed him by.

He felt warmth wash over him while he waited, coming from right in front of him. Unable to help it, he opened his eyes. A shining bare foot with a white rose atop it stood before him. She'd descended the steps to him when he'd declined to ascend to her.

*"No!"* he whispered, squeezing his eyes shut again.

He'd doubted her existence. He'd doubted *her Son's* existence! A hand caressed his cheek, moving under his chin to raise his head.

*"No! No! No! Unworthy!"* he kept whispering in the deep recesses of his mind, which he soon heard verbalized aloud thanks to incorporeal sight.

He was facing her now. His eyes were still closed.

"Oh my son," he heard a new voice speak deep within his mind where his protests had started.

A voice he would have described as pure, untouched femininity. The perfect model all women's voices were inspired by, but none of which could replicate. At last, he opened his eyes and met her gaze. A bliss he thought could only be embraced by those with the simplicity of a child's mind enveloped him. The doubts and fears plaguing his own inhibited him from succumbing to it all the way and he cast his glance downward again, unable to gaze long on the sheer innocence before him. Silent tears ran down his cheeks. Long forgotten sins returned to his memory in droves. The Virgin reached down again anyway, cupping his face in both her hands this time.

"All has already been forgiven, my love. Rise."

She lifted him to his feet, and the angels around them gasped. Dathiel beamed with what looked like pride. Everyone was staring at him as though he were an exotic animal in a zoo. Confused, he looked back at Mary. She smiled, pulling his mirror from beneath his wrist bracer and holding it up. He surveyed his reflection. His features had grown more handsome, and his soul was shining brighter. His tears had taken him to new heights of virtue and his appearance was manifesting it.

Replacing the mirror on his arm, the Immaculate Mother reached beneath her cape and detached a gold-chained, white-beaded rosary from her belt. Jack noticed it looked identical to the one Monsignor Bamonte had pulled from his pocket when he'd first told him the sacramental's power. Mary took its crucifix in hand and it began to grow. The bottom of the crucifix extended into a silver blade, while the top became a white hilt. The beads became diamonds and gold trimmings decorating it. The rosary had morphed into a broadsword. Mary held the weapon before her, its blade pointed downward into the grass.

"Tonight, you take up my very own prayer, Jack." She nodded toward the castle. "My servant is ready for you."

He felt someone sit down next to him in the pew and switched to corporeal sight.

"Merry Christmas, Jack!" Monsignor Bamonte greeted. "Bring your new rosary with you?"

Taking a moment to get his bearings and wipe away any tears clinging to his face, Jack said, "Got it right here." He pulled the black pouch from his pocket, but before he could hand it over, the monsignor handed him a wrapped package.

"Brought a little gift for you."

Jack smiled. "You didn't have to do that, Monsignor. I don't have anything for you!"

"Nonsense. It was no trouble. But, if it makes you feel better, I had extra copies."

"I'm guessing it's a book then," Jack said, untying its bow.

"Could be . . . Could be . . ."

Removing the wrapping paper, Jack flipped the book over to see the front cover. It featured the Angelic Prince striking down the Devil with the title, *Saint Michael and the Blessed Angels*, printed in bold underneath.

"This is the perfect gift for me! Thank you!"

Monsignor Bamonte beamed. "Glad you like it. Now, before I get going, what do you say we bless those beads?"

"I just met her, Monsignor!" Jack exclaimed, handing over his rosary. "She's here! The Blessed Virgin Mary!"

The priest nodded, as though he'd expected the news. "I hoped she would be. I've been praying for her protection over you, and she never fails her sons and daughters who ask for things in sincerity."

While the cleric opened the *Rituale Romanum* and proceeded to bless his rosary in Latin, Jack opened his eyes to the incorporeal and found himself still standing outside in the garden before the Blessed Virgin. She'd sheathed her sword in her belt and was holding his own rosary in her hands. It looked the same as it did through corporeal sight. But, as it was transformed into a sacramental by the priest's blessing, it began emanating white light and morphed into a small wreath of red roses. The Blessed Mother handed it to him just as he felt the monsignor physically place the beads back in his hands.

"Receive my crown, Jack Dacre."

As he took it from her, it morphed again, this time into a bouquet of roses with a larger version of the papal crucifix rising from its center, forming the base from which he gripped it. Before he could respond, he heard the priest saying something to him and switched sights again.

"—another appointment to be off to, Jack. But I hope this helps you in battle. Remember, contact me if ever you need."

"Thanks, Monsignor . . . for the gift too."

The clergyman rose and made his way through the crowd to the back of the church. Jack browsed through his present a moment. The book had pictures of the angels throughout. He liked the style in which they were illustrated. Skimming the first few pages, a passage about them caught his eye.

*We should befriend them, for no earthly friends can compare to their love or loyalty. Saint Denis delighted in assuming the title "Philangelus." That is, "Friend of the Angels."*

Jack smiled at the thought of the title, but felt unworthy of it. He brushed off the distraction, remembering the Queen of Angels herself awaited him. He got up and walked down the right side of the church, kneeling before her statue and switching back to his new sense of sight. He beheld her real face again, far more resplendent than any statue could capture. All the intelligences gathered around, anticipating what was coming. Jack began the Rosary.

"In the Name of the Father, and of the Son, and of the Holy Spirit," he prayed, feeling his skin harden as he always did when making the sign of the cross.

Hundreds more angels emerged from every nook and cranny of the garden to join him. As he went through the first decade, he watched them take the giant lily formed when he prayed the Lord's Prayer and plant it in the garden. Each rose formed by the subsequent Angelic Salutations were taken to Gabriel, who in turn either handed them to the Immaculate Mother or placed them on her person himself. Some he added to her clothes, others to her veil, eventually forming a crown around her head.

When Jack reached the final Salutation, Mary approached and allowed him to give the last rose to her himself, after which she placed it in her hair. He finished the decade with the *Glory Be*, and it formed a ruby instead of a ball of light this time. Mary took it and held it between her hands, closing her eyes. It began shining brighter than Jack could ever make it, at which point she handed it to Gabriel. The prince flew it up to a section of the cathedral's wall containing similar stones and placed it in an empty hollow among them.

Jack stood from his kneeling position as he made the closing sign of the cross, and the rosary transformed in his hands once more, into a broadsword of his own. It had a red hilt that matched its beads. Jack stared down at it, speechless, until a mischievous smile spread over his face.

Mary leaned close to his ear. "They will be treasured in my gardens forever, son," she whispered, indicating the flowers the Archangel had placed on her head and clothes. She turned and addressed all the angelic spirits present. "The prayer of the Philangelus has supremely pleased me tonight!"

They all cheered. Jack jerked his head up to look her in the eyes, wondering if he'd heard right.

She confirmed her affirmation by smiling down at him before adding, "May he now forevermore wield it as a weapon against Satan and the forces of evil!"

The angels cheered louder. Gabriel raised the hand in which Jack gripped his sword, as though declaring a champion. After several minutes of revelry, Mary took Jack's arm and walked with him up into the gazebo. He was speechless such a pure being courted him so familiarly. He didn't know what he should say to her, so he kept silent. She broke the silence for him when she stopped and took his rosary in her hands, studying its hilt and blade.

"This sword has the power to destroy vice and beget virtue in those who wield it and in those on whose behalf it is wielded, my son. It will defeat heresies wherever it finds them and conquer hearts to the desire of eternal things. The soul who fights with it will never perish or be overcome by misfortune, but will enjoy my special protection, receiving the greatest of graces.

Its bearer will become worthy of everlasting life. I promise that whosoever is truly devoted to it will not die without the Sacraments of the Church, but will possess the illumination of God throughout their lives. At the hour of their death, I and the entire Celestial Court will stand as their intercessors, granting them participation in the merits of the saints in Paradise."

She looked up, meeting Jack's eyes, which were fixated upon her face. He couldn't divert his gaze now if he tried.

"Through your battles with this weapon, *you* can merit a high degree of glory in Heaven, Jack. You can obtain anything you ask of me, for all who use it faithfully are my sons and daughters and brothers and sisters of my Only Son. Wear it always, along with my garment, the Scapular, for the two are inseparable companions."

Bringing himself to form words at last, Jack asked, "Wear it?"

Mary smiled, a gesture that pierced his heart. "My Rosary takes many forms, Philangelus. It may be used for both assault and protection. Besides a weapon that cuts down evils, it is a most powerful armor against Hell."

She raised the sword, pointing its tip at him, and the blade split as it morphed into a rose vine. The vine grew towards him, wrapping around his arm, snaking its way about his whole person, as if it were going to strangle or suffocate him. But he didn't feel panicked. It brought him a feeling of security, like it was the arms of Mary embracing him.

The vine covered every inch of him except his cloak and wrist bracers, which it slithered beneath. It began laying petals from its roses flat against his form. Soon he was covered in them. The petals changed their color and texture, thickening and hardening into the armor of which Mary had spoken. Dathiel and Gabriel approached, watching as the rosary finished dressing him.

The Archangel's face lit up with a gleeful expression. "Now the creatures of darkness will fear the knight."

Charleston's Market Street Saloon often attracted a young, promiscuous crowd

in its night life.

Profanity observed it escalating into a normal evening of fun for him, despite being Christmas Eve. The Lowcountry never did grow very cold. Snow was seen about as often as a herd of unicorns. That meant the bar would draw the usual drunks and loose women. Any demon's playground.

The bar was a small but strong fortress of black stone, guarded tonight by five spirits from Blasphemy's party. Two were stationed on the corners of its rooftop, armed with black bows and flaming arrows. The other three were posted at the front door, armed with daggers.

Spotting a spirit of lust slithering out from a dark crevice at the base of the wall, nearing a pair of men chugging their eighth beers outside the Saloon, Profanity stalked across the street. The drunkards' souls were already dead. It wouldn't even be a challenge for him to work with Lust and incite them to make lewd comments at the women coming and going, but most of the women were dead too. More than likely, the demons would succeed at provoking nothing more than a verbal confrontation. At best, it would make the humans uncomfortable. It wouldn't kill any souls, and it wouldn't be as offensive to the Enemy as a direct insult.

Profanity was more interested in aiding one of the demons of blasphemy with drawing out violations of the Enemy's Second Commandment from their mouths. It too would be easy work with souls such as these, but it would be more satisfying to him, especially on this particular night. His personal little "fuck you" to both the White Hoc and His cunt Mother.

Profanity signaled one of the demons by the door to come over, indicating the humans. Blasphemy looked to his two comrades standing with him, then back at Profanity, communicating the go ahead. Profanity approached one of the drunks and held his hand over him, slowly piercing his claws into the side of his head, attempting to access and influence the parietal lobe of his brain. This gave him access to the subject's imagination. From there, he introduced images down into the occipital lobe, successfully manipulating its mental images. This would help with steering the human's decision making.

Once he'd discerned the drunk's whims were obeying him, he started introducing more profane language into his thoughts, delighting as he repeated his phrases. When this process had gone on a few minutes, Blasphemy walked over, ready to feed greater curses into the man's vocabulary. The larger demon raised a finger and jabbed a single claw through his forehead, digging into his neocortex to use his memories against him. At the same time, he jammed a claw up through his throat until he reached his amygdala. He stirred the claw around to arouse his sexual appetite, joining this with what Profanity was presenting in his imagination. Together they dragged the soul's language down from simple vulgarities into sacrilegious conversation.

Profanity reveled in their success, cackling with orgasmic pleasure every time the drunk took the Christ's Name in vain. As he howled, he heard Blasphemy's own laughter cut short with an abrupt squeal. He opened his eyes. His partner in crime wore a pained expression.

Both spirits looked down at a blood-red arrowhead protruding from Blasphemy's chest, just before the demon was yanked backwards into an alley by a red chain attached to it, disappearing like a fish on a hook being pulled from a pond. Profanity snarled, wrenching his claws from the drunkard's soul, hunching his shoulders forward, ready for a fight. The two demons of blasphemy who'd remained guard at the door hastened over, demanding what had happened as they drew their knives.

*"There's something in the alley!"* Profanity hissed. *"I didn't get a good look, but it dragged Blasphemy off!"*

The guards proceeded into the darkness. Profanity cowered behind, preferring to let the more powerful intelligences handle the threat. He jumped when he heard a scream from behind him and turned as something rolled up to his feet. It was Lust's head. He caught a glimpse of the serpent's body lying in front of the entrance to the bar before it disintegrated. One of the demons who'd entered the alleyway came rushing back.

*"Lust!"* was all Profanity managed to shriek.

*"Signal the archers!"* Blasphemy barked at his partner.

Getting no response, he turned to lay into him for being slow on the uptake, but realized his comrade hadn't followed him back out of the alley. He was now nowhere to be seen.

*"Where the fuck did he—"* Blasphemy was interrupted by a screech from Profanity.

He jerked his head around in the gangly demon's direction, in time to see him dragged into the abandoned market across the street. A crimson chain with diamond-shaped links as sharp as shurikens had pierced his ankle. There was a flash of white light from inside the market, and the swine's shrieks were silenced. Blasphemy's eyes widened. He recognized those chain links. He knew what kind of prayer formed them. Someone was using the chain of the White Lady against them!

The bar was under attack by Catholics. The kind who actually used the Rosary. And, judging from the number of demons who'd been taken out without a sound, who was to say how many of them were out there? He shot a fireball up to the roof himself. There was no reply from the archers. They were missing in action too, no doubt already extinguished by the bead-mumbling papists. He was alone.

Raising his knife, he prepared to summon more aid from the depths, when he felt a sudden searing pain on his shoulder. He glanced down to watch his own arm disintegrate on the ground, still gripping the knife in its hand. His shoulder was now nothing more than a dripping black stump. Roaring in agony, he attempted to flee the scene. Another fireball shot out of the darkness, destroying the bottom half of one of his legs. He landed on what was left of the knee, as a gliding shape descended on him from above.

It knocked him to the ground so hard, his head cracked the cobblestones. His attacker crouched atop his chest, a cloak settling around him. Apparently, the Immaculate's chain wasn't enough. The fucking bead-mumbler was employing her Brown Scapular too!

"I'm afraid the archers were the first to go," the Catholic said in a metallic voice through the mask of his rosary.

He held up the decade he was praying and jabbed the arrowhead at its end into Blasphemy's throat, wrapping it around twice. The demon felt its links digging into his neck. The armor-clad warrior used the chain and a nearby street lamp like a pulley system to hang him. The spirit grabbed the decade with his remaining hand to keep himself from being beheaded altogether, squeezing his eyes shut in torment as he did. Like all sacramentals, the rosary was scorching to his touch. This torture still being insufficient to satisfy the pious prick, he was backhanded hard enough to make him spin in place. His eyes were forced open by the blow and he got a good look at the soul who'd single-handedly felled every dark intelligence inhabiting the Market Street Saloon.

The man's rosary had formed a protective suit of silver armor around him. It covered every inch of skin. The only things on its outside were the cloak of the Scapular and the wrist bracers of Saint Benedict. Even his eyes were concealed by blue reflective lenses in which Blasphemy could see his own image staring back at him. The mask was round and had no visible mouth, nostrils, or ears on it. But it wasn't smooth. There were grooves going down to the chin that gave it an angular angry look.

The rest of the suit was much the same, resembling robust metal that made the papist appear tall and bulky, but the demon knew it was light and flexible enough to enable the soul within to move about with agility. He'd demonstrated as much by how fast he'd eliminated the other spirits in the area. The only place besides the eyes where the armor's silver color was interrupted was by several slits over the chest and abdominal area, through which Blasphemy could see blue armor beneath. He gritted his teeth tighter, realizing the rosary's centerpiece must be the accursed Medal of the Immaculate Conception! As the rose-proffering bastard stepped back from him, he even noticed that, from farther away, the slits resembled an engraving of a capital A and M overlapping each other.

*Ave Maria!*

Knowing it couldn't be a coincidence, Blasphemy attempted to roar his hatred for the phrase. He couldn't manage it with his attacker dangling him by the neck. Unable to speak, the demon put all his loathing into his stare instead.

"Good," the Catholic said. "I have your attention. You're going to relay a message to your master for me."

Blasphemy tried to answer. The chain was still too taught. The warrior raised the hand in which he gripped his end, allowing the demon's remaining foot to touch the ground just enough for him to speak.

"You're wasting your time," Blasphemy croaked. "I'm from the Ninth Order. You really believe an intelligence of my status has access to the Lord of Hell himself?"

His attacker yanked the chain, pulling him back up into further waves of anguish.

"Wasn't talking about Satan. I want you to deliver a message to Racism, and any other demons who've made themselves at home in the Charleston Diocese. Tell them they better start looking over their shoulders. They're not the only ones going bump in the night anymore." The warrior's masked face drew in close to Blasphemy's. He raised his free hand, forming a ball of fire in it, holding it beneath their chins. "Think that's burned into your memory enough, or should I write it down?"

Understanding the papist meant to brand the message onto his person, Blasphemy struggled to back him off with reassurances of obedience. His words were coming out as nothing more than gurgles through the bladed chain links cutting into him.

The soul turned his head, bringing his ear closer to Blasphemy's mouth. "What was that?"

He pulled the chain tighter, silencing the demon's attempts to speak altogether. Blasphemy's face contorted in rage. He wished every hellish torment on this human who dared treat him as an inferior. But his pride was forgotten when the fireball was smashed into his face, burning half of it beyond recognition. He pleaded for mercy, looking his tormentor in the eyes with his only remaining one, assuring him with a glance he'd do whatever was asked of him if he'd just make the pain stop. The fire was withdrawn, and the demon felt his legs hit the ground as he was dropped. He loosened the links around his neck, panting like a parched dog.

*"Who . . ."* Blasphemy paused, rubbing his throat. It still hurt to communicate. *"Who the fuck are you?"*

The Catholic brought his boot down on Blasphemy's throat, forcing his head to the ground. The movement was so swift, the demon didn't see the blow coming. The warrior crouched over him and answered.

"The Philangelus."

# CHAPTER XIX

## ILLUMINATION AND THE ART OF ANGELIC WAR

Racism landed on Market Street among several of his henchmen who were working on putting out the fire.

So far, their efforts had been useless. What was left of the Saloon continued to blaze no matter what they did. Scowling, the demonic Principality threw his shoulders back in the face of his underlings.

"Well," he demanded, "can someone tell me how the fuck an entire stronghold is destroyed in my territory without any forewarning or leads to show for it?"

"There was one survivor, sire," an Archangel of betrayal spoke up. "We found him hanging by the neck from a streetlamp when we arrived. He met the malefactor. Even spoke to him."

Racism turned to him. *"Where?"*

Betrayal led him away from the crumbling bar to a group of demons gathered around a spirit of blasphemy lying in the road. He was missing a leg and arm, his neck was mangled to the point of near decapitation, and half his face had been burned away.

"All he's said thus far is a name unfamiliar to any of us, mi-lord," Betrayal said. "Thought maybe you'd know something we didn't. The assassin called himself, the Philangelus. Apparently, he was working alo—"

Racism cut him off with a raising of his hand. He looked down at the marred guard of the now-destroyed prison for alcoholics, rousing him with a kick to the side.

*"Who did this?"*

Blasphemy coughed up black blood as he struggled to speak. "It . . . was a Catholic."

*"No shit!"* The infernal prince kicked the familiar again. *"What other type of soul could have pulled this off? Which Catholic, damn it? All those from surrounding parishes with enough humility to destroy a fortress on their own have been accounted for. Do you know how much effort it will take to re-establish our presence here?"*

As if on cue, daylight reigned down on them from the Christ's castles. Blessed angels descended with it. The demons screamed in fear and rage, scattering outward to stay in the shadows.

Racism made sure to grab Blasphemy and drag him along with them to continue the interrogation elsewhere. Once they were safely inside the empty market across the street, he threw the cripple behind him, glaring out at the heavenly spirits. They were guiding the drunks out the bar and back to their homes, no doubt encouraging them to regain their sobriety.

"They'll all be *mine* again by tomorrow night," Racism whispered his seething contempt.

"Don't depend on it," called a voice all-too-familiar to the demonic prince. "This area belongs to me now."

Racism watched his nemesis, Avdiel, land on the border where night met day. Racism approached the edge of darkness, and the two Principalities stood face-to-face.

"You think this pathetic attempt of a conquest anything more than a short-lived victory, bread-worshiper? We'll have regained the Saloon by the end of the week!"

"Maybe . . . maybe not," Avdiel said, smiling. "Still, you might want to allot new guards. I believe the others are on an extended smoke break downstairs. No telling when they'll return."

Racism's temper boiled. He couldn't decide who he'd love the ability to harm more at the moment. The papist who'd robbed him of a stronghold, or the papist-coddler before him.

"We'll see how this new protégé fares when I find him."

"I'll be looking forward to that myself," Avdiel said. "In the meantime, I'd appreciate it if you'd stay away from my bar."

Avdiel spread his wings. Sparks of lightning flew off them. Racism grabbed Blasphemy, and he and his minions fled through the market emerging into the block on the other side. He hurled the handicapped spirit down and harassed him for more information.

*"I want a name for this, Philangelus! A real name! Was it a visitor from another territory of whom I was uninformed? Was it a new convert? Who? Speak, or what he did to you will only be the beginning of your agony tonight!"*

Blasphemy coughed up more blood. "He was armored in a rosary. I never saw his face. But . . . he's left a message for you." The maimed spirit reached up to his neck and indicated several shards of the red chain still embedded in it that the other spirits had been unable to remove. "He said he wouldn't allow me to escape from this pain into the Abyss until I'd personally delivered it to you."

Blasphemy raised his middle and index fingers. They ignited, and he shot the flame at a nearby brick wall. Racism watched with the others as the fire traced out a symbol. A cross with wings for arms that extended straight out then turned downward, making it look like a capital M at the same time. Racism saw the threefold meaning in it. A cross for Christ, an M for Mary, and wings for the angels.

"He said it was his calling card," Blasphemy said, "and that we should grow accustomed to it, because we'll be seeing it again . . . many times. He said that, from now on, you, my baal, should be looking over your shoulder."

Racism spun around, ready to vent his rage upon the familiar, but was surprised to find him smiling.

"I've kept my end of the deal," Blasphemy breathed, and was obliterated by a ball of lightning shot from a nearby rooftop.

The Principality and his minions spread out, drawing their weapons. But Blasphemy's attacker, who'd apparently been watching the whole time, vanished over the ledge. Racism only had time to glimpse a figure with glowing blue eyes, hooded and cloaked in a scapular.

A new player in town.

Jack awoke violently to what he thought must be an earthquake.

It was Chloe shaking him. She stood over him, bouncing up and down like she was dancing on hot coals.

*"It's Christmas! It's Christmas!"* she sang.

While Jack threw on a green T-shirt and red pajama pants, the previous night's exploits came back to him. In the half-conscious state that comprised his usual morning disposition, he couldn't recall the details at first. It was like trying to remember a dream that was vivid at the time but faded more with every second after waking. By the time everyone was downstairs handing out gifts from under the tree, the adventure came back to him in all its glory.

He'd felt unstoppable in the new armor. He thought he might possess a tool powerful enough to rout the demons at school. Maybe even powerful enough to overcome Mephistopheles. And the Blessed Virgin! How could he forget meeting her? Surely her face would pierce any darkness.

"This one's from me, Jack." Chloe handed him a small wrapped box, drawing his attention back to the present with its presents. "Hope you like it! I got it from Song of the Angels. One of the nuns there actually gave it to me when she heard I was shopping for you. She remembered your name."

Jack looked up at her. "Sister Jane?"

"Yeah. That's the one."

Jack smiled, opening the box to find a gold papal crucifix for wearing on a necklace.

"She said it was blessed by Saint John Paul the Great," Chloe told him.

Jack's eyes widened looking down at it, and he laughed.

"Seems like something she'd have handy. Thanks, Chloe!" He hugged her. "I'll put it on my chain right now."

He went to the garage to find needle nose pliers in his dad's tool box, lifting his necklace off and exchanging his cross for the crucifix. He switched to incorporeal sight and drew the mirror from beneath his wrist bracer to see what difference the new sacramental would make. The garage was dirtier than it was through corporeal sight. Its walls were black with soot, like there'd been a fire. It looked and smelled more like a stable than a twenty-first century parking area.

He didn't care. He was anxious to view his gift, even if he wasn't in the sanctified part of the house. He leaned the mirror against the wall and it grew to his size. The crucifix appeared as a gold breastplate and boots rather than silver ones. He pulled his rosary from his pajama pants pocket, watching his soul draw the sword sheathed at his hip in the mirror and hold it toward his reflection. He looked as though he were challenging himself to a duel.

"Not bad, Jack," he said. "Fully armed for war now."

He stuffed the rosary pouch back in his pocket, sheathing it behind his back through incorporeal sight this time. Part of its crimson chain grew from its hilt as he held it against his shoulder blade, wrapping itself over his shoulder and across his torso to reattach itself to the blade near the bottom, securing the weapon in place. He couldn't help laughing at the phenomenon when it happened.

"That's so fuckin' cool!" he said.

Admiring the weapon in the mirror made him want to put it to use once more. He also couldn't wait to see Mary again.

It would be a long time before he did.

Jack visited the cathedral on Christmas Day and every day afterward for the rest of Christmas break looking for the Blessed Virgin, but she was never there.

His heart would always flutter before he stepped through the cascade of holy water at the castle's front doors, hoping she'd be waiting on its other side. He was disappointed every time. The castle's festive mood was at least something to enjoy. Angels and saints flew about singing Christmas hymns that evoked some of his happiest childhood memories. They made him long for the simple faith in the existence of the supernatural he'd possessed then. On New Year's Day, during one of his usual afternoon visits, he knelt in a front pew near the tabernacle to pray for such faith for about the thousandth time in the past few months.

A figure materialized out of the tabernacle's light to stand at the right of the altar before him. It wasn't Jesus or Mary as he'd hoped, but it was one of the next best people. Michael stood barefoot, dressed in his short-sleeved crimson robe and silver breastplate with the tennis-ball-sized ruby embedded on the chest. He'd forgone the crown and cape this time.

"Merry Christmas, Jack."

"And a Merry Christmas to you, my prince," Jack said, as the experience of the supreme intelligence's presence engulfed him.

"I see Our Lady has given you her gift." Michael looked over the weapon attached to Jack's back.

Jack stood and unsheathed it, the chain across his torso flaking into rose petals when he grabbed the hilt. They floated around a moment before disintegrating into crimson sparks, giving off the sweetest of scents. Jack proceeded to flip the broadsword around his wrist several times, as though he'd been an expert dueler for years.

"It's amazing how light it feels!" he said. "I can tell it's heavy by the amount of devastation it inflicts, but you'd think it was made of plastic the way it handles for me."

"It would feel heavy to souls weak in virtue. But don't let it go to your head. Your enemies can wield their weapons with superhuman speed too. You'll need formal training if you're to use that sword properly."

*"Properly?"* Jack swung the blade in front of Michael's face. "I think it was put to pretty proper use on Christmas Eve."

Michael thrust a foot out in front of him, kicking Jack's wrist at just the right point. The blow went through his bracer as if it weren't there, forcing his fingers open, sending the sword flying hilt-first into the intelligence's hand.

"Now," Michael said, waving the blade back in Jack's face, "if I were Mephistopheles, what would the next move be, boss?"

"Okay! Okay! Point made," Jack said, taking a second to process what had happened.

Michael tossed the sword back to him. "Don't misunderstand. You were impressive on Christmas Eve. But you'll need more skill to challenge the greater tempters in the world. That's why I've come. I won't have our Philangelus falling short."

Jack straightened, not only elated the Angelic Prince himself had honored him with his new title, but wondering if he'd understood him right. "Are you saying you'll be . . . *training* me?"

One side of Michael's lips quivered. "You can put it that way if you want. We all have a vested interest in the success of your birthright, and I intend to ensure Mephistopheles fails to stand in its way."

"My birthright? Another vague reference to my 'destiny,' I'm guessing? What is it I'm meant to do in life anyway?"

"When you do it, then I suppose you'll know, won't you?"

Jack sighed. "Yeah, that sounds like the kind of answer I guessed I'd get."

The prince smiled, turning and heading up a spiral staircase to one of the railed walkways. Jack followed.

"In the meantime," Michael said, "we must solidify your faith. You won't be able to accomplish anything without possessing that first. But you're in luck. The Queen of Angels is the most powerful advocate with God you could have asked for in Heaven. She's His highest creature, second only to the Almighty Himself."

They ascended to one of the balconies near the peak of the castle's dome, and Michael took flight up to a doorway that had no stairs leading to it. Landing, he turned and looked back down, beckoning Jack to follow. Jack lifted his sword and morphed it into a red clamp over his wrist bracer, raising his arm and shooting the chain from it like a grappling hook. It pierced the wall just above Michael's head and retracted, pulling him across the castle to join his patron saint on the alcove. When he landed next to him, he threw the chain across his chest. It wrapped itself over one of his shoulders to connect to its opposite end at his hip, fastening itself to his person. The Archangel opened the door, and they stepped into a gigantic round room. There were no windows, but the Eucharist's light pervaded the walls enough that its stone might have been mistaken for a tent.

"This'll serve as a good place to hone your meditation," Michael declared.

*"Meditation?* What am I training to be? Some sort of ninja?"

"Not exactly. Eastern meditations entail emptying the mind of thought in order to reach a higher form of consciousness and connect with an inner divinity, understood in a pantheistic sense. There are several reasons that's both impossible and misleading. At worst, it opens the door to demonic possession. No, what I'll be teaching you is quite the opposite of the pagan practices. The kind of meditation that drives away the evil spirits. The kind attached to the Rosary."

"I didn't know there was any meditation attached to the Rosary."

"I know. A gross negligence on your parents' and past teachers' parts. But, have you never wondered why there's so much repetition in the prayer?"

"Of course. Every time we used to say it at Divine Savior. It's no great secret why most Catholics I know haven't stuck with it. Before incorporeal sight, I'd have called it tedious and boring myself."

"Too true, but the lack of appreciation Catholics have for it stems from their failure to understand it. What you've witnessed so far is only the beginning of the secrets and treasures to be found through it, the majority of which will come to you through the meditation. You wondered what Our Lady was doing on Christmas Eve when she took your *Glory Be* prayer in hand? She was adding the power of her own meditation to it, to make it more glorious before God. A Rosary without meditation is like a body without a soul. The whole point of repeating the same formulas over and over is to allow time for pondering the scenes from the lives of Jesus and Mary. The very climax of salvation history."

"So how do I do it?" Jack asked, anxious to begin his training and rectify past neglect.

The Archangel placed his hands behind his back, circling him as he spoke. "Simple. Choose one of the Mysteries and pray the decade. While reciting its designated prayers, try to think deeply about the event you've chosen. Since sight is the sense humans rely on most, I suggest closing your eyes in order to put yourself there alongside Christ and His Mother. That will help you delve into the meaning of the occasion. Try and discern how it relates in any way to what's going on in your own life."

Jack complied, deciding on one of the Sorrowful Mysteries since he was more familiar with those. "The First Sorrowful Mystery," he prayed. "The Agony in the Garden."

During the *Our Father* and ten *Hail Mary's*, he tried to picture Jesus praying in the garden of Gethsemane before the Jewish soldiers showed up to arrest Him. He thought about how Jesus started sweating blood from the anxiety of knowing what was coming, and his personal relation to the Mystery struck him. It was the kind of agony he felt when trying to work out whether or not God existed, knowing a battle was coming either way. His anxiety had even built upon itself, just as the Messiah's had, because now he questioned his sanity too. Before he knew it, his fingers had reached the tenth bead. Never before had a decade of the Rosary felt so swift and yet unhurried to him.

"Excellent," Michael praised as he finished, startling him into reopening his eyes.

The Archangel was standing before him holding up the crown he'd made with his prayers. The roses were glowing brighter than any he'd produced before.

"See how much more powerful prayer is when it's meditative?"

The prince released his fingers from the wreath, and it levitated above his hands as the roses changed into the largest fireballs Jack had seen. They spread out across the room, acting as ten torches surrounding them.

"Now, try praying another decade like that."

Jack obeyed, beginning the Second Sorrowful Mystery, but was taken by surprise when Michael drew down on him. The Archangel charged, reaching up and grabbing the gold-hilted broadsword from his backside, the blade of which must have been five feet in length. Jack raised the bouquet in his hand, and it morphed into his own broadsword as he attempted to block the attack. He was knocked down on one knee beneath the sheer force of the blow, but had managed to keep his grip on his weapon, holding it against Michael's.

"Well done with maintaining your recitation," the prince commended. "But you allowed me to disrupt your meditation."

*"What are you doing?"* Jack demanded, shocked an angel of Heaven had assaulted him.

"I told you we'd be training. Don't expect the Devil will sit idly by when you recite the Rosary. Not with how much destruction it rains down on his kingdom. He and his minions will do anything they can to distract you from contemplating the Mysteries. You need practice ignoring their temptations. I'll be providing that part for you."

Jack stared at him, astonished. The Archangel smiled, an expression Jack didn't like being on the receiving end of this time.

"Don't worry. As a saint, I could never tempt you toward any sin. But I can deliver mental distractions. You must exercise your mind at blocking out all disruptive thoughts when engaged in Mary's Prayer." He withdrew, allowing Jack to rise to his feet again before raising his weapon. "I'm sure you look upon this sword as a precious relic. The very weapon that defeated Lucifer at the climax of the war in Heaven. But, remember, intelligences don't have bodies and therefore have no need of corporeal instruments. Your charism reveals us wielding weapons only to indicate when we're on the attack. What you see as my broadsword is my intellect. That's what spirits use to engage in battle, and that's why you lost your fight with Mephistopheles."

Jack stared at the giant sword, then looked up at Michael, confused. Michael returned his gaze with a stern expression.

"You've been trying to overcome an angelic intellect by relying on your own. Do that, and you'll fall every time. That's why Mephistopheles laughed when he read you thinking that fighting with him was a mere battle of wits."

Jack remembered the demon's reaction. At the time, he'd thought it was a bluff for his having figured out how to engage in spiritual warfare. Michael nodded, reading his remembrance.

"Only by the Mind of God can a human mind ever hope to conquer an angel's, and His Spirit only enters the heart through the gateway of humility. Humble yourself and He'll inform you of the answers to your opponents' arguments. You'll never outwit them on your own."

"But it isn't just with arguments Mephistopheles keeps beating me. All it takes is his presence to weaken my resolve. It's hard to describe in words, but I get this . . . overwhelming sense of dread and despair when he's nearby, especially if he covers me in that mist of his."

Michael nodded. "Illumination. At least, that's what it would be called if he were still a member of the blessed. It's the primary mode of communication for intelligences."

"And what is it exactly?"

"Angels don't need words to speak. Words are just the symbols of ideas vocalized through bodies and may not convey the thought in its purest form or entirety. Being incorporeal, we commune without such signs and express our ideas in their totality. In this process, an angel opens his mind to another, transferring the whole of an idea directly, without the need for crude mediums. And he doesn't just transfer the idea. He communicates his joys, affections, desires, gratitude, and overall opinion about it in a single moment. So there's more given than through speech. You've experienced it yourself, every time you've met one of the blessed angels. What did you think those overwhelming sensations you've had were? We were speaking to you, in our own way."

"In that case, keep talking!" Jack encouraged.

Michael's lip curved into a half-smile. "The point is, when one of us greets you, we're giving you a foretaste of Heaven, since you momentarily share a portion of our happiness. But, when one from Lucifer's party greets you, you're receiving a taste of his domain. Your charism opens you to all angelic communications. That was why Our Lady granted you the dispensation to speak back to the demons when needed, to cast them away."

"So why's it so radically different every time?" Jack asked. "Even between you and Gabriel, your illuminations don't feel anything alike."

Michael nodded. "The experience will always vary from angel to angel. Remember, we're each a unique species. Do not the various species of animals on Earth each sound different?"

Jack raised his eyebrows and nodded. "Fair point."

Michael tapped the blade of his sword against Jack's, raising it before their eyes. "You needn't worry about being overwhelmed by any devil's threats once you've mastered this weapon. You now bear the sword of Mary Immaculate herself. Keep it always on your person. Wield it every day. And Satan's hordes will fear *you* as you walk this world."

With that, the Archangel swiped the rosary aside and swung for Jack's head. Jack ducked just in time and redoubled his meditation on Christ's scourging, bringing his own sword up to clash with his opponent's. Every time Michael broke through his defenses and struck him, he'd remember something he forgot to do at home, or think some other extraneous thought that had nothing to do with his present endeavor. As soon as he would catch himself and focus again on the Rosary's Mystery, he'd gain the upper hand in the duel. When he reached the end of the decade, he kicked Michael over.

"Very impressive," the prince praised from the floor. "You've picked it up faster than most souls." He kicked Jack's blade aside and back rolled onto his feet.

"Indeed," a gruff voice barked from behind Jack.

He turned to see Saint Benedict had entered the room. The elderly monk was carrying a version of his own medal at his side as large as his person. It looked like a giant shield.

"I haven't seen someone master the art that quickly since the Montfortian," Benedict said.

"If he's such a swift learner, let's see how he fares if we up the game," Joan of Arc said, materializing with Dathiel from the rays of light shining into the room.

"Sounds fun," Dathiel said, extending his knuckle blades.

When Jack began the Third Sorrowful Mystery, Michael, Benedict, Joan, and Dathiel all moved in and attacked him at once. Jack jumped and twisted in midair, avoiding their strikes and contending with swings of his own. Benedict and Joan were even faster than the angels. The little old monk ducked and leapt around like a pinball, even bouncing off the blades of Jack's and Michael's swords. At one point, when Jack thrust his weapon straight toward him, he jumped and ran up its flat side, kicking him in the face, as he sailed over his head to land behind him. Jack spun, bringing his sword slicing around through the air. Benedict split his shield vertically down the middle, creating two semicircular shields on each wrist. He used one to block Jack's blow and the other to ram him backward. Jack lost his grip on his weapon, and it flew from his hand as he landed hard on the stone floor.

He flipped himself to his feet, scrambling to retrieve it. Joan blocked his path. Jack used hand-to-hand combat on her, which he thought might be an even fight since she was unarmed too, but he couldn't land a punch. He wasn't sure he wanted to. He felt strange trying to hit a girl.

"Really?" she whispered, punching him in the neck and kicking him over onto his back again. "Think about that should you try to pull your punches with me again, Philangelus."

Jack didn't get back up for a few moments. The whole fight couldn't have lasted more than twenty seconds.

"Very impressive indeed," Michael mused.

"Doesn't feel that way from down here," Jack grunted, accepting a hand from Dathiel.

"You fared longer than most would have against all four of us," Benedict said, slamming his shields back together.

"I'm sure you were all holding back."

"Did that feel like I was holding back?" Joan asked.

Jack turned on her. "I've seen Dathiel move faster, when he fought the demons at Wando."

"True," Benedict said. "But even at the rate we were going, a beginner shouldn't have held their own against that level of distraction for more than five seconds. It seems you've a natural talent for shutting out the noise of the world and entering an inner spirit of solitude where the whisper of God may be heard. In the cloister we called it, the Monasticism of the Heart. Keep practicing it every day and the demons won't be able to block you from peace for long."

Jack slipped his boot under his sword and kicked it up into his palm. "Still, if I'm to defeat the master of demonic Powers, I'll need more intense training won't I?" He looked at Joan. "Best two out of three?"

She extended her hand outward and drew a sword from the light beams in the room.

Without warning, Jack commenced the next *Hail Mary* and laid into the four saints at once, spinning his blade in circles before him. They were ready. They fanned out in separate directions, forcing him to choose one opponent to pursue.

He decided to go for Michael, figuring he was the biggest threat since he was the largest person. He realized his error a second too late. Michael was the largest but not the most powerful. Benedict and Joan charged him from the sides, disarming and slamming him to the floor together. Without hesitating, Jack launched himself back into the air, hitting Dathiel away, who was coming in swinging. He refocused on his meditation and his sword came hurtling back into his palm.

He clashed blades with the guardian. The angel attempted to use one set of claws to hold the sword, while swiping the other at his throat. Jack met the strike with a block from one of his wrist bracers, locking them into a standstill. Seeing the other three closing in through his peripheral vision, knowing he couldn't stay in the deadlock for long, Jack ran up Dathiel's legs and chest, kicking him under the chin and backflipping out of their way.

All four spirits adapted as swiftly as he had, coming at him from the front in a phalanx next. Jack knew he couldn't stop them all at once. Not as long as his rosary was in the form of a sword. He willed it to morph into the chain and swung it out like a whip, halting their advance. Reaching the *Glory Be* at the end of the decade, he thrust it out to his side. A ball of lightning, ten fireballs, and a ball of white light lit up along its links. The chain now resembled its corporeal form, albeit with shuriken links, lightning, flames, and a blinding star in place of beads and metal circlets.

Jack flung it toward his attackers. The balls launched from it all at once, forcing the saints to scramble in every direction. The explosion of the *Glory Be* didn't seem to have any affect on them. Jack figured its flash only blinded the damned. On the other hand, the lightning and fireballs flying through the air disoriented them long enough to allow him to throw himself feet-first at Michael. He knocked him into the wall, bouncing back off the Archangel into Benedict and Joan, pummeling them to the ground for a change. He looked to Dathiel. The guardian whet his blades up and down against each other, a deviant smile on his face, daring him to attack.

"Now, this is interesting," he taunted.

Jack knew he was stalling to give the other three a chance to regain their footing. He waited until the moment they made their move before throwing out his chain and catching one of Dathiel's arms. He pulled him around in a circle like a wrecking ball, swatting the others away, after which he hurled the guardian into the wall. Dathiel vanished into light before ever making contact, exiting the battle.

"One down," Jack whispered to himself.

"But three to go," Michael bellowed, flapping his wings and rising into the air.

The Archangel rained havoc from above, shooting fireballs and streaks of lightning down, forcing Jack to either dodge or block with his bracers. Benedict split his weapon in half again, charging him, while Joan shrieked a battle cry, bringing her sword to bear. Jack's chain morphed into his suit of armor just in time to protect him from her blade and the sharp edges of the monk's shield.

As the minuscule saint swung its corners at his neck, he ducked and blocked with his own version of the medal. The three earthbound warriors traded blows a few minutes, each side countering most of the other's. Jack would swing his chain upward from his wrist to slice at Michael whenever he could. During the scuffle, the Archangel kept darting down any time an opportunity presented itself, striking him from behind.

On the Fourth Sorrowful Mystery now, Jack focused his mind on Christ bearing the Cross through the streets of Jerusalem, trying to find an opening toward Calvary through the jeering crowd surrounding Him. At last, Jack spotted an opening in his own opponents' defenses. Benedict was about to split his shield into halves again. When he did, Jack grabbed their edges, gripping each with all his might. His suit's gauntlets protected his palms against cuts. With both the monk's arms occupied, Jack headbutted him in the face, repeating the motion several times, his armored mask protecting his own face.

Soon the saint fell to his knees, subdued. And with no time to spare. Jack heard the gust of Michael's wings and the swish of Joan's sword descending on him. He turned to meet the attack, his armor morphing into his broadsword as he did. He slammed it against both their blades so hard, sparks flew.

"Two down, *two* to go," he said.

Michael smiled, a gesture that again made Jack grateful they weren't in a real fight. He leapt, spinning three hundred and sixty degrees into the air, bringing the heel of his gold boot around in a kick. Michael dodged, but Joan took the blow full in the face, disappearing into the light rays of the room as she fell backward.

"Don't think she'll complain of my holding back that time," Jack said. He looked at Michael. "But you've all still been holding back, haven't you? No way

I legitimately defeated saints as powerful as Benedict of Nursia and Joan of Arc. Not when I could barely touch Mephistopheles."

"You underestimate the power of the Rosary," Michael said. "But it's true. We've been going easy for your first time."

"And how intensely would I need to train in order to conquer disbelief entirely? I'm tired of living in doubt."

Michael pulled his sword back, standing upright. Jack did the same.

"Well, if you insist, I could always go harder against you."

The Archangel pointed his sword upward, and its blade changed into pure fire. He flipped it around, leaving a trail of flame in its wake. Jack stepped backward, taken off-guard, feeling the waves of heat wafting off the weapon, almost singing his hair and eyebrows.

"This is how you'll see intellects when their masters are focusing all of their wills against you. The blessed's are aflame when we're at our most loving, zealous, or angry. The damned, when they're at their most wrathful."

"How are the blessed ever angry?" Jack asked. "Isn't that sinful?"

"No. Anger over injustice is a gift from God that compels us to right wrongs. Unbridled anger leads to sin. Just remember, passions must always be ordered by reason and the will to be virtuous. If ever they exceed their control, they become disordered and dangerous."

"So can I do that with my sword then?" Jack lifted his blade and tried to focus it into flame.

"When you've wholly embraced divine faith in your heart. As you already know, that's what sacramentals require to work. You'll be capable of flight at that point too, through your scapular."

*"What?"* Jack looked him in the eyes, then down at his cloak.

"That robe is capable of more than gliding, for the wearer who believes."

Jack attempted to will his scapular into doing just that. It only flared up and billowed as though there were a breeze in the room.

"Your lingering doubts keep you grounded," Michael observed. "I'm confident the frequent use of the Rosary will shake them loose."

"So teach me," Jack challenged. "Teach me how to repel the strongest of temptations against the Faith."

He raised his broadsword and assumed a warrior's stance, preparing to pray the final Sorrowful Mystery. Michael did the same, hunching forward in his direction. When he came at him this time, he was much faster and stronger. Jack's defenses fell and he was laid out on the ground before he even knew they'd begun dueling again. Undeterred, he jumped back into battle the moment he'd recovered his senses, slashing at the Archangel with all his might.

The prince was unperturbed. He countered every one of Jack's strikes as though he were seeing everything in slow motion. He displayed such prowess, it made Jack wonder if he wasn't reading his thoughts and foreseeing each of his moves before he made them.

When the prince ceased countering and began attacking himself, Jack was helpless. He couldn't manage to block a single swing of the intelligence's giant sword. He morphed his rosary back into its armor form just to protect his skin and stay in the fight at all. Even that was of little use. Michael reared his weapon back and took a full swing at his chest, sending him sailing toward the ceiling and crashing through it, landing on the roof of the castle outside. He'd reached the end of the decade, but hadn't managed a moment of meditation on the Crucifixion of Christ. Each strike of the inflamed blade had bombarded his mind with a plethora of distractions.

Michael flew up through the hole he'd left in the roof before it resealed itself. Jack staggered to his feet, feeling the full weight of his mental strain now. They were standing on a large platform, higher than every other section of the castle's rooftop except the steeple and towers. Hundreds of angels circled overhead, guarding the airspace against winged intruders. Seeing the two warriors emerge, they began landing along the towers and walls to watch the duel. Some flew off to alert spirits on the ground of the spectacle. Jack could hear them whispering among themselves, calling out to those at the bishop's house.

"Prince Michael's fighting the Philangelus!"

Hearing the call, more saints and angels scrambled up to the castle. His zeal renewed at the prospect of giving them a show, Jack faced down the Archangel once more, raising his hands in a fighting stance. He slowed his breathing, attempting to regain his concentration before beginning the *Hail, Holy Queen* and concluding the Rosary.

Reading what he was feeling, Michael laughed. *"Show off!"*

*"Says the one holding the flaming sword?"* Jack yelled back.

Laser beams shot from Jack's suit. Wasting no time, he lunged forward, colliding with Michael a moment after the rays hit him. He used his wrist bracers to counter the prince's weapon, and—though he by no means won the battle—he remained on his feet this time. When he made the closing sign of the cross, the Archangel sheathed his broadsword across his back, extinguishing its flame. The spirits around them cried their enthusiasm, as though cheering on a favorite sport. Both Jack and Michael glanced around, chuckling at the scene.

"'Merry Christmas, ya filthy animals,'" Jack quoted *Home Alone* under his breath.

"'And a Happy New Year,'" Michael finished the quote in a perfect imitation of the elderly gangster's voice from the movie.

Taking half a second to recover from being spooked by the prince's trick, Jack glared at him and bellowed a laugh. "Don't do that again!"

He jumped as he felt a vibration on his leg, worried it had caught fire without his notice. But when he looked down, there was nothing there. He realized the sensation wasn't coming through incorporeal sight. It was his phone ringing in his pocket.

Switching to corporeal vision, he pulled it out to see it was his father calling, probably wondering when he was planning to come home. He couldn't blame him. He was astonished at the time he saw on the phone's clock. He'd been kneeling in the church for a straight hour. He rose to leave, but his legs felt as though they'd been plastered in place by a cast. He had trouble unbending them. He hadn't even noticed the pain with all he'd been doing through his beads. He sat back down to rest a minute. Glancing to ensure no one else was in the church, he answered the phone.

"Hey, Dad. Sorry, I lost track of time."

"You're still at the cathedral?" Dale asked.

"Yeah, but I'll head home now."

"No rush. Dinner's not for an hour. Just checking to see where you were."

"Thanks. I'll be home soon. Love you!"

"Love you."

Jack hung up, massaging his knees. They were still as stiff as boards. He decided to pray one more decade of the Rosary while they recovered. Switching back to his other sight, he found himself inside the castle before the tabernacle again. Michael was gone.

He raised the crown of roses in his hand, closed his eyes, and attempted to quiet his mind, directing his thoughts to choose one of the Twenty Mysteries. Before he could pick, one was announced for him. Hidden somewhere within the light emanating from the tabernacle, Dathiel's voice rang out sonorous and solemn. Jack had never heard him speak in such a manner before.

*"The First Joyful Mystery. The Annunciation!"*

Jack's vision went black and he seemed to lose all connection with his five senses. He slipped physically out the pew and slumped to the floor.

# CHAPTER XX
## THE LOCUTION

The darkness surrounding Jack seemed impenetrable, as though no sights, sounds, or smells could ever reach him through it.

He had the distinct impression it stretched onward for eternity. No light! There was no light in this place! Panic grabbed hold of his stomach and started twisting. At least he could feel that. So he couldn't be dead. He wanted to scream out for help, scream with all the power in his lungs. He couldn't muster the slightest sound. It was as if he didn't possess a body to do it. He felt trapped in his own mind.

After a minute of nothing but this insanity inducing blackness—or maybe several minutes, or hours—some form of perception returned to him. He thought he could see something. An outline in front of him. Of what, he wasn't sure. It was big. Maybe brown in color. It towered over him, stretching in all directions. It originated from the ground, if there was a ground in this void. It had multiple arms, like a giant octopus. A sea monster emerging from beneath the depths of the blackness to consume him. But there were hands at the ends of its tentacles. At least, he thought they were hands. They had too many fingers, and the fingers were growing more arms and hands from them.

And they were reaching for him!

But, they weren't moving. They were stiff, as if they'd been paused by some cosmic remote control.

*Wait,* Jack thought. *They are moving a little.*

The longer he stared, he saw them sway back-and-forth as though there was a breeze. They weren't arms or tentacles. They were branches. He was facing a gnarled tree, ancient looking and bigger than any he'd ever seen, even the redwoods outside San Francisco he'd visited as a child. The tree came more into focus and he saw multicolored fruit hanging from its branches. All dull in color. The fruits were rotten. He was surprised there were any fruits growing from it at all. The tree had no leaves on it.

*The Tree of the Dead,* he thought.

That was the impression it gave off. He felt as though the nothingness of the void was emanating from it. It reminded him of how he'd felt staring into Delusion's open cape. The tree grew clearer still and he realized it was being lit by something behind it that was growing brighter. He couldn't move his legs to walk around and see what or who it was. At last, the silence too was broken for him. But the moment it was, he wished for the dead hush of nothingness again. The voice that spoke was so terrible, he knew neither the deepest darknesses of an abyss nor the luminescent heights of the heavens would ever be able to escape it if they tried.

*"I WILL PUT ENMITIES BETWEEN THEE AND THE WOMAN, AND THY SEED AND HER SEED! SHE SHALL CRUSH THY HEAD, AND THOU SHALT LIE IN WAIT FOR HER HEEL!"*

When the voice issued its threat, a comet of light exploded into the darkness through the tree. It shot over Jack's head, almost singing his hair, pulling him in its wake like a minnow that had just been passed over by a thrashing great white shark. He was dragged along at what he felt must be the speed of light. Once more he wanted to scream, but it was taking all his focus just to manage his equilibrium. He didn't know which way was up, down, or sideways. After an indeterminate amount of time being hauled behind the comet, he slowed to a stop. He'd been squeezing his eyes shut, but they popped open at the sound of thunder erupting below him.

No, not thunder. Crashing waves. Waves rising hundreds of feet high to swallow him. He was hovering in midair over a vast ocean. He kicked his legs and flailed his arms, managing a scream at last, his senses returning to him in full now. He thought he'd fall atop the rolling mountains, but he stayed suspended thirty feet above their white caps. He couldn't get used to the feeling of dangling from nothing. He screamed a few more times. It was like falling without ever hitting a bottom. Yet he wasn't moving at all.

*"Help! God help me! God, please, help!"* he screamed.

*"He is, Jack!"* a familiar and oh-so-welcome voice yelled back from somewhere behind him. *"That's why you're here."*

Dathiel flew around to his front, hovering in place above the waves with him. Jack reached out for him.

"You don't need me to hold you up. You're not really over an ocean right now. Just seeing it. You're having a locution."

*"What location?"* Jack yelled, not hearing him well over the roiling sea.

*"A locution,"* Dathiel corrected. *"A divine vision."*

Jack kept flailing and reaching out for the angel. Dathiel flapped himself nearer, taking him by the hand and flying them higher, away from the sound of the crashing waves. The wind was still loud, but Jack could hear better now.

*"Where are we?"* he demanded. *"What's happening?"*

"In the past," Dathiel said. "Seeing it anyway."

Jack's adrenaline was still pumping. He couldn't think straight, much less listen. Dathiel put a hand on his chest, and Jack felt his pulse slow to a normal pace within three seconds. There was no way he could have calmed it so quickly on his own.

"Feel better now?" the angel asked.

"Yeah." Jack gulped his breaths slower. "That's a handy trick."

Dathiel chuckled, shaking the hand he'd touched Jack's chest with. "You don't say."

Jack laughed. He needed it after the adrenaline crash. He looked down at the waves beneath them.

"So . . ." he gulped another breath of air, "you said this is a vision?"

"Yes."

"That voice I heard, and the tree I saw . . . was that . . . was it . . .?"

The guardian nodded.

"So what was the comet? Don't remember that in the story."

"The Promise of Redemption moving across time to find the one worthy to fulfill It."

"Where's this then?" Jack indicated the ocean beneath them.

"The better question would be, when is this. And it's easier if I just show you."

The angel held Jack's shoulders from beside him and spread his wings, moving them over the waters, in what direction, Jack couldn't say. There was no land in sight. Dathiel sped them up, the waves soon becoming a blur beneath Jack's feet, until they reached a reef, stopping to hover thirty feet offshore. An enormous wooden ship had crash-landed among its rocks with several people standing outside it, one of them an elderly man bowing before a makeshift altar. There was a fire burning something on top of it. Jack's eyes widened. He knew where in history he was now.

"The only people left to carry on the Promise," Dathiel said.

Jack initiated incorporeal sight, curious if it would work within what was already a vision. It did. It revealed hundreds of angels surrounding the small band on the shore. The Promise hovered over the altar, now in the form of a Luminescent Orb. It entered the man before It, and Jack's head fell back on his shoulders. His mind felt like it was being inundated with new information which seemed to come out of nowhere. He understood that God established a covenant with the people on the beach. The World Covenant.

Unlike the one He would make with the Patriarch Abraham centuries later, this one was to be between Him and all of humanity. Its symbol would be the rainbow. Its object, the bestowing of material blessings upon mankind. Rains and the four seasons would be provided for the crops, to give people nourishment to their hearts' desire. This was so humanity would recognize the Deity's presence and laws through nature alone.

Time sped up around the two gazers from the future. Jack would have started panicking again, but he didn't have time. He was too busy taking in all the new information flooding his brain. He saw the blessed angels taking part in the World Covenant. The Principalities were assigned as guardians to the various nations and cities after their dispersion from the Tower of Babel. Along with the Archangels and Angels, they were to lead pagans to God through natural revelations, so as to prepare them for His eventual arrival into their own flesh.

Jack understood this was the answer to an objection he'd had about belief in the God of the Bible the day he'd learned of Chuck's death. That ancient pagan mythologies had similar creation and redemption stories to the Sacred Scriptures of Catholicism, which they predated. Jack saw it was the blessed intelligences who were responsible for this. Knowing what God had planned, they'd prepared men and women's imaginations to accept the strange truths of the future Revelation by influencing them into coming up with similar tales beforehand.

They accommodated primitive peoples by leading them to contemplate God as best they could, through worship of the sun, moon, and stars—objects holding the most preeminent place to corporeal sight. The sun was to be held in particular esteem, for it gave light, warmth, and life to the body, as the Son of God would later do for souls. Thus, the elements of astronomy were to serve as natural sacraments for mankind, to whet his mind for the supernatural ones to come.

The heavenly spirits also had a hand in the principles of occult philosophies, such as those of Ancient Egypt and the astrology of the Chaldeans. Even the most perverse pagan practices contained vestiges of divine truth thanks to their intervention. In his mind's eye, Jack witnessed the angels deliver philosophy to the Greeks, enlightening in particular the minds of Socrates, Plato, and Aristotle. Afterward, they brought the Romans their ideas of law, who then spread it across the known world by their conquests. They civilized it, securing the highways and political connections between kingdoms that would one day be taken advantage of by Saint Paul and the Apostles to spread the New Faith like wildfire.

Jack understood that, as horrible as so much of world history was, without the ever-vigilant guidance of the blessed intelligences, it would have been far more tragic. Every person's life far worse. He laughed as the centuries played out before him, thinking again of Satan's unoriginality. Even the most depraved belief systems he'd managed to instill in mankind hadn't escaped his Enemy's fingerprint. No matter how hard the demons tried, they couldn't pry their Creator's influence out of human nature all the way. But Jack's laughter was cut short when his vision pulled back to give him a bird's-eye view of history.

He saw how much more successful the devils were than the angels at keeping humanity's attention. The diabolic intelligences distorted the holy ones' victories at every turn, inciting humans to instead worship them as divine idols, practicing the most abominable rituals in their honor. Sometimes they'd even induce them to sacrifice their children to them. Jack saw in the most literal sense the desperate need for the Promise to find Its Promised Woman. Man's corrupted nature was too easily induced to darkness. It needed aid from within. That was where its wound festered. Aid from without, even from angelic beings, was never enough.

Dathiel grabbed Jack's shoulders again, speeding them through time.

When the blur around them died down, Jack and Dathiel were hovering over an island in the middle of a wide river.

Intuition, or whatever this automatic knowledge was, flooded Jack's mind once more. He understood he was seeing a time eight hundred years before Christ, during the lifetime of the Prophet Isaiah. But this island was far from the Land of the Israelites. It looked tropical. Dathiel propelled them downward, and they glided weightless into a strange looking building, semicircular at the back and triangular at the front. It had moss growing on its roof and down its walls. There were hundreds of people standing below them inside, dressed in foreign attire. They might have been Indian. Jack wasn't sure.

"Can they see us?" he whispered.

"No. You're seeing things that have already happened. Just think of yourself as Scrooge right now, if I were the Ghost of Christmas Past."

"So who are these people?"

"Pagans. This is their temple, where they worship a false god I believe you'll recognize."

Dathiel turned him to face a giant statue against the wall while the worshipers below all knelt before it. Jack drew a sharp breath. The idol was a decrepit looking crow, but he couldn't mistake the resemblance to the demon who'd clearly instigated its construction. Switching to incorporeal sight, he saw Mephistopheles himself standing before his adorers, wearing the grin Jack had come to fear and despise so much. Information flooded Jack, and he learned the people had just won a great battle, attributing the victory to the evil spirit. They were planning to build a new temple in his honor. Mephistopheles was about to speak through the statue and instruct them on what to make, when Michael crashed through the ceiling.

The Archangel carried a gold staff with him, which he used to strike the demon across the back and force him facedown onto the stone floor. The prince of fallen Powers writhed under the Prince of Heaven's strength, but he couldn't get out from under him. Michael coerced him to instead tell the people to consecrate the temple in honor of a Virgin who would one day appear on Earth. It was to her the victory against their oppressors was due.

Time jumped, and the two visitors from the future beheld the new temple years later. The statue of the crow had been torn down and replaced with one of a winged virgin bending over a small ship that contained a child wrapped in swaddling clothes. Jack watched the pagans below him bowing to their new statue and felt a great swell of pride in his patron saint for bringing them that much closer to a worship truly divine. He took a look through incorporeal sight to see if Mephistopheles was witnessing his loss and smiled. The demon was present, held from the shoulder by Michael, who was forcing him to look.

Time shot forward again, disorienting Jack.

When he recovered, Jack found himself looking at a forty-four-year-old Nazarene woman, again not knowing how he knew these details, but feeling sure of them nonetheless.

It was midnight. The woman was kneeling under an oak tree that overshadowed her house. The tree curved over her, Jack, and Dathiel to form an arch, its branches meeting the ground to sprout more branches, framing numerous arbors around the area. The light of a full moon illuminated the scene in white. Other than that, the only light around came from a lantern hanging on a branch beside the woman.

It was enough for Jack to see her sadness. She'd been crying. He could tell from the red around her puffed out eyes. Her husband had suffered a recent humiliation at the Temple, rebuked by one of the priests for his lack of children. She wiped more tears from her eyes, feeling at fault.

She'd taken him to bed when he arrived home to console him. Now that he was asleep, she'd snuck outside to weep her own humiliation away at her favorite spot under the oak. Her weeping became a prayer of lamentation to God. Though it was in a different language, Jack understood it as though it were spoken in English.

His whole form went rigid when he heard a sonorous voice answer it. The woman's head popped up in fear too. Gabriel appeared atop the highest branches of the tree, his words echoing from everywhere at once.

"Don't be afraid. The Virgin Mother whose womb will open the Heavens is now yours."

The moment he said this, Jack saw a blinding light begin to radiate from within the woman next to him. The same shade of light he'd seen emanating from the gazebo in the rose garden on Christmas Eve.

He realized he'd just witnessed the Immaculate Conception.

Dathiel genuflected at the moment, and Jack followed suit.

A reverential hush had fallen over nature itself. All the birds and bugs had stopped their sounds at the same time. The world was silent.

It was several minutes before Dathiel spoke. "The Almighty Trinity exerted more care in the forming of the New Eve's tiny body than in the forming of the stars, planets, and moons across all the galaxies of material creation." He glanced up at the arbors curving around the scene like protective arms. "Fitting she should be conceived beneath an oak tree too. Oak's an old symbol for the Father that represents strength."

Jack watched the pulsating light shining from within Saint Anne's womb, mesmerized. He imagined its rays would warm him at their touch if it wasn't a vision he saw them through. He felt privileged. The wonder was unseen by all human eyes but his own. Not even the Blessed Virgin's mother could see it. But he wasn't alone in being its witness, for her conception hadn't gone unnoticed by the spiritual realm.

He saw a host of one thousand angels from what must have been all the Nine Orders surrounding the scene. They were led by Gabriel, who was visible only through Incorporeal sight now. All but the Archangel were wearing badges of various symbols on their chests and glowing wreaths of flowers on their heads. Many of them resembled young men. Others were less humanoid. The eleven closest to Gabriel stood out most. These wore crowns of either precious metals or stones and carried palms.

Jack recognized Monsignor Bamonte's wolf-like guardian, Lupe, among them. Another was a burly giant of at least twenty feet, with a wingspan that must have extended beyond forty. His limbs were as broad as tree trunks. A third had blue skin, white hair, purple wings, and yellow eyes, more resembling a visitor from Mars than an angel. This one appeared more feminine than masculine. A fourth appeared as a living rosebush, sporting wings made of branches with leaves in place of feathers. It moved about on its roots instead of legs, using them like tentacles. Even its face was composed of different types of shrubbery.

There was a Cherub too, but unlike those Jack had met on Christmas Eve, this one had only one face, that of a man. He stood upright on two legs, with his abdominal area covered by a lion's mane. His arms were covered in short hair of a lighter brown, and his hands were clawed. His legs and feet were that of an ox, and he had four golden eagle wings on his back.

Despite the outlandish appearance of these five, Jack's attention was drawn more to the Seraph of the group and three feminine looking Archangels. At least, he guessed they were Archangels, considering they had gold hair like Gabriel. The Seraph looked Jamaican to him. He had cream-colored skin and dreadlocks made of flame hanging down past his shoulder blades, with the goatee on his chin burning as well. His serene demeanor was hypnotic, and Jack couldn't help staring. The Seraph's eyes would change color on occasion, followed by his robe, hair, and goatee. They cycled through every shade in the spectrum, including the new ones incorporeal sight had introduced to Jack.

"Mary Immaculate's guardians," Dathiel said, noticing where he was looking. "Each selected to be her protector based on his love and reverence for her from the first we intelligences learned of her coming."

Jack looked at him. "She had a *thousand* guardian angels?"

"We're talking about the creature Satan would do his utmost to murder upon learning her identity. So, yes, the Father spared no expense when providing for her safety." Dathiel turned to the crowd of his angelic brethren. "Of the first nine hundred, a hundred were selected from each of the Nine Choirs. Eighteen more were tasked with carrying messages directly from her to God and vice versa. Your spiritual director's guardian, Meriel, was among that group. Our Lady employed their services when she was unsure what to do in a given situation.

The next seventy were some of the highest Seraphim, among them the Sixty Strong Ones mentioned in the Song of Songs, who guarded the chamber of King Solomon from the terror of the night. Monsignor Bamonte's guardian, Jehoash, was among those. They also distinguished themselves by their valiance during the war with Lucifer and his apostates. The remaining ten bore a deep love for the Word in His Humanity. Nuri was part of that group.

Last of all, Gabriel and the eleven you see standing with him would become Our Lady's closest confidants. They'd later be mentioned in the twenty-first chapter of The Apocalypse as guarding the twelve gates of the Holy City. In the modern day, they protect any souls who call upon the intercession of the Blessed Virgin."

"They have some strange appearances," Jack said. "Just when I was starting to think I'd already seen the weirdest ways you intelligences could look. No offense."

Dathiel smiled. "Hardly. Those eleven look so eclectic because there's at least one angel from each of the Nine Orders in their group. The one who looks like a living rosebush is a Throne. The giant, one of the Dominations. And the one you thought an extraterrestrial, a Virtue. They're each the Heads of their respective Orders. That's why you feel most drawn to Cordignis there." Dathiel indicated the Jamaican looking Seraph. "He's Prince of the Seraphic Order."

Jack was astonished at being privileged to see the mightiest angels from God's kingdom altogether. He wondered how overwhelming their presence would feel if he were meeting them in the present. He was also surprised to learn Lupe was the highest of Heaven's Powers. No wonder the wolf had affected him so much when he'd met him! How had Monsignor Bamonte come by so many of the most powerful angels as his personal bodyguards? And all four of them selected from the Blessed Virgin's personal band?

Jack gazed at the saint whose child shined from within, pondering these questions. He must have stared for several minutes, but Dathiel didn't seem to mind. He kept quiet while Jack meditated. The scene was peaceful.

Jack found himself not wanting to leave it, but the vision shifted, taking the future gazers out into the night.

Jack and Dathiel circumnavigated the planet, the angel showing Jack many of the spiritual reverberations caused by Mary's Conception.

Their first stop was the pagan temple where Mephistopheles had once reigned. Five virgin prophetesses hastened to the priests, announcing they'd received visions of a Virgin arriving on Earth whom many gods had descended to greet, while other gods were fleeing before her in great lamentation.

Mephistopheles was there. He too fled at hearing the prophetesses, intending to raise an alarm across the demonic kingdom. He stopped on the river's shore before taking flight. His demonic comrades already knew. Even nature itself stirred with excitement. He sensed its change, not only in the animal kingdom but the plant.

Jack witnessed similar reactions happening everywhere on Earth. He and Dathiel visited nations of diverse religious beliefs. They were all affected in one way or another by the ripple effect emanating from Nazareth. Pagan oracles attested to either visions or dreams of a powerful Woman descending from the heavens. The hearts of the just sang for a reason they didn't understand. Notorious sinners were agitated within their minds by either fear or sorrow. The entire world had felt the arrival of its Mistress.

Jack could see why. Angels who'd held back their indignation toward their fallen brethren for millennia while they deceived and tortured souls were now driving the demons out all over the globe. Entering the Promised Land again,

Jack saw demoniacs running through the streets, their possessing demons stirred up by the angels' activity. The demons were hurling their vessels' bodies from side-to-side, shrieking and raving.

Growing up a horror fan, Jack had seen demonic possession portrayed in plenty of movies. Some had even disturbed him, despite how desensitized he'd become to the genre over the years. But he'd never seen any real possessions before, especially not up close.

The faces of the men and women running past him and Dathiel kept shapeshifting into animalistic countenances. Some of them crawled and contorted their way across the streets, drooling spittle like ravenous hyenas. When they came close, Jack would draw back and squeeze his eyes shut. It didn't help. The locution was being presented directly to his mind's eye. He couldn't look away from the scene, no matter how much he wanted.

Some of the demoniacs' voices were shifting between human and subhuman. Sometimes they'd howl. Other times they'd speak at pitches too high or low to be natural.

One woman bounded past Jack on all fours like a cheetah, squealing, *"We must surrender! We must go out!"*

Nearing a large edifice Jack understood to be the Temple of Jerusalem, Dathiel ushered him into a building down the street from it that served as a prison for madmen and the possessed. Its caretaker was a tall, white-haired man with a long beard and mustache. The current high priest of the Temple. He hardly seemed priestly at the moment.

He was running about trying to calm the inmates, half of whom had begun wailing at midnight. A prophetess who served as a teacher for the young girls living at the Temple had roused him to the disturbance, and they were both now trying to quell the uproar, to little success. The demoniacs kept riling the insane back up every time they'd subdued them. At last, the priest approached the main instigator's cell, questioning him about his unrest.

"I must flee!" the possessed man cried in a high-pitched voice.

"All of us must flee!" a different, guttural voice said from his mouth.

Multiple voices then screamed from his throat together, "A Virgin has been conceived! Don't you understand? *A Virgin has been conceived!*"

Curious as to what the demons meant, the priest decided to humor them. He opened the cell.

The man dashed past him, running into the streets, his possessors thrashing him about all the while, continuing to cry out in unison, *"There are too many angels! So many angels on Earth! They torment us! We must go out! We must go out now! Nevermore! We may nevermore enter into men! Fear the Virgin! Fear the Virgin!"*

Pursuing him outside, the high priest prayed over the man. The spirits left him after only a moment of this, lifting him several feet into the air and throwing him down on the road as they did. Simultaneously, all the other spirits possessing people in the prison departed. The building fell silent.

Approaching him afterward, the prophetess confessed to the priest she suspected the demons weren't lying. She'd had a vision of her own just before their commotion began that a child of great importance was being granted to Israel that night. The priest pondered whether or not she was right.

In all his years, he'd never seen such activity in Israel as he'd seen on this night.

Time passed before Jack's eyes, as the vision moved him and Dathiel up the street to the Temple itself.

The huge shrine crowned the top of a hill with a steep cliff to one side that dropped into a dark gully below. It was rectangular and had courtyards around the main building. It had high thick walls surrounding it lined with porticoes and lookout towers, giving Jack the impression more of a fortress than a house of worship.

He entered with the angel into this shrine and was led up thin windy passages and twisting staircases to a small corner room. It was plain and contained a single lamp that was no more than a candle. Jack realized years must have passed in the time it had taken him and Dathiel to come up the street, because the Blessed Virgin was sitting in the room reading. She was younger than when he'd seen her on Christmas Eve, but he recognized her.

The locution acted on his brain again, and he knew what Mary was studying. The writings of the Prophet Isaiah, about the Virgin who would be with Child. She couldn't figure out how God was going to enact this wonder. It had been the focus of many meditations through her years as a Temple Maiden. She'd often asked her guardian angels about it, but it was the one question for which she never received a satisfactory illumination from them.

At the moment, she was praying she'd be worthy to live in the time when this Holy Virgin walked the Earth. She longed for the opportunity to kneel before her and adore the Divine Hero in her lap. The very reason she'd vowed to remain a virgin herself was because God would choose one for His Mother. She wanted to imitate her, even serve as her slave if God would permit.

Jack smiled at the irony of her prayer. He was glad to see her again, if only in a vision. She exuded such simple innocence. He wanted to stay here with her. He turned to ask Dathiel if they could, but the angel had disappeared from his side.

Jack went out into the hall looking for him, glancing down over the balcony beside it. It overlooked the main chamber of the Temple, where several priests were praying their evening devotions. This too was a peaceful scene. Fires burned from torches on the walls. Maidens went about the last of their duties before retiring. Everything was calm.

When the last of the priests left the chamber, all the torches extinguished at once.

Jack blinked a couple of times, thinking the vision had shifted again, but it was just taking a moment for his eyes to adjust to the darkness. The one remaining source of light was now the candle burning inside the Virgin's room. It flickered violently, but stayed lit.

Jack didn't like the feeling of foreboding that came over him. His insides started doing full somersaults when a hiss echoed off the walls. It sounded like a serpent at first, but became the snarl of a wolf. He saw something move in the chamber below. Maybe just a shifting of shadow. He couldn't tell. Whatever it was, it ascended one of the spiral staircases leading to his hall. Then another. Jack thought it might be one of the priests come out to investigate the sudden dousing of the torches. But he was wrong. Very wrong.

He stepped backward into Mary's cell toward the candle's light when the hissing silhouette reached the top of the staircase. It was standing at the opposite end of the hallway from her door now. All Jack could tell in the dim light was the specter was hooded and tall, so tall its head nearly scraped the ceiling. Eight feet maybe.

He wasn't cold, but a shiver sprinted up and down his flesh. A shiver with talons for toenails. Despite knowing all he saw was only a manifestation of the past, he didn't want the thing in the hall to draw any closer. The wraith approached the cell, hunched forward and stalking, as though it were sniffing out prey.

It made no sound with its footfalls. When it reached the threshold, Jack had drawn several feet back into the room. The specter's frame filled the doorway, blocking out any moonlight leaking its way in from outside. Jack could see it more clearly now. It wore a black robe, its face shrouded from sight under its hood. There was a red hue glowing where a face should have been. Blazing red eyes stared out from the haze, dark pupils in their centers. The eyes were the only other source of light besides the candle in the room. They were wide, boring down on Jack with a look of malicious insanity. His own grew wide, fearing the wraith could see him after all.

It towered over him like some fantastical villain from a primordial nightmare. The only sound he heard was its ragged breaths. They filled his ears, rattling his eardrums before traveling down his spinal cord to tickle the back of his neck, sending the hairs there fleeing outward. The fiend sounded rabid, ready to move in for the kill at any moment. Jack jumped back to the corner of the room, drawing his sword, ready to slash his way out if he had to. The wraith's glare hadn't tracked him. He followed its trajectory and realized the monster had been staring through him, into the eyes of Mary knelt on the floor. The Virgin had been granted an angelic visitor, but not the kind who came bearing consolation. She stared back at the wraith, no hatred in her expression, but no fear either.

"Accuser," she said in a neutral tone that matched her gaze.

Jack couldn't tell if it was a greeting or a mere acknowledgment of the dark figure's presence. The enemy's eyes squinted, perhaps in fury at her lack of dread, perhaps in pleasure at his reputation preceding him. When the visitor from Hell tilted its head, Jack thought it was smiling under its hood, as if savoring the moment.

The menace reached an arm across its torso. When its hand passed through the candle's light, Jack saw it was humanoid but had blood-red skin and sharp, two-inch black talons for fingernails. The monster pulled a black-hilted sword that formed from all the shadows in the room. Its blade solidified into shiny onyx before morphing into pure flame, throwing the fiend's shadow up on the walls and ceiling of the hallway behind it.

It lunged across the room past Jack and brought the broadsword down with all its might on the Blessed Virgin's head.

The child closed her eyes as its fire broke over her face. But, although her attacker applied more and more pressure on it, attempting to split her skull down the middle, the weapon couldn't break her. The strike appeared to have no effect on her soul. The wraith lifted the sword and slammed it down again, and again. Its opponent remained unmoved, unscathed . . . and unafraid, resigning herself to silent prayer. After several more futile efforts on its part, Mary opened her eyes, sending the monster retreating back into the hallway by the gesture.

*"Who are you?"* Jack heard it whispering in a guttural voice. It backed farther down the hall. *"WHO ARE YOU?"* it kept demanding, until it sunk out a window.

Hardly believing his own courage, Jack ran after it and looked down the Temple's outer wall. The wraith climbed backward all the way into the gully below, disappearing into the shadows.

Jack sensed it wouldn't be the creature's last attack on Mary.

The locution accelerated time, shooting Jack skyward through moonlit clouds.

Dathiel rejoined him, and they stopped before a pair of golden gates. Jack recognized them as the same ones where he'd met Michael. He wanted to ask

Dathiel why he'd disappeared on him. But before he could, the gates opened and full noon poured down into the night sky. It wasn't the sun illuminating the clouds. Jack closed his eyes and covered his face at the sudden transition.

"Gabriel," he heard three voices that sounded like three cracks of thunder call in unison.

Jack's muscles stiffened, recognizing one of them as the voice he'd heard at the beginning of the locution. He couldn't say whether the other two sounded young or ancient. The three together evoked a sense of agelessness. Gabriel sped past, making Jack jump, before disappearing through the gates into the light.

"The time has come to heal the folly of Adam and Eve," Jack heard the voices tell the angelic prince. "To break the hold of the fallen Lucifer over the Earth. Go now to the Virgin Mary in the house of Nazareth. She it is whom we choose as Mother of God. But . . . she must choose this fate of her own accord. As the fall of man was a free act begun with the consent of a woman, so his Redemption must also begin with feminine consent."

The first voice spoke the next sentence alone. "My Word is to have a Mother without a father on Earth, as in Heaven He has a Father without a Mother."

The third voice followed up. "Therefore will I conceive Him, for she is My Bride, and Mine alone."

The second voice spoke the final proclamation. "As Eve bore a forbidden fruit to man to condemn him, so Mary shall bear Me as the Promised Fruit of her womb to save him. From this union, humanity will inherit thrones even My Nine Orders know not."

Gabriel came skyrocketing back out the gates in a downward glide and Jack's breath caught in his throat. The Archangel looked more godlike than any other time he'd seen him. His bearing had become grave but majestic. Even his flying seemed more elegant. He now wore a diadem around his head and his robe was shifting through sharp shades of the rainbow. There was a gold cross encased on his breast, shining too much for Jack to look at long. As he soared over, Jack's head filled up with his mood. He'd never been so joyful in all his existence before that night. He'd never imagined it would be him who'd get to announce to the Immaculate Lady her destiny. And not just the announcing of a destiny, but the most joyful message an intelligence had ever delivered to Earth.

He'd been certain that, if not given by God Himself, the privilege would have fallen to Michael. Yet the Father had sent him. The Deity's voice had followed on his heels during his descent through the worlds of angels, proclaiming the time of the Incarnation had arrived at last. Jack heard the Nine Orders cheering their response, sounding like a crowd of billions at a concert. When Gabriel passed over the future gazers, Mary's other nine hundred and ninety-nine guardians flew out the gates to join his flight. They accompanied him until he reached Nazareth, where they spread out to clear the town of any demonic spirits. The Archangel himself approached the home of the Virgin.

It was the same one her parents had lived in. Jack recognized the oak tree beside it. He guessed she was its owner now. Entering the oratory at its center where Mary had been born, Gabriel, Dathiel, and Jack saw she was just standing up from her customary midnight meditations. She was older than when Jack had seen her a few minutes ago. Her olive face was now more oblong than round, with a spotless complexion and symmetrical features. She was taller than most maidens her age, but evenly proportioned. At the moment, she was dressed in a white robe and veil with a blue cloak wrapped over her shoulders and arms. She'd placed a low narrow table in the center of the room with scrolls of Scripture atop it and a small cushion in front of it for kneeling. Jack gazed at her a long moment. Gabriel did too. She hadn't noticed his entrance yet, still deep in prayer.

*So, this was the Woman—the Girl really—who would shake the realms of Heaven, Earth, and Hell together by one choice,* Jack pondered.

This was the only creature who could catch the Comet of a Promise he'd seen without dying. It wasn't hard to recognize her as the Queen of Heaven on this night. Not with the dignified serenity her features displayed as she emerged from her meditation. When she opened her eyes, she finally saw her guardian standing on the other side of the table. His bearing was so much more glorious than any time she'd seen him before. She wanted to kneel back down in greeting, but the prince stopped her, not even allowing her to bow her head to him. He held her body erect by his preternatural power. This confused her.

She'd never experienced any of her angelic acquaintances preventing an act of humility before. She was even more astonished when the visitor, in all his splendor, instead genuflected and bowed his head before her. Never in the history of the world had an intelligence greeted a human as though they were the royalty.

*"Hail, thou who art full of grace,"* Gabriel exclaimed in his usual jubilant fashion, *"the Lord is with thee! Blessed art thou amongst women!"*

Mary's suspicion grew. Now she wasn't just astonished, but concerned she might be seeing an illusion of evil. Perhaps the Accuser had disguised himself as her guardian and was greeting her as a superior to incite her to pride. After all, the visitor bore a cross on his chest. Why would Gabriel be wearing an instrument the Israelites' pagan oppressors used to execute their criminals like it was a badge of honor? It was shining so brightly it hurt her eyes. Was it a false light borne by a false angel?

Gabriel discerned her thoughts and knew he needed to overcome her hesitancy posthaste. Not only must she know it was him, he'd need to prepare her virginal mind to accept the idea of maternity. The salvation of the entire race of men was depending on him, and him alone, in this moment. If he failed to evoke her consent, all was lost. The Lord would never act without it.

*"Mary,"* he entreated, and immediately saw the effect of addressing her by name.

Confidence at his identity now showed on her face. Her enemy had always hated her name and feared to speak it. In all the years he'd oppressed her at the Temple, she'd never heard him say it aloud.

"Don't be afraid," the Archangel said. "You've found favor in the sight of God."

Interiorly, Mary heard the Father's voice illuminating her that she was to be the Mother for His Son. That He wished all others to show her the reverence she'd been willing to show the Christ-Bearer herself.

"I want you to have Him," the Deity whispered into her mind, "so that you may give Him to whomever you wish."

Still not daring to believe what she was hearing, and inclined to plead her unworthiness, she looked to Gabriel for guidance. He only looked into her eyes with a solemn expression and nodded, confirming aloud what was being spoken to her heart.

"Behold, you will conceive in your womb and bear a Son and call Him, Jesus," he announced. "He will be Great, and men will know Him as the Son of the Most High. The Lord God will give Him the throne of His father, David, and He shall reign over the House of Jacob forever. His Kingdom shall never have an end."

Mary knew the gravity of what was being asked of her. The fulfillment of the Promise. The realization of the most important prophecy foreseen by the Prophets and Patriarchs across the ages. From her studies and locutions of the past provided by her guardians over the years, she understood that, should she accept the invitation to mother the Christ, one of many things she would have to endure was watching Him suffer a humiliating death. This insurmountable task threatened to overwhelm her. Jack knew any other human would have fainted from the stress, and the awe.

Mary wasn't any other human. And she had a thousand angelic minds around the town upholding her own, the most powerful of which stood before her. She knew that, if God willed it, she would have the strength to endure the hardships that came with any destiny He offered. Still, she hesitated in answering Gabriel.

Her oldest unanswered question held her at bay. How was she to reconcile her virginity with motherhood? How were she and Joseph to keep their vows of celibate marriage and conceive a Son? Perhaps God was unbinding them from their former promises. But why would He take from her the chance to offer Him her virginity, the gift He knew she'd always desired to give Him most?

Although willing to submit to anything He requested of her, and knowing He had the power to do whatever He willed, the burning desire of her heart to finally learn for herself His method of the Son's Conception overpowered her enough to first ask her messenger, "How will this be done, since I have no knowledge of man?"

Gabriel smiled at her inquisitiveness, happy to be able to provide her most coveted answer at last. "The Holy Spirit will come upon you and the power of the Most High will overshadow you."

Mary's eyes widened and her breathing stopped, understanding. She'd never dared imagine the Infinite Himself would unite with a finite creature in such a way as to form a child with it. But she couldn't deny it was the only way the prophecy of Isaiah—always such a paradox to her—made sense. She would remain unknown to man and yet be with child . . . Her Beloved's Child.

Seeing she'd understood and was coming around to the idea of what he presented, Gabriel nodded and smiled again, his eyes taking on their usual lighthearted expression. Although he possessed the Beatific Vision, making it impossible for him to experience anxiety, he realized he'd have been quite beside himself for the last minute without its comfort. Never before in his long existence had he been entrusted with something so momentous as he'd been just now. The closest thing he could compare to it was having to decide between serving either God or Lucifer at the dawn of creation.

Hoping with all his heart Mary was about to accept the Trinity's invitation, he emphasized once more, "Thus . . . your Holy Child shall be the Son of *God*."

Based on the smile that slipped across her face, he knew his answer had revealed what she'd wanted. In his enthusiasm, he was inspired to offer her yet another sign of her Beloved's care.

"And your cousin, Elizabeth—she's also conceived a son in her old age!" he exclaimed, his words spilling out of order in his excitement.

He took half a second to compose himself. He really would be an anxious mess if not for beatitude.

"She who was reproached with barrenness is now in her sixth month, to prove nothing's impossible for God!"

Mary hadn't needed the gratuity, but she was grateful nonetheless. She'd been won over by the miracle of God bringing forth a Child from the womb exclusive of the nuptial act. For the first time, she felt the desire to be Mother to the Son. To hold Him in her arms. To nurture Him to Manhood. To be united to her Bridegroom in an intimate, life-giving union. To join the Father in His Parentage of the Word and become the only other being in the cosmos who could call Him "Son." Though inclined to draw away in humility, she instead allowed herself to feel drawn toward this privilege since it was the Father Who beckoned her. Upon embracing and relishing this desire, she let herself fall prostrate to the floor with her arms spread to the sides.

"Behold, the Handmaid of the Lord," she answered Gabriel. "Let it be done to me according to thy word."

The room evaporated into light around them, revealing the heavens above. A white cloud rumbling with thunder and lightning descended. There were orange spots glowing within it Jack realized were Seraphim after a moment. They were sinking in and out of it, their forms aflame. They were using their middle wings to fly and their top and bottom pairs to veil their faces and feet. Jack had to cover his ears from the deafening thunder and avert his eyes from the brightness of the cloud. Mary didn't.

She was caught up in an ecstasy. Jack couldn't look at her face, the reflection on it of what she saw in the cloud being too much for his mind to bear. He was only able to peek enough to see a muscled arm the size of a tree trunk reach out from the cloud toward her. Like the triune voices, Jack couldn't place its age. The skin on the palm of the hand was smooth, but there were veins protruding from the back and on the bicep and forearm. It curled its pinky and ring finger inward, pointing its thumb, index, and middle finger toward Mary. A beam of the brightest light shot out of them. Before it reached the Virgin, a Winged Form grew from its center, standing an equal distance between her and the giant hand. Jack couldn't have described the Person Who appeared in the beam. He had to shield his eyes again, the Form's luminescence too bright. But he knew enough about the story he was witnessing to guess Who it was. The Third Person of the Trinity.

He squinted his eyes back open, careful to avoid looking at the Holy Spirit, and saw from his peripheral vision that He split the beam of light into three beams, shooting them into Mary's right side. They engulfed her, raising her to her feet, and she began shining as brightly as her Bridegroom, forcing Jack to avert his eyes from the scene altogether. The locution filled him in on what was happening. Mary was undergoing the most profound spiritual ecstasy inside the light, far exceeding the physical orgasms experienced by lovers during sexual intimacy. At that moment, the Almighty became Flesh and dwelt within her. Mary closed her arms over her midsection like a rose enfolding its petals around a drop of life-giving dew. His task complete, Gabriel turned and departed.

The room grew back around Mary, and Jack opened his eyes to see only one outward sign remained of the supernatural visitation. A shower of closed white roses fell around the Virgin, materializing from the ceiling and disappearing before ever hitting the floor. Through incorporeal sight, he saw the Archangel Michael standing beside the Mother and Child and understood he was the Son's guardian.

Before he could take in the beauty of the scene, he was plunged backward through a dark tunnel. He moaned in surprise. It felt like being on a backwards roller coaster that had taken off without warning. He squeezed his eyes shut, then jerked them back open, trying to fend off dizziness. When he did, he found himself back in the cathedral of Charleston, lying on the floor next to the pew in which he'd been seated. He bolted upright, and felt lightheaded from sitting up too fast.

He reached up to rub his forehead. His hand was clutching something. His rosary. His thumb and index finger were holding the bead at the end of the first decade, as though he'd just prayed the ten *Hail Mary's*. There was something in his other hand too. His phone.

Panicking as he remembered his father calling him about dinner before the locution started, he checked the time on it. Hours must have passed since then! He'd be in a load of trouble when he got home. He was surprised no one else had visited the church in that time and found him on the floor.

When the phone's screen lit up, his breathing stopped. He furrowed his eyebrows. All he could hear now was his heartbeat, which drummed in his throat and ears at an intoxicated pace, refusing to slow down. There was some mistake. He even checked the phone's log to compare when his father's call had come in. It aligned with what the clock said.

According to the phone, only ten minutes had passed since the call.

# CHAPTER XXI
## ENEMIES BEFORE THE GATE

Fearful of what his so-called locution might actually have been, Jack had dialed the monsignor for days, with no answer.

He wasn't too surprised. It was the Christmas season. The priest must have had family or friends to see as much as he did. In the meantime, he kept practicing with the rosary almost every day, reciting a decade slowly for ten minutes while thinking on whichever of the Twenty Mysteries caught his fancy. Most often, it was the Annunciation, his vision having provided plenty on which to meditate. For details on other Mysteries, he'd dug up and dusted off the old family Bible.

Sometimes Dathiel, Michael, or one of the others would show up and substitute distractions for temptations, helping sharpen his skill at drowning them out. Every time he started to think he was getting better at resisting them, the saints' prowess would increase, keeping him ever the underdog in their fights. He still couldn't inflame his sword or fly, though he kept trying, tired of his demonic adversaries having an airborne advantage in battle.

His latest concern was the prospect of returning to school. Thanks to his new-found weapon, he'd been giving Racism and his legions a run for their money all over the diocese. He'd attacked various demonic strongholds, leaving the symbol he'd made up burning at each one of them. They still didn't know who was doing it.

Once he returned to Wando, he didn't see how he'd conceal his identity from them any longer. Delusion would no doubt inform Racism of his use of the Rosary. From there, it wouldn't take long for the Principality to make the connection. Since he couldn't remain under the radar forever, Jack decided to make his return to Wando one that couldn't be missed.

On January eighth, two days before second semester classes were scheduled to begin, he approached the campus after nightfall through its surrounding forest. Not that the time of day made much difference. Seen through his second sight, Wando was always dark. But Jack figured Delusion and his rabble wouldn't expect him to visit the grounds he now loathed so much at night, when he had no business at the school. He'd even chosen to conduct his reconnaissance two days before the start of term instead of one, guessing that if the demons suspected any surprises from him, they'd look for them on the last day before the start of classes.

The woods were denser than corporeal eyes revealed, full of hellish creatures in addition to its wildlife. Jack was armored in his full suit, making no sound with his footfalls. Thick as his rosary's boots were, they were quiet when he needed them to be, even with all the sticks and leaves on the forest floor. That was lucky, because he'd seen several small demons as he'd stalked among the trees.

They looked like oversized toads brooding on logs or perched on low hanging branches. He could have missed them easily if he wasn't looking for them. They blended in well with their surroundings. They must have been sentries posted to spot enemies doing exactly what he was there to do. Jack kept his hood up, both to disguise himself more and give him more protection from behind if any tried to sneak up on him. A branch snapped on his right.

His heart heaved in his chest. He didn't stop to think, just brought his fist swinging around at whatever had managed to get the drop on him. His wrist was caught halfway, by a strong arm. After a couple of seconds, he exhaled his relief.

*"What are you doing here?"* he hissed at Joan, then thought better of his accusatory tone as his adrenaline spike wore down. "Not that I'm ungrateful for the company."

"Here to help," Joan said, releasing his wrist. "You're doing reconnaissance aren't you? That happens to be within my field of expertise. It'll be better to use the trees." She nodded her head upward. "You'll be harder to spot there, just like them." She turned and went back the way Jack had come. "Follow me. There're too many of them around here. They'll see you on the ground if you move any farther forward. We'll double back and climb."

Jack followed. "Will they be able to see you if they do spot us?"

"No one's going to spot us."

"I guess you've done this a lot, huh?"

"In both my lives."

"Right, I forgot. You were a soldier in life too. I guess you'd have done your fair share of spying on . . ."

He let his sentence drop, realizing with some shame he didn't know much about Joan of Arc's life. He'd never read any books on her. He couldn't even remember which country she'd fought against. She was French. So he guessed it was the English.

"It was," she said. "Specifically, the Burgundians."

"Sorry," Jack said, realizing she could read what he was thinking the way angels could. "I should have taken time to look more up about you after meeting you—"

"You've had enough on your mind," she interrupted without looking back.

"So, the Burgundians. You spy on them a lot before battles?"

"Plenty. Especially before the Siege of Orléans. That was my and my men's first and hardest won victory in our campaign to expel them from France."

"And you led the army for the king because God appointed you directly right? You could see saints like me? And they told you they wanted you to lead France?"

"I rarely saw them. Mostly I just heard them. I called them, my voices. And it was always the same three saints. Margaret of Antioch, Catherine of Alexandria," she turned to look back at Jack, "and Michael the Archangel."

Jack smiled. "I thought I remembered there being some connection between you two. So did he accompany you in your battles? Is that how you won?"

She nodded, turning to lead him through the shrubbery again. "He and his angels even physically helped us win sometimes, appearing before our enemies on the battlefield to terrify them." She turned around, slapping an oak tree next to her. "This should do."

She leapt up the first few branches. Jack did the same.

"So how was it you died, I mean, if Michael was with you? You were killed in battle right?"

"No," she said from several branches above him. "Captured. I was martyred later. Burned at the stake with a fabricated accusation of witchcraft by Burgundian bishops."

*"What?"* Jack said, too loudly.

He gripped a branch and looked around at the other trees to make sure he hadn't given away their position. There was no movement in them.

*"Bishops?"* he hissed, turning back to the saint.

Joan looked down at him. "They needed a reason to kill me. Their political interests were tied up in England's retainment of France. My voices gave them their opportunity, even though the theologians of both countries could find nothing diabolic in my story. My captors trumped up false charges when they couldn't trip me up in interrogations, led most by one particularly evil man. Bishop Cauchon. He was being influenced by a devil, as were my executioners." Joan perched herself into a sitting position on the branch above Jack's. "It was a militant spirit who'd helped the Burgundians conquer and oppress France in the first place. I'd seen him fighting alongside them during my men's campaigns. I saw him for the last time through the flames as I burned to death." She looked Jack in the eyes. "The commander of the demonic military, the prince of their Powers."

Jack stared up at her. She shot him a half-smile.

"Guess now you know why I took an interest in your plight."

"Yeah, I guess I do," Jack said. "So . . . technically . . . Mephistopheles murdered you. At least, instigated your murder."

She nodded. "And he continues to pay the price for it, because now I'm going to help you defeat him, and his soldiers." She pointed toward an area of the wood outside Wando's wall to its left. "We'll want to go that way to learn what you need."

"Lead on then, Maid."

Joan had been right about his ability to blend. The trees around the demonic fortress were all dead. So his brown cloak served as a perfect camouflage within them. It wasn't long before he heard voices as he climbed through the boughs, recognizing one of them. He and the Maid slowed their pace, crawling on their bellies atop two thick branches that were next to each other, before Jack peered down to see a gathering of Wando's demons in a clearing below. Delusion was hosting a counsel. After eavesdropping a few seconds, Jack realized they were strategizing about him.

"I want you all stationed three blocks away, ready to intercept him before he reaches the stronghold," the minotaur said. "Pride," he barked at a demon who'd been holding his head high with his nose turned up, "I want you to make the first move against him, but from a distance. Get him thinking about his accomplishments thus far. How he's learned so much more than the other students about what's really happening here. Bigotry," the chieftain turned his attention to another, "follow up Pride's arrow by making him feel he's different than the rest, set apart by the Enemy from these ignorant and lowly pagans. Retaliation," he turned to a third, "rile his passions over their stupidity at playing directly into the Master's hands. But do it subtly, only enough to whet his emotions, not enough to make him sin. That'll prime him for the rest of us by the time he gets here."

"And what if his guardian alerts him to our presence?" Pride inquired. "It would only increase his virtue if he were to notice my attack and commit it to prayer."

"Thank you, Pride, I hadn't thought of that!" Delusion said, angering his minion into silence. "Now, if I may continue, should the ambush fail, bombard the boy with temptations from a distance anyway. It should still rile him, and I want him flustered by the time he returns. Remind him this is *my* territory and there'll be no peace for him here."

*"Sire!"* A newcomer came running out the trees from the direction of the campus.

*"What?"* Delusion demanded. *"Didn't I tell you we were not to be disturbed?"*

"You should come immediately!" the underling said. "The main gate, sire! On the main gate!"

Delusion and the others followed the hysterical demon around to the entrance of the school and the chieftain almost threw a fit.

*"Summon Baal Racism!"* he ordered Bigotry. "Tell him his coveted quarry seems to have chosen Wando as his next target."

Bigotry flew off toward the south.

"The rest of you, find out if any of our party are missing!" the minotaur commanded.

Jack shook his head, watching with Joan from within a bush across the street. Delusion hadn't made the connection by his little gesture. He guessed he'd have to wait a couple more days to see the look of surprise on the demon's dolled up face.

He hoped it would be priceless.

Jack had already scouted out his usual driving route through incorporeal sight, with his rosary.

He'd risen from bed earlier to leave himself time. He parked the Jeep a few blocks away from campus, hopping out to hike the rest of the way to school.

*"Jack! Hey, Jack!"* he heard someone calling.

He turned fast, ready for an attack, his hand closing over the rosary pouch in his pocket as he started to draw the sword. Naomi was climbing out of April Evans' car. He breathed easier, relinquishing his second sight. April drove on to Wando, while Naomi joined him.

"You walk all the way here?"

"No, I parked back there." He pointed over his shoulder. "Just thought I'd stretch my legs a bit today."

She chuckled. "Yeah, like *you* really need the exercise." she said, looking him up and down.

Jack wanted to smile at her words but his facial muscles performed some other unknown dance instead, as if his brain wasn't sure how to direct them. It'd been Naomi's first blatant flirt since Thanksgiving.

"So what classes you have this semester?" she asked.

Jack rattled them off, and they realized they'd be in most of the same periods again. While they chatted, a downpour started, and they were forced to take refuge under a large tent in a field beside the road. It looked like it had been left up from a community picnic on New Year's Day.

"That came outta nowhere," Jack said, brushing water from his hair.

"Think it'll stop long enough for us to get to school?"

He looked out at the sheets of water blanketing the grass, forming mud puddles beneath the green blades. "Not by my guess."

*"It's freezing!"* Naomi's lips quivered as she began to shiver.

She moved in closer to Jack, putting her arms around his torso. Soon she was leaning her head on his shoulder. He put an arm around her, trying to warm her up, aware they hadn't been this close since his botched opportunity to kiss her.

Feeling his heart speed up, he wondered if she wouldn't notice the manic flapping from under his shirt as it stuck to his chest, or the increased puffs of condensation coming out his mouth.

Glancing over, he saw her face was downcast. He felt drawn to stroke her cheek. From there, he could lift her lips up to meet his own. She'd probably consent, especially after her reaction when he didn't take the hint last time. His nerves ran away with his pulse, and he worried his heart would come storming out of his chest if it punched against it any harder. He contemplated his next move, and felt the same pull he had on the previous occasion he'd been in this situation. A pull that told him to decline from taking the kiss. Even more irritated than then and determined not to let the irrational feeling ruin his second chance, he reached up and lightly caressed Naomi's cheek.

She didn't stop him.

After a moment in which he held his breath, she lifted her own hand and pressed his palm down against her skin. He pushed gently, and she offered no resistance as he slowly raised her head. Their lips met. She moved her hand to stroke his cheek. He was careful to only kiss her lips, holding his tongue back. He didn't want to come on too strong. The whole thing was over before he knew it, probably because he'd been so focused on technique he'd forgotten to enjoy the moment.

Naomi kept her forehead pressed against his chin after. He wasn't sure what was supposed to happen next. The movies never did seem to showcase what to do right after a first kiss. Thankfully, she was the first to speak.

"I've been wondering if we were ever gonna do that."

"So have I."

She raised her head, and they stared into each other's eyes a few moments.

"Still wondering how I feel?" he asked.

She smiled. "How'd you know I was?"

He smiled. "Oh you were making it pretty obvious. Besides that, you're not a hard read."

"So you *were* picking up on that then. Why'd it take you so long to respond?"

He grinned wider and shrugged. "Had to make it dramatic, didn't I?"

She popped him across the face.

*"Was I that bad?"* he asked.

She laughed. The rain had slowed almost to a stop now. The two of them continued their walk to campus.

"I hear you've a papist control problem," Racism spat, landing beside Delusion, who'd been awaiting his arrival for hours.

"It appears the prize you've been chasing visited us two nights ago," Delusion said, leading him to the front gate.

The Principality stood before it, grinding what was left of his teeth. Upon Wando's entrance burned the winged cross he'd come to know so well over the past two weeks. This time, it had the words "To resist and to conquer" ablaze beneath it.

"Yes, this is it," Racism confirmed. "The cross of 'the Philangelus,' as he's calling himself."

"Think he's law enforcement or military in his day job?" Delusion asked. "Given the language of the threat?"

Racism said nothing, just kept staring at the burning symbol.

"Either way," Delusion continued, "the message seems to indicate your 'Philangelus' has chosen my school as his next plunder."

"That's right," said a metallic voice from behind them.

Both demons spun around, drawing their weapons. The Philangelus stood next to a large oak, the Angel Dathiel sitting in the tree above him.

"So you might want to think about vacating it now," the agitator continued. "It'll be far less painful than my method of eviction."

Recognizing the guardian angel, Delusion's eyes widened. The armor-clad warrior threw a chain at their feet and they widened more. Its links were lined with the impaled heads of the soldiers he'd sent to intercept Jack Dacre on his way to school.

"I'm afraid your boys here were underqualified for the job you sent them on this morning," the Philangelus addressed the minotaur. "They decided to quit." He spread a hand over the severed heads. "Consider this their letters of resignation."

The heads disintegrated as the chain evaporated into rose petals of the most offensive smell to the two fallen angels.

*"My baal,"* Delusion turned to Racism, *"it's—"*

But before he could finish his sentence, he was cut off by a swat to the throat from the Principality's index finger. He crumpled to the ground in a coughing fit.

"So . . . the Philangelus," Racism greeted. "At last we meet."

"I thought it was time," the warrior said. "You've been seeking me with such vigor. Hope you've been getting my love notes in the meantime." He nodded to the burning cross behind the Principality. "I made sure to sign them all for you."

"Indeed," Racism said. "You seemed desperate for my attention. I'd say you've earned it. Who are you?"

The Philangelus laughed, his chuckles echoing through the metallic mask. "If you lent more of an ear to your underlings, you'd already know."

He looked down at Delusion, still on his knees heaving. Racism glanced down too, then back at the Philangelus. The warrior's hood came off by itself, and his mask receded down his face, shedding rose petals into the air. The demon shied away, repulsed by the smell. The armored suit transformed into a crimson-hilted sword across the soul's back, attached to his person with a chain of the same color. The chain rotated continuously around his torso like a snake, annoyingly reminding the demonic prince that his enemy's weapon was the *Living* Rosary. At last, he looked on the face of the soul who'd been causing so much trouble in his territory. It was a fully matured soul, as he'd expected, but it was a young man in body.

"Jack Dacre," the youth greeted.

Racism stood in silence a moment, then began to laugh.

*"This* is the warrior who terrifies my familiars? *The boy* from Mt. Pleasant who struggles in his faith?"

"Sounds like your minions know something you don't," Jack said. "Maybe they should be running the territory."

The humor on Racism's face vanished. He let his whip extend to the ground. Jack gripped the chain on his hip, which stopped circling his abdomen, ready to lash out in defense. Before either of them moved against the other, a raspy cackle rained down from above.

Both opponents looked up to see Mephistopheles standing atop Wando's wall above the gate. He was leaning on his staff with both hands, his head tilted to one side, looking like a curious crow perched atop the entrance to Hell. Jack's breath grew shallow, betraying his concern over failing to detect his greatest adversary's approach.

"If the dick measuring contest is over, pups," the Master of Powers said. "Allow me to declare a winner. That'd be you, Jack. We don't have dicks." He grinned the awful smile Jack hated and feared so much. "Pepping yourself up?" the Power asked him. "If you're that concerned, why don't you just drop your pants for Naomi? Let her be your judge."

Hearing Naomi's name dragged through the sewer of his enemy's mouth sparked Jack's courage back into action. "Mention that name again, demon, and I'll be sure to tear the forked tongue from your mouth before sending you on your merry—"

"Oh let's not waste one another's time with idle threats, Jack," Mephistopheles interrupted. "If you could send me anywhere, you'd have done it already. As it stands, you won't stop clinging to me." The Power winked at him. "And, in any case, if I'm but a figment of your unconscious, it was you who thought of her as a slut just now."

*"Really?"* Jack raised an eyebrow at the monster. "This is what it's come down

to? The demon who claims to be the voice of reason stoops to insulting my romantic interest to rile me? No actual arguments today?"

Mephistopheles threw a hand up and shrugged his shoulders, a feat that looked all the more abnormal because of his permanent hunch.

"I've already given you all the answers you need," he said. "It's up to you to accept them in your heart now. But, if you'd like another demonstration this is all a product of schizophrenia . . ." The Power leaned over to gaze down at the winged cross aflame below his feet. "'To resist and to conquer,' is it? Well, you're certainly doing quite a bit of resisting truth. And here I thought you Christians were supposed to embrace it." He pointed a taloned finger at Jack. "To quote your own, beloved Scriptures on which you all hang so desperately, 'it's hard to kick against the goad,' boy."

With that, the monster leaned his staff forward and poured black mist from its red orb. The fog crept downward toward the cross like the shadow of a hand about to snuff out a candle. After masking it, it receded back to its source. Jack's symbol had been replaced with an upside down pentagram traced in black flames. Beneath it, his motto had been replaced with the words: "To seduce and to ravish."

"As you can see, Jack, or Philangelus—whatever childish nickname you wished to be called by these days—all that you see is relative to your own hopes and fears. If I'm a demon, would not the cross repel me? How then have I overcome it?"

Jack didn't answer. He wasn't going to play into his enemy's cons this time. He'd been warned enough against that. Instead, he raised a hand and shot a fireball at the pentagram. Racism and Delusion dove to the sides like frightened squirrels. The ball reached the satanic symbol. But, rather than replace it with the winged cross again, its fire was lost amid the black flames of the Power's conjuring. The pentagram remained.

Mephistopheles cackled. "You could make it disappear if you truly wanted to, child. You could make this all disappear."

"I'll make you disappear, demon." Jack glared up into the Power's dead white eyes. "Like you said, it's hard to kick against the goad."

His armored suit grew around him and he leaned forward, shooting lightning from both hands. Several streaks hit the gate, obliterating it altogether. Two more of them skyrocketed up to Mephistopheles' position. The demonic lord vanished into black mist just before the prayer reached him. With Racism and Delusion having fled outright the moment he'd gone on the offensive, Jack walked through the fortress' now open entryway to his first class of his final semester.

It would be physics with his oh-so-favorite science teacher, Mr. Wilkerson.

# CHAPTER XXII
## CHLOE'S SECRET

"What's wrong, Jack?" Naomi asked, bringing him out of his brooding.

He'd been staring off into space, tapping his fingers across his thumb. They were seated on her living room floor in front of the fire place, which had been stoked to a blaze by her father. They'd been dating for just over a week now, doing their homework at her house almost every day. The living room was much smaller than his own, but he found it cozy.

"Sorry," he said. "Just have a lot on my mind."

"Like what?"

"Like, my family."

"Yeah? Speaking of which, when do I get to meet them as your girlfriend? We never go to your house."

"Well, my house is . . . a little crazy right now."

That was the partial truth. The whole of it was he preferred her place to his because he'd never encountered any demonic activity there. Her home felt like a safe haven from his insane life outside its doors.

"How so?" she asked.

Jack paused again before answering, wondering how to include her in his affairs without telling her about incorporeal sight

*—or was it schizophrenia—*

and all he'd been dealing with through it.

"The truth is . . . I've felt a bit . . . severed from my family lately. It's like we live in two sharply divided worlds that don't mix."

"Sounds about right," she nodded.

Jack laughed. It felt good to laugh. She always managed to bring more humor and normality into his day.

"I'm not talking about teenage rebellion," he said. "I love my parents. And it's not like they're abusive, or uninvolved, or overbearing, or anything."

"What is the problem then?"

Jack stopped to think again, choosing his words carefully. "A few months ago

. . . I . . . found out my parents and sister did some . . . awful things in their pasts. Things they've never told me about. They don't know I know—" Jack cringed for a split second, doubting whether he really did know the spiritual state of his family, "—and I've tried to get them to fess up for themselves. But they've refused, and I keep coming out looking like the bad guy when we argue. They make me feel like a religious bigot for asking. But I only ask because I care about their well-being. I don't know how to make them see that though."

"So . . . I take it these, awful things, you found out about are moral faults then? Like . . . sins?"

"Yeah, but they either don't care they've committed them, or I'm just the last person they want to discuss them with. My parents always end up silencing me when I bring it up. And my sister acts like she doesn't know what I'm talking about."

"Does she?" Naomi asked, and Jack felt his cheeks heat up. "Wouldn't it help if you told them how you found out so they'd stop denying it?"

Jack brushed a hand through his hair. "I wish it were that simple, but explaining that would be . . . complicated."

"Because . . . ? Would it get you into trouble somehow? Wait, you didn't read their diaries or something did you?"

Jack laughed again. "No, not exactly. Although I've *seen* things I'm sure they never thought I'd see."

"Like old pictures or videos?"

Jack shook his head. "No. Not like that."

"Okay . . . What then? How are you so sure they've done anything wrong?"

"I'm not a hundred percent sure!" Jack exclaimed, surprising himself by how agitated he sounded. "That's part of the problem! But if I'm wrong, it means I'm just crazy!"

It was Naomi's turn to laugh. "Crazy? Crazy how?"

"Just . . ."

Jack shook his head, veering off into silence again, unsure how to proceed without going into details. Monsignor Bamonte had told him to keep his "ability" between the two of them and his family for the present, and he didn't wish to disregard his spiritual director's instruction.

"Jack," Naomi said in a much more subdued tone than before.

He looked her in the eyes.

"I don't know what you've seen that makes you think your family has somehow betrayed you. It's not really my business to ask now that I think about it, if you're not ready to share. So I'm sorry if I pushed you. But—and I'm only speaking hypothetically here—don't you think it's possible you're angry with them over nothing? What if you're wrong?"

Jack stared at her, clenching his teeth as he braced against the thought that came to him. He tried not to let it enter his mind, but it was too late. The thought had kicked in the front doors of his emotions, leaving jagged splinters in its wake, and it was now making itself at home on the couch of his will, looking up with a grin and a wave at his intellect. He *hoped* he was right about his family, simply because he hoped incorporeal sight was real. He was hoping his family was spiritually dead, all because he didn't want to be the one deluding himself. He balled his hand into a fist, unsure how he should feel about that, but knowing it was what he thought nonetheless.

"I can't be sure," he answered Naomi at last. "Still, I won't know until I can work out my own problems."

"Okay . . ." Naomi nodded, looking confused by his logic. "And what are those?"

She sounded more cautious in her words now, probably afraid she'd hit a nerve before and wishing to avoid upsetting him further. He felt badly for that. It wasn't her prying that upset him. He wished he could tell her everything. The only reason he was being ambiguous was out of obedience to his spiritual director. She probably wouldn't believe him anyway. How could he expect her to when he wasn't sure of it himself? Deliberating a few more seconds, he decided it wouldn't be violating Monsignor Bamonte's wishes if he confessed his struggles to Naomi in a way that excluded any mention of supernatural occurrences. He turned to face her.

"You wanna know the truth?"

She nodded, an expression of hopeful curiosity splashing across her face that he found endearing.

"I've been having doubts about the existence of God," he said, pausing a moment to gauge her reaction.

Her face retained its listening expression, encouraging him to go on.

"That's why I've been so sensitive to moral issues lately, and why I sometimes feel like I'm insane. The world just doesn't make sense to me if there's no Higher Being ordering it. If God doesn't exist, then everything's temporary and based only on chance, and that will never sit well with me."

Naomi was silent, digesting what he'd said. "So, that's why you look so down all the time?" she asked. "Because you doubt if there's a God?"

"Yes."

"I'm sorry," she said, an expression on her face Jack hadn't seen before.

It looked like anger, or maybe pain. He couldn't read it.

"That must be hard."

Giving up on figuring out what emotion her face was expressing, Jack gave her a tired look of his own. "You have no idea."

"When did it start?"

"Last year, the day I found out Chuck had . . ."

She nodded after his pause, not making him say it.

"If you remember," he went on, "that was the same day Mr. Wilkerson declared there was no Creator in class. It was the day I realized I'd always taken Christianity for granted."

"So, how is that connected to doubts about your family?"

Jack wasn't sure how to answer that without saying too much. "I'd rather not go into that for their sake. It includes their private stuff. But I can say my main problem is that I thought they were all more devout Catholics than they apparently are. And it angers me, because they should know better."

"Maybe it doesn't just anger you," Naomi said. "Maybe it saddens you too."

He looked her in the eyes, then looked away when he felt emotion well up inside him at their gaze. "Yes, that too, I guess. I'm disillusioned."

"Realizing the people closest to you aren't everything you thought they were growing up."

Jack couldn't tell if it had been a statement or a question, but he pointed at her. "Yes, exactly . . . That."

She nodded, lowering her head. "I guess we all go through that at some point." She raised her gaze again. "But you said if you were wrong about your family, it means you're crazy. I don't follow. You mean crazy like, in the sense of being paranoid for no reason?"

Jack tilted his head back, thinking. "You could put it that way I guess, but only if I'm wrong. Regardless, all I can think about when I'm around them now are what dark secrets they might be hiding from me." He paused and thought another moment. "I suppose if I am crazy, there's an upside." He started laughing. "At least it'd mean my parents and sister aren't in as bad a place as I feared. That the real problem lies in me. So, as my ever-so-perfect mistake-free mother would say, the glass is half-full!" He laughed harder.

"Stop being cynical! That won't help. And you're not crazy! You should just talk to them and find out if you're right."

"Like I said, I've tried! It always turns into an argument! They're my parents and older sister. They get condescending when I try to give them advice, and it ends up chipping away at my patience."

"Is this why we haven't been going to your house for homework? Because you're resentful of them?"

Jack looked her in the eyes. "Maybe. I don't—yeah. Maybe, now that I stop and think about it."

*"Jack!"*

"What?"

"How bad can they really be? They seemed laid back enough when I met them at Halloween."

Jack took a few deep breaths to calm down before speaking again. "It would be funny to see Chloe's reaction to the news that I'm dating."

*"You haven't told them we're dating yet!"* She popped him.

He grinned. "Only because you abuse me."

"You embarrassed by me or something?"

He chuckled. "Actually—if you want the real reason—it's because I'm protective of you. I don't like the idea of putting you in a house that's always under siege from demo—" he caught himself mid-sentence, "from . . . demonstrations of such hostility."

She guffawed. "You haven't told your family you have a girlfriend because you *argue* a lot?" She laughed harder. "You think my family never argues? Honestly, unless they're abusive or something, I don't think you have to worry, Jack."

Jack breathed again. She hadn't caught his fumble before. "That's . . . not exactly what I meant. I have other reasons besides my family for not being ready to bring you to my place."

"Like what?"

Jack felt he was backing himself into a corner. He'd come out looking like an idiot if he didn't think of some concrete answers he was allowed to give her soon. Brainstorming hard, beginning to feel desperate, a way to articulate his feelings blew into his mind like a breath from the Holy Spirit Himself.

He said, "You're the one part of my life right now that's untouched by any problems. I just want to enjoy that sanctuary for myself a little longer, before my two worlds are mixed."

The look that came over Naomi's face told him he'd said the right thing. She tackled him to the floor in a hug.

"So, I'm like a whole new world for you, huh?" She smiled down into his eyes.

"Sure, like a new world. Unexplored, possibly hazardous to breathe on, and potentially containing germs I've never encountered before that could either kill me or change me into something else." He nodded and stuck his thumb up at her. "Yeah, good analogy."

She smacked him, then kissed him.

The first thing Jack did after getting home that afternoon was go up to his room and kneel in front of the wall.

He'd framed the holy card of Jesus and Mary on it. He began his prayers with the *Glory be*, watching how it manifested through incorporeal sight when there were no demons around. A precious stone formed in his palm, this time a sapphire the size of a tennis ball. Dathiel took it, carting it off anywhere the divine kingdom needed brightening up. He did the same with the flowers, after Jack had said the Lord's Prayer and Angelic Salutation, delivering them to the gardens. When Jack arrived at the *Creed*, instead of the shockwave he always saw in battle, his hands produced an assortment of building implements. Stones, wood, pieces of fence or railing, gold, silver, or iron grating—these were just some of the elements he materialized from thin air.

Dathiel had explained to him the first time he'd seen all this that he and the saints used the prayer to either build or repair the blessed kingdom wherever needed. This was the purpose Jack intended for it this evening, directing the implements flying from his hands to reinforce his household. His section of it anyway. Reciting the *Hail, Holy Queen*, he used its light rays like lasers to weld the pieces together, making his bedroom impenetrable from the outside. At least, he hoped so.

He closed his eyes, pulling his rosary from the pouch in his pocket, gripping it tightly. Before learning the prayer, he'd have been running the fingers of his right hand over his thumb in this state of mind. Now, he ran them over the beads. He prayed the First Joyful Mystery, meditating on what he'd seen in his vision again. Several minutes of blessed silence passed. Then he heard a faint scraping from the hallway outside the door. It sounded like someone dragging fingernails along the walls and floor.

*One, two, Freddy's coming for you*, he thought. *Time to go to the boiler room, Jack. Come on now. Best be cooperating.*

He tried to ignore the sound and stay focused on the Mystery. His fear overruled his concentration and he turned to look at the door. The scraping stopped outside it. There was a haunting pause, before an ominous knock broke the silence. The horrors had arrived. Jack had reinforced the door with a wooden brace and bolts.

*Three, four, I locked my door.*

If not for the brace, the door probably would have given way to the crash from the other side as something rammed into it. Jack had been expecting it, so it didn't make him jump. What did was the hoarse cackle that sounded from behind him a second later.

*Five, six, grip your crucifix*, Jack thought, gripping the bottom of his rosary tighter.

Mephistopheles' smile wasn't the only thing that could unnerve him to the point of wanting to huddle into a fetal position. His laugh did the trick too. He was outside, on the terrace. Jack had prepared for an attack from there as well. He'd built a wall of sapphire in front of the curtain leading out to it. He heard his enemy tapping his spear on it from the other side.

*"Seven, eight, gonna keep you up late,"* the Prince of Powers sung, unnerving Jack all the more. *"Nine, ten, until the loony bin. Oh, little piiiig? Little piiiig? Let us come iiiiiiiin!"*

Jack drew his rosary up to his chest, gripping it in both his trembling hands.

*"Not . . ."* he cleared his throat to level his voice, "by the hair of my chinny chin chin," he whispered.

He began the *Apostle's Creed.* This time the prayer sent out the shockwave. It seeped through the walls. He listened to hear if the demon had been chased away.

The fiend laughed, sounding like he was standing in the same spot as before. "Stop it, Jack! That tickles!"

Jack kept praying, but he had trouble concentrating on the meditation because the walls around him exploded with noise as if a hurricane was battering their outsides. Pounds, groans, growls, and howls made it sound like his efforts had only drawn more beasts out from Hell. The howls were the worst part. They weren't the soothing sounds made by the mammals of Earth. They were a feral noise that could only come from creatures condemned to eternal misery, hungry to drag more souls into their company.

If Jack were to compare it to anything, it most resembled the grunting of wild boar. He'd heard such sounds when deer hunting with his uncle as a kid. They'd scared him shitless, but not like this. That childhood scare had been nothing to the fear that had become his daily life now. Judging from the sounds, there must have been twenty beasts outside. Their growls sounded like what he'd heard behind him in his bed the night Ruby had fled from his room.

He'd yet to see what these beasts in the shadows looked like. Any glimpses he'd caught of the outside through the holes they eventually made in his defenses on previous nights had been of nothing but black mist. He doubted they were the demons from school. Their presence stirred more dread in his heart than he'd felt from Delusion's brood in some time.

These monsters were the main reason he'd been so insistent on keeping Naomi away. The last thing he wanted was to attract their attention to her, a soul seemingly at peace and one of his few escapes from their oppression. While the spirits continued bashing and thrashing the room from the outside, looking for a weak spot, Jack kept repeating the *Apostle's Creed*, hoping his faith was strong enough to keep them out. If they broke through, he knew their attacks would fill his mind with doubts and depression again. His lessons with the monsignor about objective reasons to believe had been going so well, he wanted to see them through to the end without interruption.

He rebuilt his reinforcements as fast as the fallen angels tore them down from the other side. He could hear them climbing around inside the walls, scratching and hacking. All the while, he heard Mephistopheles goading him from among them.

*"Jackooo?* Won't you come out and play?"

The pounding on his surroundings grew in frequency. Jack closed his eyes, trying to keep up with matching the demons' rate of destruction with construction. He was slipping. Holes started appearing where the creatures clawed the walls. He saw a dead white eye appear through one of them.

"Ready or nooot . . ." Mephistopheles teased, *"here we cooome!"*

Jack changed his tactic, employing the Lord's Prayer, firing off lightning bolts from his palms through the holes. The Prince of Powers moved just in time.

*"Missed!* Would you care to try again?"

The demon scraped his spear along the walls, moving around to the one made of sapphire. Jack could see his hunched silhouette on the terrace through it.

"You can put up all the mental barriers you like to protect your world of pretend, Jack." The dark prince pointed his spear toward the sapphire. "But, reason will always break through in the end."

Jack saw red lightning strike the wall from the other side. Cracks began forming on it. Growing more desperate, he initiated another decade of the Rosary. He combined the flaming balls of the Angelic Salutations into one continuous stream of fire, using it to heat the wall from his side, fusing it back together to keep it in one piece.

It still looked like it was about to explode inward by the end of the decade. He held out his hands and prayed the *Apostle's Creed*, forming a stone wall up against the sapphire, double layering the barrier. When the sapphire gave, Mephistopheles rapped his spear twice on the new obstruction . . . and silence followed.

It sounded like the demons had left. The world outside Jack's bedroom was quiet. He wouldn't be fooled. It was a ruse to get him to let his guard down. He held his sword by his hip, ready to swing it up at anything that broke in from the terrace.

A hand crashed through the bedroom door behind him and grabbed his head. He hadn't been standing far enough away to avoid the beast's reach, even though he was several feet into the room. He felt claws pierce his forehead as the monster's grip tightened. He swung his sword up, gashing the arm, stunning the brute enough to wriggle free and retreat to the opposite side of his chamber. But that turned out to be the real trap.

Mephistopheles' spear broke through the wall from the terrace, extending half a meter into the room, trapping his neck in between its two prongs. He was pulled face-first toward the wall, his chin slamming into its stone. He was stuck staring through the hole the scepter had opened.

Mephistopheles' upside down face lowered before him. He must have been clinging to the wall on the other side like an overgrown bug. Adding to Jack's horror, the head of the impish, bat-like creature who'd recited the dark poem about the Power on Halloween popped up below the demon's head.

*"Eeny, meeny, miny, moe!"* the imp sang. *"Catch a Catholic by the toe! If he hollers, kill him slow! Eeny, meeny, miny, moe!"*

Fury rose in Jack's chest despite his pain. He couldn't wait to inflict the Rosary upon this particular little sprite. He struggled against the pull of the spear. Mephistopheles held him fast.

"Now, now, Jack," the fallen prince taunted. "Behave yourself, or I and the pups will have to take out our displeasure on Miss Ackermann."

Jack's fist tightened, angered as always when his enemy dared even mention his girlfriend. He pushed harder against the wall, attempting to free his neck.

*"Jack! Don't be rude! I said hold still, damn it!* Relax and you might even enjoy this."

Black mist started issuing from the red orb on the spear beneath Jack's chin. He morphed his sword into the suit of armor to cover his mouth. As it grew over his neck, it broke the hold the two prongs of the weapon had on him. He wasted no time, forming another barrier between himself and the mist to trap it outside before it infected him.

"How disappointing," he heard Mephistopheles saying on the other side. "Well pups, if the Philangelus won't oblige to entertain us this evening, maybe his family will."

Jack heard the Power and those with him scamper away from his room, climbing down the walls to Chloe and his parents' section of the house.

*"No!"* he whispered, turning and tearing the brace off his bedroom door and charging out after them.

When he rounded the corner at the end of the stone hallway, Mephistopheles stood waiting for him in the wooden section. Jack almost crashed into him.

"Heroes," the demon mused. "So unoriginal and uninteresting. The same threats work on every one of you."

Jack lunged forward to attack first, having no choice but to fight now. His opponent was quicker, jabbing the bottom of his staff on a rotten part of the floor in between them, opening a hole. Jack fell through, landing on his back in the hallway below. He watched the demon leap down after him, kicking him out of his way into the wall, heading for the living room. The rest of the Dacres were in there, watching television.

"You had your chance to be my only prey tonight, dreamer. Now, your loved ones'll have to suffer for your stalling." The Prince of Powers turned back and smiled. "For a demon's always true to his word, eh?"

He winked and turned the corner into the living room. Jack struggled to get to his feet, but was slowed by a cramp in his ribs where the fiend had kicked him. It made him feel like despairing, making his incorporeal movements sluggish. When he hobbled around the corner, Mephistopheles was holding the pronged end of his spear before his parents, while the sharp arrowhead at the end of his tail was poised to slit Chloe's throat.

"They're already slaves of your master, demon. Why waste your time with them when I'm the one he wants?"

The Power turned, wearing his grisly grin. "The fact they belong to us is exactly why we torture them, pup. Of course, if you're offering to take their place . . ." He spread a hand out over the living room floor. "By all means. Throw down those malodorous beads and submit yourself before me. I'll let them be. I promise."

Jack felt panic constrict his chest. He'd never relinquish his weapon in the face of the enemy, and both of them knew it. He also knew the demon intended to drag his loved ones farther from the Light whether he submitted or not. It was a standstill. One he couldn't see a way out of. Where was Dathiel when he needed him?

His mind raced, trying to think of a way to get to Mephistopheles the way he got to him. But he'd never been able to do that, no matter how much he'd tried. He didn't know of a single weakness—

Wait.

There was something he knew about the Power the demon likely wouldn't want him knowing. A humiliation he'd witnessed.

"Give up my veneration of the Blessed Virgin to worship *you*, Mephistopheles? Why should I? It didn't work out that way for the people of the river."

Jack saw for the first time ever an expression of confused agitation on the demon's face. He had his attention. The grin faded.

"As I recall," Jack continued, "they gave you up for her at your own command. Of course, Prince Michael helped, didn't he?"

The Power's next move was so swift, Jack would have missed it had he blinked. His tail wrapped once around Chloe's throat, tightening and yanking her from the couch to stand before him like a human shield. The tail's arrowhead hovered in front of her forehead, ready to stab. Mephistopheles stared over her shoulder.

"Who told you that, *boy?*"

Chloe's soul fretted under the influence of the creature holding her. *"That bitch better get here on time!"* Jack heard her murmuring. "I'm not going to be late! I swear, every fucking time I leave Lisa in charge of the carpool—"

The walls began crumbling around the scene as Chloe's thoughts further corrupted their surroundings. With larger holes opening to the outside, Jack heard more hellbeasts enter the room. He couldn't see them in the shadows, but he heard their snarling. Scared though he was, his anger at his tormentor presuming to threaten his family superseded his fear for the moment.

"Let her go now," he said with icy calm, "and when I finally do send you screaming back to Hell, I promise I'll make it quick."

"I'll tempt her to more than a few wrathful thoughts before I'm done with her, Jack," the dark prince threatened, beginning to pierce her head with the tip of his tail, "unless you care to reveal what you think you know about me."

A suggestion entered Chloe's mind to sleep with one of the guys at the party she'd be attending later. Jack saw her hungrily accept it, rashes and sores spreading on her soul's rotten skin as she did. He leaned forward, ready to charge.

Mephistopheles leaned his spear forward, ready to counter him. "Come any closer and you're all getting a face full of my special recipe."

"What do I care?" Jack bluffed. "If you're just a figment of my own concoction, you can't affect anyone but me, can you? And if you're really a demon, rest assured, I'll make you suffer tenfold whatever you do to them." His armor started glowing brighter as he prepared to pray the *Glory Be.* "Either way, I'm coming at you within the next five seconds, and if you haven't released her by the time I get to you, I'll shove that tail up your ass until it cuts its way through your lying tongue."

Neither spoke for a moment, sizing up what the other would do next, searching for any opening. Neither offered any. The silence between them was only broken by Chloe's incessant babbling, whether it was about her friend who was late to pick her up or the guy who'd invited her to the party.

Jack finally glanced at the writhing corpse. *"Will you shut up already, Chloe! The sister I thought I knew doesn't carry on like that!"*

"You're right," she said, taking a deep breath. "I need to calm down."

Mephistopheles hissed, almost losing his hold on her. Jack stood erect, shocked at what had just happened.

"Chloe?" he called.

She turned her head to face him and would have been looking him in the eyes if she'd had any herself.

*"Chloe!"* he shouted. *"Stop thinking like that! You're better than sleeping with any guy who opens his eyes at you. You've made it this far without sacrificing your virginity."*

She laughed bitterly, and Mephistopheles regained his grip.

*"Wrong thing to say, Jack!"* he cackled. "But I guess now you know what killed this little cunt, eh?"

His laughter was joined by his victim's. Having heard enough, Jack charged forward. The bat-like imp glided through a hole in the ceiling and plopped on the couch in between his parents' souls, distracting him.

"Hoho, Jack! Let's *all* play!"

Growling echoed all around them in the darkness. Jack felt the ground tremble beneath him a moment too late, as a beast stalked up behind him. He wouldn't have time to turn and fight before it lunged. He squeezed his eyes shut, bracing for the inevitable impact of its clobbering. A different collision occurred. Something very bright crashed through the ceiling, landing atop the monster about to tackle him.

Mephistopheles disappeared into a puff of black smoke. His comrades weren't so lucky. They whined like wounded animals as they were driven off the property, the light radiating from Jack's rescuer shining through the walls, illuminating every corner of the household like a giant flash grenade. When the luminescence lessened, Jack opened his eyes to see who'd interceded. Dathiel stood with his blades extended, his appearance magnificent.

"Thanks." Jack bowed his head.

"My duty," the guardian said.

Jack sat down on a musty armchair across from his family, needing the rest as his adrenaline rush receded. He let his suit of armor recede off him, changing into the sword, which he leaned on for support. Despite incorporeal sight's dulling of his other senses, he could feel his legs shaking.

"Something . . . just happened," he said through deep breaths.

"You discovered you can do more than see and hear peoples' souls with your charism. You can also communicate with them. Influence them, like we angels and demons do."

"So Chloe did hear me just now!" Jack stood back up, approaching his parents. "What mortal sins have you committed in your pasts?" he asked.

They said nothing. He repeated his question, still receiving no response.

"Souls will only hear you inasmuch as you ever heard me before last Halloween," Dathiel said. "And the degree to which they perceive you will depend on their state and willingness. Those in death are the least likely to be listening. You'll find that—the same as when speaking audibly to people—your effectiveness at guiding them will depend more on your prayers than your words."

Jack sat back down in the rotting armchair. "So Chloe . . ." He trailed off, unable to finish his question.

Dathiel nodded, knowing what he was asking.

Jack sat brooding a moment before speaking. "When? With who?"

"When she was your age, with Ricky Garcia. You remember him?"

"*Yeah!* That foreign exchange student at her school. Left after a couple years. But he never dated Chloe."

"Didn't have to. He charmed her into bed at a party one night. Since it was consensual, her sin became grave. On top of that, the demon who tempted them was clever. The next day, it persuaded Ricardo to tell one of his friends Chloe wasn't very good in bed, which spread like wildfire through their school. This, of course, made your sister ashamed of what she'd done, and she denied the whole thing, claiming to her friends that Ricardo had lied about everything to gain popularity. Her story was she'd rejected him and he'd started the rumor to put a blotch on her reputation as a way of getting back at her.

To her credit, she's never slept with anyone since. But, because she clung so desperately to her version of events, she never breathed a word to anyone of what really happened that night. Not to her parents, a confessor, or any friends, and her soul stayed locked in the dark kingdom. Because of this, her conscience has been stifled into silence regarding moral matters over time, eventually becoming indifferent to them."

Jack sat in silence through Dathiel's story, still brooding. What felt like a thousand conflicting emotions raged through his body clamoring to be heard all at once, like reporters barking questions at a person giving a public statement. He felt anger toward Ricky Garcia, but also his sister. At the same time, he felt pity for Chloe's humiliation and zeal to bring her back from her folly however he could. Most of all, he felt outraged such a stupid fuck up had robbed her of eight years of happiness. He looked over at the corpse sitting across from him hardly resembling his sister. When he spoke, it was through gritted teeth.

"I want the name of the demon who did this to her."

"And I have no doubt you'll get it," Dathiel said. "But not before getting through the demon who has his sights set on your soul, and your faith must be won if you're to overthrow him."

"Then I have all the more reason to keep fighting." Jack stood up, facing Chloe, staring hard at her, as though it would help connect the two of them. "Don't go to the party tonight, Chloe."

The dead soul snorted. "Yeah, like I'd miss this!"

Relieved she'd at least heard him, Jack kept trying to reason with her. "You're *not* the object of someone else's pleasure!"

She laughed again. "Sounds like something Jack would say."

"Yes, it does," he pressed. "And what's so wrong with that? Maybe your brother has a point putting his values above his whims."

"Well, I have been thinking about this for a while now. And Ryan's a nice guy!"

Jack knew he wasn't getting anywhere. He needed to change his tactic, come at the problem less directly. He was just pushing her closer to going through with her choice.

"You make decisions based on what you believe, even if it doesn't align with what you feel like doing," Dathiel said to Jack, who paused to look at him. "She makes decisions based on how she feels in the moment. So, how do you think you can convince her not to do something she feels like doing?"

Jack stared at him, thinking. "By . . . helping her to feel something else."

Dathiel nodded. "And what feeling would prevent her from repeating a past mistake influenced by the same feeling she's experiencing now?"

The answer clicked in Jack's mind. "What she felt like after she made it."

"Which was?"

"Hurt," Jack said.

The angel nodded. "So, what do you need to do?"

Jack looked back at Chloe. "I don't want to hurt her. That's the whole point. I'm trying to prevent her from getting hurt." He stared another moment. "Maybe I need to . . . somehow remind her of the hurt?"

He looked back to Dathiel, who nodded again, and an idea came to him. "You're right," he said to Chloe. "Ryan's a nice guy. But so was Ricardo."

Chloe looked up in his direction.

"As I recall, he was charming too . . . right up until he wasn't."

She recoiled, but he kept pressing.

"That started at a party too, didn't it?"

*"Nice, Chloe!"* she spat. "Why'd you have to bring *that* up?"

Jack was about to hammer home the reverse psychology, encouraging her to screw this "Ryan guy" too and see if things turned out any differently this time, when Dathiel grabbed his shoulder, stopping him, instead suggesting more questions. Jack repeated them to Chloe.

"What happens if you get hurt again? Do you really know Ryan well enough to trust him with that kind of vulnerability?"

Jack held his breath for several heartbeats.

"Fuck it," Chloe caved. "He's not getting any unless he asks me out first. Matter of fact, not even 'til he makes it an official relationship. We'll see how much he really wants me."

Jack breathed. "Well," he turned to Dathiel, "another mistake stalled at least. Maybe if I keep pressuring her, she won't do anything with this 'Ryan' at all."

"I'd be careful about that. Understand, her past sin is also a deep psychological wound associated with a traumatic experience. Push her in the manner you were about to and you may inflict more hurt and end up pushing her to do more damage to herself than originally intended. The real trick with guiding souls is to know which tactics to use at which times and juggle them according to the person's state of mind. Nice maneuver though. The one-eighty worked well for tonight. Not half bad for your first time being a spiritual guide."

"Wouldn't have done as well without your help, and it never woulda worked face-to-face."

"That's the advantage of being unseen and unheard except by the mind. Now you've had a taste of the dance we guardians have to do all the time. Nice when the soul finally lets you lead, isn't it?" He winked.

"If you're so inclined to lead my soul, how about leading me in pursuit of the spirits you chased outside?" Jack lifted his sword to rest the flat side of the blade on his shoulder, ready for a hunt.

"They're gone and won't be back tonight. But they'll return in time without your needing to seek them out."

Dathiel ushered him upstairs to his bedroom instead. The place was still in shambles from the attack it had suffered. They stepped over the former door brace and broken pieces of wall until they reached the terrace, looking out at the horizon. Jack saw daylight shining down on the front yard and held his sword by his hip. It sheathed itself by growing part of the chain around him, forming a belt.

"More of the locution making sense to me tonight," he said.

The first time he'd spoken to Dathiel after his vision, he'd asked him why God had shown him all He had. The angel's only answer had been a question.

"Why do *you* think Christ and Mary showed you their origins at this point in your life?" When Jack had stared, waiting for more of an explanation, the guardian had just said, "Think on it."

Now Dathiel's eyes met Jack's, the aqua orbs piercing his soul with their gaze. "Yes," he said, "good use of what you learned about your enemy against him."

"There is one question I haven't been able to work out about the whole thing. Hope you'll answer this time, since it's a how and not a why question. How was it I knew certain things throughout the vision?"

Dathiel tilted his head, making Jack think he wasn't going to give a straight answer once again. But he did.

"Infusion. God was supplying knowledge directly into your mind, without going through the medium of your senses."

Jack's eyes roamed the multicolored horizon. "That's . . . awesome. Think he'd mind doing that when I have exams at school?"

Dathiel laughed. "Hey, you could ask Him!" The guardian stepped up on the railing, about to depart.

"One more question before you go," Jack pleaded, grabbing the back flap of his outfit.

He didn't want the angel to leave him. He was the only one in the house he could open up to all the way. Dathiel looked back.

"I saw how the thousand angels prepared to be Mary's guardians for generations of her family beforehand. I was wondering if you did the same thing with me? I noticed the names Dathiel and Dacre are similar. Am I the first Dacre you've protected?"

The angel shot a half-smile at him, turning like he was about to dive off the railing without saying anything.

"Stop dodging my questions!" Jack gripped the railing with his free hand and yanked a chunk of stone out of it the size of his palm, chucking it at the back of the angel's head. "I'm just curious!"

Dathiel flicked the stone from the air with a finger without turning to look, as the railing repaired itself.

He glanced back. "No."

"No what?"

"No, I haven't protected any Dacres before you. I waited from the dawn of creation just to guard *you,* Jack. Ensuring the salvation of the Philangelus is my vocation."

Jack released the angel's garment and took a step back, forgetting to breathe for a few seconds. He didn't know what to say to someone who had that level of dedication to him. Surely it was greater even than the dedication husbands and wives were supposed to have toward each other.

"So you always knew about the title I'd choose then," he said after a moment.

Dathiel's half-smile returned. "What makes you think you chose it?"

He dove from the terrace, gliding off under the branches of the trees. Jack stood where he left him for a long time, wondering who in Heaven had first thought of his new name. God, Mary, Michael, Dathiel, Joan, or someone else? Mary was the first to say it. So maybe it had been her. Thinking of her brought his vision to mind again. He pondered how he'd seen her attacked by a dark spirit in her bedroom at the Temple. He turned to look back into his own bedroom, debris strewn across the floor from Mephistopheles' attack, and he realized the Queen to saints had been forged the same way they were. Through fire.

He turned back to the horizon, watching night and day vie for dominance across it, thinking about his favorite Scripture passage. He'd had to write an essay about it at thirteen, before his Confirmation. It was about a pregnant Mary who appeared clothed in sunlight, and how Saint Michael the Archangel had defended her from the Devil, represented as a seven-headed dragon. Remembering it in the context of his locution made him ponder it in an all new light. The Woman clothed in the sun had never not been battling with the Dragon, for all of her existence. She'd been a Woman conceived into war. The same war into which he'd now been thrust. Another person might have considered these thoughts scary or depressing. Jack found himself smiling.

He was looking out on a spiritual world with ever-shifting allegiances, seeing it for the first time as an endless array of gardens. Gardens that belonged by right to his Queen. But, in the dark places, it was being invaded and ravaged by infernal pests. He gripped the hilt of his broadsword.

He was happy to serve as his Queen's exterminator.

# CHAPTER XXIII
## THE COSMOS AND THE CAUSE

Ever since Jack had seen what the Rosary could do, he always walked the halls of Wando with it tucked inside his pocket, imagining the very air within the den of demons a noxious vapor.

He felt if he let it touch his soul, he'd be infected by the deceptions of the place. He wore it in suit form at all times when on school grounds, shielding every inch of skin. Even if it was overkill, at least he'd be better protected should the demons attempt to jump him. He doubted any spirit besides Mephistopheles would try. Since he'd shown up for the new semester bearing the Rosary, none of the demons from Delusion's rabble had dared approach him. They'd been steering clearer of him than ever. A welcome change. It made his days more bearable, which was needed given how hard his nights were now. He'd lost a lot of sleep defending his room from nocturnal assailants.

Heading back from the bathroom through the science wing, Jack scanned the hallways through his second sight. He'd made a habit of using it when on a break to keep track of who was where and what his enemies were doing. He didn't like surprises. The school was quiet for the moment. As quiet as a demonic fortress ever got. He was about to flip visions when he stopped outside one of the chemistry dungeons. He'd overheard a familiar voice. Two actually, speaking in near unison.

"Now the bodies of humans," Mr. Wilkerson lectured, Delusion guiding him in what to say, "being nothing more than another mammal that evolved from the elements making up the planet, are composed of four main elements. Oxygen, hydrogen, carbon, and nitrogen."

Jack heard the teacher writing out the elements on the board. Without noticing, he started tapping the fingers of his right hand over his thumb.

"Yes, Miss Ackermann?" Mr. Wilkerson called on Naomi.

Jack stopped tapping.

"You mentioned how humans are mammals," she said. "I was just wondering, what makes us different than other animals? I mean, we've advanced, developing things like technology over the centuries, while other species are still living the same way they have in every other time period. What's the thing that separates us as so unique?"

Jack heard Delusion grunt in annoyance before giving Mr. Wilkerson an answer, which he repeated almost verbatim to Naomi.

"Good question. I'm glad you asked. The structural differences between our brains and those of any other species, coupled with our opposable thumbs, enabled us to build and invent our way to the civilizations we see today."

Jack balled his hand into a fist, wanting to scream out counterpoints to the answer. He and Monsignor Bamonte had discussed his exact point in one of their meetings. He cocked his head when he heard Naomi give them herself, as though she'd taken the words straight from his own head.

"But plenty of monkey breeds have opposable thumbs too. And human brains aren't even the largest in the animal kingdom when considering brain-to-body mass ratio, nor do they have more neurons or synapses than some other animals. Also, our brains' nerve centers are only slightly more complex than those of other mammals. Yet we possess metacognition and appreciate abstract things like humor, time, morality, beauty, and death. How is all that explained if we're just a summation of chemical elements from the periodic table?"

Jack heard a shuffling of chairs, as though a bunch of people in the class had turned to look at Naomi, no doubt with looks of astonishment on their faces. He remembered sharing some of what the monsignor had been teaching him with her after revealing his struggle with belief three days before. She must have been paying closer attention than he'd thought. She'd just quoted his exact words from their discussion on the soul. More than that, she'd perfectly set Mr. Wilkerson up to play into her making the point. He couldn't have done it better himself!

"Human brains may not be the largest among mammals or have the greatest amount of connections within them."

Jack drew a sharp breath that felt like it burned his throat as it went down when he heard who was answering through the teacher now.

"But our frontal lobes are bigger than any others," Mephistopheles continued. "That's why we're the most intelligent, and why there's no need for notions like an invisible soul. Remember, the brain has many parts. It's which of those parts are bigger that determine an animal's intelligence level."

Jack turned in fury toward the classroom door. Before he could do anything, Delusion appeared at the end of the hallway to his left, his silhouette illumined by torchlight. It was enough for Jack to see the blue grin glowing on his pale face. His features looked like they kept going from sad to gleeful as the reflection of flames flickered over them from different directions.

"Quite the protégé," he said. "I'd say she needs more work before sending her against us though. Speaking of which," he frowned, his painted grin stretching downward into an awkward shape on his cheeks, "sad really, sending your girlfriend to fight your battles for you."

"A disappointing match was she?" Jack shot back. "Yet Mephistopheles had to rely on outright lies to publicly discredit her."

Delusion spread his arms in a gesture of innocence that didn't look innocent at all given his misshapen figure. "Well, if we are what you insist we are, lying would simply be what we do to accomplish our ends, wouldn't it?"

"Keep peddling your deceits through the school system," Jack said. "See what happens."

"Truth'll shine through?" the demonic Archangel asked. "That's what we keep hoping for, Jack. For your sake."

The final bell rang, and students poured into the hallways from multiple doors, blocking the two enemies from each other's sight. Paviel accompanied Naomi, who spotted him.

"Jack!" she called. "I was just thinking about you! I tried using some of your stuff on Mr. Wilkerson just now."

"I would have guided her with another comeback," her scarlet-haired guardian told him, "but Delusion went and prompted the main office employees to ring the bell a few minutes early today, to cut us off."

Jack nodded to the angel, then answered Naomi. "I heard. You were great!"

"You heard?" She looked puzzled. "How did you—"

"Happened to be passing by."

"Yeah? Well I thought I had him cornered this time. But, like always, he had an answer ready—"

"His answer was a line of bullshit," Jack interrupted. "Scientists have already concluded the size of our frontal lobes isn't what determines our intelligence. Wilkerson was wrong, either because he was lying or misinformed. I can't be sure which, even with my ability to see who's really behind . . ."

Jack let his sentence fade. The heat of the moment had almost made him slip up in front of Naomi again. He needed to be more careful.

"Behind what?" Naomi waited.

They pushed their way through the crowd, heading back to Jack's last class so he could retrieve his backpack.

"What I mean to say is, it's hard for me to see beyond my distaste for the man because of my memory association with him. I can't be sure if he's lying to push an agenda or doesn't believe just because he's ignorant of certain facts. If his only problem is ignorance, I should go easier on him I guess." He grimaced. "It's just not easy for me to do that. Not with him."

Naomi laughed. "So passionate! You really get bothered by all this, babe."

Jack smiled, but the smile didn't reach his eyes. "Truth is important to me."

*"Jack!"* someone called from behind them.

They turned to see Kevin elbowing his way through the crowded hall.

"Where you been, man? Ain't seen you in ages! You start dating, and the best friend gets leftovers?"

Jack and Naomi chuckled, and Jack noticed something different in Kevin's face. He looked happier than he'd seen him in a long time.

"It's her fault." Jack jammed his thumb toward Naomi. "She won't let me see my friends. And when we're alone, she beats me."

Naomi elbowed him.

"See!" Jack exclaimed.

Kevin laughed. "Guess we can commiserate being off the market together then," he said, cocking his head backward and turning to look behind him.

Becky Hall was pushing her way through the crowd. When she got to their group, she stopped and stood next to Kevin.

Jack looked back-and-forth between them. "Wait . . . you two . . .?" He pointed his middle and index finger at them in a fork, joining them together.

Kevin nodded, a big smile on his face, putting his arm around Becky. She smiled too, flicking his cheek.

"When did this happen?" Jack asked.

"Told you, you ain't been around much lately," Kevin said.

"Sorry," Jack said. "But, congratulations!"

"Thanks," Becky said in her sultry tone. "I'm thinking about keeping him."

"Don't," Jack said. "You'll never get rid of him. I've been trying for years. He's like a stray puppy."

"Fuck you, whore," Kevin said.

"I like puppies," Becky said.

"Congratulations," Naomi said.

Becky nodded at her.

"So when did this start?" Jack asked.

"Only just made it official," Kevin said. "Went on our first date last weekend." He smiled toward Becky. "Finally got the courage up to ask."

Becky smiled back. "Really? I didn't know it was something you'd been thinking about a long time . . ."

Jack chuckled. "Yeah, I could tell you stories."

"None of which you'll actually be telling her," Kevin interjected.

"Wait, I might I want to hear some of these," Becky said. "I think you and I should talk, Jack."

"Only when he's not around to stop me."

"No, no, no. I don't think so!" Kevin said, grabbing Becky by the shoulders and pretending to steer her away from Jack.

"Wow, secrets already," Jack mused. "You should hit me up for relationship counseling. Got a lot of experience with my week-long head start."

"Sure," Kevin said. "I mean, I see so much of you these days, it shouldn't be a problem nailing down a meeting time."

"Touché," Jack said. "We should hang out soon."

"Yeah, I don't even remember the last time I've seen you online," Kevin said. "You've missed a few games."

"Yeah. Haven't even turned my system on in a while."

"You gonna get *Biohazard* when it comes out?"

Jack squinted. "Remind me which one that is again."

"Man, you have been out of it!" Kevin exclaimed. "The new *Resident Evil*."

"Oh yeah. Yeah, I don't see why not."

"Shit, you better!" Kevin said. "This one looks like it gets back to the basics of the franchise finally. Survival horror. Wandering around eerie locations with stuff popping out at you. Everything a growing boy needs!"

Jack wondered if Kevin would feel the same way were they to switch lives for a day. He thought he'd just summed up his last few months pretty well.

"Anyway," Becky interrupted, sounding bored. "I have to get to my locker. Great talking with you guys!"

"Same," Naomi said.

"Yeah," Jack said, half-distracted.

"Guess we'll see you two around," Kevin said, following Becky.

"Yeah, you should," Jack said, still distracted.

He gazed after the new couple. He was shocked his friend had somehow managed to get Becky Hall of all girls. Even now, he saw a few guys turn from their lockers to stare after her when she passed, noticing the sway of her curves as she moved. Kevin was lucky. Even Jack could admit he wasn't that easy on the eyes. He thought back to what he'd said during their conversation the day after Chuck died, about his dating intentions. Given Becky's reputation, he guessed she'd have no problem obliging them.

As they joined hands, Jack flipped to incorporeal sight. The rashes and sores on their zombified souls had increased. They were spreading even as he watched. He saw serpentine demons slithering after them, some leaving trails of slime behind them, and knew he'd been right about what he'd suspected three nights before, when he saw the same phenomenon occur on Chloe's skin as Mephistopheles tempted her.

The rashes, boils, and sores on souls were the symptoms of lust, and the serpentine spirits no doubt the demons who specialized in the vice. He'd thought as much at the bar on Christmas Eve. Now they were set to tempt his best friend to fall in the same way his sister had, if they hadn't already. Jack's jaw clenched until it flexed. If he could just revitalize belief in Kevin's heart somehow, maybe his conscience would stop him. It was a long shot. He could barely sustain faith in his own heart despite all he'd been through. How was he supposed to convince anyone else of it?

"Give yourself a little more credit," Naomi's guardian said behind him.

Jack turned to look at him, realizing his musings weren't private. The angel had been reading them.

"With all you've been learning of late from Monsignor Bamonte, you know much more than most. You're ready enough to challenge the objections of someone like Kevin. And your actions may yet make a difference. You won't know unless you try. Trust me, it'll be better for you to stand before the Lord at judgment and be able to say you tried than to say you stood by and did nothing."

"But I don't know how," Jack said. "I'll just end up driving him farther away from the Light. I mean, look what happens every time I try to talk to my own family about this stuff!"

"We going anytime soon, Jack?" Naomi asked. "Or are you still busy staring off into space?"

Jack flipped to corporeal sight. "Sorry. Just . . . thinking."

"I'm used to it," she said, turning to head in the opposite direction from Becky and Kevin.

Jack's feet stayed hammered to the spot. Deciding fast, before he lost sight of them in the crowd, he called after the new couple while they were still in earshot.

*"Hey, Kev!"*

Kevin turned, and Jack hurried after them. Naomi followed.

"You're getting *Biohazard* when it comes out this week right?"

Kevin nodded, his face lighting up.

"Why not bring it by my house on Friday? We could take turns playing. You should come too, Becky. All four of us could play. It'd be a fun double date."

Kevin looked more than down for the idea. So did Naomi, from what Jack saw out the corner of his eye. It was Becky who looked half-sold.

"Of course," Jack said, "probably not the most interesting activity for you ladies. What if I threw in pizza and ice cream?"

Becky's eyes brightened.

"Works for us!" Kevin said. "I don't think we had any plans, did we, baby?"

Jack had already seen the answer in her eyes before she shook her head. "Great!" he said. "I'll see you Friday, about 3:30?"

Kevin fist pounded him and he and Becky left.

"So . . ." Naomi said, as she and Jack went their own way, "going to your house at last then, huh? Is your family going to know me as your girlfriend when I'm there, or is it just your friend's privilege to introduce those to them?"

"Alright, alright! I get it!" Jack said. "I'll tell them about us. Today. Soon as I get home."

And he would. He didn't see a way around it this time. Naomi was coming to his house. He'd have to take the risk if he was going to try and rescue his best friend. He hoped Paviel would at least protect her if he couldn't.

After all, he'd acted at the guardian's prompting.

"Look who's emerged from his room for once," Chloe said after arriving home that afternoon.

Jack smiled. "Guess I have been a bit reclusive lately."

"Just a bit, huh?"

"Well I've had my reasons."

"Yeah, like a girl?"

"What?"

Jack didn't know what his face had done, but it must have been funny, because Chloe started laughing.

"Spending almost every afternoon over at 'a friend's house' for 'help with homework,' but it's not Kevin? What? Did you think we were stupid?"

Jack was silent.

"Shit," he finally said. "So I guess everyone knows?"

Chloe raised her eyebrows. "Amateur. If you wanted to keep a secret, you should have come up with a better excuse. Like you've ever needed help with homework." She rolled her eyes.

Jack leaned his head back on the couch, chuckling. "Noted. Become a good liar. Have any other big sister tips for me today?"

"Always. So . . . what's her naaaame?" She drew out the last word.

"Naomi. You already met her once. Remember the girl that came to the Halloween party?"

Chloe plopped on the couch next to him, her face alight, like she'd just hit her favorite drug. He stifled laughter. This was by far her favorite kind of conversation.

"*Yes!* So you were interested in her. I knew it! You made a move yet?"

"A little more than that. You're being brought in a little late to the party. We're kinda already dating."

"*What!*" his sister exploded. "How long has this been going on? When did— How did you— *Have you—*"

Jack was laughing at the roller coaster of expressions passing over her face. Once she refocused herself from the entanglement of her thoughts, she smacked him.

"*Ow! The fuck?*"

"How could you not tell *me* something like this!"

"I'm telling you right now!" She went to smack him again, but he dodged this time. "Watch it, or I'll start fighting back!"

"So what have you two been doing? You kiss her yet?"

"Well . . . yeah," he said, moving from the couch to a separate armchair for safety.

"No," Chloe shook her head. "My baby brother doesn't know how to do that. No, no, nope." She kept shaking her head. "What was it like? Tell me every detail! Wait, maybe not *every*— "

"Sssslimy," Jack interrupted.

*"Gross!"*

"Don't ask then."

Chloe sat back on the couch. "Jack . . . kissing a girl. My little bambam's getting all growed up!"

"Shut up." Jack laughed. "Like you've never done anything like that."

"Me? *Never!* So, you bringing her over soon? I want to meet her! Officially this time."

"Friday," Jack said.

"I'll be here."

"What about you? Anyone special on the horizon?"

"Not at the moment. But we're talking about you, little sneak. Don't go changing the subject. What's Naomi like?"

"She . . . puts my mind at ease."

"That's quite the compliment. You should tell her that."

"I have. And I feel like I can tell her things. Most things anyway. You have anyone like that?"

"Why do you keep asking about me? I told you, there's no one."

"No, I mean, do you have anyone you feel you can confide *anything* to? Even something embarrassing?"

"Sure. My friends. Plus I have you guys."

"So you'd tell me if there was ever anything bothering you right? Even if it was really private or hurtful, or if it happened a long time ago?"

"I should hope so! But, why are you asking me all this? Did something happen to you?" She tilted her head. "Has Naomi been beating you?"

He snorted. "No. I just wanted you to know you can tell me things. Anything. Even if it's humiliating."

She smiled. "Aw, dating's made you so mushy. Well," she saluted him, "I'll be sure to report if there's ever any trouble. What's with all this serious talk anyway? You sound more like an older brother."

"Hey, I may be younger," he said, puffing his shoulders up, "but it's still my job to defend my sister's honor! And don't you forget, I'm still the man of the house when Dad's not around!"

She chortled.

"Seriously though, there's nothing you've ever felt you couldn't tell the rest of us? No embarrassing stories from like, a party or something? Nothing in high school? Like having to deal with rumors spread about you?"

She looked confused. "No. You can rest easy, Jack. I'm fine."

"Okay. Well, here if you need me."

She nodded, smiling, but with a look of concern on her face. "I know. You said that."

"Well, I tried," Jack said mentally to Dathiel, switching his sights as Chloe switched on the TV. "Looks like it won't be easy getting her to admit anything."

The angel said nothing. He looked like he was praying. Jack let him be, clenching his teeth at a thought he couldn't help. If everything he could see right now was bullshit, it was no wonder Chloe seemed oblivious to what he'd been talking about.

What if the whole story of her tragedy had been made up by his own mind?

By Friday afternoon, Jack felt like he was walking on egg shells.

He'd been an anxious mess the day before too, worried demons would move in as soon as Naomi arrived in his home. None did. Naomi came home from school with him to meet his family before the others arrived. Introductions went without incident. Once Kevin and Becky got there, they were all soon upstairs with pizza, drinks, and controllers in hand. Still, no demons showed up.

The scariest thing around was their video game of choice. The opening cut scene featured a woman everyone joked looked like Becky. Kevin and the girls enjoyed themselves taking turns playing. Jack didn't. He'd volunteered to go last, claiming that, as host, he wanted to give everyone else a chance to play first.

In truth, the game reminded him too much of his life after all. Tiptoeing down decrepit hallways in a haunted house trying to escape a possessed girl. Being held hostage there by a cannibalistic family who didn't seem to mind losing limbs any more than zombies did. Crawling through tunnels under floorboards to avoid getting caught by a demonic sadist.

*So much for escapism,* Jack thought.

Not only did the game's content refuse to let him take his mind off what he'd been through. The real reason he'd invited Kevin over weighed on him. It would sit on him until it either suffocated his thoughts or he did something about it. He kept waiting for the right opportunity, hoping it would come up naturally. It never did. How was he supposed to segue pizza, ice cream, coke, and screaming at the TV screen every time there was a jump scare into a conversation about the existence of God?

When they paused the game for the girls to take a bathroom break after an hour of playing, Jack guessed it was as good a time as any. He took a deep breath. His heart rate didn't slow. He ran his right fingers over his thumb. Index to thumb, middle finger to thumb, ring finger to thumb, pinky to thumb. Backwards. Rinse. Repeat.

He guessed the only way to calm his pulse now would be to say what he had to say. Once he got going, maybe he'd forget to be nervous. He checked his surroundings one last time through incorporeal sight. The room was bright, no demons present. The only rotten thing around was Kevin's soul. Dathiel and Paviel were there. They both nodded at him, signaling it was his window of opportunity. He took one more deep breath, and his soul rose from its sitting position to tap Kevin's on the shoulder.

"You know," he said aloud to Kevin, "I've thought a lot about what you said the day after we lost Chuck."

Kevin looked at him, both physically and spiritually, swiveling the desk chair around, his face going serious at the mention of their former best friend.

"Which thing you talking about?"

"When you were telling me why you didn't believe in God anymore. Because He wouldn't have created us if He was really Perfect on His own, and how it's a contradiction to say He's All-Powerful."

Kevin nodded. "Right, right. 'Cause He'd have to be able to create something more powerful than Himself which, if He could, would show He's not the Most Powerful Thing out there. And, if He couldn't, then He's obviously got limits. Been working for you then?" He jerked his head in the direction of the doorway. "Get into it with your folks too?"

"No, I found it failed. I got an answer to it, from a priest actually."

Kevin looked surprised. "Yeah? What'd he say?"

Physically, Jack leaned his head back on the foot of his bed from his spot on the floor. His soul remained standing, ready for resistance should any show up.

"It does seem a clever argument," he mused. "But he gave me an answer without even having to think on it. Apparently, the same argument was put forward and debunked as far back as medieval times. Although they phrased it a little differently than you. They asked whether God could create a rock so heavy, He couldn't lift it. The answer was that theology has never taught God has the power to do anything, only all logically possible things. Asking if He can create something more powerful than Himself is the same as asking if He can create a square circle or a three-sided square. He can't, because the circle and square would both cease being what they were if those changes were applied to them. In the same vein, since God's Infinite Perfection Itself, it's logically impossible for there to be more than one Infinite Being or anything more perfect than Perfection."

Kevin was silent a few moments. His brow had furrowed. He was looking down at the floor, processing what Jack had said. Jack watched his soul get up and start pacing the room, appearing disturbed. Soon, it stopped, and he physically looked up again.

"Still, seems like God wouldn't be All-Powerful in that case, since He can only do all logically possible things and not anything we're able to imagine."

Jack raised his eyebrows. "Can you imagine a square circle or three-sided square?"

Kevin went silent again, his face looking dumbfounded. His soul started biting its fingers.

"Besides," Jack said, approaching the soul and trying to soothe it, taking the hand from its mouth, "saying God can do all that's logically possible doesn't limit His limitlessness. It confirms it."

Kevin raised his eyebrows this time, his spirit looking up into Jack's eyes. "How do you figure that?"

"Well, I can name one thing God can't do right off the bat. He can't sin. But that doesn't demonstrate any lack of power on His part. He can't sin, specifically because He's Almighty. Like we were taught at Divine Savior, evil's a deprivation of good. A lack of something that's supposed to be present. Since God's lacking in nothing, there's no evil present in Him. So, He can't commit a sin."

Kevin sat without saying anything. His soul pulled free of Jack's grasp and resumed its pacing. It took a great deal of self-control on Jack's part to allow the silence to rest between them and not to interfere with the soul again, giving his words time to sink in. When he thought enough time had passed, he recapped.

"In other words, since God's Absolute Perfection Itself, there can never be an imperfection found in Him. It only compliments Perfection to say He can't commit an imperfection. It doesn't show any weakness in His power, only how nothing compares to it."

Kevin continued to sit in silence, stewing on his words. The girls came back in, sitting between the two of them, ready to start playing again. Kevin seemed to have forgotten about *Resident Evil* for the moment. Suddenly, his soul jerked its head in Jack's direction and ran at him. Jack stepped back in surprise. He'd been prepared for an attack, but not from any living person's soul. None of the zombies had ever assaulted him before.

"That still doesn't answer my other argument," Kevin said, his words manifesting as a strike to Jack's breastplate.

Naomi and Becky looked at him.

"If God's Infinite and Perfect on His own," Kevin went on hitting him, "why'd He need to create anything, like this universe, and us? What was the point of creation? It seems like that's adding something to God. And wouldn't it be impossible to add something to Infinity?"

"Yes, it would," Jack nodded, and Kevin's fists bounced off his armor like a human's who'd just tried to punch Superman.

Jack calmed back down, enough to keep his head. The zombie was much weaker than his soul. The girls looked at them, their expressions displaying intrigue at what had happened during the few minutes they'd been out of the room. How had the boys gotten from bullets and limbs flying across the television to a conversation like this?

"And you're right," Jack said, taking the zombie by the shoulders and trying to calm it. "God didn't *need* to create us. But the priest I spoke with had an answer for that too. I'm guessing you're imagining God created us because He was lonely, or bored, or something? Like He needed the company? But that's forgetting again that He's Infinite Perfection. We experience things like loneliness and boredom because of our imperfection, but it's impossible for God to experience those things. The reason for our existence is completely gratuitous. You have to remember God's also identified as Love, and love is selfless. It was out of His self-giving, superabundant love that He created the universe. He didn't have to, and it added nothing to Him. But He did it anyway, just so we could share in *His* existence."

Kevin was quieted again, still with a brooding expression on his face. His soul wriggled free once more, fleeing to a corner of the room like a caged and frustrated animal. But Becky's soul approached Jack's, almost like a puppy that wanted to make friends.

"That's interesting," she said. "I've never heard anything like that. Are you guys Christian?"

Jack and Naomi nodded.

"What about you?" Naomi asked her. "Any religious beliefs?"

"Not really," Becky said. "Wasn't raised with any, and have never heard any good arguments in their favor. But I've never heard what you were just saying, Jack. What are we talking about here?"

"Oh just something Kevin and I were talking about last year after what happened to Chuck Nelson."

Becky nodded her remembrance, her eyes darkening.

"Basically the question of whether or not God exists," Jack said. "I've been trying to look at the arguments for and against it lately."

"Really?" Becky asked, her eyes lighting up. "You know, something I've always wondered myself is whether or not Jesus even existed. I mean, the Bible seems to be the only place we hear about Him, right? But what if that's a fable? What other evidence would the world have that He was a Real Person?"

"Oh there's other documentation for that," Jack said, and watched her spirit draw closer to him, assuming a stance he could only describe as pining. "I had a problem with that too and looked into it. Jewish historians, and even some pagan writers who lived in Jesus' time, wrote about Him.

Tacitus, who's regarded as the greatest Roman historian, wrote about 'Christus,' Whom he named as Founder of the new religion they called Christianity. He said Christus was executed during the reign of the Emperor Tiberius under the Procurator, Pontius Pilate, which lines up with the Bible. Then there was the biographer of the Caesars, Suentonius, who thought of the Christians as just another Jewish sect and wrote how they were expelled from Rome in 51 A.D. because they were causing disturbances under the instigation of Christus. Most likely, those 'disturbances' entailed their refusal to offer tribute to the pagan gods.

Also, the Jewish historian, Flavius Josephus, who lived from 37 to 100 A.D., mentions Christ in two places in his *Jewish Antiquities*. He wrote about a Wise Man Who could work miracles and Who was condemned under Pilate to execution by the cross. He also mentioned the sect known as the Christians was named after Him." Jack stopped and thought a moment. "There are other examples, but I can't remember them off the top of my head. Still, that's enough to prove Jesus of Nazareth at least existed."

While he'd been speaking, he'd been astonished at how Becky's soul had stepped more and more into the light shining in from the terrace outside, for once not avoiding it the way zombies tended.

"I never knew any of that," she said. "What else have you learned?"

Confidence began to rise in Jack's chest at the results he was seeing with one of his zombie listeners, even if it wasn't the one he was trying to reach.

"A lot actually," he said, flipping back to corporeal sight. "I've been talking to a Catholic priest who's made me hesitate before writing off the existence of God too quickly."

"Like what?" she pressed him.

Feeling confidence swell through his chest at the look Becky had just shot him, Jack opened the floodgates of his mind all the way, letting the knowledge Monsignor Bamonte had poured into it drain into his listeners' ears. "Ever heard of the Cosmological Argument?" he asked.

"No. What is it?"

"It posits the existence of a First Cause that set the cosmos itself into motion.

It states that you can't have an infinite per se series of causes going back forever—which would be an 'infinite regress'—but that there must be an Uncaused Cause at some point. And we call this Cause 'God.'"

Becky laughed. "Okay, you lost me there."

The others chuckled and nodded agreement.

"Yeah, what she said," Kevin voiced.

Jack smiled with them, but checked Kevin through incorporeal sight. He was standing in the corner, hunched forward in an aggressive posture, looking ready to charge at the first sign of an opening from Jack.

"I didn't understand it at first either," Jack said. "But, here's how it was explained to me. First, you have to understand what a per se series of causes is. An example would be a baseball player, a baseball bat, and a baseball. The ball is hit by the bat, which is swung by the player. The player *causes* the bat to swing, which *causes* the ball to change direction. But, both the ball and the bat are dependent upon the player. Neither the ball nor the bat can cause themselves to do the action the player causes. They're both *dependent* causes, in the sense that they both depend on the prior cause for each of their causal powers. So, a per se cause is a dependent cause. And you can't have an infinite series of dependent causes, because you eventually need to get to a *first* cause of the many causes that can't cause themselves to have effects. In this case, the first cause was the baseball player. In the case of all the movement in the universe, which couldn't have set itself into motion, the First Cause was God."

Becky and Naomi looked mystified, both their souls standing in the light shining from Jack's. Kevin pressed further, his spirit charging out the corner and leaping onto Jack's, who caught him and held him at bay with one arm. The zombie clawed at the arm holding it.

"So what started God?" he asked. "Why should we just accept that He had no cause?"

The sleeve of Jack's scapular rendered Kevin's clawing ineffective.

"That's exactly what atheists usually object against the Cosmological Argument," he said, tossing Kevin back a few paces. "The answer kind of relates to what we were talking about before. Understanding a little about God Himself. Catholicism doesn't just profess Him to be the Supreme and First Being, but Being Itself. It's His nature to exist, in the same way it's a square's nature to be four-sided and it's fire's nature to be hot. If He's literal Infinity, He can't have a beginning. If He had a beginning, or end for that matter, He wouldn't be what we call 'God,' and He would then require a cause."

Everyone was silent. Naomi's soul was basking in light from an illumination by Paviel. Becky's had sat down to rest in the light given off by Jack and Dathiel. If Jack wasn't mistaken, it looked healthier than it had moments before, though it still wasn't breathing. Kevin's soul had gone back to pacing the room, careful to avoid anywhere light shined into it from outside or the living spirits present. His appearance was growing more decrepit by the moment. His skin was flaking off as though Jack were watching months of decay put on fast-forward. Jack didn't know what to do. He seemed to be helping Becky, but only hurting Kevin. He looked to Dathiel for guidance. The angel nodded him onward and he proceeded, hoping he could change his friend's mind by the end of the conversation.

"The objection of God needing a cause also supposes He's part of the universe He created. But He's not. He existed before the universe, in the sense that He exists outside or separately from it. That's another reason He doesn't need a beginning. The word 'beginning' implies time, and time's a part of this universe, starting with its creation, because time's just a measure of change. In other words, time is movement. And anything that changes in any respect exists within time. God's Unchanging, since He's already Perfect and requires no change. So, He exists without time, or timelessly. This implies He's outside this universe. Besides, if He created space and time, He's clearly not a part of them and therefore can't be bound by either, anymore than a painter is a part of his painting."

Light had emanated from Jack's soul as he'd spoken, but Kevin kept receding farther back into the shadows the more he shined. Naomi and Becky didn't.

"That's . . . pretty awesome!" Naomi said.

"You're telling me!" Becky seconded. "I've never heard anything like this from Christians before. I might have taken them more seriously."

"I hadn't heard any of this before either, until I asked," Jack said. "Of course, I was lucky to find a priest who happened to know the answers. Like I said, they've given me pause before disregarding Christianity, or the virtues it asks of us."

Kevin pursed his lips. His soul started hissing and moaning.

"Virtues?" Becky asked. "Like what? What do you mean?"

"I mean the precepts God asked His followers to live by. Like not lying, not stealing, not murdering each other, not having sex outside of marriage. Things like that."

Becky laughed. "Wait, Christians don't have sex?" She looked at Kevin with a raised eyebrow.

Jack chuckled. "Nah, nah, I didn't say that. I said they're not supposed to have sex with anyone they're not married to. Seems an outdated notion in today's society, I know. But then, so does God's existence for a lot of people, until you stop and think about it like we just did."

Naomi laughed. "You mean like *you* just did. I think the rest of us were just trying to keep up."

Becky nodded her agreement.

"Point is," Jack said, "if God exists, and He's the Cause we can thank for the existence of the universe, we can also attribute the laws that govern it as His design. And He did clearly establish laws within it. Inanimate bodies like planets and stars are governed by physical laws like gravity. Animals are governed by instincts. But, for the one type of creature in this solar system to whom He gave an intellect, which would be us, why wouldn't He provide laws for that too? Like laws for behavior? After all, humans are the only thing in the material cosmos that can think abstractly. If everything else that was created has a law that naturally guides it, why wouldn't our intellects have a law? The moral law? Besides, the human brain is more complex in itself than the entirety of the universe, and it's the brain our intellects use to operate the body. If God has so ordered every detail of the rest of His universe, from the largest stars to the smallest cellular arrangements, why should we assume He stopped when it came to the ordering of the human brain and the mind controlling it, His greatest and most detailed creation within His material cosmos?"

"But laws like gravity, or friction, or hunger can't be broken just because we don't like them or believe in them," Becky objected, though her soul didn't attack Jack's like Kevin's had, just pined for more light from it. "They're not man-made like moral rules are. If I stop believing in things like gravity or hunger, I'm still going to fall if I walk off a building or starve if I stop eating. But people break moral precepts all the time. Some even have a natural aversion to them. So how can it be natural for us to follow them?"

Jack smiled. He'd had no idea Becky Hall possessed such intelligence. She was exactly the type of person he'd been interested in debating.

"The fact we can break from the laws of morality is yet another way to show how unique we are in the universe," he said. "Not just a bunch of insignificant specs on another insignificant spec in the middle of space. Our ability to choose to go against what's naturally good for us shows how we're godlike."

"Godlike?" Becky looked both half-amused and half-fascinated.

"Yes, we're like God. Or, as Christians put it, created in God's image, because, like Him, our wills are free to do as they please. It's because we have free will we can go against the law of morality. If we couldn't choose to disobey, we wouldn't be free in our wills. There aren't any other beings like that in our physical world. So, just because our consciences can go against objective morality doesn't prove it's not there. The fact we have any type of conscience in the first place shows there is something there, dictating right and wrong to us."

"Hang on," Kevin said, charging out the corner again to attack Jack. "Back up a second. Even if the universe was created by a Higher Being of some kind, why does it have to be a Being like the One Christianity describes? Why couldn't the universe have been created by a superpowered Force or something?"

"Because forces can't choose," Jack countered the zombie's blows before they connected this time. "Only persons can. A force couldn't think or put laws into the universe the way we've been talking about. If it was a force that created the universe, and that force were eternal like I've been saying about God, then the universe would have to be eternal too, because it would be as old as the force that's constantly causing it to exist. So, the universe in that case wouldn't have had a beginning, which we know ours did, at the Big Bang.

A Divine *Person*, on the other hand, could choose to create a universe when there wasn't one there before. Plus, based on their study of the galaxies, even many scientists have come to admit they reveal something about their Creator. He's clearly a Being with intellect, because everything from the arrangement of our solar system down to Earth's ecosystem is perfectly ordered to sustain life as we know it."

Kevin leaned back, while his soul slumped down into a cowering position below Jack's, unable to fight anymore.

"So," Jack grinned, trying to lighten his friend's mood, "despite what Obi-Wan might teach, I'm afraid I'll have to agree with Han Solo on this one, and say there's no all-powerful *force* controlling everything. There is obviously a Cause behind the world though."

As everyone laughed, Becky's phone rang.

"Oh shit, it's my dad," she said before answering, going out into the hallway to talk.

Kevin was about to say something, but his phone rang too. "Hey, Mom," he answered.

"Well done," Dathiel praised Jack.

"I'll say," Paviel seconded. "You've got your enemies scrambling!"

"Kevin's not my enemy," Jack protested. "At least . . . I don't want him to be."

"That's not who I meant," Paviel said. "It's the demons who prompted your friends' parents to call them home just now. They've been listening from a safe distance outside and want to get your listeners out before you create anymore work for them." He smiled. "But it doesn't matter. You've already played your part."

"I'm not done yet!" Jack said. "The only change I've effected in Kevin's soul so far is to make it worse!"

"*Kevin* made Kevin's soul worse," Dathiel said. "But he wasn't the soul we arranged for you to work with today." He nodded toward the doorway. "The seed you've planted in Becky's mind can be nourished by the Father now. You've begun a good work He's sure to bring to perfection."

Jack looked at Paviel. "I thought my goal tonight was helping to rescue Kevin . . . You said I was ready to help draw him back to the Light!"

"I said you could beat his objections and that your actions might make a difference. They did, with Becky. You can't force anyone to accept the truth. You can only show it to them. Every soul must choose to embrace or reject it for themselves. Kevin's obstinate, a doubter. Becky's open-minded, an inquirer."

"You might have forewarned me! I could have focused on her from the start."

"Then you'd have tried too hard," Dathiel said. "Your disposition as it was was exactly what she needed from you."

"Remember you're but a pencil in God's hand," Paviel said. "The pencil knows not what it will write or when. It just needs to let the writer do his work, without breaking."

Becky came back into the room looking annoyed. "Dad's calling me home," she told Kevin.

Without any complaint or hesitation, Kevin rose to eject his game from the console.

"I'm sorry to break up the party early," Becky apologized to Jack and Naomi.

"No, no! No problem!" Jack said. "When you gotta go, you gotta go."

"We should talk more at school!" she said, gathering her things. "You should hang out with us more often. I never knew Jack Dacre was so interesting once you got him talking."

"Yeah, me neither," Naomi teased. "See, babe! I told you you should speak up more."

"I agree!" Becky smiled at him. "How come you've never said anything like this to Mr. Wilkerson? He makes comments in class all the time about there being no scientific evidence for God."

Naomi stared at Jack with an *I told you so* expression on her face.

He laughed. "You're not the first person to point that out, so . . . maybe someday."

"You ready to go, baby?" Kevin asked.

"Yeah. Well, thanks for having us!" She waved to Jack and Naomi.

"It was fun! Thanks!" Kevin waved too, hastily ushering Becky out the room.

Jack and Naomi got up and waved them goodbye out the door from the top of the stairs, afterward returning to Jack's room.

"That was cool," Naomi said in a half-whisper, taking a seat and swiveling back-and-forth in the desk chair.

Jack let a long breath out through his nose and shook his head, kicking the bean bag chair Becky had been using back into the corner and plopping down. "Yeah I doubt there'll be any more game nights for a while."

"What? Why?"

Jack snorted. "You didn't see that? Couldn't get away fast enough could he? Pretty sure I scared him off." He shrugged. "Becky seemed interested at least."

"It was interesting, babe! No one talks like you. If Kevin found it offensive, maybe you shouldn't invite him over. He was the one who wanted to hang out in the first place. Plus I thought you guys were old friends. He's not used to this? I figured it was just what you guys normally talk about."

Jack shook his head. "No. I've changed since Chuck died." He paused. "So has he. And I think we've been coping in very different ways."

"You think he's mad at you?"

Jack tilted his head, staring off into space, and raised his hands in a shrug. "People don't like feeling preached at, which is how I guess he felt. I tried my best not to sound preachy, but at a certain point you just have to say what you think even if people aren't going to like it. I don't know any better way to do it. I just keep thinking about a quote Monsignor Bamonte gave me."

"What quote?"

Jack looked at her. "How much would you have to hate somebody to believe everlasting life is possible and not tell them about it?"

Naomi smiled, nodding. "Good quote."

"It is, isn't it? Guess what, it wasn't a believer who first said it. It was an atheist."

# CHAPTER XXIV
## THE SIEGE OF THE CASTLES

*"Monsignor! Monsignor Bamonte!"* Jack called, hurrying across the cathedral's front steps.

The priest turned in front of the bishop's residence, waved, and crossed back to his side of the street.

"Jack! I'm glad I ran into you. So sorry I've been missing you on the phone. I've been running back-and-forth to Savannah for weeks." He leaned a hand on the stair railing. "What was it you've been wanting to tell me?"

"I don't really have time to go into details now," Jack said, breathing heavily, leaning a hand on the railing too.

The short jog across the stairs had winded him more than it should have. He must be falling out of shape. Maybe the constant stress he'd been under for almost half a year was starting to get to his health.

"I was heading into Mass when I spotted you. We do need to meet though. I've recorded everything in my journal, but I don't have it on me."

"I'll call you tomorrow when I've got my schedule in front of me to set one up," the monsignor said. "Are you alright? Is there any emergency?"

Jack shook his head. "No, I guess not. I could be better, but I could be worse too. I'm definitely stressed, and there have been new developments I need to tell you about. But, when is that ever not the case, right?"

"You tell your therapist? He should be able to help you with the stress part."

Jack's eyebrows rose. "Oh, I thought you knew. I never went back to Dr. Rasput after the thorazine fiasco. I think my father was on the verge of suing him. In any case, he told me stuff in our first meeting that made me think he was the wrong doctor for me."

"Like what?"

Jack shook his head at the memory. "He had weird ideas about miracles. On the one hand, he claimed to believe in them. But, when I questioned him, he always had some way to explain them by a natural means instead of a supernatural one."

The monsignor furrowed his eyebrows. "Can you give me any examples?"

"Yeah, plenty. He said things like the parting of the Red Sea was just an unusually strong wind that moved the tide back more than usual. That the feeding of the five thousand was just the," Jack raised his fingers in the air to make punctuation marks with them, "'miracle of sharing,' whatever that means, and that angels and demons were just biblical literary devices and not actual creatures."

Monsignor Bamonte laughed, shaking his head.

Jack laughed with him. "Like I said, weird! I mean, those ideas would be considered heretical, right?"

"Yes, that's heresy," Monsignor Bamonte chuckled. "I'm sorry you had the trouble. So you've been without any mental health care since, what, November of last year then?"

"Yeah, that sounds right."

"You never looked into any other therapists?"

Jack shook his head. "No. The reason I chose Dr. Rasput in the first place was because he was the only Catholic counselor in the area I could find."

The priest grinned. "I'll have to let Austin know he needs to market himself better. I'm sorry you had trouble with your search, but I happen to be good friends with a Catholic psychologist in the area. He has offices here and in Savannah and bounces back-and-forth between them. I'm sure he'd be happy to see you for an evaluation. And don't worry, this one's no heretic."

Jack was flabbergasted. "Yeah . . . That'd be . . . pretty great actually! I'd still wanted an unbiased opinion on what's going on with me from a professional in mental illness. So, yeah, that'd be awesome!"

The priest nodded. "I'll give Austin a call this evening and see when he can schedule you in. Hopefully I'll have some news for you when I talk to you tomorrow."

"Have *you* formed an opinion on what you think's happening to me yet?"

The priest's face went serious.

"Sorry to keep pushing," Jack said, "but I haven't asked in a while."

"No, it's alright. It's an important question for you. That's why I didn't want to say one way or another too early and risk misleading you."

"Well," Jack sighed, "I don't know how you could do more damage to my mental state than the monsters I've been seeing already have."

The priest nodded, and, after a moment, he answered the question at last. "I'm not a mental health professional. So don't take what I say as any official diagnosis. I'll leave that for the psychologist. But . . . no. I don't personally think you have any form of mental illness. I think what's happened to you is something either preternatural or supernatural. That's the main question I've been focused on in listening to you and reading your journal entries. Whether incorporeal sight's of Heaven or Hell."

"You don't think I could just be crazy?"

Monsignor Bamonte shook his head.

"Why not?"

"I don't think schizophrenia's something your family would have missed. It's quite the debilitating disease. You probably wouldn't be able to function normally in a day-to-day routine if you had it. Just carrying on a conversation with someone who has it can be difficult, because their thoughts tend to be sporadic. They'll say things at random that make no sense to the people around them."

"You sound like you've met people who have it before . . ."

"I have."

Jack raised his eyebrows.

"I've referred them to the same doctor I'm referring you to."

"Well," Jack said, "at least I know he's seen other people with it. So he'll know what to look for. But . . ." He still wasn't ready to let the priest's point go. He wondered if his spiritual director would change his opinion once he told him he'd had a full blown vision in which he'd lost track of real time and any sense of his physical surroundings. "I don't think my family failing to notice anything is enough to prove my sanity to me. I read in my psychology textbook last semester that there are different kinds of schizophrenia. What if I'm a paranoid schizophrenic? Then I'd be hiding what I was really thinking from others, because I'd believe they were out to get me, or wouldn't believe me, or whatever other reason. And I've certainly become more paranoid since all this started happening."

"True," Monsignor Bamonte nodded. "But it's a completely sane reaction for someone who sees what you claim to see to become more skittish. And just the fact that you're able to evaluate your own mental state in such an objective manner as you are right now demonstrates to me you're thinking rationally. If you were truly mentally unstable, you wouldn't likely be aware of it. Still . . . this is what I warned you about when we first met."

Jack looked him in the eye with a dubious expression. "What are you talking about?"

"I told you, even if you experienced a miracle, it might not be enough to solidify divine faith in your heart. And look how hard it still is for you to believe, even with all you've been through. Like I said, you can't rationalize all the way into having divine faith. You can only receive and accept it, which requires the consent of your will."

Jack nodded. "And my will won't consent until I stop finding reasons to doubt."

The monsignor nodded back. "Hopefully getting an official diagnosis from a doctor who specializes in mental health will help you with that. That's why I want you to see him."

"Thanks for that by the way!"

"You're welcome," the cleric said, jerking his head back toward the bishop's residence. "In the meantime, I've got a meeting."

"Talk to you tomorrow!" Jack waved him goodbye, heading into the church, feeling better than he ever had about his faith and his so-called charism, despite his few lingering doubts.

"In the Name of the Father, and of the Son, and of the Holy Spirit," Father Murphy began Mass in his signature drone. "Today we celebrate the Feast of the Presentation of the Lord in the Temple . . ." His voice trailed off for Jack, who'd switched his sights.

Without seeing the wonders his second vision revealed to him at Mass, Father Murphy would just succeed at putting him to sleep. For a guy whose whole life was supposed to be dedicated to lifting the veil between this world and the next for people, the priest's sermons never enlightened Jack about what was really happening at the altar more than one quick glance through incorporeal sight did. But there was something different when he looked this time.

The castle hadn't opened to the clouds above or begun extending outward for eternity. The structure had retained its normal shape, despite the Mass. Jack didn't even see any angels or saints lining the staircases and walkways along the walls. The only thing that had stayed consistent with his other experiences was Father Murphy's transformation into the Blinding Figure, at which he could never directly gaze for long.

Jack looked around for Dathiel to ask him why nothing else had changed to signal the Mass was in progress, but his guardian was missing in action too. He'd always seen him attending Mass at his side. Jack's soul left his pew, wandering the aisles, looking for any sign of blessed attendees. He stopped at the Good Shepherd Window. It featured Christ and an angel tending a bunch of lambs. Staring into the face of the Savior, as he often did with the picture on his bedroom wall, he observed how it was different through incorporeal sight.

The hair and beard were darker and thicker. The skin was tanner. The nose longer. The eyes gold. Jesus now resembled the Woman Jack had met on Christmas Eve. As he continued to stare, he focused on the eyes. Just like at home, they always seemed to follow him wherever he went. Even now, they shifted . . . and morphed. They became a dull gray. The face changed with them, darkening, the lips drawing upward into a sneer. Before Jack could register the changes, the window exploded inward.

He was blown backward several feet, landing hard on his back. His scapular cushioned his fall, its hood forming around his head before it hit the floor. He was still disoriented, squeezing his eyes shut in pain. He heard what sounded like a flag blowing in the wind and felt raindrops hit his face through the open window. There was something off about the rain. Its drops were warm instead of cold. Acid rain maybe? He wouldn't know. He'd never seen acid rain. The incessant flapping filled his ears, irritating him enough to cover them after wiping his face on his sleeve. When a most unwelcome voice broke through the sounds of flapping and rain, Jack's eyes flew open.

"How rude to have a party and neglect to invite us, Jack."

Jack lifted his head to see Racism hovering outside the window he'd broken. It was the monster's wings Jack had heard flapping. The droplets pelting his face were flecks of his black blood spraying from where the wings were sliced down the middle. He had to flap them twice as fast as most of his comrades to stay airborne, making up for their missing halves. Disgusted, Jack wiped his face more vigorously on his robe's sleeve, forming his rosary into his suit of armor. The gray eyes that had peeked through Christ's on the window tightened, as the demon smiled again.

*"Oooh, Jack, we've miiissed yooou!"* Racism drew the words out in a singsong looking like a hummingbird from Hell.

Black blood leaked onto the floor all around Jack, as if the demon were vomiting nectar drunk from infernal flowers. Jack rose to his feet, ready to blast the intruder away. Before he could, the front doors of the castle burst inward behind him. He jerked his head around. A one-horned silhouette stood on the other side of the holy water cascade, as though a broken church gargoyle had sprung to life.

"My, my!" Delusion said, his voice muffled through the water, though not enough for Jack's comfort. "What delightful delicacies this buffet has to offer."

"Yes, it's been too long since we've fed from this garden," Racism agreed. "And oh, how you've kept the crop ripe for us, Jack!" He spread his arms in the air. "Bon appétit, niggas!"

Several other windows and walls crashed inward as numerous demonic spirits entered, laying siege to the castle. They swooped down, howling and cackling, grabbing up souls, whose attention drifted away from the Liturgy when they did. Some of the more powerful demons were even so bold as to shoot fireballs and streaks of red lightning at the more attentive attendees, tempting them away from protecting the weaker ones by their perseverance. Jack shot a crimson arrowhead from his wrist into his palm, ready to throw his chain and snag the dissenters. Before he could raise his arm, Racism and Delusion shot red lightning at him, knocking him to his knees. He felt his limbs lock up.

"Now, now, Jack," said Racism, "it's rude to interrupt others' meals. You have to wait your turn. There'll be leftovers for you."

Jack felt his head being forced to look a certain direction, as though the demons had control over his movements through the lightning. His gaze settled on the gangly soul of a thirteen-year-old boy in a nearby pew. He looked sickly, but alive. Several evil spirits were enticing him toward a nearby broken window from outside, offering more sensual thoughts than he was getting from the Scripture readings at the pulpit. The boy started moving toward the monsters, as eager as a mosquito drawn to a bug light.

"Besides," Racism continued, "we've taken such pains to make this special for you. Dinner and a show."

Fury building in his chest, Jack slowly but surely stood back up, seeing Racism and Delusion struggling to maintain their hold on him out the corners of his eyes.

*"You think you can paralyze me with temptations when armed with this weapon?"* he demanded, his voice ringing through the metal of his mask. *"Temptations to . . . What is that?"*

Jack closed his eyes, paying attention to what was going on internally. His thinking was being clogged by an emotion. But which one?

*"Ah! Fear!"* he said, turning his head to look at Racism now. *"So, you think I'm still afraid? Of you two?"*

His words echoed across the castle with the metallic vibration his mask added to them. The Principality and the minotaur each applied both hands to their lightning streaks, trying their best to hold him. But Jack was now coming toward Racism with slow, steady steps.

*"You think . . . you can stand against me with the Ark of the Covenant and the entire divine family at my back?"* His voice rose with his form, as he finally stood erect. *"You dare . . . invade . . . THE MASS!"* he roared louder than he'd ever done.

The demons' hold broke and they cowered backward, Racism's features unable to hide his fear from the realization of how powerful Jack had become since he'd last seen him.

"It's hard to kick against the goad," Jack said in a near whisper, and unleashed a slew of lightning bolts from his hands.

Every demon who'd ventured inside the castle was hit. They were sent screaming back out the openings through which they'd entered. Jack sealed them with a single *Apostle's Creed*. The boy who'd been wandering toward a broken stained glass window was now faced with a repaired one, into which he gazed at the eyes of Christ and Mary. His attention was recaptured by something that stood out to him in the Scripture reading echoing through the church and he turned back to the pulpit.

Jack turned his attention to the front doors, stalking toward Delusion's silhouette. More stones and iron rungs materialized from his hands, and he directed them to fly at the minotaur, who was knocked to the ground and pinned in place by their weight. Passing through the holy water, Jack grabbed the demon by his remaining horn without stopping, dragging him along behind him to the top of the castle's front steps. Racism stood at the far end of the drawbridge. Jack hurled Wando's chieftain toward him, and the minotaur bounced and rolled all the way to his baal's feet.

"Take back your rejects and *GET OUT!*" Jack bellowed, his voice shaking the whole drawbridge with the magnification the rosary added to it.

The Principality was scared. Jack could see that. But he was proud too, and not willing to be humiliated in front of his soldiers without more coercion. He spat on Delusion before responding.

"Enjoy small victories while you can, boy! Did you think we were retreating?" The demon smiled a nearly toothless grin. "For every step you help a soul take toward the Light, we will drag it backward into the dark another ten!"

Jack smiled beneath his mask. "Becky Hall's not molding to your will so easily anymore, is she?"

Racism's face stayed neutral at the comment, which told Jack it had probably gotten to him. Why else would he give zero reaction, unless he were masking his real one? The demon spread his arms to indicate the castle they stood before.

"You think this place can act as a hovel of minds forever? No place in the cosmos is beyond our reach, Philangelus! *No place!* We will tear your Church down brick-by-brick." The fallen prince raised his head and snarled, summoning what must have been thirty additional demons from every street and alleyway Jack could see around the castle's moat. "We will have our souls, child, even if we have to drag you all kicking and screaming from the bosom of the Enemy Himself!"

The newcomers dive bombed a few souls hurrying toward the church, late to Mass. They bit and tore at them like hungry lions, fueling anxiety, distracting them from reaching a calm state of mind before walking into the Liturgy. Jack sent a few fireballs their way, dissuading them, then turned back to their leader.

"You want in, demon?" Jack asked, stepping aside from the waterfall behind him. "We're not the ones with Something to fear within the walls of the Catholic Church."

Light from the tabernacle shined out, hitting Racism like a spotlight. He flew up out of its path, shielding his eyes. Upon recovering his vision, he glared at Jack, grabbing the whip off his loincloth and cracking it in the air.

*"Take them!"* he ordered.

The other evil spirits rushed forward. Jack shot his chain from his wrist to the drawbridge's mechanism. It wrapped itself around the wheel several times. He yanked, spinning it. The bridge flew up.

The demons who'd already made it on went flying off into the moat of holy water. Most disintegrated. Some made the swim back to land before that happened, their skin scalded and red, their cries making the rest of their comrades hesitate. Jack spread his arms and fired two lightning bolts behind him down both sides of the castle, striking the mechanisms of all the side bridges. They raised to a closed position. St. John's was now an island, cut off from the mainland of the dark kingdom.

Racism swooped back-and-forth behind his gang, whipping their heels toward the moat. *"Get going! We all know it burns! I don't give a rat's ass! Get the souls!"*

The earthbound demons were forced into the luminescent river, most of them melting before ever reaching Jack's side. The winged spirits sailed over the moat. Jack lifted his chain, swiping and swinging it around to cut down any who came within a close enough radius. They got the message and kept their distance.

*"Leave the Philangelus, curs!"* Racism barked. *"Take the weak!"*

The demons spread out to assail the castle from multiple directions. Jack jumped meters into the air, waving his chain around to catch them before they could. He couldn't get them all. Most flew above his reach, laughing.

*"Too bad! So sad!"* one of them jeered.

Jack recognized the bat-like imp he'd run into twice alongside Mephistopheles.

"If only the Friend of Angels could fly like one," it said, circling above just out of Jack's grasp, daring him to give chase.

Angered at the very sight of the pigmy, Jack shot a fireball. The bat barely dodged in time, abandoning its game and darting toward the castle before he fired another. It took shelter somewhere in the bell tower. Jack launched his chain up to a turret, using it to grapple himself to the roof and flip onto its corner. He climbed to the bell tower. The imp was nowhere in sight, having given him the slip yet again.

Hearing the other spirits pounding on the walls, he turned and ran along the rooftop's perimeter, swinging his chain down in circles over the edge, launching fireballs off it at the flying menaces in rapid succession. The fanned out formation of balls left the demons no openings in which to approach the windows. They roared and hissed, until one of them finally lunged at Jack from behind to get his accursed prayers out of their way. A sorry mistake on its part.

Jack swung his chain around behind him and snagged the monster's ankle. It flew upward again, screaming at the burning touch of the rosary. As it dashed to-and-fro, trying to shake the sharpened links from its leg, Jack swung from it in circles, kicking several other demons to the ground now that he was airborne. To those still outside his reach, he shot fire and lightning balls from his free hand, backing them even farther away from their target. Realizing what was happening, the spirit Jack was hanging from dove, no doubt in order to pull up just in time to smash him into the ground.

He released his hold on it before they'd descended too far, spreading his cloak and gliding back onto the roof of the castle. Landing, he turned to face the flock of enemies, a fireball burning in one hand, a ball of lightning in the other, daring them to attempt another assault. They all held their distance.

Infuriated by their fruitless efforts, Racism cracked his whip in the air, calling off the attack. They descended back to the ground on the far side of the moat. Racism landed next to Delusion's still crippled form, kicking the minotaur awake. Jack walked off the edge of the roof, spreading his scapular to land at the top of the castle's front steps. Through the entire feat, he'd never taken his eyes off his enemies.

"Do we need to continue," he asked, "or have I made myself clear?"

Racism grinned and bowed in a theatrical manner. "Very impressive, Philangelus. Very impressive. You've made sport of us."

Jack shot a fireball at him while his face was turned down. The Principality slashed it away into nothing with a crack of his whip.

*"Alright!"* he shouted. "You're not much for games. So be it."

He threw his head back and whistled, summoning minions from the surrounding city again. There must have been a hundred of them this time. Jack wasn't sure he'd be able to hold them all at bay by himself.

"If you don't wish to deal with me," said their master, "why don't you work with him?"

Racism cocked his thumb backward. Jack's gaze followed the gesture up to the roof of the bishop's house behind him. Mephistopheles stood atop it. Jack wondered how long he'd been there, frustrated once more that he hadn't detected his greatest adversary's approach. Then again, he'd been busy.

After a moment, the Power clucked his forked tongue. "Jack, Jack, whatever am I going to do with you? Playing hero in your daydreams like a child. The great defender of the Church! The last son of a dying religion making a final stand for it. Aren't you supposed to be listening to the sermon right now? I thought this silly little ceremony was what you've been insisting you need for your mental well-being instead of me."

Jack didn't bother engaging in a dialogue. He let the spearhead of his chain slip silently from his wrist into his palm, which was faced away from his enemy, ready to lash it out at a moment's notice. Mephistopheles tapped his spear on the ground a couple of times and multiple streaks of red lightning shot from its orb. They struck the mechanisms of every bridge leading to the castle, which all fell back down.

*"Feast, pups!"* he commanded.

The demons rushed the fortress again.

*"Get in there, curs!"* Racism drove them on with pleasure. *"Rip them all from the milking breasts of that bitch of a Mother they call Queen!"*

What happened next was so fast, it took a moment for Jack to register it. Racism was struck to the ground by a lightning bolt shot from somewhere above him, while Mephistopheles receded, hissing into one of his clouds of black smoke. The strange thing was, Mephistopheles had reacted before Racism was struck, as though he'd been expecting it. Jack didn't have time to consider why. Something landed next to him with a thud that shook the ground. He turned, ready for a fight. There was no need.

"You can try," Avdiel said to Racism, brandishing a decorative scimitar in his hand.

"Try your damnedest," Dathiel added, emerging through the shower of holy water at the castle's front doors to stand at Jack's other side, knuckle blades extended. "After all, your first attempt to lay siege to Heaven went so well."

Angels exited the castle from every door. More emerged from hidden passages along the roof. Others rose out of the moat, their numbers matching the demons' now.

"You've done valiantly!" Avdiel whispered to Jack. "It's not often a single parishioner is able to fend off an entire wave of invaders without aid from the castle guard!"

"Did my best," Jack breathed, without taking his eyes off their opponents.

"That's all God asks," Avdiel said.

Mephistopheles reemerged from his mist, while Racism climbed back to his feet, helped by several of his underlings. He glowered at Avdiel, then resigned himself.

"You know, boys, I think this place is a bit pricey for our budget today. Let's eat elsewhere."

He took flight, flapping his wings so fast they almost disappeared, making Jack think of an incensed hornet. The other winged spirits followed through the air, with the earthbound demons running behind on foot down Broad Street. When their leader switched direction, they climbed over buildings like giant beetles to keep up. Mephistopheles grinned and winked at Jack before spreading his own wings and following the crowd like a hellish buzzard waiting to scavenge the other demons' kills.

*"Luther's loot it is!"* Jack heard Racism yell from a distance.

"They're going to hit a Lutheran service!" he said, turning to his guardian and Avdiel. "The Blessed Sacrament won't be there to protect them! We have to help!"

Avdiel ordered several of his soldiers to tail him and took off after the demonic gang. Dathiel grabbed Jack and flew him up with them. They spotted the dark spirits gathered around St. John's Lutheran Castle on Clifford Street. Jack remembered how he'd once mistaken it for the cathedral on his first venture through incorporeal sight. Now he knew who'd torn the walls asunder.

His guardian flew him downward, releasing him in time to dive headfirst through a hole in its wall left by the pillaging intelligences. He rolled forward over his shoulder, coming up on his feet in one swift motion. The demons were already wreaking havoc, looking far less hesitant to move about the interior of this castle than the one they'd just come from. They circled the ceiling, tossing souls they'd grabbed from the pews to one another, as though playing a game of catch. The earthbound demons laughed various thoughts of vice into the worshippers' minds on the ground. Teenagers seemed their favorite targets. So malleable to their suggestions, they welcomed thoughts of sensual distraction over the sparse stimulations offered by dusty hymns and dry sermons.

Avdiel's band flew in through the front doors, and, together with Jack, laid into the hellish horde. But Jack and Avdiel's soldiers may as well have held back, because Charleston's guardian landed in the center of the floor and emitted an entire storm of lightning from his person. The bolts extended in all directions, driving every single demon back out onto the street. Jack gazed in awe, but quickly recovered himself, following Avdiel outside to keep the marauders from returning. Racism was rallying his troops back into formation. They charged forward in a phalanx. Avdiel and his soldiers ran out to meet them. Angelic and demonic intelligences clashed together like a thunder clap rolling over the road.

When Avdiel reached Racism, Jack watched the two Principalities square off. Racism lashed his whip out at his nemesis. Avdiel caught it on the blade of his scimitar, ripped it in half, and pummeled the bigoted spirit to the ground. Dathiel spun into Delusion, his knuckle blades sparking against the minotaur's machete. Jack engaged three other fallen Archangels who were approaching to grab him, felling every one of them before they landed a blow. Even he was shocked with how much he'd advanced in prowess. Mere months before he'd had to use all his skills to challenge Delusion alone. More spirits moved in to strike at him, but were called off at the last moment.

"Stay your blades, pups. You're only indulging his fantasy."

Jack turned and spotted Mephistopheles. He was perched on a nearby crumbling wall like the vulture Jack thought him to be, enjoying the chaos. Jack raised a hand, beckoning the demon come down and fight him himself. The Power chuckled.

"Does brave, bold Jack feel he's ready to face me then?"

He took a hand off his spear, flipped it palm up, and raised it slowly, as though summoning something from below. Jack leapt backward in horror when a hand broke through the road from underground, grabbing at his ankle.

"How about a puppet show before the main feature?" Mephistopheles asked.

The subterrestrial figure finished breaking its way out from under the street to tower over Jack by several inches, loose dirt falling from its form. It was a damned soul. Jack was sure of it with how much it reeked. Its white hair was long, but it must have been male. There was a beard and mustache hanging off his decayed skin. This only served to make his face more grotesque, because it drew attention to the fact he had no lips, leaving his rotten teeth exposed. The red of his frayed robe made Jack wonder if he'd been royalty in life.

*"Faustus!"* Mephistopheles commanded. *"Drag this insolent soul to the depths. Teach him the taste of worms."*

He flung his spear toward the old man, who stuck out a gnarled hand and caught it, leaning on it for support rather than attacking Jack.

"Faustus?" Jack wondered aloud, looking at the old soul. *"Marlowe's* Faustus? The man who sold his soul to the Devil to have Mephistopheles at his beck and call?"

The fallen Power cackled from his perch above them. "Who looks to be at whose beck and call, boy?"

*"Gl-ory,"* Faustus half-coughed in a voice that sounded like air trapped in a maggoty carcass for centuries was finally escaping.

Jack thought he heard a German accent underlying it.

"You promised me . . . *glory!"*

"And I'm offering it to you," Mephistopheles rebuked. "Glory in the conquering of the Philangelus."

Mephistopheles raised both hands, folding in all his fingers except the thumbs and pinkies, as though holding puppet strings. To Jack's surprise, Faustus swung the spear at his neck in an attempt to decapitate him. He ducked.

"That's right, pup," Mephistopheles encouraged. *"Dance!"*

Faustus began imitating his master's movements and fighting style.

"Afraid to face me directly, demon?" Jack demanded, dodging more strikes from the soul. "Almost as afraid as you were when Michael made you destroy your statue? How about when Joan of Arc burned rather than bending to you?"

The jabs at his pride got his attention, but not in the way Jack had hoped. It was still through Faustus he viciously swung the spear at him. Jack blocked with both wrist bracers, but couldn't hold his opponent back long. It seemed the soul was remotely receiving its master's strength too. Jack shifted the spear to his side and flipped out of its way, redirecting it instead of trying to overpower it. Faustus swung it back up at him. He ducked aside again. He was able to counter most of his opponents moves, but not all of them. His suit of armor held strong against those he couldn't, but the blows that connected still discombobulated him more than he was comfortable with. He formed the suit into his broadsword and clashed it against the spear, tired of playing defense.

He pushed as hard as he could back against Faustus, then released his tension, stepping to the side. His enemy overstepped and stumbled forward. With this opening, Jack slashed his blade upward at the soul's chest, gashing a wound across his abdomen from hip to shoulder. The condemned soul and Prince of Powers screamed together, Faustus sounding like a clogged steam whistle. He dropped the spear and fell backward, clawing his way across the road to the hole he'd made in it with his emergence. It was as if he swam back into the dirt, sinking from sight in moments. Jack figured the injury must have broken Mephistopheles' concentration and thus his hold on his surrogate, freeing him to flee back to Hell.

"Well . . ." Mephistopheles still sounded like he was recovering, "that was underwhelming." He thrust his hand out, and his spear came flying back into it.

"Still wish to hide behind men, demon," Jack challenged, "or are you ready to face me like one?"

The decrepit prince shot him his signature grin. "Emboldened out here in the daylight among your imaginary friends, aren't you, Jack? You forget, I've seen you in the night, when your real character is unmasked."

"Come down here and maybe I'll unmask how I got my information on your little embarrassment with the river people."

"You mean your locution?" the Power asked.

Jack couldn't help the reaction that passed over his face, giving away his surprise.

The fiend's smile widened. "I'm part of you, remember? How do you expect to keep secrets from me? Even in a compartmentalized brain such as yours, all knowledge eventually comes under the light of reason. Now, regarding your challenge," his wings rose over his shoulders, then spread wide, "I've never been one to back down from an honest summoning. Just ask Faustus."

Jack bent his knees, ready to move in whichever direction he needed once his enemy dove. An attack came, but not from Mephistopheles. A white blur rushed past him from behind as Lupe bounded into the battle. Jack heard Monsignor Bamonte's voice trailing him on the wind, issuing prayers on his behalf. In response, the winged wolf grabbed Racism in his jaws, flinging him forty feet into the air. He then proceeded to bite and claw his way through the whole demonic horde, even using his wings to slash opponents in half. The demons who had time scattered into the shadows. Delusion took one look at who'd arrived and dropped his machete, taking off as fast as he could in the direction of Wando. The hound of Heaven took flight, chasing Racism and what airborne minions he had left all the way into the clouds. Once it was clear they weren't coming back, the wolf returned to land between Jack and Mephistopheles.

"Well, if it isn't the pup the Enemy thought could lead the Powers more gloriously than I," Mephistopheles sneered.

"You're not welcome here, fallen one," Lupe growled. *"Begone!* Or I'll put you back in your hole myself."

"Oh yes? As when you betrayed me in the first war, thief?"

"This isn't a debate," the canine angel threatened. "Leave, or I'll demonstrate what a Power's duty was meant to be, firsthand."

As though echoing through a tunnel, Jack heard Father Murphy reciting the Eucharistic Prayer at the altar. Faced with the divine Prince of Powers and the approaching consecration of the bread and wine, the fallen prince backed toward the shadows. But he turned to Jack as he did.

"Looks like our little wrangle will have to wait, boy. But don't worry." He grinned one last time, lowering his voice to a whisper as he vanished. "I'll be back! For now . . . get some rest."

# CHAPTER XXV
## GOTHIC MOONLIGHT

Knowing Mephistopheles' final words at Mass had been a threat of another attack on his bedroom by night, Jack barricaded his chamber all the more that evening.

He went up and began his prayers right after dinner, losing count of how many times he recited the *Apostle's Creed*. He stayed awake long after it sounded like everyone else had gone to bed, awaiting the inevitable onslaught of his defenses. The anticipation was the worst part. He was on edge, jumping at the slightest noises. Most of them were just Ruby moving about the house. The rest were the sounds a creaky house such as he saw through incorporeal sight was bound to make. When the grandfather clock downstairs chimed midnight, the rickety floorboards creaked with them. Then silence. Jack jolted when he finally heard a tapping on the wall blocking the terrace.

"It's the witching hour, pup," the Russian accented voice called from outside. "Time to unmask."

Jack's door burst into pieces behind him. His barriers hadn't held for a moment this time. A gigantic, snarling beast rammed into him, and together they crashed through the wall to the terrace. Jack found himself writhing in pain at Mephistopheles' feet, the beast that tackled him scampering over the railing and down the wall before he ever got a look at it.

"Well, you certainly know how to make an exit," the dark prince said over him. He grabbed his face with one of his pawed feet, his claws gripping the grooves on his mask. "Come on, Jack. The mutts are dying to finally meet you."

He carried Jack through the air, flying over the roof of the house and dropping him into the backyard. Jack had recovered enough by the time he landed that he only went down on a knee and hand, standing back up to defend himself. The backyard was a place he didn't explore when employing his second sight. It was always shrouded in night. Mephistopheles landed inside his mother's gazebo, tucking his wings beside him like a cape, looking like a deformed version of Jack's first sighting of Gabriel or even the Blessed Virgin Mary. A blasphemous mockery who dared to taunt him at his own home.

"At long last," the demon said.

"Yeah . . . at long last," Jack seconded, ready to rid himself of his tormentor once and for all.

Mephistopheles grinned. "Always so defensive, Jack! It's no wonder it's taking so long to get through to you. Your obstinacy is rivaled only by the craftiness of your overactive imagination."

"And your pride's rivaled only by your stupidity at challenging an Almighty Being."

The Power hadn't liked that. His grin became a snarl of broken teeth. He raised his spear toward the sky. The clouds parted to allow the moonlight to shine down. Jack thought it was strange a demon was the one welcoming light, since it was reflecting off the moon from the tabernacles around the world, but he soon saw why he'd illumined the yard for him.

They weren't alone. Jack now got his first good look at the band of demons that had been attacking his home almost every night. Humanoid hulking beasts with canine heads and dark shades of fur. Some of them had wings, both the webbed and feathered kind. A few were skinny, their fur mangy, like they were rabid or had been bullied by the others. Their common trait was the feral ferocity displayed in their eyes. There was no mistaking what they were.

*Werewolves*, Jack thought. *Fucking. Werewolves. That's why they feel so much worse than the others! They're the fallen Powers!*

"That's right," Mephistopheles said in response to his thoughts.

The Prince of Powers alone was enough of a challenge. Jack couldn't take his Order on with him. He felt very alone and exposed all of a sudden. The hounds of Hell circled, smelling his fear as surely as their earthly likenesses smelled blood.

"Powerful are you, Philangelus?" Mephistopheles taunted. "Enough to stand against the Powers of Hell?"

The werewolves stalked toward him. Jack crouched down and prayed another *Apostles' Creed*, emitting a shockwave. The beasts were only slowed, forcing their way through the barrier within moments. They shoved him facedown into the dirt under their weight, biting and clawing at him. His suit and robe held strong, but he couldn't overpower them. He tried praying a *Glory Be.* They closed their eyes when it flashed, ignoring their singed fur, continuing to pin him down until they could tear through the rosary and scapular.

"Your Master sicced his bitch, Lupe, on me before, Jack," Mephistopheles said. "Now I return the favor in kind."

Jack's frustration rose to meet his fear. He prayed the Lord's Prayer, letting its lightning bolts shoot out in all directions. The wolves piled atop him yelped, moving back a few paces. It was enough that Jack was able to move one of his arms. He shot the chain from his wrist, whipping it around to slice any monsters he could. At the same time, his cloak sprung up from behind his back, wrapping itself around the head of one werewolf and spinning it to whack the others away. It got enough of them off him that he was able to shimmy out from under the rest and climb to his feet.

There was still a beast clinging to his ankle. He let the rosary morph into his sword, swinging it around to decapitate it with one cleave. It crackled as its form disintegrated back into the shadows. There wasn't a moment to stop and relish his victory. The lycanthropic intelligences recovered more quickly than those he was used to fighting. They were moving toward him again. He morphed his weapon back into his suit to guard against their teeth and claws, launching himself into battle. He attempted to ricochet his way around the group, punching and kicking them to the ground like he'd done in his first fight at school, but this gang was more experienced with battling the virtuous. He was struck out of the air by a powerful arm after landing only a few successful blows. Before he could recover, the wolves bounded over and pummeled him into the dirt again. His armor held up, but their blows hurt more than those of other demons, and some of their master's temptations began to break through to him.

"Do you still not recognize this as a story of your imagination's concocting, Jack?" Mephistopheles' voice echoed through his minions. "Saving drunks from drowning their sorrows at a corner bar by fighting off their demons? Then spying from the rooftop like a vigilante as a demonic gangster shows up to survey your damage? *Werewolves?*" He laughed. *"Seriously?"* A wolf stomped its paw on Jack's masked face, smashing it deeper into the earth. "And how else do you explain my knowledge of your locution, if I'm not part of the brain that made it up in the first place?"

Jack ejected the arrowhead of his chain into his hand again, stabbing the werewolf's ankle, launching himself into the air above the crowd of beasts when it howled and released him. "You inferred it," he kicked, "then intuited it based on my reaction. Angels are the greatest of psychologists."

His mental resistance took him closer to Mephistopheles through the horde, but there were still too many skilled opponents in his path. For any progress he made, they kept beating him back farther than he'd been.

"You've been trying to find irrefutable proof of the immaterial for months now," the werewolves brought their leader's words bearing down on him with each swipe of their claws. "Yet every time you thought you'd discovered it, was I not able to throw doubt on its reliability? That's because you can't trick your own brain, Jack. Your rational side's always going to see the holes in proofs you make up for yourself. *Stop being a fucking child and start listening to reason already!*"

Jack hammered back against the Powers' assaults with fireballs, but the beasts just kept coming.

"If you're a part of me," he threw another one, "why didn't you know about my locution from the beginning? Doesn't add up."

A beast was struck to the ground with that one.

"You know well from your study of both schizophrenia and dissociative identity disorder," another werewolf came in, "that one part of a brain can hide things from another . . . for a time."

Jack shot out a continuous stream of lightning at his opponents. They were still only slowed.

"You also know all knowledge can be shared between the different parts of the brain eventually," they pushed, "with medicine and counseling. If you visualized me confirming your delusions at any time, or had visions of things I'm unaware of, it's only because you're slipping further from reality to where even I can't reach you anymore. You're that much closer to full-blown insanity, Jack! I warned you about the danger of ignoring me! I told you I'll only remain so long as your sanity stays intact."

The wolves were close now. So close.

*"No!"* Jack put more effort behind the lightning bolt firing from his palms. *"You only remain so long as I hold on to any bit of doubt, monster!"*

All the werewolves were knocked to the ground together. They recouped and gathered for another charge. Mephistopheles called them off with a wave of his spear.

"Enough, bitches. If the Philangelus is so determined to face me, he'll have his wish."

The wolves parted, forming a row leading to their prince. Jack stalked forward. As he did, Mephistopheles transformed. His eyes grew red irises with black pupils. His wings became a black cape with a crimson interior. His skin turned white. The top of his head sprouted black hair as the length of it in the back receded. His teeth filled in. The canines sharpened, and his spear turned into an ornate broadsword with a gold hilt, the red orb shrunken to appear as a red jewel encased at its center. He'd morphed into Count Dracula.

A decrepit figure crawled toward the villain from out of the darkness to rub against his leg like a cat. Faustus had emerged from the ground again. Something moved on the ceiling of the gazebo too. It was the pygmy bat, hanging upside down above the demon's shoulder. The smile the imp shot at Jack looked like a toothy frown from his angle. The Power glanced down at himself, then back at Jack.

"Tired of facing a character from Marlowe's play?" he asked. "Now you wish to face Bram Stoker's vampire? Complete with a Renfield and giant bat for accessories?" He gestured out to the wasteland of Jack's backyard. "Werewolves aren't enough for you? You have to visualize every representation of rationality as a creature from Gothic literature?"

Jack ignored the accusations, charging forward. He would defeat his adversary in whatever form he chose to take. It made no difference to him. The vampire spread his cape and black mist swarmed out, covering the yard like a fog. It shrouded both the prince and his Powers. Jack stopped his advance, calming down, trying to focus on pinpointing Mephistopheles. If he could take him down, maybe the blinding mist would go with him.

As the cursed fog whirled around him, he could feel its effect even through his armor. He tried praying the *Glory Be* to light his way. It failed to penetrate his blanketed surroundings. To make matters worse, he could hear the werewolves prowling around him in the darkness. He resorted to the *Hail, Holy Queen*. Its beams would at least keep the beasts at bay while he figured out where his target had gone.

The lasers spun the fastest when he reached the words, "to thee do we send up our sighs, mourning and weeping in this vale of tears."

When he reached the end of the prayer, the mist swirled around him once more, discouraging him from praying it again. It wasn't that it filled his mind with specific arguments against belief, just a feeling of nothingness. Of oblivion. Like the black hole on Delusion's chest had done. Perhaps it was what death would be like. This was an atheist's outlook for sure. Pointless.

*Depression*, Jack identified, trying to shake off the demons' subtle attack.

"Not quite," he heard Mephistopheles whisper through the raspy vocal chords of a wolf as it thudded past him in the dark. "Despair," he said through another beast from just over Jack's shoulder. "A subtle distinction, but different nonetheless."

Jack swung his arm around to backhand the lupine puppet. It was already gone.

"As far as you're concerned though," the Lord of Power's voice echoed from several directions, "yes. I suppose you could call it depression. Not the temptations of incorporeal beings from some dark realm," Jack heard from near his feet, which he assumed was Faustus crawling around, "but the chemical imbalances of a teenage brain in need of medical attention," he heard from above him through the bat.

Jack swung his chain around blindly hoping to hit something. He didn't.

"If you don't address your problems," Mephistopheles' voice continued to rain on him from above, "you'll end up just like Chuck, taking a gun to your head to drive me out instead of a pill."

"Tried pills," Jack swung the chain. "Didn't work. Because you're not in my head." He snagged something with that thought. *"You're right here!"* He yanked.

Instead of pulling his opponent toward him, the chain was pulled back and he was the one who found himself flying off his feet. Michael hadn't been kidding when he'd told him the fallen Powers were adept at combating the devout. Jack was punched from the air by the wolf he'd caught, who then ripped the chain links from its arm and threw them back at him. He lay facing up at it from the ground. The hellbeast leaned over to maul his face, but Jack pulled the mirror of the Holy Face from under his wrist bracer and turned it toward the monster. It expanded to cover him. The Power leapt back, howling in misery.

Jack stood up and spun around a few times, seeing the mirror was shining a beam of light that penetrated the mist. Not only that, it seemed to repel it. After a few seconds, the yard was clear. Any werewolves who'd been close enough to catch a glimpse of themselves in the mirror were sent whining back to the shadows of other yards. Mist only remained in the gazebo now. Jack approached, toting the mirror like a shield to shine it out. Instead of dissipating, it materialized into Mephistopheles, still disguised as Dracula. He snarled, lunging forward. Jack held the mirror before him, but the Prince of Powers wasn't driven away like the others. He attacked it in a rage, breaking it to pieces and knocking Jack to the ground.

"Reflection won't get rid of me, Jack. You've been trying that for months. I'm still here."

"Hope will drive you out," Jack muttered from the ground. "You might be blocking faith, but you haven't robbed me of hope." He smiled up at the fiend. "Bet that's been frustrating, huh?"

Mephistopheles crouched beside him, his cape spreading around him like a puddle of blood and shadow. "I'm trying to give you hope, my boy."

"Your plot will fail in the end. You know that right?" Jack's words lifted him onto a hand and knee as he struggled to regain his mental footing. "Predications based on falsehoods never stand forever. They collapse in on themselves. Why are you still trying to kick against the goad?"

The fiend stood erect, sighing deeply, his cape settling around him. "I agree, Jack. Why are you?"

"Someday . . ." Jack's breaths came in gulps, "I'll see the truth with perfect clarity and my will can stop fighting it. When that day comes, demon," he finally stood, staring the vampiric spirit in his red eyes, "neither hellbeasts, mist storms, nor the deepest hovels of the Inferno will be able to shield you from what I'll bring against you."

The Power backhanded him across the face with such swiftness, Jack didn't see it coming. The words of the blow sunk in only after he'd stumbled backward several feet.

"They won't have to. At that point, you'll see me no more."

The words made Jack's mind want to sink toward despair again. His anger helped him keep his footing. He continued to stand tall.

"I'm getting close aren't I?" He smiled in the fiend's face. "Felt a tickle of desperation in that little love tap."

Mephistopheles raised the sword from his side, pointing it at him. "If you're so close to ending this, then do it. Destroy me." The Victorian villain flung his pale hand with its sharpened fingernails around to indicate their surroundings. "Destroy all of this!"

In the brief moment his enemy's eyes left him, Jack brought his fist swinging up in a roundhouse punch. The vampire dematerialized into black mist before it contacted his face, swirling around and solidifying behind Jack. He kicked him in the rear, making him stumble forward, to the amused howls of the spectating werewolves. They circled the duel, ensuring Jack wouldn't escape, some of them crouching to all fours and snarling, daring him to try. They needn't have worried. He wasn't about to run. It was time to end this.

Jack turned back toward his opponent, swinging his chain out. It morphed into his own sword. Mephistopheles clashed his blade against it, holding it at bay, and the two of them proceeded to parry and thrust at each other with seeming equal skill. Every time Jack managed a successful swing at the monster himself, he would transform into mist, and Jack would hit nothing but air.

"Swordplay now, Jack? You would imagine problem-solving that way. The broadsword was always your favorite weapon when you played with your friends growing up, wasn't it? Don't you see this is just a coping mechanism for missing Chuck?"

The reference to his dead friend brought Jack swinging his blade even harder against his opponent's weapon, trying to ignore the words that entered his mind with every hit he took.

"So many times you've told yourself you'd rather believe a painful truth than a comforting lie," the Gothic monster went on. "You're full of shit, Jack!"

"Says the one who's not even showing his true face, *Count,*" Jack whacked back against his blade.

"Deflection, Jack," the demon countered his thrust. "You already know you control how you visualize me. Stop avoiding the point."

"Stop avoiding *this point!*" Jack sliced his sword tip through the air, barely missing the vampire's throat this time. *"I'll stake it through your cold dead heart!"*

*"Enough! I'm done arguing with you, you stubborn little fucker! If you won't allow reality to enter your mind, I'll force it in! No more games!"*

Mephistopheles proceeded to display a degree of skill far beyond what he'd been showing, as though he'd been toying with Jack before. Jack realized he was still far from ready to best the Prince of Powers one-on-one. He pulled his weapon back into an armored suit to shield himself, using his wrist bracers to parry his enemy's swings instead. They hurt, even through the double layer of the Rosary and Medal of Saint Benedict.

"The fact you're hallucinating things that aren't even based on the blueprint of your surroundings anymore shows how your mind is slipping further from reality, Jack," Mephistopheles beat him away. "And your supposed infusions of knowledge were the same experience of knowing certain facts in a dream regarding its story and context."

Jack fell to his knees beneath the onslaught.

"They only seem believable until you wake. Your mind wasn't just the spectator of what you called a locution. It was the author."

Jack dropped his arms, exhausted. He couldn't resist the argument. Mephistopheles was just voicing what he'd already thought of himself

*—redundant, Jack; you are Mephistopheles—*

regarding his vision.

The demon kept up the battering, slashing at his breastplate now. "As for the, illumination, of your angelic figments, it's a simple dopamine rush. A high! The same chemical release in the brain alcoholics and drug addicts experience when they hit their substances, as you read about last semester in your psychology textbook."

Jack fell backward to the ground under the barrage of blows. He heard a loud crack and glanced down to see a fissure forming on his armor. The demon was beginning to pierce the rosary! He'd thought that impossible!

*"NO!"* Jack shouted, catching the Power's sword, stopping it mid-swing. *"The experience was too profound to have been anything of Earth!"*

"How would you know, you fucking, naive idiot? Your over-sheltered, dumb ass has never done drugs or been drunk has it?"

The blade sliced through Jack's palm, a thin crack forming on his gauntlet where he'd gripped it. Mephistopheles placed the point of the weapon in the fissure on his chest and began prying, attempting to widen it enough to stab into his heart.

*"NO!"* Jack protested again, using his cloak to push himself off the ground from behind and fly up into the demon's face.

His opponent stumbled back, almost tripping over his cape.

*"BULL,"* Jack punched him across the face with all his might, *"SHIT!"* he finished, punching him again with his other fist.

The monster turned his head back toward him in a smile that displayed vampiric fangs. "A bit of fight left in you after all. Good, because I have more to tell you before you'll know enough to be free."

Jack moved in to punch again, but the vampire countered both his fists with his free arm and kicked one of his legs out from under him, throwing him off balance. He brought his sword up with his other hand and slashed him across the torso. Jack reeled backward, squealing in more mental anguish than he'd ever felt. He fell to his knees, the demon's blow having pierced his armor. It echoed through his head.

"I'm sorry, but I have to fight hard tonight," it reverberated. "Your schizophrenia's far more rampant than we realized at first. It's not just active when you have visions or use your so-called charism. It's happening all the time, Jack, to the point you're barely able to tell the real world from your imaginary one anymore!" The fallen angel with the face of an undead human looked down on him in what Jack couldn't deny was an expression of pity as its words sunk in. "Now focus, Jack. Try to remember. Remember how disappointed you were by Father Murphy's dry, unintellectual preaching. Remember . . . how you then visualized the optimistic side of your reason into a better priestly mentor."

*"Wha-at?"* Jack half-coughed, half-whispered. *"What did you say?"*

The expression of pity remained on Dracula's face as he shook his head. Jack saw a red tear running down his pale cheek.

"Hadn't you figured it out yet? Jack . . . Monsignor Bamonte's not real. He's just another figment you made up to reinforce your deluded worldview. And now you've even invented a Catholic psychologist friend for him—when you know you scoured the internet before, finding no such doctor in Charleston—all so you can tell yourself you're not insane."

The words weighed on Jack like a bag of bricks tied around his neck. They kept looping and jumbling in his head.

*Not real. Another figment. Just another figment you made up. Monsignor Bamonte's not real . . . not real . . . No!* Jack protested against himself.

The demon pressed onward anyway, with no respect for his breaking heart and mind under their shattering armor.

"He's the positive to my negative, Jack. Optimism to cynicism. Why do you think he's so laid back and filled with joy all the time? Why do you think he's always ready with the exact answers you're looking for and seems to remember everything—even obscure quotes—off the top of his head? Why do you think you're the only one you know of who's ever seen him?"

Jack was silent, near tears. Then he glowered up into the fiend's face.

*"Lie!"* he stood back up, his legs wavering. "I'm *not* the only one who's ever seen him! I saw him helping hand out Communion at the Christmas Eve Mass!"

"No," the count swatted him back to the ground with his sword and black mist started spewing from its red jewel, covering the wolves around them in a swirl, leaving only the two of them visible at its center, as though they were in the eye of a hurricane. "You saw a layman helping Father Murphy hand out Communion. You *projected* the monsignor onto him, as usual, seeing what you wanted to see. Your senses have become untrustworthy. That's the affliction of schizophrenia. There is no visiting priest at St. John's. Your disease started before Halloween, Jack. It started at Chuck's funeral when you couldn't face your grief. When you first visualized the priest into existence. Who knows, maybe it even started sooner."

The demon raised his sword over his head and brought it downward in a chopping motion. It struck across Jack's forehead and chest, spitting sparks, breaking his suit into pieces. His bare skin was now exposed to the poisonous mist. His mind swirled with the fog, desperately searching for answers as it had on Halloween. But he was distracted. Something had broken in his physical hand when his armor shattered. It was his rosary. He felt it swinging from his fingers like a hypnotist's yoyo, no longer in the shape of a necklace. He must have pulled on it too tightly—

*No, a demon broke it!*

*No, that was . . .*

"Wishful thinking," Mephistopheles said for him. "The equivalent of a sweet old lady looking for answers in a cup of tea leaves." He stared down at him with his glowing red eyes. "But we're not a gullible old maid, are we? We're smart. We are Jack Dacre! And we will rise out of this delusion, together."

Jack turned over and tried to crawl away, to escape the thoughts flooding his head. He forced the Miraculous Medal to surface from beneath what armor he had left and shoot its beams out at his attacker. The vampire pinned him down beneath his heel, either not feeling the burning rays or choosing to ignore them. They didn't seem to pierce his skin like they did other spirits.

"Oh no, Jack! Not this time! You've avoided facing your fears long enough. This time, you're going to hear what I have to say without throwing up any more defense mechanisms."

Mephistopheles kicked him back onto his back and sheathed his sword at his hip, reaching down and jamming his clawed fingernails into the teenager's face and neck. He pulled his head to one side, exposing his throat, and Jack knew what was coming next. He moaned, kicking his legs, trying to push the vampire away with his arms. He might as well have been pushing against a hydraulic press. The fiend laughed, as though enjoying the resistance. His undead tongue slithered across Jack's throat, leaving a trail of slime behind it like a slug. The monster had whet its appetite. The teeth penetrated Jack's jugular like two razorblades. There was a sharp pain, and Jack felt warm blood stream from the puncture wound of the violation.

At the same time, fury toward Mr. Wilkerson fired through his mind. He was the bastard who'd started all this chaos in his life! He wished the teacher were here now so he could beat the shit out of him! And Chuck! Why'd he have to solve his problems with suicide? The jackass could have reached out, asked for help, sought a professional like he had. Instead, he had to leave everyone behind to feel guilty. *Fuck him!*

Mephistopheles moaned against Jack's throat at these thoughts, and Jack couldn't help the tears of frustration and shame that bled from his eyes. He tried closing them. That didn't help get his mind off what was happening. He opened them again. Tried focusing on something else instead. Anything else! But there was nothing around except the swirling mist, and it only made him dizzy staring at that. He couldn't even see the stars. It would have been nice to try and count them. After a time Jack wouldn't have cared to measure, the demon stood back up, smiling down at him, blood flowing over his chin.

"Delicious appetizer!" he complimented. "I think I'm ready to indulge in the entrée." He drew his sword again, ready to impale Jack, much as the historical figure connected to his present manifestation had done to his enemies in life. *"At last,"* he gasped, raising the weapon over Jack, *"the truth shines forth!"*

Jack tried remembering the faces of those he'd come to know—or thought he'd known—over the past months. He had a feeling whatever Mephistopheles was about to do, it would take the remembrance of their countenances away forever. Mary, Dathiel, Michael, Joan, Gabriel, Benedict, Avdiel, Paviel. Jack cycled through all of them as he closed his eyes, trying with whatever mental strength he had left to see their features one last time.

A specific memory of his guardian's face flashed across his consciousness. It was of the angel looking back at him from across a chasm. From across . . . a turret on the corner of the cathedral's roof. He'd been about to take flight but he was telling Jack a story first. Jack remembered now. The memory was from the day he'd first met his patron saint. Dathiel's story had been of the war in Heaven. He'd told him about—

Jack's eyes jumped open.

*"Mikha'el!"* he shouted with the last of his energy.

The effect was instant and wondrous. The mist around him dispersed. The werewolves whined. Mephistopheles' hair fell out, showing a bald, decrepit Dracula for a moment, before his skin changed black and the cape spread into his feathered wings. The monster drew back, hissing. Jack heard the werewolves around them start howling in pain, like they were being attacked. He couldn't see exactly what was going on. He was too worn out even to lift his head. But he could see Mephistopheles' reaction to it. The fiend was glancing off to Jack's right, fear evident all over his features. Not a sight Jack had often seen. A white blur flashed over him, pummeling Mephistopheles off him, and he knew who'd arrived to give the fallen Powers hell. He started laughing, but it turned into a cough halfway out his mouth.

"Somebody's . . ." he coughed again, "gonna get an ass-beating now!"

As though on cue, Mephistopheles screamed like he was being tortured on the rack.

In the next moment, silence settled around Jack like a comforting blanket.

Jack might have dozed off for a minute with how fuzzy he felt.

All he knew was the next thing he remembered was a glowing light approaching him out the corner of his eye.

"I don't think I can rise just yet," he croaked to the hound who'd rescued him.

Lupe lay down next to him instead, licking his wounds, beginning with the worst ones on his torso and neck. Jack's pain was alleviated, but the true harm of the battle was much more deep-seated. The white wolf slipped one of his wings under him and lifted him onto his back, carrying him gently through the house back to his bedroom. Jack hardly noticed. He was too preoccupied with the numbness coursing through him.

"I can't go on like this," he said, as the heavenly Power rolled him onto the decorative canopy bed, and he rolled over on his physical bed.

"We will protect you," the wolf assured. "Monsignor Bamonte has prayed for your relief. You won't have to face Mephistopheles again for some time."

He sat down next to the bed so as to be on more of an eye level with Jack. His gigantic form still put his head a foot above Jack's pillow. Jack was silent a long moment.

"It doesn't matter," he said. "His damage is done. How am I supposed to conquer doubts about the Faith and my sanity if I can't even be sure of what basis to judge reality itself from?" He turned over on his pillow, putting his hands on his forehead, digging his fingernails into his hair. "What can a person do who can't trust their senses? What even is reality?"

"The fallen Powers are clever liars, Philangelus," the lupine prince soothed. "Mephistopheles most of all. And the most effective lies are half-truths. Demons love blending what you know to be fact with the deceptions of their agendas. Only the humble, prayerful, persevering man will be able to separate reality from their fictions."

"I've tried," Jack said in a barely audible voice. His wounds were still festering angrily. "But it's always one step forward, two steps back. And both sides claim to offer the truth."

"Hence, only one side can be telling it."

Jack turned and looked the angel in his yellow eyes, which were gentle at the moment despite their usual fierceness. The wolf displayed an untamed beauty, contrasting the feral looks in the eyes of the fallen ones he'd just fought. Jack felt the beginnings of what he'd been told was illumination at beholding their gaze. He turned away from it.

"Both sides seem to make sense when I hear them out. I have no idea who or what to believe!"

"You will, when you're ready."

"The demons seem to offer evidence for their arguments. Your side seems to only ever give me just enough to . . . *hope! Not know!* I'm sorry," Jack said quickly. "If you really are an angel, I don't mean to be disrespectful. It's just . . ."

"It's alright. You seek the truth in honesty. There's no shame in that."

"And I am ready!" Jack said. "You angels keep telling me I'll possess belief when I'm ready, but how could I be more ready than I am now? All my happiness hinges on whether or not God exists. If your side is really the one with the truth, what're you waiting for? Make me know it!"

"If God wanted you to know in the sense you're thinking, He wouldn't ask you for faith. He values trust, Philangelus. There is no faith in Heaven. We have no need of it. You'll have the knowledge you're longing for in the next life. For now, in this one, all we're waiting for you to embrace is faith, and after that, your destiny. They will be enough to sustain your happiness in this world. They are what will lead you to the direct knowledge of God we call, Heaven, in the next."

"Which Mephistopheles would say sounds like just the hippy-dippy bullshit he'd expect from charlatans trying to pull one over on the gullible. Or, in this case, the overactive imagination of a teenager who grew up watching too many movies. And I have to say, I'd agree with him! I still have no way of knowing you're real. So, how can I trust anything you tell me? How do I even know Monsignor Bamonte's real? What can be known, beyond the shadow of any doubt?"

"Seek the answers to these questions and you'll find them," the wolf advised. "Then your belief in reality will not only be saved, but your mind guarded against future assaults on its perception."

*"That's just putting it off! More stalling!"* Jack protested. *"More Yoda-speak!* Why don't *you* just tell me, if you're really an angel who holds the secrets of an immortal lifetime?"

"I could. But, as you just said, you'd write it off as more you're telling yourself through hallucination. You already question my existence. And now you're doubting what your senses tell you even more than before." The Power shook his head. "No. You need to discover these answers through a natural means you know you can trust. Not anything perceived through incorporeal sight."

Jack stared at him, spreading his hands in a *how do I do that* gesture, wishing he could sink down into his pillow and sleep for weeks. "I don't even know where to begin," he said. "If I can't be sure of anything I see, hear, or touch . . ."

"By relying on something else that's intangible," the wolf said, "but that you already know is real and reliable."

"There's no such thing."

"Sure there is. You've been using them since you were a child. Abstract concepts you don't need the five physical senses to comprehend."

Jack stared, not getting it.

"In this case, logic," the prince said. "Use simple logical deduction to solve the dilemma of reality for yourself."

The advice seemed sound, regardless of its source. But Jack didn't know how he was supposed to follow it. He wouldn't be able to think his way around his problems at the moment anyway. He was too tired and his head ached too much. Before he could let himself sleep, there was another concern he had to get off his chest.

"How did a fallen angel break through the armor of the Rosary if it's really powered by the Queen of Angels herself?"

"Sacramentals are partially powered by the user's faith. You know that. After their consecration at a priest's blessing, your weapons are only as strong as you make them."

"Then I might as well be naked before my enemies." Jack jabbed his chest. "There's no faith left in here."

"If that were true, we wouldn't be talking. And you certainly wouldn't still harbor such hatred in your heart for everything Mephistopheles stands for. You've not succumbed to despair yet, Philangelus."

"Don't call me that," Jack said, massaging his forehead again, deliberately avoiding the wolf's eyes. "It's either just a name I made up for myself in pretending I'm something I'm not, or it's a title I'm unworthy of."

Lupe laid his head down on Jack's chest like a pining dog, the gesture making Jack look down into the glowing yellow eyes despite himself. Tears formed in them, and more formed in Jack's own.

"Don't give up, Jack. Even God Himself experienced His darkest moment just before the Final Victory."

# CHAPTER XXVI
## BEYOND THE CURTAIN

The following morning, Jack updated his journal, thinking it might help him see things more clearly if he wrote everything down.

He was mistaken.

None of the answers he sought were obvious. Lupe had said logical deduction could solve the question of reality, but Jack didn't know what dots he was supposed to be connecting and his tortured mind went unappeased. After school, he drove out to the cathedral, determined to see Monsignor Bamonte in the presence of others. When he walked into the office lobby, there was a different receptionist at the front desk than he'd seen before. It was a broad bearded man instead of the elderly lady.

The receptionist looked up. "Can I help you, sir?"

"Yes," Jack said after a moment, realizing he was staring. "I was wondering if Monsignor—are you the only receptionist who works here?" he altered his question mid-sentence.

"Yessir," the man said.

"There wasn't an older woman working here recently? Wore thick glasses?"

The receptionist furrowed his eyebrows. "No . . . Don't think so. I've been the receptionist here for years."

Jack's head throbbed with a sudden headache. Had he invented a fake priest and the receptionist who'd introduced them? He turned and dashed back out the door. In the sunlight, the cathedral stood imposing before him. Its sight usually brought him comfort. He felt only how small and insignificant he was in its shadow now, the silhouette of the steeple tracing its cross over him.

He couldn't take anymore surprises. He'd deliberately been holding out from incorporeal sight all day until he could see his spiritual director and make sure he was real. Now, with the realization he may have dreamed up more people than just the priest, he felt at a crossroads. Should he use incorporeal sight to seek answers from one of the angels he'd surely see on the castle grounds, or be done with the whole thing now, swear off its use forever, and check himself into a home for the insane?

He couldn't do the latter. Not until he was sure he'd gone crazy. But he feared to do the former, perhaps because it would confirm that for him. Maybe Mephistopheles was right. Maybe he was a hypocrite who refused to seek the truth when the truth didn't appeal to him.

The fuel of that angering thought drove his mind into making its decision.

He switched to his other vision, and screamed in horror.

Jack was standing in the rose garden under the gazebo with Mephistopheles stalking toward him from behind a bush, his hunched form and segmented legs making him resemble an ostrich that had escaped Satan's zoo.

*"No! No! No! No!"* Jack screamed. *"No more! Leave me alone!"*

He ran toward the castle, but his pace was slowed by pain. His soul still bore the wounds from the previous night's thoughts. They stung as though they'd just been inflicted, still bleeding, not having healed at all the way physical wounds did with time.

"Won't do you any good to run, Jack," the monster called from right behind him. "You can't escape me any longer. I'm going to dissect that brain of yours until it operates properly, even if I have to pull it apart synapse by synapse."

He spread his wings, taking flight. Jack could see his shadow on the ground in front of him, closing the gap between them. He ran in zigzags across the paths of the garden, ducking under tree branches to keep the wretch away. The Power broke through them, hardly slowed from reaching his prey. The moss-covered wall of the garden appeared before Jack when he rounded another corner, but he wasn't sure he'd be able to scale it before his enemy snatched him. Not with his injuries. He rolled forward, narrowly escaping a swipe from Mephistopheles' clawed feet. He felt like a mouse running from a hawk. The demon circled around for another try, coming at him from the front now, blocking his path to the wall and the castle beyond. Jack fell to his knees, squeezing his eyes shut, feeling hopelessness begin to cloud his mind as the personification of all his nightmares closed in for the finish.

It was over.

Mephistopheles—whatever he was—had won.

Nothing happened. After several moments of waiting for the inevitable strike, during which his heart went to work on his chest like a sledge hammer, Jack opened his eyes. Mephistopheles was lying on the ground a few yards in front of him, an arrow protruding from his shoulder. The demon rose, looking winded. He shook himself off like a wounded dog as he reached up to grab the arrow. He winced when it burned his fingers but managed to yank it out anyway, throwing it aside.

A bright figure jumped down from a tree branch, standing between Jack and the monster, unsheathing a sword, a gold-embroidered white flag in the other hand. The flag bore a picture of the Blessed Virgin with an angel kneeling before her and presenting her with a lily. Below them were printed what looked to Jack like the names of Jesus and Mary, but they were written in a different language. The demon looked up to see who'd shot him, and his expression of fury became one of horror.

"Remember me?" Joan asked.

Mephistopheles didn't say anything, just turned and fled. When he shot a fireball from the orb of his spear at a wall of bushes to make a hole for escape, Joan was waiting on the other side of it. He turned to run back the other way. She stood before him again, this time only feet away. She smashed the butt of her sword into his face. He fell to the ground screaming. He couldn't outrun her, and she was keeping him from teleporting. He had to face her. He rose, holding his spear out, ready for a fight.

"You wish to stand against me? Again?" the Maid asked, her flag swimming through the wind as she flipped it around.

She charged forward, engaging the damned intelligence with both sword and flag, using the flag like a spear of her own. Its cloth scalded the wretch at its touch like a towel of fire the saint was using to swat him.

*"This isn't your fight, Pucelle—"* The demon was kicked to the ground hard before he could finish, rolling for several meters.

"Nor was France and England's yours, pup," Joan said.

Jack couldn't help smiling at seeing Mephistopheles so outmatched for once, even if it was all in his imagination. It was the first time he'd smiled since at the church the day before. Mephistopheles used the momentum of the blow to roll back to his feet, and the two spirits flew toward each other. The demon couldn't land a hit on the saint.

"You used to be faster," she said. "Satan sent you back up with this level of training?"

*"Fuck you, bread-worshipping whore, and all the other bitches who work the castle corners with you!"*

Joan brought her flag swinging toward the fiend's ribcage, but flipped its back end up when he brought his spear around to block it, hitting him in the throat instead. "How's that for turning a trick?"

Mephistopheles limped away, gasping for breath. Or at least, Jack thought he was gasping. It was a grating sound. The demon's version of coughing, he supposed.

"Oh, please," Joan rolled her eyes. "I didn't hit you that hard."

The demon turned and came charging back, head hunched forward and snarling. Joan swung the flag around again, connecting it with her opponent's head. She'd hit him hard this time. Mephistopheles sailed up into the trees, screaming in agony when he came in contact with the flowers growing from them. They'd transformed into the forms they took in the presence of the fallen. The fireballs caught on his feathers and the lightning balls sent him knocking back-and-forth across the branches like a pinball. When one of them burst him through the top of the trees, he flapped his wings so as not to fall back among them, skyrocketing away from the cathedral, raining glowing feathers behind him like a newborn phoenix. It took him several seconds to get up to enough speed to extinguish the flames engulfing him, but he was soon nothing but a glowing spark on the horizon.

Jack's breathing came in deep gulps. He hadn't realized he'd been holding it for most of the fight. Joan planted her flag in the grass, sheathed her sword at her hip, and came over, lifting his arm over her shoulder to help him walk.

"Let's get you inside," she said.

"Thanks," Jack whispered, the words stinging his injured throat.

"Believe me, it was my pleasure," Joan said.

They exited the garden and Jack saw Gabriel perched on the castle's steeple beside the cross. He was holding a gold trumpet. When he raised it to his mouth and blew, Jack heard a sonorous echo, as though the blast of the instrument was coming from all around him. It was like the crashing of waves in his ears and yet a harmonious melody. It reminded him of the voice of God Himself as heard in his locution, though there were no words to it. It tugged at his heartstrings, terrible and beautiful, joyful and sad, all at once.

It must have been a different sound to the damned, because Jack heard them crying out in agony from blocks around. Some fled their dens. Others cowered where they stood. He even saw some of those closest to the castle disintegrate into pieces when the sound wave hit them. As for the zombies lining Broad Street, some looked up as if they'd heard the horn and were drawn to it. Others fled alongside the demons, covering their ears. Jack, for his part, was drawn. He felt the sudden urge to attend Confession, thinking it had been too long since his last. As Joan walked him across the castle's front drawbridge, other souls both living and dead walked with them, looking up at the trumpet blower as though answering a summons.

"Is that a call to repentance?" Jack asked his rescuer.

"Yes."

"Heard by people who don't have my ability within their consciences, as a still small voice, right?"

"Right again."

Jack nodded, hanging his head down in exhaustion. His neck had stung again when he'd craned it upward to look at the Archangel. He coughed, both the bite on his throat and the wound on his chest protesting when he did. Joan dipped her hand in the holy water cascade at the front door and rubbed it on his injuries at the same time Jack dipped his fingers physically into one of the fonts and made the sign of the cross upon entering the church. The water brought relief to his wounds.

"Holy water erases sins?" he asked, watching some of his cuts shrink and disappear.

"Venial ones," Joan said. "But these have gone deep. A confession will heal you completely."

Jack looked around through corporeal sight and saw he was in luck. Confessions were in session. Gabriel's trumpet blast must have been some sort of spiritual announcement, for those who had the ears to hear. That was why Joan had brought him here. Maybe it was even why Mephistopheles had tried to block his path.

There were two confessionals in the back of the church. They had sectional enclosures with red curtains and screens covering them. Both had signs in front of them at the moment. The one to Jack's left read "Father Murphy." The one to his right, "Father Bamonte." Refusing to trust his senses and knowing it would just be him and the monsignor alone again, Jack jumped in Father Murphy's line. He knew he was real. He could ask him about the other priest, if there was one. There were less people in his line anyway.

When he switched back to his other sight, he looked up and down both lines. Guardian angels and saints accompanied the penitents, even the dead. They were holding some of the weaker souls up, much as Joan was holding him. When the green lights went on above the confessionals to signal the start of the penance service, a bright angel in emerald robes with long flowing hair the same color as Michael's and Gabriel's flew past the two lines. Jack had never seen him before, but he felt almost as powerful as the golden-haired Archangels he resembled. He was tall and tan like them, but leaner. His stride gave Jack the impression of a youthful personality, like a child who'd just set out on a quest as yet untouched by the cynicism of the world.

What happened next made Jack do a double take. He blinked to see if his eyes were playing tricks on him. The angel split in two and what appeared to be twin angels walked apart from each other in opposite directions, each entering a different confessional.

"What the . . ."

Joan laughed at his confusion. "Angels are powerful minds, Jack. They can focus their attention wholly on more than one place at a time."

Jack shook his head, wondering if there'd ever be an end to the strange phenomena incorporeal sight exposed to him on a daily basis. Every time he'd thought he'd seen everything, something would turn his perception of the world upside down again. As he watched, the penitents started taking their turns behind the curtain.

The first one in his line was a living soul, wounded like him. When he emerged, his injuries were gone and he was brighter than before. The next in line was a zombie. Jack was glad when he took his stench ducking behind the curtain with him. After a few minutes, he reappeared looking like a different creature, not shining as brightly as the first penitent, but looking human. When he exited the box, Gabriel descended from one of the upper balconies of the castle, carrying a large lily with him. He placed it over the penitent's chest, and it dissolved into him, helping his soul shine brighter. The Archangel took the horn slung over his shoulder and blew a single note into it that resounded pure joy around the nave.

"What was the deal with the flower?" Jack asked, after recovering from the effect of the music. "He didn't give one to the other guy."

"That soul wasn't dead," Joan said. "He hadn't lost Gabriel's gift."

Jack looked at her.

"Gabriel's patron of Baptism," she said.

"Yeah, he told me that. I don't know what it means though."

"At every Baptism, he gives the soul a special grace to help it on its journey. When they lose the life of grace, they lose his particular grace. So he gives them a new one when they're resurrected."

While Joan was speaking, another zombie who'd entered a confessional reemerged. It was still a walking corpse. More than that, it looked worse than when it had gone in. Jack cringed at the new rotten scents wafting over from it. Gabriel gave this one nothing, flying away.

"What happened with that one?" Jack asked. "Why didn't the Sacrament work?"

"The Sacrament always works," Joan said. "When the soul cooperates with it. That one held something mortal back, and Confession's never meant to be a partial healing. You can't choose among grave offenses to confide. You have to confess them all. Otherwise a new one's added for the sacrilege of the Sacrament."

Jack glanced over, his face turning pale with fear.

"You've got nothing to worry about," Joan reassured. "Just never hold back."

The penitent who'd been in front of Jack exited the confessional, and Dathiel lifted the curtain from behind him, smiling at his charge.

"Your turn, Jack!" He looked at Joan. "Thank you for bringing him. I can take him from here."

The Maid handed him off to his guardian. "See you around, Jack," she said, and disappeared before he had a chance to say goodbye.

Dathiel helped Jack across the threshold beyond the curtain, and Jack's eyes widened at all he saw before him.

The confessional was a much bigger room on the inside than the little wooden nook it appeared from without.

It looked like it would hold ten people inside it now. The vines growing around the walls of the castle were much denser, filling the space with the scent of their lilies, making Jack feel he'd stepped into a tropical vacation. The only scent overpowering them was that of roses, exuding from the person Jack had most wanted to see for a long time.

The Blessed Virgin Mary stood to Father Murphy's right, beckoning him forward. He wanted to come. He wanted to throw himself into her open arms. But he was hesitant to approach the priest next to her. There was no screen between them, and the cleric had taken the Blinding Form of white light he always did at Mass. He was also standing and facing him instead of sitting and facing away from him. Thankfully, others were present to help Jack forward through his hesitation.

As Dathiel supported him, Michael took his other arm, and the two angels half-carried him to the kneeler before the priest. The Archangel's touch alone brought more relief to the bruises on Jack's bicep. When he'd drawn near enough to kneel at the priest's feet, he saw the lean angel who'd split himself in two. He was crouched on one knee to Father Murphy's left. The light coming from the clergyman had blocked him from sight before. Jack now noticed his golden eyes, matching his hair in color. He smiled at Jack, taking his hand to help him kneel down, while Mary took his other hand. Jack gave her a longing look since Father Murphy was too bright to look at directly. He felt tears well up in his eyes when she gazed into them. She wiped them from his face.

"In the Name of the Father, and of the Son, and of the Holy Spirit," Father Murphy intoned, reminding Jack what he was there to do.

He crossed himself, feeling more relief come to his bruises as he did. "Bless me, Father, for I have sinned. It's been about . . . a few months since my last confession, I guess."

Father Murphy didn't say anything, so Jack went on.

"I had wrathful thoughts about a teacher of mine I don't like . . . and about an old friend of mine. And . . . I've also been questioning the existence of God. He seems to have blessed me with gifts, but I question their validity too . . . I'm not sure what to believe anymore."

Jack waited, hoping the priest would offer some sort of guidance.

"Is that all?" the cleric asked from inside the light.

"Yes," Jack said after blinking. "I haven't committed any big sins I can think of," he added, fearing the omission of anything mortal.

"Okay," the priest said. "For your penance, say one *Our Father* and three *Hail Mary's*. Now say your act of contrition and I'll give you absolution."

Jack blinked again, astounded by the priest. But he didn't argue, just prayed the formula printed on top of the kneeler. It was only when Father Murphy raised his hand to absolve him Jack was brought back to awe. He saw his hand extend from the light. It was bloody. Pierced with a large wound on the palm that had gone all the way through. It placed itself on Jack's forehead, the blood from it dripping down his cheeks and nose, feeling like liquid fire, both cold and hot.

"I absolve you from all your sins," Father Murphy said, but alongside another voice; one Jack had heard before, in his locution, "in the name of the Father, and of the Son, and of the Holy Spirit."

At the voices' words, two rays of light extended farther out than the other rays emanating from the priest. They looked like they were coming from where his chest would have been. One was white like the others. The second was crimson, the same color as the blood. Mary raised a hand and placed it into the white ray. It parted into five rays extending from her fingers out to Jack. The two rays engulfed him, blood raining all over him from within them until he was covered.

Instead of leaving him drenched and dripping, the blood seeped into his skin and armor, even into his sword. His muscles expanded. He took in a deep breath. He felt rejuvenated, the way he did when receiving Holy Communion. The wounds on his neck and across his chest had sealed themselves. He was healed. He stood.

As the blood soaked in all the way, the angel at the priest's left stirred. Remaining on his knee, which still left him tall enough to reach Jack's forehead, he unfastened a jug tied to his belt. It was no bigger than the palm of his hand, but when he poured its sweet smelling ointment over Jack's head, it flowed out like it would never stop, as though the jug were bottomless. The ointment soaked into Jack's skin like the blood, and he burned with a desire to crush Mephistopheles' head beneath his heel. He couldn't remember the last time he'd felt such anger toward the demon instead of fear. Looking around, he thought he saw other figures in the confessional, outside the light rays. One of them might have been

Avdiel, but he couldn't make them out to see for sure.

"Have a nice day, sir," Father Murphy said.

The two rays vanished, taking the emerald-garbed angel and his jug of mystical ointment with them. The only saints who remained were Dathiel and Mary. Jack didn't want to leave the Blessed Virgin's presence, but the priest was shooing him out. He almost stood and left, but stopped himself, remembering what he still had to ask him, preferably not while using incorporeal sight. With the reluctance of someone who had to exit a hot shower on a cold morning, Jack relinquished it, seeing nothing more than a screen in front of his face with the priest's side profile on its other side.

"Father, can I ask you a question?"

"Go ahead," the priest said, sounding annoyed.

"Is there . . ." Saliva caught in Jack's throat. He swallowed. "Is there a visiting priest staying at the parish?" He held his breath.

"No," Father Murphy said. "It's just me."

Jack's heart wanted to explode. He almost fell backward out of the confessional. He looked over at the sign in front of its twin. It still read, Father Bamonte, to his eyes. He hurried from the church, near tears, feeling like a child who'd been out with his parents who'd just realized he was lost.

It was all bullshit!

Beginning that night and persisting over the next several days, Jack received a number of missed calls and voicemails from Monsignor Bamonte.

He ignored them, deleting them as soon as they popped up on his screen, refusing to trust his senses just as he'd been refusing to use incorporeal sight since Confession. If insanity was going to consume him from the inside out, he wasn't going to help it do so by indulging any possible fantasies. In the meantime, he'd been trying to find answers to what he called, the question of reality, on the internet and in books at the library. But to no avail. Finding stuff written about the question of God's existence or schizophrenia was easy. Finding stuff about what to do when you questioned the existence of everything perceived through the senses. That wasn't so easy.

He didn't understand how he was supposed to "use logic" to think his way around the problem either. Of course, Lupe had suggested that, and Lupe had been part of the fantasy he was no longer indulging. This left him back at square one in solving his existential paradoxes and appeasing his tormented mind. As he sat at the desk in his room perusing yet another philosophy book from the library, his phone rang.

The screen read *"Monsignor Bamonte"* again.

He held the phone out over the floor as though it burned his palm like a hot potato. He was more tempted than ever before to answer it this time, his own search for answers having come up so fruitless. He resisted. He would answer the question of reality and then God before he let schizophrenia take him down. At least then he'd have the peace of mind to know there was a better life waiting for him after this one. It was the only way he'd be able to accept the prospect that the rest of this life would be spent living in some facility doped up on meds all day to keep from hallucinating.

Just when his resolve was about to falter, the phone stopped ringing. He took a deep breath. His heart was racing. He could see the *thump-thump thump-thump thump-thump* of his chest beneath the buttons on his shirt. The phone's screen lit up.

*New voicemail.*

Jack's will failed him. He clicked on the voicemail, putting the phone to his ear.

"Hello, Jack," Monsignor Bamonte's voice greeted.

Jack felt a pang of sadness sting him. It had been less than a week since he'd last seen him, but he missed talking to the priest.

"I've left you a few messages already, but I don't know if you've been getting them, since I haven't heard back from you. I tried looking for you around the cathedral, but had no luck catching you. Anyway, I was hoping to meet with you one more time before I left town just to make sure you were okay, but I don't think there'll be time now. I've got an early flight out tomorrow.

I've been called to Rome for a seminar the bishops want me to present at, and I'm not sure yet how long I'll be gone. I probably won't have cell service to the States, but you can reach me there by email. And I've got the psychologist's name and number I told you about here. Just tell him I referred you. I talked to him about you. So he'll know who you are when you call. His name is Austin Vonhagen and his number is—"

But Jack's mind had gone numb and he barely listened as the monsignor provided the doctor's information and his own email address. His mental disease was removing his block to truth now that he'd recognized it for what it was. He could already picture Mephistopheles smiling with an, *I told you so,* expression in his dead eyes, claiming the illness he was there to battle was in full retreat.

The monsignor really wasn't real!

*No!* Jack rebelled at the thought, wanting to hold onto one of the few good things in his life from the past several months.

But he couldn't deny the convenience of this mysterious trip's timing, just when he'd begun questioning the priest's existence. An international trip at that. One where Jack would never be able to see or hear the cleric and would certainly never be able to have someone else present to say whether he was there or not. Jack could show email correspondence to Naomi or his family to test the validity of their existence. But, if he really was crazy, what if he went into a fugue state or something and composed the emails himself, to himself? There'd still be room for doubt in his mind.

Jack rolled his chair back a few feet, hanging his head down. He'd made the whole thing up! He'd made a *person* up! What else might his mind make up? What if it got so bad he got himself hurt? What if his illness deceived his senses enough that one day he walked out in the street and got hit by a car, having never seen there was a car coming? He had to solve his existential questions now! Monsignor Bamonte or no Monsignor Bamonte, he had to figure this shit out!

*Well,* he reasoned, *if the monsignor is real, I need a way to stay in contact, don't I? Plus I can check if that psychologist is real or not. Lose the email address and doctor info, and I'll have nothing to go on.*

He nodded his head, picking his phone back up to replay the message and copy it all down.

*"No!"* he shouted. *"No! No! Shit! Shit! FUCK!"*

He'd accidentally pressed the delete button instead of replay. The voicemail was gone. He wracked his brains, trying to remember the name of the psychologist. The monsignor had just said it, but he couldn't for the life of him recall it. He tried redialing the monsignor. It went straight to voicemail.

He threw the phone across the room. *"SON OF A BITCH!"*

There was a timid knock at the door. It opened.

"Jack?" his mother called, concern in her voice.

Naomi stood with her, an expression of equal concern on her face at overhearing his outburst. "What happened?" she asked.

Jack just sat there looking at them, shaking his head, not knowing what to say. Unable to take the looks of worry on their faces, feeling like it was the only expressions he'd ever see once confined to an institution, he turned to look out the window instead. But all he saw was darkness.

It was night.

# PART III: NOON

# CHAPTER XXVII
## HORN, SERPENT, AND BONE

Out in the shadows, a few miles from Jack's house, Delusion tromped through the mud.

He stopped when the familiar sound of wings beating quicker than they should need to passed above his head.

"And I thought your outpost was a pathetic place to meet," Racism grumbled, landing ahead of the minotaur.

Delusion didn't say anything, just kept marching on, taking what pleasure he could in Racism's discomfort. Though he tried to mask it with anger, he could tell the Principality was scared more than anything. Why else would he have landed to walk the rest of the way with him instead of flying all the way there?

"Why he insisted on meeting now," Racism ranted. "I was on the verge of convincing a cracker to rape a nigger bitch upstate. The motherfucking Power better have some damn good news to—"

Racism paused mid-sentence. Delusion had stopped walking too. There were howls coming from the direction of Mephistopheles' camp.

"He tell you he was bringing in werewolves?" Delusion asked.

*"No he fucking didn't!"*

Once again, Racism felt his authority over his own territory had been usurped. His rage cracked under the weight of his trepidation when the shadow of a winged wolf passed over them. Delusion saw him flinch. They were close to a den. Emerging through the next tree line, they saw the growling, salivating crowd that awaited them. They were gathered near the mouth of a cave. A cave not dissimilar to the one before which Jack Dacre had first met the two of them in a nightmare. Except this one wasn't in some distant desert. It was in the middle of a now wolf-haunted forest near Wando High's grounds.

The pack didn't appear willing to part when the two visitors approached to enter the cave. Delusion kept his head down and facing forward, refusing to meet any Power's eyes and give it a reason to engage. Racism on the other hand kept his head held high, trying to present an air of self-importance. It wasn't working. The wolves snapped their jaws over his cranium forcing it down into a bow, as the two lesser demons tried to elbow their way through them.

"Far enough," one of the monsters barked in a voice that sounded as though it was never meant for human speech.

He was the most hulking of the werewolves, standing on hind legs with immense webbed wings on his back that were wrapped around him like a cape. The den's second-in-command.

"Your baal summoned us here," Racism said, watching his tone. "He's expecting us."

Snarls resembling laughter swept the crowd. Delusion feared they weren't gaining entry without first paying a toll of torture.

"Indeed," the big wolf said. "And this gives you leave to enter his domain?"

Racism and Delusion braced for what would come next, but the beast only raised his head and howled. Mephistopheles emerged from the cave at the summoning like a cockroach crawling out from a corpse's gaping mouth. He perched himself on a boulder before it, looking down on the two underlings surrounded by his pack of Powers.

"Ah, comrades," he greeted. "How good to see you're still with us." He turned to address the other wolves. "That will do, pups. Guard the perimeter."

The werewolves spread out to encircle the meeting.

"Now," Mephistopheles turned back to the local demons, "I've called you here as a courtesy, to keep you informed on the Philangelus. A contact of mine in Europe came through and, thanks to his efforts, the boy's spiritual director has been removed from his life for a time. Our prey is vulnerable. Enough that we should be able to finish our work before the priest's return. The pooches and I have already been wearing him down. I want you two to . . ."

Mephistopheles broke off, seeing a damned soul emerging from the ground between Racism and Delusion.

*"Faustus!"* he yelled, as his slave finished pushing his way out of the mud. "I did not summon you! Do I appear unoccupied?"

The spikes on the Power's spear sparked with red lightning as he prepared to lay his wrath over the interruption upon the wretched spirit. To his amusement, Faustus looked petrified. But, when the soul announced his reason for the intrusion, Mephistopheles suspected his terror was not of him, but of where he'd just come from.

"I've been sent with a message, my baal . . . from Baal Satan."

All the den members stopped their activities and gave the fallen human their full attention.

After a hush in which an almost tangible chill ran through the pack, Mephistopheles answered. "Well? Let's have it then!"

"It is addressed to you, my baal," Faustus informed. "The Dark Master is here, in town. He demands a meeting with you immediately."

All eyes looked to Mephistopheles. Yellow ones, red ones, green ones, black ones. All marked with fear, but also relief it was only their master the Devil wanted to see. Delusion and Racism suppressed smiles at seeing Mephistopheles' hesitation. At last it was his turn to suffer the scrutiny of a superior.

*"Where?"* the Prince of Powers hissed.

Faustus pointed, and the demon knew the answer just from the direction.

"Is that all?" he asked, a coldness in his tone.

Faustus nodded. Mephistopheles formed a fireball in his hand and threw it at him. The damned soul was struck to the ground and incinerated amid screams of pain, banished back to Hell. The demon looked to his pack of Powers.

"Our meeting is postponed, pups. If you wish, you may amuse yourselves with our guests until I return."

He took flight, leaving a stupefied Racism and Delusion surrounded by his bloodthirsty brutes.

Speeding through the air, the Prince of Power's thoughts were agitated and haphazard.

Why would *he* have come to the little shit splat town of Mt. Pleasant just to speak with him? If he wanted a progress report on the situation, why wouldn't he have sent a representative? It was rare Mephistopheles had been summoned to an audience with the Baal of baals himself. The occasions he had spoken with him had left enough of an impression. He was glad to let more powerful intelligences deal with him directly. He flapped his wings faster, propelling himself more quickly through the air, knowing the Dark Master did not like to be kept waiting. He'd heard rumors the last spirit who'd dared be late had been tortured for what the fleshlings would reckon a decade, and that demon had been from a much higher Order than the Powers. Of course, Mephistopheles could have used his agility to teleport straight to his destination, but he wasn't yet sure how he should present himself.

No matter how he assessed the situation, if the Devil had come to town in person, it wasn't because he was pleased.

Far sooner than he would have liked, Mephistopheles arrived at the shadowy fortress in which his lord awaited him.

Unlike the bastions of Wando High School, this castle was singular, enormous, and had no windows whatsoever. Only a front and back door. It didn't have any cracks in its walls, but stood strong against attacks from without. Landing before it, the Power noted the devils who tended the place were bustling about their business with even more promptitude than usual. Hosting such a distinguished and feared guest inside would light a fire under the ass of any evil spirit. They didn't even acknowledge him as he approached the front entrance. Not that they would have on any other occasion. Most of them hailed from a superior Order.

At long last he came to stand before the castle's threshold. It wasn't sealed by a door. The opening, shaped as a gaping mouth with sharp teeth, was covered by rungs. It was more like the door to a prison cell, except the rungs weren't placed across the entryway in vertical or horizontal lines. They formed a symbol.

Two beams in the shape of sharpened horns rose from the bottom of the threshold, extending outward in a V to touch both sides of the doorway halfway up. Two additional beams, shaped to resemble bones, crossed them at the sides and leaned towards each other to meet at the doorway's top, pointing upward. In the center of the four beams was a curved rung in the shape of a serpent rising above its coils to strike. These three symbols depicted the unholy trinity of the Devil, sin, and death. They were portrayed in that order from the bottom up to exhibit Satan offering sin and thereby death to man from below as a mockery to the Holy Trinity, Who descended down to him offering redemption and life from above. Poised before them, the Prince of Powers spoke the three passwords that unlocked the symbols, as they did for every door similar to it across Satan's kingdom.

"Enslavement, Oppression, Hatred," he whispered.

The bones and horns withdrew, sliding into the top and bottom of the entryway, freeing the snake to swing inward and allow the demon access to the fortress. The gaping mouth led down a dark tunnel that took Mephistopheles a minute to stalk through before reaching the foyer. This area contained spiral staircases and doors all around it, heading off to various sections of the fortress. At the moment, there were no other spirits occupying the enormous room. Mephistopheles knew why. They were shying as far away as they could from such an odious intelligence as their visitor.

Cursing the fact he had no choice but to draw nearer to him, the Power paced straight across the foyer toward the main double curved stairway on the opposite side. This was the imperial staircase that ascended to the throne room, where the Master would doubtless be awaiting him. At their top stood a set of black double doors with a sculpture of a winged two-headed dragon protruding from them. Each head stuck out a forked tongue from its mouth. Pausing one last time to collect himself before entering, the demon pulled the tongues down like levers, opening the doors into the room. The duel-headed monster separated to appear as two single-winged dragons facing each other.

Mephistopheles stepped inside.

The central chamber was crowded, with three thousand demonic Thrones standing about the place.

The Devil often enjoyed surrounding himself with such a train. It was in mockery of the Blessed Sacrament, Whose every tabernacle on Earth was perpetually surrounded by three thousand celestial Thrones. Mephistopheles knew such a hellish crowd should have been boisterous. But, in the presence of the loathsome superior who'd come to see him, they were silent.

These devils, like their angelic counterparts, appeared in diverse forms, many resembling things that would be inanimate on Earth. Some looked like statues. Others boulders. Others trees and bushes. Others, of course, appeared as chairs or thrones. Even the ostentatious black throne on the far side of the room, upon which Satan reclined, was a fallen angel from the Order. The most powerful of those present. Standing at his sides were what appeared to be black marble statues holding staffs. They were devils too, quite conscious and alert. The two next in command to the one supporting the Prince of Darkness.

Mephistopheles observed them turning their heads almost imperceptibly as he approached the center of the room to genuflect and bow before his lord. The one on the left had thin goat horns protruding from its forehead and curving around behind its cranium to point straight down. Its eyes, filled with disdain for the Power, were jet black with yellow irises. The spirit on the right appeared even more bizarre. It had two faces, melded together next to the nose, leaving only two eyes between them, but two noses and two mouths. Its goat horns grew from the middle of the two foreheads. The eyes appeared less human than the other guard's. They were yellow, with black catlike slits for pupils. The two statuary spirits had their wings wrapped around their shoulders as capes, naked other than the red skirts hanging from their wastes down past their feet. These draped over the steps leading up to their master.

The Evil One himself was slouched in his seat, clothed in his black robe and the shadows. Not even his eyes were visible beneath his hood. This was helped by the fact that his head was tilted back and to the side, as though he'd dozed off. A feat impossible for an intelligence. Still, Mephistopheles could dream. More likely, the Master was making some statement by his posture. Saying Mephistopheles wasn't worth the time to sit up and face when addressing. At least that might mean the baal wasn't so angry he'd reprimand him, just give him whatever message he'd come to town to deliver and be gone. Mephistopheles could dream.

Satan's staff leaned against the wall next to him. The black scepter formed three sharp spikes at its top, the longest point in the center. The two shorter spikes slanted out before turning to point straight up on the sides. Mephistopheles knew those spikes would often emit a flame from their top like a torch, which would change color based on the Master's mood. An orange flame meant his temper was normal, as normal as could ever be with him. A black flame meant he was brooding on something. Blue occurred when he was taking pleasure in tempting souls or plotting their destruction. Red meant he was especially pissed off.

The Power hoped never to be around when the trident burned that color. He couldn't tell what mood the Master was in at the moment. The staff wasn't aflame. Perhaps this meant he'd get by unscathed . . . He could dream.

"Hail Your Malevolence, Baal Satan, King of the World and Master of the Infernal Hordes!" Mephistopheles saluted, remaining silent and on his knees with his head down until being instructed to rise.

No instruction was given. He grew more nervous with each passing moment. At last, the binary-faced Throne addressed him, which was an odd sight, considering he had two mouths that moved together. His voice was as cold and high-pitched as wind rushing through desert ruins.

"His Malevolence, Baal Satan, extends his greetings to His Highness, Prince Mephistopheles."

The Power discerned the obvious contempt the Throne held for him in his tone, as though he didn't think he deserved to be saluted with any title attached. He stood back up to address the Lord of Hell, but the guard continued to speak for him.

"I didn't tell you to rise, pup," the Throne threw his phrase of choice at him.

Mephistopheles froze, unsure what to do.

*"On your knees!"* the marble devil commanded.

The Power lowered himself to the floor again, to the amusement of the surrounding crowd.

"Now," the guard said, "the Master would like to know why he still feels the pinch of the thorn he sent you here to deal with five months ago. The Catholic boy should have been removed by now. Yet, reports have come in that your harassments have not only failed to yield desired results, but have been met with inverse effects. His Malevolence hears the young soul has grown stronger, upsetting his kingdom far more than he ever did before you were assigned to him."

The only thing Mephistopheles wanted more at that moment than to throttle the Throne who berated him was to reveal the reasons his work was taking longer than expected. Surely the Master would understand, perhaps even send him more aid. But the bind that had been placed on him by an ambushing spirit on Halloween restrained him from speaking of things such as incorporeal sight, the boy's locution, or the fact Monsignor Adrian Bamonte had become his spiritual director. He labored against its hold to find something he could report.

"The boy's faith is weak enough," he managed. "But his hope keeps it flickering every time it's about to die. I have him beaten down though, even to the point of questioning the existence of reality itself. He won't last much longer."

"You've had him questioning reality for two weeks already," the Throne rounded on him. "Yet there are no indications to thoughts of suicide, or even abandoning his Faith to live a life of debauchery while he still has his youth. What is your excuse for his perseverance in the Enemy's Religion?"

Mephistopheles tried again to choke up the full gravity of the situation. "His will is stubborn in its hope!" was still all he was able to say.

He grew terrified at not being able to give more details. It was making him look like a fool before Satan himself! He'd be dragged through the raping rabbles of the deeper Abyss if he didn't find a way to offer better explanations soon.

"But things are going our way," he said. "I've taken him from questioning his faith, to questioning his sanity, to questioning everything he senses. I trust he'll break soon."

"Trust?"

A tremor of disquiet rippled through the crowd. The Master had spoken, his guttural voice as unnerving as Mephistopheles remembered. None of the Thrones dared move an inch now. Satan turned his head toward Mephistopheles. His face was still cloaked by shadow, but his red eyes with their midnight pupils became visible.

"Is my kingdom built upon trust now, Mephistopheles?"

The Power was silent and trembling under the weight of the baal's focus.

Satan shrugged his crimson hands which had been hanging lazily over the sides of his throne. "I must have missed the memorandum. To my knowledge, it was still founded on results centered around a common goal held among enemies." The Devil gripped his armrests and leaned forward in his chair, appearing to sniff the air. "Do I smell hope in your statements as well? Yes, it's there. Hope that you'll soon have the boy's soul ready for me. Will I find the seeds of faith and charity growing in your mind next? Are you thinking of converting to the Enemy's

Business? I could put in a good word for you if you like. I was well acquainted with management before resigning. We would all gladly attend your Baptism. Of course, I doubt the Enemy would have us invited."

Fits of laughter erupted from the crowd. Mephistopheles said nothing.

"Are trust and hope all you've come offering me then, in place of the assiduous calculations you know I expect from an intelligence of your stature? Am I to understand the Alpha of my Powers feels . . . overmatched by a Catholic teenager raised in Protestant country?"

No one was going to speak between them now, but Mephistopheles found himself wishing he could discourse further with Satan's decorations instead.

"No, my lord," the Power said. "But, you should know, the boy has educated himself more in his Faith since I first moved against him. He now substitutes the time he once used for entertainment with . . . reading. Books on philosophy, theology, even angelology, and . . . the Sacred Scriptures."

Mephistopheles heard the vicious intake of breath through the Master's nostrils and wanted to squeeze his eyes shut in reaction to what was coming. But he knew that would only make it worse for him. Satan didn't take up his weapon, nor did he strike the Power down where he stood. He just let the silence hang between them a few moments, dangling the Power over the precipice of anticipation, letting him go on unsure whether he'd thrust him down its sheer drop into terror.

"And you have allowed this change?" the Devil almost whispered.

"I've roused doubts within him to which he won't find answers in the books he's using, my lord."

"Yet you allow him to study answers to other questions we may have had use for in the future. *Angelology!*" Satan spat the word. "Does this mean he's become suspicious of your presence, or remembered that of his guardian?"

Mephistopheles' panic rose over how much Satan didn't know due to his inability to report it.

"He suspects it, my lord. But he hasn't confirmed anything beyond doubt. And I have, of course, told him it would be insane to entertain such a notion as the existence of angels and demons, because it would discredit him as a religious simpleton before anyone reputable."

"All that's needed is a hint of suspicion to lead a skeptic into becoming a saint," the Devil derided. "Too many souls have I watched slip through my fingers all the way into the Enemy's bosom, thanks to that abhorrent abomination of His. Why do you suppose your prey grows in knowledge of the metaphysical after months of temptations?"

Mephistopheles didn't answer. He couldn't. He was trying again to reveal the news of Jack's charism, but was unable.

"Because," Satan ranted, failing to notice his underling's struggle to tell him something, "you track his movements everywhere, but never follow him into it. The place he's most likely to escape my grasp!"

"I've never found it necessary, my lord. I always manage to rob him of any answers he believes he's discovered there. He is ours!"

"Obviously, if he believes he finds answers there, then it is necessary to tail him inside! Your excuses only reveal your fear of doing what's necessary. And *your* temptations against belief have been found wanting ever since the Aquinas disaster."

"My lord, how am I to hold the boy's mind in the Presence of the White Hoc? He—"

Mephistopheles fell silent. Satan had stood from his throne. The Power thought he perceived a subtle pulling away of the devils nearest him. The Master took up his trident from against the wall, and its three tips ignited at his touch. A red flame.

The baal stepped down the stairs toward the Prince of Powers, coming to stand before him, towering over his knelt form from his eight-foot height. Mephistopheles braced as much as he could for the scourging. The Master didn't strike him. His eyes were glowing from beneath his hood a more intense red than usual, their blaze increasing with his temper. At least the pupils hadn't expanded to make them completely dark. Mephistopheles knew once that sign was visible, the Master was at his most murderous. When he flicked his black, forked tongue out, as though to taste and savor the Power's fear on the air before striking, Mephistopheles didn't think he'd need to be at full wrath to inflict a beating the Power would feel for the next century.

"Have we not dragged souls from the Enemy's Sacramental Presence before?" Satan asked. "Weaker spirits than you have done it."

The Devil relinquished his grasp on the scepter, which continued standing erect on its own. He paced around his subject, reminding Mephistopheles of a lion circling its prey. The staff's flame bent in the Devil's direction every time he passed in and out of its light and the Power's line of sight. Mephistopheles dared not rise or turn his head.

"How do you expect to keep him from growing attached to that loathsome castle if it's the only place he feels relief from your influence, you ignorant cur?"

"I can assure you, my lord—"

"You can assure me, from now on, you'll follow the boy anywhere he goes and keep his thoughts shrouded in the dark," the Devil whispered, passing across Mephistopheles' line of sight and back into the dark himself.

"Permit me, my lord! The cathedral isn't the only place the boy feels relief. I've seen to it no attacks are made on him while with his girlfriend. We've been careful to leave her and her family alone. He sees them as a sanctuary and remains distracted from what you ordered me to keep him from. He believes her presence is a detriment to me and distasteful to us all. So he stays close to her."

"All the more reason for you to stay on him when before the White Hoc," the Devil's words circled. "Lest he be made aware of what I suspect." Satan passed before the Power's eyes. "And your tactic of drawing back anytime his cunt is around has disrupted our hold on two more souls!"

"With all respect, my lord. Our claims over Kevin Ross and Becky Hall remain strong. I thought it the lesser of two goods to allow him to speak with a pair of your slaves unimpeded than to soil the comfort he takes in his whore."

"But seeds were planted. Seeds to perhaps enter the Enemy's Camp someday, especially in the bitch."

Satan extended a single taloned finger, telekinetically tilting his scepter forward over Mephistopheles. The Power felt the flame's heat above his face.

"That will be on your head should it ever occur."

"I saw to it the boy was punished for his attempts, Master! I sent a horde to attack his people at their castle in retaliation."

"Indeed." The Devil let the scepter stand erect, circling again. "And I've heard tell he defended them all too well. That not a hair was harmed on a single soul's head in the end."

Mephistopheles was about to speak, but the Evil One held up a hand from behind his back, stifling his words before they ever left his throat.

"For which you retaliated against him again that night . . . with a pack of your Powers no less." The Devil glared down as he passed in front of him. "Such a show of force shouldn't be necessary if this boy is as simple a case as you claim. Yet, even accompanied by your werewolves, he thwarted you and has continued his resistance ever since."

Mephistopheles struggled with all his might to reveal who had stopped that attack on Jack, and who'd sent him. But the bind on him held strong. He thought it must have been a very powerful spirit who'd placed it.

"I thought it excessive to send in the Head of my Powers before," Satan went on. "But your lack of expedient results makes me ponder . . . Does this case perhaps require someone of more formidable skills? Do enlighten me, why has such an infinitesimal thorn in my side as Jack Dacre inflicted the damage I would only expect from a sword through my heart?"

Mephistopheles was horrified at the prospect of being replaced in his mission. Not just because it offended his pride to be thought defeated by a South Carolinian teenage shit stain, but because to return from a mission such as his empty-handed meant he would have to suffer the torments intended for his prey. Yet, to admit the answer to his baal's inquiry would surely bring the beating he feared down on him. There was no way out unscathed.

"Because," he said, having no choice, "he does possess a sword, my lord."

The Devil paused, looking down into the Power's eyes. Though they were white and dead, the fear in them was legible to all in the room. Mephistopheles finished the revelation, sealing his doom.

"In late December, he began wielding the Weapon of the White Lady against us, praying a decade almost daily. *But—*"

But the rest of the demon's words were drowned in fire and fright. It was sudden, violent, and traumatic. The Devil raised both hands to his head, lowering his hood, unveiling his face at last. His short, ink-black hair stood erect, as though electricity coursed through it. The Power wouldn't have been surprised if he saw a spark traveling between the horns on his head with how angry he looked. They resembled little lightning rods enough, between their dark color and the way they protruded out from his forehead for three inches, then turned to point upward for another three. The Master's hooked nose pulled up with the rest of his countenance as he snarled, the feat almost making his cheeks appear as pointed as his ears, stretching the skin even tighter over his cleft chin. The snarl exposed his sharpened canines, and Mephistopheles indeed felt like a downed antelope below the mercy of a hungry lion.

Satan grabbed his staff and slammed its burning spikes down atop the Power's head. Even through his screams, the demon knew the routine. If he resisted, his punishment would be worse. He had to hold still and allow the flame to scald him.

*"HOW . . . IN HELL . . . WAS HE EVER ALLOWED TO TAKE UP THOSE MOTHERFUCKING BEADS?"*

Mephistopheles trembled with pain, doing his best to speak over the flame's sizzle, beginning to smell himself cooking. *"I'm still winning, Master! The last time he tried to use them against me, I broke the armor into pieces, and he hasn't used them since! He's abandoned much of his reading too! He's afraid too much thought on mystical matters will retrigger the schizophrenia he's now convinced he has. He's been throwing himself into what he calls, real life. Spending time with his girlfriend, his family, at the movies. Trying to hold onto his sanity as long as he can before his disease takes him. He's been ignoring all this. Both the Enemy and us!"*

Satan lifted the staff, and Mephistopheles gasped for breath.

"Interesting," the Devil said, using the staff like a walking stick as he began circling his servant again. "So, you've made him put the Weapon down of his own accord." He gazed down at the writhing Power with his first approving look. "Impressive. Finally the manner of result I expect from the Prince of my Powers."

Mephistopheles' breaths sounded like a choking vacuum. He put all his might into staying still, despite the scalding. He didn't dare reach up to tend or even touch his head.

"Rise, my servant," the Devil said, shooting what looked like a white wisp of cloud from his free hand.

The burn atop the demon's bald pate healed at its touch. He felt instant relief. Unable to believe his luck, he rose to his full height, still dwarfed by his master's.

"Now," Satan said, "tell me. What do you plan to do should La Pucelle descend again to help him take it back up?"

Mephistopheles glanced up into the Evil One's crimson gaze.

"Oh yes, pup." Satan smiled. "I'm quite aware of your little skirmish, and how you fared. You fled a battle, letting the boy avail himself of a *Sacrament.*" The Devil spat the word like it was distasteful in his mouth.

"My lord, how could I have—"

The flame went out on Satan's trident and he speared Mephistopheles' neck between two of its prongs, lifting him off his feet, bringing their faces parallel to each other.

"You could have stayed and fought to the end of your strength, Power. Perhaps then the boy would have been dissuaded from entering the castle."

"My . . . lord," Mephistopheles struggled to speak with his feet dangling below him, "it . . . was impossible for me to . . . get close to him with . . . La Pucelle blocking my every attempt—"

"You didn't abandon your attempts because she forced you. You deserted because you were afraid." Satan caressed the demon's cheek with a talon even darker than the underling's skin, moving his hand below his chin and gripping it between his thumb and index finger. "Perhaps you lack the proper motivation to keep the boy from becoming a threat to my designs at all costs." He squeezed the Power's face tighter. "But you'll give everything you have to end the little papist now, won't you, pup?"

"My lord," Mephistopheles hissed as best he could while hanging from the trident, "nothing else occupies my endeavors. I will serve up his soul for you to feast upon forthwith."

"Oh I have little doubt of it." The Devil smiled, his eyes glowing brighter. "In the meantime, I grow hungry for an appetizer. And since you've delayed my entrée . . ."

Satan's face lunged forward. He tilted his head, opening his mouth, biting Mephistopheles over his own mouth and exposed nasal cavities.

The sight was too appalling to watch, and Jack jolted, screaming himself awake from his nightmare.

# CHAPTER XXVIII
## REAL LIFE

Swinging his legs over the side of the bed, Jack sat up and rubbed his eyes, the dream he'd been having slipping away the moment his brain regained consciousness.

He could remember a few details. Satan had been in it. He'd even seen his face this time. That crimson countenance with its burning blood eyes stood out most in his memory. He didn't think he'd soon forget it. Mephistopheles had been there too. And there were other figures surrounding them. Statues, or gargoyles, or something. Had they been meeting in a museum? Jack didn't think so. An old church or castle? Sounded more like something he'd dream up. What had Satan and Mephistopheles been talking about? He looked up, opening his eyes all the way, hearing sleep crust crunch through his eyelashes. The picture of Jesus and Mary hanging on the wall drew his gaze like a moth to lamplight. He concentrated on remembering the nightmare. His enemies had been discussing . . . him.

But what had they been saying? He hung his head, closing his eyes again, rubbing the crust from them while he racked his brains. Naomi's face flashed across the back of his eyelids like heat lightning on a pitch-black night. His eyes jumped open with the thought, his gaze landing on the rosary and Saint Michael card lying on his nightstand. He stared at them in earnest, as though they could change what he now remembered. Mephistopheles had indicated he'd planted his girlfriend in his life. That she was a distraction from . . . something. That he was using her to keep him from . . . some kind of knowledge? Jack couldn't remember.

He thought it was something Satan didn't want him to realize. Something in which Naomi played a part in keeping him ignorant. But ignorant of what? And how was she keeping him from it? That part Jack didn't know. He couldn't remember if either spirit had ever said it in the dream.

*So what?* he thought. *It was just a dream. No more real than any of your other experiences.*

He couldn't make sense of it.

*Of course you can't! Because it was a fucking dream! Dreams don't have to make sense.*

He stared harder down at his rosary. It was still broken from when the chain had snapped in half the last time he'd used it. The dream might have been his diseased mind's way of trying to trick him back toward insanity, by getting him away from the person who kept him grounded. After all, he hadn't had any weird experiences since he'd stopped trying to engage in them two weeks before. He'd refused any use of incorporeal sight since his confession. He'd put the rosary down on his nightstand as soon as he'd gotten home and hadn't touched it since. He'd put all his focus on Naomi, spending his free time with her, avoiding isolation, not allowing himself to be alone with his thoughts any more than he had to be. And he'd been happily spirit-free ever since. No zombies. No dark castles. No demons! Nothing but normal, tangible, everyday life. Real life.

That was, if anything at all outside himself was real. Jack brushed his fingers through his hair, shaking his head, getting up to get ready for school. This was why he didn't let himself be alone if he could help it.

These were the kind of thoughts that could drive a person crazy.

Over the next five weeks, Jack continued resisting a daily urge to take up the rosary again.

His prayers had been limited to grace before meals and an *Our Father* and *Hail Mary* before bed. He didn't want to allow his overactive imagination too much leeway. Meditation on the Mysteries of the Rosary might give it enough to run away with his sanity again. It seemed to be working. Other than his nightmare about a demonic counsel, he still hadn't had any weird experiences.

He'd tried not to dwell on the dream. It might affect how he looked at Naomi, and he didn't want his view of her soiled. She was all he had left to hold onto now that so much else he'd held close to his heart had been ripped from it in a single afternoon. Yet, despite his attempts to repress it, he'd catch himself looking suspiciously at his girlfriend now and then, wondering what knowledge she was somehow holding him back from discovering. He'd shake off the thought once he realized what he was doing, but his temptation to turn to the Rosary for answers only grew.

He thought he knew why. He was getting bored of hanging out with Naomi and her friends all the time. Between Darris and Brad's football talk, Brad's amusing failures to win Jenny back when she was around, April and Naomi's fashion discussions, and even the philosophical discussions he, Naomi, and Becky would sometimes have while Kevin politely listened, Jack's mind would wander back to thinking about incorporeal sight. He missed the adventures he'd had with Dathiel and other imaginary friends. At least the ones that didn't involve demons. He missed jumping off rooftops and scaling walls like a superhuman. He missed the monsignor, a much more interesting priest than the one he had to sit through at Sunday Mass. Most of all, he missed what he used to see at Mass and the few times he'd seen the Blessed Virgin Mary.

It was getting harder and harder not to turn to the Rosary where he could at least visit them in his memory. But, if he indulged their memory, the hallucinations might return and throw his brain off-balance again. In all he'd read on schizophrenia, he hadn't found any indication it was a disease that could be fought off by willpower alone. Every source indicated it required meds. Yet he seemed to have avoided slipping into its delusions by keeping himself surrounded by people and activity all the time, and by staying away from too much thought on the mystical.

Maybe he could avoid being committed after all. It had worked for the guy in *A Beautiful Mind,* hadn't it? Jack would catch himself when this thought went through his head. That was a movie. This was real life. He wanted to stick to what the real science said, not Hollywood. Still, he'd never breathed a word about schizophrenia to any of his friends or family, and none of them seemed to think he ever acted strange when around them, from what he could tell. But he didn't know how long he could hold out against the temptation to think about his past hallucinations. Even though imaginary, they'd been so . . . so much better than what his life was now! That was it. That was what ate at him.

Dating Naomi, hanging out with the popular crowd through being associated with her, even being accepted by them—none of this compared to how he'd felt when surrounded by the friends who'd turned out to be imaginary. He'd sworn to himself, and several of them, that he preferred the truth, even if it was less comfortable than a lie. That he preferred real life to an imaginary one. But he couldn't deny that real life was turning out so much less fulfilling than the one he'd conjured up in his head.

It was just a bunch of eating, shitting, fucking, making fun of people, the occasional genuine laugh or enjoyable experience, sleeping, then getting up to do it all over again. There were no grand adventures, no destiny to fulfill, no kings and queens to serve, no monsters to slay, and no eternal life to win at the end of it all. At the end, it was just the weight of the earth from six feet under.

These thoughts, when they came, would either send Jack back into distracting activities with others or back to the library or internet to try and solve his existential questions. His findings never left him satisfied. He hadn't found adequate answers to the questions of God or reality. This left him pining more and more to try the Rosary again, wondering if it would lead him where books and the internet had failed.

He'd had profound insights through its use before, even if they'd been from imaginary persons. Didn't that mean the answers to his questions at those times had come from his own head? Maybe he could find the ones he sought now there too, if he allowed himself to ponder more deeply . . . Maybe he could think his way around his present dilemmas through meditation.

*No!* Jack protested to himself as he walked into his room. A protest he'd had to renew several times a day. *I'm not slipping back into insanity! Someone's gotta have the answers I'm looking for. Surely I'm not the first person in the world to ever ask these questions. The Matrix did. Where'd the writers for that get their ideas?*

He sat on his bed, looking down at the broken rosary on his nightstand for about the thousandth time. Maybe he could just do half a decade. And forego the meditation part. Just ask the Blessed Mother to guide him through his troubles. Just a few *Hail Marys*. No different than what he did before falling asleep at night. Jack squeezed his eyes shut, feeling like an addict who'd tried to go cold turkey from his chosen substance but knew he was about to give in again after weeks of sobriety.

*Half a decade. No meditation,* he promised himself. *Just a plea for help.*

Feeling the last moments of struggle seep from his muscles, his shoulders fell. He picked up the rosary. It slithered up and down through his fingers as he twisted his wrist. Though broken in half, it felt familiar in his hand, the clinking of the beads reminding him of the shuriken chain links he'd once used to lasso monsters from his head. It felt like . . . home.

Jack crossed himself in a single motion, as though getting through the whole thing fast would be safer. He settled on the Fifth Sorrowful Mystery, since he felt as abandoned as Christ and Mary must have on Calvary. But he never had the chance to begin.

*"The Second Joyful Mystery,"* Dathiel's voice boomed into the room.

Jack's reaction to it was mixed. It startled him. But, after the initial shock wore off, he felt joy and dread intertwine his intestines like warring serpents.

*"The Visitation!"*

Jack fell backward on his bed, losing all sense of his surroundings.

His hands stayed active, his fingers traveling over to the second set of beads along the chain, passing each one slowly through them, as though directed by his unconscious.

# CHAPTER XXIX
## THE DEVIL'S NIGHTMARE

As at the beginning of his first locution, Jack found himself facing a tree.

It was the oak tree outside the Blessed Virgin's house, under which she'd come into existence. Jack jolted when Dathiel stepped up beside him.

*"No!"* he screamed. *"You're not real! None of this is real!"*

He bent over, holding his head in his hands, trying to concentrate on waking himself up, if he was even asleep. Had he fainted or was he hallucinating? Either way, he wanted to snap out of it. He felt a flick on his ear.

*"Ow,"* he protested.

That pain was real, wasn't it? It had to be. It felt real. But he knew it wasn't. He knew his confused brain could make him think he was feeling pain when he wasn't.

"Isn't it funny how people trust pain more than bliss in measuring the reality of an experience?" Dathiel asked.

It was he who'd flicked Jack's ear. Jack looked up at him with furrowed eyebrows, his hand over his ear, which was now very warm.

"That *hurt!"* he complained.

"Did it? How could I have hurt you, Jack? I thought I wasn't real."

*"You're not!"* Jack stood his ground.

"That's rude, Jack. And, were I not in beatitude, it'd be rather hurtful to hear."

*"You're . . . Not . . . Real!"* Jack shouted again. "And I won't be guilted into believing you are! You're only doing that because you're me, and it's how I'd get what I wanted from someone. I learned it from Mom. She's the queen guilt-tripper! But I won't be tricked! I'm not falling for it! I won't be tricked! I won't be tricked!" Jack put his head in his hands again, rubbing his eyes, trying to close out the vision and see his bedroom, continuing his chants as though they were a prayer that would make it happen. "I won't be tricked! I won't be tricked!"

"I'm sorry you think that," Dathiel said. "When you're ready, your other Royal Mother has sent you a gift. So you might want to pay attention."

Jack stayed down, ignoring the angel's words, hoping everything would go away if he ignored it. He'd awoken from nightmares that way as a child. The delusions only had the power he gave them . . . he hoped. After a minute, he opened his eyes and looked up. He was still in what he knew to be Nazareth, and the figment he'd known as his guardian angel still stood with him.

*NO!* he thought.

"Yes," Dathiel answered it. "Believing I'm not real doesn't negate my existence. Takes more than that to get rid of me, Jack. Now, come on." He held out his hand. "The only way out is forward. You've a lesson to learn. Since you're still losing fights, and telling you how to win hasn't changed that, Mother's decided to show you."

Not knowing what else he could do, and unable to help that part of him wanted to hug Dathiel upon seeing him again, Jack took the angel's hand.

"Hold on tight," he said. "What happens next is going to be big."

The Archangel Gabriel burst out of Mary's house cheering and blowing his horn.

He was shouting something over the flower-covered hills of the land, lighting them up by his glow. Other angels started celebrating after hearing him. Before Jack could make out their words, a great light exploded from the house into the night, knocking him and Dathiel along with it as though it were a tidal wave.

It took them across vast deserts and bodies of water. Jack felt like he had when the Comet had exploded from the tree at the beginning of his last vision, struggling to hold his eyes open at the speed he was flying. Dathiel flapped his wings, dragging Jack along behind him, propelling them farther ahead of the light wave so their ride would be smoother. He kept flapping them faster, until they were several miles ahead of it. Soon they arrived in a vast city, which Jack's second sight revealed as a swarming kingdom of pagan decadence. Zombies paced the streets, tailed and tortured by their guardian demons. Jack hadn't missed these sights in his weeks of normality.

Dathiel flew him over to a graveyard on a hill near the center of the city, and the vision informed him they were in Rome. In the future, this graveyard would become the place of Saint Peter's crucifixion and burial, and later the construction site of Vatican City. On the highest point of the hill, perched in a tree, overlooking the city as its true emperor, a cloaked and hooded figure brooded.

Satan ignored the wealth of souls already enslaved beneath his feet in the empire's capital. He was still preoccupied with how best to get at Mary of Nazareth.

He would be forever unsatisfied with any of his other accomplishments until he'd dragged her despicably pure soul through every vice imaginable in the dregs of Hell. When the light emanated from the direction of the Holy Land, he was distracted for the first time in months. Just as he perceived it, and before he had time to comprehend it, he felt smitten by something.

The tree he crouched on split beneath his feet down the middle all the way to the ground, as though lightning had struck it. Jack heard him let out a long, disturbing croak of pain. An inhuman sound. It was as though the reality of his everlasting sentence had only just hit him. A tumultuous sense of foreboding arose in his mind. He sensed the Presence of the only Being naturally superior to angelic natures. Sensed it closer than it had been to him since his curse in Eden. He felt the way he had when struggling beneath Michael's heel at the climax of the war in Heaven. The feeling that precipitated being flung down from his throne.

Had the Enemy done it?

Despite all his efforts to instigate enough vice in man to prevent it, had the Enemy still done it? That ridiculous plan to become one of the disgusting intellectual beasts for Himself? And, if so, what did that mean for his earthly kingdom? He wanted to fly toward the land of the Enemy's Chosen People. Investigate. But . . . found he couldn't. He was paralyzed. Never since the fall of the first thinking fleshlings had he felt such a deep dread to move about in his own world!

As the realization came to him, he noticed the rest of his kingdom had ceased all movement too. Rome was quiet. Not one of his minions was speaking or performing preternatural wonders through their respective idols. Angered, he moved at last, spreading two jet-black batwings that emerged from the folds of the cloak over his back. Their wingspan looked the same size as Michael's to Jack. The moon spread their shadow over the graves on the hill, as though the lord of the dead were laying claim to his territory.

The Devil flew southeast.

While he flew, Satan listened for any demonic activity outside the capital, discerning none.

As Jack's vision followed the route of his travels, he too heard nothing from the demonic spirits on Earth. Not even the oracle at Delphi in the land of Greece was active. The devil Satan had assigned to feign prophecy there was as petrified as he'd felt when the light had shone from Israel. The Evil One found him cowering in his temple, prevented by some higher force from approaching the priestess to speak his deceptions through her. The fallen angels were all on edge for a reason they couldn't understand. But they were each convinced that, should they attempt to perform any phenomena through an idol, they would be struck down to the lowest depths of the Inferno faster than lightning could travel to the ground. The false gods of the world had been silenced, and Jack's locution informed him they would remain so for the next thirty-three years, while the Real God walked the Earth.

Jack started chuckling, watching Satan's perplexity, until it turned into a full laughing fit. "Not so fun is it?" he said from behind the cloaked fiend, while he glared out the doorway of Delphi's temple in the direction of the Holy Land. "When your enemy comes in and turns your whole worldview upside down?"

Suddenly, Satan and the Delphi oracle's possessor screamed like banshees, vanishing through cracks in the floor.

*"Whoa shit!"* Jack jumped at their dramatic departure. "What was that about?"

"The Devil and his followers were bound to the Abyss for three days following the Incarnation," Dathiel said. "A little Christmas present from Christ to the world."

The vision sped up time, and Jack watched the sun pass by the doorway three times. As night fell on the third day, the Devil slunk from the shadows at the back of the temple, ready to brave the Earth once more. He stalked past where Jack was standing and glared outside again, lowering his hood. He threw his head back and howled. The sound wasn't like those the Powers had made. This howl was deeper. It sounded more dangerous. It reminded Jack of his favorite *Twilight Zone* episode, from the times he'd done a deep dive into classic horror. *The Howling Man*. At the time, he'd had fun with the unabashed cheesiness of the episode, which was still enjoyable despite itself. Now he pondered it in a whole new light. There was nothing enjoyable about the howling he heard from the real Devil's mouth.

He covered his ears, wanting to get away. The howl was going on forever! It echoed across the land, summoning all demons in Greece to Delphi. Jack saw them arriving in droves through the air. The Devil flew out of the temple to meet them.

*"Carry the message to all my hordes around the world,"* he commanded in a voice that projected for miles. *"I want the source of our overthrow identified! All former missions are secondary."*

Dathiel grabbed Jack and they took flight, tailing Hell's prince as he traversed the globe, hunting his New Enemy.

The Devil began in the Holy Land, his first suspect being Mary of Nazareth.

But God blinded him from finding her, steering his suspicions elsewhere. He departed Israel almost as soon as he'd entered it. Along the way, millions of other fallen spirits crossed paths with him, always reporting the same thing. Nothing of interest found yet. When angelic perceptions failed, they riled up the demoniacs, using their physical senses to search. After three days, they'd still come up short.

Furious, Satan himself dove into one of their possessed. A formerly virtuous woman whom the demons had twisted to their ways after years of hounding. She was so bruised from what she'd been through now, she almost looked elderly to Jack, despite being twenty-one. She walked with a hunch, but when the Devil assumed the helm of her body, he twisted it into an even more bent shape. He thrust her onward, forcing her to run on all fours through the trees of the forest in which he'd found her. Jack thought she looked like an emaciated gorilla.

As he watched, more of her possessing demons spread out from her, forming a phalanx through the woods as they charged. There must have been hundreds of them. Some were Principalities. Others he recognized as the werewolves he'd fought in his backyard. They were being led by Mephistopheles. He was running behind the girl, while Satan drove her. Jack figured the Prince of Powers had been the possessor in charge of her before the Evil One commandeered his post.

When she emerged from the trees into a clearing, Jack saw they'd reached a small city. Most of its houses stood in groups atop hills and along their slopes. It was filled with overhanging boulders, caves, and lush valleys of flowers, the midday sun embellishing their colors. A beautiful scene, soured by the appearance of the new arrivals.

The locution informed Jack that the city rested over the ashes of Old Testament Patriarchs. It was where King David had once left the Ark of the Covenant to dwell for three months. A hundred yards farther down from where the demoniac had emerged from the tree line, Jack saw a bearded man step out from the trees. He was leading a donkey with a passenger atop it. The possessed woman crouched down among the bushes, as though afraid to be seen by these people, preferring to spy on them from the shadows. Walking ahead to take a closer look, Jack saw who the passenger on the donkey was, which meant the man leading it must have been her husband.

Saint Joseph.

The Holy Family's appearance was simple.

Saint Joseph was thirty-three, tanned, handsome, with curly black hair hanging over the tops of his ears. His countenance carried a note of solemnity, as though an older man's wisdom had been placed in a younger man's body. He was dressed in a plain gray robe with a pale blue coat over it. Mary wore her usual white robe with a blue, hooded cloak. Incorporeal sight revealed a much more complex scene to Jack's eyes.

Genuflecting beside Mary at the outskirts of the forest, Gabriel welcomed her to the city by blowing his gold trumpet. Her other guardians nested among the trees, some perched on branches, others hanging from them. The Dominations stood as tall as many of them. The thousand were glowering at Satan and the band of demons who'd arrived.

Mary hopped off the donkey and rushed ahead of Joseph, heading for a house near the center of town. It rested on the highest peak. The echo of Gabriel's horn reverberated among the hills, heard by the townspeople in their minds. They marveled at the beauty of the Woman they saw passing their homes, moved by the horn to shy away, retreating indoors. They thought it was because of the sublime air of dignity the Lady gave off. In reality, it was her guardian angels. Riding the voice of their leader into town, they were shoeing the bystanders inside, all the time watching the edge of the forest.

The Devil had relinquished his grip on his vessel, handing her off to Mephistopheles as he put his hood up. Jack watched him pace back-and-forth grunting, flapping his wings like a pissed off bird of prey. He knew the disturbance would have something to do with Mary of Nazareth. *He knew it!*

He grabbed a boulder that looked to Jack like it would have taken ten men to lift and hurled it into the forest, breaking several trees in half. He sensed an even more powerful presence coming from Mary than he had the last time they'd met. He was unable to penetrate it to discern its meaning. She was . . . different. He bent down and crawled in her direction, sniffing. The fact so many angels attended her had always disturbed him. Their present increased vigilance—more than he'd ever detected from them—alarmed him all the more. But not as much as the overpowering force proceeding from Mary herself.

He'd never been able to exercise authority over her soul, but something was worse about her now. He surmised she wasn't the cause of it. Maybe a secondary cause. Still, he couldn't be sure of that either. Something was amiss, dammit! *Something!*

Jack had to reach up and massage the sides of his head. The locution was pouring so much hatred from the Devil's mind into his own, to call the experience disturbing wouldn't have covered it. But he didn't want it to stop. The aspiring military tactician in him had been roused. He wanted to get a sense of how his enemy thought.

*If the enemy's real,* he reminded himself.

He brushed the thought aside. He didn't have time to wonder right now. All he could do was pay attention to what was playing out before him. The Devil was still pacing, trying to edge closer to Mary, but being warned off by her guardians when he drew too close.

Mary neared the house on the hill, and an elderly woman emerged from it at her approach, looking excited to see her. The two women embraced at the base of the house's outer court. There was a garden of colorful flowers to one side of them and a large tree with a fountain at its base on the other. The women said nothing at first. The older one just led Mary through the outer court into her home.

When they reached the threshold, Mary finally extended a verbal greeting. "The Lord be with you!"

"The same Lord reward you for having come so far to see me!" the elderly woman said.

Mary smiled, staying on the front step. The other woman turned back, beckoning her to follow.

"May God save you, Elizabeth," the Virgin prayed. "May His Divine Light give you life!"

Knowing for sure what story he was seeing now, Jack looked through incorporeal sight for what happened next. When Mary said Elizabeth's name, a ray of light extended from her womb, engulfing her cousin, so bright it made her partially transparent. Another soul, inside the elderly matron, came to life. Elizabeth's unborn son had been baptized.

The infant inside her reached back toward the Source of his sanctification, in Mary's womb feet away. Gabriel, who'd stayed by Mary's side on her journey up the hill, stepped forward, bestowing the most gorgeous luminescent lily Jack had ever seen into the newborn's heart. When he drew back to stand by his charge again, Jack noticed the slender, golden-haired angel who'd attended Confession with him standing next to Elizabeth now. Jack hadn't seen when he'd appeared. Much like at the confession, he'd been blending unnoticed within the light radiating from the two women.

Jack didn't have time to consider his presence, because an ugly moan behind him interrupted the tranquility of the scene. He turned to look at Satan standing at the bottom of the hill. He'd sensed his authority over Elizabeth's son had just been nullified. Somehow, Mary of Nazareth's infection was spreading. Unable to contain his unstable wrath any longer, the Devil let out a roar, signaling the horde of demons behind him to charge the women on the hill. They dropped their hold on the demoniac, leaving her swooning in a stupor, and bolted out of the woods.

Gabriel signaled his own soldiers, and the Prince of Dominations led several other members of his Order out from the trees. They swatted the werewolves and demonic Principalities aside with clubs like giants from a fairy tale. The Prince of Virtues flew out and tackled Mephistopheles from the air. As they engaged each other in ground combat, Jack felt like he was watching some bizzarre mix of fantasy and science fiction. Mephistopheles looked like a crow enchanted to be the size of a man, while the Virtue looked like an invader from Mars fighting with him. The demonic horde was driven back with ease, never nearing Mary, her cousin, or their unborn children.

Satan glared up at Gabriel with utmost malice. The Archangel stared back, an expression of challenge on his own features. The Devil's staff appeared in his hand and he flung its head out to his side, spreading a wall of fire across the grass behind his followers. The demons were prevented from retreating. He commanded them to drive forward again. When they complied, Nuri, Jehoash, and another Seraph from the Sixty Strong Ones intercepted them. All the Seraphim had to do was spread their wings. The fire burning within and around them spread, forming a second wall of flame before the demons, trapping them between two barriers.

Infuriated, Satan relented his, letting his minions return to his side. All the while, he'd never taken his eyes off Mary. She was protected behind her guardians' fire. Thanks to it, he couldn't hear what she was saying anymore. But Jack could. He was on the wall's other side. Elizabeth had taken a step back from her cousin when she'd felt her son move. The baptism in her womb had infused within her mind the knowledge of what had occurred in Nazareth. She was looking at Mary with reverence in her eyes now. When she spoke, it was in a near whisper.

"Blessed art thou amongst women," she repeated Gabriel's words, hearing them echo to her from the night of Christ's Conception, "and Blessed is the Fruit of thy womb!" she added. Saying it out loud made her almost frantic with excitement, and her voice rose. *And how have I deserved to be visited by the Mother of my Lord? When I heard your greeting, the infant in my womb leapt for joy. Blessed are you for believing the message brought to you from the Lord would be fulfilled!"*

While she spoke her last sentence, she led Mary into the room to the right of the front door. Her household oratory. She offered it for the Virgin's room during her stay. Once inside, Mary released herself from Elizabeth's grip and crossed her arms over her chest to show humility, desiring all her cousin's praise be offered to God rather than her. She spoke in a soft voice Jack found endearing.

"My soul magnifies *the Lord*," she emphasized. "My spirit rejoices in *God my Savior*, for He has looked with favor upon the humility of His Handmaid."

The Virgin's words pleased the Child within her so much, He inspired her with a prophecy.

"Behold, from henceforth *all* generations will call me blessed, because He Who is Mighty—He Whose Name is Holy—has done great things to me, and His mercy is from generation unto generations upon those who fear Him. He has done valiantly with the might of His arm, driving the proud astray in the conceit of their hearts. He has put down the mighty from their thrones and exalted the humble. He has filled the hungry with good things and sent the rich away empty-handed. He has come to the aid of His servant, Israel, remembering His promise of mercy. The promise He made to our forefathers, Abraham and his seed, forevermore."

Elizabeth had stood mesmerized by Mary as she prophesied. So had Jack.

*My soul magnifies the Lord. My soul magnifies the Lord.* The words kept repeating in his short-term memory, inscribing themselves onto his long-term memory. *My soul magnifies the Lord.*

Jack realized he wasn't repeating the words to himself. It was the locution. It was like it wanted to drill them into his head. Before he had time to consider why, he heard a roar from outside and stepped back through the doorway. The Seraphim had dropped their wall of fire. Satan was free to resume his assault on the hill. He spread his wings, looking like an enraged dragon as he charged forward himself this time.

Gabriel flew out to meet him, the trumpet in his hand morphing. It emitted light from within itself and expanded like a flower blossoming in fast-forward. Yet the process was fluid. The end of the horn sharpened, growing into the head of a gigantic, double-bladed battle ax. The Archangel swung it around like a baseball player going for the Hall of Fame. He batted Satan in the face with its flat side, sending him crashing back into the forest. Jack stared at the spectacle. Gabriel had always come across so gentle and laid back to him. He'd never seen his countenance look the way it did now. He was downright terrifying.

Jack was so caught up in the moment, he hadn't noticed Mary step back outside. She was standing next to him. The Devil came screaming out of the woods like an angry warthog. Sighting her, he took hold of the demoniac woman. She charged from her hiding place in the bushes. The other demons joined their master in his ride as he passed them, helping direct her toward the Virgin. All the power of each of their wills was fueled into a singular desire to have the demoniac strangle the life from Mary, no matter the consequence.

The thousand angels were about to intervene again, when the Virgin directed them to let the enemies pass. They obeyed, and Mary and Jack stood watching the hunchbacked girl shriek her way toward them. Jack would have been terrified, but he knew it was just a vision. Besides that, Mary was so regal in her composure next to him, it put him more at ease. She seemed to have accepted her queenly authority since he'd last seen her at the Incarnation. Her serenity was infectious. Her expression for the possessed woman one of pity. Her Divine Son moved inside her when the demoniac reached the outer court of the house, and she spoke.

"Begone, apostates."

It was a soft tone but one of authority. Satan and the demons detected the coercive finger of God the moment she gave the order. They were dispossessed of their puppet, violently.

*"Who is this weak Woman who oppresses us with such power?"* the Evil One screamed as he let his victim go. *"What authority is this that revokes my claim?"*

As the demons fled the hill country, Jack heard the Devil whispering to himself.

"We must hold a counsel. We must unite to find a weakness in her defenses. *We must slay her!"*

Upon being freed, the hitherto possessed woman stood erect. Her bruises had been effaced. Her form now appeared well-nourished. She glanced around, spotting a man standing with a donkey several feet away, looking from her to a beautiful lady standing in the doorway of the house she was facing. He wore an astonished expression.

"Persevere in prayer always," the lady told her, "and never again allow doubt to sway your heart."

The words hit Jack as though Mary had tossed a sack of stones into his chest. They bothered him. He looked away from the scene, occupying himself with tracking the black cloud of fleeing demons across the horizon. They were miles away now, but he could still hear them screaming like dying pigs.

He sensed it wouldn't be Satan's last attempt on the Virgin's life. He could feel how much the wretch longed for her murder. His pride exceeded his power too much to give up yet. He wouldn't admit defeat, not even to himself. He would wander the countryside day and night for as long as it took to devise a way through her angelic guard.

"Ever the tactician," Dathiel said next to Jack, making him jump.

He'd almost forgotten his guardian was there.

"Well, come on then," the angel said. "Let's follow the demons and see how their plot plays out."

Dathiel flew Jack to a faraway land, touching down between the entrance of a dark cave and some ancient ruins.

There were broken pillars, stone squares carved in the ground that had been used for baths, and decrepit statues of half-human, half-animal creatures. Jack wondered if they hadn't gone back to Greece.

"Welcome to Hierapolis," the guardian said.

"Where's that?"

"In what you know today as, Turkey. This was a Greco-Roman worship site for Hades." He indicated the cave. "The ancients believed this an entrance to the Underworld, because animals always died the moment they entered. In truth, they died because the cave emits a poisonous gas. Still, seems a fitting entry point for where we're headed."

"Which is?"

"Straight to Hell."

*"What—"*

Jack was pulled along by the angel before confirming he'd heard him correctly. Smoke spat on them from the cave as they entered, descending into a pitch-black tunnel. The glow of their own forms was soon their only light. The tunnel eventually dipped straight down into the Earth, forcing them to either turn back or jump.

"Don't worry," Dathiel said. "The tunnel will open into a cavern before you hit rock, giving you room to glide."

Without further explanation, the angel jumped off the edge, diving headfirst into darkness. Jack didn't hear him hit a bottom, his glow fading within seconds. He took a deep breath. Then another, not feeling ready. None of this was real, but what did that matter? He didn't like the idea of leaping off a ledge with no rope or parachute, imaginary or not.

He remembered his scapular. Right. In dreamland, he had powers. Ways he could get around that were superhuman. It had been a while since he'd been able to play with them. He took one more deep breath, and jumped.

Air whizzed past his ears like a spectator whistling his admiration for the daring feat. He tried to spread his cloak and slow the fall but couldn't spread it out all the way yet. As he plummeted, he thought he saw something open beneath him at one point. A circle glowing red around the edge. It might have been a portal. He fell through it too fast to get a good look. The moment he did, the tunnel opened into an immense circular cavern. To his horror, its entire floor was made up of an iron grate. A carving of the same symbol he'd seen on the door to Satan's fortress in his nightmare five weeks earlier. He spread his cloak out all the way, parachuting toward it. Dathiel shot out from somewhere beside him to grip his arm, stopping his descent, and they hovered a hundred feet above the symbol.

"Do the three passwords have to be spoken for it to open?" Jack asked. "'Cause I won't humor evil."

"Nor would I," the angel agreed. "But you forget, this is a vision. We're not really entering Hell. Just seeing it."

The giant grate opened. The bones and horns receded into the walls, and the serpent slithered into them as though it were alive. The moment the seal moved aside, sulfurous smelling smoke and blasphemous shrieks wafted up to greet them. Some of the wails were of pain. Others of anger. It reminded Jack of Wando's gate opening before his carriage every school morning. Only now, he was about to go to Hell. Jack whispered a quote he'd learned the previous year in English class.

"Abandon all hope, ye who enter here."

They descended through various realms of the damned, flying at such super-human speeds Jack didn't have the chance to examine them like the character in Dante's poem.

They slowed only when they'd neared the lowest caves of the Abyss. The whole way there, Jack had heard its master summoning every single condemned spirit to a counsel. When they finally reached the destination themselves, Dathiel flew them over a putrid ground of lava and raven rock.

Human souls screamed amidst flames in the lava. They were tossing about like burning popcorn kernels, their sporadic movement out of their own control. They burned unceasingly, yet were never destroyed. The demons didn't fare any better. Not those caught in the lava. Numerous monsters lined the lava-free areas too. They seemed more in control of their movements, but steam still rose off the rock, burning their feet. It was clear there were no pain-free areas.

Despite the chaos, Jack saw how the demons were separated into their Nine Orders, gathered in what appeared to be an endless crowd. They were all looking up, awaiting their baal's proclamation with as much attention as they could muster. It was like seeing an infernal inverse of a crowd waiting to hear the pope speak in Saint Peter's Square. Standing atop the highest ridge, Satan had his hood down and his trident in hand. The flame on its spikes burned black. Dathiel landed them on a lower cliff not far from the Master of Shadows. After a moment spent overlooking his gathered hordes, the Devil addressed the assembly, bellowing enough to be heard in every corner of the Abyss.

*"My subjects, you are all well aware with what stupendous avidity I have sought to avenge myself and destroy the Almighty's power ever since He cast us out from our rightful dwelling and deprived us of our full might!"*

The demons howled their approval.

*"Although I can in no way injure Him, I have spared no time or endeavor in spreading my dominion over the humans He so loves. By my own strength have I peopled my reign. Now, multitudinous nations and tribes obey and follow me. Day by day, I draw to myself innumerable souls, depriving them of the Most High, that they may never enjoy the happiness we have lost. I ensnare them toward these eternal pains we suffer, and they blindly follow my teachings. Upon them do I wreak the*

*vengeance I swore against their Creator!"*

The infernal throngs roared their approbation once again. Jack, for his part, found himself fascinated by the speech. Were what he was now seeing real, what valuable intelligence it would be for an enemy of the Devil to hear! The tactician in him was eating it up.

*"But,"* Satan raised a finger to silence the crowds, *"this all appears of little consequence to me in the face of the overthrow we have recently experienced."* He paused for effect, and the demons nodded, grumbling among themselves. *"An attack so tremendous has not devastated us since we were first hurled from Heaven. My power has felt the same shock as yours. This fresh defeat must have a new cause in the world. I fear our present weakness may be the beginning of our ruin . . . the coming of the End Times!"*

He paused again, allowing a wave of fear to sweep across the multitudes. When everyone stopped muttering, he continued.

*"This matter will require redoubled diligence, for my fury remains unquenchable. My vengeance insatiable. I have personally scoured the Earth, observed all the humans, and discovered nothing of consequence . . . except in one."*

Panicked whispers rose from the hordes. They knew which human he meant. Satan raised his hands to quell them, waving his staff.

*"I know what you fear. But I find no reason to believe the Nazarene is the Woman of the Curse. I have discerned no sign that Maiden has yet been born. None on Earth possess the marks destined for her. The Nazarene troublemaker concerns me with her numerous virtues. But she is married now. And the Enemy's Prophet foretold His Mother would be a Virgin. Nevertheless, I am disquieted over this Woman. Such a pious Israelite may give birth to the Man-God's Mother, or another Prophet. To this hour I have failed to conquer her in anything, and of her life I know less than that of any other fleshling. And there has been a new incident with her. She dispossessed me of a demoniac . . . not through prayer . . . but as though she wielded God's authority for herself!"*

A gasp was followed by a hush across Hell. It was such a stark difference from its former noise, Jack thought he'd lost his hearing for a moment.

*"Rest assured, I will consider this matter rigorously,"* the Devil said. *"In the meantime, her defiance demands reprisal! My wrath will not be satisfied until the Nazarene grovels before my feet. I command your aid in this enterprise. Bring all your strength and malice to bear. Any who distinguish themselves in her conquest will receive lavish rewards at my hand."*

Jack had to cover his ears at the noise that rose to bite them now. Mobs shouted out strategies. Others just mockeries of the new enemy.

*"There is no need to fear this woman, Master,"* Jack heard a voice call in a Russian accent from below him on the mountain. *"We will overthrow her posthaste. You will*

*have your triumph. Your great power rules the world!"*

Jack looked down to see Mephistopheles hunched among his Powers. A gang of Principalities stood near them, conversing among themselves.

"Could the Nazarene be the Woman of the Curse?" They quivered.

"No, she can't!" a Power barked at them.

Jack recognized him as Mephistopheles' second-in-command from his dream.

"You heard the Master," the winged lycanthrope went on. "The Nazarene is married. And neither she nor her husband have public esteem among the fleshlings."

"Why should public esteem matter?" the Principalities demanded.

Mephistopheles rounded on them himself now. "It matters, curs, because the dignity to be expected from the Mother of God would never be united to such impoverished wretches as the Couple in Nazareth. The Almighty will enter the world a King with a great show of strength, to humble the royalty of Earth."

An uproar distracted the Power and his pack from saying more. Jack looked over the caverns to see fights were breaking out across the crowds everywhere. Similar arguments must have arisen among them. He laughed. Even in Hell, politics got heated. The chaos was spreading through the ranks like wildfire, until several streaks of red lightning descended on all of them from the high mountain.

*"That isn't helping, vicemongers!"* the Devil roared, lowering his trident to his side again.

A crimson flame burned on its spikes. Rallied back to their common goal, the hordes of Hell plotted more constructively. They even started encouraging one another in their attempts to outthink the difficulty of getting at the Woman of Nazareth. Nobody could come up with anything, and skirmishes continued to break out when frustrations rose to peak level. Satan kept having to send out his more high-ranking devils to smite the troublemakers into refocusing on the dilemma at hand instead of each other's company. In the end, no new stratagems were contrived Satan hadn't already tried against Mary in the past.

It was the Devil himself who thought of the one thing he'd never attempted. Overwhelming her by their numbers. Hunting the Woman of the Curse had always been the top investigation of Hell, and he'd only ever entrusted himself with it. Whenever any female fleshlings displayed enough virtue to merit suspicion, he'd persecute them alone, never allowing any underlings to have a go. He'd feared they'd fuck it up. But perhaps it was time to open Hell's floodgates all the way on his present foe.

He'd wanted to see the Nazarene fall by his power alone ever since he'd first attacked her with no effect. But, though he'd admit this to no one, he was getting desperate now. Desperate enough to call on the aid of other devils. He summoned seven legions of his most powerful generals to the base of his mountain.

"We're going to Nazareth," he said. "I will see my enemy's downfall tonight."

The devils roared their assent, taking flight behind their master. They passed from the mountain over Jack's head like a swarm of angry hornets emerging from their nest. He felt Dathiel take his shoulder again.

"Now you'll see how to win a fight."

Jack's guardian teleported him to the Virgin's side.

Months had passed since her visit to the hill country, and she was back in her home at Nazareth. Her belly was showing her pregnancy now. She was shining bright as a tabernacle, making Jack shield his face. The change of surroundings from Hell's deepest abysses to the house of the Holy Family stung his eyes more than looking directly at the sun after being blind for a lifetime. Once he recovered, his second sight showed him the light's source. He could make out the Divine Fetus' tiny figure inside Mary's womb as though through a curtain. While he watched, Christ looked to stand up within her, and Jack heard Him speak into His Mother's mind. He recognized the voice from the night of the Annunciation.

"Mother," He said, pausing, looking out through the walls of the house, sensing what was coming, "the fallen Lucifer approaches. He brings seven legions of devils against you."

Jack saw a fire begin to blaze from the Christ, fanning out to consume His Mother. She didn't burn, and Jack felt like Moses gazing at the burning bush.

"The Infernal Dragon vomits wrath against My Holy Name and all who adore It," Christ said. "With daring presumption, he attempts to blot It out from the land of the living before the Redemption ever takes place. Come to the defense of My cause. He brings his underlings to aid him. Very well. You too will come with aid. I am with you more intimately this time. Do battle in My Name against the Ancient Serpent! Magnify Me."

Mary looked like a Seraph now, burning within and without. Jack had never seen her face so fierce. Her Son was fueling her with zeal for the fight. He thirsted for conquest, so she did too. She glanced out the window, saw the evil spirits approaching, and her expression hardened. She summoned her thousand guardians with an act of the will and signaled them retreat several miles behind the property. She and her Son would handle this themselves. Jack took several steps backward, looking at her in awe, grateful he was on her side.

He was moved outside by the locution to stand near the devils. Satan halted his band, perceiving the house suddenly vacant of the thousand, finding it suspicious.

His coveted prey had been left vulnerable for the first time since their final feud at the Temple. Was it a ruse?

No. Mary was stepping outside to face them. He salivated, whetting his appetite to consume the cunt's soul at last. To his delight, she came forward willingly. He raised his hand to signal an onslaught of all seven legions at once, but paused, leaving it suspended in the air.

Mary had stopped beneath the oak tree next to her house and raised her own right hand. She then performed a feat he'd never witnessed a human soul enact. Not since humanity's fall in Eden. She produced a grace from God. From her palm grew a luminescent rose that shifted from white, to gold, to red, to every shade under heaven. It smelled more potent than any prayer he'd encountered before, from enemies below or above the firmament. Not even his age-old nemesis, Michael, had brought such power against him as he now sensed from this Nazarene Woman's little flower.

Satan squinted his blazing eyes, scrutinizing the wonder. To his horror, it transformed further. Mary let it slip down through her fingers, holding it by the petals, and its stem grew into a blade, while the petals became an ornate white hilt. The broadsword was bejeweled with diamonds and adorned with gold trimming.

This Woman was wielding a weapon like unto those only the intellects of angels had hitherto forged!

And the Devil's nightmare didn't stop there.

Vines grew from the hilt of the weapon, slithering up her arm and chest. She'd been barefoot and dressed in nothing but a sleeveless blue dress, cape, and veil before. The vines formed a gold belt and gold-trimmed white breastplate, wrist bracers, and boots over them. Jack's eyes widened at the spectacle. He realized he'd just witnessed the origin of the Rosary. The sword was the same one he'd seen Mary bearing in the garden on Christmas Eve.

It had been forged from her meditation. She'd been focused on the One inside her the whole time it grew, contemplating His story as she understood it from her Scripture studies at the Temple. She glanced up at the enemies before her. Her expression displayed the fearlessness of their presence Satan had come to despise so much over the years. The way she was looking at them, Jack would have thought they were no more than a swarm of pesky gnats buzzing around her while she was out gardening.

Infuriated more than hesitant now, Satan resumed his legions' march toward her. She strode out to meet them, sword held at her side. She closed her eyes as she walked, her meditation growing deeper. It was so profound she hardly seemed to notice the monsters bearing down on her more than the One she felt moving about inside her. Jack was enchanted watching her. He'd never meditated deep enough to ignore evil spirits when they attacked, and he could only imagine how disturbing the presence of such powerful devils as those facing Mary must feel.

There was a burst of light from the Child within her. It spread across her members, illuminating her form. When it reached her eyes, they snapped open. They were as gold as the Archangels' hair now. They locked onto Satan's, and she broke into a run across the grass, raising her sword. Satan sent the most powerful of the seven legions to the front line, preferring them to test her unprecedented weapon's power so he could observe. They fired flaming arrows at her head. Preliminary temptations meant to stir up her passions and throw her inclinations into disorder. They were supposed to prepare her mind for being more easily influenced as their assaults progressed. They failed.

Mary flipped her weapon up, deflecting every single arrow with the blade, not slowed at all in her charge. She even managed to ricochet some of them back at the archers who'd fired them. The front line froze in its tracks. They'd never been so perfectly countered by a human before. Mary took advantage of their hesitation and let her soul shine out its virtues. Its blinding brightness tormented the legion more than the flames of Hell already consuming them. They wanted to shy backward, flee all the way back to the Abyss, but their master didn't permit it. He and the other legions pushed forward behind them. They were trapped.

Mary leapt forward into the army, bringing her sword down upon them. Its blade sliced through their weapons like a chainsaw through twigs. They clashed back with their claws. That sent their limbs flying in all directions. The spirits' screams penetrated Jack's ears to the point of pain. He'd never seen spiritual warfare like this. It was terrifying and exciting at the same time. God's Ark was paving the field with the fallen forms of His enemies.

Satan brought his own sword against her once he could get to her through the hordes. She kicked him in the chest before he could swing it down at her head, sending him flying back, his sword spinning out of his grip. After that, she felled every one of his generals, along with their underlings. In the end, she was the only one left standing on the battlefield.

Satan was the first to rally himself, seeing Mary reenter her home when none had been left to challenge her. Fuming, he flew after her, howling a battle cry through the air. When he neared the domicile, he breathed a stream of hellfire from his mouth, incinerating a hole in the wall. He didn't find her in the first room. Turning toward the area of the house he figured she'd retreat, he broke through the wall of her oratory. She was waiting for him, standing in the calm state he always found her, not a trace of fear on her face. He paused at being this close to her again, remembering what happened the last time he was. His smoking breath trailed behind him like tendrils of an infernal grapevine as he looked her over, sizing her up.

His eyes widened, and Jack thought for a second they'd disappeared altogether.

But their pupils had just expanded to make them completely dark beneath the hood. God had finally let him perceive what was different about Mary. She wasn't alone. She was . . . *pregnant!*

The Girl who'd humiliated him more thoroughly than any child of Eden ever had, with child herself.

*NO!*

He'd watched both Mary and Joseph's family lines produce enough malefactors in his kingdom already. He wouldn't suffer another. He wouldn't!

It was the Child! The Child was the Source of all this new power flowing through her. Another realization struck him. The light! This Child's Conception must have been the source of the light that had emanated from Nazareth when he was in Rome. That, or Mary's climax during copulation. Regardless, what was he to make of this new creature that had entered his world? He sensed his lack of authority over It, much the same as he had Its Mother's soul before It. The trait of immunity had passed to her Offspring. Every other descendant of Adam and Eve had been conceived into his slavery before this Woman. How were she and her Child immune? And how had they spread it to Elizabeth's child?

This son or daughter must be destroyed while still in the womb. He wouldn't allow it to come to fruition and rain down even more havoc on his kingdom than had already been done. Never! It being Mary's Child, he'd love the chance to corrupt It after Its birth, to spite her. But he couldn't take that chance. If It were even half like Its Mother, the Child of Mary could become one of the greatest threats ever known to him on Earth. It had to go. Now.

His wrath kindled more than it had ever been against her, the Devil lunged toward the Virgin, drawing his sword from the shadows in the room. He was ready to rip the Fetus screaming from her womb and slice it in half then and there. Let the wisdom of Solomon reign on! The Nazarene was ready for him, raising her own weapon to parry with his. Their blades ignited into flame when they clashed, producing a unique sound. The best description Jack could give to it was nails scratching a chalkboard combined with a thunderclap.

*"You were lucky last time, Whore!"* the Evil One spewed. *"This time, Daddy's not here to save you. Now you'll at last be subjected at my feet, as is my right!"*

Mary said nothing, responding only by countering every swipe and thrust of his sword with expert skill. It was the fastest dueling Jack had ever witnessed. The two opponents struck with a precision that made him and every intelligence he'd ever seen fight seem like toddlers swinging toy clubs. As the battle raged, he observed Mary wasn't exercising her best effort, whereas Satan was giving it his all. The Virgin was only being defensive, deflecting, ducking, and sidestepping. At first, the Devil attempted temptations to melancholy, but found her joy too difficult to touch. He tried the other deadly vices of wrath, lust, sloth, gluttony, greed, envy, and pride, all to humiliating failure. And since terrifying her never worked, he drew back to the hole he'd made in the wall.

*"You will grovel!"* he screamed. *"YOU WILL SUBMIT!"*

He flipped his sword around in his hand so the blade pointed downward and it grew, morphing into something else. The transformation was an eerie sight to see. Unlike when Jack witnessed celestial weapons change form—always a luminescent and beautiful phenomenon—the Evil One's weapon seemed to move through shadow, as though a black, rippling liquid were slithering around it. He soon recognized what it was turning into, as Satan drew his hand away from the sword's handle in pain. The hilt had become the three spikes of his trident, alight with a red flame. He pointed the spikes toward Mary, shooting a continuous stream of red fire and lightning at her. It was a regurgitation to her mind of every heresy and blasphemy he'd ever thought of against God's Truth, from the beginning of the world to the present age.

The Immaculate Mother stood strong, holding her flaming sword before her. It absorbed the Devil's onslaught, as she in turn directed every answer to his claimed errors from her mind, along with hymns of praise to God's glory. It more than counteracted the dark prince's sacrilegious protestations. No matter how hard he labored, he couldn't tempt her to the slightest falsehood. Mary began walking forward, her weapon's fire swallowing Satan's stream the closer she came. His eyes widened.

She reached him and battered his staff aside before swinging her sword around, sending him crashing through the walls with a slap of its flat side. He flapped his wings to stop his tumbling and regain control, but he was overwhelmed. He didn't stop until he smashed into the oak tree beside the house. Jack followed through the holes in the walls to watch. The seven legions had recovered enough to see their leader thrown from the Virgin's presence. They panicked. Some wanted to return to Hell. Others argued they stay and continue the battle. Frustrated over the evident futility of either option, they started fighting among themselves, as their lesser comrades had done at the counsel. Jack was distracted from their fueds by a voice he heard from inside the house. Jesus was speaking to Mary again, laughing, if he wasn't mistaken.

"Lucifer's inability to touch you has served as a sign that none can stand against My Father's will. End this. And see to it he and his legions never again forget what happens to the unworthy who presume to touch the Ark of My Covenant."

Jack looked over at the Devil stumbling to his feet beneath the tree. He had to use his staff to hold himself up. Livid at the division in his battalions during this crucial moment, he turned it on them, frying them all with lightning.

*"Enough!"* he ordered, his voice hoarse from his beating. "We're . . . not . . . finished . . . yet!" he choked out.

"Yes, you are," Mary said.

She'd stepped out of the house behind Jack, who moved as though he was in her way. Really, he just didn't want to be the one in front of her gaze when her face looked like it did at that moment. Her countenance still displayed a zeal for combat. She went on the complete offensive, unleashing her full power.

*"Who is like unto God, Who dwelleth on high?"*

It was a question, but she made it sound more like a command. The devils hadn't missed that. Their eyes widened in horror at the sound of the ancient angelic battle cry. The cry of their first downfall. They found themselves pulled up beside their master under the tree and paralyzed, compelled to slam themselves down on their knees before their Queen. Even Satan wished he could escape back to Hell now. But the White-Armored Lady held them all present by some unknown power.

She approached the Devil, at eye level with him while on his knees. She stood before him, meeting his terrified gaze with . . . pity. That was what it looked like to Jack. She shook her head at him, speaking in a near whisper, so that only he could hear. Jack had to move closer to pick it up. She sounded so sad and sincere.

"What a heart filled with bitterness, Fallen Lucifer. Had you but venerated the will of God, it would then be *I* kneeling to venerate *you.*"

Satan's fearful expression was replaced in a flash with one of ferocity at the reminder of what might have been. He would have ripped her throat out in that moment if he could. As it was, he couldn't even speak. The Nazarene seemed to hold sway over his very voice with a mere wave of her hand.

"Prince of Darkness, author of sin and death, in the Name of the Most High, cast yourself with your legions back into the infernal caves where your place is appointed."

The Devil and his followers screamed. A crater had opened in the ground beneath the oak tree. It looked like a black hole to Jack. Like it would suck light itself away. It started sucking in the fallen angels. Satan reached out a clawed hand, scraping his fingers into the dirt to save himself. He couldn't. He was swallowed with his minions, the crater closing over them. It was over.

In all, the battle between the Mother of God and the legions of Hell had lasted months. She was nearing the end of her pregnancy. Jack felt a hand land on his shoulder and figured Dathiel was about to plunge him forward in time again. He wished he could stay and enjoy the victory with Mary, but he couldn't control locutions the way he could incorporeal sight. He closed his eyes, trying to counteract any dizziness before time raced past him. He didn't feel anything.

He opened his eyes and found himself standing alone in his bedroom.

# CHAPTER XXX
## THE SECRET OF SUFFERING

Good Friday was always a day of penance for Catholics, but Jack didn't need to self-impose suffering that year.

It found him when Naomi walked out his backdoor and compounded when she crossed back over its threshold. Jack was sitting on the steps of Lorelai's gazebo enjoying the first colors of Spring, thinking again about all he'd experienced since the Fall, when his girlfriend found him. More than anything else, he was thinking about his so-called divine visions. His latest hadn't changed his mind about his condition, just reinforced his caution against the Rosary.

When it ended, he'd promptly put the beads away in the drawer of his nightstand, out of sight so as to be out of mind. He was afraid at first that by taking them up he'd reopened the door in his head that had kept schizophrenia locked out for so long. But, once more, he'd had no weird experiences as long as he'd stayed away from contemplating anything mystical. In the three weeks since his hallucination about the Visitation, life had been normal again.

Now his mind was wandering back to the locutions, having still failed to find any answers to his existential questions in books. He'd never been able to figure out what the Blessed Virgin Mary—that is, the version of her he'd made up in his head—had been trying to tell him through the second vision. Dathiel had said it was to show him how to fight, but Mary had fought her demons the same way he always did. She'd just done it better. He didn't see any new lessons to be taken from what he'd been shown.

She'd meditated deeper than him, but the locution hadn't told him how he was supposed to reach her level. Besides that, Mary was Mother of God. He couldn't be expected to match her in holiness. As for figuring out reasons for the first locution, Jack had already seen the parallels between his life and what he'd observed of Mary's. He even saw the similarity between their quiet temperaments. But he'd always felt there was some other point he was supposed to glean from the whole thing that he'd missed.

He got that he was supposed to imitate Mary as the greatest of Christians and that the locutions were showing him her life for that purpose. But there had to be more to it than that. Why him? Other Catholics weren't shown Mary's life through visions. Why was it so important for him to see what he'd seen? There must be a greater purpose there. At least, that's what he would have suspected if he hadn't already realized it was all hallucinations. He didn't have to try and make sense of it now. The only reason his mind was going to work analyzing these questions at the moment was because he was bored and daydreaming again. It therefore seemed right on cue when he saw Naomi arrive. She was still the person who best got him out of his head and grounded him. He smiled and waved her over. She waved back, but there was no returning smile, and there was something off about her expression. Jack couldn't place what it was.

"Hey," she said, sitting on the steps next to him.

"What is it?" he asked.

She looked thrown off for half a second. "Can we talk?"

"Yeah, what's wrong?"

Naomi looked down, like she was having trouble finding her next words. Jack's heart palpitated. Whatever it was she had to say, it wasn't good. She looked up after another moment.

"Sorry. I've been trying to figure out how to say this. I thought I had it figured out. But . . . I guess not."

Jack didn't say anything for a second, feeling the hard beating of his heart against the inside of his shirt. "What's wrong?" he asked again. "Something happen?"

"I guess so."

"To who?" Jack asked. "Your dad? Your mom?"

He almost found himself hoping it was something like that, not what he suspected she'd come to say. But whatever hope he allowed for it to be about something other than them was minuscule. He knew when a woman asked a man if they could "talk" it was going to be about their relationship, and it was never something the man was going to like hearing.

Her forced chuckle answered his question before she did. "No, nothing like that."

Now he just wished she'd get it over with, knowing what was coming.

"It's about us actually."

*No shit, Naomi. Say it already.*

"I think I need a break."

*A break . . . Why did people always call it a break? Just finish the fucking word already! It's breakup!*

"A break," Jack said. "From our relationship?"

Why was he asking for such an obvious clarification? He knew the answer. It just made him look like he was begging. She didn't answer immediately, just sat not looking at him again. She looked like she was about to cry. Why the fuck was she the one near tears? She was the one doing this! He hadn't asked for it. She looked at him, finally nodding her head.

Jack raked in a deep breath through his nostrils. "I know this is what everyone asks at this point, but I guess I'll go ahead and keep the cliché going. Why?"

Naomi looked away again, like she was fighting back a sob. "You've been distant lately. You've changed."

*Ask the cliché question, get a cliché answer, I suppose.*

"Whatever," he said.

Her head sprang back up to meet his gaze. *"That, right there."* She pointed. "You've been taking everything lying down. What happened to the passion you used to have? The most I see it come out now is when you and Becky get into one of your heady conversations. And, even in those, the spark I used to see from you has died. Where did the Jack I used to know go?"

"I'm right here in front of you! You're the one asking to leave me!"

"See, there it is! This is the most emotion I've seen from you in weeks! Maybe months! I haven't been able to draw it out any other way."

Remembering emotional blunting and social withdrawal were both symptoms of schizophrenia, and knowing he was losing the one person he thought had been keeping it at bay, Jack felt the sudden urge to tell her about it. But what good would it do? Wouldn't telling her he thought he had a sickness as serious as schizophrenia just put the final nail in the coffin of their relationship? Sure, she might stick around for a little while longer. She was a nice person. She'd be there for him all the way up until he was committed. But for how long after? How long would treatment last? What teenage girl could be expected to wait for him through all that? It wasn't as if they were married. No, telling her about schizophrenia wouldn't help anything, just make things worse.

"Even now, you're closed off," she said.

He looked up, realizing he'd been zoning out.

"You want to say something," she said. "What is it? What are you not telling me?"

He stared into her eyes a long moment. He did want to tell her. But, he wouldn't.

"Nothing," he said.

She stared back at him for another second, then nodded her head, the tears filling her eyes now, but not spilling over yet. She stood and turned to leave. But before she'd made it two steps, she stopped.

"Oh, here," she said through a half-formed sob, turning back. "I thought you might want this. I found it cleaning my room the other day."

She dug through her purse and handed him a book. *Saint Michael and the*

*Blessed Angels.* Jack stared at it in disbelief. He'd been convinced the book was part of his hallucinations. He hadn't seen it since before giving up incorporeal sight. He flipped open the front cover to see it was still signed to him by a "Monsignor Bamonte." And the Christmas note was not in his handwriting!

For one brief moment, he felt a touch of the joy he hadn't known in over two months. An exhilaration at the possibility his spiritual mentor was real. And maybe, just maybe, it was all real. Then rationality returned, slamming the sledge hammer of a reasonable explanation down on the feeble wall hope had started to build up in his mind.

The handwriting, although different from his normal handwriting, could still be his. He'd read enough about conditions like dissociative identity disorder to know a person's handwriting could change as they shifted through different alters. Who was to say the same thing wasn't possible in schizophrenia? His handwriting might have changed during a fugue state. He could have bought and addressed the book to himself during one of those. Wouldn't be the first time he'd lost complete touch with reality. He had no idea what he did physically when having full-blown hallucinations.

This book, with its inside cover signature by a mysterious visiting priest no one else he knew had ever met, wasn't proof of the world he'd made up, only more proof he'd made it up. It also proved he needed help. If his mind was so far gone he'd sent himself gifts from imaginary persons, he needed to find a cure, and he needed to find it fast. He needed Naomi.

At this thought, a door slammed, making him glance up from the alien signature. It was the backdoor to his house. While he'd been pondering over his lost book, Naomi had left.

Watching the screen door swing back-and-forth on its hinges a couple of times before settling, he remembered how it had been through that same door Naomi had walked into his backyard last Halloween. That had been the first night he'd immersed himself in the delusion of incorporeal sight. The imaginary friends he'd made through it were gone now. His childhood best friend was gone. He was losing his still-living best friend. His fake spiritual director was gone. And, with the closing of the backdoor, his girlfriend—now ex-girlfriend—was gone.

Everyone was gone.

Jack's bedroom door slammed back against the wall as he burst into his room. He liked the loud bang it made. It hurt his ears, and he wanted to feel something other than the pain of his breakup, even if it was physical pain. He hadn't paid attention to where he was going when he stomped out of his backyard, into the house, and up the stairs, until he found himself before his nightstand. About to grab its drawer's handle, he stopped, realizing what his subconscious mind had pulled him toward. He stood stock-still a moment.

"Fuck it," he said, grabbing the handle and pulling the drawer open.

His rosary's iridescent beads shimmered up at him in the afternoon sunlight pouring through the window like found pirate treasure. He hesitated, then leaned over to pick them up.

*"Don't do this, Jack!"*

He stopped halfway there.

"Why not?" he whispered to himself. "It's the only consolation I've got left."

*"Come on! There are plenty of better ways to handle this. Why not ask for help?"*

Tell his family about schizophrenia? Yes, it would come to that now. But he wasn't ready quite yet. He'd just lost Naomi. He wanted something to make him feel better first. Then he'd bite the bullet and get himself committed for treatment. He picked up the rosary.

*"It's not too late! Put the rosary back, Jack. You can still turn this whole thing around. Call her! Fight for her!"*

He thought about that for a moment.

"And what? Let things go on the way they have for months? No. Even when I was with Naomi, I was bored. There was something missing in her world. I want a better one. Sometimes, you've just gotta take matters into your own hands."

He tightened his grip on the rosary, feeling an adrenaline rush from the expectation of praying it. He longed for the inspiration it brought to his imagination again. He wanted to think on the Divine Hero. If He was real, He could end Jack's misery. He began to sweat. His determination rose . . . and all the arguments against the supernatural he'd ever come across entered his thoughts at once, almost as if they were being pressed into his mind whether he liked it or not.

*"A wonderful little bedtime story to keep kids happy when they go to sleep at night. A Divine Hero to inspire their imaginations. A Fictional Character in a cosmic joke, like Mr. Wilkerson's always saying at school! You have a chance to experience real freedom here, Jack! Not the imagined freedom of religion!"*

Jack closed his eyes and stood still, trying to ignore the arguments, or discern his way through them. He breathed slowly and listened. As he sat pondering them, something else started ringing through his thoughts. He tried concentrating on it and realized it was one word.

*"Delusion . . . Delusion . . . DELUSION, JACK!"*

Jack gasped and his eyes snapped open, before he opened them farther, to what he'd always known as the incorporeal.

Delusion had him by the throat and was pulling him over the side of his terrace.

With one hand, Jack gripped the railing. With the other, he was trying to hold back the minotaur's machete from slicing his throat. The demon's feet stuck to the side of the house as he pulled with all his might, trying to take Jack's head. Jack was losing the struggle, his arm weakening under the pressure. He wasn't as powerful as he used to be. He guessed his neglect of the Rosary for two months had done a number on his soul's strength. Even if the monster didn't succeed in decapitating him, if he managed to pull him over the railing, Jack didn't think he was strong enough to survive the fall in his weakened state.

He needed his weapon. But the sword was propped against the wall by his bed, as though the beads were still in his nightstand and not in his hands. He tried to start the prayer, but found he couldn't bring himself to speak the first words of the *Apostle's Creed* again.

*I believe! I believe in God! That's all I need to say! That's all it will take!*

He couldn't pray the words in good conscience. He still wasn't sure if he did believe. Not with incorporeal sight being proved a fiction. Not with Monsignor Bamonte being a part of the delusions. The priest was where he'd gotten all his arguments for the existence of God outside of his charism. If God was real, why would He come to his aid if he prayed the words of His *Creed* to Him falsely? He was trapped. Trapped by a paradox in his own mind. Trapped by a demon of his own making.

"That's right, Jack," Delusion hissed in his ear. "And this demon's going to take your head the way you took my horn, you little prick!"

The minotaur sliced his blade back-and-forth, drawing blood from Jack's throat. Jack squealed in pain. He hooked his ankle around a rung of the railing to keep himself from falling and lifted the hand that had been gripping it, reaching out for his sword, trying to summon it into his palm. It wouldn't come. Not until he'd initiated its use with the *Creed*. He squeezed his eyes shut.

"This . . . isn't . . . real!" he said through gritted teeth.

"That's right," Delusion repeated. "So why don't you relax? Let yourself fall? You can't die if it's not real. Why're you fighting me?"

Jack didn't answer, just kept trying to pry the demon off him.

"You're still wishing it was real, aren't you? Even in this pickle I've got you? Unbelievable! Alright, Jack. Clearly the principal needs to take you back to school. Lesson one, how many atheists does it take to convince a Catholic he's one of them?"

"Not . . . an . . . atheist," Jack choked out. "Never . . . have . . . been."

After he'd said the words, their full meaning struck him. If he wasn't an out-and-out atheist, why couldn't he pray the first words of the *Creed* with intellectual honesty?

*Because,* he reasoned, *though not a strict non-believer, I doubt.*

So, he was an agnostic maybe? No, he wouldn't call himself an agnostic either. He was a Catholic. That hadn't changed. A struggling Catholic, but a Catholic nonetheless. But, if he was struggling with belief, did that give him a right to say the prayer of belief?

He wasn't sure. He couldn't say he believed in God wholeheartedly. But, didn't that mean he believed in Him partially? The *Creed* didn't specify the level of belief, as long as there was some present, he supposed. Hadn't Christ said somewhere that faith the size of a mustard seed could move mountains? If not enough to move a mountain, was whatever faith Jack had enough to move a sword into his hand?

But Jack didn't think he had any faith. He had hope God was real. Plenty of hope. But did he really have faith He was real?

*Wait! I must have some! Why else have I kept saying my prayers every night? That's faith, isn't it?*

Maybe. Maybe not. Probably not. That seemed like just another manifestation of hope.

He felt like he'd missed something. Like he'd had the answer for a moment, but then it had eluded him again as fast as it had appeared. He circled back to his original thoughts, trying his best to concentrate despite the monster at his throat. If he wouldn't call himself an atheist or an agnostic, then he had some belief. He wouldn't say he doubted fully, which meant he believed partially. Which . . . meant he could pray the *Creed* honestly.

Jack's eyes jumped open. He stuck his hand out again. The broadsword came flying into it.

*"I believe in God,"* he brought the blade up, cutting Delusion's machete in half. The demon shrieked as he lost his grip on him.

*"The Father Almighty,"* Jack continued, swinging the sword around to decapitate his would-be executioner right back.

He missed his head. The minotaur was already half-falling, half-crawling backward down the side of the house. But Jack saw he'd managed to slice off his other horn.

*"Creator of Heaven and Earth,"* Jack gave chase down the wall. *"I believe in Jesus Christ, His Only Son, Our Lord!"*

Jack raised the sword over his head, bringing it down in a chopping motion to slice the demon in two. Delusion teleported from his place on the wall to avoid the strike, but only managed to make it as far as the ground below his attacker. Jack's prayer was holding him present. He couldn't teleport off the property. He could only flee on foot. He scampered toward the outer darkness at the edge of the front yard.

*"Who was conceived by the Holy Spirit,"* Jack hit the ground and ran after the demon, *"and born of the Virgin Mary!"* He closed on him, almost catching his cape. *"He suffered under Pontius Pilate,"* Jack swung his sword, slicing a piece of cape away, *"was crucified, died, and was buried,"* Jack nicked the back of Delusion's shoulder this time. *"He descended into Hell,"* Jack gashed his leg near the hoof, and the demon screamed. *"On the third day,"* Jack jumped and pummeled Delusion to the ground before he reached the edge of the yard, *"He rose again from the dead!"*

Delusion lay facedown under Jack's boot.

*"He ascended into Heaven and sitteth at the right hand of God, the Father Almighty,"* Jack raised his weapon. *"From thence He shall come to judge the living and the dead!"* he brought the sword down to slice the wretch in half.

Delusion managed to wriggle around and face upward before he could finish him, opening his cape as he did. The black hole of his chest spewed out a vomit-scented black slime all over Jack, making him close his eyes and lose focus for half a second. It was long enough for the demon to slip out from under him.

*"I believe in the Holy Spirit,"* Jack yelled, focusing his angry reaction into his prayer.

As he did, he swung the sword back upward, slicing it across Delusion's chest while he clawed his way backward across the ground. The monster roared in pain. Jack realized the black hole was tangible. It could be struck by a rosary at least. The minotaur wrapped his cape back over it, turning to crawl toward the wall of night only feet in front of him now.

*"The Holy Catholic Church,"* Jack stomped after him, *"the communion of saints,"* he stepped on the demon's cape, halting his escape, *"the forgiveness of sins,"* the cape tore again, and Delusion kept going, *"the resurrection of the body,"* Jack held his sword out to his side for one final swing.

It was his last chance if he didn't want to chase Delusion into the demonic kingdom. The fallen Archangel was almost at the border.

*"And life everlasting!"* Jack swung . . . and missed.

The baal of Wando disappeared into the night, the clip-clop of his hoofed foot fading fast.

Jack couldn't believe it!

He'd had him! How many fucking times could the fucking clown-faced minotaur-magician fucking escape his comeuppance? He hesitated in indecision about whether to follow the demon where he'd fled. He didn't like the idea of entering the dark in his current state. His muscles weren't as big or strong as they once were. The sword felt heavier in his hands than it used to. That was why he'd missed his target so many times.

As he stood deliberating, he stiffened. He'd sniffed something that took his mind off his problem. A strong scent of fresh roses blowing past him from behind. A painful lump clamped his throat. He knew the scent. And he knew who gave it off. When she spoke, tears streamed down his face to accompany the lump. He hadn't realized how badly he'd needed to hear her voice again.

"Well done, son! I'm so proud of you!"

Only that voice could dispel his disappointment so swiftly. He turned to see the Blessed Virgin Mary standing in a globe of light atop the highest boughs of the oak tree in his front yard. She was clothed in all white this time. An ankle-length dress and a mantle hanging from her head to her feet behind her like a cape. The mantle was edged in gold. From her neck hung a sphere of gold light. Every shade of her form shined. He'd missed seeing beings like that. Her brilliance should have made him squint his eyes, but it didn't. She was like a sun that did no damage to the optic nerve. Of course, that could be because she was only in his head. But he didn't care about that right now. He was too glad to see her again, imaginary or not.

At the sight of her, the strength in his legs failed him, and he fell to his knees before her. She was reaching toward him, a rosary of white pearls on a gold chain hanging from her wrist. Beams of light emitted from her fingers and enveloped him, intensifying the smell of roses. He felt his muscles strengthen again as he breathed it in. The wound on his neck left by Delusion's machete healed.

She turned the hand with the rosary hanging from it, shining its beams into the darkness surrounding the house, and fire combusted out of nowhere. Jack thought for a second Mary's light had started it, wondering why she'd set it. Then he realized the fire was a person who'd appeared. A soul engulfed in flames. It was naked and was being carried into the yard by two angels. One of them was Dathiel. The other he'd never met. They supported the soul under the arms and brought him up next to Jack, who rose to his feet to see who it was. He looked familiar. When the spirit glanced up, looking him in the eyes, Jack took a step back, almost choking on his next word.

*"Chuck?"*

Chuck smiled at him. It was a happy expression, but it looked like he was trying not to grimace in pain at the same time. Flames were still licking up his nude form like a hundred dragon tongues. They didn't seem to burn the two angels, but they were hurting Chuck. He didn't smell damned to Jack. There was almost no scent to him at all. And he certainly didn't look as miserable as Faustus had, or any of the walking dead Jack saw so often on the streets.

"Are you . . . are you in . . . *Purgatory?"* Jack asked.

Chuck nodded, a sad expression passing over his face, but it was intermingled with what Jack thought was hope.

"How?" Jack asked. "I thought you were in . . . in Hell!"

Chuck shook his head, trying to speak. It looked painful for him.

"Not . . . d-dead," he whispered, sounding far away. "S-s-saved at the last . . . m-moment. Regretted . . . p-pain . . . from sh-sh-shooting . . . right before . . . d-d-dying. W-w-wished S-S-Someone c-could s-save me. Enough . . . f-f-for rescue."

Jack nodded, getting the picture, not wanting Chuck to strain himself anymore than he already had. He was just glad to see him again. He let his sword fall from his hand and embraced him, not worried about the flames anymore. They both fell to their knees as the angels let Chuck go.

Chuck strained to speak a few more words anyway. "T-Thank you for your . . . s-s-s-sufferings! They've . . . b-b-been bringing m-me r-r-relief."

Jack's eyes opened in shock, looking up into Dathiel's to confirm. His guardian smiled down at him from over Chuck's shoulder and winked.

"S-s-sorry I s-sc-scared you that day in class w-w-when I . . . m-m-moved the b-back of your ch-ch-chair. I w-w-was j-just t-t-trying t-to g-get y-your a-a-attention s-s-so you could p-p-pray f-for m-me."

Jack remembered the day he was talking about. So, he had felt something kick his chair!

"It's okay," he said. "I'm sorry I didn't get the message. I would have prayed for you sooner if I'd known you weren't lost forever."

"B-B-But y-your prayers ha-have b-b-brought m-me r-relief." Chuck smiled through his pain. "S-s-sorry I . . . w-w-wasn't able t-t-to . . . b-bring *you* m-m-more r-relief."

"You've been interceding for me?" Jack asked.

"I ch-ch-chased Delusion a-and th-th-the others away f-from you a-a-at th-this v-v-very s-spot the day you f-f-first m-met him."

Jack thought back, remembering the incident to which Chuck referred. It was the day Mephistopheles, Racism, and Delusion had attacked him together alongside several of their underlings after he'd arrived home from school. The day Dathiel had explained the so-called dilemma of creation to him. Dathiel had told him it was another of his patrons that had rescued him that day and that he'd eventually meet him. He remembered he'd been excited that day because . . . because he'd just repaired things with Naomi the first time she'd been mad at him and secured a date with her. The memory stung him. The moment it did, he saw

Chuck's grimace of pain change to a look of relief as he took several deep breaths.

Jack drew back. "Did I just . . . Did that . . .?"

"Yes," Chuck answered. "Your pain at her loss is helping repair the damage my choices inflicted on me."

The angel who'd brought Chuck to him with Dathiel reached down and placed a hand on Jack's shoulder. "And now—if you don't mind finishing that Rosary, Philangelus—my charge is ready to be freed from Purgatory."

Jack looked up at him, almost not daring to believe he'd heard him right. The angel's smile and nod confirmed he had. He looked Chuck in the eyes, who nodded and gave his own smile, the most hopeful one Jack had seen him give yet. Jack's tears stopped, his face growing solemn. He nodded his assent and took his sword back up, standing. He faced the Blessed Mother in the tree, held his sword pointing downward into the grass before him, and initiated the *Lord's Prayer*.

The weapon grew into a bouquet of roses in his hands. He went through the decades, as the angels carried his prayers up to Mary one-by-one, then back down to squeeze their nectar over Chuck. Every time they did, Jack watched the flames licking Chuck's form lessen more and more, until they disappeared altogether during the *Hail, Holy Queen.*

Chuck was shining bright now. The angels flew him up to the top of the tree, the rays from Mary's hands dressing him in white robes as they passed over him during the ascent. When Chuck turned to look back down at Jack from her side, the bliss on his face told him he now beheld the Beatific Vision.

Jack realized his childhood best friend had just become a saint.

Leaning on his sword, Jack genuflected and bowed his head before the wonder.

"Thank you, Jack," Chuck said, sounding like he was right in front of him.

Jack jerked his head back up. The new saint was standing a few feet away. He'd descended from the tree so fast, he must have teleported.

"I'd have suffered the flames of Purgatory many more years if not for your efforts. I owe you Heaven."

Jack's eyebrows fell inward with his face. "You don't owe me anything. I should have been there for you while you were alive."

"I owe you all, Philangelus. And, as a first show of thanks, I present your enemy at your feet."

Chuck indicated for Jack to look behind him. When he did, he saw Gabriel had dragged Delusion back to the edge of the yard. Mary's guardian had the demon by the back of the neck, his giant ax poised under his throat. Jack wondered if he hadn't been there the whole time, forcing Chuck's murderer to watch Mary crown him. With both his horns cut short, the minotaur looked like a combination of the Joker and Hellboy.

"Found this miscreant hiding in the Old City Jail in Charleston," Gabriel said. "Thought you might want to finish with him."

The giant Archangel dragged the minotaur over to Jack and Chuck beneath the oak tree. Jack looked down into Delusion's petrified white face. He was shaking as though it was thirty below outside, looking from Jack, to Chuck, then almost all the way up the tree, afraid to look directly at who stood atop it.

"Time to go home, Delusion," Jack said, bringing the demon's attention back to him. "Consider yourself retired from the teaching profession."

He lifted his sword to decapitate him at last.

*"NO! DON'T!"* the monster begged.

After a moment, Jack said, "You're right."

The demon looked at him, confused, but glad he was still around, whatever the reason.

"It's no coincidence I've missed delivering your final blow so many times before. It's not fitting I be the one who banishes you. I'm not the one you deceived into killing himself." Jack flipped his sword around and offered the hilt to Chuck. "He's yours. I only ask that you send him where he tried to send you."

Chuck accepted the weapon, gazing down into the minotaur's terrified eyes, staring for a long time. He looked deep in thought.

"You held me in the prison of depression for years," he said to his former tormentor. "Always whispering from the shadows. Always suggesting. Always so subtle with your lies."

Chuck lifted the sword before him, gazing at the blade. It would be his first use of a rosary.

"Rest assured, this won't be subtle, demon."

Delusion struggled again in Gabriel's vise of a grip. *"Let me go! LET GO OF ME, CRUMB-WORSHIPPER!"*

Chuck felt his determination rise with those words of encouragement. The last beating he'd received from the demon flashed through his mind. That was the final push.

"What are you afraid of?" he asked the monster. "I thought this was just a delusion."

With that, he flipped the sword around, slicing the minotaur's cape open from the bottom up, exposing the black hole beneath it and jamming the sword down into it. Delusion wailed, sparkling and smoldering as he was sucked into his own chest, disappearing at the sword's tip. Jack stepped back when it happened. He'd never seen a demon go like that. It was like he'd consumed himself. Chuck brought the sword up, holding the hilt out to him. Jack took it, and Chuck thanked him one last time before ascending back to the top of the tree.

The three angels joined him, and Jack watched them all ascend toward the sky in the white globe surrounding Mary. The Blessed Virgin had looked him in the eyes and smiled before they'd departed. Jack tried to hold onto the memory of her face, not knowing when or if he might see her again. He relinquished incorporeal sight, staring down at the broken rosary in his hands.

Everything he'd seen might not have been real, just another projection of wishful thinking on his part. But, if reality was real, then the Rosary had to be. He hadn't made that one up. Catholics had been praying it for centuries. It had brought him comfort, even if the Chuck he'd just seen had been another hallucination. If reality was real and Catholicism was too, then, for all he knew, the real Chuck needed him praying for his soul. He decided to start carrying the rosary with him again. He might not use it every day, but he'd have it with him, just in case.

Maybe he was being superstitious at this point. He felt like Jonathan Harker in *Dracula* again. The Englishman had wanted to keep the rosary a Transylvanian peasant had given him around his neck in case Dracula and his brides really were lurking around the next corner. As a Protestant, Harker had wondered if he was being superstitious too. It hadn't stopped him from wearing the rosary. It wouldn't stop Jack from carrying it either. He would keep it in his pocket on the off-chance the monsters were real and he needed a sword ever ready to draw against them. But a broken sword was no good.

He reached down and took the open links, bending them back around each other. It would have been easier to use pliers from the garage for such minuscule, meticulous repair work, but he preferred fixing the rosary by hand. The little pinch it gave his fingers could be his first offering for the souls in Purgatory.

He finished. The rosary was whole again. He put it in its pouch and slipped it into his pocket. As he did, his phone vibrated in his other one. He pulled it out, and forgot to breathe when he saw the name written across its screen.

"Hey, Jack—"

Jack jumped as his door burst open behind him.

"You have any laundry in here?" his mother asked.

*"Jeez, you scared the crap out of me! Don't you knock?"*

"Sorry!" Lorelai laughed. "Any laundry?"

"No, I don't—hey, Mom?" He walked toward her, holding his phone out in front of him like it was a hot potato he wanted to pass as soon as he could. "Can you answer this for me and tell me who it is?"

She furrowed her eyebrows, looking down at the piles of clothes in her arms.

"I'm kind of busy. You can't do that yourself?"

"Just humor me. Please! I'll hold the clothes for you."

He switched with her, gathering the laundry from her chest to his. She gave him a dubious look, glanced down at the phone, looked back at him, and shrugged her shoulders.

"Hello?" she said. "Yes, this is his number. This is his mother. His hands are full at the moment. He should be—yes, lovely to meet you too! I've heard a lot about you . . . Oh yes? Well," she looked at Jack, "I hope it's all been good things." She winked. "Hold on a minute. He's right here."

She held the phone out to Jack.

"It's who the caller I.D. said it was," she told him, still looking confused by his request. "Monsignor Bamonte."

# CHAPTER XXXI
## SOLIPSISM

If everything Jack saw was a projection of his own mind, it had shown him the monsignor and the psychologist he'd recommended were both characters in the story after all.

Jack sat in the doctor's waiting room, tapping the fingers of his right hand across his thumb. He was staring at a painting of a lone monk on the opposite wall. The monk was hooded in a brown habit and praying before a window. Sunshine filtered in through the window, its beams divided by a stone column in its center. They projected the monk's shadow on the wall of the stone corridor behind him.

The shadow stood taller than he did, its towering hooded form looking like Death himself approaching the religious figure at his back, always one step short of catching him. Jack wondered what prayers the brother was muttering under his breath. His hands were folded and his head bowed so the viewer of the painting couldn't see his face. Was he trying to hide from his fate? To escape the reality of oblivion ever chasing him to his final breath? Would it be Heaven that awaited him on its other side, or the stark blackness of nothing?

Jack tried looking away from the painting to enjoy the others lining the walls of the waiting room. There were scenes of beaches and boat docks, lush forests with squirrels and deer scampering through their trees, even pictures of warm cottages with fires exhaling smoke through their chimneys. But Jack kept finding his attention drawn back to the painting of the lone monk. He supposed it was intended to evoke feelings of tranquility too. A reminder one needed to find a quiet place to be alone with God during the day, even if it was just to stop and enjoy the view from a window in an empty hallway. This was not what it succeeded in doing. Not for Jack.

It just reminded him of his quest to answer that most ancient and frustrating question of the ages. Where do I come from and where am I going? Of course, answering that question had been further complicated for him, by more questions being piled atop it like stones atop his chest. Am I crazy? Is any of this real? What is reality anyway? How does one define it? Do I even exist?

Jack was aware of how stupid some of these questions sounded when asked aloud. Yet he'd been unable to come up with any easy answers for them. So had all his research. Most books didn't even address them. This had surprised him time and time again, because they seemed like the first questions that needed answering when beginning the pursuit of any knowledge. He'd expressed as much to Dr. Vonhagen in their first meeting two weeks ago.

The psychologist hadn't reacted with judgment. He'd sat before Jack quietly, meeting his eyes through his thick glasses, resting his mouth on the back of his fingers for most of their session. The doctor exhibited a calming persona different from Dr. Rasput's. This one came across to Jack like a curious but intelligent listener. In that sense, he reminded Jack more of Monsignor Bamonte. He could see how the two would get along.

When Jack had told his mother he wanted to try therapy again and that his priest friend had recommended someone he knew, she'd been happy to pay. So the monsignor had volunteered to drive him to his first session and introduce them. During the ride, Jack had learned why Father Murphy had said there was no visiting priest at St. John's when he'd asked him. The monsignor had moved to St. Mary's parish rectory in Greenville shortly after Christmas. The bishop had asked him to train the pastor there in a new ministry.

Jack couldn't believe his neglect to clarify with Father Murphy if there had *ever* been a visiting priest at the cathedral. That simple oversight had resulted in so much time spent thinking his spiritual director was a figment of his imagination. He could have even gotten Monsignor Bamonte's Rome contact information from the cathedral's rector, if he'd bothered to inquire. All this, because he'd been too isolated. That had fueled Jack into seeing Dr. Vonhagen as soon as possible now that he knew he was real.

He couldn't solve his problems alone. They were too big. Isolation had just compounded them. He knew that now. He'd already been on the verge of bringing his family into his secret the day Monsignor Bamonte had called to tell him he was back in the country. But he'd waited a little longer, to learn the results of his psychological evaluation first. At least he'd be sure he was schizophrenic when he told them now. He'd have a professional's findings to back him up. The road to treatment would already be underway too.

Dr. Vonhagen had greeted him and the monsignor in a subdued voice when he'd finally come out to the waiting room to welcome Jack to his first session. He was a middle-aged man, well put together. His dress had been professional, but not so dressed up he'd been intimidating or made Jack feel he'd interrupted him on his way out to the ball. He struck Jack as a man who'd be just as comfortable at a gala as he was out fishing on the Cooper River. But that may have just been the theme of the waiting room's paintings influencing his thoughts.

Jack had told him everything once in his office. His story from the day of learning about Chuck's suicide and Mr. Wilkerson's declaration, to his most recent experience of witnessing Chuck's supposed entrance into beatitude, including every detail he remembered of his life since October. He'd even left his journal with the doctor to cover any parts he'd forgotten. Jack had been anxious two weeks ago sitting in this waiting room with his spiritual director, waiting to meet the non-heretic Catholic psychologist at last. A person who could finally provide an unbiased opinion on his whole situation. But the butterflies that had swarmed Jack's stomach then nowhere near matched the size of the ones flitting about and tickling it now.

He felt himself quiver. He was about to get a breakdown of what exactly was happening in his brain. The question of his sanity—a doubt he'd wrestled with so long—was about to be answered, with no room left for doubt this time. That was, of course, no room left for doubt beyond his questioning of everything as a fantasy. If only the psychologist could somehow eliminate his doubts of reality too. Then he could move on with his life, maybe even find a way to embrace Catholicism despite the loss of incorporeal sight as its proof. Still, he'd be happy enough for the doctor to put his questions about that phenomenon to bed. In all, he and Dr. Vonhagen had talked for ninety minutes, with Jack doing most of the talking. When the therapist did speak, one of the things he'd asked Jack was to walk him through his experience of incorporeal sight.

"What happens right before you 'step into' the spiritual world you see? What is it like? How does it feel physically?"

Jack had given a detailed description, repeating a lot of what Dathiel explained to him the first time they met.

"Would you describe yourself as being in a trance state when you employ the ability?"

"No," Jack had said. "In fact, I use it when I'm around people all the time. And they've never said anything, like that I look different or something. I've never had them stare at me or give me any weird looks or anything. I've even recorded myself on my phone while doing it, and I don't look any different."

The doctor had made a note in his pad. "Have you ever done any illegal drugs or abused substances of any kind?"

"No."

"Have you ever abused alcohol?"

"No, sir. I've had sips of wine and beer. Never been drunk though. Never even had a full glass of anything."

"When you see and hear persons and things no one else can, would you describe them as coming from somewhere else, or inside you?"

Jack had given him a puzzled look.

"From . . . outside me. I see and hear them the same way I see and hear people through my regular sight. The same way I see and hear you right now."

The doctor wrote another note to himself. Despite all his odd questions, the one Jack had pondered the most for the past two weeks was his last one of the session.

"I want to ask you what therapists sometimes call, the miracle question. It's phrased differently for everyone, but I suppose I'll phrase yours like this. If you could go to bed tonight, have God miraculously change your life while you slept, erasing all your problems, and wake up tomorrow to find your circumstances exactly as you wanted them, what would they be?"

Jack had sat for a second. "You mean, if everything was made ideal in my life in one instant? No explanation as to how it got that way, other than, it's a miracle?"

"Yes."

Jack had thought another moment. "Well . . . I'd know for sure reality was real of course . . . I'd know God was real, or at least have a perfect divine faith in His existence. I'd still be dating Naomi. Chuck would be alive, or I'd at least know for sure he was in Heaven . . . I suppose I'd like it if incorporeal sight had been a real charism from Heaven and that all my experiences through it had been real . . ." He'd paused and thought again. "That seems like it's everything I'd want, but . . ."

Jack had put his hand to the side of his head and massaged it.

"Was there something else?" the doctor asked.

Jack looked up. "I can have anything I want in this scenario, right?"

"Yes. It's *your* dream scenario."

"Then . . . I'd wish there was a great external miracle, witnessed by a bunch of people, not just me this time. A public miracle, like the ones we read about in the Bible. Like the plagues of Egypt, the parting of the Red Sea, or the miracles it says Jesus performed. And this miracle would be witnessed by *a lot* of people, atheists and believers included, in the *modern* world, not something that happened two thousand or more years ago and is hard to verify now. Documented with modern technology. With no natural explanation that could explain it away. Everyone would *see* the proof of God's existence for themselves. Not just me. And it would end the age of materialistic skepticism. Everyone would be a believer. If I was granted all that, I suppose I'd finally be happy."

The doctor had looked impressed by his answer, writing it down in his notepad. Jack had the impression he hadn't heard an answer like it before. After their session, Jack had spent the next six-and-a-half hours being put through various psychological tests. He'd taken the WAIS-V, which he'd been told was an intelligence test for measuring his IQ. He'd done one called the RISB, where he'd had to look at incomplete sentences and finish them. He'd taken one called the TAT, in which he'd had to look at cards with pictures on them and tell stories, filling in what had happened before, during, and after the images.

He'd done the Rorschach, where he'd had to glance at ink blots on paper and say what they most resembled to him. He'd been asked to draw a picture of a house, a tree, and a person, then answer questions about each. And finally, he'd taken two tests, called the MMPI-II and the MCMI-III, the first consisting of five hundred true or false questions and the second involving two hundred regular questions. These had been probing for depression, anxiety, and personality disorders. Jack could tell that much even as a layman. But the test that had scared him came last.

Learning its results was what had him so anxious in his seat at the moment. Dr. Vonhagen had a neurologist on staff in the office, and he'd done a brain scan on Jack. It was to check for any physical causes of hallucination, like tumors. The mention of that word had made Jack sweat. He could feel cold perspiration licking his forehead now just thinking about it. The thought of having schizophrenia was bad enough. The idea he might have brain cancer . . . Suffice it to say, he'd been trying not to think about that one, praying it was the former. At this point, he'd feel relieved if it was the former.

Dr. Vonhagen's reassurance he was only ruling out all possibilities and that he didn't think it was likely that Jack had cancer had made Jack feel better . . . a little. If not for the psychologist's calming demeanor, Jack thought he would have been even more worried over the last couple of weeks. From the death of his friend, to concerns about receiving visions from either God or the Devil, to thinking he was crazy, to questioning reality—add on top of that getting his first girlfriend who'd then broken his heart—and Jack had thought his woes couldn't possibly be increased. He'd been wrong again. Another stone had been placed atop his already suffocating chest. Now he'd spent fourteen days wondering if cancer was eating his brain.

When Dr. Vonhagen opened the door to the waiting room to take him back for their follow-up session, Jack didn't know if he felt more comfort or dread at the moment of truth's arrival.

Dr. Vonhagen's office was on the second floor, up an antique stairwell.

Like so many other buildings in Charleston, his was a converted house from an older period. His chosen therapy space must have been a master bedroom before, because the brick fireplace that started in the downstairs lobby rose up through the floor to exit the ceiling. The psychologist had taken advantage of the brick structure jutting into the room by making it into a mantelpiece. He'd stuck an antique clock in the center and hung a painting above it.

This painting was Jack's favorite thing in the building. A giant portrayal of Saint Michael slaying Satan, while other angels chased the rest of the demons from Heaven in the background. When Jack asked if it intimidated any of his other clients, Dr. Vonhagen said he covered it up before some of his younger and more timid clients came for sessions. Jack was no such client. He loved it. When he'd asked why he'd chosen this picture for the focal point of his therapy room, the doctor had said it was to keep him mindful of where his work took place.

Therapy, in his view, was a battle for peace of mind and therefore peace of soul. The same battle the angels had fought. He'd said that, for him, the painting represented good thoughts casting out bad ones. It also reminded him to ask clients' guardian angels to help him before every session, aware they had a far keener insight into what was going on in a person's head and life than he ever would. Besides all that, he figured he owed Saint Michael some kind of tribute within the offices. In looking for a workplace close to the center of town that was still an affordable lease, this building had been the only one, and it was located on St. Michael's alley. A detail Jack had taken for a sign himself when the monsignor had first brought him here. He hadn't even known there was a street named for his patron saint in Charleston. It had been easy for Jack to relay his story to the psychologist after their discussion of the painting.

Upon entering the room for his second visit, Jack took courage from the painting again. One way or another it represented his battle today, whether purely mental or against real spiritual creatures. God-willing, Dr. Vonhagen's test results would help him discern which it was. Jack sat himself on the end of the couch farthest away from the painting so he could keep it ever in view of his peripheral vision while looking at the therapist in his armchair.

Dr. Vonhagen crossed his legs. "It's good to see you again, Jack!"

"You too," Jack said.

"Before I forget, I've got this back for you." The doctor handed him his journal. "Hope it helped."

"It certainly did! Thank you for being so open and willing to share all the details of your story. It backed up what I and the tests concluded."

Jack braced himself for the diagnosis.

"Before we get into your results," Dr. Vonhagen said, placing the folder in his hands on a round mahogany table beside his chair, "I wanted to speak briefly about one of the crises you told me about last time. It was really a philosophical problem as much as a psychological one. Solipsism."

Jack furrowed his eyebrows. "I've never heard of it. Which crisis are you referring to?"

"Your doubt of the existence of reality. You were right. You're not the first person ever to struggle with the position. Solipsism's the philosophical term for it. It's a theory positing that only the self exists, or can be proven to exist, since the solipsist believes he can't know for certain the reality of things beyond himself. It's a terrible affliction to suffer, because it makes a person feel trapped in their own mind, unable to reach out and have a true relation with anyone or anything else."

Jack nodded his head, sighing. "Tell me about it."

Dr. Vonhagen nodded back. "Another difficulty with it is, due to its nature, it might seem impossible to disprove its claims, since it involves the mistrust of one's own senses. It sounded to me like this was part of your own difficulty. Not knowing who or what you could trust to help you out of it."

Jack nodded more emphatically, leaning forward on the couch.

"The position can be disproved though," the psychologist affirmed, "through the use of logic, which doesn't have to involve the senses."

All of Jack's muscles tensed together. He couldn't believe what Dr. Vonhagen had just said. He wondered if he'd see Lupe standing with the therapist whispering what to say into his mind were he to use incorporeal sight.

"One thing to realize," Dr. Vonhagen went on, "is that, if solipsism is true, there can only be one solipsist in existence. Imagine two people meeting who both believe they're the only one who exists. The first solipsist would have to convince the second that he was the one projecting reality and the other person was a projection of his mind." The doctor smiled. "A tough thing to do when the only existence the second solipsist is certain of also happens to be his own. So, solipsism can never really be more than a private belief, because good luck convincing other people they aren't real."

Jack laughed, feeling some of his tension subside, but only some. His shoulders were still tight and wouldn't let him rest on the back of the couch.

"That doesn't disprove it as a valid philosophy," Dr. Vonhagen said. "Just shows why there are few adherents to it out there, which is probably why you had such a hard time finding any information on it."

"Makes sense," Jack said. "But it sounds like you know about it . . ."

"I do. I've had clients struggle with it before. Some of them called it 'the Matrix Syndrome.'"

Jack chuckled. "Yeah, I thought of that movie too. So, have you ever helped any of your other clients get over the problem?"

Jack had leaned farther forward. He hadn't expected Dr. Vonhagen to have answers about his reality doubts, just his sanity ones. His knowledge on the subject was an unexpected and most welcome surprise.

"I have," the doctor said.

Jack's heart skipped a beat.

"One thing to consider if you're a true solipsist is that you're making yourself

God."

Jack leaned back, feeling gut punched. "What do you mean?"

"If you, the self, are responsible for the existence of everything else, then you've made yourself the Creator."

Dr. Vonhagen paused. Jack didn't say anything. Silence hovered between them for several seconds like a wall of suffocating smoke.

"But," the psychologist dissipated the silence at last, "if that were true, it seems odd you don't have an inherent understanding of all that's in the universe and that you're not omniscient. If everything's only a projection of your own mind, why aren't you able to will anything you wish on a whim? Seems you'd be able to abandon limits like time and space whenever you felt like it. But, you can't. Even the ability you told me about last time, incorporeal sight, has rules you aren't able to break. You're not able to do anything you wish through it. If you're the one who established the rules of reality, why can't you break them?"

"I . . . didn't think about it that way," Jack said.

The doctor tilted his head, still looking at Jack, but appearing in deep thought. "If you'll bear with me a moment for a hypothetical scenario. Perhaps the all-powerful self created the universe in its own imagination, established unbreakable rules for the figments within it, then entered that universe itself as part of some private game. Perhaps it even deprived itself of the memory of creating the cosmos and of its omniscience over it in order to pass the time and avoid boredom. This scenario might hold up if the conscious self were ignorant but its subconscious were still aware of its infinite knowledge and power, holding the rules of reality in place against the conscious self. It would be sort of like what happens in a dream, when you accept certain facts while the dream is running, but they seem strange to you after you wake up."

Jack nodded his head, following the doctor's line of reasoning, but unsure where he was going with it. The tightness in his shoulders was still clamped down hard.

"But the scenario falls apart when you remember its ultimate purpose," the doctor said. "To entertain the self and keep it from boredom. As you wrote in your journal, Monsignor Bamonte already explained why it's impossible for an Infinite, Almighty Being to experience boredom. And, if the conscious self had become aware of what its subconscious was up to, the whole purpose behind the illusory game would be defeated. What's the point of a recreational distraction where the self is supposed to be residing ignorantly among its own projections if the solipsist is claiming to be aware that he created reality? It seems, once he'd made that realization, the game would end. Yet your life, Jack, has gone on just the same, even in asking yourself these questions. So, logic has to conclude you're not the sole reality after all."

Jack's shoulders loosened a little, like they were coming untied. He felt the butterflies move in his stomach again, but they were flying in exhilaration now, not fear. His doubts over the existence of things outside his mind seemed more hilariously stupid than ever before. More importantly, they were ebbing away the more the counselor spoke.

Dr. Vonhagen uncrossed his legs and shifted in his chair. "The fictitious scenario I just described is similar to the belief systems of some pantheists, including Buddhists."

"Really?" Jack met his eyes. "I didn't know that." He looked back down, thinking a moment, before meeting the doctor's gaze again. "I'm no pantheist. And I never thought I was God! At least," he spread his hands in a shrug, "not consciously. But I see your point. I guess I was kind of making myself out to be creator by doubting reality. It would mean the illusion of reality at least was my doing, because it would mean nothing and no one else existed."

Dr. Vonhagen smiled. "It's okay, Jack. Sometimes it takes an outside view to help us see things more clearly."

"Which is pretty hard to get, when you don't believe outside views exist." Jack smiled.

The doctor laughed. "Touché! It's funny how many solipsists come to therapy anyway."

It was Jack's turn to laugh. As he did, his shoulders dropped more. He was starting to feel better than he had in a long, long time.

"Another reason I draw your attention to the relationship between solipsism and pantheism is because the questions my little scenario leads to are the same ones Catholicism and any other form of theism has to address at some point. How and when did the self come into existence? Was it always there, or did it have a beginning? Why did it create the universe, and why in the way that it did?" The therapist paused once more to watch Jack think before answering. "Insert the word 'God' in place of the word 'self' and you'll still have to ask those questions as a Catholic. But, from Catholicism's perspective, you wouldn't be asking about yourself, as though you'd made the world up in your imagination and then decided to play a cruel joke on yourself by placing a part of your consciousness as a character in that world. Instead, you'd be asking about a Being Who isn't you. In that scenario, it would make sense you didn't have all the answers, because you're not the Omniscient One. It's also a lot easier to make the First Cause Argument about God than yourself, seeing as you don't have memories going back infinitely. You had a beginning."

"Again, I never thought of it that way," Jack said, his inward jubilation growing.

"Well, compare everything I just said to Jesus of Nazareth and tell me if you notice anything."

Jack didn't have to think long. He'd started to see where the psychologist was leading him.

"Jesus did enter His own creation as one of its Characters," he said.

"There you go," Dr. Vonhagen said. "And, unlike the rest of us, He did claim memories going back before His Conception. He also demonstrated an omnipresent knowledge of things happening apart from Himself while serving as a Character in His own drama. So, Jesus Christ is the One who can claim the titles of both Author and Protagonist of the same story."

Jack settled all the way back into the couch now, the cushion billowing up around his shoulders like a soft cloud. He looked up at the painting of Heaven's war. Had the angels just cast the demons from his mind at last?

"Back to your particular situation," Dr. Vonhagen said, "another proof against solipsism lies in the question, if your mind produces everything for itself, why do you experience things like pain? If you don't want suffering to occur—which is obvious in your case—then why is your mind producing it? Aren't you in control of your mind? If not, then you're clearly not the one who can claim responsibility for all that exists. Someone or Something else must be shaping how things go and allowing misery to be a part of life."

Jack shook his head slowly.

The doctor smiled. "Sorry. Am I losing you?"

"No! I'm following you fine. You're just blowing my mind!"

The doctor's smile widened. "There's one more thing I could say about it, if you want me to keep going."

Jack leaned forward in his seat. "Please! I want to know everything."

"I can't promise you everything, but I can offer you one final thought. If all reality is your own projection, then whatever you declared to be true or untrue should have to be so. Agree?"

"Yes . . . that follows."

"But that opens the door to a glaring paradox. If you were to state and believe, solipsism is false, then either your belief in it was indeed false, or—if your statement was false, and solipsism was actually true—you'd be contradicting your own mind, which is supposed to be what's creating all. If solipsism is true, everything should cease to exist upon your statement of its falsity. But it doesn't. So you see, the philosophy is disproved either way."

Jack leaned back again, saying nothing. There was nothing left to say. He was still shaking his head. He'd begun to think he'd never find the answer to the question of reality after so many fruitless weeks of research. And he hadn't expected that, if he ever did, it would come from a mental health professional. But his doubt over the existence of reality was gone. In the end, it had been purged from his mind in a matter of minutes. He felt a blissful release.

Reality existed. Which meant Monsignor Bamonte existed. Which meant his proofs for God's existence could be considered again. Besides all that, Dr. Vonhagen was about to provide the professional opinion on his psychological state, clearing up the question of his exact medical diagnosis too.

"I wish you'd been there to explain all this to me months ago," Jack said. "It would've saved me a lot of anguish. I can't believe I duped myself into a pagan belief."

"Don't feel too badly," Dr. Vonhagen said. "You're not the first Catholic to wrestle with solipsism. G.K. Chesterton did for a while."

"Don't know him."

"He was an author who influenced J.R.R. Tolkien and C.S. Lewis. You've probably heard of them, if you're a *Narnia* or *Lord of the Rings* fan."

"Oh yeah! I know who they are."

Dr. Vonhagen nodded. "I think Chesterton was even a major influence on Lewis' conversion from atheism to Christianity. But I'm getting sidetracked." He lifted Jack's folder off the side table. "Let's review your test results, huh? That's why you're here."

Jack's muscles tightened again, and he realized how relaxed they'd been. Time for the moment of truth. The doctor flipped open the folder. The butterflies in Jack's stomach did laps like they were in a NASCAR race. Dr. Vonhagen looked up and must have seen his distress.

"You can breathe easy and relax, Jack! To sum up the findings, there's nothing clinically wrong with you. There were no indications of schizophrenia or any other mental illnesses. And your MRI was negative for any brain defects or tumors."

Jack felt lightheaded. He didn't think he'd heard the doctor properly.

"I'm sorry," he said, raising his hand and spinning it next to his head. "There's just a lot going through my mind right now. Could you repeat that?"

Dr. Vonhagen smiled. "I was saying, you're not crazy like you thought. You're quite sane. The MMPI-II and MCMI-III tests you took revealed no forms of psychosis, no borderline personality disorder, no bipolar disorder, and no schizophrenia. On the depression and anxiety scales, you ranked a 62, and you'd have to be at least at 65 for there to be any clinical concern.

Don't be alarmed by there being some depression and anxiety present. Yours would be the result of your situation and a completely normal reaction given the circumstances you described to me. In other words, you were depressed and anxious, because you thought you might be crazy or may be seeing demons. Those are catalysts enough to cause depression or anxiety in the sanest of minds."

Jack nodded, still wary of what he was being told.

"On what we call 'the bizarre scale'—which measures what we identify as 'bizarre thought processes'—you ranked a 60, which is somewhat high, but was also to be expected given the nature of your experiences. I'll come back to that in a moment. Here are the pictures we had you draw."

He handed Jack the house, tree, and person.

"As for the details we looked for in those, notice how you gave the house a foundation, a chimney with smoke coming out of it, and windows, even illustrating one of the windows as open. These were all indications your home life is open, honest, stable, and warm. To me, this meant your family situation is a happy one. On the tree, you didn't draw any knots. Another positive indication. And you gave the person hands, again signaling openness to communication."

Jack looked at his drawings. "That's strange you concluded all that." He looked up at the doctor. "Because I've kept everything I told you hidden from my family."

"Only because you didn't want to worry them and wished to be certain about the experiences yourself first, not because you didn't trust them with your secrets. So that wouldn't have necessarily shown up in your tests." The doctor glanced down. "I see your IQ measured, 116." He looked up again. "That's high, especially for someone your age. A superior intelligence level."

Jack raised his eyebrows.

"To give you a perspective," the doctor said, "average intelligence falls between 90 and 109. Genius levels are 140 and above. It's believed Einstein's IQ was 160. I'm guessing you're a quick study."

Jack shrugged his shoulders. "I guess. School's never been that interesting to me."

"Ah, so you're bored with it, huh? But have you ever struggled in school?"

Jack bulged his lips and shook his head.

"That's what I'd guessed. Sounds like you're bored because it's not stimulating enough for you. You'd probably have liked specialized programs better. I'm surprised your parents never had you skip any grade levels."

"Never asked them to. I've always preferred learning stuff on my own. I never felt very involved with school. My parents were just happy I brought home straight A's."

Dr. Vonhagen chuckled. "That explains the full scholarship to the Citadel. No wonder they want you."

Jack shrugged again. "Always had a good memory."

The therapist stroked his chin. "A high IQ and a good memory. So, it's probably not likely you'd have forgotten much you've learned in school over the years then."

"No," Jack said.

"But you told me last time that Mephistopheles tells you all the seemingly new information learned through your incorporeal experiences is just unremembered lessons from your time at Divine Savior School."

Jack was silent, seeing the contradiction the psychologist had uncovered. The doctor let the silence hang between them again. He didn't seem uncomfortable with it, just gave Jack time to process.

After a long enough pause, Dr. Vonhagen said, "Highly unlikely a brain with a 116 IQ would forget such an extensive amount of material, in my professional opinion."

"Yes," Jack acknowledged. "I guess it is."

Dr. Vonhagen flipped through the folder again. "Well, since there were no indications of any type of schizophrenia spectrum, dissociative disorders, or other psychotic disorders, there was no diagnosis of any psychological disorders. My professional conclusion, based collectively on these tests, is that there are indications of spiritual experiences due to your rank on the bizarre scale, but nothing that merits the need for any therapeutic or pharmacological intervention."

The doctor looked up and smiled. Jack's body still felt tight.

"Are you saying you've concluded scientifically that incorporeal sight is supernatural? That I'm not crazy?"

"To conclude definitively whether an occurrence is supernatural or not isn't for my practice to determine. You'd have to take that up with your spiritual director and the Church. But I can state definitively you're not crazy, yes. I suspected as much based purely on our initial session before you even took all the tests."

"Really? Why?"

"Reality testing. You don't display any outward indications of having schizophrenia. If you did, you'd most likely appear strange to those around you. And your family and girlfriend definitely would have noticed something was off."

"That's what Monsignor Bamonte thought," Jack said. "But what if I'm a paranoid schizophrenic?"

"No person with schizophrenia—of any type—can hide it well when unmedicated," Dr. Vonhagen said. "And you have no vocal or motor tics present. You don't make word salads, where sentences break off in the middle and you veer into other random ideas. In addition to all that, you identified the voices and appearances of creatures you meet through incorporeal sight as coming from outside of you. A lot of people with schizophrenia identify voices they hear and things they see as coming from an inward source.

You also mentioned using incorporeal sight in front of other people and not being in a trance state when you do it. This evidences a lack of dissociative symptoms. Most importantly, you can reason objectively about whether or not you have a mental disorder. If I were to even suggest to a person with schizophrenia that he was deluding himself, he'd most likely react by denying it tooth and nail, regardless of what proof I offered him to the contrary.

People with schizophrenia are adamant about sharing what they're seeing with others and grow frustrated when people claim they don't see anything. You, on the other hand, are the first to question what you see and don't broadcast it to any and every person you meet, because you know it would sound crazy, even if it isn't. You're as adamant about questioning the reality of your experiences as a person who has schizophrenia is about defending theirs. That objective reasoning simply isn't present in the mentally ill of the kind we're talking about. People with a mental illness as debilitating as schizophrenia usually don't realize they have it on their own."

"But Mephistopheles has claimed I am fighting it tooth and nail," Jack said, "because I keep resisting him, and he claims to be the manifestation of my reason."

"Yes, which is another reason I wondered if he's not a real demon after all."

Jack stared at the psychologist, not believing what he'd just admitted. Dr. Vonhagen smiled back and elaborated.

"If he's a real demon, it would mean he possesses the intelligence of an angelic being, right? So he'd of course weave a deception clever enough to seem true, to get you to trust him. Wasn't getting the human to trust him the first thing the Serpent did in Eden, specifically by getting Eve to question her own knowledge about things?"

Jack nodded, marking the painting in his peripheral vision again. This meeting wasn't going how he'd expected at all. It was going much, much better.

"But," the doctor continued, "since we've now proven clinically you don't have schizophrenia and that you don't have any brain defects that could cause visual or auditory hallucinations, there's only one conclusion left to draw about the validity of your experiences . . . Well . . . two actually. You'll want to rule out whether their source is divine or diabolic."

"Monsignor Bamonte's been vetting that," Jack said. "He told me that, in his opinion at this point, they're a gift from God."

"Well," the psychologist held out his hand, "there you go. Like I said, that determination is in the realm of your spiritual director and the Church. But, if that's the monsignor's conclusion, I'd say trust it. I've known Monsignor Bamonte a long time, and he's no fool."

"No," Jack said smiling. "He isn't."

Suddenly, it hit Jack all at once. Even incorporeal sight had been proven as real. To the best of human ability anyway. He fell back on the couch, looking up at the Saint Michael painting one last time.

"I can rest," he breathed.

"Yes," Dr. Vonhagen said, "I'd say if anyone deserves to, it's you, Jack."

Jack felt his whole body decompress as though a snake that had been coiled around it since October was finally letting go.

Unseen by either counselor or client, the third attendant of the session reacted to its conclusion. Mephistopheles had tried clinging to his prey throughout his time in front of his therapist. In the moment Jack felt his body was unbound, the demon perceived his own bind lift. He was now free to tell his master everything he knew about Jack Dacre.

He departed Charleston with the speed of a thought.

# CHAPTER XXXII
## FATIMA

*The Peace Plan from Heaven.*

It was a strange title.

Jack wasn't in the habit of taking holy cards or pamphlets off the back tables in the nave. They'd been the same ones for months. He'd gotten used to passing them without a second thought. But his eyes had been drawn to the stack of blue booklets on the table the moment he entered the cathedral this time. The sign at the foot of the stack said they were free—"one per family please"—and something about the booklets made him look twice at them on this occasion. He grabbed one on his way up the center aisle without hesitation, almost as if it had been a subconscious decision.

He thought it was the title that struck him. It came across presumptuous. He was all for Marian devotion, which he assumed the book was about, given it had a statue of Mary pictured on the cover. Still, for a simple devotional booklet to claim it had a message directly from Heaven . . . It made him curious to see how it backed up such a claim. Unless Mary had appeared and dictated its contents to the author, what book but the Bible could boast divine inspiration?

Jack offered prayers of thanksgiving in one of the front pews for such a successful therapy session that afternoon, and it wasn't until after he'd finished he looked down at the booklet again. He'd almost forgotten about it in his excitement of embracing his faith. He picked it up, figuring he'd thumb through it, and noticed what had drawn his attention in the first place. It wasn't just the title. It was the cover photo. The statue of Mary was dressed the same as Mary herself had been the last time he'd seen her in person, atop the tree in his front yard for Chuck's deliverance. He noted a subtitle for the book at the bottom of the front cover. *The Story of Fatima.* He sat back in the pew and began reading.

What he read changed his life forever.

*The story of Fatima begins in the Spring of 1916 when three shepherd children in the small mountain village of Fatima, Portugal were visited by an angel. Lucia dos Santos, age nine, and her cousins, Francisco and Jacinta Marto, ages eight and six, would be visited three times by the angel between the Spring and Fall of that year. In his subsequent visits, he identified himself as the Angel of Peace and guardian angel of their country. His visits heralded events that would transform the young shepherds into three of the most influential figures of our modern age, though they would remain unknown to most.*

Intrigued, having never heard of these children himself, Jack skimmed farther down the page.

*What the angel's visits had prepared them for would become apparent on May 13, 1917, when the children were visited by another celestial figure. The shepherds were out tending their parents' sheep near midday in a valley known as the Cova da Iria when a white light flashed twice across the sky. Believing it to be lightning, the shepherds began rounding up their animals and heading home. On their journey, they came across a small holm oak tree in their path. Atop it hovered a white globe, much like the one that had first borne the angel to them. Within this globe was a woman whom Lucia described as being "more brilliant than the sun." She was clothed in a white gown and mantle that hung from her head to her feet, appearing as though she were made of light. Around her neck hung a sphere of gold light. From her right arm, a rosary of white pearls.*

*"Do not be afraid," the woman said. "I will do you no harm."*

*Inspired to trust her from the expression of tenderness on her face, Lucia asked, "Where are you from?"*

*"I am from Heaven."*

*"What do you want of me?"*

*"I have come to ask you to come here at this same hour for six months in succession on the thirteenth day. Later on I will tell you who I am and what I want."*

Jack flipped back to the booklet's cover photo, noting Mary's clothing again. So it had been the Mother of God who'd appeared to them, clothed in the same outfit in which he'd last seen her. Sensing there was some connection between himself and these children, and beginning to suspect it wasn't a coincidence he'd picked this booklet up today when he could have on many previous occasions, he flipped it back open, devouring its contents.

As promised, Mary kept appearing to the shepherds above the holm oak in the Cova da Iria at noon on the thirteenth of every month. More people showed up with them each time, but only the three children could see her. Sometimes others would witness supernatural phenomena, such as a shower of white rose petals falling from out of nowhere around the holm oak and disappearing again ten feet above the ground. Some even saw the white globe of light in which Mary appeared atop the tree, bending its branches as though someone was standing on it. Afterward, they saw it depart into the sky toward the east from where it had descended. During her apparition in July, Mary promised the children she'd work a great public miracle on her final visit so all might know she'd appeared and believe her message. Ravenous to know what happened after reading that bit of the story, Jack skipped ahead to the apparition of October thirteenth.

*Over seventy thousand people showed up in the Cova on October 13, 1917, atheists and believers alike. The secular press had come to scoff and disprove the children's claim a miracle would take place, their cameras ready. It had rained all night of the twelfth, and torrents of rain continued pouring on the pilgrims through the morning of the thirteenth, sinking them up to their ankles in mud. When the apparition arrived, the children were once more the only ones who could see her.*

*"What do you want of me?" Lucia asked her.*

*"I want to tell you a chapel is to be built here in my honor. I am the Lady of the Rosary. Continue to pray the Rosary every day."*

*As the Blessed Virgin departed to the east, she pointed toward the sun, with Lucia repeating her gesture. The incessant rain ceased. The clouds parted. The sun appeared from behind them, and all were able to look on it with the naked eye. It had turned into a silver disc, more resembling the moon. It glowed, then dimmed, until suddenly it went into a mad whirl, spreading rays of multicolored light across the heavens. Blue waves, green waves, yellow waves, violet waves, and red waves of light all washed over the horizon for miles around. The phenomenon ceased after three minutes, started again for another three, ceased, and occurred a third time, extending for a span of twelve minutes in all. The sun spun faster with each return to its rotation. During this time, it also danced across the sky, moving back-and-forth over the Cova as though it had come to life and gone wild.*

*The thousands of witnesses stood mesmerized, their upturned faces flashing the various colors the twirling, bouncing disc was throwing off. The world appeared aflame with a rainbow. Fear mixed with wonder in the minds of the spectators, until terror rose from them as a unified sentiment at the miracle's finale. The disc turned blood red and tore itself from the firmament, hurling toward Earth, aimed to crush humanity under its fiery weight. Many cried, pleading the Virgin's intercession. Others screamed they not be made to die in their sins. Still others fainted. Most feared it was the end of the world. All fell to their knees, praying.*

*Before the sphere of fire fell upon them, when it appeared just above the ground, the miracle ended. The sun retreated, shining from the sky again, bright and distant as ever it was. The crowd stood, discovering their clothes to be clean and dry, despite their being knelt in the mud after being rained on all morning. The ground itself was sun-cracked, as though it hadn't rained all season. Many crippled and ill among the pilgrims had been cured of their ailments. Though a number of atheists had entered the Cova that day, none left it.*

*All were now believers.*

Jack looked up from the booklet, astonished.

It was his answer.

Fatima was God's answer to the miracle question Dr. Vonhagen had asked him. The hair on his skin rose across his body as a wave of warmth washed over him. He felt as though the Holy Spirit Himself was breathing down on him in that moment. Mary's clothes when she'd appeared to these three shepherd children. How she'd stood atop an oak tree when appearing to them. How she'd appeared on it within a globe of light. The flowers falling during one of her visits, appearing out of nowhere and disappearing before they'd hit the ground, just like what he'd seen in his first locution after the Annunciation. There was so much in this little booklet's story that matched his own.

And the sun miracle. A great public miracle. Witnessed and documented by believers and atheists alike. Thousands of them. Exactly like what he'd described in his ideal dream scenario to Dr. Vonhagen. He felt God was speaking to him, goosebumps continuing to sweep across his skin. After restoring his belief in reality, bestowing on him divine faith, even showing him incorporeal sight's validity, God was giving him yet another gift on the very same day. His coveted public miracle, biblical in its breadth.

Fatima's story seemed like a fairy tale. Then again, so did his, if he considered the things he'd seen through his charism. But Fatima was a public story, with so many witnesses. If it were true, how could he have never heard of it before? He whipped out his phone to look it up on the internet, but stopped when the screen lit up and he saw the clock. His hand started shaking as his goosebumps increased. He almost dropped the phone. Below the time was the current date.

May 13, 2017.

It was one hundred years to the day from the date Mary was supposed to have first appeared in Fatima.

If he was encountering God in that moment, Jack felt He'd just breathed on him again. Still trembling, he opened the internet and typed in a single word. Fatima. The first several links to pop up included the words, *Our Lady of Fatima*, in their titles.

It took only minutes of reading from various websites for him to see the story was true. Numerous books had been written about the events of 1917 too. Lucia, the eldest of the visionaries and last to die, had only passed away in 2005. She'd lived during his lifetime. Goosebumps washed over his arms again. God had given him everything he wanted and so much more besides.

He felt overwhelmed, his skin heating up with his emotion. Tears began welling in his eyes. For the first time in a long while, they weren't tears of sadness. He closed his eyes and bowed his head, letting them fall.

After a minute, he jerked his head up, staring into the sanctuary, looking at what was next to the ever-burning red candle. The angel of 1916 had revealed to the Fatima children that the little box behind the altar was indeed the House of a Living Inhabitant. He'd brought them Communion on one of his visits, and the Host and chalice had levitated in midair before them, the Host bleeding into the chalice. If Fatima was fact, there was no denying the truth of Christ's Real Presence in the Eucharist. Jesus was in the tabernacle before him.

So long had he wondered if his God dwelled behind its little door. He'd been concerned it was a doorway into fantasy. The entrance to a little leprechaun's house who didn't exist. Now he knew the truth. The guardian angel of an entire country, even the Queen of the World herself, had descended from Heaven a hundred years ago to remind the world of it. Two millennia ago, people had traveled from faraway lands and shoved their way through crowds just to get a glimpse of the Nazarene Miracle-Worker. God in the Flesh. Jack could visit Him every day if he wanted. See Him. Touch Him. Even receive Him into his body.

He fell to his knees in the pew, bowing his head again, squeezing his eyes shut. More tears hit the floor. The cathedral was so quiet, Jack thought they'd echo like mini-waterfalls across the nave alerting everyone to his weeping. He didn't care. He'd grown up a Catholic. But, even before the past year when his faith in Catholicism had been fine, the reality of the True Presence had never struck him as it did in that moment. He'd never take it for granted again.

He prayed in silent thanksgiving several minutes before he opened his eyes. When his head rose, a question arose in his mind along with it. What did God want in return for this gift of Fatima He'd given him today? He flipped the booklet back open, his eyes falling on the heading of a section near the back. *What Can You Do?* His eyes scrolled.

*"Pray the Rosary every day in order to obtain peace for the world."*
*These words were spoken by Our Lady during her first visit on May 13, 1917. The*

*Rosary is the Church Militant's weapon, distributed to us by Our Queen herself. It is our sword which can be wielded to slay the evils of the world. It has been used for this mission in ages past and can be used so again in the modern age.*

Jack sucked in a breath through his nose. He couldn't believe what the booklet had just compared the Rosary with, wondering if its author knew how accurate incorporeal sight revealed him to be. He'd also never heard the Catholics on Earth referred to as the Church Militant. He liked the name. He skimmed more of the booklet's pages, looking at what else it had to say.

*Atheistic reporters who had come to the Cova the morning of October thirteenth to disprove the promised miracle instead produced testimonies and photographic evidence of it. Copies of these can be found in the U.S. Congressional Library. Yet the vast majority of the world did not listen. Newspapers outside Portugal ignored the story, and we continue to see organized attempts on every level of society to deny the existence of God, even in our schools.*

Jack's fist tightened, his pulse rising with his temper, his nostrils flaring as he yanked in another breath. He thought of Mr. Wilkerson and shut the booklet. He'd read enough for now. He was sold. He vowed in his heart to pray a complete five decades of the Rosary every day, for the rest of his life. Until now, he'd rarely prayed a complete one and it hadn't been every day. It would be now, forevermore.

Everything was real. That meant Mephistopheles was real. As was his master. And the demons occupying Wando High. If they thought they could ravage the world any more than they already had without his having something to say about it, they were mistaken. Sorely mistaken. Not while he had his faith. Not while he had his sword. He'd ensure they heard his response in every *Hail Mary* and *Our Father* he prayed from thenceforth. The hairs on his skin stood in unison again, like soldiers rising in a battle formation. If that was a nudge from God to begin then and there, he'd answer Him.

He pulled his rosary from its pouch.

Thinking of the demon who'd stalked and tormented him for the past seven months, he whispered, "Coming for you this time, pup."

When he put his focus into locating the most hateful presence in creation, Mephistopheles was drawn far from South Carolina, to the Cova da Iria in Fatima,

Portugal.

*Of course,* he thought. *The centennial.*

All Hell had been smart enough not to speak of it in the Master's presence. They'd gone about their business as usual, ignoring the approaching date. He supposed Satan had been unable to ignore the dreaded day any longer. No one knew what was going to happen, but every one of the damned had figured something would.

The Master was there. Mephistopheles sensed it. No doubt he was plotting the destruction of the thousands of Catholic pilgrims gathered at the site for the anniversary, or at least plotting some way to disturb them if he couldn't destroy them outright. If Mephistopheles knew anything about the Enemy, He'd probably prevent the Master from doing even that much. After all, the pope—that papist of papists—was among those gathered.

When he sensed the Prince of Power's presence, the Devil emerged from whispering into the mind of a cardinal beside the supreme pontiff and flew up to meet his minion in the air. "Not here. Too hot with so many of the Enemy's angels present. Follow."

Mephistopheles obeyed, and they settled elsewhere.

"What the fuck are you doing here?" Satan demanded. "You're supposed to be in Mt. Pleasant. Have you finally conquered the *boy?*"

He made the last thought into an insult, stinging Mephistopheles' pride. The Power swallowed it. There was nothing he could do. Not against this intelligence. And there was no reason to piss the Master off more than the news he bore was already going to.

"With permission, my lord," Mephistopheles communicated, and relayed all in a single thought.

The wrath that emanated from Satan's person in the next instant threatened to overwhelm the Power, the way he'd often overwhelmed Jack Dacre's mind with his own presence. The Devil was so furious he didn't know which part of his minion's story to rage at him about first. Finally, he settled on something.

*"That priest?"* he roared in reference to the identity of the bead-mumbler's spiritual director. *"THAT . . . DAMN . . . PRIEST?"*

Mephistopheles was unsure if he should answer or keep silent. He was terrified he was the only one around to endure the brunt of the Master's outburst. He had Satan's full attention focused on him for the first time in centuries.

"He's a prime reason for my delay in shackling the putrid youth, Master. Him, and the boy's ability to see through the material veil now."

"He goes by a title?" Satan fretted, as though he hadn't perceived his underling's disclosure. *"A title?"*

Mephistopheles didn't know why that particular detail attracted so much of his baal's attention. He'd always chalked up Jack's assigning himself an alias to his love of comic book movies. A teenager's typical self-glorification. The Power had no more time to consider this, because he was struck down in the next instant.

*"WHY DIDN'T YOU TELL ME THAT BEFORE?"* the Devil demanded.

Mephistopheles struggled to answer after the blow. "The . . . b-bind, my lord!"

"The Enemy has hidden much about this one," Satan went on, ignoring Mephistopheles again. "Much! He planned this. *He planned this whole thing!* Adrian Bamonte. Incorporeal sight. Locutions. *And a title! Another fucking title! What does it mean?"*

The Devil cast his attention back to the Cova, wondering if this was a ruse to draw him away. His instincts had told him to keep watch here of all places on this day. Then again, hadn't his inattention to this unimpressive spot off the beaten path a century ago resulted in the poisoning of his hundred-year plan? Was the White Lady doing it again? Distracting him with all these pilgrims swarming the Cova with their bread-worshipping leader, only to be pulling another con on him half a world away in a new backwater nothing of a town? It sounded like her. She and her whore-loving Son had always favored the nothings of this world. Always spiting his pride by turning grime into gold, after turning the gold of his own perfection into grime. Well, this time, he'd be ready. He'd think like his Enemy for once. He wouldn't be blindsided again. He redirected his attention to the fallen soldier before him.

"Convalesce yourself, cur. We're going to Charleston!"

# CHAPTER XXXIII
## BIRTH OF A HERO

Jack knelt before the statue of Mary in front of her side chapel.

The statue he'd once thought had smiled at him the day he'd met Monsignor Bamonte. As he knelt, he thought he saw it smile down on him again. He didn't bother analyzing whether or not it was a trick of the light this time. Just accepted the experience and moved on to his prayer.

Before beginning the Rosary, he flipped through the Fatima booklet. He'd seen a prayer of consecration to the Immaculate Heart of Mary he wanted to make at the outset. He found it and began the formula. While he prayed, he switched to incorporeal sight to see the real Mary standing before him. She was dressed again as the Lady of Fatima. The Lady of Peace. His peace. A peace of the mind he'd worked so long to obtain. The thought gave him chills again, even as the warmth of the white and gold light flowing off her person washed over him. She accepted his offering with a smile and open arms.

When he began the Rosary, he was given another treat. Her thousand guardians emerged from the light of the tabernacle to join him in proffering its flowers. As he'd suspected when he'd first seen them in a vision, the feeling of their real presence was overpowering. It was only thanks to the familiarity of the prayers he was reciting he was able to keep going and not be distracted into silent awe by the strength of the illuminations coursing through him. He picked the Joyful Mysteries on which to meditate. They were easiest since he'd witnessed the events of the first two for himself. The meditation was made easier still by his present company. They'd all participated in the salvific events, and their illuminations brought him more firsthand knowledge of them.

That got him thinking on his two locutions. Despite all his mind had been opened to in the past several hours, he still didn't know why God had revealed those particular Mysteries to him when He had. He wondered again if there wasn't a larger purpose behind what he'd seen. This became the focus of his meditation during the first decade. When he finished the *Glory Be,* Gabriel approached and paused him, telling him to look one more time in the Fatima booklet before moving to the next decade. He complied and found what the Archangel had clearly wanted him to find on the first page his eyes scanned.

*At the end of each decade of the Rosary, Mary requested that the children, and by extension all who would heed their message, recite the following prayer.*

Jack prayed the formula as he read it. "O my Jesus, forgive us our sins, save us from the fires of Hell, and lead all souls to Heaven, especially those most in need of Thy mercy!"

The prayer manifested in his palm as a luminescent apple. Staring into its deep red glow, he remembered seeing such fruits on the trees in Mary's garden and asking Gabriel which prayer they were.

The golden-haired prince took it from his hand once it had finished growing, grinning at him. "Told ya you'd learn this prayer soon enough."

He flew off to hang the apple from one of the vines growing up the castle wall.

"So," Jack looked up to Mary before starting the second decade, "this was your plan all along then. To have me read of Fatima, when the time was right."

Mary's only answer was a smile. It was enough for Jack. He initiated the next decade. When he neared the end, he heard movement in the sanctuary behind him. Switching sights, he turned and saw altar servers were setting up for something. He guessed there was a Mass coming up at three o'clock. He moved from his kneeler so as not to be in their way.

A family of three had taken his former spot in the front pew, so he sat in the one opposite them. He noticed the family looked unhappy to be there, especially the son, like they'd all just gotten a whiff of something foul. Jack wondered why they'd come. It was only a daily Mass. There was no obligation to attend. Trying not to judge by appearances, he realized he'd just found an opportunity to "make everything he did a sacrifice," as the angel of Fatima had taught the children in one of his apparitions. He decided to pray his next decade for this family, for whatever their problems might be.

Taking his seat, he was surprised when it was Monsignor Bamonte who emerged from the sacristy a moment later. He realized he'd never seen his spiritual director celebrate Mass. The servers had set him up on the high altar at the back of the sanctuary. This would put him face-to-face with the tabernacle instead of facing the people in the nave. Jack had never seen a Mass celebrated like that. He didn't even know the high altar was ever used. Father Murphy always celebrated on the free-standing one closer to the sanctuary's front steps, facing the people.

Utilizing his charism, he saw the monsignor's hair go from white to black, his thumbs and index fingers begin to shine, and all four of his guardians appear, flanking him at the altar. He wrapped up the second decade of his prayer and reached into his pocket to put his rosary away until after Mass, when his hand locked up. Gabriel's hand had fallen over it. At his touch, Jack's fingers latched onto the next bead.

*"The Third Joyful Mystery!"* the giant declared in a voice that thundered up into the rafters and rolled across the balconies above them. *"The Nativity!"*

Overtaken by a locution for the third time, Jack was surprised when he didn't lose all sense of what was happening around him.

He remained aware of the Mass, while simultaneously viewing events from the past. As the congregation made the sign of the cross with the monsignor, Jack saw an edict from Caesar Augustus go out across the Roman Empire, calling its citizens to attend a census at their birthplaces. The entire civilized world was stirred into motion, all so the God-Man would be born at the prophesied location. Monsignor Bamonte led the faithful through the opening prayers and readings of the Liturgy, while Saint Joseph led a donkey with Mary seated atop it across nearly a hundred miles of the Holy Land, from Nazareth to Bethlehem.

When it came time for the sermon, Jack was excited to hear the monsignor preach about Fatima and its centennial celebration. But he didn't catch much of the homily's content, because Mary was also teaching. She and Joseph had set up camp in an abandoned shed along their journey, and several children from a nearby village had found them. Taking an opportunity to practice her mothering skills, the Blessed Virgin had begun giving them religious lessons. She used metaphors and typology to explain the workings of the spiritual worlds, veiling them in stories with fantastical creatures and characters that kept the children entertained. Jack realized where her Son must have gotten His own teaching method.

Before Jack knew it, Monsignor Bamonte was stepping away from the ambo and over to the altar, preparing for the second half of the Mass. While he did, the Holy Family reached the outskirts of Bethlehem, stopping first at the courthouse for the census. As the scribes took down Joseph's occupation and checked his ancestral line, the Roman soldiers posted there sneered remarks at him. They mocked him for marrying so far below his age just so he could parade to the world he was still being pleasured by the young and beautiful.

Embarrassed, Joseph hurried Mary away from the building as soon as his legal obligations were done, searching for an inn. As he went from street to street and house to house, it became clear there were no vacancies in town. Bethlehem was full of Romans and wealthy merchants from the East who'd come for the census. No room was offered in creation to Him Who'd created it and Who would Himself soon be the Inn for all homeless hearts within it.

"Holy, Holy, Holy Lord, God of Hosts," Monsignor Bamonte led the congregation in prayer.

Jack recited the words with them, watching the Holy Family wind up in a more rural part of town. The houses there were built into the sides of the hills and the roads were unpaved. It reminded Jack of the hill country where he'd witnessed the Visitation. Joseph had remembered a cave where he used to play as a boy when he wanted to be alone. It was the best he could come up with, since every house had failed them.

It took some time, but he and Mary found it. It was almost fully hidden behind an oak tree. The cave's entrance led through a narrow passage into a wider chamber, half semicircular, half triangular. There were three grate-covered openings on the ceiling and walls of the east side, allowing air to flow. The rock walls were naturally formed and rough. A stone bench had been installed low on the wall to line the cave's length. Joseph saw the place was now used for feeding and watering cattle. A manger had been placed under one of the grates. Moonlight shined down on it like a spotlight.

The Virgin immediately chose it as the best option for her Child's crib. She set about making it as comfortable as she could with blankets. In the meantime, Joseph set out to clean the cave, fastening a lamp to the wall. His head hung low while he worked, trying to hide silent tears. He was ashamed of the shabby shelter. Ashamed he couldn't provide better than this for his family. Chosen to guard the Promised King Whom King David himself had longed for, and he couldn't even put a proper roof over His head for His birth. He apologized to Mary several times for that. Even her sincerest of reassurances couldn't extricate his guilt. When he was done cleaning, he moved outside to make a fire at the cave's entrance for cooking and keeping warmth trapped inside.

There was no sign of any shepherds, but their animals were in the cave. Four beasts. An ox, a donkey, a goat, and a lamb. They'd instinctively retreated from Mary when she arrived, sensing the Presence inside her, showing more reverence to It than most people she'd encountered on her journey.

"In communion with those whose memory we venerate," Monsignor Bamonte prayed, "especially the Glorious Ever-Virgin Mary, Mother of Our God and Lord, Jesus Christ, and blessed Joseph, her Spouse . . ."

At midnight, the Father cast Joseph into a deep sleep at the mouth of the cave. It was a rest more peaceful than Adam's had been during Eve's creation. In turn, Mary was lifted into the air above the manger, experiencing an ecstasy even more intense than the one at Christ's Incarnation.

While she levitated, Jack watched the monsignor extend his hands over the bread and wine on the cathedral's altar, praying, "Be pleased, O God, we pray, to bless, acknowledge, and approve this offering in every respect. Make it spiritual and acceptable, so that it may become for us the Body and Blood of Your Most Beloved Son, Our Lord Jesus Christ."

Mary was so beautiful, Jack thought she no longer appeared human, but a divine being. He understood why the pagans could mistake such a person for a god. The roof of the cave opened and the storm cloud of the Trinity descended with her thousand guardians. She didn't seem to notice in the midst of her bliss. Beginning faintly and rising in volume, the angels began to sing.

*"Let all mortal flesh keep silence*
*and with fear and trembling stand!*
*Ponder nothing earthly minded,*
*for with blessing in His hand*
*Christ our God to Earth descendeth,*
*our full homage to demand.*

*King of kings yet born of Mary*
*as of old on Earth He stood,*
*Lord of lords in human vesture,*
*in the Body and the Blood;*
*He will give to all the faithful*
*His Own Self for Heavenly Food.*

*Rank on rank the host of Heaven*
*spreads its vanguard on the way,*
*as the Light of Light descendeth*
*from the realms of endless day,*
*that the powers of Hell may vanish*
*as the darkness cleareth away!*

*At His feet the six-winged Seraph;*
*Cherubim with sleepless eye,*
*veil their faces to the Presence,*
*as with ceaseless voice they cry,*
*Alleluia! Alleluia!*
*Alleluia, Lord Most High!"*

Jack couldn't have held back the tears that came rolling out from his eyes like red carpets to greet the angelic voices. He didn't think he'd be able to enjoy the contemporary music on any of his playlists anymore. Not after hearing Heaven's choirs. Nothing of Earth could compare. He'd felt both a longing and a foreboding at the song's melody. It was beautiful and haunting at the same time. He'd had to grip the handrail in front of him to keep from falling over into the center aisle.

The thousand angels had encircled Mary in the air. The cloud had come to rest in front of her, and she looked like she was hovering above the altar. Jack could no longer distinguish between his vision and his surroundings. When Monsignor Bamonte leaned over the altar, resting his elbows on it, holding a large host before his face with his glowing fingers, the Father's arm reached out from the cloud to the Virgin above him.

"Take this, all of you, and eat of it," the priest declared, "for This is My Body, which will be given up for you."

Instead of the emanation of blinding light Jack sometimes beheld at the moment of consecration, he witnessed the Father place the shining Fruit of Mary's womb beneath her in the manger, which rested in the same spot as the altar where the priest was placing the Consecrated Host before genuflecting. The Infant Deity allowed His Soul to be seen through His Body for His Mother's first sighting of Him, appearing brighter than any sun. Jack couldn't look at Him. But the Ark of the Covenant could. She gazed down, mesmerized, unsure at first if she was dreaming or if the Messiah had indeed been born. She'd experienced no labor pains.

For the first time in the history of creation, someone looked down on Heaven instead of looking up to it. Mary descended from her levitation to adore the Luminescent Child, Who promptly hid His Soul, assuming the appearance of a normal baby. He shivered and cried out. Monsignor Bamonte gathered him up in his arms, turning toward the congregation.

"Behold, the Lamb of God," the priest intoned, "behold Him Who takes away the sins of the world. Blessed are those called to the supper of the Lamb."

"Lord, I am not worthy that you should enter under my roof," the congregation responded, striking their chests, with Jack forgetting to join them, so wrapped up in what he was seeing, "but only say the word and my soul shall be healed."

The thousand angels were lying prostrate around the manger, their wings spread out on the ground over those of their fellow intelligences. There seemed no end in sight to the worshiping spirits. The cave now extended for eternity in the Blessed Mother's eyes, just as the church appeared to do before Jack. Jack didn't need an infusion from the locution to tell him the significance of what he was seeing. It had shown him.

The Incarnate God had chosen to be placed from the sanctuary of His Mother's womb straight into a trough where animals ate, making it clear He was the Bread come down from Heaven to feed the intellectual animals the demons loathed so much. Busy pondering this, Jack hadn't noticed it was time for Communion, until Mary met his eyes from beside the manger that was now the altar. He stood and stepped into the center aisle. As he approached the kneeler at the foot of the sanctuary, Mary and her angels escorted Monsignor Bamonte down to him, the priest still bearing her Child in his arms.

"The Body of Christ," he said, offering Jack to hold the Infant.

"Amen," he choked out in a whisper, taking Jesus into his own arms.

He swallowed and his muscles grew. He felt more power course through his soul than ever before. The Christ's touch had not only restored the strength he'd lost during his months of neglecting the Rosary. He'd made him stronger. Jack stood in awe after receiving, until the monsignor had to give him a look to move on so others could too. He walked back to his seat, staring down into his God's eyes. They were a warm chestnut, like His Mother's. A calming color. They were possessed of a memory extending back through eternity. Jack saw a glimpse of their agelessness as they pierced his own eyes with their gaze.

When he knelt down, Mary and her band of one thousand surrounded him. He was careful to support the Baby's head. In all the time he'd spent wondering what it would be like when he finally saw God Himself through his charism, he hadn't expected it would be in His Infant Form.

*God always surprises,* he mused. *Always coming down to meet us in the most unexpected ways. The hidden ways.*

Jesus tilted His head, probably listening to his thoughts.

"Baby steps, Philangelus," He said.

The shock of this phenomenon made Jack's heart jump, but he kept his arms steady so as not to drop the Child. Hearing an Infant's vocal chords produce articulated words was perhaps the most bizarre yet beautiful sound he'd ever heard. Like Gabriel had said at His Conception, nothing was impossible for Him. Christ laughed at Jack's reaction. Another adorable sound.

"No need to fear anymore, Jack. The time for hiding is over. It's the time for courage now. I need you to be for Me in this time what the children of Fatima were in theirs. A hero."

Jack raised his eyebrows, images of Iron Man, Batman, and Spider-Man flooding his mind at the word. He knew Christ had meant what He said in a spiritual sense. But, still . . . a hero? Like Joan? Or even Michael? How was he to match the saints in glory?

"I'm willing," he said at last. "But, what in your eyes is a hero?"

Christ's all-knowing orbs pierced his soul again. "One who's willing to lay down his life for the good of souls in My Name."

*Martyrdom!* Was that what Christ wanted of him? Who was out to kill him? Not understanding, but deciding to trust, Jack nodded. Neither said anything more for the next ten minutes. They just looked at each other while Jack held the Infant, meditating on all He'd given him over the past year. Finally, the Christ nodded toward the doorway.

Standing up, Jack noticed he was the last one left in the church. At least, corporeally. He turned to look through the cascade of holy water at the entrance and saw a silhouette on its other side that turned his blood hot. He looked back into Christ's eyes, then up to Mary's. They both nodded. His doubts and despair had been conquered, but there was one impediment left in his soul. It was time to master his fear.

He handed the Child to His Mother and dashed toward the exit, ready for spiritual combat.

When he burst through the glowing doorway of water, Jack attempted to hit his opponent with its spray.

He missed.

Mephistopheles had taken flight as he'd emerged. Jack swung his sword around off his backside and slashed at him. The demon was already too far overhead. Undeterred, Jack gave chase. With his focus so heightened by the sight of his former tormentor, his stamina was increased. He ran across the drawbridge faster than he'd ever run, flinging his weapon out into a chain and attempting to snag the demon's heel.

The Power dove over the rooftop of the bishop's residence, and Jack only caught the ledge. He grappled himself up, continuing the pursuit. His enemy taunted him, flying slow enough for Jack to keep him in his sights, but never slow enough that he was able to catch him. He'd flash his hideous grin back at Jack every chance he got.

"Too bad you've never mastered flight, eh, pup?" he goaded from a story below, while Jack raced along the edge of a rooftop.

When Jack reached its corner, he dove off it toward his quarry, hands extended. The intelligence rolled out of the way, and he was forced to tumble onto the street, flipping himself over to continue the hunt. He shot the chain from his wrist into the side of the building and ran up the wall of another, forcing himself into an upward swing when he came to its end, releasing it from the wall at just the right moment. He was propelled upward by the momentum and spun around to relaunch the arrowhead at the Power himself. The demon dodged, and Jack landed on top of a lamp post in a crouch. It was the same lamp post where Dathiel had first spoken of his destiny to him.

He spread his scapular and glided off, shooting his chain out to catch another post. He continued in like manner, snagging the arrowhead on lamp posts and window ledges to keep up, swinging his way over the streets, feeling indeed like a comic book superhero. The demon twisted and turned in his flight, leading Jack into the dark kingdom. Jack didn't slow. He wasn't afraid of the demonic realm. Not with all the strength his Communion had just poured into him. He ignored the chill he felt in the air when he passed over its border.

As Mephistopheles crashed through dead houses and glided over backyards, agitating a few family pets along the way, Jack was reminded again of the first night he'd used incorporeal sight. He'd chased Dathiel across town much like this. He wondered if his guardian hadn't been training him for this night during that pursuit, the way Mary had apparently been preparing him for months for all that had already happened today.

The mood of this chase couldn't be more different than that night of fun and games. He felt nothing but raw anger coursing through him as he chased his target this time. He was going to hammer every hurt and hardship the demon had ever inflicted on him right back upon his own head when he got a hold of him.

The demon dove through a narrow alley. Jack ricocheted himself across its walls to increase his speed. He was almost there. A little closer and he'd have the wretch in his grip.

"Hot for me, huh, Jack?" The demon cackled. "Then come and get me!"

Mephistopheles sailed down into St. Philip's Graveyard, perching atop a headstone. Jack smiled from the rooftop he stood upon. Chuck was buried here, and he himself had received absolution beside the burial ground the day he met Monsignor Bamonte. He glided down into the cemetery, which appeared much larger through incorporeal sight, and landed before the damned intelligence. This was the perfect place to expel his nemesis.

"Now we end this!" he declared, drawing his chain into a sword and marching forward.

He stopped cold when a guttural voice spoke behind him. It was a familiar voice. One he'd only ever heard before in visions and nightmares.

"Hello, Jack."

# CHAPTER XXXIV
## GRAVEYARD GUILES

Jack whipped around, realizing he'd allowed his enemy to lead him straight into a trap.

Satan was seated atop a mausoleum hanging his clawed, blood-red feet down in front of its doorway. It was Chuck's mausoleum. The Harbinger of Death's bat wings draped over its sides like a satanic internment flag. His hood was up. He gripped his trident, holding it beside the grave, a blue flame flickering atop it as though he was claiming victory for the nature of Chuck's death.

Jack willed his sword into his suit to hide his soul and what he did next, hoping the armor would be enough to hide it. For the first time, he felt what he'd only known in theory before. The presence of the Devil himself. Now he understood why even other demons avoided his company. The stench of every deadly sin wafted over from him. Sulfur, rotten and burning flesh, vomit, excrement, sewage, skunk spray, stale sweat, bad breath, and so many other horrid odors. All intwined together to attack Jack's nose at once like the tentacles of some mad mythical creature, each vying to be sniffed first. Yet the smells were the least of the experience.

The Evil One's fallen illumination conveyed sentiments of doubt, dread, and despair, also clamoring to enter Jack's mind together. With how powerful the force behind them pushed, he almost let them. It made the mist of Mephistopheles seem like a refreshing breeze at high noon. Even the barrier of his rosary couldn't altogether block out the negativity of the presence before him. His former zeal to at last put an end to his nemesis froze into stagnating fear.

Satan tilted his head. "Or should I say, Philangelus? I believe that's the name you prefer these days, don't you?"

Jack said nothing, still wrestling his terror.

"I see you know who I am," the Devil said. "Good. That saves us the need for introductions."

Jack had to will with every ounce of his strength to appear courageous, even if he didn't feel it. He would have failed if not for his recent Communion. The happiness of that union kept him balanced enough to stay on his feet. Courage against fear. That was what Christ had asked of him, and he remembered his first lesson from Michael on battling the demonic. Without fear, there'd be no such thing as courage. This was his moment to prove himself a hero. There was no greater villain in the cosmos than the one facing him now. He concentrated on calling up a mental image of Christ's face, or at least Mary's. Once he had one, he stood tall. But he was still shaking. He hoped it wasn't perceptible through his suit.

"I was wondering if we'd ever meet," he said in what he hoped was an assertive tone.

"Congratulations," Satan praised. "You've stirred up enough of my kingdom to rouse my attention."

Jack's trembling increased the more he tried to hold still. There was no way it wasn't perceptible to the two enemies.

"Attack me," he said, "and you might stir Someone Else's attention. Someone Whose attention you spend all your time avoiding."

The Devil raised a taloned hand. "Relax, Philangelus. I'm only here to talk, which is all the Prince of Powers here should have done." He waved the hand toward Mephistopheles. "It seems you gave challenge to him when he employed force against you. A rare feat, even for a Roman Catholic. Again, congratulations! Very, very impressive!"

Jack let himself breath, but he stayed vigilant, keeping both spirits in his field of vision. If he could keep the monsters talking, that was good. It would buy time.

"Wouldn't have needed to cause the uproar had your minions left me alone in the first place," he said, fighting to keep his voice steady now too.

The Devil chuckled, his hood shifting as he did. The red haze from under it looked like it was bobbing in and out the way rays from a street lamp did if a person squinted their eyes at it.

"Yes. I suppose life would be much easier for your race if they weren't such an uproarious horde."

"They?" Jack demanded. "I suppose you're the even-tempered one?" He cocked a thumb toward Mephistopheles. "Someone else send him against me?"

Satan threw his arms out in a theatrical gesture. "You caught me, Jack! Yes, I'm the instigator of your recent miseries. But hardly their author. If you want the Cause, look to your God. He's the One Who placed you here in my domain and left you vulnerable to our attacks. Tell me, what kind of a Loving Father is it Who abandons His children among strangers to be beaten and robbed of their happiness? Seems your Master's no better than me."

Anger rose in Jack's heart, backing his fear out of it a few paces. "My Master doesn't force His underlings to serve when they don't want to."

The Devil shifted his head again, and Jack saw his hooked nose poke out from under his hood. His glowing red eyes became visible. The monster had bared his teeth at the comment. Jack could see the white of the fangs. Or so he thought at first. After a second, he realized Satan was smiling beneath the hood.

"Is that so?" The fiend sniffed the air. "Ah, that's right," he whispered. "You've seen portions of our pasts. Carefully selected memories that paint us out as the villains of the story."

Jack couldn't believe it. He wanted to smile, even laugh, feeling more of his fear ebb away at the sentiment.

"Let me stop you right there," he said, holding up his hand. "Don't tell me you're about to do what I think."

Satan was silent. He stared at him.

"You're not about to pitch yourself as the hero of history and offer me the classic join me proposal? Please no." Jack did start laughing under his breath then. "Let me guess, it's a one-time-offer, and you'll kill me if I refuse?" He laughed louder, unable to help himself. "Unoriginal. *Unoriginal, Satan!* Once again, so very unoriginal. I expected a little less of a cliché from the villain of all villains!"

For a moment, Satan didn't speak or move. Jack sobered, ready for him to lash out, despite what he'd said about just being there to talk. Jack wasn't ready for that yet. He needed more time. But the fiend surprised him, throwing his head back and cackling, his entire face exposed by the movement.

"Touché, my little prince! You'd of course never believe my followers and me to be the real champions of right. And I freely admit, I loathe your race's existence with all the might of my being. *God's little favorites."* He spat on the foot of Chuck's grave, his spittle burning into the earth. "Skipping along in the belief He'll never grow tired of you and create new creatures, casting you out like forgotten toys." The Devil lowered his head, hiding his face in the shadows as though brooding on a bad memory. "But . . ." he met Jack's eyes again, "I was personally never much for being His bitch. You can have Him, bread-worshipper."

"Funny coming from someone who'd like nothing more than to make me his bitch," Jack threw back.

"Oh, I don't want your alliance, Philangelus, much less your, friendship. Your compliance on the other hand is, unfortunately, something I'm forced to bargain with you for by that Master you claim doesn't force servitude. Don't worry, I've not come to ask that you bow before me. Not even to try and convince you to abandon your Roman beliefs, injudicious though they be. I simply must ask you to stay out of the dark kingdom. Do whatever you want in your scalding kingdom of light. But leave my domain. Do that, and we'll stay out of yours. I'll withdraw Mephistopheles from Charleston and you'll never see him or me again. I'll even forbid any more attacks on your loved ones from my familiars. And," he paused, "I will concede Wando High School to your angelic friends. You leave us be. We'll leave you be. I believe that's what you good creatures call, fair?"

Before Jack could answer, Satan thrust his staff out, shooting red lightning from its head before he could react. His heart jumped, but not from electrocution. The blast never touched him. It went past him, and he heard Mephistopheles scream. The Power was blasted through a gravestone. Jack had let him slip out of his field of vision for a moment, and he'd almost gotten the drop on him.

*"I didn't tell you to strike!"* the Devil barked, his staff's flame burning red. "We're here to negotiate, not wage war. There's been enough of war, for both our kingdoms."

Jack seethed, turning back to Satan. "You think I'd ever compromise with evil spirits? You picked the wrong soul to approach. Especially after trying to block me from knowing what lies beyond death."

Satan extended his wings to their full twenty-foot width and flapped them once, propelling himself down from Chuck's grave. An odorous gust of wind rippled out across the surrounding headstones, sending leaves crunching over the ground. The Devil lowered his hood as he came to stand over Jack. The entire movement was so fluid, it took Jack a second to react, stepping back now that his enemy stood so close.

"If you believe you have what it takes to put me down, Philangelus, by all means, have at me. Otherwise, we can talk."

Jack didn't move. Panic had stiffened him. But he still had the presence of mind to try again what he'd tried when he first saw the Devil had come to town. *What was taking so long?* Clearly, he needed more time. He had to keep stalling.

"What's the difference?" he asked. "You always have an agenda, whether you're trying to present it through temptation or conversation. You're so wrapped up in your war, the two are indistinguishable with you."

Satan pointed a claw at him. "The pot calls the kettle black, Philangelus. Unless you can claim every action you take in regard to me doesn't relate to my ruin."

"Touché." Jack nodded. "So why waste your breath asking me to leave your kingdom alone? We both know we'll never stop until the other one's lost everything. Why pretend either of us could ever trust the other with a bargain?"

Satan leaned back, resting his head against his staff, which burned blue again. He grinned at Jack.

"'Until the other one's lost everything' . . . Interesting way to put it. And what does that look like to you, Friend of Angels? All souls captured from my kingdom back into your Master's? Restored companionship with the guardians He assigned them instead of the ones they chose here? You know, they only live here in the dark because they want to. They like it. The light of your Master's countenance blinds them. But, for the sake of argument, let's say you managed to convince them all otherwise, and you all one day reach Heaven. What then? Do you imagine life with the Deity is going to be peaceful?"

Satan rolled his eyes.

"That's a lie He's had His slaves pushing since day one! A lie I've tried my damndest to shout from the rooftops to all His blinded followers before it's too late for them to do something about it. And you Catholics are the worst when it comes to propagating it. You poor, brainwashed, stubborn, naive little bunch of souls! Your priests talk a lot about going to Heaven, don't they? But they never talk much about what happens when you get there. That's because they don't know.

I know. I know what the Enemy has planned for you. I've been there. I've seen it for myself. It was the same thing He had planned for us. Your pope and bishops weren't there to see how my fellow intelligences and I were treated in the First Heaven. What we were expected to spend our eternal lives doing. Why do you think I left? I chose the Inferno over what the Enemy offers. What does that tell you?"

Jack didn't say anything. The Devil gave him time to think.

After several quiet seconds, he asked, "Still think there's nothing to my side of things, boy?"

"Servitude?" Jack asked, looking up into his face. "Is that what repulses you so much? I'm well aware we'll all be servants forever, Satan. How could we not be when every moment of our existence depends on the Omniscient holding us in it? What's always so offensive to you in simply acknowledging yourself as inferior to the Almighty Being Who made you?"

The Devil let his head fall back on his shoulders as he shook it. *"Agh! Still* stubborn! *Still* being naive! It's so simple in your infinitesimal mind, isn't it, human? Okay then, tell me this. What's so offensive to you in falling prostrate before me and acknowledging your inferiority to my higher nature?"

"You'd love that, wouldn't you?"

Satan pointed a clawed finger at him again. "There it is! There's the rebellious response I expected. The same kind I gave your Master when he requested that of me. And why won't you? Because you think me a tyrannical monster?"

"I *know* you're a tyrannical monster, devil. I've experienced firsthand how you and your kind treat other creatures."

"Yet you lovingly serve *the Creator?* Everything you hate about me applies to Him infinitely more! At least I have the excuse of having learned it all from Him!"

The Devil started pacing back-and-forth before Jack, who took the opportunity to step away another few paces himself, making sure to keep both villains in front of him. Mephistopheles had recovered and was leaning on his own staff off to Jack's left, staring downward at nothing in particular with his dead white eyes. He looked more like a Halloween decoration than a living thing. The only parts of him moving in the wind were the gray rags that clothed bits of his form and the feathers of his wings. If the expression on his face was to be trusted, he didn't like the topic of his master's ranting.

"You Catholics," Satan went on, "with all your theology and philosophy, never bother to sit down and actually read the Bible do you? You wouldn't identify the God you find in it as, Love, if you did! How do you hate me so when worshiping such a Bloodthirsty, Vindictive, Misogynistic, Homophobic, Filicidal, Infanticidal, Pestilential, Sadomasochistic Megalomaniac as the Lord of the Israelites? A Cruel Tyrant, proud of His jealous disposition, Who endorsed genocides and slavery for hundreds upon hundreds of years! But you're right, Jack. I must be the villain for having refused to worship such a Control Freak. I, the philanthropist who liberated man and woman from their garden of imprisonment with its rigid law of intolerance and have been encouraging every inclination of their hearts since. I, the realist. I, the romantic. I, *the social worker of souls!*"

Jack burst out laughing, unable to help himself. The Devil stopped his pacing, turning to him, his eyes glowing brighter. His trident swirled a few red flames among the blue ones. It cut Jack's laughter short.

"Sorry," he said. "That last one was just, too much!" He chuckled again.

Satan stepped toward him, and Jack felt his stomach muscles quiver. He'd read somewhere once that the Devil couldn't bear to be mocked. Apparently, it was true. He tried for a third time what he hoped would save him, praying again the suit could conceal what he was doing. He flicked his eyes upward for half a second, careful not to let his head follow, so the Devil wouldn't see where he was looking. In the meantime, he let the arrowhead of his chain drop from his wrist a few links and started swinging it back-and-forth before him. That caught his enemy's attention. He halted.

"You leave me alone, I leave you alone, right?" Jack mashed his nose against the interior of his mask so his words rang through it with even more of a metallic zing than usual.

Satan didn't say anything, but he didn't stalk forward anymore either. The rosary had intimidated him, for the time being.

"You think . . . you can threaten . . . the highest creature in the cosmos, boy?" Satan seethed in a near whisper. "Your mind is less than an atom compared to mine."

Jack knew his stall tactics couldn't last much longer. He was surprised he'd made it as far as he had without provoking an attack. It would have to come eventually. He'd need it to come for what he was attempting to work. But not yet. He wasn't ready yet. He had to keep the Evil One talking.

"'The highest creature,' huh? Now I know why they call you 'father of lies.' You even delude yourself."

Satan straightened, then smiled. "Ah, something else your angelic friends never told you, eh? They are selective about the details they give and the ones they hold back, aren't they?"

"What's that?" Jack asked, glad to keep the conversation going.

"You don't know who I was. What I am. They only told you half the story of our first war."

"You're the creature who's labored for my race's extinction with every choice you've made since the beginning. What more do I need to know? Satan means 'Adversary' in Hebrew."

"That's the name I chose, Philangelus. But you never bothered to look up the meaning of the name your Master gave me, did you?"

Jack didn't say anything, just kept swinging his chain at the ready. Satan flaunted his sharpened canines in another smile.

"I didn't think so. You really know very little of what passed between me and Him at the dawn of creation, don't you?"

"I know enough," Jack said.

"Hardly," Satan whispered, glancing up at the flame flickering on his staff.

He appeared to be reminiscing. The fire started to burn white.

"I suppose I'll go against my usual nature and enlighten your ignorance. Help you see things clearly. Perspective is everything. Wouldn't you agree?"

He looked back at Jack, who remained silent.

Undeterred, the Devil went on. "My original name, Lucifer, is Latin for 'Light-Bearer.' Or as the Hebrews pronounced it: 'Halal.' 'To shine.' I was the Morning Star long before the Maiden of Nazareth ripped off the title from me."

Jack spun the chain he'd been swinging before his legs up into a full circle. Mephistopheles winced behind his master. Satan, for his part, didn't wince, but he was silenced by the gesture.

"Careful, devil," Jack threatened, surprised at his own courage. "Blaspheming God already landed you in Hell. Blaspheme His Mother, and the fury that rains down on you will make you long to hide beneath its flames."

Jack wanted to put his foot in his mouth as soon as he'd said it. The goal was to keep the Devil talking, not attacking! Why was he issuing threats? It wasn't time to provoke him yet. But he'd been pissed off by the insult of Mary. It was laughable Satan had actually tried to play the whole "I'm really the good guy who's just misunderstood" card after Jack had met her. How did the Evil One expect him to fall for any proposal that painted her out as a false advertiser? To his surprise—and relief—the Devil grinned at his reaction, the flame on his trident staying white.

"Perhaps," Satan said, "if I were lying."

Jack saw something moving beneath Satan's cloak. It was one of his wings. After a second, Jack blinked. Satan's wings were hanging behind him at the moment, outside his robe. This was a third wing. A fourth joined it from the other side and they spread out, throwing the cloak off his form. The Devil spread all his wings, and Jack counted twelve protruding from his backside in all.

The monster stretched them to their full extent, and he saw they were each the same size. It looked like a gang of giant bats were spreading their wings in formation, one behind the other, like they'd burrowed themselves into Satan's form from behind. Clothed in nothing but a black loincloth now, Jack saw the Evil One was as bulked out as Michael. Huge pectoral muscles, biceps, triceps, shoulders, abs. Everything. A perfectly formed bodybuilder's body with the head of a monster atop it and the wings of six dragons behind it. Satan's form combusted, burning within and without, flames licking him from head to toe. Jack stepped back with a start. The Devil grimaced in pain, and Jack guessed the flames were hurting him.

"You see, boy?" the fallen intelligence asked, flame and smoke exhaling from his mouth as he did. "I never ceased being your Lord's fiery angel. Only now, the Sadist makes the flames hurt. I held *the* position in Heaven before He grew tired of me. I bore the light of all knowledge down to every other creature directly from Him, just as your White Lady does now. I was His favorite, Philangelus . . . The Prince of Angels . . . *The Head of the Seraphim!*"

He flapped all twelve wings together and put the fire out, but the misery on his face didn't change. Jack had the impression he was still burning, though he couldn't see it.

"If your spiritual director's seraphic guardians possess three pairs of wings to signify their place in the Celestial Court, how high a throne do you suppose I was favored to occupy with six?"

Jack said nothing.

"That is," Satan spat, "before the Deity betrayed me and incited others to do the same,  to war against me constantly, blocking me from reclaiming my right to rule, right down to you. Your Master has a habit of raising His friends above all others for the mere pleasure of watching them plummet when He casts them down to be trampled under their feet. Like I said, He's a Child playing with toys. Occasionally, He likes to throw the toughest-looking ones out the window, just to see if they'll break on landing."

Jack stared at the Devil, and—though he couldn't see his eyes through the reflective lenses of his mask—Satan knew he'd caught his attention. Jack had stopped swinging his chain. It was hanging suspended by his side.

*"Liar!"* Jack finally whispered.

The Devil smiled. "Think so?"

"You think just because you put on a wing and fire show, I'll believe you were a Seraph? You're the master of illusion. Besides, I've already met the highest angel. *Michael* is Prince."

Jack saw the Evil One wince when he said his patron's name. He couldn't read at first if the expression that came over his face was one of fear or rage, but it was clear which when he saw his pupils expand until his eyes were black and his trident roared red.

*"THAT USURPER STOLE MY THRONE, YOU BLIND ACOLYTE!"*

The reprobate intelligence's explosion was so loud, pieces crumbled off the decrepit headstones and even some of the condemned buildings surrounding the graveyard.

*"AN INSOLENT AND COVETOUS ACT OF DISLOYALTY FROM A POWER-HUNGRY VASSAL! A VASSAL WHO SAW AN OPPORTUNITY TO CAPITALIZE ON MY DISAGREEMENT WITH THE CREATOR'S IN-SANITY AND PRESUMPTUOUSLY INTERPOSE HIS OPINION WHERE IT DIDN'T BELONG!"*

Jack tried not to flinch at his enemy's shouts. It wasn't easy. His words were so thunderous, he could feel them pushing him backward.

*"To defend the honor of Our Father is never presumptuous!"* he yelled back.

His zeal was channeled through his sacramentals as he did. His scapular flared up to flap threateningly around him. The glow of his suit intensified. Even Mephistopheles took a couple of steps away from the two raging foes. Jack saw it out the corner of his eye. The Devil hunched forward, snarling, commanding his full attention again.

"He'll betray you too, Jack. I was only His first victim. The moment He grows bored of you, He'll forget you as an afterthought and move on to someone else. It happens every time. You think His relationship with you is anything more than utility? Don't feel too secure in your position as His, *Philangelus!*" Satan spat the name. "It bemuses me you've held His fascination this long!"

Jack looked the deformed angel up and down and shook his head. "I have no pity for you, Satan. Dathiel told me how you fell. Of this 'dilemma of creation.'"

Satan's eyes focused, boring into Jack's.

Jack met his gaze without blinking, nodding his head this time. "You see, I'm not so stupid. You'll never get me to act on it."

After a long pause of intense silence that sounded loud in Jack's ears following their deafening outbursts, the Devil nodded back, shooting him a wide grin. Jack saw more of his teeth this time, from both the top and bottom rows. It was like watching an animal try to smile.

"At least there are no atheists in Hell, *doubter,*" Satan emphasized the last word. "We all believe in God down here."

Jack chuckled, letting the metallic ring of his laughter echo through his mask across the graveyard. It wiped the smile from Satan's face.

"Yes," he said. "And that tortures you, doesn't it?"

The Devil lowered his staff as though about to shoot its fire at him. Jack assumed a battle stance, ready to swing his chain out at last.

Satan eyed it. "You think those beads have any power over me, Mama's boy? God is dead! I killed Him! Just look at what hangs from the bottom of your little necklace there."

"If He's dead, why do you still tremble before His image?" Jack asked, physically swinging the crucifix hanging between his legs in the church's pew back-and-forth like a hypnotist's pendulum. "Still fearing the Woman who brings Him to crush your head?"

Red lightning sparked in the flame atop Satan's trident. Several bolts shot out, obliterating surrounding gravestones, but none touched Jack. Yet. He was almost out of time. *What was taking so long?* He couldn't stall the Devil much longer. His wrath would overrule his tactics soon, just like in the locutions.

"I'll let you watch the day I rip Him from her embrace to rend Him limb from limb before her eyes!" Satan promised.

Jack's own anger flared again. He looked the Devil in the eyes. He wanted to rip him limb from limb where he stood. At last, he saw what he'd been waiting for. And none too soon. It was time to provoke the attack, and he'd do it with pleasure.

"What a heart filled with bitterness, Fallen Lucifer," Jack quoted.

The Devil's eyes widened in fury. Jack had his undivided attention, which kept him from noticing what was coming. He completed the quote.

"Had you but venerated the will of God, it would then be *her* kneeling to venerate *you.*"

The flame on the trident turned its deepest crimson. It looked like bloody tongues were waggling at Jack from it, before Satan fired them off. It all happened so fast, Jack didn't have time to duck. Everything in front of him flashed red, then gold. When it was over, he found himself crouched down with his scapular held up over his face to protect him, though he didn't remember crouching. He'd never felt the impact of the Devil's blow.

"Well, well," he heard Satan muttering, a slight apprehension in his tone now, if Jack wasn't mistaken, "speak of the Archangel, and he shall appear."

# CHAPTER XXXV
## JACK'S DISCERNMENT

A flurry of luminescent white feathers shifted before Jack as Michael withdrew his wing from shielding him.

The wing was afire with red flames but wasn't burning. When Michael flapped it outward, the flames were dispelled. Jack's patron had landed in front of him in the nick of time. Though his sword was sheathed across his back, Jack would have thought he'd caught him unawares. He was barefoot and dressed in a short-sleeved blue robe. His only armor was a gold breastplate with a giant sapphire embedded in the chest. He either didn't realize who Jack had called him down to protect him from, or he wasn't worried about it and not at all afraid to show his nonchalance. Jack hoped it was the latter.

*"Thank . . . God!"* Jack exhaled. "I invoked your prayer three times! You had me worried you weren't coming!"

Michael turned and smiled down at him. "I've been here the whole time. He was never going to lay a hand on you. Just wanted to see how long he'd embarrass himself trying to recruit you."

The Devil looked livid, but Jack could see fear mixed with the rage in his expression at the sight of his age-old rival.

"Once again, you interject yourself where you don't belong, *Standard-Bearer,*" Satan hissed.

Michael smiled at him. "Not when you try to steal one of my charges."

The Evil One raised his eyebrows, then turned to glower at Mephistopheles. The Power, who was already gazing in terror at who'd arrived, looked all the more afraid with his master's anger directed at him.

"You neglected to inform me *the usurper* was his patron saint! Slip your mind?"

Mephistopheles found his voice, but it was shaky. "I swear, my baal! I didn't know!"

"He's telling you the truth," Michael said. "Of course, I know how much you like denying that."

Satan glared at him, unsure whom he loathed most out of all those present.

"You never should have sent him against Jack Dacre," the Archangel went on. "You'll be regretting that choice for the rest of his life. And you shouldn't have come here." Michael drew his sword, the blade morphing into fire. "You'll regret that choice even sooner. It's time you know the fear you've been inflicting on my apprentice."

Jack looked from Michael to the two monsters, his heart beating in exhilaration. He felt like a boy who'd been bullied on the schoolyard whose older brother had just shown up. Satan grabbed the center spike on his staff, swinging it around as it transformed into his own broadsword, its blade likewise igniting into flame.

"You won't win this time," he declared.

The two titans of the spiritual realms faced each other, poised as preternatural gladiators in a post-apocalyptic arena. Jack couldn't believe what he was about to see. A battle between the most powerful angel and devil in creation. Neither moved at first. They'd gone as motionless as statues, their weapons flickering. As if at some invisible signal, both flew at each other, holding their swords before them. The blades collided, rippling a clap of thunder across the graveyard. Its reverberation knocked Jack and Mephistopheles off their feet.

Jack stayed on the ground upon recovery, watching the Herculean intelligences dueling in midair as they circled each other, spiraling back down among the tombstones. His ears adjusted to the thunder claps of the blazing blades, mesmerized more by the speed and skill of the fighters' swordsmanship. Now he saw how much Michael had held back during their training sessions. The fight's prowess was comparable to the fight Jack had seen between Satan and Mary. The intelligences ducked, jumped, backflipped, and performed all manner of superhuman feats to avoid each other's thrusts. But there was a stark difference to their methods. Satan was vehement, appearing to put all his aggression behind every blow. Michael seemed calm, his movements more fluid, like he was in a half-meditative state. At the same time, he looked like he was having fun.

The Devil swung his weapon down to slice Michael's face open, dragging a trail of fire through the air. The Archangel flapped his wings, propelling himself backward several meters to avoid it. He flapped them in the opposite direction, shooting himself toward his enemy again at three times the speed, surprising him with an uppercut to the chin. Satan went sailing. As he tumbled upward through the air, Michael took off after him, catching up and bashing him again, and again, every time he was about to regain his equilibrium. Before Jack knew it, they were hundreds of feet above Charleston. Finally, Satan met Michael's strike with a block, and they circled again, looking for an opening.

Every time their swords met, roars of thunder resounded across the sky, shaking the entire city below. Jack heard the cries of both living and dead souls as they were affected by what was going on above them. Through his corporeal sense of hearing, he discerned actual thunder as it started raining outside the cathedral. He sucked in a breath through his nostrils, still not believing what he was witnessing. The battle of good and evil as it unfolded on this thirteenth of May had caused a thunderstorm over the Tri-County area. He stood up, watching the airborne skirmish. But he'd forgotten about Mephistopheles. He regretted that as he was clobbered through a gravestone.

"Your protector looks occupied, pup," the Power jeered, kicking him through several more headstones before he could get up. "Now . . . finally, I'm going to finish what I was sent to this damn town to do!"

The demon raised his spear, its two prongs pointed at Jack, and brought it down to impale him. Jack rolled over and caught the spikes just above his chest. Mephistopheles put the pressure of his full strength behind it.

"I pierced your armor once, boy," he grinned his terrifying smile. "I can do it again. This time, I'll penetrate all the way to the deep recesses of your heart. There'll be no room for faith there anymore!"

The red orb of the staff issued the monster's signature mist. It flowed over Jack. This time, it seeped through his rosary. His thoughts were inundated. He felt afraid to trust in all he'd learned, all he'd seen.

*"Delusion. Illusion. Insanity. A child's overactive imagination. Winged gladiators in the sky? The forming of yourself into a fucking superhero? Daydreams, Jack!"*

Jack tried to remember Christ's face. When he did, the mist receded. The Power redoubled his efforts. The mist proceeded up over his face again.

*"You're forming a hazy mist to block out the ugliness of reality! Stop fighting it!"*

Jack remembered Mary's face. The mist receded. He had trouble holding onto the image. The mist proceeded. Mephistopheles was too strong. Despair threatened to poison his confidence. The mist would swallow him. When it was about to cover his eyes, Jack saw Michael perched in a tree above the Power.

*"Philangelus,"* the Archangel called down, making the Power waver in his effort to stab him, *"end him."*

It wasn't an encouragement. It wasn't even advice. It was a command. And his commander would never order him to do something he was incapable of doing. The saint's words penetrated his heart's depths faster and deeper than Mephistopheles' mist had managed to do. He was ordering him to banish the evil from his life. Now. A zealous anger rose in his heart such as he'd never known before. He was sick of the monster that had held him back for so long.

*No more!* he thought, and the mist receded.

"You want this finished, Mephistopheles?" he asked, his mask amplifying his voice into a metallic zing across the graveyard. "Fine. I'm done despairing. I'm done doubting. I'm done being afraid. And I'm done with you."

Strength coursed through him, warmth arose around him, and he began another Rosary.

At the words, "I believe in God," his form erupted in fire.

What mist remained over him was dispelled. The head of the spear was thrust off him. And Mephistopheles stumbled backward. Jack reached out and grabbed the red orb of the demon's weapon, squeezing. It was crushed to pieces in his palm. Mephistopheles grimaced in pain. Jack screamed his indignation, his scapular raising him off the ground. The recitation of the full *Apostles' Creed* shoved the Power into Chuck's mausoleum. The demon disappeared through its smashed door. Other than his cloak and the lenses of his mask, Jack appeared composed of fire now. The suit burned like his mentor's sword. He was Heaven's blazing avenger. Michael marveled from where he crouched on the tree branch.

"Now you know what it is to have divine faith," he said.

Satan dove from the darkness above the graveyard, holding his sword out before him, hellbent on Jack's destruction. The Archangel shot a bolt of lightning from his palm without even taking his eyes off his inflamed protégé. The Evil One was knocked off course into a building beside the cemetery. Michael glanced at Chuck's mausoleum, then back at Jack. Before flying off to reengage his own nemesis, he issued another command.

"Show him what it is to be like God."

While Michael hurled lightning bolts into the building where the Devil had crashed, drawing him back out into the open, Jack turned his full attention on Chuck's grave.

Mephistopheles emerged gripping his orbless spear. He looked dazed at first, until he saw the burning specter before him. He spread his wings and leapt into the air.

"You're stronger than the last time we met, Jack. Breaking you down just got a lot more interesting! But you forget, I'm prince of the Order known for . . ."

He broke off. The sleeves of Jack's robe had receded up his arms, but the cloak wasn't burning off him. It had spread and parted behind him, forming a pair of brown wings. Jack flapped them, headbutting the monster from the air. The demon was sent rolling down the city streets. Jack flew after him.

As he flew, he pondered the realizations entering his mind through his prayer. He understood now why God had sent him his locutions. They weren't just to prepare him for Fatima. They were for this last battle. Meditation on what he'd been shown was what had cast Mephistopheles and his putrid mist off him, and it was what fueled his fire now. The second vision had shown him that, when fighting devils, Mary never engaged them in dialogue except to rebuke them. She never argued with them. She never even spoke to them beyond what her prayers manifested. She just magnified the Lord in their presence. Monsignor Bamonte and Michael had tried to warn him of the dangers in speaking with the demonic. The Archangel had even told him his soul would fall if he challenged the wit of their intellects with his own. He hadn't understood how to implement their advice, and the evil spirits had continued drawing him into debates. So Mary had shown him the lesson instead of repeating it.

Now he understood the significance of what he'd seen. When faced directly with demons, all he needed to do was pray and meditate. That was their rebuke. That was all the argumentation it would take to topple their defenses and drive them off. It would break their minds and illuminate the Truth down on their lies.

The greatest lies were half-truths. So Lupe had once told him. He'd learned that lesson from experience too. But he knew something else from experience now. Sincere meditation would lead him to discern which parts of demonic deceptions were true and which false. He'd wondered why, of all Catholics, he'd been given an aid to meditation as great as divine visions, knowing it couldn't have been solely to aid his personal struggle for faith. He understood the reason behind that now as well. Other people didn't have to face such foes in their lives as had come into his, and they never had to see them as he did.

"To whom more is given, more is demanded," Dathiel had told him the night they met.

*But,* Jack thought, *to whom more is demanded, more graces are given. Enough to meet the demands.*

There was still one more reason Jack now suspected God had given him the locutions. The holistic and simplest reason. So he'd have the memory of them while he meditated. It was making his meditation that much more potent. So potent, the mental images could block out Mephistopheles' attacks the way Mary had blocked Satan's. It was such potency that was about to banish Mephistopheles from his life. He flew faster, ready to keep his mouth shut this time and let God use him however He willed to rain His wrath down upon their enemy.

He would magnify the Lord.

Mephistopheles stopped skidding only when he hit the Pineapple Fountain in Waterfront Park.

He'd lost his scepter somewhere along the way. He hunched over on hands and knees, struggling to climb to his feet. When he managed, it was to spot what looked like a winged firecracker hurtling toward him. The warrior landed atop him, beating him into the fountain. His head was slammed into it so hard, chunks broke off it.

Mephistopheles shoved back, regaining his footing, proceeding with hand-to-hand combat. He used his greatest skill, but the fucking teenager displayed more prowess than he'd ever known, and his flaming armor kept scorching his knuckles with each punch. Jack countered all his blows, even slapped him back-and-forth across the face at one point just to humiliate him. He screeched like a mad owl, jabbing at him with his tail. The warrior dodged that too. He launched a fireball from his palm. Jack shot his own. It snuffed his out, before bouncing across the Charleston harbor.

The warrior swung a chain of fire out from his wrist and sliced off the bottom half of his tail. Mephistopheles screamed, in agony this time. His scream was cut short when the chain's arrowhead harpooned him by the neck.

He was lifted off his feet and spun around the warrior's head several times before being hurled down the road.

Satan barreled into the clouds, spinning out of control, ricocheting off the floating mountains.

He landed face-first on one of them, sliding forty feet before he stopped. It took him a moment to recover. Once he had, Michael appeared over the edge of the nimbus and landed in front of him. He'd lost his grip on his weapon at some point. The Archangel sheathed his own, as though he wished to keep the fight fair. Satan seethed. He hated this intelligence . . . *so* . . . *fucking* . . . *much!*

They'd landed in a celestial section of the sky. Heavenly Principalities lorded over the fortress next to them. They looked surprised by the abrupt arrival of the Princes of Heaven and Hell, but they adapted fast, drawing their blades to come to their captain's aid. Michael raised a hand and bid them stay back. This just pissed the Devil off more.

*"You can't protect the boy forever, usurper. He lives in my domain! My world!"*

He flew at his nemesis, ramming his horns into his forehead, and another thunder clap roared across the Charleston sky. Together the two angels careened through the walls of the castle on the next cloud, emerging from its opposite side and continuing to catapult for miles. They smashed into the Third Gate where

Jack had met Michael, and the Evil One drew his head back, slamming his horns into the Archangel several more times. When his opponent's skin refused to break and he didn't even looked phased, Satan resorted to punching, trying with all his might to break his enemy's will. It was fruitless. He brought his fist forward for the fifth time, when Michael surprised him with a punch of his own. The damned spirit was knocked off-balance and stumbled backward.

"Done whining?" Michael asked.

Satan snarled, the growl clawing its way up the cocoon of his throat, metamorphosing into a full roar by the time he was running forward again. The Archangel caught his throat and cut it short, lifting him off his feet and body-slamming him into the cloud they stood upon.

"So that's a no?" Michael asked, before kicking him forward fifty feet off the edge of the cliff.

The Devil spiraled downward several hundred meters before he recomposed himself. When he did, he flew toward the darker clouds. Sensing their Master's approach, forty demonic Principalities swarmed out of the fortress he neared like angry wasps emerging from their nest.

Satan landed and beckoned them over. *"Give him hell!"*

The demons were bewildered at first, until Michael burst through a gray cloud across from theirs. He landed before them with a thump that shook the entire floating mountain. Another clap of thunder rumbled through Charleston. The demons weren't keen on getting involved in whatever situation they'd just been thrust, but Satan pulled his sword from the air, flinging streams of flame at them from its blade like lashes of a whip. Lightning bolts lit up the sky over the city. The ten Principalities closest to the Archangel charged, wielding axes and spears against him. The celestial intelligence walked forward, his countenance calm. When the fallen spirits leapt to strike, he drew his flaming sword and sliced through all of them with a single swing, continuing his march forward, not slowed at all. The remaining thirty gaped, backing up.

*"With me,"* Satan ordered, flying toward their opponent.

He swung his own sword around. Michael caught his wrist with his free hand and yanked the Devil down to the ground, stomping his foot over his back to pin him. He looked up at the other demons, spreading his arms, daring them to come at him. They didn't.

*"Move, bitches,"* Satan's muffled voice commanded from the ground. *"Take him now! He's only an Archangel!"*

The Principalities ran forward. Michael sheathed his broadsword and engaged them with hands and his one free leg. Without taking his foot off Satan, he tore them all to pieces before they could land a blow. Afterward, he shot a dozen fireballs at the black tower they'd been guarding, obliterating it. Evil spirits from surrounding clouds witnessed the demolition, but they didn't dare approach the presence they sensed was doing it. Not the one they'd seen hurl the Baal of baals himself from Heaven. Satan roared his frustration and punched the cloud he lay upon, flapping what wings he could, beginning to tunnel down through the mountain and escape out the bottom.

As the Evil One disappeared beneath him, Michael tightened his own wings to his sides and dove through the hole he'd left.

Jack stopped breathing and listened.

Mephistopheles wasn't far away.

They'd been fighting across the rooftops of Charleston's Rainbow Row when he'd kicked the demon over the side of the buildings and he'd disappeared. But Jack knew the feeling of his presence well enough to track him. It had led him to the Battery Carriage House Inn.

He walked its hallways without making a sound, having extinguished his armor to mask his approach. The feeling of despair the Power gave off was pulsating the strongest from Room Eight. He sniffed, recognizing his enemy's scent. Jack listened outside the door. He could hear a faint scraping, like the claws on Mephistopheles' paws scraping across the ground. Jack kicked the door in, his armor igniting to illuminate the room. His quarry was hunched over a sleeping guest of the hotel, probably about to poison her mind with some nightmare. She must have been a tasty morsel to make Mephistopheles careless enough to try and seduce her while he was still trying to escape town. Regardless, he wasn't going to escape. Not today.

"Boo," Jack whispered when the demon turned in surprise at his entrance.

He charged, spreading his cloth wings to envelop the room, and rammed the demon through the wall. They rolled through the air and crashed into a group of souls on the sidewalk below. Some were living. Some were dead. The souls stopped their conversations a moment as the unseen warriors tumbled through them, a few getting a negative feeling from the demon's presence, others feeling a jolt of joy at Jack's.

The enemies kept rolling, all the way into Battery Park across the street. Jack made sure to land on top when they stopped. He started punching the demon, hammering his every indignation onto his repugnant face. He broke his teeth worse than they'd already been. Mephistopheles stuck his scepter between them and tried to push his attacker off. Jack grabbed it and pushed back, making his enemy work for it. The Power had to press with all his might to regain his footing.

*"Fucking bread-worshippers!"* he yelled. *"Why couldn't you just behave yourself? You could have had an easy life, filled with the pleasures of the flesh!"*

Jack didn't say anything, just kept pushing. The Power got the sense of his response through his prayers. It was a promise he'd burn him and the whole satanic operation to the ground before he ever relented.

"You think you'll have time for peace if you dedicate yourself to resisting Satan's regime?" Mephistopheles demanded. "Hell will never stop warring against you! We don't take vacations, boy. There will always be another battle. Then another. And another. Until you crumble to dust in the wind, forgotten!"

Jack's arms weakened for half a second, enough for Mephistopheles to move the weapon's spikes closer to his face. He edged them toward a stabbing position under his chin. Jack shoved the spear back at his own face, smashing it into where a nose would have been. The warrior had feigned weakness to catch him off-guard and get in another hit. Mephistopheles felt what this prayer said too.

The boy didn't care. Every time a demon was stupid enough to poke its head up from Hell, he'd bash it back down, just like his. He'd tear Satan's kingdom down brick-by-brick if he had to, until the day he died. The demon barked.

"You want conquest, Philangelus?"

He shoved the spear back and hit Jack in the nose this time, stunning him for a moment. It was enough for him to backflip away from the warrior and land in a crouch atop one of the park's cannons.

*"What do you know of conquest?"* He clutched his paws tighter on the cannon, leaving imprints on it. *"You've not lived millennia to witness the wars I have! You know not of what you speak in welcoming the pandemonium my kind can bring against you!"* He smiled, his grin even eerier with the new chips in his teeth. "But you will, Jack. We will never cease to—"

His words were cut short by Jack flying forward and punching him. He slid backward across the grass, using his momentum to backflip onto his feet again, growling all the way. He flew forward to impale the impudent little shit on the end of his spear. Jack recited the Fatima prayer at the end of the Rosary's first decade. As he did, his hands joined together and formed a ball of water that he launched at the demon's head. It attached itself and started drowning him. Mephistopheles veered off course, landing and clawing at his face to get it off. It wouldn't cooperate, no matter how much he swiped at it or shook his head. It stayed in its balled shape. He felt like an astronaut whose helmet was suffocating him instead of providing air.

When it finally poured onto the ground, the demon couldn't be sure how long he'd been suffocating, but it was long enough for Jack to close the distance between them. The warrior almost kicked him across the park. He dodged just in time, flying backward away from him. He threw his spear at him. Jack caught it. He'd never been this fucking fast before! Mephistopheles found himself dodging his own weapon as it was thrown back at him. He twisted, grabbing its bottom end after it sailed past, swinging it back around at Jack yet again. The warrior was flying toward him. He blocked the strike with his inflamed wrist bracer. The spear bounced off it, repelled by an invisible force.

Mephistopheles didn't like the way this battle was going. Not at all. It wasn't fun anymore. He brought his fist toward Jack's chin to uppercut him. Before he managed, something huge and heavy slammed into him from above.

He and the unidentified object smashed through the trees across the park.

"You're doing very well, Jack," Michael praised, landing next to him.

Jack beamed, then realized the Archangel couldn't see his smile of gratitude through his flaming mask. He willed his suit off into a flaming sword in his hand. Mephistopheles came stumbling out of the mess of fallen trees. Even Jack had jumped back in surprise when the Devil had come tumbling into him.

"The end is nigh!" Jack said to Michael.

*"Say that again, boy!"* Satan bellowed, cutting away the branches of the tree he was tangled in and landing next to his Power. "I dare you!"

He stood shoulder-to-shoulder with Mephistopheles. Michael stepped up and stood shoulder-to-shoulder with Jack. The four fighters stared each other down. The trees behind the evil spirits were burning from their contact with Satan's blade. It looked like they'd just emerged from Hell itself. Each pair of fighters began walking forward, closing the distance between them. Soon, they broke into a run, everyone taking flight and colliding in midair.

Mephistopheles pushed Jack backward, until the youth backflipped and pulled the Power around with him, kicking his upside down form to the edge of the park. Michael had shoved Satan into the grass, plowing a deep trail through the dirt. When they stopped, the Archangel held the Devil's sword at bay with his own and used his free hand to pummel him farther into the earth. Satan's whole form ignited as he screamed in rage, burning the soil around them, widening the crater they'd made.

He shot red lightning from his hand to back Michael off. The Angelic Prince caught the bolts in his palm and threw them skyward. It gave the Evil One enough time to get to his feet and ram his shoulder into his opponent. He drove him backward into the gazebo at the park's center, swinging his broadsword out and slicing toward the celestial champion's neck. Michael blocked with his own fiery blade, and they stood under the gazebo's roof, testing each other's strength.

Satan bared his teeth, growling louder than a lion. Michael's countenance was still calm but it had a silent, threatening edge to it. After a moment, Mephistopheles bounced off the Devil, breaking the tension. Satan glanced down at his fallen underling, and Michael uppercut him on the chin. He stepped back, dazed.

"Just returning the favor," Jack shouted to Michael as he flew past the larger warriors to attack the Power.

Mephistopheles thrust with his spear, Jack swung with his flaming sword, and Michael and Satan thundered their weapons, as all four spirits leapt, ducked, and flipped through the gazebo. Amid the chaos, Jack was careful to avoid grappling with Satan. Likewise, Mephistopheles evaded Michael as best he could. Dodging between the two titans of the fight was half the smaller warriors' effort. Both had several close calls of being cut in half by the giant swords swinging about the place. The structure started weakening from all the collateral damage the battle was inflicting. When one of the weapons slashed through the last stable pillar, none could have said whose it was, but it didn't matter. The place was coming down on top of them.

Michael reacted first, spreading his wings at different speeds. With his right, he pushed Jack out of harm's way, careful not to shove him hard enough to hurt, only to clear the roof. His left slapped Mephistopheles, who went rolling to the seawall bordering the harbor. When he closed his wings, their flap propelled him backward, and the structure caved in atop the Evil One's head. Satan shoved the wreckage off him a moment later, in time to see Michael swinging one of the park cannons toward him from its barrel as though it was the world's largest tennis racket.

It sent him hurtling through several dilapidated buildings of his kingdom.

Mephistopheles rose to his feet on the seawall moments before Jack slammed into him and sent them both tumbling into the harbor.

Neither would relinquish their grip on the other while they sank. Jack realized it didn't matter. He couldn't drown in the ocean when only projecting himself into it through his charism. But it was getting darker the deeper they descended. He'd lose sight of his enemy if he managed to get even a few feet away from him. He willed his sword back into his suit to give him more light. It was still aflame. Seeing fire burn underwater was about the one hundredth strange sight he could add to what he'd seen in the past seven months. As though the demon knew what he was thinking—which, Jack realized, he probably did—Mephistopheles yanked himself free and propelled away, using his wings like fins. He faded into the dark within moments.

Jack formed his scapular back into its normal shape and willed it to move in waving motions like a dolphin's tail, propelling him through the water. The Power had vanished. Frustrated, he spread the cloak back into wings and crashed through the ocean's surface. It was still no use spotting his enemy. Not only was this area surrounded by night, but Charleston's waters were always murky. He reached the end of the second decade and prayed the *Glory Be,* shining the bright ball it formed in his hand down on the waves as a searchlight. He flew in ever-widening circles, feeling like a pelican hunting fish. He saw nothing.

He dove back under the waves to shine the light. Still nothing. He'd lost the wretch. He was not going to get away! Not this day! He slowed his breathing, trying to calm down, exiting the surface again. He morphed his suit into the sword, closed his eyes, and focused his senses, trying to smell or hear his prey. There was nothing.

Fine. If fishing for him wouldn't work, he'd smoke him out. He raised his arms, sword in one hand, the other with the palm open, and prayed the beginning of the third decade. Streaks of lightning sprayed down into the harbor, followed by fireball after fireball. They fell everywhere, exploding under the waves, illuminating the coast. Mephistopheles shot up from right below him, howling through the air, striking him square in the chest with his spear.

Stunned, Jack fell backward and hit the water, feeling like he'd landed on a stone slab. The demon dove, grabbing his ankle and flinging him across the ocean's surface. Jack skipped on it for several hundred meters before crashing into a beach. He lay motionless facedown on the sand, his sword beside him. Its flame was extinguished. Mephistopheles glided toward him, descending like a vulture that had just spotted an easy meal. Right before he pounced on the youth, Jack's hand shot up and grabbed his leg.

"Gotcha," he cried.

He grabbed his sword, its blade igniting at his touch, and chopped it into the demon's leg. It didn't slice through, but there was a nasty crunch and the bottom third of the leg dangled at an odd angle. Mephistopheles screamed such as Jack had never heard before. He hobbled away as Jack stood. When he turned to look back at him, Jack saw an expression on his face he'd never seen directed his way before.

Sheer terror.

Michael and Satan busted through a wall inside a condemned building together, the impact doing nothing to slow their brawl.

They hacked at each other's swords, sending out shockwaves of both devastation and restoration to their surroundings. The Devil was powerful and obstinate. But, even through his anger, he knew he could do nothing against a will reinforced by the Almighty's, and Jack wasn't even close by anymore. There was no point to fighting here. As soon as he was free of the Archangel's grip, he flapped all twelve of his wings and rocketed through the ceiling. Michael was on his tail in an instant.

They zoomed through the streets, entering the blessed kingdom. The Archangel saw where his ancient nemesis was headed and sped up. But the Devil still made it. He tore down the alley named after the heavenly prince, entering Dr. Vonhagen's building. The psychologist was busy helping to conduct a group, trying to bring healing. *Always healing!* The Prince of Hell slashed his blazing blade about the room, upsetting the process for the moments he had until Michael caught up to him. He dove out the window, just as the Archangel entered.

Michael flapped his wings three times, putting the fire the Devil had started out, restoring the session to equilibrium before continuing his chase. The unquiet spirit had broken into a home of living souls next. He was slashing the adults' heads, riling up their tempers against each other when Michael entered.

"Yours might be an untouchable will," he taunted the Archangel. "But how willingly your lackeys here follow my lead!"

He cackled, dashing through the house to attack the children next. Michael moved past the parents, restoring serenity to their minds with slashes of his own sword as he flew by, and delivered a high kick to the Devil's head before he reached his targets. The monster sailed through the roof, dragging a trail of fire behind him into the sky from his sword. He turned back to Charleston miles below and spewed a stream of hellfire from his mouth down over the city. It was drawn and absorbed into a singular point of impact. The fire of Michael's sword. He was holding it in front of him as he flew up toward the fuming Dragon.

Satan concentrated all his might into keeping his enemy at bay. Michael never slowed. He stopped only when his face had broken through the flames of Satan's breath to stare him in the eyes. The Devil's eyes widened as their glow dwindled. A sharp pain had paralyzed him. He looked down. Michael's sword pierced his chest where a human's heart would have rested.

He looked back up into Michael's sapphire eyes. The Archangel's expression was one of pity. Satan would have been furious at that were he able to muster the strength for an outburst. Instead, he fell backward, flipping over and over in the air as he dropped toward Charleston. Another tremendous pain burst through him, and he saw a golden beam protrude up through his chest from behind, halting his descent.

*It burned!* He felt two more beams burning behind him, one on the nape of his neck, the other going down his back to where a tailbone would have been. Although seeing it upside down, his angelic mind at once calculated where he'd fallen in the city. He'd landed atop the steeple of the Baptist's Castle. He was impaled on its gold cross. He reached up to pull himself off the scalding symbol, when Michael landed on him, pinning him in place, one heel on his stomach, the other on his neck.

"Somehow, you and I always end up in the same disposition," the Archangel said.

He brandished his sword over the Devil's face, forcing his head backward to again view the upside down city.

"I want you to see this."

Below the giants on the steeple, Mephistopheles was flying as fast as he could past the castle, trying to find a hiding place in the city.

His wings flapped haphazardly. Jack collided into him from behind, pinning him in the middle of the castle's front drawbridge. He slammed the demon's head repeatedly into the stone ground. Cracks began slithering out from beneath him in all directions. The flaming sword sheathed across Jack's back grew around him into flaming armor, flooding his memory with every lie the Power had ever inflicted on him. Every ridiculous belief he'd deceived him into. He screamed a primal sound, rolling the monster over and beating his indignation into his skull of a face.

*"You tried to rob me of belief!"* Jack punched him. *"Of happiness!"* he punched again. *"You made me think I was crazy!"* came another punch. *"You and your kind will pay for it, forever!"* he drove his fist down one more time, driving the last of the fight from the prince of demonic fighters.

He grabbed the demon's spear from beside him, holding it in both hands and straining. It snapped in two. He threw the remaining halves into the moat to burn. Mephistopheles lay unmoving under him, black blood leaking from multiple wounds on his crippled form. Jack crawled off him, hanging his head between his arms, gasping for breath. He had to lean physically forward in the pew he was sitting in too. He willed his armor back into a sword on his back, and its fire extinguished. His brain was fried. His mind exhausted.

After a full minute, a gurgling sounded from Mephistopheles' throat. He spit up blood. It kept coming. But soon the sound under the gurgling changed. Jack realized he was laughing. He lifted his head to look back at him. Mephistopheles was staring at him with one white eye. The other was swollen shut.

"You're still my bitch, pup," the demon spat at him.

Jack's anger returned, renewing strength in his muscles. He stood, grabbed Mephistopheles by the scruff of white hair growing from the back of his head, and started dragging him toward the castle's front doors.

*"You have no idea the hell we'll bring on your life, angel-fucker!"* Mephistopheles yelled through grimaces of pain.

"I got something for you that'll burn better than Hell," Jack breathed as he dragged.

Mephistopheles realized where he was taking him. *"No!"* he yelped. *"NO!"* he screamed louder.

He struggled, kicking Jack with his good leg just before they reached the cascade of holy water. The blow freed him from the warrior's grip. He started crawling away. He flapped his wings and lifted off the ground. Jack caught him by the leg before he'd risen five feet, slamming him back down. He squeezed the leg and stomped on it. It snapped, hanging off the demon as loose as the other leg. Mephistopheles howled. Jack grabbed his hair again, yanked him around in front of him, and forced him to face the doorway of water. He drew his sword. It ignited, and he raised it behind the monster.

"It's hard to kick against the goad," he whispered, and stabbed the demon in the back, the blade extending out through his chest.

Mephistopheles tried to scream, but he lacked the power. His mouth just hung open in silent trauma. Jack lifted him off his feet with the weapon and walked him through the waterfall. The demon writhed as he passed under its heat. It was a mere preview to the burning he suffered inside. Jack stepped through the water after him, raising him higher, basking him in the sacramental sunlight, taking him all the way up to the foot of the sanctuary. Mephistopheles found his voice at last, and screamed. Screamed with all the might he had left. The pain was excruciating, but he screamed more from terror at the Shining Deity before him.

*"NOOO! NOOOO! NOT THE WHITE HOC!"* Mephistopheles caught fire. *"LEAVE ME ALONE! LEAVE ME BE! BID ME NOT INTO THE ABYYYYYSS!"*

Jack lifted the writhing, flaming wretch above his head, waving him back and forth as though waving a flag of surrender. It was slow at first, but it was working. Mephistopheles was being sliced in half down the middle. Jack yanked the sword into one final long arc. His enemy split above him, his two halves flying off in separate directions. They disintegrated into nothing before they ever hit the floor. The only proof there'd been a demon in the castle a moment later was a hail of smoldering black feathers raining around Jack.

Mephistopheles was gone.

Satan perceived the Prince of his Powers descend from Earth back to the Inferno, knowing who'd sent him on his way.

He coughed up black blood, trying to speak.

"A trifle," he sputtered. "So he defeated a Power. So What!" He looked up at Michael. "Small fish, usurper! I have more to offer him than Mephistopheles! I'll—"

His words were cut off as his head was yanked down by the hair. Jack's eyes stared into his upside down face. The youth was hovering before them. Satan growled, snapping his fangs like a caged animal at the insolence of this mortal.

"*YOU DARE TOUCH ME!*" he roared, lashing his forked tongue at him.

His wrath returned some of his strength despite the cross still impaling him. But he couldn't get at the boy. Michael was right there.

"*You think you can stand against all of us with how much trouble it was for you to overcome the Prince of our Sixth Order?*" the Devil demanded. "*You're just a thorn in my side, Philangelus! Not a sword! We will—*"

His words were cut short again, by a blow to the face from the butt of Jack's sword.

"This thorn in your side's going to fester until it infects your whole kingdom," Jack said in words barely above a whisper. "I'll wreak havoc across it every chance I get for the rest of time. I'll dedicate my life to helping others you presume to torture in the dark. After death, I'll come back to do it again, with all Heaven at my heels. Wherever you go, whatever schemes you attempt, I'll be there to look you dead in the eyes," Jack pulled their faces closer to drive home the point, "*as a priest!*" he declared.

He released his grip. What had he just said? He hadn't intended the words. They'd seemed the natural thing to say.

"There it is," Michael said. "My task here is done."

Jack looked up at him. The Archangel shot him a half-smile and winked as he bent under Satan and tore the gold cross from the steeple. He flew off into the eastern horizon carrying it and its impaled catch with him, leaving Jack alone to ponder what had just happened.

# CHAPTER XXXVI
## THROUGH THE TABERNACLE

What had just happened?

Jack relinquished incorporeal sight and looked to the tabernacle. He didn't know why he'd said what he'd said. It was like the words had been planted on his lips before they'd gone through the filter of his brain. He felt something tickling the top of his head and reached up to see what it was. There was nothing there.

He dropped his hand. The tickle returned. He reached up again. Nothing. Every time he moved his hand away, he felt it again. It was similar to the feeling of static electricity, but different, and there was nothing near his head at the moment to make the hair stand on end. He wasn't even sure the hair was standing up. He just felt a tickle. And only on the top center of his scalp. Nowhere else. He tried brushing his fingers through his hair again. No change. He decided to ignore the phenomenon. He had bigger things to consider.

He went back over his declaration again, sitting with the words. Was that the "destiny" the angels had been alluding to all this time? Was he meant to be a priest? Was that even why Naomi had left him? He remembered how he'd felt pulled away from her when he'd almost kissed her the first time, and again, right before he had kissed her for the first time. He'd always wondered if that pull had been an angel or demon. If he'd always been destined for the priesthood, and if the angels knew about it, it would make sense they'd try to stop him from dating. Why waste his and Naomi's time if the relationship was doomed to end in a breakup from the start? Was that it? Was he meant to be a Catholic priest?

He opened his eyes to the incorporeal again. His soul stood on the castle's roof where he'd been before. The city and surrounding countryside were brighter now. The battle had shifted the daylight into more areas than he'd ever seen. He caught a sweet scent of roses blowing in on the east wind and turned to it. There was a white globe floating down toward him over the city. When it came to rest in front of him, he genuflected and bowed. The Blessed Virgin stood inside it on a small cloud, clothed in her Fatima raiment.

Light from another Catholic castle shined behind her, giving the impression she was stepping out of a sunrise as she alighted on the roof before Jack. He smiled, feeling emotion stab his throat at seeing such a welcome sight after all he'd just been through. He looked her in the eyes, squinting while his eyes adjusted to the luminosity of her countenance.

"Mother," he whispered.

She took his hands and pulled him up on the cloud with her, into a hug. He returned her squeeze.

"I'm so proud of you, son! You faced the Dragon and stood."

Jack closed his eyes, his emotion manifesting in a single tear that paraded down his cheek. After a full minute, he drew his head back to look at her and saw the cloud had taken them hundreds of feet above Charleston. He'd never felt them move. He looked down, getting an even better view of the divide between the kingdoms of light and darkness, confirming the light now prevailed in more places than the dark. But he could already see night returning to the homes where the dead's choices welcomed it back, as though a bunch of lamps that had been set up sporadically throughout the city were dimming. Between the zombies and the glowing spirits of the living, he felt like he was looking down at a giant ant farm into which someone had thrown lightning bugs.

"Saving souls always comes at the cost of sacrifice," Mary said, bringing his attention back to her.

He saw she'd been looking down at the city with him.

"And the sacrifice the Lord wants of me . . . Is it the forswearing of a future wife and children, to enter the priesthood instead?"

She looked at him. "Would you be willing to make that sacrifice if called?"

He looked back down over the city, not sure how to answer a question as momentous as that, especially when it was the Queen of Heaven and Earth asking him. He thought long and hard. It was no light undertaking. He would have to forgo a future family. Forgo his plan to attend the Citadel and pursue a career in the military. His life would be at the total disposal of Christ's Church . . . which he now knew was Christ's Military. Other than a corporeal marriage, maybe the priesthood wasn't so different from the future he'd already planned. Just the supernatural version of it. He could be a military tactician in the most fateful war with the highest stakes.

He crouched down on the edge of the cloud, observing the shifting borders between the celestial and diabolic kingdoms like a general overlooking a map of battle, planning how to organize his soldiers. He watched the angels, the demons, the heroes, and the sinners all mingling together in the world below. He thought about what he'd seen of Mary's earthly life when she'd lived among them. He thought about the sacrifices she'd had to make to win against evil. How could he do any less?

A charism such as the one he'd been given demanded by its very nature that he help souls get to Heaven with it. What better way could he do that than if he possessed the ability to enact the Sacraments too? But . . . giving up having a family someday. He'd never considered that before. Never once thought about the priesthood in his life. Now, he had to. He didn't want to be like Father Murphy. That was for sure. But, what if he could be like Monsignor Bamonte?

That was an inspiring thought, and a goal he didn't think he'd ever reach. But he wouldn't mind trying. Still . . . to forswear marriage and parenthood . . . Even if he was willing, would he be able? He pondered further. A priest's life was one of moving around. Meeting all kinds of people. All kinds of souls. All kinds of sinners. It would provide him ample opportunity to apply his gift on their behalf, probably far more than he'd find as a family man. But would he be able? Could he make a sacrifice of that high a cost?

A hundred years ago, the Mother of God had descended from Heaven to ask three shepherd children to make sacrifices to help save the people in danger of damnation. Now, the same Mother had descended again, to stand before him and ask the same favor for the same reward. This was his chance to be a hero, as Jesus Christ Himself had asked him to be not an hour before. And what else had Christ said? That to be a hero meant to lay down his life for the good of souls in His Name. Jack had thought He was talking about martyrdom. Maybe He'd meant the priesthood. Losing his own life in the Church so others could regain theirs.

Would he say yes?

Could he say yes?

How could he say no?

He couldn't.

And he'd just made a promise to the Devil. One he intended to keep. If being a priest meant more trouble for him and his demons than his becoming a husband and father, he was down. He stood, never taking his eyes off the half-fallen world below him.

"Too many," he said. "Too many souls fall prey to the Devil and his armies every day. And they don't even know it. They don't even believe in devils."

He looked back into Mary's golden eyes. She was so beautiful, he wanted to weep every time he did. How could he say no to anything she asked of him?

"Too many ignored your warnings a century ago at Fatima. It's time people's eyes were opened to the war they're already involved in . . . Whatever I can do to help you and your Son accomplish that . . . I'll do it."

Mary smiled at him. His heart leapt.

"That's all He'll ever ask of you," she said.

Jack heard water pouring behind him and turned in surprise, knowing it wasn't raining. The cloud had floated them down to the ground without his noticing anymore than he'd noticed its ascent. They were in front of St. John the Baptist's Castle. Mary took his arm.

"Come," she said. "Accompany me into the castle. He'll want to see you."

When he and Mary passed through the holy water, Jack sensed a different mood in the castle than the hustle-and-bustle to which he'd grown accustomed.

The angels and saints were standing still, some lining the balconies along the walls, others perched on statues. All silent. All watching him and Mary. The Virgin's little cloud floated them to the foot of the sanctuary. She knelt on the bottom step, with Jack following her lead. He was surprised when the vines growing along the walls came to life and slid cushions beneath their knees before they hit the floor. Mary took his hand in hers, bowed her head, and closed her eyes.

Jack had a flashback to the first time he'd visited the church through incorporeal sight. He'd knelt with Dathiel in this very spot. If he'd thought he was blessed with great company then, it paled to the one he was privileged to pray with now. He was about to bow his own head and join her when the door of the tabernacle opened before them.

After the myriad times Jack had wished that door would open and God Himself would speak to him, he'd begun to give up on it ever happening. As the shadows shifted over the walls of the castle while the Source of its light stepped across the altar, he got his wish at last. Thanks to the intercession of she who'd first made Him seen in the world, Jack looked for the second time that day at Jesus Christ Unveiled.

He was in His Adult Form this time. He wore a white robe with a red toga draped over His shoulder and held a gold staff crowned with a cross. He shared His Mother's eyes, skin tone, hair color, even her long nose. It was the same face Jack had seen on all the windows and paintings around the kingdom. He'd spent hours almost every night looking into that face, on the picture in his bedroom. He'd knelt before it in prayer, using it as a focal point while he reinforced his home through months of demonic attack. Now that he finally saw it in person, he let his eyes fall, feeling unworthy as he had when he'd met the Deity's Mother.

Christ stepped forward off the altar, and the living vines extended themselves again. They tied themselves together, looking like strings twisting into rope, which then joined to make thicker ropes. The kind thick enough to tow a barge. These lined themselves into steps for the Lord. Mary rose to her feet and she and her Son kissed on both cheeks. Jack stayed kneeling and bowed before the King and Queen.

He saw the holes in Christ's bare feet before him, red rays shining up from them, contrasting with the tan rays of his skin.

"Rise, Philangelus," Jesus called, His voice matching the one Jack had heard in his locutions this time. He extended a hand, which had a hole in it like His feet. "Let Me have a look at my newest seminarian."

Jack rose to his feet, but kept his head down. He was surprised to find he was taller than the Lord by several inches. He wouldn't have expected that, had he ever thought about what Christ's height might be.

"I'm sorry . . . sorry for doubting Your existence," he whispered, trying to lower his gaze enough to avoid the Lord's eyes, which was awkward with his being taller.

"I'm not. You were valiant in the struggle. It helped you grow. It led you here, to this moment. I'm proud to call you family, Jack."

A smile tore itself across Jack's face. Christ grabbed him by the shoulder, patting his arm like an old friend.

*"There's a smile!"* He exclaimed, hugging him to His side and laughing. "Why so somber? The demons are gone. You can relax now."

Jack was shocked, not expecting Christ to seem so down-to-earth. Gabriel hadn't been joking in his description of His sense of humor. He looked Him in the eyes.

"Sorry," he said.

"You already told me that. No need to apologize when there's nothing to apologize for."

Jack almost said it again. "Sorr—ah," he paused. "Thank you for everything you've given me. Especially for incorporeal sight!"

"You're very welcome! But gratitude's also due to Mom here." He nodded toward Mary. "She's the one who asked the charism for you."

"Thank you, Mother," Jack nodded.

Mary smiled at him.

"I don't know if I'd have been able to accept divine faith without it."

"You would have," Mary said. "Your gift wasn't given for that purpose alone. Jesus and I have other designs for your life. It will aid you in fulfilling them."

"The priesthood," Jack said, turning to Christ, Who still had an arm around him. "I'm guessing that's the destiny the angels kept mentioning You had planned for me?"

"Maybe," Jesus said, giving a half-smile that reminded Jack of Dathiel's. "But whichever vocational state you discern My voice calling you into, trust there will be great demands put on your shoulders." His face went more serious. "The destiny I've set for you isn't always going to be an easy one."

Jack was silent, exchanging a long look with the Christ before nodding his assent. "Anything you care to tell me about it now?"

"Yes, there is. That's why I've come out today. I've something to show you." He turned and walked up the vine steps to the altar looking back at Jack and beckoning. "Come up here."

"You want me to stand on the altar with you?"

Jesus smiled. "If it doesn't offend your sensibilities."

Jack looked at Mary. She just waved a hand toward her Divine Son.

"Do whatever *He* tells you."

She kissed his forehead, and he stepped up next to Christ. The Deity put a hand on his shoulder, facing the open tabernacle with him. It was big enough to fit Jack inside it if he ducked his head.

"Step through," Jesus said.

*"What?"* Jack looked at Him. "Into Your tabernacle? I shouldn't even touch it!"

Jesus tilted His head. "Who're you talking to here? You have my permission today."

Christ nudged him onward, and Jack stepped up to the little house. He couldn't see to the back of it. He couldn't see much of anything inside it, the gold of the interior was shining so bright.

"Once you're inside, look for the smallest of the white doors. It shouldn't take you long to find. What you see when you step through it you will have to work out for yourself, with fear and trembling."

# CHAPTER XXXVII
## SATAN'S CENTURY

Jack wanted to look back at Christ with raised eyebrows on hearing His final words, but the door to the tabernacle had already swung shut behind him.

It was so bright inside he had to close his eyes and feel in front of him for the back of the little house. He didn't find it. After walking more than five steps, he started wondering just how far back it went. He reached out for the walls instead. He didn't feel them either. Impossible! The tabernacle was bigger through his charism, but not so big he shouldn't be able to touch at least one of the walls with his arms outstretched.

He opened his eyes and found himself in a round room that must have been forty feet in diameter. It looked like it extended upward for eternity. There were stone spiral staircases twisting around each other, going higher and lower than where Jack stood. The most common sight was doors.

There were doors filling every space possible. Staircases leading to doors. Doors lining the walls like windows that could only be reached by flying up to them. Even doors posted along the railings of the staircases. These looked like they led nowhere. Like if someone opened them and stepped through, they'd fall over the side of the stairway. If Jack knew anything about the unpredictability of the mystical world into which he'd awakened last October, he guessed that wouldn't be the case. He turned around to look at the door he'd entered through and confirmed his suspicion. It looked similar to the others. He was looking at the inside of the doors to all the tabernacles throughout the world.

A straight staircase across the room from him led into a tunnel lined with more doors. He couldn't see its end, but there was a white twinkle shining out of it, like it was beckoning him. Remembering what Christ had said about the smallest white door, and not seeing any white doors in the room he was in now, he ascended the staircase and followed the light. The hallway looked like it went on for miles. Other tunnels broke off from it on both sides along the way. Some of these twisted out of sight so that Jack couldn't see how far they went. But there was never more than a few feet of space on any wall that was door-free.

He couldn't be sure at first, but he thought the doors were shifting. Or maybe it was the tunnel itself. Either way, something around him was moving. The more he walked down the tunnel he was following, the faster the doors beside him seemed to pass by, like his journey was being hurried for him. He reached the end of the tunnel, exiting into another round room, this one bigger than the last, and the white light twinkled from a tunnel off to his right now.

He didn't know how that was possible. How had he seen it from the first room if it was originating from such an angle through this room? He didn't question it. He'd seen enough strange phenomena through his charism not to do that anymore. He just kept following the winking light. It led him down another tunnel to yet another round room, larger still. In this room lay the white door.

As he'd guessed, it was what had been shining. It was beautiful. It was on the bottom row of doors, smaller than any other he'd seen. He'd have to crawl to fit through it. He crouched down and saw there was an engraving on it. A boat in a stormy sea that was being weighed down on the waves by a giant rock at the foot of the mast keeping the vessel from upending. The door's handle was a carving of two keys in the shape of a cross.

Jack turned it and crawled through, almost screaming at what he saw.

Half a second later, Jack wanted to laugh at the ridiculousness of what had startled him, but in the moment of fear rationality was never present.

Rationality was what returned after, making the moment funny.

The white light Jack had thought was coming from the white door wasn't. It had been shining through the door, from the Blessed Sacrament Himself. The Host was being elevated above the altar out onto which Jack had crawled. He was being held up in the hands of a priest, who was celebrating Mass the same way Monsignor Bamonte had, facing the tabernacle. His position had put his face right in front of Jack's as he'd emerged from the room of doors, their eyes inches apart. That was what had startled him.

The priest's elderly countenance bore an uncanny resemblance to the Emperor's from *Star Wars*. For that half-second, when his face had materialized through the sacramental light, Jack thought he'd come face-to-face with the Lord of the Sith. He'd had stranger experiences at this point. He'd tangled with Dracula and the Wolf Men not four months earlier.

Jack moved to the priest's side. It didn't look like he could see him. His eyes didn't follow. They remained on the Host, which he put down to elevate the

Chalice of the Precious Blood next. Jack let out a loud breath, relieved at his invisibility. It had been enough of a scare for him. He couldn't imagine how much he'd have scared the priest if he'd seen a glowing, armor-clad warrior crawl out of the tabernacle right when he lifted the Host up in front of him. He'd probably have keeled over from a heart attack then and there, scattering the Lord across the floor.

Jack kept crawling to the side and off the altar, feeling even more awkward being on one while Mass was being celebrated on it. Stepping away from the priest and through his several altar servers, he stopped to get his bearings once among the attendants of the Mass. These were made up of several more priests and—Jack couldn't believe it—several cardinals! He'd never seen one in person, but he knew their clerical colors. And this wasn't his last surprise. As he looked up at the altar he'd just climbed off, he recognized the painting on the wall above it. He'd never known the original was so large. He looked above him at the ceiling to confirm. There he saw what he considered the most famous painting in the room, maybe in the world. He'd crawled out of the tabernacle into a Mass being celebrated in the Sistine Chapel. He was in Vatican City.

He looked around at the clergymen surrounding him again, seeing if any were wearing a white robe. They were all in full robes, but none of them were white. He saw only black clad priests and the cardinals, with their red sashes, buttons, and caps. No bishop in white. He looked again at the celebrant on the altar. He might have been wearing a white robe under his Mass vestments. Jack couldn't tell for sure. But the celebrant couldn't be the pope. Jack had gotten a close look at his face when he'd crawled in through the tabernacle—a closer look than he'd have cared for—and it wasn't the pope's face. At least, not the current one's.

Jack took an even closer look at the clothing of those standing around him. They didn't seem to mind. It appeared he was invisible to everyone in the room like he'd been in his locutions. The priests' and cardinals' clothing did look a little different from how Jack thought the modern ones dressed, but he couldn't be certain. He was no expert in clerical attire. Other than Monsignor Bamonte, he'd seldom seen any clad in a full robe. Maybe the man celebrating Mass was a pope from a different time period. Maybe he was seeing something from the past, or even something prophetic, from the future.

Giving up on figuring it out, he decided just to pay attention to everything that happened. He knew Christ wanted to show him something by what he was seeing. Something that had to do with his mysterious destiny. It must be important if He'd sent him into the Sistine Chapel to find out.

Nothing out of the ordinary occurred. At least, not out of the ordinary for what Jack was accustomed to see at Mass. The celebrant brought Communion down for everyone and they lined up along a railing at the foot of the sanctuary.

Still nothing of significance happened. Jack took the opportunity to take in the room. He'd never been to the Vatican. The collection of paintings on the walls and ceiling seemed to have no end. Michelangelo had been an extraordinary master of his craft.

The history of the world, from its beginning, to its climax, to its end, spread out before him. Mystics, martyrs, sinners, kings, traitors, prophets, pagan oracles, the old, the young, Mary, Christ. All gathered under one ceiling. Sanctity, sexuality, violence, peace, the rise of empires, the fall of empires, the war of angels and demons, the creation of the world, its condemnation, its Redemption, its Last Judgment, Genesis and Apocalypse. All of time and a glimpse of eternity, present in one room. The awe, horror, and joy of it flowed through Jack's mind, and his soul glowed brighter. He welcomed the feeling, smiling, wondering all the more what part in the drama the Lord of History had reserved for him.

He stared up at the creation painting on the ceiling that had identified for him where he was. The Father, His angels beneath His arms, stretched forth His hand to form Adam on Earth. Adam reached back toward the Father from the world. The forefingers almost touched. Jack was reminded of what he'd seen at the Visitation, when the unborn John the Baptist had reached from inside his mother's womb for his Cousin in another womb.

He shifted his gaze to the giant painting above the altar again. The Final Judgment. Christ was painted to look like Adam from the creation painting. Mary sat beneath His right arm, much as Eve rested below the Father's left in the creation painting. The angels blew trumpets and collected saints. The demons fled, some dragging damned souls with them to the Abyss painted at the bottom above the altar. One of the demons, a ferryman, beat the human sinners into a boat with a paddle to take them on their journey to the Underworld.

Jack looked closer at Mary. She was looking down to her right. He tried to trace the trajectory of her gaze to see what—of all that was happening in the painting—held the Mother of God's attention most. His own gaze landed on an angel below her. The celestial intelligence was pulling two souls up onto his cloud with a beaded rope, rescuing them from the damnation below them. Jack had seen copies of Michelangelo's Last Judgment before, but he'd never known the Rosary was part of it. Was that the message Christ wanted him to get out of his visit to the chapel today? Keep praying the Rosary so you can help the angels rescue souls from Hell? If so, it was enough for him. He didn't need to know more about his future than that.

The celebrant finished giving out Communion and completed the Mass. Still nothing out of the ordinary occurred. Jack saw he'd been right in his suspicion about the celebrant himself. After he'd divested and returned to the chapel, he wore a white robe and cap. He was a pope.

The pontiff gathered with the cardinals near the center of the chapel, while one of the priests present began celebrating his own Mass on the altar below the Final Judgment. Jack stepped nearer to listen to what the cardinals and bishop of Rome were saying, wondering if it was their conversation Christ wanted him to hear. But they were speaking Italian and the locution wasn't translating their words for him like the others had.

They spoke in hushed tones for half an hour, the priest on the altar nearly finished his own Mass. Still, nothing of significance had happened. Jack was beginning to wonder how long he was supposed to wait around. Maybe he was supposed to do something. Maybe go somewhere else in the Vatican.

Then something happened.

The pope straightened, looking up from his conference with the cardinals at the altar where the Mass celebrant was elevating the Host at consecration, his face turning pale, his expression one of mixed wonder and horror.

Jack looked up with him. He'd heard it too, although it looked like no one else in the chapel had. The roar of a lion that soon became a more humanoid scream of pain and disgust. At the bottom right corner of the Last Judgment there was a rabbit-eared devil pictured standing in the midst of other demons, not unlike the pope surrounded by his cardinals at the moment. He was naked and had a serpent wrapped around his form that was latched onto his penis. This figure on the painting moved. Or so Jack thought it had at first. After a moment, he realized something was moving over it. Something growing from the shadows in the corner of the room beside it.

A figure cloaked and hooded in a black robe with glowing red eyes that stretched out six batwings on each side. They soon encompassed the entire bottom of the painting from wall-to-wall. Jack wondered what he was doing there.

Satan stepped onto the altar, something that really got Jack's blood boiling. But he was distracted when the menace yanked his right wings in, away from the center of the altar where the tabernacle sat, as though something had stung them. Jack saw the tabernacle—together with the Host in the celebrant's hands—had transformed into a gold throne upon which sat Christ in His Adult Form.

He looked as Jack had seen him earlier, except now He wore a gold crown on His head bedecked with jewels of all colors. The pope was gazing with intensity at the two figures, his expression at seeing Christ's appearance one of amazement, his witnessing of the Devil's emergence turning his skin paler. The cardinals were approaching him with caution now, looking in the direction he was looking, seeing nothing, then waving their hands before his eyes. The pontiff didn't react. He never even blinked. He wasn't seeing them, only the vision Jack was sharing with him.

Satan's face emerged through the red hue under his hood as he turned his head toward Christ, the glow of his eyes illuminating it. He looked at the enthroned Deity, placed the foot of his trident down on the altar beside his clawed feet, and smiled. His white fangs stood out to Jack and the pope against his red skin.

The Devil couldn't remember the last time he'd spoken to his Enemy. But it seemed, with all he'd set up, it was time again. The dominos were ready to fall into place. This time, he was going to win. This time, he was finally going to prove the folly of the Deity's trust in humanity.

"I can destroy half Your Church," he boasted in his guttural voice.

"You can, can you?" Christ asked in a subdued, gentle tone.

Satan interpreted the tone as boredom. Good.

"And . . ."

The monster paused for effect, knowing he had to be tactful in his proposition. His Enemy was proud and liked to watch. If He was bored, all the better. He would undoubtedly accept his challenge, but only if he presented it in just the right manner.

"If you gave me a little more freedom, I could destroy the whole of it!"

Christ's eyebrows rose. It had worked! Satan had His interest.

"That would be a sight to see," Christ said. "The Church is imperishable. If you're able to destroy her completely, why don't you?"

"To do so, I need more time."

"How much time?"

The Devil looked out at the chapel where Jack, a pope, the cardinals, and the priests all stood. He fought to hold back a satisfied smile. This was going very well! He tilted his head while he looked about, as though appraising the worth of the room.

"Sixty to seventy years would suffice," he said, looking back at the Sacramental Lord, careful to keep his expression neutral, "and a greater power over those who would give themselves to my service. Granted those allowances, I would show you what I could do to Your Militant!"

Christ exchanged a long look with him. Satan didn't avert his eyes. Their red glow stared right back into the Lord's golden orbs. Christ's expression looked pitying and determined to Jack at the same time. The Devil saw only the challenge in them. The King nodded, waving his right hand.

"You are granted the freedom, the time, and the power. Do with them what you will. We will see what happens, and speak again at a later time."

Satan's grin widened. He laughed a harsh cackle, spreading his wings, rising up off the altar. The pope trembled. So did Jack. And it wasn't even his first time being inundated with information by a vision. As the Devil's wings unfurled, Jack and the pontiff saw a story unfold under them. The story of a century.

They were immersed in it, seeing nothing else of their surroundings. The century began with the Devil leading hordes of demons into a gathering on the Eternal City. Jack recognized many of the spirits as the ones who'd helped lead the attack on the Blessed Virgin during her pregnancy. They paraded up and down the streets of Rome as they marched about, even into St. Peter's Square and the halls of the Vatican itself.

Among them were human evildoers helping the demons hold up black banners. Some of these pictured Lucifer with the Archangel Michael crushed under his heel. Others bore the demonic symbol of the horns, serpent, and bones Jack had seen in his nightmares ever since his nightmare about Satan and Mephistopheles' meeting. The men and spirits shouted antipapal slogans together, including a claim that the Devil would rule in the Vatican by the year 2017 and that the pope would serve him as a doorman. More black banners proclaimed the same statement, as did propaganda pamphlets that the hellish horde threw about the streets and at the Vatican's windows. Some of the windows broke since the pamphlets were wrapped around little rocks. It was chaos and it threatened to overwhelm the two visionaries who witnessed it. But the vision was only beginning.

Years blew past them. They saw with what rage the Devil let devastation loose upon the Church and the world. How he and his minions raved, going around seducing and ravaging all they could get their claws on, in every land. The attack was universal. At the height of the distress, a great light emanated over the heart of the Church just before she was swallowed by the chaos. Michael the Archangel appeared with his own armies under his wings, humans and angels alike. Any who would follow him. Jack recognized the armor of the Rosary on many, but there were other luminescent weapons and armor he'd never seen. Under the Prince of Heaven's command, these armies cast Satan and his followers back into the Abyss of Hell, restoring peace. The whole vision lasted thirteen minutes.

For its duration, the pope stood stock-still and unblinking. When it ended, he collapsed, his face ashen. Several cardinals caught him. When they laid him down on the floor, they feared he was dead. There was no sign of a pulse. His fragile body was stiff. Doctors who'd been summoned by other cardinals soon rushed into the room to look him over, creating a flurry of activity as the cardinals and priests stepped out of their way. They didn't look dressed like modern doctors. Their clothing was archaic.

Jack wondered again what year he was seeing. Part of the vision had spoken of 2017 as the future. So he knew at least some of what he was seeing had to be the past. But was all of it? Had the vision he'd just shared with the pope included things that were yet to happen? Had its sight killed the pontiff? He'd never read of a pope dying after fainting in the Sistine Chapel, not that he'd ever looked up how every pope had died.

The vision's content was terrifying for sure, but Jack had seen his fair share of the terrifying over the past year. This vision didn't shake him as much as it seemed to have shaken the elderly cleric. He guessed he'd had more experiences to get him used to the supernatural dropping into everyday life without warning. More than this poor old man anyway, pope or not.

After a minute of the doctors checking him over, they couldn't find any natural explanation for his trance and fainting. As they were about to lift him and take him to a hospital, the pontiff came to with a gasp when a doctor touched his hand to move it. He still looked frightened, but he rose to his feet faster than any of the cardinals had seen him move in years.

*"Horrible!"* he shrieked, and this time Jack understood him. *"What horrible vision! What horrible things to know! To see!"*

The doctors and clergymen looked confused, and frightened. But, as the pope got his bearings and realized where he was, his own expression of fear was replaced with one of determination. He marched from the room. His friends and assistants followed him. So did Jack.

"Holy Father!" the others called behind the pontiff as he stomped down hallways lined with paintings. *"Holiness!* Do you feel alright? Do you need anything?"

"No," the pope said without turning or slowing. "Nothing."

He reached his private study and closed himself in. Jack waited with the others. Time sped up. He could tell, because the people around him started moving faster than normal. After half an hour, the pope reemerged carrying two sheets of paper. He handed one to the cardinal closest to him.

"Have copies of this made. I want it sent to every ordinary in the world. It's to be recited at the end of every Low Mass."

The cardinal looked down at what he'd been given, his face one of astonishment. *"Every* Low Mass, holiness? Everywhere?"

"You heard me, eminence," the pope said. "I want it circulated to every parish as soon as possible."

"What just happened in there?" the cardinal asked.

The pope closed his eyes, massaging the side of his head, and shook it. "Not today. I can't speak on it yet. But I will tell you soon. In the meantime, ensure *that,"* he pointed at the paper, "is delivered as ordered. Let not a word of it be altered."

Jack peeked over the cardinal's shoulder to read what was on the paper. It was written in a different language. Probably Italian or Latin. He didn't get a good look before the cardinal tucked it into a pocket, and the locution didn't supply him with a translation.

"Return with me to the Sistine Chapel," someone said, stepping up next to him.

He would have jumped in surprise if not for the tenderness of the voice. Mary had come to him, the white and gold rays of her garments making him squint as they illuminated the room far more than the candles in the alcoves of the walls. Jack wondered if she'd followed him here through the network of doors or just teleported. He didn't care. He was always glad to see her.

She held her arm out from beneath her veil that was hanging down like a cape, and he took it on his. Their surroundings changed, and they were standing back where the visions had taken place. Jack noticed the lighting in the chapel was different. So was the arrangement of the furniture and the paintings. Their colors were brighter, like they were newer. He wondered if they were in the same time period as whatever one he'd been seeing over the last hour or if they'd gone even farther back in time.

Mary released his arm and stepped up to stand at the right of the altar, turning to face the entrance on the far side of the room. Christ was again seated on His gold throne atop the altar. Jack couldn't help but notice the King and Queen's positioning was similar to that on the painting behind them, except this time Christ was sitting while Mary stood. The doors of the entrance opened, and Jack turned to see Michael dragging something behind him into the chapel. It was Satan, still impaled on the giant gold cross of Jack's home cathedral. The Prince of Heaven stalked across the room past Jack and genuflected to his Master and Mistress. While he did, the Devil saw Jack, his expression going from groggy to angry.

Jack figured he wasn't having a vision anymore. The Devil could see him this time. So could everyone else in the room. Michael slung the twelve-winged monster around before his conquerors, and he retched out a disgusted sound from his throat, vomiting black blood onto the floor in front of him. Michael used the cross to hold him up off the floor, dangling his feet above it, and grabbed him by the hair with his free hand. This not only kept him pulled backward and impaled on the cross, but forced him to face Jesus and Mary. He averted his eyes from them, staring at the corner of the room from where Jack had seen him emerge before.

"What's the matter, Accuser?" Jesus asked in a quiet but stern tone.

Satan said nothing. Jack found himself holding his breath for the confrontation. The only sound was the dripping of black blood onto the floor from the Devil's wounds and mouth.

"Were you not even going to approach of your own accord this time?" Christ asked. "You needed Michael to come and fetch you?"

Satan looked at him now, his dark pupils expanding to cover his eyes as he snarled. Christ raised His right hand off His armrest, and the Devil's growl was silenced like a dog whose chain had just been yanked.

"You claimed you needed only sixty to seventy years to destroy My Bride," Christ said. "Yet your empire warred against her sixty-seven, falling in but seven once the Ark of the Covenant was carried into the battle. I've even bequeathed you thirty-three more years, allowing you a full century of war. My Bride lives on . . . What now do you have to say, My fallen star? What now is your boast?"

Satan said nothing, writhing on the cross, flailing his legs and pulling on its head to get free. Michael held him fast. Christ said no more. It was Mary who stepped forward next. Jack hadn't thought it possible, but the Devil shot her a look of abhorrence greater than the one he'd thrown at her Son. The Queen's own countenance reminded Jack of the expression she'd worn in battle during his second locution. He again found himself glad he was on her side.

"You claimed the power to destroy my Son's Church?" she demanded. "I will show you and all the world the heart of a true Morning Star. In a shadow of the time you boasted to need, I will destroy yours! You know my chosen number. When as many years have unfolded, I will act, and your temple will fall in but three."

She turned to step back up to Christ's side, but paused, turning to the Devil one last time.

"Beware my Epitheta," she warned.

Michael turned and shot Jack a half-smile, winking again, before swinging the impaled Satan around in a full circle. He let the monster's hair go at just the right moment. The Devil was hurled off the cross toward the shadow in the right corner of the room from which he'd come in the vision. The Evil One half-screamed in terror, half-roared in fury as he fell into the shadow and disappeared.

Michael slung the cross around toward Jack. Jack hadn't been ready for the throw and took the full weight of the cross in his chest, knocking him backward off his feet. But he didn't fall to the ground. He fell backward for what felt like several meters, the room in front of him disappearing until he landed on his back looking up at open sky. He sat up, shifting the cross over his shoulder. He was back on the roof of St. John the Baptist's Castle next to the steeple.

After sitting there several moments, trying to make sense of everything he'd just seen, he stood up, lifting the cross with him. He flew it up to the top of the steeple and restored it to its rightful place, as he supposed Michael had intended. He hung off its side by a hand, looking out over the divided horizon.

His destiny was still a mystery to him.

# CHAPTER XXXVIII
## THE DEBATE

Wando High looked like a post-apocalyptic ghost town.

Jack had even had to lift the gate out of his carriage's way, as it had stopped automatically opening. With their chieftain missing for a month now, a good portion of the demons had flown the coup. Those who remained had been fighting among themselves over who was going to take up the leadership role. No one was very agreeable as to who it should be. Jack observed several factions had risen up, each supporting a different candidate. They were warring against each other in the central bastion as he entered it for class. Satan and Racism must have been a little too busy to bother appointing a new leader to this "backwater outpost," as they called it.

Passing argument after argument in the hallways, Jack would have laughed at the monsters' inability to come to an agreement if he had the energy. As it was, he hadn't gotten much sleep over the weekend. He'd stayed up all night Saturday, energized over everything he'd seen. He hadn't told anyone about his decision to pursue the priesthood yet. He was still digesting it himself. He wanted to talk about it with the monsignor first. Plus, now that he knew incorporeal sight was real, he had to figure out how to break that to his family too.

He descended a dark spiral stairwell into the dungeon. A few of the demons who looked up and saw him coming ran away. Others whispered among themselves as he passed, shying away from the glow of his suit. Before the weekend, rumors had floated that Jack might be the reason Delusion was missing. With the stories coming out of Charleston about what had happened there Saturday night, those who remained at Wando knew it must be true. If this teenager had bested Mephistopheles, their chieftain wouldn't have stood a chance. If all the stories about what happened in Charleston were to be believed, Jack Dacre had even stood up to Satan himself. Whether that last part was accurate or not, none of Wando's possessors were going to approach Jack to find out. They were scared to raise a ruckus over anything when he was around, afraid they'd draw his attention.

Jack had fun with their fear. He'd randomly shoot a glance at gathered packs just to watch them scuttle like cockroaches he'd turned a light toward. When he walked into Mr. Wilkerson's classroom for physics, the reaction was no different. The few demons present in the medieval laboratory scampered down into holes in the floor like spooked rabbits. Some even dove into the fires burning on the ground, preferring to pass through their heat to what the Philangelus might do to them. One imp hadn't noticed his arrival. He was busy scratching something into one of the lab tables between the cobwebbed jars of green and red liquids. Jack figured it would be a pentagram. That was the demons' most common form of graffiti. But it wasn't. It was the symbol from his visions and nightmares. The horns, serpent, and bones.

Annoyed at seeing it again, Jack blasted the entire counter away with the little sprite before he'd even known he was under attack. The glass jars shattered and the wood of the table splintered, evaporating into dust from the heat of Jack's prayer. The imp never had the chance to scream out before it was gone. The warrior took his seat at the back in front of the new crater he'd made in the floor, satisfied.

While he shoved the chains on his oversized chair aside to get comfortable, Naomi walked into the room. This was the first time her sight didn't bother him since their breakup. He smiled at that. She smiled back, and he guessed she'd thought he'd been smiling at her. He dropped his grin and looked the other way. Paviel nodded at him, and he nodded back.

"I guess you always knew we'd end in a breakup, huh?" Jack asked him.

The guardian angel shrugged, giving Jack a side-smile. Jack chuckled. Even his ex-girlfriend's guide wasn't going to say anything that might give away his vocation. It was for him to discern over time.

"Alright, e'erybody shut up now," Mr. Wilkerson called the class to attention, walking into the room.

No demons accompanied him, and Mephistopheles' mist wasn't there to en-shroud him this time. Jack got the first good look he'd had at the heavyset zombie in months. There was no mistaking it for Mr. Wilkerson. The hair and goatee were the same. The face was the same. There was no flesh rotting off him like so many others. The only differences between his body and soul were the pale skin, raggedy clothes, and empty eye sockets. Jack still didn't know what that implied as far as his ability to discern people's vices was concerned.

"As I hope you all remember," the science instructor started his lesson, "we covered on Friday how the space that contains our sun, Earth, and the other seven planets is a solar system. Our solar system is contained in the Milky Way, which is our galaxy. Our galaxy contains multiple solar systems. And the space that contains the billions of galaxies out there is the universe. So, from the biggest to the smallest," he reiterated, seeing Monday first period faces looking back at him, "the universe contains billions of galaxies within it, which contain billions of solar systems within them." He paused to allow any students diligent enough to copy the information down. "We also covered the Big Bang Theory. But, today, we'll be discussing more about how the universe operates now. Matter's motion through space and time. So—"

*So you'll probably neglect to mention how the movement of the universe is perfectly ordered to sustain life on our one tiny spec in it, just like you neglected to mention the actual person who discovered the Big Bang on Friday,* Jack thought to himself, remembering his lesson on reasons to believe with Monsignor Bamonte the previous week.

Mr. Wilkerson stopped talking, and his soul looked straight at Jack. At least, it would have been, had it possessed eyes. Jack leaned forward in his seat, realizing the teacher had heard his thought. Mr. Wilkerson had never been able to hear him through his charism before. The demons must have been blocking him. But there were none present to block Jack anymore.

"So . . ." the instructor shook off his hesitation and moved on, "if you could all turn to page thirteen in your books. Remember, the Big Bang Theory began with Albert Einstein and his theory of relativity."

That was it! Jack had tolerated listening to Mr. Wilkerson get things wrong for the last time.

"Yes, Mr. Dacre?" the teacher called on his raised hand.

"Don't you mean Father Georges Lemaître?" Jack asked.

"Pardon?"

"The Catholic priest and physicist who actually discovered the Big Bang. The one who first brought it to Einstein's attention. Einstein was skeptical at first. It was Lemaître who convinced him of the theory that the universe began with the expansion of a single primordial atom. Shouldn't we be writing that on our tests Friday?"

*"What the fuck?"* he heard Mr. Wilkerson say in his thoughts.

"Y-yes," the teacher stuttered aloud, "that's correct. But, for our purposes, knowing Einstein's publicizing of it will suffice for its origin."

"Why?" Jack demanded before the teacher could turn back to the board.

Naomi turned to look at him, her expression one of excitement, like the face of a kid who'd just been told Christmas had come early. It bolstered Jack all the more.

"Why not teach us the true origin of the theory? We'd look like idiots later in life if we went around saying Einstein discovered the Big Bang when he didn't."

Several more students turned to look at him now, Becky and Kevin among them.

"Alright," Mr. Wilkerson chuckled. "Fair point. Since you asked, sure, I can elaborate. Georges Lemaître was the first to propose what he called 'the Primeval Atom Theory.' Funny story, it was actually one of his opponents in the field of physics who first called it 'the Big Bang,' as a mockery. That physicist adhered to the opposing view of the Steady State Theory of the universe, which is now rejected by modern astrophysicists and astronomers.

Anyway, like Jack said, Einstein was skeptical at first, but he later called it one of the most beautiful theories he'd ever heard. Lemaître developed his model of the Big Bang based on Einstein's equations of gravity in his theory of relativity though. So," Mr. Wilkerson looked at Jack, "that's why I was saying Einstein's the only one relevant to this course, Jack. If you all remember to put his name on Friday's test, I'll accept the answer. But, if you put Georges Lemaître's, I'll accept that too, I guess."

While the teacher was speaking, Jack had been watching his soul. Its face was displaying very different expressions than his body's. They were more telling of his attitude on the subject. He looked disgusted with Jack, and afraid of him. The eyeless face kept shooting either angry or timid looks his way.

"Keep pushing," Paviel advised next to Jack.

"Seems the only acceptable answer to me," Jack challenged, "seeing as the theory originated with him and Einstein only helped him refine and publicize it later."

Jenny, Brad, April, Darris, and the rest of the class turned to look at him now. The argumentativeness in his tone was obvious. It couldn't be glossed over by the teacher this time.

"I see your point . . ." Mr. Wilkerson said, letting the annoyance in his own tone be heard. "Was there something you needed to get off your chest, Jack?"

Corporeally, the teacher appeared angry. Incorporeally, Jack saw how nervous he'd made him by his objections.

"He's not used to being challenged by someone who's both outspoken and knowledgeable," Paviel informed. "He's never met a Christian like you. He's only ever argued with those who throw Scripture at him to defend their positions. This has made him think there are no rational believers. Keep pushing."

Jack bowed his head to the angel and obeyed, all fear of public debate gone. With how tired he was, and with all he'd been through that weekend, he had no fucks left to give about speaking up in front of a crowd on a controversial subject.

"Just wondering why you tried to hide the fact that a Catholic priest is responsible for one of the most impactful discoveries in the history of astrophysics," he said. "And, I was thinking, maybe it has something to do with the fact you mock and belittle Christianity every chance you get."

Every student in the room was looking from Jack to Mr. Wilkerson. Naomi, Becky, and Darris had grins on their faces, enjoying the controversy that was brewing, waiting to see what would happen.

"Well," the instructor said, "I apologize if I've offended—"

"Oh yes, you've done that plenty," Jack cut him off. "But I'm not asking for an apology. Had your assertions been correct, you shouldn't be required to give one. My being offended would be my problem in that case. No, I'm more interested in discussing your claims themselves. Facts are what matter in science, not how people feel about them, and I've found your atheistic comments to be fallacious."

The room was silent, until Mr. Wilkerson found his voice again.

"Well, we can talk after class if you wish to—"

"Why?" Jack interrupted again. "Maybe you misunderstand. It's not a theological debate I'm interested in. It's a scientific one. And this is science class. Isn't this the time and place to discuss science?"

"Well still, like I said, we can speak after class if you like."

"Why? Why rob my classmates of the opportunity to learn the facts too? Why should getting to the truth be a private discussion between you and me?"

Paviel whispered an instruction in his ear, and Jack did as he advised.

He smiled at the teacher and said, "Are you afraid I'll embarrass you by outsmarting you in your own field?"

A few students laughed. Others looked toward Mr. Wilkerson with horrified expressions on their faces. Still others looked at him with challenging expressions, wanting to see how this discussion Jack was suggesting would play out and not wanting to be excluded from it. But Jack wasn't paying attention to any of that.

He was too busy handling the effect of his comment through incorporeal sight. A stench of burning flesh had wafted toward him from the science teacher's soul, mercifully blocked for the most part by his mask, and the zombie had run at him, moaning a sound Jack guessed was supposed to be a cry of rage. The corpse was slow and clumsy. Jack was on his feet and had shoved him back to the front of the room in an instant without exerting much strength. The teacher's spirit stumbled backward while he fumbled to find what to say out loud. He'd never had to deal with something like this before, especially from a quiet student like Jack Dacre.

"This isn't the time or place for this, Jack," he managed at last.

*"Oh, come on!"* Kevin piped up. "He just told you why it is!"

Jack looked at Kevin, feeling like they'd just connected better than they had since learning of Chuck's suicide.

Mr. Wilkerson looked at him too, bewildered by what was happening. "Look, if you all want to stay a few minutes after class, you're welcome to."

"We have another class after this," Jack objected, "and only so much time to get to it. We're in science class now, sir. Why are you so averse to discussing it? Weren't we already reviewing? I'd like to review some of what you've taught us. Or is school no longer the place to ask questions and be enlightened?"

Jack spoke his next words through incorporeal sight alone. "Unless you feel you're unqualified to debate a seventeen-year-old high school student."

Another whiff of burning flesh wafted over to him, as Mr. Wilkerson's nostrils physically flared. "Frankly, Mr. Dacre, you're coming across belligerent and threatening."

"You say belligerent. I say forthright. The same way empirical science is, presenting reality to us regardless of how we feel about it. And I'm not threatening you, sir. I'm disputing you intellectually."

*"Shrewd, smart-ass little shit!"* the teacher thought.

Jack's soul stepped up to the front of the room, standing before the zombie. "Yes," he said through his charism, reaching out and flicking the corpse's forehead. "And calling your bluff."

The zombie moaned again. Jack thought he was trying to snarl.

"What exactly is it you want to discuss, Jack?" the teacher asked aloud.

"How empirical science provides ample evidence for the existence of a Higher Being. The same kind of Being Whose existence you've claimed it disproves."

"And you think that's not a theological debate?"

"Not at all, sir. I won't be throwing the Bible at you. The claims I've heard you make don't require anything other than logic and scientific observations to discredit. And, since we're in physics class at the moment, and I don't want to waste your or the other students' time, I'll keep the discussion with physics."

*"You've almost got him!"* said a welcome voice from the doorway to the dungeon.

Jack turned to see Dathiel. He stepped inside, leading Joan, Benedict, and Gabriel behind him. Jack's heart leapt at seeing his friends.

"Time this trafficker of false teachings is put in his place," Benedict declared.

Jack smiled beneath his mask as the saints and angels spread out across the laboratory. Benedict stood next to Brad. Joan with Jenny. Gabriel with April and Darris, while Paviel began illuminating Kevin, Becky, and Naomi. Dathiel stood with Jack at the front of the room, facing Wyatt Wilkerson. Jack stared down the eyeless corpse that resembled his teacher, as Dathiel whispered into his ear from behind. He stepped up to his opponent to repeat his guardian's words.

"You really think he'll be able to make you look like a fool in front of your class by *scientifically demonstrating* the existence of God?" Jack whispered into the teacher's mind. "He's just a student! And he's made you look like a fool so far by calling out your sidestepping for what it is. If you shut this thing down now, it'll just make him look like a martyr or some shit. I say, give him a chance to embarrass himself. What could it harm but to prove you right and teach him not to disrupt class like this again? Quit deflecting and let him say whatever it is he wants to say. He is asking for it. Use his own logic to humiliate him like you always do. You really think he can outsmart *you?*"

Jack stepped back and watched his manipulation take effect. The teacher slouched back to sit on his desk both corporeally and incorporeally, feeling more comfortable. He smiled.

"Alright, Jack." He spread an arm out in a gesture of invitation before the class. "What did you want to say?"

"Have at him," Dathiel commanded, beginning the debate that had been so long in coming.

Jack stepped toward the slouching zombie, who laughed. It sounded like sandpaper being scraped across concrete.

"But you should know," the teacher said in his mind, "I've debated your kind before on scientific topics, and you're never able to answer any of my objections."

"You've never debated my kind," Jack said in his metallic voice.

The zombie shuddered at the sound of it, hunching into a less confident stance.

"Much," Jack said aloud, jabbing the teacher's soul as he did.

He shocked its chest with a small bolt from his glove's fingertips, attempting to defibrillate the zombie back to Truth.

"First, let me ask, where is all this supposed proof you have that God doesn't exist, sir? What clinical evaluation or trial did He fail to show up for that proved beyond doubt He wasn't there?"

Mr. Wilkerson said nothing, still feeling the effects of Jack's shock. A cold sweat had physically broken across his forehead. He felt under duress. Some of the other students chuckled, seeing Jack's point.

"You see?" Jack said, after the teacher failed to give an answer, giving his soul another jolt. "Your belief in atheism is as much a matter of faith as Catholicism is for me, sir. Empirical sciences like biology, chemistry, and physics are concerned with the natural world. They can't do anything to test or explain things about the supernatural realm if there is one. It's beyond their scope.

God, angels, and demons can't be tested in a lab experiment. If they exist, they're intangible and invisible. Beyond the physical laws of this universe. That's what believers profess to believe about them. So, if the empirical sciences find no physical evidence of them, that does nothing to prove they're not there. It just aligns with what we profess about them."

The zombie teacher shuffled off the side of the desk, trying to get away from Jack, then changed its mind halfway across the room and ran back toward him, taking a swing at his face.

"But if it's impossible to test a hypothesis through experiments and observations, then it's not technically a scientific hypothesis," Mr. Wilkerson countered in front of the class. "So the question 'does God exist' isn't a scientific one."

The punch never connected with Jack's face. He dodged, sticking his boot out and tripping the zombie on his own words.

"Exactly! Thank you!" Jack praised aloud. "So, you admit empirical science can neither prove nor disprove the existence of God, because it's not even a matter for scientists to study. It's inherently a matter for philosophers and theologians to spin their wheels over. Which means all your claims that science has disproved God's existence were a mistake on your part."

Mr. Wilkerson pursed his lips while his soul face-planted next to Jack's.

Several of the students let out a long, "Ooooh," in Jack's favor.

The zombie struggled back to his feet. "Well, if God did exist," his mind and body echoed together, "don't you think there'd be *some* evidence He was there?"

"Oh I've found there's plenty, sir, if one bothers to look."

Mr. Wilkerson gave him a skeptical smile. "Really?"

Jack smiled politely back. "Yes. But, just to make sure we're on the same page, I'm guessing the evidence you'd want is the Giant Figure in the sky Who opens up the clouds and wishes a good morning and good night to the world every day? Something or Someone you could wrap your mind around?"

"That would help," the teacher said.

A few students laughed, and Jack laughed with them.

"Yes, I suppose it might. Though I wouldn't call that definitive proof of God's existence, because that wouldn't necessarily be God. Not the God Catholics like myself profess to believe in. What we call God is an Infinite, and therefore Incomprehensible, Being that a finite intelligence like the human mind could never fully wrap itself around. A Being a limited human science could also never hope to fully comprehend. If we could fully grasp the man in the sky, he wouldn't be what I call 'God.'"

The teacher had been silenced into thought again.

"And given that idea of God, by the way," Jack pressed, "skeptics shouldn't be pouting about how little we understand of Him, but how much we have had revealed to us about Him."

The zombie scurried backward over its desk and climbed under it.

Outwardly, Mr. Wilkerson chuckled. "Where is it He's revealed Himself in the world, Jack? I've never seen him. Have you?" He glanced around at the other students. "Has anyone?"

Some of them laughed, and Jack laughed with them again.

"A trick question, wouldn't you say, sir?"

Everyone looked at him, the teacher with an annoyed expression.

"If any of us said they had, you'd automatically label us schizophrenic, don't you think?"

The students laughed at him this time, while Mr. Wilkerson allowed himself a chuckle with them. But Jack could read the apprehension he was trying to disguise behind it, even through his physical senses. Besides that, his soul was still hiding under its desk like a frightened dog in its crate.

"Touché," the teacher said. "Still, the point is, if God existed and wanted us to believe in Him, why would He choose to be invisible and intangible like you said?

Why wouldn't he just appear to disprove atheism?"

"If He did appear to you, do you think that'd be enough, or would you just think *you'd* contracted schizophrenia, or a brain tumor, or something like that?"

More students laughed. Others looked at Mr. Wilkerson with honest curiosity. The teacher himself smiled and waved a hand.

"Again, touché. But, the nature of the proof aside, first there has to be some. And there aren't any documented cases of supernatural phenomena occurring anywhere outside of books written thousands of years ago by the ignorant and superstitious."

Jack shook his head, pursing his lips. "No. That's not true," he said, his voice as calm and even as ever.

As he spoke, his soul ripped the desk in front of it from the floor, tossing it against the far wall where it splintered to pieces. The zombie was again exposed to the light of Jack's armor from which it had hidden. It trembled on the floor in a fetal position. Looking down, Jack felt pity for the poor creature, so afraid that, if it acknowledged the light before it, the change in its worldview would break its mind rather than bring it to life. But Jack wasn't about to stop admonishing it now. All the other students were not only looking at him corporeally, their souls were looking at him too. And the saints and angels present were shining their own light down on them, with some of the dead hungrily accepting it.

"You've joked on several occasions about how modern society would've documented miracles if they'd happened," Jack said. "But, have you ever gone looking for documentation, or have you just been assuming none exists?"

The teacher again said nothing.

"If you'd checked, you might have come across reports on the events at Fatima, Portugal."

"Fatima, Portugal," the teacher repeated, his tone making it unclear as to whether it was a question or just an echo of what Jack had said, while his mind attempted to latch onto something that made sense to it.

Jack could see his soul was beginning to go mad, hitting the floor like a toddler throwing a tantrum.

"Don't worry about that," Dathiel said. "This one has to be broken down first, like you did. Push through it."

"Yes, Fatima," Jack said. "A little town where apparitions of an angel and even the Mother of Jesus Christ took place in 1917, in front of multiple witnesses. There's plenty recorded about those events. There was even a public miracle, witnessed by more than seventy thousand people, where the Virgin Mary made the sun spin around and shoot across the sky for twelve minutes. The crowd of thousands who saw it included many atheists, by the way. Journalists who'd come to disprove the apparitions were happening. They ended up writing articles about the miracle they saw. You can find the documentation online and in the Library of Congress."

Several students gave him either astonished or skeptical looks. Gabriel was blowing lightly over the horn in his hand, his lips almost touching it. The curious souls were moved by its sound and presented themselves closer to the blessed spirits' illuminations.

"That's one example," Jack said, prodding the zombie crouched before him with the tip of his boot. "If you read the lives of Catholic saints, you'd find more. Tons of reports of miracles occurring throughout the centuries, including the twentieth. The point is, supernatural phenomena didn't cease after biblical times like you've said. And they didn't cease with the dawn of modernity either. But, I promised I wouldn't get theological, so I won't say more about that. Besides, I don't need the miracles to dispute atheism.

Since the Real God transcends matter, seeing or touching Him isn't necessary to demonstrate His presence. And," Jack stooped down to coax the dead soul to its feet, "because of that, a skeptic is justified in asking if He exists. I'd just ask that he be honest in his pursuit of truth from that point. I've found myself that, though God transcends matter, He still left His fingerprint on it as its Creator. And a close, unbiased examination of it reveals this fingerprint."

"Okay," the instructor challenged, his soul shoving Jack away as it rose to its full height, "so tell us, where is all this evidence for God in science?"

Jack slammed the obstinate soul back against the stone wall where the white board would have been, defibrillating it on the chest again.

"Beginning at the beginning—the Big Bang," the current in Jack's gauntlets electrified the spirit. "I've found it lines up with the Christian belief in creation in every major way. As you explained in our last class, the Bang was a cataclysmic explosion approximately thirteen point seven billion years ago that resulted in the existence of the universe we know. That was backed up by astronomer Edwin Hubbell when he invented his Hubbell telescope and saw that the galaxies are moving away from each other at an increasingly faster rate.

What you didn't mention were Father Lemaître's and Einstein's more apt description of the Big Bang as more of an expansion of space, energy, matter, and time than an explosion. Explosions are chaotic, uncontrolled events. Astrophysicists and cosmologists find the universe to be incredibly well-ordered and predictable, governed by laws. The laws of physics. All indicating the Bang was a finely calibrated event.

The *reason* these laws exist in the universe has not been answered by science, by the way, but I'll come back to that in a second. For now, it's enough to point out that, if the Big Bang was an expansion of the material universe in all directions, it logically follows it all started from a definite point. Physicists have concluded this point as the beginning of time. You can't say there was any 'before' the Big Bang, because time is a measure of change or movement which began with it."

The teacher's forehead was really sweating now, as Jack continued to shock his soul with his fingertips.

"Until the Bang, nothing physical or temporal existed. When scientists have attempted to determine what caused the event using the laws of physics, they've always encountered a singularity. A point where the laws break down. They've come to admit that Something which transcends temporal existence is what has to suffice as an explanation. So," Jack shoved one last jolt into the zombie's chest, "what the Bible describes as God commanding 'Let there be light' could be its way of describing the astronomical event we call 'the Big Bang.'"

Mr. Wilkerson's lips were tight, his expression one of strain. He'd been attempting to push Jack's spirit off his the whole time, with no success. On the other hand, most of the students in the room were staring at him with expressions of fascination or admiration. Some still wore looks of skepticism. But, when they turned to the teacher, ready for him to break down Jack's arguments, they found nothing but hesitation and trepidation in their mascot. The saints and angels in the room defibrillated their souls in their moments of doubt.

"In other words, sir," Jack said, "the Big Bang shows the universe came into existence from nothing, just like Christianity teaches. Science lines up with Genesis."

He let his words hang in the air, as he let the zombie he'd been shocking fall to the floor at his feet. It didn't move, and Jack kicked it.

"Get up," he commanded through his charism. "I'm far from done with you yet."

He heard a hiss to his right and looked over to see demons gathered outside the door. They were looking in at the saints with hesitation. The bigger ones coaxed the smaller ones on, determined to put a stop to what Jack was doing. They charged into the room. The leader was a spider-like demon not unlike the one who'd mocked Jack the first time he'd seen this dungeon through his gift. It was clicking its pincers at him in fury. Several of the other demons had arachnid features too, some of them appearing no different from real spiders, but two feet wide in length. Jack held up a hand, signaling the saints to stay and protect the other students. He'd put down the wretches himself. He wanted a crack at the big one.

"Also," he went on aloud, striking the leader with his electrified gauntlet and sending it flying back atop its underlings, "the six periods of creation it talks about show that God created things in a specific order," he stomped one of the two-foot wide spiders, crushing its middle with his boot. "First the Earth," he stomped another, "then plants," he stomped, "then animals," stomp, "then humans," stomp. "Science lines up with this too," he grabbed a humanoid demon by the neck, spinning the head on its axis and breaking it. "Discoveries tell us the universe developed over periods. First, clouds of hydrogen pulled together by gravity formed stars," he swatted a small flying demon aside. "Some stars exploded and their remnants formed planets," he swatted another. "Then sentient life developed on one of them, beginning with simple organisms and evolving into complex ones," he swatted another. "First plants," another, "then sea animals," another, "then land animals, and eventually intelligent land animals. So tell me, sir," Jack grabbed the lead demon again, who was the last one standing, "where is this discrepancy between my religion and science you've so often referenced? You say science disproves Christianity. But," Jack grabbed the demon's mouth by the pincers and tore the head from the body, tossing it aside, "after looking into it, I've found it continuously confirms it."

The teacher said nothing, his spirit still collapsed on the floor by the wall. Out of his peripheral vision, Jack saw Paviel prompt Becky to say something he'd read on her mind.

"Could all that be coincidence though?"

Jack looked at her and shrugged. "It could. But how long can a person keep chalking things up to 'pure coincidence,'" he made quotation marks with his fingers, "before they have to acknowledge intelligent, unseen forces are at work influencing outcomes? Personally, I've noticed that, the more I pay attention, the more coincidences seem to happen when people pray." He raised his eyebrows and tilted his head. As he did, he turned his soul's head and shot bolts of lightning across the room over Becky's soul and several others'. "Don't take my word for it though. I'm already a believer. So I must be biased, right?"

Becky and the others smiled, experiencing the effect of his incorporeal activity.

"Go to the scientists," Jack said. "They've drawn these conclusions for themselves. British physicist Edmund T. Whitaker wrote that there's no ground for supposing matter and energy existed before and were then suddenly galvanized into action. He said it's simpler to postulate creation out of nothing by a divine will. Allan Sandage, one of the world's leading astronomers, said we can't understand the universe in any clear way without the supernatural. And world-renowned astrophysicist Robert Jastrow, who was a former agnostic, wrote that the essential elements in the astronomical account and the Biblical account of Genesis are the same. He said the chain of events leading to man commenced suddenly and sharply at a definitive point in time in a flash of light and energy.

He also said that astronomers are now finding they've painted themselves into a corner, because they've proven by their own methods that the world began abruptly in an act of creation that you can trace the seeds of every star, planet, and living thing in the cosmos to. That this moment happened as a result of forces they can't offer a natural explanation for. And that what people would call supernatural forces at work is now, in his opinion, a scientifically proven fact."

Jack stopped shooting the lightning to see the effect it had on his classmates' souls. Instead of burning and smoking from resistance like Mr. Wilkerson's was, theirs were looking healthier, like they'd been brought closer to the threshold of life. They were bathing in the light shining from Jack's armor and the supernatural creatures around them. They were all quiet, digesting what Jack had said.

"These aren't popes or preachers I'm quoting here," Jack said. "They're non-religious scientists. To quote Jastrow again, he said that for the scientist who's lived by his faith in the power of reason, the story of the universe's origin ends like a bad dream. Such a scientist scales the mountain of ignorance. He's about to conquer the highest peak, and when he pulls himself over the final rock, he's greeted by a band of theologians who've been sitting there for centuries."

Several students sat back in their chairs. Some of them looked confused, like they hadn't kept up with Jack. But all of them wore expressions of astonishment, confused or not. Jack thought it must be what his face looked like when he sat in the presence of Monsignor Bamonte. Mr. Wilkerson's soul roused and stood back up. Jack looked at him, electrifying his gloves' fingers, ready for the fight to continue if it must.

"But," the zombie moved forward to strike, "as Miss Hall said, these parallels between science and religion could be coincidence," the corpse punched Jack, who didn't bother to block it. "They're not enough to convince atheists," the zombie punched again. "Otherwise, there wouldn't be any," he kicked. "Personally," the zombie joined its hands to slam them down atop Jack's head, "I find it highly convenient that the statements in Genesis are ambiguous enough to be interpreted pretty broadly!"

The skeptical students who'd been waiting for Mr. Wilkerson to come up with some brilliant counterpoint nodded their heads. Others turned to see if Jack could best the teacher again. He obliged their curiosity, not having felt any of the zombie's blows through his suit.

"That's because Genesis, like many other parts of the Bible, contains allegory," he backhanded the zombie. "It's written that way on purpose, precisely so it can be interpreted in multiple ways, depending on the need of the reader. For the purposes of this conversation though, I'd answer that, unlike science, which is concerned with how the universe is, Genesis is concerned with why it is. The study of physics deals with the way creation functions. Religion wants to tell us the purpose behind it. Science can't tell you the goodness of the world or the meaning of life. At the same time, Genesis wasn't written as a scientific manual. So it needs the empirical practices to compliment it. Science and religion together help us come to a full understanding of the universe we find ourselves in and our origin as a species."

The zombie went sprawling across the floor from Jack's blow. He watched it struggle to come up with rejoinders and get back up.

*"Come on, Wyatt!"* he heard it encouraging itself. *"How the fuck are you letting this little shit make you out to look like an idiot?"*

"Still," Mr. Wilkerson said aloud, finding his spiritual footing and charging again, "seems too convenient. And saying something's supposed to be convenient doesn't change the fact that it is."

"Then I guess you'll find all the aspects of teleology convenient too," Jack said, absorbing his blow.

*"Oh shit!"* the instructor's soul gasped, stepping back from Jack and trembling.

"Ah, so you know a little about that, huh?" Jack interrogated mentally, stalking forward and shoving the zombie back to the ground. He leaned down over the corpse. "And yet you continued to preach to your students there's no evidence in science for God." He stood and put a boot down on the dead soul's throat. "You call yourself unbiased? You call Christians the pretenders? I'm going to make you wish you never met this Christian, Wyatt."

The zombie moaned under his heel. *"There has to be a way to impressively counter his argumen—"*

"Scientists have discovered evidence of deliberate fine-tuning in the universe," Jack interrupted his thought with a shock running from his glove to his boot, "from the largest stars down to Earth's ecosystem, all designed to enable the evolution and sustaining of organic life."

Jack took his foot off the corpse and turned to the more receptive ones in the dungeon. But the teacher's soul rose to its feet as soon as he'd stepped off it, lunging at him, desperate to shut the debate down. Jack kicked the uproarious soul's feet out from under it, grabbed it, lifted it over his head, and slammed it down on Chuck's empty desk, which collapsed to the floor with it.

"That's what I was talking about when I said all I needed was physics to showcase God's existence," he continued aloud. "It's also what the physicists I quoted were referring to when they spoke of the supernatural being a clear scientific find. Their discoveries render it highly indefensible for any logical person to attribute the existence of life on Earth to a random assortment of atoms anymore."

The instructor's spirit lifted itself onto a wobbling elbow. "I think it's time we wrap this up—"

"What discoveries?" Darris interrupted at Gabriel's prompting.

"We can talk about it later," Mr. Wilkerson insisted, trying to regain control of a situation that had grown entirely out of hand.

"He's talking physics," Kevin said at Paviel's encouragement.

"Yeah," Jenny spoke up at a nudge from Joan. "Why not hear what he has to say?"

*"Yeah!"* Brad rushed to agree with her without Benedict having to persuade him at all.

"We should put it to a vote," Naomi suggested. "Who wants to see the end of the debate?"

Every single student in the class voiced their assent. Jack looked over them through his charism as he stood before them. They were all reaching for the light shining in the darkness of the dungeon from the blessed spirits now. Some might have just been thirsting for controversy, but he could see many were thirsting for the truth. He smiled beneath his mask, almost ready to weep at what was happening, but holding himself together. He'd been granted his moment. He had to stay sharp. He had to carry this through to the end. Physically, he looked Mr. Wilkerson in the eyes. The teacher didn't appear amenable, even with the whole class rallying to Jack's side.

"Honestly, sir, I think everyone's more awake and attentive than they've ever been in first period . . ."

Kevin, Brad, and Darris cheered their agreement. The teacher's zombified spirit rose from the floor, growling and scratching at Jack. Jack didn't have to do anything this time. Dathiel stepped between them. He grabbed the corpse and shoved it to the back of the room, forcing it into Jack's chair, strapping it down with the chains attached to it. The soul looked like a death row prisoner about to be electrocuted. Jack and his teacher had incorporeally switched places from their corporeal positions in the room. Dathiel placed his fist over the zombie's forehead, his blades extending from his wrist bracer. The outer two shot past the corpse's ears, piercing the back of the chair on both sides of its head, holding it in place. The middle two extended just enough that their tips touched the instructor's forehead.

"Move again," Dathiel dared. "Move . . . again."

The zombie stayed still, stifled into silence under the intelligence's influence as, physically, the teacher slouched back on his desk, a defeated look on his face.

"So what's fine-tuning?" Becky asked Jack.

He looked into her savvy chestnut eyes.

"It's when someone plans or tampers with something to make it occur or operate in a specific way. Physicists have found evidence of it throughout the makeup of the universe. They've uncovered a number of constants and conditions that, if altered at all, even by a fraction of a percent, would render life within it impossible."

"Constants and conditions?" Darris asked, he and Brad looking like they were straining to keep up harder than they ever did in school.

"A constant is a letter within a scientific equation that always remains the same or 'constant' no matter what equation it's applied to," Jack said. "The cosmic conditions in the universe are the amounts of matter and energy that were present at its beginning. All of them were almost incalculably fine-tuned so as to ensure life would evolve. And scientists have been forced to ask, how and why? They've concluded that a universe with constants and conditions that permits life instead of prohibiting it should have been extremely unlikely. And yet, life occurred."

Brad and Darris didn't look like they'd kept up fully, just enough to be impressed. The others were with him.

"So what are these constants and conditions?" Becky asked.

"There are a lot," Jack said. "Over twenty cosmological ones alone, that I know of. But I only need name a few to demonstrate that Someone clearly planned out the cosmos.

One would be the universe's weak gravitational force. In comparison to other forces of nature within atoms, gravity is ten to the thirty-sixth power times weaker. If stronger, only large stars would have formed, and they burn too quickly for biological life to evolve. Also, planets would be smaller, and any lifeforms larger than insects would be crushed. In order for life as we know it to come about, gravity's strength and the expansion rate of space had to balance with each other to within one in a quadrillion at exactly one second after the Big Bang. An alteration in this gravitational force by even one part in ten to the fortieth power would mean stars like our sun couldn't exist."

"What the fuck . . ." was the general response Jack heard through his charism, from both students who had and hadn't kept up.

Mr. Wilkerson's soul just moaned under its restraints. Naomi, Becky, and Kevin were paying the closest attention. The saints present helped expand everyone's minds so they could continue without being overwhelmed, illuminating those falling behind to help them catch up. They did this by repeating Jack's words to them until their significance sunk in, the souls thinking it was an echo in their short-term memories.

"On the other hand," Jack continued once the saints signaled his listeners were ready, "if gravity were slightly weaker, stars either wouldn't exist or would be too small to possess energy enough to fuse hydrogen and form the heavier elements necessary for life. Things like carbon, the building block of life. So, gravity had to have a measured force of exactly the amount it does in order for humans to exist. Any other measurement would have prevented us."

He paused again to make sure everyone had kept up. The saints signaled him to keep going.

"Another fine-tuned constant is the strong nuclear force that binds protons and neutrons together inside the nucleus of atoms. The protons have a positive charge and should repel the neutrons like the positive ends of two magnets, but a strong nuclear force holds them together. If this force were only two percent weaker, the protons and neutrons would repel each other. This would mean hydrogen atoms would repel each other. Which would leave nothing but hydrogen atoms in the universe. Which would mean there'd be no heavier elements like carbon. Which would mean there'd again be no us. But, if the nuclear force holding the protons and neutrons together were only two percent stronger, all hydrogen atoms would attach to one another and there'd only be helium in the universe. No hydrogen. And without hydrogen, there'd be no water. Again, no us. Our bodies are about sixty percent water and need it for survival. There'd also be no heat in stars, because it's fueled by the nuclear fusion of hydrogen. So there'd be no heat in the universe. Again, no us. We need warmth for survival too."

Some of the students were stifling laughter at Jack's clear superior knowledge, looking at Mr. Wilkerson's dumbfounded face. But the saints kept them focused, not allowing them to distract themselves by the humor of the situation.

"Fine-tuning's also found at the atomic level," Jack said, "in the electromagnetic force. This binds electrons into orbits around the atomic nucleus that forms atoms in the first place. The building blocks of molecules. If this force's strength were altered, the number of elements able to exist in nature would be different, which would render impossible the complex biological molecules that make evolution possible."

Jack paused for a second, glancing into the teacher's eyes, enjoying the fact he'd just used the concept of evolution to demonstrate God after the instructor had tried to use it to disprove Him.

"For example," he said, turning back to the other students, "if the electromagnetic force were stronger, heavier elements like potassium, calcium, and iron wouldn't be here, all of which are necessary for sentient life."

Mr. Wilkerson's soul struggled again under Dathiel's hold, trying to speak out. His mind was too overcome by the intelligence, and he quieted.

"The next condition and constant are closely related and *really* could have screwed things up if they weren't fixed exactly the way they are. The density of matter in the universe and the rate of its expansion. If matter had differed in density by more than one in one quadrillion in the first seconds after the Big Bang, our universe wouldn't be here. Had matter been more dense, there would have been a Big Crunch instead of a Big Bang. A collapsing of a universe, instead of the formation of one. Had matter been less dense, the universe's expansion would be too fast for the galaxies to form. So there'd be no stars, no planets, and, once again, no life.

But, even with matter being exactly the right level of density, the strength of gravity had to be precise enough to perfectly affect the universe's rate of expansion too. Had that rate differed at all, it would have ruined things. The expansion rate was originally thought to be zero, but has since been discovered to be fine-tuned to the one hundred and twentieth power. The smallest deviation from that would result in disaster on a cosmic scale, so much so that physicist Alexander Vilenkin noted this constant as the most notorious and perplexing case of fine-tuning in all of physics. Other physicists have further noted that unless this constant had been fine-tuned," Jack made quotation marks with his fingers again, "'statistically miraculous events' would be required for our universe to sustain biological life. Alter the rate of expansion by one in a quintillion and life becomes impossible."

After a moment, Darris asked, "What's a quintillion?"

"A one with eighteen zeros behind it," Jack said.

Several eyes around the room widened.

"To get an idea of how big a number that is," Jack added, "imagine every grain of sand from every beach on Earth. That's probably a quintillion. So, if the expansion rate of the universe that supports life is represented by that exact amount of grains, all I'd need to do to destroy the possibility of biological organisms existing in it is add or subtract a single grain of sand. That's the level of exactitude required for us to be here."

Jack's classmates were speechless. Even Darris and Brad had sat back in their chairs in understanding this time. Naomi was beaming at him.

"Those are only some of the constants and conditions required for the evolution and sustainment of life," Jack said while he still had everyone's rapt attention. "The more general, universe-wide ones. My favorite ones—the ones that most point out to me that there has to be Someone behind our existence—are the ones found right here, in our local solar system."

"And what are those?" Becky pressed.

She, Jenny, and April were looking at him with almost hungry fascination.

"For starters," Jack said, "Earth is placed at exactly the right orbit in exactly the right solar system. One that has a star capable of providing for life. Our sun. And our planet, rather conveniently, orbits at all times within the circumstellar habitable zone."

Jack saw Darris' and Brad's souls begin to grow paler. He was losing them. He clarified.

"That's the circular band around a star like our sun with temperatures enabling water to form. So, it's the only area in the solar system biological life is able to exist. The zone's very narrow. Only Earth has the nearly circular orbit that keeps it always within it. The next closest planet to the sun, Venus, has a surface temperature of over eight hundred degrees. And Mars, the next farthest from the sun, is too cold for liquid water. So, we're in the perfect area. If Earth were only five percent closer to the sun, it'd be too hot for us to live. If twenty percent farther, too cold."

Brad and Darris came back, their skin turning pinker as their souls warmed to the saints' illuminations again. Everyone except Mr. Wilkerson was looking less affected by the demons' intellectual poison now.

"Another factor protecting us is the moon. There are multiple reasons its orbit is important for life, and I only need to name one to show why. Without the pull of its gravity, Earth would teeter on its axis, affecting when and for how long sunlight reached the poles. That would affect Earth's surface temperatures, causing them to vary by about ninety degrees. Not the most hospitable environment for humans."

Everyone was nodding their heads. Their souls were approaching to touch either him or one of the other living spirits present. Dathiel rose to greet them, removing his hand from Mr. Wilkerson. The zombie struggled against the chains, but remained restrained.

"As for the last bit of fine-tuning I'll identify in our solar system. My favorite one of all. Not only is Earth at just the right position relative to just the right type of star with just the right size moon, but it's protected by the other giant planets from comets and wandering asteroids. Those would be quite hazardous for evolution. Jupiter and Saturn's gravitational pulls act as comet catchers, guarding any from getting through to the inner solar system. Once more, Earth is shown to be, coincidentally, in exactly the right place for life out of all the rest of the billions of solar systems in all the rest of the billions of galaxies throughout the universe."

The zombified Mr. Wilkerson finally found his fight again, tearing the chains from the chair and bringing them swinging around, gnashing his teeth at Jack. Jack stared him down. All the other souls gathered behind him, as though for protection. Dathiel and the saints moved them farther back into the laboratory, giving Jack and the teacher a wide berth.

"That still sounds like blind chance to me," the teacher objected aloud, bringing a chain swinging toward Jack's face, "if, out of all this expansive universe, life only evolved on this one tiny spec in it!"

Jack blocked the chain with a wrist bracer.

"If it was planned," the zombie swung it at him again, "it seems like a great waste of space! How can you say a universe so little occupied by life is fine-tuned for it? Wouldn't God have either made a smaller universe or filled this one with a greater amount of intelligent beings?"

*Well there are angels,* Jack thought as he swung a red chain out from his own wrist, slicing the teacher's in half.

But he didn't want to get into angelology and how many other kinds of intellectual creatures indeed existed in creation. He wanted to keep things focused on physics.

He addressed the teacher aloud. "Are you saying that, if God had made only our local solar system, you'd then believe in Him, sir, or would you then be objecting exactly what you're now arguing against? That an *Infinite* Being would have surely created something grander?"

The chain Mr. Wilkerson had been swinging fell to the floor. Tired of playing defense and growing even more tired of the teacher's obstinance, Jack went on a full offensive. He shoved his hands into the soul's chest again, defibrillating it so hard it flew back into his desk chair. Jack was on him in a flash, sending shockwave after shockwave through him. Outwardly, the teacher's cold sweat returned and a slight headache started building up behind his eyes.

"If the human brain is the most complex thing in the universe," Jack asked aloud, "as we learned here in the study of both biology and psychology, why wouldn't the Designer have made an expansive universe worth exploring for it?"

The zombie gasped, but Jack went on shocking it.

"Our planet even happens to possess a transparent atmosphere, enabling us to discover the galaxies beyond our own." He shocked again. "What we find hardly discredits a Creator's existence. It reveals His Breadth, His Power, and His Majesty." Jack punched him in the face. "Also, if this Creator is a Loving Being, as most major religions attest, why wouldn't He have provided an enjoyable view in the sky for the creatures He's so enamored with? Billions of years of cosmic expansion seem worth it to me for a view as beautiful as ours."

Several of the ladies looked at Jack with swooning expressions, liking his poetry and how unapologetic he was in expressing it. Mr. Wilkerson still resisted, biting Jack's wrist.

"Why'd this universe exist for so many billions of years without the presence of humans then," the teacher asked aloud, "if we're really God's crowning achievement, like Christianity teaches?"

The bite was absorbed by Jack's wrist bracer.

"Because, as you well know, sir, evolution takes time. Why should God have needed to hurry if—as Christianity also teaches—He exists outside of time in an eternal present and never experiences being rushed? Why wouldn't He take His sweet time in preparing a universe, galaxy, solar system, and planet to be nothing less than perfect for His crowning jewel? Does a spouse not meticulously prepare a homecoming party for their beloved when they're returning home from a long journey?"

The enthralled expressions of the ladies in the room intensified.

"I'd also add that science hasn't definitively determined when exactly homo sapiens dawned on Earth," Jack slammed the zombie's head on the back of the chair, wrapping the remaining chains around it to restrain it again. "Its guesses range from twenty-five thousand to one million years ago. So," Jack tied the rest of the corpse's form in place, "who's to say exactly how long the Earth was barren of intelligent life?"

The zombie was held in place, but still obstinate. A gang of demons leapt up from the holes surrounding them on the floor, carrying his arguments forward for him. Jack backed up, taken off-guard.

"The apparent design in the universe is the result of the accidental coming together of atoms!" the first monster clawed into Jack. "Nothing more! Evolution and natural selection are all that are needed to explain our origins."

Jack let the rays of his Miraculous Medal shine through his suit, slicing through his attacker, which fell screaming off him.

"Even if that were true," he said, "they don't explain the extreme unlikeliness of this universe being able to support a planet where they could occur in the first place. How can you say natural selection's responsible for the intelligent design found within the human species, and yet deny the possibility of a God Who put the process into action in the first place? Where one finds order and obvious planning, an intelligence has clearly been at work."

Dathiel came to Jack's aid, slicing demons out of his way with his knuckle blades as he continued addressing the teacher.

"Are you telling me that, if you continuously poured the twenty-six letters of the alphabet out of a bucket, you'd expect them to eventually form a book for you without your having to tinker with them yourself?"

Kevin and Becky chuckled at that, seeing his logic.

"No," Jack sent a lightning bolt at the zombie strapped to the chair, "obviously not. You claim humanity evolves according to natural selection, as though nature thinks. But, if nature's not a conscious being, how does it think to design itself? Your explanation of why things are ordered and develop as they do is even more far-fetched than the Christian's!"

The other students all looked to Mr. Wilkerson for his comeback, feeling like they were watching a boxing match. If they could see what Jack could, they'd have seen how accurate that comparison was. A battle royal in fact. Several demonic fists flew toward Jack's face at once. They were sliced out of the air together by Gabriel, who'd swung his horn out and let it morph into his ax for an instant. The swing left one demon in the dungeon. He didn't bother engaging Jack or the angels, just broke Mr. Wilkerson's chains for him and fled back into the ground. The zombie rose and ran at Jack. Jack didn't bother to block this time. He changed his tactic, lowering his arms. Maybe if he let the resistant spirit exhaust itself instead of struggling with it, it would bring itself around to seeing reason in the end.

"If the universe was fine-tuned by a Higher Being, then who fine-tuned God?" the zombie rammed into Jack, bouncing off his armor without the warrior having moved an inch.

"So you admit there could be a God then, huh? Well, you don't have to ask that question about Him, sir. Religion teaches He's the simplest Being imaginable. An Infinite but Undivided Mind that possesses no moving parts. He doesn't fragment or multiply His thoughts like we do. So He required no design. He's Ever-Existent Being Itself."

"It's true there's a delicate balance to the universe," the corpse pounded Jack's chest with both fists. "But the reason for all the apparent fine-tuning was already solved hundreds of years ago, by Isaac Newton."

"But who put the laws of motion Sir Isaac Newton discovered in place, sir?" Jack stood like a brick wall against the opposing mind's attacks, sparks flying off him and shocking the corpse when it hit him. "Laws don't cause things. So they don't serve as a substitute for God. In orthodox physics, the fact that nature conforms so elegantly and efficiently to mathematical principles is left unexplained."

"The mathematical principles were simply decided by physicists and mathematicians based on the world they found themselves in," the soul pounded, despite the electrocution of its hands. "They don't prove the presence of a Fine-Tuner!"

"A fallacious description of the origin of mathematics," Jack corrected, the zombie's fingers breaking against his mask as it yelped in pain. "Mathematicians and physicists abstracted the laws through discovery," Jack kicked the corpse in the groin, sending it doubling over. "They were already there," he kneed it in the face, forcing its head back up to eye level, "written into nature itself, implying it was *designed* according to mathematical principles."

Jack lifted the zombie and slammed it down on a lab table, dragging it through volumetric flasks, test tube holders, and distillation equipment, each filled with body parts or liquid gold. The laboratory implements shattered on the stone floor as Jack mopped the teacher across his own work space.

"And this has forced physicists to acknowledge the work of an Intellect," he slammed the teacher through a few more implements before sliding him off the edge of the table and onto the floor. "Stephen Hawking himself—one of the most notorious atheists of today, whom you yourself have quoted before as one of the most intelligent astrophysicists of both Oxford and Cambridge Universities—has had to admit that the laws of science as we know them at present contain many fundamental numbers, and that the remarkable fact is that the values of these numbers seem to have been finely adjusted to make possible the development of life." Jack towered over the soul lying at his feet. "That's *Hawking,* sir. Every science teacher's idol. You gonna argue against him too?"

Mr. Wilkerson's soul climbed slowly to its feet, then turned suddenly to bite him in the face. Jack caught it by the throat and lifted it up, dangling its feet off the ground. He wasn't going to win it over, but he could still humiliate it. Its humiliation would be its own fault at this point.

"Ready for my royal flush?" he whispered to it mentally, then spoke aloud. "If you really want to argue numbers with me, sir, I'll counter with another of those universe-wide constants. The fact that the cosmos isn't a disordered place after such an explosive event as the Big Bang that caused it. The odds it would be organized enough for life, versus a chaotic place, is one tenth of ten to the one hundred and twenty-third power. That number's zeros, if written out in long-form, would extend across the Milky Way."

There were audible gasps and "wows" across the room from the students.

The teacher stood muted, unable to think straight because of Jack's mental chokehold.

"Don Page of the Institute for Advanced Study at Princeton actually calculated the odds against a life-sustaining universe as one in ten billion to the one hundred and twenty-fourth power. To get a more practical idea of those odds, a person would have a better chance at winning two thousand five hundred lotteries in a row, while being struck by four separate lightning bolts each time they did, than by betting on life evolving in this universe. Yet, they'd have won that bet, because life is here. Taken as a whole, the constants and conditions required for the evolution of organisms are so near incalculable that cosmologists like Michael Turner have had to fall back on an even more striking analogy to best describe them. The chance of complex life being able to evolve is equivalent to the chance of throwing a dart across the universe and hitting a bullseye one millimeter in diameter on the other side of it."

Kevin was looking at Jack like someone he didn't know.

"And yet another analogy I could use. My favorite. Poker's royal flush."

Jack paused for half a second to watch Mr. Wilkerson's spooked expression when he said the words that had crossed his mind moments before. He must have felt like Jack was reading his thoughts. Not a total inaccuracy.

"If you were playing poker with a friend and he came up with a royal flush, you'd probably chalk it up to chance. But, if he got ten or twenty royal flushes in a row, you'd suspect cheating. In other words, you'd never believe your friend wasn't fine-tuning the game in his favor.

Well, the odds of our universe forming to have its constants and conditions all line up perfectly to sustain life is less than the odds of getting fifty royal flushes in a row without cheating, sir. Since no one would believe a person being dealt fifty royal hands consecutively wasn't the result of a plan, why should any of us believe this life-permitting universe wasn't planned? Someone rigged its constants and conditions in our favor."

Jack lowered the flailing spirit to hold it before his face and look it straight in its empty eye sockets.

"All this is to say, sir, that astrophysicists—some of the world's leading minds in the area of empirical science—are finding reasons to believe in God by studying nature according to their own practice. Let the universe speak for itself! It's manifesting evidence of a Creator at every turn. If you want proof, throw all your efforts into seeing if you can disprove it. I guarantee you, you won't be able to. Science hasn't disproven God like you've claimed, sir." He threw the soul onto one of the fires burning from the floor. "It's led us straight to Him."

Naomi appeared ready to clap. So did Becky and several other students. It was Darris—always glad to open his mouth at Mr. Wilkerson—who stated the obvious out loud.

"Sounds like a K.O. to me, sir."

Everyone laughed. While they did, Joan approached Jack and whispered an instruction in his ear. Jack looked at her, lowering his mask off his face and raising his eyebrows. She nodded at him, confirming what she'd said. The zombie on the floor issued a spine-chilling sound of pain and anger at the flames licking it.

"I've had about enough of your disrespect, Jack!" the teacher said aloud.

"No disrespect intended, sir. Not to your dignity. But when I detect bullshit being offered me in place of an education at school, I'm going to call it out for what it is, no matter who offered it. Unless you can explain how I'm mistaken in anything I just said . . ."

The students all looked at Mr. Wilkerson with daring expressions.

"This is *my* classroom, Jack!" The zombie struggled to get off the fire, but it was too weak to rise anymore. *"I* decide what's taught in here."

"Oh, I see," Jack let the sarcasm flood into his tone. "Well, you'll forgive me for not taking instruction from an ego-tripping dictator."

The teacher jumped up from his desk and lunged forward like he was about to physically assault Jack this time. Naomi and several of the ladies squealed in disbelief. Mr. Wilkerson caught himself at their frightened reactions before he'd made it past the front row of desks. But Jack escalated, standing physically from his own seat.

*"And maybe,"* he shouted, startling everyone even more, *"if you'd offered your students a more optimistic worldview, I'd have let that slide! MAYBE IF YOU HADN'T SHOT YOUR MOUTH OFF ABOUT ATHEISM BEING A FACT, CHUCK NELSON WOULDN'T HAVE SHOT OFF HIS!"*

Naomi and the ladies put their hands to their mouths. Kevin's jaw had dropped. Even the football players, Darris and Brad, looked intimidated, whipping their feet under their desks as Jack passed them.

Mr. Wilkerson had been stunned into silence.

He didn't say a word or make a move when Jack stomped by, slamming the door behind him as he left the class.

# CHAPTER XXXIX
## RECKONINGS

Jack stepped out into the hallway, forgetting for a moment what Joan had just told him to do when he saw everything that was happening.

How long had they been in the office? Hours? Maybe. It felt like it could have been hours. He hadn't been watching the clock. He'd been too busy coordinating everything the Maid of Orléans instructed him to do.

First she'd told him to make the belligerent statement that had gotten Mr. Wilkerson's blood boiling so much. Then to throw Chuck's death in his face and storm out of his classroom, while she protected him from any physical retaliation on the teacher's part. From there she'd guided him to the principal's office, sword drawn, like she was prepared to fight off resistance on the way. None of the demons dared.

Joan was up to something, but Jack hadn't known what. He was starting to get an idea of it now, seeing all that had been happening while they'd met with Dr. Stopes. Everyone was still talking in the principal's office. Although he'd been sent outside, he kept reentering through his second sight, listening to what was being discussed. Joan was still there, guiding the conversation from all sides. Jack stepped back out into the hall every few minutes to watch the spiritual ripple effect rolling over the campus.

When Joan had first taken him to see the principal, she'd directed him to say that he and Mr. Wilkerson had "had a disagreement" and that he should probably call the teacher and his father to the office to join them. She'd emphasized that if Dr. Stopes wanted to call Jack's mother too, that was fine, but he at least needed to call his father. Dr. Stopes had tried asking for more details of what had happened in physics class, but Joan had bid Jack say nothing until both the science teacher and his father were present.

"I don't know that it's necessary to call your parents, Jack," Dr. Stopes had said.

He'd never had Jack Dacre sent to his office before. He hadn't even been sent this time. He'd come of his own accord.

"Let's talk with Mr. Wilkerson first, and—"

"I've talked with Mr. Wilkerson all I need," Jack had interrupted. "If you don't want to call my dad, I will. He needs to know what's happened and I'd prefer he hear it firsthand. Just tell him I'm in your office because I was in a fight with a teacher. That should get his attention."

Seeing Jack's determination and getting nothing more out of him, Dr. Stopes had made the call. Dale Dacre couldn't believe what he was hearing on the other end. He'd volunteered to come down to the school himself before Dr. Stopes even suggested it was necessary. Joan had winked at Jack when the principal hung up, making Jack wonder whether there weren't saints on his father's end too, putting the idea to come to the school in his head for him. Heaven had been coordinating something. Jack marveled again at just how much.

The debate he'd been prompted to start in physics class had only been the spark. The spark had lit a wildfire that was burning across the school, and beyond it. When Dale Dacre had arrived at the office, Jack and Mr. Wilkerson were both waiting. Dr. Stopes had kept them in separate rooms until his arrival, leaving Jack to wait for him while he talked with his employee. During his wait, Jack had listened to what the two men were saying in the other room through his gift, curious if Mr. Wilkerson would spin the events contrary to how they'd occurred to his boss. To his credit, he didn't lie about anything, just didn't give a very detailed account.

"It wouldn't matter if he lied," Joan had told him.

"Why?" Jack had asked. "I mean, I think my father would believe me. But, still, that'd make things harder. My word against his and all."

"It wouldn't be."

"Why?"

She'd given a half-smile, showing again she was up to something. "You'll see."

When Dale arrived twenty minutes later, he, his son, Mr. Wilkerson, and Dr. Stopes all sat together in the principal's office.

"Want to tell me what happened?" Dale had demanded of Jack, a mixture of anger and curiosity on his face, not sure yet which reaction he'd go with until he heard the story.

Jack had narrated, Joan helping him behind the scenes with exactly what to say. Mr. Wilkerson then gave his side, also under Joan's unseen direction. The saint even influenced Dr. Stopes' and Dale's reactions. Jack saw how she set certain perspectives up against others, wondering how she was planning to have the dominos fall in the end. Mr. Wilkerson emphasized Jack's disrespect and disruption of his class in his story. Dale's face had grown angry while listening. But, when Dale spoke his piece, Jack realized Joan hadn't been stoking his father's anger against him.

"So," Dale said, looking at both the principal and teacher when Mr. Wilkerson finished, "if I'm hearing things correctly, my son was attacked for defending his religion, by a faculty member no less, who openly slandered it?"

Mr. Wilkerson looked panicked at the reaction, but not as panicked as Dr. Stopes. It was Jack who spoke first.

"No, Dad. He didn't attack me. This wasn't a fight, or even an argument. Not until the end anyway. I want it understood it was a debate. It got heated at the end, but that was more my doing. But it was still *a debate.*"

Dale turned to him. "A debate about science versus religion it sounds like." He turned back to the teacher before Jack could answer. "So, you were attacking my son's religion?"

"Not at all, sir," Mr. Wilkerson said. "I was—"

*"Really?"* Dale interrupted him.

Mr. Wilkerson recognized the challenging, unafraid tone. He'd heard it not an hour earlier, in his physics class.

"Because it wouldn't be the first time he's told me you did!" Dale said. "He's mentioned your anti-religious comments before. It sounds like you've been making a habit of this."

Dr. Stopes eyed his employee, but Dale turned on him next.

"As for any behavior problem I'm hearing here, it sounds to me like Wando's fishing for a lawsuit over religious discrimination. My firm will be more than happy to take up the case. If my son's felt persecuted for his beliefs by an employee of your institution, I think we'd have a field day with it."

Dr. Stopes had raised his hands to complete his deer-in-the-headlights body language. "That's not at all what we want here, sir! I have no plans to enact disciplinary action against Jack. I never did. He came to my office and requested I call you."

"Yes," Mr. Wilkerson joined in, "and I didn't send Jack here, sir. He came of his own volition."

Jack was about to speak up in their defense, but his father was already retaliating, and he knew better than to interrupt him on a tirade.

"So I've wasted my time leaving work and coming down here then? Are you telling me my son stops by the office when he feels there's no problem in school?" He looked at the principal. "He come here to hang out with you often, Doctor?"

Dr. Stopes had tried placating next. "What can we do to fix this situation for you, sir? I don't see a need for it to extend beyond today."

"For starters," Dale jerked his head toward Mr. Wilkerson, "I think you can fire your employee here, unless you want that lawsuit."

*"Dad!"* Jack spoke up, careful not to yell too loudly at him, "I'm not looking to get Mr. Wilkerson fired."

His father turned to him. Jack didn't want his heat directed toward him at that moment, but he didn't want a man to lose his job over this thing either. He'd intended to put Mr. Wilkerson in his place and shut him up from making anymore flippant comments about matters in which he wasn't knowledgable, but he'd never intended to oust him from his livelihood.

"And what is it you want, son?"

He'd said it with less fire than Jack had expected, like it was an honest question. It surprised Jack, and he had to think about how to respond for a moment.

"I just want him to stop making uninformed statements about theism and to make sure he teaches things accurately in the future."

"Oh," Dale turned back to the other two, "so there's been inaccurate teaching going on too? I think I and the other taxpaying parents would like to know what kind of an education our children are receiving here."

*"Dad!"*

"Why don't you step outside, son?" Dale suggested in a not-so-suggestive tone. "I think the three of us need to speak further."

Jack had obeyed, not only because he knew better than to argue with his father in this state, but because Joan had nodded him out too. Jack guessed this was how she'd wanted things to go, because she hadn't been calming his father. She'd kept stoking his anger, touching his soul with flaming hands at pivotal moments during the conversation.

"Check your phone," she'd advised him on his way out.

Jack had planned to comply, but that was when he'd been distracted by all the spiritual activity going on outside the office. Angels and saints were driving the remainder of Delusion's hordes off the campus. The billowing black smoke of the place was dissipating, banished by the flaps of so many celestial wings. Avdiel was leading the charge. He and his Principalities had the demons screaming in terror. Music to Jack's ears as his soul wandered the campus. Now he saw how much Heaven had been planning for the day.

Talk of his challenge and humiliation of Mr. Wilkerson was spreading about the school on the lips of the other students, many of whom hadn't even been in the room when it happened. Jack's name was suddenly on everybody's mind. So was what he'd pointed out to Mr. Wilkerson. Most were laughing about how he'd tripped the science teacher up on his own words, making him fumble and show Jack's points to be that much more obvious. Others were discussing the debate in more serious tones, blown away by how Jack had demonstrated the existence of God through science. His actions were the talk of the school.

Rays of light from the tabernacles pierced the clouds of Wando and rained down on the campus, welcomed by numerous zombies for the first time and feeding even more illumination into the souls already living. This inspired them into discussing Jack's story that much more, with the angels helping to spread it. It gained rapid momentum under their guidance, and several of the dark fortresses of Wando were slowly transforming into pristine outposts.

*But how?* Jack wondered.

How had the story spread so fast across campus? And how had it stayed so intact? The rumor mill usually ground up the facts into an embellished version of a true event.

He remembered Joan's last instruction about checking his phone and dropped incorporeal sight. He'd missed several texts and calls. Kevin, Naomi, Becky, and the others were all wondering where he'd gone. But those weren't the messages Joan had wanted him to see. According to some of the texts, April and a few other students who'd been in class had filmed the whole debate on their phones. Kevin and Naomi had both texted him to check April's Instagram for some of the best clips, but the whole video had been uploaded to YouTube, by everyone who'd filmed it.

Jack had missed phones being out during his challenge. Of course, he'd been rather busy through his charism. He guessed Mr. Wilkerson had missed them too. Otherwise he probably would have made the students put their devices away, or stopped engaging in the debate. Jack wondered if it had been the saints and angels present who'd prompted the filming and then guarded the students doing it from being noticed. Either way, it was too late now. The debate was out there for all the world to see.

According to some of Jack's texts, the video was trending. Other texts informed him Jenny, Becky, and April were busy peddling the story across the student body through word-of-mouth. He could see their success with what was going on spiritually before him. He leaned back on the lockers in the hall, his muscles relaxing for what felt like the first time since the debate had begun. He let his head fall back, closed his eyes, and allowed a smile to blossom across his lips. He offered a silent prayer of thanksgiving for being chosen as God's instrument in conquering a demonic stronghold as immense as Wando. The weight of seven months' worth of troubles felt lifted off his shoulders.

No wonder Joan hadn't supported him in the office. Dr. Stopes would fire Mr. Wilkerson whether his father demanded it or not now. The debate was on the internet. With the kind of publicity that was about to flood Wando, he'd want to look like he'd done something about the incident. There might even be boycotts outside the school from activist groups. Jack could imagine it, judging from the number of views the video was getting online.

He leaned his head back against the lockers again, watching Heaven's wildfire rage. There was nothing else to do now. It was lit, and it would burn as long and as far as God intended. He didn't know how long or far that might be, but it was out of his hands. He couldn't believe he'd helped start such a blaze.

Joan came out of the office.

"So, I guess getting Mr. Wilkerson fired was always your plan?"

"That, and more," she said. "Gabriel and I were the ones who encouraged your classmates to film the debate."

Jack nodded, smiling. "I wondered."

"The story being on the internet for all to witness will have Dr. Stopes replaced before long too."

Jack looked at her in shock. "Man, you take no prisoners do you?"

"Not when they forfeit surrender," she said, her face hard. "The next principal will ensure nothing like this ever happens at Wando again. He won't want anything to do with even a whiff of discrimination against the Faith. We will hold the fortress as celestial territory now."

Jack shook his head. "Very impressive, Maid."

He paused, trying to think of something else to say. But there was nothing.

So, he repeated, "Very impressive . . . I never expected to be a part of something this big."

Joan smiled a smile of which Jack never wanted to be on the wrong end. "I reconquered a country in life," she said. "You think I couldn't lead a coup to reconquer a school from the afterlife?"

Jack chuckled. "Well when you put it that way, it makes me feel foolish for being overwhelmed by all this."

"This will not be your last or grandest conquest, Philangelus. But, you've earned a reprieve from battle for now."

He and the Maid watched the angelic rout, saying no more.

Soon, voices called down the hallway snapping Jack out of incorporeal sight. *"Jack! There you are!"* Naomi yelled.

Kevin, Becky, April, Brad, Jenny, and Darris all followed her.

"Where've you been?" several of them asked.

"Principal's office," Jack said. "If you get the chance, you might want to say goodbye to Mr. Wilkerson. I don't think we'll be seeing him around Wando anymore."

*"What?"* Darris and Naomi yelled together.

"He's being fired as we speak," Jack told them.

Everyone was silent, their faces in shock.

"Fuckin' A!" Brad said.

Jack shrugged. "I tried to stop it. But, even if Dr. Stopes had listened to me, he'd probably have changed his mind once he saw the videos.

"You seen them?" April asked.

"No, haven't had a chance to look yet. But I was there. I know what happened."

"But you should see the comments they're getting!" Jenny said.

"Yeah?" Jack asked. "Are they positive?"

"Most. Most people are finding the whole thing hilarious." She laughed.

"I can't believe what you did!" Kevin exclaimed. "You fuckin' outsmarted Mr. Wilkerson, man! *Mr. Wilkerson!*"

Jack shrugged again. "Helps to be prepared."

"Where'd you get all that stuff anyway?" Becky asked. "It was fascinating."

Jack smiled. "The priest I've mentioned before. Monsignor Bamonte. I should introduce you two sometime. You'd like him."

"I'd be curious to meet him myself," Kevin said.

"Yeah? Well, I'll try to invite him to dinner at my house or something. You can pick his brains. He's where I get my best arguments. And that in there today," Jack jerked a thumb toward the science wing, "was only stuff from one meeting. I told you two about the Cosmological Argument before. That was the Teleological Argument. My new favorite when it comes to debunking materialism."

"You have more stuff?" Becky asked. "That story about what happened in Portugal. Was that true?"

"Yeah, I was wondering about that myself," Jenny said.

The others all nodded, and Jack's smile widened.

"Yeah, it's true. I've only started learning about it recently, but I've been finding tons of books on the subject. Already ordered some. Like I told Mr. Wilkerson, there's evidence of the supernatural out there, if one bothers to look for it." Jack thought he heard his father's voice near the office door next to them. "I'd love to chat more about it, but I think I'm about to have to leave. My father's in there." He nodded at Dr. Stopes' door. "He came down to help sort everything out with Mr. Wilkerson. Why don't you all come over to my place tonight? We can hash out everything that happened."

Everyone looked agreeable.

"Actually," Jack said, "let me text everybody a little later to make sure it's a good time. I've got to find out what's waiting for me at home first."

"You think you'll be in trouble?" Naomi asked.

"I don't know. My dad's pretty angry. I don't know if any of that's going to get directed at me. Either way, I'm going to have to explain everything to them before I bring guests over. I'm not in trouble with the principal. That should help."

Dale Dacre's voice grew louder. He sounded like he was right inside the door. Jack looked at it.

"Time to face the music I guess."

"I'll stay with him," Naomi said, turning to the others. "You guys don't have to be here for this. We can all catch up later."

As everyone cleared out, Kevin reached out and shook Jack's hand. "I never thought anyone could do that," he said. "You beat Mr. Wilkerson . . . at his own science."

Jack's face turned serious. "It was for Chuck."

Kevin's smile slipped off his face, his hand stopping mid-shake.

"I'm not so sad anymore myself," Jack said, seeing his friend's eyes. "I think he still exists. That he's still with us, in a new way."

Kevin's eyes reddened. He turned and walked away before he spilled any tears in front of people. Jack would have to talk more with him later. Kevin didn't yet have the closure over Chuck he did. He wanted to find a way to give it to him, without telling more than Monsignor Bamonte had bid him tell about his gift. First he had to talk to his father. He had to talk to his whole family and find a way to tell them everything. They needed to know about his decision to seek the priesthood. Not to mention, he had to figure out how to tell them he had a supernatural ability. No big deal.

Naomi was the only one left standing with him.

"You don't have to stay," he said. "My dad might be fuming when he gets out, but I can handle it. This isn't your problem."

"You were brilliant today!" she said, hugging him. "I knew you could beat him if you stood up to him. I knew it! You finally got your passion back, huh?"

Jack smiled, but took her arms off him. "Yeah. Guess I did."

She looked hurt when he pulled out of the hug. "Jack . . . could we talk—"

"We can't get back together," he interrupted.

She looked hit by his bluntness. "It's okay," she insisted after a moment. "I'm sorry I—"

"It's not that," he said. "You did the right thing. It was what we both needed at the time. And it's not because I wouldn't want to try again." He looked over his shoulder at the principal's office, ensuring his father hadn't come out yet. "Look, you'll be the first I'm telling this too. So keep it quiet for now. I haven't told my family yet. But, I decided over the weekend to become a Catholic priest."

She smiled at him. "That's awesome! I think you'd make a great preacher!"

Jack stared at her. She didn't seem to get it. She frowned as he kept staring.

"What does that have to do with us getting back together?" she asked.

Jack raised his eyebrows and took a deep breath. She didn't know.

"Catholic priests don't marry," he said. "So, there'd be no reason for me to date if that's what I think God's calling me to."

She looked like he'd slapped her. "Oh."

He hated putting that expression on her face. His instincts told him to hug her.

His mind told him otherwise.

Why did this feel like a breakup all over again? They were already broken up, and she was the one who'd done that! He thought he'd been spared this conversation by realizing his calling after their relationship had ended! He switched to incorporeal sight. Joan was watching them. She was standing on Jack's other side, as though representing the two women between whom he was being pulled. Naomi or the Bride of Christ? Dathiel and Paviel walked up next to the group.

"Can you help me get her out of here?" Jack asked Naomi's guardian.

"Working on it," he said.

"I'm not trying to hurt you," Jack said to Naomi aloud. "When God calls, I have to answer. He comes first."

"I know," she said, looking back up. Her face had gone so pale. "But, I don't understand. The minister at my church is married . . ."

Jack tilted his head. This was not a conversation he wanted to have, ever. And he definitely didn't have time for it at the moment. His father's voice was getting closer to the door.

"The Catholic Church is different," he said. "Priests are celibate, in imitation of Christ Himself. It's so they can be completely at the disposal of His Church's needs."

"Okay," she said, her voice breaking a little. "Am I still going to see you tonight?"

"That's up to you. You're welcome over. That is," he nodded his head backward toward the door, "depending on how much of a storm I have to deal with from my parents. I'll text you all to let you know."

"Can we talk more later though?" she asked, her voice getting shakier.

Jack just wanted to get her gone before his dad came out.

"Sure," he said. "We will. For now, I've got to handle this. You'd better make yourself scarce. I don't want you catching any of his frustration. If he's still mad, I want it aimed at me."

She hugged him again before leaving, tightly, as though afraid to let go. As though afraid it would be their last hug, which, Jack supposed, it might be. With that thought, he couldn't help embracing her back.

"Take care of her will you?" he asked Paviel.

"As ever I have, Philangelus. And you, take care of the Church. Tell the devils I said hello." He reached out a hand, and Jack shook it. "It was an honor to accompany you for a time."

"No," Jack said, more emotion swelling in his throat. "The honor's mine when I get to be in the presence of a prince of Heaven."

Paviel placed a hand on his shoulder, imparting a silent blessing, then coaxed Naomi to leave with him.

As soon as she'd turned the corner of the hall, the door opened behind Jack.

Jack opened the door to the cathedral offices, stopping when his heart felt like it had dropped into his stomach at who he saw in front of him.

He'd convinced his father to wait until they arrived home before they discussed what had happened at school. He'd told him he had something to tell the whole family. Something important. Something that would affect the rest of his life.

That had gotten Dale's attention enough to wait. That, and the look on Jack's face when he said it. Jack had also told him he had to stop at the church first. To Jack's surprise, his father hadn't argued.

As he'd climbed into his Jeep, Jack had looked back at Wando one last time through incorporeal sight. Avdiel had been standing atop the front gate as the school's new Principality, tracing a cross onto it beneath his feet. A cross with wings. Mephistopheles' pentagram was finally replaced. The angel had smiled and waved Jack away. Jack had ridden on air the whole way to the parish.

He felt like he'd crashed now, gaping at who sat before him. For a moment—one brief moment—he feared he was crazy again. The receptionist at the front desk was the broad bearded man he'd seen the day he began doubting Monsignor Bamonte's existence. The man looked up at him.

"Can I help you, sir?"

"Yes," Jack said after a moment, realizing he was staring. "I was wondering if Monsignor—"

"Hey, I recognize you," the receptionist interrupted. "Didn't you ask me once if there was another receptionist who worked here?"

"Oh . . . yes, that was me," Jack said.

"Yeah, I remember," the receptionist said. "You dashed out of here like you'd seen a ghost last time."

"Yeah . . . sorry about that. I was dealing with a lot that day."

"Well your visit made an impression. You got me curious. I found out they'd used Mrs. Crandall as a substitute a few times when I was out sick. She's from another part of the staff. Kind of our unofficial cathedral historian. Got short gray hair and thick glasses. That sound like who you saw before?"

"*Yes!*" Jack said with a little more force than he'd intended. "That must have been her. I thought she was the regular."

"Nope, that's me," the receptionist said, holding out a hand. "Lloyd Delain."

"Jack Dacre." Jack shook. "I was here to see Monsignor Bamonte, if he's in. He's my spiritual director."

"Yes, he's in."

"I was wondering when you'd figure it out," Monsignor Bamonte laughed.

"You knew?"

"Of course not! No one but God knows. But, I suspected that might be the vocation He intends for you. I've just been waiting for Him to whisper it into your mind Himself." The cleric rose from his armchair and grabbed a notepad off his desk, writing a name and number down. "This is the deacon you need to call at the Vocations Office. He'll know what you need to do to start the application process." He tore the top sheet off and handed it to Jack. "You'll meet with him first."

"Thanks." Jack took it. "Should I tell him or anyone else about my charism?"

"I wouldn't. There's no need." The priest paused as he took his seat again. "I take it things went well with Dr. Vonhagen then? You look different. And you don't seem to be doubting incorporeal sight anymore."

Jack shook his head, smiling. "No, I'm not. He didn't find any mental illnesses. He even showed me some video footage of people who actually have schizophrenia before I left his office." He chuckled at himself. "I definitely never had it."

"That's good to hear." The monsignor smiled back. "You look more at peace than I think I've ever seen you."

"I guess I am." Jack let out a heavy breath. "There is something I need your advice on though. I don't know how to tell my family about the charism."

The priest leaned forward in his chair, a stunned look on his face. "You've never told them?"

Jack shook his head. "I wanted to make sure it was genuine first. Maybe not the smartest move. But . . . I just didn't. I wanted to be sure I was right about their souls. Now that I am . . . I still don't know what I'm going to say."

Monsignor Bamonte's eyebrows rose and he nodded his head, leaning back. "Yes, I can imagine."

"I also haven't told them about this yet." Jack indicated the paper in his hand. "I wanted to tell you first, to see what you'd say."

"Well you have my blessing there. Hopefully you'll have theirs too. I think you'd make an excellent priest."

Jack felt like he glowed as brightly as his soul did when viewed through his gift at the monsignor's affirmation.

The priest stood. "I'll give you a blessing that things may go well with your family. You have a lot you're about to put on them today."

As Jack bowed his head under the cleric's sign of the cross, he flipped to incorporeal sight to watch its unseen effect. Seeing the four bright figures who stood in the room with them, he flipped back to regular sight.

"Hey! You never told me if I was right about your four guardian angels the day we first tested my charism."

The priest looked at him with an expression Jack couldn't place, one he'd never seen on his face before.

"I didn't? . . . You're right!" He shook his head, as though he couldn't fathom how he'd forgotten. "I'm sorry, Jack. Could have saved you a lot of trouble!"

"I was right then?"

The monsignor sat back down. "You were right about when I'd last heard confessions and attended the Sacrament myself, right down to the detail about the bishop hearing it. And I believed I had four guardian angels at the time, but I didn't know for certain. That was the point I knew you weren't schizophrenic though. I knew incorporeal sight had to be something otherworldly. I just didn't know yet if it was from God or His enemy. The angels who identified themselves hadn't told you what I'd confessed."

"What did that indicate?" Jack asked.

"It's believed sins that have been confessed are blotted out from the fallen angels' memories, or at least bound from use in some way so they can no longer accuse us of them before God. So, you see my reasoning. The angels you were seeing could have been diabolic ones posing as my guardians who knew the externals of my sacramental activity but not what was spoken in Confession. On the other hand, the answer that they'd forgotten what I'd confessed could just as easily have been an indication they were my real guardians."

"Why?" Jack asked. "That answer always confused me. I didn't think an angelic intellect could forget anything?"

"It can't," the priest said. "It was a tongue-in-cheek answer on my guardians' part. It meant they were no longer acknowledging my sins since they'd been confessed. Christ had drowned them in the ocean of His Divine Mercy, after which He acted as though they'd never happened. So my guardians were following suit, in a sense 'forgetting' them too. Though 'ignoring' would have been a better way to put it. Either way, you can see how the answer left room for doubt as to the source of your ability."

Jack laughed. "Sounds like the angels to me. Dathiel's got the same teasing sense of humor."

Monsignor Bamonte smiled. "Well, I have to thank you for clarifying how many protectors I have. I had faith before, but your gift brought me knowledge."

"How had you come to suspect you had four before I told you?" Jack asked.

The priest's face went serious a moment, like he was considering something.

But his smile soon returned.

"One I'd have had since conception, the same as everyone. Another would have been bestowed the day of my ordination. It's an ancient tradition that priests are given a second guardian to help them with such a momentous task as Holy Orders."

"Really? I've never heard that. That's awesome! So, if I become a priest . . ."

The monsignor nodded. "If you become a priest, you'll receive a second yourself, if you don't already have more than one by then."

"Yeah? How else do you acquire more?"

"It's also a belief that you can ask God for more guardians as you advance through the stages of holiness, or that they're automatically given to you the more you advance. I myself don't make such a grand request except for very solemn reasons. One of those was on the occasion I consecrated myself totally to Mary as her personal slave. I asked her to grant me a new guardian to help me fulfill the consecration every day. The fourth angel . . ." The monsignor paused. "Well, the fourth angel I asked for to help me in the same task I was planning to ask your help with the next time I saw you. I think your charism will come in handy with it."

"What?" Jack asked, intrigued.

The monsignor had never asked a favor from him that involved using his gift on his behalf before. He guessed things were going to get very interesting now that they'd discerned it was from God.

"It can wait," the priest said. "You've already got a lot on your plate today. I don't want to burden you with something else."

"You're not a burden, Monsignor! And I owe you a lot. It's about time I was able to do something for you for a change."

The priest sighed. "Alright."

He told him the favor.

Jack hadn't seen it coming at all.

Jack stepped out of the office into the sunlight, the gold cross of the cathedral's steeple tracing its shadow over him, still in shock from what the monsignor had revealed.

But he had to focus. He still had a lot ahead of him today. He squinted up at the steeple, smiling in the warmth of the afternoon, and opened his eyes to the incorporeal, flying up to the castle.

"Father Wannabe's come to join us," Gabriel said, spinning his ax under his fingertips like a top as Jack alighted on the balcony before him.

The giant Archangel, Dathiel, Joan, and Benedict were all congregated on the high terrace where he'd stood looking out over the city with Joan on Halloween. Jack had forgotten how peaceful it was up here, so far above the noise of the streets. The only sound besides Gabriel's spinning blade was the trickle of the holy water in front of the doorway into the castle.

"You know," Jack said to the Archangel, tilting his head and grinning, "I think I could get used to that."

"You better," Benedict said in his usual gruff tone. "Especially if you want help getting into the seminary."

Jack stepped off the balcony to join them. "Well, if you're going to be that way about it, I'll be sure to only call on *you* when I'm desperate."

The wizened saint did something Jack seldom saw him do. Smiled. Jack stood next to Dathiel, facing the other three.

"Thanks for all your help today, especially yours, Maid," Jack bowed his head to Joan. "Couldn't have conquered the school without your backup."

Joan smiled, and Jack saw the look in her eyes he'd seen before. A look that said she wasn't done yet.

"Also," he paused, "I'm sorry for doubting that all of you existed for so long. I hope I can make up for it in the future."

"With the vocation you're going to be discerning . . . you will," Dathiel said.

"It's a good time to be a priest," Benedict mused. "Better to be one in dark times for the Church than in peaceful times. It's when Hell's on the attack the best heroes are forged."

Jack smiled, drawing his sword off his back, spinning its blade on the ground under his fingers, mimicking Gabriel. "Sounds like my kind of adventure," he said.

"Good," a voice said behind him.

He turned to see Avdiel land with a few of his soldiers on the balcony.

"Because there's a flock of demons on the horizon who're intending to try and retake Wando," the Principality continued. "Have a few minutes to aid their welcoming party?"

Physically, Jack entered the church to say a quick prayer before leaving. "What do you know?" he said. "My schedule just cleared up all of a sudden."

"Good," said another deep voice from above everyone.

They all looked up to see Michael perched on the archway above the door of holy water.

"Because mine did too."

Jack smiled, spreading his robe into wings.

"Have fun," Gabriel bid everyone.

Michael, Jack, Joan, Benedict, Avdiel, and his Principalities took off.

Less than a minute later, several miles away, a gang of evil spirits found themselves scattered and chased across the marshlands by what seemed like a wrecking ball as bright as a sun barreling into them. Once they recovered enough to see who'd attacked them on their way into town, they were even more horrified. Saints! The Prince of Heaven himself! The Principality of the territory, with his angels! And their legendary new friend.

The Philangelus.

# Coming Soon!

The journey of *The 13 Tales* will continue in
SEPTIMUS: THE SECOND TALE

If you are enjoying this series,
you may also enjoy Brian Prater's
forthcoming series,
THE LEVITE

Licia Asaju has looked death in the face and lived to tell the tale. Saved from kidnapping and ritual sacrifice by a dark figure, Licia and her sister are swept into the midst of a criminal conspiracy involving the Ku Klux Klan, an Egyptian who fancies himself a modern-day Pharaoh, and a Nazi who escaped justice following the Holocaust. Her rescuer claims to be on a mission from God to hunt and execute devil worshippers. While he asserts his mysterious abilities are a gift, Licia fears the vigilante who saved her may be just as insane as the cults he hunts. Is he monster, man, or something else entirely . . .

A new action-horror story from the mind that brought you *The Philangelus.* Prepare to meet *The Levite.*

# ACKNOWLEDGEMENTS

The first person I must thank is my lovely bride for doing the most work on this novel after me. She was my first and harshest editor, and she is the reason it has now come out in much better shape than it was when she first joined me on the project. A thank you to our friend, Zach Smith, for serving as final editor of the book. Thank you to two more mutual friends, Dr. Emily Dowdell, Psy.D., and Dr. Cate Bergmann, Psy.D., for their contributions to making Jack Dacre's clinical evaluations in the novel authentic. My thanks to the writings and recorded debates of apologist Trent Horn, which helped me better conceptualize the arguments between atheism and theism. Thank you to Dr. John Cuddeback, Ph.D., of Christendom College and several of its philosophy majors for their help in my developing the concept of incorporeal sight, as well as to Dr. William Marshner, Ph.D., for his theological insights on the concept. On that and other philosophical and theological elements of the novel (which were important to me to portray in an authentic manner) there were also several Catholic priests I interviewed. I am sure I may forget some, but I will attempt to remember everyone. My thanks to: Monsignor Anthony La Femina, Father Jerome Fasano, Father Jack Durkin, and my good friend, Father Mark Moretti. Thanks to my friend, videographer Jason Loughry for his insights during the brainstorming phase of the novel. Thanks to my friend, film writer and director Joe Duca for his editorial insights and advice on whether or not the book needed a prologue. Thanks to my parents, sister, and friend Joe Brizek for serving as a few of my beta readers, some of them even taking the time to allow me to read aloud to them. Thanks to my friend Galilee Bürger for serving as my interior illustrator and drawing up the symbol of the Philangelus. I think I can speak for the both of us that we had fun going back-and-forth arguing over how exactly it should look. Lastly, thanks to all my readers for taking the time to read the novel! You could have read anything, but you chose to read this. I hope you enjoyed it.